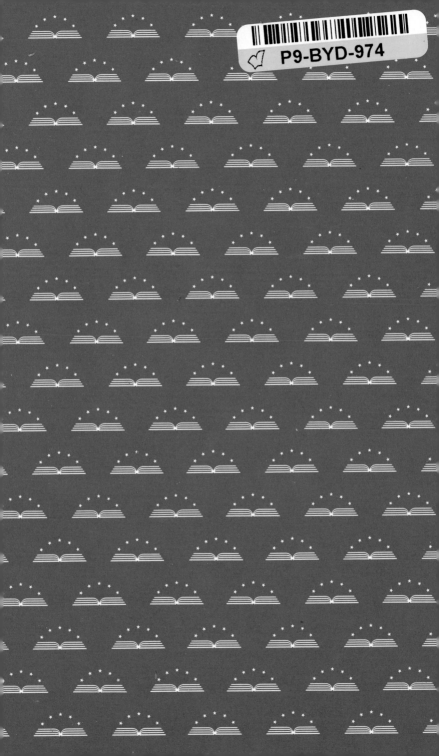

HENRY JAMES

Henry James

COMPLETE STORIES
1898–1910

THE LIBRARY OF AMERICA

The paper used in this publication meets the
minimum requirements of the American National Standard for
Information Sciences—Permanence of Paper for Printed
Library Materials, ANSI Z39.48—1984.

Distributed to the trade in the United States
by Penguin Books USA Inc
and in Canada by Penguin Books Canada Ltd.

Library of Congress Catalog Number: 95-23462
For cataloging information, see end of Notes.
ISBN: 1-883011-10-8

First Printing
The Library of America—83

Manufactured in the United States of America

DENIS DONOGHUE

WROTE THE NOTES FOR THIS VOLUME

Contents

John Delavoy 1

The Given Case 36

"Europe" 62

The Great Condition 81

The Real Right Thing 121

Paste 135

The Great Good Place 152

Maud-Evelyn 178

Miss Gunton of Poughkeepsie 206

The Tree of Knowledge 220

The Abasement of the Northmores 235

The Third Person 255

The Special Type 287

The Tone of Time 306

Broken Wings 326

The Two Faces 345

Mrs. Medwin 360

The Beldonald Holbein 382

The Story in It 403

Flickerbridge 421

The Birthplace 441

The Beast in the Jungle 496

The Papers 542

Fordham Castle 639

Julia Bride 661

The Jolly Corner 697

"The Velvet Glove" 732

Mora Montravers 760

Crapy Cornelia 818

The Bench of Desolation 847

A Round of Visits 896

Chronology 925

Note on the Texts 940

Notes 943

John Delavoy

T HE FRIEND who kindly took me to the first night of poor
Windon's first—which was also poor Windon's last: it was
removed as fast as, at an unlucky dinner, a dish of too perceptible a presence—also obligingly pointed out to me the
notabilities in the house. So it was that we came round, just
opposite, to a young lady in the front row of the balcony—a
young lady in mourning so marked that I rather wondered to
see her at a place of pleasure. I dare say my surprise was partly
produced by my thinking her face, as I made it out at the
distance, refined enough to aid a little the contradiction. I
remember at all events dropping a word about the manners
and morals of London—a word to the effect that, for the most
part, elsewhere, people so bereaved as to be so becraped were
bereaved enough to stay at home. We recognised of course,
however, during the wait, that nobody ever did stay at home;
and, as my companion proved vague about my young lady,
who was yet somehow more interesting than any other as
directly in range, we took refuge in the several theories that
might explain her behaviour. One of these was that she had a
sentiment for Windon which could override superstitions; another was that her scruples had been mastered by an influence
discernible on the spot. This was nothing less than the spell
of a gentleman beside her, whom I had at first mentally disconnected from her on account of some visibility of difference. He was not, as it were, quite good enough to have come
with her; and yet he was strikingly handsome, whereas she,
on the contrary, would in all likelihood have been pronounced
almost occultly so. That was what, doubtless, had led me to
put a question about her; the fact of her having the kind of
distinction that is quite independent of beauty. Her friend, on
the other hand, whose clustering curls were fair, whose moustache and whose fixed monocular glass particularly, if indescribably, matched them, and whose expanse of white shirt
and waistcoat had the air of carrying out and balancing the
scheme of his large white forehead—her friend had the kind
of beauty that is quite independent of distinction. That he was

her friend—and very much—was clear from his easy imagination of all her curiosities. He began to show her the company, and to do much better in this line than my own
companion did for me, inasmuch as he appeared even to know
who we ourselves were. That gave a propriety to my finding,
on the return from a dip into the lobby in the first entr'acte,
that the lady beside me was at last prepared to identify him.
I, for my part, knew too few people to have picked up anything. She mentioned a friend who had edged in to speak to
her and who had named the gentleman opposite as Lord
Yarracome.

Somehow I questioned the news. "It sounds like the sort
of thing that's too good to be true."

"Too good?"

"I mean he's too much like it."

"Like what? Like a lord?"

"Well, like the name, which is expressive, and—yes—even
like the dignity. Isn't that just what lords are usually not?" I
didn't, however, pause for a reply, but inquired further if his
lordship's companion might be regarded as his wife.

"Dear, no. She's Miss Delavoy."

I forget how my friend had gathered this—not from the
informant who had just been with her; but on the spot I accepted it, and the young lady became vividly interesting. "The
daughter of the great man?"

"What great man?"

"Why, the wonderful writer, the immense novelist: the one
who died last year." My friend gave me a look that led me
to add: "Did you never hear of him?" and, though she professed inadvertence, I could see her to be really so vague
that—perhaps a trifle too sharply—I afterwards had the
matter out with her. Her immediate refuge was in the question of Miss Delavoy's mourning. It was for *him*, then, her
illustrious father; though that only deepened the oddity of
her coming so soon to the theatre, and coming with a lord.
My companion spoke as if the lord made it worse, and, after
watching the pair a moment with her glass, observed that it
was easy to see he could do anything he liked with his young
lady. I permitted her, I confess, but little benefit from this
diversion, insisting on giving it to her plainly that I didn't

know what we were coming to and that there was in the air a gross indifference to which perhaps more almost than anything else the general density on the subject of Delavoy's genius testified. I even let her know, I am afraid, how scant, for a supposedly clever woman, I thought the grace of these *lacunæ*; and I may as well immediately mention that, as I have had time to see, we were not again to be just the same allies as before my explosion. This was a brief, thin flare, but it expressed a feeling, and the feeling led me to concern myself for the rest of the evening, perhaps a trifle too markedly, with Lord Yarracome's victim. She was the image of a nearer approach, of a personal view: I mean in respect to my great artist, on whose consistent aloofness from the crowd I needn't touch, any more than on his patience in going his way and attending to his work, the most unadvertised, unreported, uninterviewed, unphotographed, uncriticised of all originals. Was he not the man of the time about whose private life we delightfully knew least? The young lady in the balcony, with the stamp of her close relation to him in her very dress, was a sudden opening into that region. I borrowed my companion's glass; I treated myself, in this direction—yes, I was momentarily gross—to an excursion of some minutes. I came back from it with the sense of something gained; I felt as if I had been studying Delavoy's own face, no portrait of which I had ever met. The result of it all, I easily recognised, would be to add greatly to my impatience for the finished book he had left behind, which had not yet seen the light, which was announced for a near date, and as to which rumour—I mean of course only in the particular warm air in which it lived at all—had already been sharp. I went out after the second act to make room for another visitor—they buzzed all over the place—and when I rejoined my friend she was primed with rectifications.

"He isn't Lord Yarracome at all. He's only Mr. Beston."

I fairly jumped; I see, as I now think, that it was as if I had read the future in a flash of lightning. "Only——? The mighty editor?"

"Yes, of the celebrated *Cynosure*." My interlocutress was determined this time not to be at fault. "He's always at first nights."

"What a chance for me, then," I replied, "to judge of my particular fate!"

"Does that depend on Mr. Beston?" she inquired; on which I again borrowed her glass and went deeper into the subject. "Well, my literary fortune does. I sent him a fortnight ago the best thing I've ever done. I've not as yet had a sign from him, but I can perhaps make out in his face, in the light of his type and expression, some little portent or promise." I did my best, but when after a minute my companion asked what I discovered I was obliged to answer "Nothing!" The next moment I added: "He won't take it."

"Oh, I hope so!"

"That's just what I've been doing." I gave back the glass. "Such a face is an abyss."

"Don't you think it handsome?"

"Glorious. Gorgeous. Immense. Oh, I'm lost! What does Miss Delavoy think of it?" I then articulated.

"Can't you see?" My companion used her glass. "She's under the charm—she has succumbed. How else can he have dragged her here in her state?" I wondered much, and indeed her state seemed happy enough, though somehow, at the same time, the pair struck me as not in the least matching. It was only for half a minute that my friend made them do so by going on: "It's perfectly evident. She's not a daughter, I should have told you, by the way—she's only a sister. They've struck up an intimacy in the glow of his having engaged to publish from month to month the wonderful book that, as I understand you, her brother has left behind."

That was plausible, but it didn't bear another look. "Never!" I at last returned. "Daughter or sister, that fellow won't touch him."

"Why in the world——?"

"Well, for the same reason that, as you'll see, he won't touch *me*. It's wretched, but we're too good for him." My explanation did as well as another, though it had the drawback of leaving me to find another for Miss Delavoy's enslavement. I was not to find it that evening, for as poor Windon's play went on we had other problems to meet, and at the end our objects of interest were lost to sight in the general blinding blizzard. The affair was a bitter "frost," and if we were all in our places to the last everything else had disappeared. When I got home it was to be met by a note from Mr. Beston accepting my article almost with enthusiasm, and it is a proof of the rapidity of my fond revulsion that before I went to sleep, which was not till ever so late, I had excitedly embraced the prospect of letting him have, on the occasion of Delavoy's new thing, my peculiar view of the great man. I must add that I was not a little ashamed to feel I had made a fortune the very night Windon had lost one.

II

Mr. Beston really proved, in the event, most kind, though his appeal, which promised to become frequent, was for two or three quite different things before it came round to my peculiar view of Delavoy. It in fact never addressed itself at all to that altar, and we met on the question only when, the posthumous volume having come out, I had found myself wound up enough to risk indiscretions. By this time I had twice been with him and had had three or four of his notes. They were the barest bones, but they phrased, in a manner, a connection. This was not a triumph, however, to bring me so near to him as to judge of the origin and nature of his relations with Miss Delavoy. That his magazine would, after all, publish no specimens was proved by the final appearance of the new book at a single splendid bound. The impression it made was of the deepest—it remains the author's highest mark; but I heard, in spite of this, of no emptying of table-drawers for Mr. Beston's benefit. What the book is we know still better to-day, and perhaps even Mr. Beston does; but there was no approach at the time to a general rush, and I therefore of course saw that if he was thick with the great man's literary legatee—as I, at least, supposed her—it was on some basis independent of his bringing anything out. Nevertheless he quite rose to the idea of my study, as I called it, which I put before him in a brief interview.

"You ought to have something. That thing has brought him to the front with a leap——!"

"The front? What do you call the front?"

He had laughed so good-humouredly that I could do the same. "Well, the front is where you and I are." I told him my paper was already finished.

"Ah then, you must write it again."

"Oh, but look at it first——!"

"You must write it again," Mr. Beston only repeated. Before I left him, however, he had explained a little. "You must see his sister."

"I shall be delighted to do that."

"She's a great friend of mine, and my having something may please her—which, though my first, my only duty is to please my subscribers and shareholders, is a thing I should rather like to do. I'll take from you something of the kind you mention, but only if she's favourably impressed by it."

I just hesitated, and it was not without a grain of hypocrisy that I artfully replied: "I would much rather *you* were!"

"Well, I shall be if she is." Mr. Beston spoke with gravity. "She can give you a good deal, don't you know?—all sorts of leads and glimpses. She naturally knows more about him than anyone. Besides, she's charming herself."

To dip so deep could only be an enticement; yet I already felt so saturated, felt my cup so full, that I almost wondered what was left to me to learn, almost feared to lose, in greater waters, my feet and my courage. At the same time I welcomed without reserve the opportunity my patron offered, making as my one condition that if Miss Delavoy assented he would print my article as it stood. It was arranged that he should tell her that I would, with her leave, call upon her, and I begged him to let her know in advance that I was prostrate before her brother. He had all the air of thinking that he should have put us in a relation by which *The Cynosure* would largely profit, and I left him with the peaceful consciousness that if I had baited my biggest hook he had opened his widest mouth. I wondered a little, in truth, how he could care enough for Delavoy without caring more than enough, but I may at once say that I was, in respect to Mr. Beston, now virtually in possession of my point of view. This had revealed to me an intellectual economy of the rarest kind. There was not a thing in the world—with a single exception, on which I shall presently touch—that he valued for itself, and not a scrap he knew about anything save whether or no it would do. To "do" with Mr. Beston, was to do for *The Cynosure*. The wonder was that he could know that of things of which he knew nothing else whatever.

There are a hundred reasons, even in this most private record, which, from a turn of mind so unlike Mr. Beston's, I keep exactly for a love of the fact in itself: there are a hundred confused delicacies, operating however late, that hold my hand from any motion to treat the question of the effect produced on me by first meeting with Miss Delavoy. I say there are a hundred, but it would better express my sense perhaps to speak of them all in the singular. Certain it is that one of them embraces and displaces the others. It was not the first time, and I dare say it was not even the second, that I grew sure of a shyness on the part of this young lady greater than any exhibition in such a line that my kindred constitution had ever allowed me to be clear about. My own diffidence, I may say, kept me in the dark so long that my perception of hers had to be retroactive—to go back and put together and, with an element of relief, interpret and fill out. It failed, inevitably, to operate in respect to a person in whom the infirmity of which I speak had none of the awkwardness, the tell-tale anguish, that makes it as a rule either ridiculous or tragic. It was too deep, too still, too general—it was perhaps even too proud. I must content myself, however, with saying that I have in all my life known nothing more beautiful than the faint, cool morning-mist of confidence less and less embarrassed in which it slowly evaporated. We have made the thing all out since, and we understand it all now. It took her longer than I measured to believe that a man without her particular knowledge could make such an approach to her particular love. The approach was made in my paper, which I left with her on my first visit and in which, on my second, she told me she had not an alteration to suggest. She said of it what I had occasionally, to an artist, heard said, or said myself, of a likeness happily caught: that to touch it again would spoil it, that it had "come" and must only be left. It may be imagined that after such a speech I was willing to wait for anything; unless indeed it be suggested that there could be then nothing more to wait for. A great deal more, at any rate, seemed to arrive,

and it was all in conversation about Delavoy that we ceased
to be hindered and hushed. The place was still full of him,
and in everything there that spoke to me I heard the sound
of his voice. I read his style into everything—I read it into his
sister. She was surrounded by his relics, his possessions, his
books; all of which were not many, for he had worked without
material reward: this only, however, made each more charged,
somehow, and more personal. He had been her only devotion,
and there were moments when she might have been taken for
the guardian of a temple or a tomb. That was what brought
me nearer than I had got even in my paper; the sense that it
was he, in a manner, who had made her, and that to be with
her was still to be with himself. It was not only that I could
talk to him so; it was that he listened and that he also talked.
Little by little and touch by touch she built him up to me;
and then it was, I confess, that I felt, in comparison, the
shrinkage of what I had written. It grew faint and small—
though indeed only for myself; it had from the first, for the
witness who counted so much more, a merit that I have ever
since reckoned the great good fortune of my life, and even, I
will go so far as to say, a fine case of inspiration. I hasten to
add that this case had been preceded by a still finer. Miss
Delavoy had made of her brother the year before his death a
portrait in pencil that was precious for two rare reasons. It
was the only representation of the sort in existence, and it was
a work of curious distinction. Conventional but sincere, highly
finished and smaller than life, it had a quality that, in any
collection, would have caused it to be scanned for some signature known to the initiated. It was a thing of real vision,
yet it was a thing of taste, and as soon as I learned that our
hero, sole of his species, had succeeded in never, save on this
occasion, sitting, least of all to a photographer, I took the full
measure of what the studied strokes of a pious hand would
some day represent for generations more aware of John Delavoy than, on the whole, his own had been. My feeling for
them was not diminished, moreover, by learning from my
young lady that Mr. Beston, who had given them some attention, had signified that, in the event of his publishing an
article, he would like a reproduction of the drawing to accompany it. The "pictures" in *The Cynosure* were in general

a marked chill to my sympathy: I had always held that, like good wine, honest prose needed, as it were, no bush. I took them as a sign that if good wine, as we know, is more and more hard to meet, the other commodity was becoming as scarce. The bushes, at all events, in *The Cynosure*, quite planted out the text; but my objection fell in the presence of Miss Delavoy's sketch, which already, in the forefront of my study, I saw as a flower in the coat of a bridegroom.

I was obliged just after my visit to leave town for three weeks and was, in the country, surprised at their elapsing without bringing me a proof from Mr. Beston. I finally wrote to ask of him an explanation of the delay; for which in turn I had again to wait so long that before I heard from him I received a letter from Miss Delavoy, who, thanking me as for a good office, let me know that our friend had asked her for the portrait. She appeared to suppose that I must have put in with him some word for it that availed more expertly than what had passed on the subject between themselves. This gave me occasion, on my return to town, to call on her for the purpose of explaining how little as yet, unfortunately, she owed me. I am not indeed sure that it didn't quicken my return. I knocked at her door with rather a vivid sense that if Mr. Beston had her drawing I was yet still without my proof. My privation was the next moment to feel a sharper pinch, for on entering her apartment I found Mr. Beston in possession. Then it was that I was fairly confronted with the problem given me from this time to solve. I began at that hour to look it straight in the face. What I in the first place saw was that Mr. Beston was "making up" to our hostess; what I saw in the second—what at any rate I believed I saw—was that she had come a certain distance to meet him; all of which would have been simple and usual enough had not the very things that gave it such a character been exactly the things I should least have expected. Even this first time, as my patron sat there, I made out somehow that in that position at least he was sincere and sound. Why should this have surprised me? Why should I immediately have asked myself how he would make it pay? He was there because he liked to be, and where was the wonder of his liking? There was no wonder in my own, I felt, so that my state of mind must have been already

a sign of how little I supposed we could like the same things.
This even strikes me, on looking back, as an implication sufficiently ungraceful of the absence on Miss Delavoy's part of
direct and designed attraction. I dare say indeed that Mr. Beston's subjection would have seemed to me a clearer thing if I
had not had by the same stroke to account for his friend's.
She liked him, and I grudged her that, though with the actual
limits of my knowledge of both parties I had literally to invent
reasons for its being a perversity, I could only in private treat
it as one, and this in spite of Mr. Beston's notorious power
to please. He was the handsomest man in "literary" London,
and, controlling the biggest circulation—a body of subscribers
as vast as a conscript army—he represented in a manner the
modern poetry of numbers. He was in love moreover, or he
thought he was; that flushed with a general glow the large
surface he presented. This surface, from my quiet corner,
struck me as a huge tract, a sort of particoloured map, a great
spotted social chart. He abounded in the names of things, and
his mind was like a great staircase at a party—you heard them
bawled at the top. He ought to have liked Miss Delavoy because *her* name, so announced, sounded well, and I grudged
him, as I grudged the young lady, the higher motive of an
intelligence of her charm. It was a charm so fine and so veiled
that if she had been a piece of prose or of verse I was sure he
would never have discovered it. The oddity was that, as the
case stood, he had seen she would "do." I too had seen it,
but then I was a critic: these remarks will sadly have miscarried
if they fail to show the reader how much of one.

III

I mentioned my paper and my disappointment, but I think it
was only in the light of subsequent events that I could fix an
impression of his having, at the moment, looked a trifle embarrassed. He smote his brow and took out his tablets; he
deplored the accident of which I complained, and promised
to look straight into it. An accident it could only have been,
the result of a particular pressure, a congestion of work. Of
course he had had my letter and had fully supposed it had
been answered and acted on. My spirits revived at this, and I

almost thought the incident happy when I heard Miss Delavoy herself put a clear question.

"It won't be for April, then, which was what I had hoped?"

It was what *I* had hoped, goodness knew, but if I had had no anxiety I should not have caught the low, sweet ring of her own. It made Mr. Beston's eyes fix her a moment, and, though the thing has as I write it a fatuous air, I remember thinking that he must at this instant have seen in her face almost all his contributor saw. If he did he couldn't wholly have enjoyed it; yet he replied genially enough: "I'll put it into June."

"Oh, June!" our companion murmured in a manner that I took as plaintive—even as exquisite.

Mr. Beston had got up. I had not promised myself to sit him out, much less to drive him away; and at this sign of his retirement I had a sense still dim, but much deeper, of being literally lifted by my check. Even before it was set up my article was somehow operative, so that I could look from one of my companions to the other and quite magnanimously smile. "June will do very well."

"Oh, if *you* say so——!" Miss Delavoy sighed and turned away.

"We must have time for the portrait; it will require great care," Mr. Beston said.

"Oh, please be sure it has the greatest!" I eagerly returned.

But Miss Delavoy took this up, speaking straight to Mr. Beston. "I attach no importance to the portrait. My impatience is all for the article."

"The article's very neat. It's very neat," Mr. Beston repeated. "But your drawing's our great prize."

"Your great prize," our young lady replied, "can only be the thing that tells most about my brother."

"Well, that's the case with your picture," Mr. Beston protested.

"How can you say that? My picture tells nothing in the world but that he never sat for another."

"Which is precisely the enormous and final fact!" I laughingly exclaimed.

Mr. Beston looked at me as if in uncertainty and just the least bit in disapproval; then he found his tone. "It's the big

fact for *The Cynosure*. I shall leave you in no doubt of *that*!"
he added, to Miss Delavoy, as he went away.

I was surprised at his going, but I inferred that, from the
pressure at the office, he had no choice; and I was at least not
too much surprised to guess the meaning of his last remark
to have been that our hostess must expect a handsome draft.
This allusion had so odd a grace on a lover's lips that, even
after the door had closed, it seemed still to hang there between Miss Delavoy and her second visitor. Naturally, however, we let it gradually drop; she only said with a kind of
conscious quickness: "I'm really very sorry for the delay." I
thought her beautiful as she spoke, and I felt that I had taken
with her a longer step than the visible facts explained. "Yes,
it's a great bore. But to an editor—one doesn't show it."

She seemed amused. "Are they such queer fish?"

I considered. "You know the great type."

"Oh, I don't know Mr. Beston as an editor."

"As what, then?"

"Well, as what you call, I suppose, a man of the world. A
very kind, clever one."

"Of course *I* see him mainly in the saddle and in the
charge—at the head of his hundreds of thousands. But I
mustn't undermine him," I added, smiling, "when he's doing
so much for me."

She appeared to wonder about it. "Is it really a great deal?"

"To publish a thing like that? Yes—as editors go. They're
all tarred with the same brush."

"Ah, but he has immense ideas. He goes in for the best in
all departments. That's his own phrase. He has often assured
me that he'll never stoop."

"He wants none but 'first-class stuff.' That's the way he has
expressed it to *me*; but it comes to the same thing. It's our
great comfort. He's charming."

"He's charming," my friend replied; and I thought for the
moment we had done with Mr. Beston. A rich reference to
him, none the less, struck me as flashing from her very next
words—words that she uttered without appearing to have noticed any I had pronounced in the interval. "Does no one,
then, really care for my brother?"

I was startled by the length of her flight. "Really care?"

"No one but you? Every month your study doesn't appear is at this time a kind of slight."

"I see what you mean. But of course *we're* serious."

"Whom do you mean by 'we'?"

"Well, you and me."

She seemed to look us all over and not to be struck with our mass. "And no one else? No one else is serious?"

"What I should say is that no one *feels* the whole thing, don't you know? as much."

Miss Delavoy hesitated. "Not even so much as Mr. Beston?" And her eyes, as she named him, waited, to my surprise, for my answer.

I couldn't quite see why she returned to him, so that my answer was rather lame. "Don't ask me too many things; else there are some *I* shall have to ask."

She continued to look at me; after which she turned away. "Then I won't—for I don't understand him." She turned away, I say, but the next moment had faced about with a fresh, inconsequent question. "Then why in the world has he cooled off?"

"About my paper? *Has* he cooled? Has he shown you that otherwise?" I asked.

"Than by his delay? Yes, by silence—and by worse."

"What do you call worse?"

"Well, to say of it—and twice over—what he said just now."

"That it's very 'neat'? You don't think it *is*?" I laughed.

"I don't say it"; and with that she smiled. "My brother might hear!"

Her tone was such that, while it lingered in the air, it deepened, prolonging the interval, whatever point there was in this; unspoken things therefore had passed between us by the time I at last brought out: "He hasn't read me! It doesn't matter," I quickly went on; "his relation to what I may do or not do is, for his own purposes, quite complete enough without that."

She seemed struck with this. "Yes, his relation to almost anything is extraordinary."

"His relation to everything!" It rose visibly before us and, as we felt, filled the room with its innumerable, indistinguishable objects. "Oh, it's the making of him!"

She evidently recognised all this, but after a minute she again broke out: "You say he hasn't read you and that it doesn't matter. But has he read my brother? Doesn't *that* matter?"

I waved away the thought. "For what do you take him, and why in the world should it? He knows perfectly what he wants to do, and his postponement is quite in your interest. The reproduction of the drawing——"

She took me up. "I hate the drawing!"

"So do I," I laughed, "and I rejoice in there being something on which we can feel so together!"

IV

What may further have passed between us on this occasion loses, as I try to recall it, all colour in the light of a communication that I had from her four days later. It consisted of a note in which she announced to me that she had heard from Mr. Beston in terms that troubled her: a letter from Paris—he had dashed over on business—abruptly proposing that she herself should, as she quoted, give him something; something that her intimate knowledge of the subject—which was of course John Delavoy—her rare opportunities for observation and study would make precious, would make as unique as the work of her pencil. He appealed to her to gratify him in this particular, exhorted her to sit right down to her task, reminded her that to tell a loving sister's tale was her obvious, her highest duty. She confessed to mystification and invited me to explain. Was this sudden perception of her duty a result on Mr. Beston's part of any difference with myself? Did he want two papers? Did he want an alternative to mine? Did he want hers as a supplement or as a substitute? She begged instantly to be informed if anything had happened to mine. To meet her request I had first to make sure, and I repaired on the morrow to Mr. Beston's office in the eager hope that he was back from Paris. This hope was crowned; he had crossed in the night and was in his room; so that on sending up my card I was introduced to his presence, where I promptly broke ground by letting him know that I had had even yet no proof.

"Oh, yes! about Delavoy. Well, I've rather expected you, but you must excuse me if I'm brief. My absence has put me back; I've returned to arrears. Then from Paris I meant to write to you, but even there I was up to my neck. I think, too, I've instinctively held off a little. You won't like what I have to say—you *can't*!" He spoke almost as if I might wish to prove I could. "The fact is, you see, your thing won't do. No—not even a little."

Even after Miss Delavoy's note it was a blow, and I felt myself turn pale. "Not even a little? Why, I thought you wanted it so!"

Mr. Beston just perceptibly braced himself. "My dear man, we didn't want *that*! We couldn't do it. I've every desire to be agreeable to you, but we really couldn't."

I sat staring. "What in the world's the matter with it?"

"Well, it's impossible. That's what's the matter with it."

"Impossible?" There rolled over me the ardent hours and a great wave of the feeling that I had put into it.

He hung back but an instant—he faced the music. "It's indecent."

I could only wildly echo him. "Indecent? Why, it's absolutely, it's almost to the point of a regular chill, expository. What in the world is it but critical?"

Mr. Beston's retort was prompt. "Too critical by half! That's just where it is. It says too much."

"But what it says is all about its subject."

"I dare say, but I don't think we want quite so much about its subject."

I seemed to swing in the void and I clutched, fallaciously, at the nearest thing. "What you do want, then—what is *that* to be about?"

"That's for you to find out—it's not my business to tell you."

It was dreadful, this snub to my happy sense that I *had* found out. "I thought you wanted John Delavoy. I've simply stuck to him."

Mr. Beston gave a dry laugh. "I should think you had!" Then after an instant he turned oracular. "Perhaps we wanted him—perhaps we didn't. We didn't at any rate want indelicacy."

"Indelicacy?" I almost shrieked. "Why it's pure portraiture."

"'Pure,' my dear fellow, just begs the question. It's most objectionable—that's what it is. For portraiture of *such* things, at all events, there's no place in our scheme."

I speculated. "Your scheme for an account of Delavoy?"

Mr. Beston looked as if I trifled. "Our scheme for a successful magazine."

"No place, do I understand you, for criticism? No place for the great figures——? If you don't want too much detail," I went on, "I recall perfectly that I was careful not to go into it. What I tried for was a general vivid picture—which I really supposed I arrived at. I boiled the man down—I gave the three or four leading notes. *Them* I did try to give with some intensity."

Mr. Beston, while I spoke, had turned about and, with a movement that confessed to impatience and even not a little, I thought, to irritation, fumbled on his table among a mass of papers and other objects; after which he had pulled out a couple of drawers. Finally he fronted me anew with my copy in his hand, and I had meanwhile added a word about the disadvantage at which he placed me. To have made me wait was unkind; but to have made me wait for such news——! I ought at least to have been told it earlier. He replied to this that he had not at first had time to read me, and, on the evidence of my other things, had taken me pleasantly for granted: he had only been enlightened by the revelation of the proof. What he had fished out of his drawer was, in effect, not my manuscript, but the "galleys" that had never been sent me. The thing was all set up there, and my companion, with eyeglass and thumb, dashed back the sheets and looked up and down for places. The proof-reader, he mentioned, had so waked him up with the blue pencil that he had no difficulty in finding them. They were all in his face when he again looked at me. "Did you candidly think that we were going to print this?"

All my silly young pride in my performance quivered as if under the lash. "Why the devil else should I have taken the trouble to write it? If you're not going to print it, why the devil did you ask me for it?"

"I didn't ask you. You proposed it yourself."

"You jumped at it; you quite agreed you ought to have it: it comes to the same thing. So indeed you ought to have it. It's too ignoble, your not taking up such a man."

He looked at me hard. "I *have* taken him up. I do want something about him, and I've got his portrait there—coming out beautifully."

"Do you mean you've taken him up," I inquired, "by asking for something of his sister? Why, in that case, do you speak as if I had forced on you the question of a paper? If you want one you want one."

Mr. Beston continued to sound me. "How do you know what I've asked of his sister?"

"I know what Miss Delavoy tells me. She let me know it as soon as she had heard from you."

"Do you mean that you've just seen her?"

"I've not seen her since the time I met you at her house; but I had a note from her yesterday. She couldn't understand your appeal—in the face of knowing what I've done myself."

Something seemed to tell me at this instant that she had not yet communicated with Mr. Beston, but that he wished me not to know she hadn't. It came out still more in the temper with which he presently said: "I want what Miss Delavoy can do, but I don't want this kind of thing!" And he shook my proof at me as if for a preliminary to hurling it.

I took it from him, to show I anticipated his violence, and, profoundly bewildered, I turned over the challenged pages. They grinned up at me with the proof-reader's shocks, but the shocks, as my eye caught them, bloomed on the spot like flowers. I didn't feel abased—so many of my good things came back to me. "What on earth do you seriously mean? This thing isn't bad. It's awfully good—it's beautiful."

With an odd movement he plucked it back again, though not indeed as if from any new conviction. He had had after all a kind of contact with it that had made it a part of his stock. "I dare say it's clever. For the kind of thing it is, it's as beautiful as you like. It's simply not *our* kind." He seemed to break out afresh. "Didn't you know more——?"

I waited. "More what?"

He in turn did the same. "More everything. More about Delavoy. The whole point was that I thought you did."

I fell back in my chair. "You think my article shows ignorance? I sat down to it with the sense that I knew more than any one."

Mr. Beston restored it again to my hands. "You've kept that pretty well out of sight then. Didn't you get anything out of *her*? It was simply for that I addressed you to her."

I took from him with this, as well, a silent statement of what it had not been for. "I got everything in the wide world I could. We almost worked together, but what appeared was that all her own knowledge, all her own view, quite fell in with what I had already said. There appeared nothing to subtract or to add."

He looked hard again, not this time at me, but at the document in my hands. "You mean she has gone into all that—seen it just as it stands there?"

"If I've still," I replied, "any surprise left, it's for the surprise your question implies. You put our heads together, and you've surely known all along that they've remained so. She told me a month ago that she had immediately let you know the good she thought of what I had done."

Mr. Beston very candidly remembered, and I could make out that if he flushed as he did so it was because what most came back to him was his own simplicity. "I see. That must have been why I trusted you—sent you, without control, straight off to be set up. But now that I see you——!" he went on.

"You're surprised at her indulgence?"

Once more he snatched at the record of my rashness—once more he turned it over. Then he read out two or three paragraphs. "Do you mean she has gone into all that?"

"My dear sir, what do you take her for? There wasn't a line we didn't thresh out, and our talk wouldn't for either of us have been a bit interesting if it hadn't been really frank. Have you to learn at this time of day," I continued, "what her feeling is about her brother's work? She's not a bit stupid. She has a kind of worship for it."

Mr. Beston kept his eyes on one of my pages. "She passed her life with him and was extremely fond of him."

"Yes, and she has the point of view and no end of ideas. She's tremendously intelligent."

Our friend at last looked up at me, but I scarce knew what to make of his expression. "Then she'll do me exactly what I want."

"Another article, you mean, to replace mine?"

"Of a totally different sort. Something the public *will* stand." His attention reverted to my proof, and he suddenly reached out for a pencil. He made a great dash against a block of my prose and placed the page before me. "Do you pretend to me they'll stand *that?*"

"That" proved, as I looked at it, a summary of the subject, deeply interesting and treated, as I thought, with extraordinary art, of the work to which I gave the highest place in my author's array. I took it in, sounding it hard for some hidden vice, but with a frank relish, in effect, of its lucidity; then I answered: "If they won't stand it, what will they stand?"

Mr. Beston looked about and put a few objects on his table to rights. "They won't stand anything." He spoke with such pregnant brevity as to make his climax stronger. "And quite right too! *I'm* right, at any rate; I can't plead ignorance. I know where I am, and I want to stay there. That single page would have cost me five thousand subscribers."

"Why, that single page is a statement of the very essence——!"

He turned sharp round at me. "Very essence of what?"

"Of my very topic, damn it."

"Your very topic is John Delavoy."

"And what's *his* very topic? Am I not to attempt to utter it? What under the sun else am I writing about?"

"You're not writing in *The Cynosure* about the relations of the sexes. With those relations, with the question of sex in any degree, I should suppose you would already have seen that we have nothing whatever to do. If you want to know what our public won't stand, there you have it."

I seem to recall that I smiled sweetly as I took it. "I don't know, I think, what you mean by those phrases, which strike me as too empty and too silly, and of a nature therefore to be more deplored than any, I'm positive, that I use in my analysis. I don't use a single one that even remotely resembles them.

I simply try to express my author, and if your public won't stand his being expressed, mention to me kindly the source of its interest in him."

Mr. Beston was perfectly ready. "He's all the rage with the clever people—that's the source. The interest of the public is whatever a clever article may make it."

"I don't understand you. How can an article be clever, to begin with, and how can it make anything of anything, if it doesn't avail itself of material?"

"There *is* material, which I'd hoped you'd use. Miss Delavoy has lots of material. I don't know what she has told you, but I know what she has told *me*." He hung fire but an instant. "Quite lovely things."

"And have you told *her*——?"

"Told her what?" he asked as I paused.

"The lovely things you've just told me."

Mr. Beston got up; folding the rest of my proof together, he made the final surrender with more dignity than I had looked for. "You can do with this what you like." Then as he reached the door with me: "Do you suppose that I talk with Miss Delavoy on such subjects?" I answered that he could leave that to me—I shouldn't mind so doing; and I recall that before I quitted him something again passed between us on the question of her drawing. "What we want," he said, "is just the really nice thing, the pleasant, right thing to go with it. That drawing's going to take!"

V

A few minutes later I had wired to our young lady that, should I hear nothing from her to the contrary, I would come to her that evening. I had other affairs that kept me out; and on going home I found a word to the effect that though she should not be free after dinner she hoped for my presence at five o'clock: a notification betraying to me that the evening would, by arrangement, be Mr. Beston's hour and that she wished to see me first. At five o'clock I was there, and as soon as I entered the room I perceived two things. One of these was that she had been highly impatient; the other was that she had not heard, since my call on him, from Mr. Beston, and that her arrangement with him therefore dated from earlier. The tea-service was by the fire—she herself was at the window; and I am at a loss to name the particular revelation that I drew from this fact of her being restless on general grounds. My telegram had fallen in with complications at which I could only guess; it had not found her quiet; she was living in a troubled air. But her wonder leaped from her lips. "He does want two?"

I had brought in my proof with me, putting it in my hat and my hat on a chair. "Oh, no—he wants only one, only yours."

Her wonder deepened. "He won't print——?"

"My poor old stuff! He returns it with thanks."

"Returns it? When he had accepted it!"

"Oh, that doesn't prevent—when he doesn't like it."

"But he does; he did. He liked it to *me*. He called it 'sympathetic.'"

"He only meant that *you* are—perhaps even that I myself am. He hadn't read it then. He read it but a day or two ago, and horror seized him."

Miss Delavoy dropped into a chair. "Horror?"

"I don't know how to express to you the fault he finds with it." I had gone to the fire, and I looked to where it peeped out of my hat; my companion did the same, and her face showed the pain she might have felt, in the street, at sight of the victim of an accident. "It appears it's indecent."

She sprang from her chair. "To describe my brother?"

"As *I've* described him. That, at any rate, is how my account sins. What I've said is unprintable." I leaned against the chimney-piece with a serenity of which, I admit, I was conscious; I rubbed it in and felt a private joy in watching my influence.

"Then what *have* you said?"

"You know perfectly. You heard my thing from beginning to end. You said it was beautiful."

She remembered as I looked at her; she showed all the things she called back. "It *was* beautiful." I went over and picked it up; I came back with it to the fire. "It was the best thing ever said about him," she went on. "It was the finest and truest."

"Well, then——!" I exclaimed.

"But what have you done to it since?"

"I haven't touched it since."

"You've put nothing else in?"

"Not a line—not a syllable. Don't you remember how you warned me against spoiling it? It's of the thing we read together, liked together, went over and over together; it's of this dear little serious thing of good sense and good faith"—and I held up my roll of proof, shaking it even as Mr. Beston had shaken it—"that he expresses that opinion."

She frowned at me with an intensity that, though bringing me no pain, gave me a sense of her own. "Then that's why he has asked *me*——?"

"To do something instead. But something pure. You, he hopes, won't be indecent."

She sprang up, more mystified than enlightened; she had pieced things together, but they left the question gaping. "Is he mad? What is he talking about?"

"Oh, *I* know—now. Has he specified what he wants of you?"

She thought a moment, all before me. "Yes—to be very 'personal.'"

"Precisely. You mustn't speak of the work."

She almost glared. "Not speak of it?"

"That's indecent."

"My brother's work?"

"To speak of it."

She took this from me as she had not taken anything. "Then how can I speak of him at all?—how can I articulate? He *was* his work."

"Certainly he was. But that's not the kind of truth that will stand in Mr. Beston's way. Don't you know what he means by wanting you to be personal?"

In the way she looked at me there was still for a moment a dim desire to spare him—even perhaps a little to save him. None the less, after an instant, she let herself go. "Something horrible?"

"Horrible; so long, that is, as it takes the place of something more honest and really so much more clean. He wants—what do they call the stuff?—anecdotes, glimpses, gossip, chat; a picture of his 'home life,' domestic habits, diet, dress, arrangements—all his little ways and little secrets, and even, to better it still, all your own, your relations with him, your feelings about him, his feelings about *you*: both his and yours, in short, about anything else you can think of. Don't you see what I mean?" She saw so well that, in the dismay of it, she grasped my arm an instant, half as if to steady herself, half as if to stop me. But she couldn't stop me. "He wants you just to write round and round that portrait."

She was lost in the reflections I had stirred, in apprehensions and indignations that slowly surged and spread; and for a moment she was unconscious of everything else. "What portrait?"

"Why, the beautiful one you did. The beautiful one you gave him."

"Did I give it to him? Oh, yes!" It came back to her, but this time she blushed red, and I saw what had occurred to her. It occurred, in fact, at the same instant to myself. "Ah, *par exemple*," she cried, "he shan't have it!"

I couldn't help laughing. "My dear young lady, unfortunately he *has* got it!"

"He shall send it back. He shan't use it."

"I'm afraid he *is* using it," I replied. "I'm afraid he *has* used it. They've begun to work on it."

She looked at me almost as if I were Mr. Beston. "Then they must stop working on it." Something in her decision somehow thrilled me. "Mr. Beston must send it straight back. Indeed I'll wire to him to bring it to-night."

"Is he coming to-night?" I ventured to inquire.

She held her head very high. "Yes, he's coming to-night. It's most happy!" she bravely added, as if to forestall any suggestion that it could be anything else.

I thought a moment; first about that, then about something that presently made me say: "Oh, well, if he brings it back——!"

She continued to look at me. "Do you mean you doubt his doing so?"

I thought again. "You'll probably have a stiff time with him."

She made, for a little, no answer to this but to sound me again with her eyes; our silence, however, was carried off by her then abruptly turning to her tea-tray and pouring me out a cup. "Will you do me a favour?" she asked as I took it.

"Any favour in life."

"Will you be present?"

"Present?"—I failed at first to imagine.

"When Mr. Beston comes."

It was so much more than I had expected that I of course looked stupid in my surprise. "This evening—here?"

"This evening—here. Do you think my request very strange?"

I pulled myself together. "How can I tell when I'm so awfully in the dark?"

"In the dark——?" She smiled at me as if I were a person who carried such lights!

"About the nature, I mean, of your friendship."

"With Mr. Beston?" she broke in. Then in the wonderful way that women say such things: "It has always been so pleasant."

"Do you think it will be pleasant for *me*?" I laughed.

"Our friendship? I don't care whether it is or not!"

"I mean what you'll have out with him—for of course you *will* have it out. Do you think it will be pleasant for *him*?"

"To find you here—or to see you come in? I don't feel obliged to think. This is a matter in which I now care for no one but my brother—for nothing but his honour. I stand only on that."

I can't say how high, with these words, she struck me as standing, nor how the look that she gave me with them seemed to make me spring up beside her. We were at this elevation together a moment. "I'll do anything in the world you say."

"Then please come about nine."

That struck me as so tantamount to saying "And please therefore go this minute" that I immediately turned to the door. Before I passed it, however, I gave her time to ring out clear: "I know what I'm about!" She proved it the next moment by following me into the hall with the request that

I would leave her my proof. I placed it in her hands, and if she knew what she was about I wondered, outside, what *I* was.

VI

I dare say it was the desire to make this out that, in the evening, brought me back a little before my time. Mr. Beston had not arrived, and it's worth mentioning—for it was rather odd—that while we waited for him I sat with my hostess in silence. She spoke of my paper, which she had read over—but simply to tell me she had done so; and that was practically all that passed between us for a time at once so full and so quiet that it struck me neither as short nor as long. We felt, in the matter, so indivisible that we might have been united in some observance or some sanctity—to go through something decorously appointed. Without an observation we listened to the door-bell, and, still without one, a minute later, saw the person we expected stand there and show his surprise. It was at me he looked as he spoke to her.

"I'm not to see you alone?"

"Not just yet, please," Miss Delavoy answered. "Of what has suddenly come between us this gentleman is essentially a part, and I really think he'll be less present if we speak before him than if we attempt to deal with the question without him." Mr. Beston was amused, but not enough amused to sit down, and we stood there while, for the third time, my proof-sheets were shaken for emphasis. "I've been reading these over," she said as she held them up.

Mr. Beston, on what he had said to me of them, could only look grave; but he tried also to look pleasant, and I foresaw that, on the whole, he would really behave well. "They're remarkably clever."

"And yet you wish to publish instead of them something from so different a hand?"

He smiled now very kindly. "If you'll only let me have it! *Won't* you let me have it? I'm sure you know exactly the thing I want."

"Oh, perfectly!"

"I've tried to give her an idea of it," I threw in.

Mr. Beston promptly saw his way to make this a reproach to me. "Then, after all, you had one yourself?"

"I think I couldn't have kept so clear of it if I hadn't had!" I laughed.

"I'll write you something," Miss Delavoy went on, "if you'll print this as it stands." My proof was still in her keeping.

Mr. Beston raised his eyebrows. "Print two? Whatever do I want with two? What do I want with the wrong one if I can get the beautiful right?"

She met this, to my surprise, with a certain gaiety. "It's a big subject—a subject to be seen from different sides. Don't you want a full, a various treatment? Our papers will have nothing in common."

"I should hope not!" Mr. Beston said good-humouredly. "You have command, dear lady, of a point of view too good to spoil. It so happens that your brother has been really less handled than anyone, so that there's a kind of obscurity about him, and in consequence a kind of curiosity, that it seems to me quite a crime not to work. There's just the perfection, don't you know? of a little sort of mystery—a tantalizing *demi-jour*." He continued to smile at her as if he thoroughly hoped to kindle her, and it was interesting at that moment to get this vivid glimpse of his conception.

I could see it quickly enough break out in Miss Delavoy, who sounded for an instant almost assenting. "And you want the obscurity and the mystery, the tantalizing *demi-jour*, cleared up?"

"I want a little lovely, living thing! Don't be perverse," he pursued, "don't stand in your own light and in your brother's and in this young man's—in the long run, and in mine too and in every one's: just let us have him out as no one but you can bring him and as, by the most charming of chances and a particular providence, he has been kept all this time just on purpose for you to bring. Really, you know"—his vexation *would* crop up—"one could howl to see such good stuff wasted!"

"Well," our young lady returned, "that holds good of one thing as well as of another. I can never hope to describe or express my brother as these pages describe and express him;

but, as I tell you, approaching him from a different direction, I promise to do my very best. Only, my condition remains."

Mr. Beston transferred his eyes from her face to the little bundle in her hand, where they rested with an intensity that made me privately wonder if it represented some vain vision of a snatch defeated in advance by the stupidity of his having suffered my copy to be multiplied. "My printing that?"

"Your printing this."

Mr. Beston wavered there between us: I could make out in him a vexed inability to keep us as distinct as he would have liked. But he was triumphantly light. "It's impossible. Don't be a pair of fools!"

"Very well, then," said Miss Delavoy; "please send me back my drawing."

"Oh dear, no!" Mr. Beston laughed. "Your drawing we must have at any rate."

"Ah, but I forbid you to use it! This gentleman is my witness that my prohibition is absolute."

"Was it to be your witness that you sent for the gentleman? You take immense precautions!" Mr. Beston exclaimed. Before she could retort, however, he came back to his strong point. "Do you coolly ask of me to sacrifice ten thousand subscribers?"

The number, I noticed, had grown since the morning, but Miss Delavoy faced it boldly. "If you do, you'll be well rid of them. They must be ignoble, your ten thousand subscribers."

He took this perfectly. "You dispose of them easily! Ignoble or not, what I have to do is to keep them and if possible add to their number; not to get rid of them."

"You'd rather get rid of my poor brother instead?"

"I don't get rid of him. I pay him a signal attention. Reducing it to the least, I publish his portrait."

"His portrait—the only one worth speaking of? Why, you turn it out with horror."

"Do you call the only one worth speaking of that misguided effort?" And, obeying a restless impulse, he appeared to reach for my tribute; not, I think, with any conscious plan, but with a vague desire in some way again to point his moral with it.

I liked immensely the motion with which, in reply to this, she put it behind her: her gesture expressed so distinctly her vision of her own lesson. From that moment, somehow, they struck me as forgetting me, and I seemed to see them as they might have been alone together; even to see a little what, for each, had held and what had divided them. I remember how, at this, I almost held my breath, effacing myself to let them go, make them show me whatever they might. "It's the only one," she insisted, "that tells, about its subject, anything that's anyone's business. If you really want John Delavoy, there he is. If you don't want him, don't insult him with an evasion and a pretence. Have at least the courage to say that you're afraid of him!"

I figured Mr. Beston here as much incommoded; but all too simply, doubtless, for he clearly held on, smiling through flushed discomfort and on the whole bearing up. "Do you think I'm afraid of *you*?" He might forget me, but he would have to forget me a little more to yield completely to his visible impulse to take her hand. It was visible enough to herself to make her show that she declined to meet it, and even that his effect on her was at last distinctly exasperating. Oh, how I saw at that moment that in the really touching good faith of his personal sympathy he didn't measure his effect! If he had done so he wouldn't have tried to rush it, to carry it off with tenderness. He dropped to that now so rashly that I was in truth sorry for him. "You *could* do so gracefully, so naturally what we want. What we want, don't you see? is perfect taste. I know better than you do yourself how perfect yours would be. I always know better than people do themselves." He jested and pleaded, getting in, benightedly, deeper. Perhaps I didn't literally hear him ask in the same accents if she didn't care for him at all, but I distinctly saw him look as if he were on the point of it, and something, at any rate, in a lower tone, dropped from him that he followed up with the statement that if she did even just a little she would help him.

VII

She made him wait a deep minute for her answer to this, and that gave me time to read into it what he accused her of failing to do. I recollect that I was startled at their having come so far, though I was reassured, after a little, by seeing that he had come much the furthest. I had now I scarce know what amused sense of knowing our hostess so much better than he. "I think you strangely inconsequent," she said at last. "If you associate with—what you speak of—the idea of help, does it strike you as helping *me* to treat in that base fashion the memory I most honour and cherish?" As I was quite sure of what he spoke of I could measure the force of this challenge. "Have you never discovered, all this time, that my brother's work is my pride and my joy?"

"Oh, my dear thing!"—and Mr. Beston broke into a cry that combined in the drollest way the attempt to lighten his guilt with the attempt to deprecate hers. He let it just flash upon us that, should he be pushed, he would show as—well, scandalised.

The tone in which Miss Delavoy again addressed him offered a reflection of this gleam. "Do you know what my brother would think of you?"

He was quite ready with his answer, and there was no moment in the whole business at which I thought so well of him. "I don't care a hang what your brother would think!"

"Then why do you wish to commemorate him?"

"How can you ask so innocent a question? It isn't for *him*."

"You mean it's for the public?"

"It's for the magazine," he said with a noble simplicity.

"The magazine *is* the public," it made me so far forget myself as to suggest.

"You've discovered it late in the day! Yes," he went on to our companion, "I don't in the least mind saying I don't care. I don't—I don't!" he repeated with a sturdiness in which I somehow recognised that he was, after all, a great editor. He looked at me a moment as if he even guessed what I saw, and, not unkindly, desired to force it home. "I don't care for anybody. It's not my business to care. That's not the way to run a magazine. Except of course as a mere man!"—and he added a smile for Miss Delavoy. He covered the whole ground again. "Your reminiscences would make a talk!"

She came back from the greatest distance she had yet reached. "My reminiscences?"

"To accompany the head." He must have been as tender as if I had been away. "Don't I see how you'd do them?"

She turned off, standing before the fire and looking into it; after which she faced him again. "If you'll publish our friend here, I'll do them."

"Why are you so awfully wound up about our friend here?"

"Read his article over—with a little intelligence—and your question will be answered."

Mr. Beston glanced at me and smiled as if with a loyal warning; then, with a good conscience, he let me have it. "Oh, damn his article!"

I was struck with her replying exactly what I should have replied if I had not been so detached. "Damn it as much as you like, but publish it." Mr. Beston, on this, turned to me as if to ask me if I had not heard enough to satisfy me: there was a visible offer in his face to give me more if I insisted. This amounted to an appeal to me to leave the room at least for a minute; and it was perhaps from the fear of what might pass between us that Miss Delavoy once more took him up. "If my brother's as vile as you say——!"

"Oh, I don't say *he*'s vile!" he broke in.

"You only say *I* am!" I commented.

"You've entered so into him," she replied to me, "that it comes to the same thing. And Mr. Beston says further that out of this unmentionableness he wants somehow to make something—some money or some sensation."

"My dear lady," said Mr. Beston, "it's a very great literary figure!"

"Precisely. You advertise yourself with it because it's a very great literary figure, and it's a very great literary figure because it wrote very great literary things that you wouldn't for the world allow to be intelligibly or critically named. So you bid for the still more striking tribute of an intimate picture—an unveiling of God knows what!—without even having the pluck or the logic to say on what ground it is that you go in for naming him at all. Do you know, dear Mr. Beston," she asked, "that you make me very sick? I count on receiving the portrait," she concluded, "by to-morrow evening at latest."

I felt, before this speech was over, so sorry for her interlocutor that I was on the point of asking her if she mightn't finish him without my help. But I had lighted a flame that was to consume me too, and I was aware of the scorch of it while I watched Mr. Beston plead frankly, if tacitly, that, though there was something in him not to be finished, she must yet give him a moment and let him take his time to look about him at pictures and books. He took it with more coolness than I; then he produced his answer. "You shall receive it to-morrow morning if you'll do what I asked the last time." I could see more than he how the last time had been overlaid by what had since come up; so that, as she opposed a momentary blank, I felt almost a coarseness in his recall of it with an "Oh, you know—you know!"

Yes, after a little she knew, and I need scarcely add that I did. I felt, in the oddest way, by this time, that she was conscious of my penetration and wished to make me, for the loss now so clearly beyond repair, the only compensation in her power. This compensation consisted of her showing me that she was indifferent to my having guessed the full extent of the privilege that, on the occasion to which he alluded, she had permitted Mr. Beston to put before her. The balm for my wound was therefore to see what she resisted. She resisted Mr. Beston in more ways than one. "And if I don't do it?" she demanded.

"I'll simply keep your picture!"

"To what purpose if you don't use it?"

"To keep it *is* to use it," Mr. Beston said.

"He has only to keep it long enough," I added, and with the intention that may be imagined, "to bring you round, by the mere sense of privation, to meet him on the other ground."

Miss Delavoy took no more notice of this speech than if she had not heard it, and Mr. Beston showed that he had heard it only enough to show, more markedly, that he followed her example. "I'll do anything, I'll do everything for you in life," he declared to her, "but publish such a thing as that."

She gave in all decorum to this statement the minute of concentration that belonged to it; but her analysis of the matter had for sole effect to make her at last bring out, not with harshness, but with a kind of wondering pity: "I think you're really very dreadful!"

"In what esteem then, Mr. Beston," I asked, "do you hold John Delavoy's work?"

He rang out clear. "As the sort of thing that's out of our purview!" If for a second he had hesitated it was partly, I judge, with just resentment at my so directly addressing him, and partly, though he wished to show our friend that he fairly faced the question, because experience had not left him in such a case without two or three alternatives. He had already made plain indeed that he mostly preferred the simplest.

"Wonderful, wonderful purview!" I quite sincerely, or at all events very musingly, exclaimed.

"Then, if you could ever have got one of his novels——?" Miss Delavoy inquired.

He smiled at the way she put it; it made such an image of the attitude of *The Cynosure*. But he was kind and explicit. "There isn't one that wouldn't have been beyond us. We could never have run him. We could never have handled him. We could never, in fact, have touched him. We should have dropped to—oh, Lord!" He saw the ghastly figure he couldn't name—he brushed it away with a shudder.

I turned, on this, to our companion. "I wish awfully you'd do what he asks!" She stared an instant, mystified; then I quickly explained to which of his requests I referred. "I mean I wish you'd do the nice familiar chat about the sweet home-life. You might make it inimitable, and, upon my word, I'd give you for it the assistance of my general lights. The thing is—don't you see?—that it would put Mr. Beston in a grand position. Your position would be grand," I hastened to add as I looked at him, "because it would be so admirably false." Then, more seriously, I felt the impulse even to warn him. "I don't think you're quite aware of what you'd make it. Are you really quite conscious?" I went on with a benevolence that struck him, I was presently to learn, as a depth of fatuity.

He was to show once more that he was a rock. "Conscious? Why should I be? Nobody's conscious."

He was splendid; yet before I could control it I had risked the challenge of a "Nobody?"

"Who's anybody? The public isn't!"

"Then why are you afraid of it?" Miss Delavoy demanded.

"Don't ask him that," I answered; "you expose yourself to his telling you that, if the public isn't anybody, that's still more the case with your brother."

Mr. Beston appeared to accept as a convenience this somewhat inadequate protection; he at any rate under cover of it again addressed us lucidly. "There's only one false position—the one you seem so to wish to put me in."

I instantly met him. "That of losing——?"

"That of losing——!"

"Oh, fifty thousand—yes. And they wouldn't see anything the matter——?"

"With the position," said Mr. Beston, "that you qualify, I neither know nor care why, as false." Suddenly, in a different tone, almost genially, he continued: "For what do you take them?"

For what indeed?—but it didn't signify. "It's enough that I take *you*—for one of the masters." It's literal that as he stood there in his florid beauty and complete command I felt his infinite force, and, with a gush of admiration, wondered how, for our young lady, there could be at such a moment another man. "We represent different sides," I rather lamely said. However, I picked up. "It isn't a question of where we are, but of what. You're not on a side—you *are* a side. You're the right one. What a misery," I pursued, "for us not to be 'on' you!"

His eyes showed me for a second that he yet saw how our not being on him did just have for it that it could facilitate such a speech; then they rested afresh on Miss Delavoy, and that brought him back to firm ground. "I don't think you can imagine how it will come out."

He was astride of the portrait again, and presently again she had focussed him. "If it does come out——!" she began, poor girl; but it was not to take her far.

"Well, if it does——?"

"He means what will you do then?" I observed, as she had nothing to say.

"Mr. Beston will see," she at last replied with a perceptible lack of point.

He took this up in a flash. "My dear young lady, it's *you* who'll see; and when you've seen you'll forgive me. Only wait till you do!" He was already at the door, as if he quite believed in what he should gain by the gain, from this moment, of time. He stood there but an instant—he looked from one of us to the other. "It will be a ripping little thing!" he remarked; and with that he left us gaping.

VIII

The first use I made of our rebound was to say with intensity: "What *will* you do if he does?"

"Does publish the picture?" There was an instant charm to me in the privacy of her full collapse and the sudden high tide of our common defeat. "What *can* I? It's all very well; but there's nothing to be done. I want never to see him again. There's only something," she went on, "that *you* can do."

"Prevent him?—get it back? I'll do, be sure, my utmost; but it will be difficult without a row."

"What do you mean by a row?" she asked.

"I mean it will be difficult without publicity. I don't think we want publicity."

She turned this over. "Because it will advertise him?"

"His magnificent energy. Remember what I just now told him. He's the right side."

"And we're the wrong!" she laughed. "We mustn't make that known—I see. But, all the same, save my sketch!"

I held her hands. "And if I do?"

"Ah, get it back first!" she answered, ever so gently and with a smile, but quite taking them away.

I got it back, alas! neither first nor last; though indeed at the end this was to matter, as I thought and as I found, little enough. Mr. Beston rose to his full height and was not to abate an inch even on my offer of another article on a subject notoriously unobjectionable. The only portrait of John Delavoy was going, as he had said, to take, and nothing was to stand in its way. I besieged his office, I waylaid his myrmidons, I haunted his path, I poisoned, I tried to flatter myself, his life; I wrote him at any rate letters by the dozen and showed him up to his friends and his enemies. The only thing I didn't do was to urge Miss Delavoy to write to her solicitors or to the newspapers. The final result, of course, of what I did and

what I didn't was to create, on the subject of the sole copy
of so rare an original, a curiosity that, by the time *The Cynosure* appeared with the reproduction, made the month's sale,
as I was destined to learn, take a tremendous jump. The portrait of John Delavoy, prodigiously "paragraphed" in advance
and with its authorship flushing through, was accompanied by
a page or two, from an anonymous hand, of the pleasantest,
liveliest comment. The press was genial, the success immense,
current criticism had never flowed so full, and it was universally felt that the handsome thing had been done. The process
employed by Mr. Beston had left, as he had promised, nothing
to be desired; and the sketch itself, the next week, arrived in
safety, and with only a smutch or two, by the post. I placed
my article, naturally, in another magazine, but was disappointed, I confess, as to what it discoverably did in literary
circles for its subject. This ache, however, was muffled. There
was a worse victim than I, and there was consolation of a sort
in our having out together the question of literary circles. The
great orb of *The Cynosure*, wasn't that a literary circle? By the
time we had fairly to face this question we had achieved the
union that—at least for resistance or endurance—is supposed
to be strength.

The Given Case

BARTON REEVE waited, with outward rigour and inward rage, till every one had gone: there was in particular an objectionable, travelled, superior young man—a young man with a long neck and bad shoes, especially great on Roumania—whom he was determined to outstay. He could only wonder the while whether he most hated designed or unconscious unpleasantness. It was a Sunday afternoon, the time in the week when, for some subtle reason, "such people"— Reeve freely generalised them—most take liberties. But even when the young man had disappeared there still remained Mrs. Gorton, Margaret Hamer's sister and actual hostess—it was with this lady that Miss Hamer was at present staying. He was sustained, however, as he had been for half an hour previous, by the sense that the charming girl knew perfectly he had something to say to her and was trying covertly to help him. "Only hang on: leave the rest to me"—something of that sort she had already conveyed to him. He left it to her now to get rid of her sister, and was struck by the wholly natural air with which she soon achieved this feat. It was not absolutely hidden from him that if he had not been so insanely in love he might like her for herself. As it was, he could only like her for Mrs. Despard. Mrs. Gorton was dining out, but Miss Hamer was not; that promptly turned up, with the effect of bringing on, for the former lady, the question of time to dress. She still remained long enough to say over and over that it *was* time. Meanwhile, a little awkwardly, they hung about by the fire. Mrs. Gorton looked at her pretty shoe on the fender, but Barton Reeve and Miss Hamer were on their feet as if to declare that they were fixed.

"You're dining all alone?" he said to the girl.

"Women never dine alone," she laughed. "When they're alone they don't dine."

Mrs. Gorton looked at her with an expression of which Reeve became aware: she was so handsome that, but for its marked gravity, it might have represented the pleasure and pride of sisterhood. But just when he most felt such complacency to be natural his hostess rather sharply mystified him. "She won't *be* alone—more's the pity!" Mrs. Gorton spoke with more intention than he could seize, and the next moment he was opening the door for her.

"I shall have a cup of coffee and a biscuit—and also, propped up before me, Gardiner's *Civil War*. Don't you always read when you dine alone?" Miss Hamer asked as he came back.

Women were strange—he was not to be drawn in that direction. She had been showing him for an hour that she knew what he wanted; yet now that he had got his chance—which she moreover had given him—she looked as innocent as the pink face in the oval frame above the chimney. It took him, however, but a moment to see more: her innocence was her answer to the charge with which her sister had retreated, a charge into which, the next minute, her conscious blankness itself helped him to read a sense. Margaret Hamer was never alone, because Phil Mackern was always— But it was none of *his* business! She lingered there on the rug, and it somehow passed between them before anything else was done that he quite recognised that. After the point was thus settled he took his own affair straight up. "You know why I'm here. It's because I believe you can help me."

"Men always think that. They think every one can 'help' them but themselves."

"And what do women think?" Barton Reeve asked with some asperity. "It might be a little of a light for me if you were able to tell me *that*. What do they think a man is made of? What does *she* think——?"

A little embarrassed, Margaret looked round her, wishing to show she could be kind and patient, yet making no movement to sit down. Mrs. Gorton's allusion was still in the air—it had just affected their common comfort. "I know what you mean. You assume she tells me everything."

"I assume that you're her most intimate friend. I don't know to whom else to turn."

The face the girl now took in was smooth-shaven and fine, a face expressing penetration up to the limit of decorum. It was full of the man's profession—passionately legal. Barton Reeve was certainly concerned with advice, but not with taking it. "What particular thing," she asked, "do you want me to do?"

"Well, to make her see what she's doing to me. From you she'll take it. She won't take it from me. She doesn't believe me—she thinks I'm 'prejudiced.' But she'll believe you."

Miss Hamer smiled, but not with cruelty. "And whom shall *I* believe?"

"Ah, that's not kind of you!" Barton Reeve returned; after which, for a moment, as he stood there sombre and sensitive, something visibly came to him that completed his thought, but that he hesitated to produce. Presently, as if to keep it back, he turned away with a jerk. He knew all about the girl herself—the woman of whom they talked had, out of the fulness of her own knowledge, told him; he knew what would have given him a right to say: "Oh, come; don't pretend I've to reveal to *you* what the dire thing makes of us!" He moved across the room and came back—felt himself even at this very moment, in the grip of his passion, shaken as a rat by a terrier. But just that was what he showed by his silence. As he rejoined her by the chimney-piece he was extravagantly nervous. "Oh Lord, Lord!" he at last simply exclaimed.

"I believe you—I believe you," she replied. "But *she* really does too."

"Then why does she treat me so?—it's a refinement of perversity and cruelty. She never gives me an inch but she takes back the next day ten yards; never shows me a gleam of sincerity without making up for it as soon as possible by something that leaves me in no doubt of her absolute heartless coquetry. Of whom the deuce is she afraid?"

His companion hesitated. "You perhaps might remember once in a while that she has a husband."

"Do I ever forget it for an instant? Isn't my life one long appeal to her to get rid of him?"

"Ah," said his friend as if she knew all about it, "getting rid of husbands isn't so easy!"

"I beg your pardon"—Reeve spoke with much more gravity and a still greater competence—"there's every facility for it when the man's a proved brute and the woman an angel whom, for three years, he has not troubled himself so much as to look at."

"Do you think," Miss Hamer inquired, "that, even for an angel, extreme intimacy with another angel—such another as you: angels of a feather flock together!—positively adds to the facility?"

Barton could perfectly meet her. "It adds to the reason—that's what it adds to; and the reason *is* the facility. I only know one way," he went on, "of showing her I want to marry her. I can't show it by never going near her."

"But need you also show Colonel Despard?"

"Colonel Despard doesn't care a rap!"

"He cares enough to have given her all this time nothing whatever—for divorcing him, if you mean that—to take hold of."

"I do mean that," Barton Reeve declared; "and I must ask you to believe that I know what I'm talking about. He hates her enough for any perversity, but he has given her exactly what is necessary. Enough's as good as a feast!"

Miss Hamer looked away—looked now at the clock; but it was none the less apparent that she understood. "Well—she of course has a horror of that. I mean of doing anything herself."

"Then why does she go so far?"

Margaret still looked at the clock. "So far——?"

"With me, month after month, in every sort of way!"

Moving away from the fire, she gave him an irrelevant smile. "Though I *am* to be alone, my time's up."

He kept his eyes on her. "Women don't feed for themselves, but they do dress, eh?"

"I must go to my room."

"But that isn't an answer to my question."

She thought a moment. "About poor Kate's going so far? I thought your complaint was of her not going far enough."

"It all depends," said Reeve impatiently, "upon her having some truth in her. She shouldn't do what she does if she doesn't care for me."

"She does care for you," said the girl.

"Well then, damn it, she should do much more!"

Miss Hamer put out her hand. "Good-bye. I'll speak to her."

Reeve held her fast. "She does care for me?"

She hesitated but an instant. "Far too much. It's excessively awkward."

He still detained her, pressing her with his sincerity, almost with his crudity. "That's exactly why I've come to you." Then he risked: "*You* know—!" But he faltered.

"I know what?"

"Why, what it is."

She threw back her head, releasing herself. "To be impertinent? Never!" She fairly left him—the man was in the hall to let him out; and he walked away with a sense not diminished, on the whole, of how viciously fate had seasoned his draught. Yet he believed Margaret Hamer *would* speak for him. She had a kind of nobleness.

II

At Pickenham, on the Saturday night, it came round somehow to Philip Mackern that Barton Reeve was to have been of the party, and that Mrs. Despard's turning up without him—so it was expressed—had somewhat disconcerted their hostess. This, in the smoking-room, made him silent more to think than to listen—he knew whom *he* had "turned up" without. The next morning, among so many, there were some who went to church; Mackern always went now because Miss Hamer had told him she wished it. He liked it, moreover, for the time: it was an agreeable symbol to him of the way his situation made him "good." Besides, he had a plan; he knew what Mrs. Despard would do; *her* situation made her good too. The morning, late in May, was bright, and the walk, though short, charming; they all straggled, in vivid twos and threes, across the few fields—passing stiles and gates, drawing out, scattering their colour over the green, as if they had the "tip" for some new sport. Mrs. Despard, with two companions, was one of the first; Mackern himself, as it happened, quitted the house by the side of Lady Orville, who, before they had gone many steps, completed the information given him the night before.

"That's just the sort of thing Kate Despard's always up to. I'm too tired of her!"

Phil Mackern wondered. "But do you mean she prevented him——?"

"I asked her only to make him come—it was *him* I wanted. But she's a goose: she hasn't the courage——"

"Of her reckless passion?" Mackern asked as his companion's candour rather comically dropped.

"Of her ridiculous flirtation. She doesn't know what she wants—she's in and out of her hole like a frightened mouse. On knowing she's invited he immediately accepts, and she encourages him in the fond thought of the charming time they'll have. Then at the eleventh hour she finds it will never do. It will be too 'marked'! Marked it would certainly have been," Lady Orville pursued. "But there would have been a remedy!"

"For *her* to have stayed away?"

Her ladyship waited. "What horrors you make me say!"

"Well," Mackern replied, "I'm glad she came. I particularly want her."

"You?—what have *you* to do with her? You're as bad as she!" his hostess added; quitting him, however, for some other attention, before he had need to answer.

He sought no second companion—he had matter for thought as he went on; but he reached the door of the church before Mrs. Despard had gone in, and he observed that when, glancing back, she saw him pass the gate, she immediately waited for him. She had turned off a little into the churchyard, and as he came up he was struck with the prettiness that, beneath the old grey tower and among the crooked headstones, she presented to the summer morning.

"It's just to say, before any one else gets hold of you, that I want you, when we come out, to walk home with me. I want most particularly to speak to you."

"Comme cela se trouve!" Mackern laughed. "That's exactly what I want to do to you!"

"Oh, I warn you that you won't like it; but you will have, all the same, to take it!" Mrs. Despard declared. "In fact, it's why I came," she added.

"To speak to *me*?"

"Yes, and you needn't attempt to look innocent and interesting. You know perfectly what it's about!" With which she passed into church.

It scarce prepared the young man for his devotions; he thought more of what it might be about—whether he knew or not—than he thought of what, ostensibly, he had come for. He was not seated near Mrs. Despard, but he appropriated her, after service, before they had left the place; and then, on the walk back, took care they should be quite by themselves. She opened fire with a promptitude clearly intended to deprive him of every advantage.

"Don't you think it's about time, you know, to let Margaret Hamer alone?"

He found his laugh again a resource. "Is that what you came down to say to me?"

"I suppose what you mean is that in that case I might as well have stayed at home. But I can assure you," Mrs. Despard continued, "that if you don't care for her, I at least do. I'd do anything for her!"

"Would you?" Philip Mackern asked. "Then, for God's sake, try to induce her to show me some frankness and reason. Knowing that you know all about it and that I should find you here, that's what determined me. And I find you talking to me," he went on, "about giving her up. How *can* I give her up? What do you mean by my not caring for her? Don't I quite sufficiently show—and to the point absolutely of making a public fool of myself—that I don't care for anything else in life?"

Mrs. Despard, slightly to his surprise and pacing beside him a moment in silence, seemed arrested by this challenge. But she presently found her answer. "That's not the way, you know, to get on at the Treasury."

"I don't pretend it is; and it's just one of the things that I thought of asking you to bring home to her better than any one else can. She plays the very devil with my work. She makes me hope just enough to be all upset, and yet never, for an hour, enough to be—well, what you may call made strong; enough to know where I am."

"You're where you've no business to be—that's where you are," said Mrs. Despard. "You've no right whatever to persecute a girl who, to listen to you, will have to do something that she doesn't want, and that would be most improper if she did."

"You mean break off——?"

"I mean break off—with Mr. Grove-Stewart."

"And why shouldn't she?"

"Because they've been engaged three years."

"And could there be a better reason?" Philip Mackern asked with heat. "A man who's engaged to a girl three years without marrying her—what sort of a man is that, and what tie to him is she, or is any one else, bound to recognise?"

"He's an extremely nice person," Mrs. Despard somewhat sententiously replied, "and he's to return from India—and not to go back, you know—this autumn at latest."

"Then that's all the more reason for my acting successfully before he comes—for my insisting on an understanding without the loss of another week."

The young man, who was tall and straight, had squared his shoulders and, throwing back his massive, fair head, appeared to proclaim to earth and air the justice of his cause. Mrs. Despard, for an instant, answered nothing, but, as if to take account of his manner, she presently stopped short. "I think I ought to express to you my frank belief that for you, Mr. Mackern, there can be nothing but loss. I'm sorry for you, to a certain point; but you happen to have got hold of a girl who's incapable of anything dishonourable." And with this— as if *that* were settled—she resumed her walk.

Mackern, however, stood quite still—only too glad of the opportunity for emphasis given him by their pause; so that after a few steps she turned round. "Do you know that that's exactly on what I wanted to appeal to you? *Is* she the woman to chuck me now?"

Mrs. Despard, all face and figure in the mild brightness, looked at him across the grass and appeared to give some extension to the question of what, in general at least, a woman might be the woman to do. "Now?"

"Now. After all she has done."

Mrs. Despard, however, wouldn't hear of what Margaret Hamer had done; she only walked straight off again, shaking everything away as Mackern overtook her. "Leave her alone— leave her alone!"

He held his tongue for some minutes, but he swished the air with his stick in a way that made her presently look at him. She found him positively pale, and he looked away from her.

"You should have given me that advice," he remarked with dry derision, "a good many weeks ago!"

"Well, it's never too late to mend!" she retorted with some vivacity.

"I beg your pardon. It's often too late—altogether too late. And as for 'mending,'" Mackern went on almost sternly, "you know as well as I that if I *had*—in time, or anything of that sort—tried to back out or pull up, you would have been the first to make her out an injured innocent and declare I had shamefully used her."

This proposition took, as appeared, an instant or two to penetrate Mrs. Despard's consciousness; but when it had fairly done so it produced, like a train of gunpowder, an audible report. "Why, you strange, rude man!"—she fairly laughed for indignation. "Permit me not to answer you: I can't discuss any subject with you in that key."

They had reached a neat white gate and paused for Mackern to open it; but, with his hand on the top, he only held it a little, fixing his companion with insistence and seemingly in full indifference to her protest. "Upon my soul, the way women treat men——!"

"Well?" she demanded, while he gasped as if it were more than he could express.

"It's too execrable! There's only one thing for her to do." He clearly wished to show he was not to be humbugged.

"And what wonderful thing is that?"

"There's only one thing for *any* woman to do," he pursued with an air of conscious distinctness, "when she has drawn a man on to believe there's nothing she's not ready for."

Mrs. Despard waited; she watched, over the gate, the gambols, in the next field, of a small white lamb. "Will you kindly let me pass?" she then asked.

But he went on as if he had not heard her. "It's to make up to him for what she has cost him. It's simply to do everything."

Mrs. Despard hesitated. "Everything?" she then vaguely asked.

"Everything," Mackern said as he opened the gate. "*Won't* you help me?" he added more appealingly as they got into the next field.

"No." She was as distinct as himself. She followed with her eyes the little white lamb. She dismissed the subject. "You're simply wicked."

III

Barton Reeve, of a Sunday, sometimes went for luncheon to his sister, who lived in Great Cumberland Place, and this particular Sunday was so fine that, from the Buckingham Palace Road, he walked across the Park. There, in the eastern quarter, he encountered many persons who appeared, on the return from church, to have assembled to meet each other and who had either disposed themselves on penny chairs or were passing to and fro near the Park Lane palings. The sitters looked at the walkers, the walkers at the sitters, and Barton Reeve, with his sharp eyes, at every one. Thus it was that he presently perceived, under a spreading tree, Miss Hamer and her sister, who, however, though in possession of chairs, were not otherwise engaged. He went straight up to them, and, while he stood talking, they were approached by another friend, an elderly intimate, as it seemed, of Mrs. Gorton's, whom he recognised as one of the persons so trying to his patience the day of his long wait in her drawing-room. Barton Reeve looked very hard at the younger lady, and was perfectly conscious of the effect he produced of always reminding her that there was a subject between them. He was, on the other hand, probably not aware of the publicity that his manner struck his alert young friend as conferring on this circumstance, nor of the degree in which, as an illustration of his intensity about his own interests, his candour appeared to her comic. What *was* comic, on his part, was the excessive frankness—clever man though he was—of his assumption that he finely, quite disinterestedly, extended their subject by this very looking of volumes. She and her affairs figured in them all, and there was a set of several in a row by the time that, laughing in spite of herself, she now said to him: "Will you take me a little walk?" He left her in no doubt of his alacrity, and in a moment Mrs. Gorton's visitor was in her chair and our couple away from the company and out in the open.

"I want you to know," the girl immediately began, "that I've said what I could for you—that I say it whenever I can. But I've asked you to speak to me now just because you mustn't be under any illusion or flatter yourself that I'm doing——" she hesitated, for his attention had made her stop short—"well, what I'm not. I may as well tell you, at any rate," she added, "that I do maturely consider she cares for you. But what will you have? She's a woman of duty."

"Duty? What do you mean by duty?"

Barton Reeve's irritation at this name had pierced the air with such a sound that Margaret Hamer looked about for a caution. But they were in an empty circle—a wide circle of smutty sheep. She showed a slight prevision of embarrassment—even of weariness: she had hoped for an absence of that. "You know what I mean. What else is there to mean? I mean Colonel Despard."

"Was it her duty to Colonel Despard to be as consciously charming to me as if there had been no such person alive? Has she explained to you that?" he demanded.

"She hasn't explained to me anything—I don't need it," said the girl with some spirit. "I've only explained to *her*."

"Well?"—he was almost peremptory.

She didn't mind it. "Well, her excuse—for her false position, I mean—is really a perfectly good one." Miss Hamer had been standing, but with this she walked on. "She found she—what do you call it?—liked you."

"Then what's the matter?"

"Why, that she didn't know how much you'd like her, how far you'd—what do you call it?—'go.' It's odious to be talking of such things, I think," she pursued; "and I assure you I wouldn't do it for other people—for any one but you and her. It makes it all sound so vulgar. She didn't think you cared—on the contrary. Then when she began to see, she had got in too deep."

"She had made my life impossible to me without her? She certainly has 'got in' to that extent," said Barton Reeve, "and it's precisely my contention. Can you pretend for her that to have found out that she has done this leaves open to her, in common decency, any but the one course?"

"I don't pretend anything!" his companion replied with some confusion and still more impatience. "I'm bound to say I don't see what responsibility you're trying to fix on me."

He just cast about him, making little wild jerks with his stick. "I'm not trying anything and you're awfully good to me. I dare say my predicament makes me a shocking bore—makes me in fact ridiculous. But I don't speak to you only because you're her friend—her friend, and therefore not indifferent to the benefit for her of what, take it altogether, I have to offer. It's because I feel so sure of how, in her place, you would generously, admirably take your own line."

"Heaven forbid I should ever be in her place!" Margaret exclaimed with a laugh in which it pleased Reeve, at the moment, to discover a world of dissimulation.

"You're already there—I say, come!" the young man had it on his tongue's end to reply. But he stopped himself in time, and felt extraordinarily delicate and discreet. "I don't say it's the easiest one in the world; but here I stand, after all—and I'm not supposed to be such an ass—ready to give her every conceivable assistance." His friend, at this, replied nothing; but he presently spoke again. "What has she invented, at Pickenham, to-day, but to keep me from coming?"

"Is Kate to-day at Pickenham?" Miss Hamer inquired.

Barton Reeve, in his acuteness, caught something in the question—an energy of profession of ignorance—in which he again saw depths. It presented Pickenham and whomsoever might be there as such a blank that he felt quite forced to say: "I rather imagined—till I spied you just now—that you would have gone."

"Well, you see I haven't." With which our young lady paused again, turning on him more frankly. It struck him that, as from a conscious effort, she had a heightened colour. "You must know far better than I what she feels, but I repeat it to you, once for all, as, the last time I saw her, she gave it me. I said just now she hadn't explained, but she did explain that." The girl just faltered, but she brought it out. "She can't divorce. And if she can't, you know, she can't!"

"I never heard such twaddle," Barton Reeve declared. "As if a woman with a husband who hates her so he would like

to kill her couldn't obtain any freedom——!" And he gave
such a passionate whirl of his stick that it flew straight away
from him.

His companion waited till he had picked it up. "Ah, but
there's freedom and freedom."

"She can do anything on all the wide earth she likes." He
had gone on as if not hearing her, and, lost in the vastness of
his meaning, he absolutely glared a while at the distance. "But
she's afraid!"

Miss Hamer, in her turn, stared at the way he sounded it;
then she gave a vague laugh. "How you say that!"

Barton Reeve said it again—said it with rage and scorn.
"She's afraid, she's afraid!"

Margaret continued to look at him; then she turned away.
"Yes—she is."

"Well, who wouldn't be?" came to her, as a reply, across
the grass. Mrs. Gorton, with two gentlemen now, rejoined
them.

IV

On hearing from Mrs. Despard that she must see him, Philip
Mackern's action was immediate: she had named the morrow
for his call, but he knocked at her door, on the chance, an
hour after reading her note. The footman demurred, but at
the same moment Barton Reeve, taking his departure, appeared in the hall, and Mackern instantly appealed to him.

"She *is* at home, I judge—isn't she?" The young man was
so impatient that it was only afterwards he took into account a queerness of look on Reeve's part—a queerness that
seemed to speak of a different crisis and that indeed something in his own face might, to his friend's eyes, remarkably
have matched. Like two uneasy Englishmen, at any rate,
they somehow passed each other, and when, a minute later,
in the drawing-room, Mrs. Despard, who, with her back
presented, was at the window, turned about at the sound of
his name, she showed him an expression in which nothing
corresponded to that of her other visitor. It may promptly
be mentioned that, even through what followed, this visitor's presence was, to Mackern's sense, still in the air; only

it was also just one of the things ministering, for our friend, to the interest of retrospect that such a fact—the fact that Mrs. Despard could be so "wonderful"—conveyed a reminder of the superior organisation of women. "I know you said to-morrow," he quickly began; "but I'll come to-morrow too. Is it bad or good?" he went on—"I mean what you have to tell me. Even if I just know it's bad, I believe I can wait—if you haven't time now."

"I haven't time, at all, now," Mrs. Despard replied very sweetly. "I can only give you two minutes—my dressmaker's waiting. But it isn't bad," she added.

"Then it's good?" he eagerly asked.

"Oh, I haven't the least idea you'll think it so! But it's because it's exactly what I myself have been wanting and hoping that I wrote to you. It strikes me that the sooner you know the better. I've just heard from Bombay—from Amy Warden."

"Amy Warden?" Philip Mackern wondered.

"John Grove-Stewart's sister—the nice one. He comes home immediately—doesn't wait till the autumn. So there you are!" said Mrs. Despard.

Philip Mackern looked straight at the news, with which she now presented herself as brilliantly illuminated. "I don't see that I'm anywhere but where I've always been. I haven't expected anything of his absence that I shan't expect of his presence."

Mrs. Despard thought a moment, but with perfect serenity. "Have you expected quite fatally to compromise her?"

He gave her question an equal consideration. "To compromise her?"

"That's what you are doing, you know—as deliberately as ever you can."

Again the young man thought. They were in the middle of the room—she had not asked him to sit down. "Quite fatally, you say?"

"Well, she has just one chance to save herself."

Mackern, whom Mrs. Despard had already, more than once, seen turn pale under the emotion of which she could touch the spring, gave her again—and with it a smile that struck her as strange—this sign of sensibility. "Yes—she may have only one chance. But it's such a good one!" he laughed. "What is Mr. Grove-Stewart coming home for?"

"Because it has reached him that the whole place is filled with the wonder of her conduct. Amy Warden thinks that, as so intimate a friend, I should hear what he has decided to do. She takes for granted, I suppose—though she doesn't say it—that I'll let Margaret know."

Philip Mackern looked at the ceiling. "She doesn't know yet?"

Mrs. Despard hesitated. "I suppose he means it as a surprise."

"So you won't tell her?"

"On the contrary—I shall tell her immediately. But I thought it best to tell you first."

"I'm extremely obliged to you," said Philip Mackern.

"Of course you hate me—but I don't care!" Mrs. Despard declared. "You've made her talked about in India—you may be proud!"

Once more Philip Mackern considered. "I'm not at all proud—but I think I'm very glad."

"I think you're very horrible then. But I've said what I wanted. Good-bye." Mrs. Despard had nodded at the footman, who, returning, had announced her carriage. He had left, on retiring, the door open, and as she followed him to go to her room her visitor went out with her. She gave Mackern, on the landing, a last word. "Her one chance is to marry him as soon as he arrives."

Mackern's strange smile, in his white face, was now fixed. "Her one chance, dear lady, is to marry *me*."

His hostess, suddenly flushing on this, showed a passion that startled him. "Stuff!" she crudely cried, and turned away with such impatience that, quitting her, he passed half downstairs. But she more quickly turned back to him; calling his name, she came to the top, while, checked, he looked up at her. Then she spoke with a particular solemnity. "To marry you, Mr. Mackern"—it was quite portentous—"will be the very worst thing for her good name."

The young man stood staring, then frankly emulated his friend. "Rubbish!" he rang out as he swiftly descended.

V

"Mrs. Gorton has come in?"

"No, miss; but Mrs. Despard is here. She said she'd wait for you."

"Then I'm not at home to any one." Margaret Hamer went straight upstairs and found her visitor in the smaller drawing-room, not seated, erect before the fireplace and with the air of having for some time restlessly paced and turned. Mrs. Despard hailed her with an instant cry.

"It has come at last!"

"Do you mean you've seen your husband?"

"He dropped on me to-day—out of the blue. He came in just before luncheon. If the house is his own——!" And Mrs. Despard, who, as with the first relief to her impatience, had flung herself, to emphasise her announcement on the sofa, gave a long, sombre sigh.

"If the house is his own he can come when he likes?" Standing before her and looking grave and tired, Margaret Hamer showed interest, but kept expression down. "And yet you were so splendidly sure," she continued, "that he wouldn't come!"

"I wasn't sure—I see now I wasn't; I only tried to convince myself. I knew—at the back of my head—that he probably *was* in England; I felt in all my bones—six weeks ago, you know—that he would really have returned and, in his own infamous, underhand way, would be somewhere looking out. He told me to-day about ninety distinct lies. I don't know how he has kept so dark, but he has been at one of the kind of places he likes—some fourth-rate watering-place."

Margaret waited a moment. "With any one?"

"I don't know. I don't care." This time, for emphasis, Mrs. Despard jumped up and, wandering, like a caged creature, to a distance, stopped before a glass and gave a touch or two to the position of her hat. "It makes no difference. Nothing makes any."

Her friend, across the room, looked at her with a certain blankness. "Of what does he accuse you?"

"Of nothing whatever," said Mrs. Despard, turning round. "Not of the least little thing!" she sighed, coming back.

"Then he made no scene?"

"No—it was too awful."

Again the girl faltered. "Do you mean he was——?"

"I mean he was dreadful. I mean I can't bear it."

"Does he want to come back?"

"Immediately and for ever. 'Beginning afresh,' he calls it. Fancy," the poor woman cried, rueful and wide-eyed as with a vision of more things than she could name—"fancy beginning afresh!" Once more, in her fidget, appalled, she sank into the nearest seat.

This image of a recommencement had just then, for both ladies, in all the circumstances, a force that filled the room— that seemed for a little fairly to make a hush. "But if he can't oblige you?" Margaret presently returned.

Mrs. Despard sat sombre. "He *can* oblige me."

"Do you mean by law?"

"Oh," she wailed, "I mean by everything! By my having been the fool——!" She dropped to her intolerable sense of it.

Margaret watched her an instant. "Oh, if you say it of your-self!"

Mrs. Despard gave one of her springs. "And don't *you* say it?"

Margaret met her eyes, but changed colour. "Say it of you?"

"Say it of *your*self."

They fixed each other a while; it was deep—it was even hard. "Yes," said the girl at last. But she turned away.

Her companion's eyes followed her as she moved; then Mrs. Despard broke out. "Do you mean you're not going to keep faith?"

"What faith do you *call* faith?"

"You know perfectly what I call faith for *you*, and in how little doubt, from the first, I've left you about it!"

This reply had been sharp enough to jerk the speaker for a moment, as by the toss of her head, out of her woe, but Margaret met it at first only by showing her again a face that enjoined patience and pity. They continued to look in-deed, each out of her peculiar distress, more things than they found words for. "I don't know," Margaret Hamer finally said. "I have time—I've a little; I've more than you—that's what makes me so sorry for you. I've been very possibly the direst idiot—I'll admit anything you like; though I won't pretend I see now how it could have been different. It couldn't—it couldn't. I don't know, I don't know," she wearily, mechanically repeated. There was something in her that had surrendered by this time all the importance of her personal question; she wished to keep it back or to get rid of it. "Don't, at any rate, think one is selfish and all taken up. I'm perfectly quiet—it's only about you I'm nervous. You're worse than I, dear," she added with a dim smile.

But Mrs. Despard took it more than gravely. "Worse?"

"I mean you've more to think of. And perhaps even *he's* worse."

Mrs. Despard thought again. "He's terrible."

Her companion hesitated—she had perhaps mistaken the allusion. "I don't mean your husband."

Mrs. Despard *had* mistaken the allusion, but she carried it off. "Barton Reeve is terrible. It's more than I deserve."

"Well, he really cares. There it is."

"Yes, there it is!" Mrs. Despard echoed. "And much *that* helps me!"

They hovered about, but shifting their relation now and each keeping something back. "When are you to see him again?" Margaret asked.

This time Mrs. Despard knew whom she meant. "Never—never again. What I may feel for him—what I may feel for myself—has nothing to do with it. Never as long as I live!" Margaret's visitor declared. "You don't believe it?" she, however, the next moment demanded.

"I don't believe it. You know how I've always liked him. But what has *that* to do with it either?" the girl almost incoherently continued. "I don't believe it—no," she repeated. "I don't want to make anything harder for you, but you won't find it so easy."

"I shan't find anything easy, and I must row my own boat. But not seeing him will be the least impossibility."

Margaret looked away. "Well!"—she spoke at last vaguely and conclusively.

Something in her tone so arrested her friend that she found herself suddenly clutched by the arm. "Do you mean to say you'll see Mr. Mackern?"

"I don't know."

"Then *I* do!" Mrs. Despard pronounced with energy. "You're lost."

"Ah!" wailed Margaret with the same wan detachment.

"Yes, simply lost!" It rang out—would have rung out indeed too loud had it not caught itself just in time. Mrs. Gorton at that moment opened the door.

VI

Mrs. Despard at last came down—he had been sure it would be but a question of time. Barton Reeve had, to this end, presented himself, on the Sunday morning, early: he had allowed a margin for difficulty. He was armed with a note of three lines, which, on the butler's saying to him that she was not at home, he simply, in a tone before which even a butler prompted and primed must quail, requested him to carry straight up. Then unannounced and unaccompanied, not knowing in the least whom he should find, he had taken, for the hundredth time in four months, his quick course to the drawing-room, where emptiness, as it proved, reigned, but where, notwithstanding, he felt, at the end of an hour, rather more than less in possession. To express it, to put it to her, to put it to any one, would perhaps have been vain and vulgar; but the whole assurance on which he had proceeded was his sense that, on the spot, he had, to a certain point, an effect. He was enough on the spot from the moment she knew he was, and she would know it—know it by divination, as she had often before shown how extraordinarily she knew things—even if that pompous ass had not sent up his note. To what point his effect would prevail in the face of the biggest obstacle he had yet had to deal with was exactly what he had come to find out. It was enough, to begin with, that he did, after a weary wait, draw her—draw her in spite of everything: he felt that as he at last heard her hand on the doorknob. He heard it indeed pause as well as move—pause while he himself kept perfectly still. During this minute, it must be added, he looked straight at the ugliest of the whole mixed row of possibilities. Something had yielded—yes; but what had yielded was quite most probably not her softness. It might well be her hardness. Her hardness was her love of the sight of her own effect.

Dressed for church, though it was now much too late, she was more breathless than he had ever seen her; in spite of which, beginning immediately, he gave her not a moment. "I make a scandal, your letter tells me—I make it, you say, even before the servants, whom you appear to have taken in the most extraordinary way into your confidence. You greatly exaggerate—but even suppose I do: let me assure you frankly that I care not one rap. What you've done you've done, and I'm here in spite of your letter—and in spite of anything, of everything, any one else may say—on the perfectly solid ground of your having irretrievably done it. Don't talk to me," Reeve went on, "about your husband and new complications: to do that now is horribly unworthy of you and quite the sort of thing that adds—well, you know what—to injury. There isn't a single complication that there hasn't always been and that we haven't, on the whole, completely mastered and put in its place. There was nothing in your husband that prevented, from the first hour we met, your showing yourself, and every one else you chose, what you could do with me. What you could do you did systematically and without a scruple—without a pang of real compunction or a movement of real retreat."

Mrs. Despard had not come down unprepared, and her impenetrable face now announced it. She was even strong enough to speak softly—not to meet anger with anger. Yet she was also clearly on her defence. "If I was kind to you—if I had the frankness and confidence to let it be seen I liked you—it's because I thought I was safe."

"Safe?" Barton Reeve echoed. "Yes, I've no doubt you did! And how safe did you think *I* was? Can't you give me some account of the attention you gave to *that*?" She looked at him without reply to his challenge, but the full beauty of her silent face had only, as in two or three still throbs, to come out, to affect him suddenly with all the force of a check. The plea of her deep, pathetic eyes took the place of the admission that his passion vainly desired to impose upon her. They broke his resentment down; all his tenderness welled up with the change; it came out in supplication. "I can't look at you and believe any ill of you. I feel for you everything I ever felt, and that we're committed to each other by a power that not even death can break. How can you look at *me* and not know to what depths I'm yours? You've the finest, sweetest chance that ever a woman had!"

She waited a little, and the firmness in her face, the intensity of her effort to possess herself, settled into exaltation, at the same time that she might have struck a spectator as staring at some object of fear. "I see my chance—I see it; but I don't see it as you see it. You must forgive me. My chance is not *that* chance. It has come to me—God knows why!—but in the hardest way of all. I made a great mistake—I recognise it."

"So *I* must pay for it?" Barton Reeve asked.

She continued to look at him with her protected dread. "We both did—so we must both pay."

"Both? I beg your pardon," said the young man: "I utterly deny it—I made no mistake whatever. I'm just where I was— and everything else is. Everything but you!"

She looked away from him, but going on as if she had not heard him. "We must do our duty—when once we see it. I didn't know—I didn't understand. But now I do. It's when one's eyes are opened—that the wrong is wrong." Not as a lesson got by heart, not as a trick rehearsed in her room, but delicately, beautifully, step by step, she made it out for her-self—and for him so far as he would take it. "I can only follow the highest line." Then, after faltering a moment, "We must thank God," she said, "it isn't worse. My husband's here," she added with a sufficient strangeness of effect.

But Barton Reeve accepted the mere fact as relevant. "Do you mean he's in the house?"

"Not at this moment. He's on the river—for the day. But he comes back to-morrow."

"And he has been here since Friday?" She was silent, on this, so long that her visitor continued: "It's none of my business?"

Again she hesitated, but at last she replied. "Since Friday."

"And you hate him as much as ever?"

This time she spoke out. "More."

Reeve made, with a sound irrepressible and scarce articulate, a motion that was a sort of dash at her. "Ah, my *own* own!"

But she retreated straight before him, checking him with a gesture of horror, her first outbreak of emotion. "Don't touch me!" He turned, after a minute, away; then, like a man dazed, looked, without sight, about for something. It proved to be his hat, which he presently went and took up. "Don't talk, don't talk—you're not *in* it!" she continued. "You speak of 'paying,' but it's I who pay." He reached the door and, having opened it, stood with his hand on the knob and his eyes on her face. She was far away, at the most distant of the windows. "I shall never care for any one again," she kept on.

Reeve had dropped to something deeper than resentment; more abysmal, even, it seemed to him, than renouncement or despair. But all he did was slowly to shake his helpless head at her. "I've no words for you."

"It doesn't matter. Don't think of me."

He was closing the door behind him, but, still hearing her voice, kept it an instant. "I'm all right!"—that was the last that came to him as he drew the door to.

VII

"I only speak of the given case," Philip Mackern said; "that's the only thing I have to do with, and on what I've expressed to you of the situation it has made for me I don't yield an inch."

Mrs. Gorton, to whom, in her own house, he had thus, in defence, addressed himself, was in a flood of tears which rolled, however, in their current not a few hard grains of asperity. "You're *always* speaking of it, and it acts on my nerves, and I don't know what you mean by it, and I don't care, and I think you're horrible. The case is like any other case that can be mended if people will behave decently."

Philip Mackern moved slowly about the room; impatience and suspense were in every step he took, but he evidently had himself well in hand and he met his hostess with studied indulgence. She had made her appearance, in advance, to prepare him for her sister, who had agreed by letter to see him, but who, through a detention on the line, which she had wired from Bath to explain, had been made late for the appointment she was on her way back to town to keep. Margaret Hamer had gone home precipitately—to Devonshire—five days before, the day after her last interview with Mrs. Despard; on which had ensued, with the young man, whom she had left London without seeing, a correspondence resulting in her present return. She had forbidden him, in spite of his insistence, either to come down to her at her mother's or to be at Paddington to meet her, and had finally, arriving from these places, but just alighted in Manchester Square, where, while he awaited her, Mackern's restless measurement of the empty drawing-room had much in common with the agitation to which, in a similar place, his friend Barton Reeve had already been condemned. Mrs. Gorton, emerging from a deeper retreat, had at last, though not out of compassion, conferred on him her company; she left him from the first instant in no doubt of the spirit in which she approached him. Margaret was at last almost indecently there, Margaret was upstairs, Margaret was coming down; but he would render the whole family an inestimable service by quietly taking up his hat and departing without further parley. Philip Mackern, whose interest in this young lady was in no degree whatever an interest in other persons connected with her, only transferred his hat from the piano to the window-seat and put it kindly to Mrs. Gorton that such a departure would be, if the girl had come to take leave of him, a brutality, and if she had come to do anything else an imbecility. His inward attitude was that his interlocutress was an insufferable busybody: he took his stand, he considered, upon admirable facts; Margaret Hamer's age and his own—twenty-six and thirty-two—her independence, her intelligence, his career, his prospects, his general and his particular situation, his income, his extraordinary merit, and perhaps even his personal appearance. He left his sentiments, in this private estimate, out of account—he was almost too proud to mention them even to himself. Yet he found, after the first moment, that he had to mention them to Mrs. Gorton.

"I don't know what you mean," he said, "by my 'always' speaking of anything whatever that's between your sister and me; for I must remind you that this is the third time, at most, that we've had any talk of the matter. If I did, however, touch, to you, last month, on what I hold that a woman is, in certain circumstances—circumstances that, mind you, would never have existed without her encouragement, her surrender—bound in honour to do, it was because you yourself, though I dare say you didn't know with what realities you were dealing, called my attention precisely to the fact of the 'given case.' It isn't always, it isn't often, given, perhaps—but when it is one knows it. And it's given now if it ever was in the world," Mackern still, with his suppression of violence, but with an emphasis the more distinct for its peculiar amenity, asserted as he resumed his pacing.

Mrs. Gorton watched him a moment through such traces of tears as still resisted the extreme freedom of her pocket-handkerchief. "Admit then as much as you like that you've been a pair of fools and criminals"—the poor woman went far: "what business in the world have you to put the whole responsibility on her?"

Mackern pulled up short; nothing could exceed the benevolence of his surprise. "On 'her'? Why, don't I absolutely take an equal share of it?"

"Equal? Not a bit! You're not engaged to any one else."

"Oh, thank heaven, no!" said Philip Mackern with a laugh of questionable discretion and instant effect.

His companion's cheek assumed a deeper hue and her eyes a drier light. "You cause her to be outrageously talked about, and then have the assurance to come and prate to us of 'honour'!"

Mackern turned away again—again he measured his cage. "What is there I'm not ready to make good?"—and he gave, as he passed, a hard, anxious smile.

Mrs. Gorton said nothing for a moment; then she spoke with an accumulation of dignity. "I think you both—if you want to know—absolutely improper persons, and if I had had my wits about me I would have declined, in time, to lend my house again to any traffic that might take place between you. But you're hatefully here, to my shame, and the wretched creature, whom I myself got off, has come up, and the fat's on the fire, and it's too late to prevent it. It's not too late, however, just to say this: that if you've come, and if you intend, to bully and browbeat her——"

"Well?" Philip Mackern asked.

She had faltered and paused, and the next moment he saw why. The door had opened without his hearing it—Margaret Hamer stood and looked at them. He made no movement; he only, after a minute, held her eyes long enough to fortify him, as it were, in his attempted intensity of stillness. He felt already as if some process, something complex and exquisite, were going on that a sound, that a gesture might spoil. But his challenge to Mrs. Gorton was still in the air, and she apparently, on her vision of her sister, had seen something pass. She fixed the girl and she fixed Mackern; then, highly flushed and moving to the door, she answered him. "Why, you're a brute and a coward!" With which she banged the door behind her.

The way the others met without speech or touch was extraordinary, and still more singular perhaps the things that, in their silence, Philip Mackern thought. There was no freedom of appeal for him—he instantly felt that; there was neither burden nor need. He wondered Margaret didn't notice in some way what Mrs. Gorton had said; there was a strangeness in her not, on one side or the other, taking that up. There was a strangeness as well, he was perfectly aware, in his finding himself surprised and even, for ten seconds, as it happened, mercilessly disappointed, at her not looking quite so "badly" as her encounter with a grave crisis might have been entitled to present her. She looked beautiful, perversely beautiful: he couldn't indeed have said just how directly his presumption of visible ravage was to have treated her handsome head. Meanwhile, as she carried this handsome head—in a manner he had never quite seen her carry it before—to the window and stood looking blindly out, there deepened in him almost to quick anguish the fear even of breathing upon the hour they had reached. That she had come back to him, to whatever end, was somehow in itself so divine a thing that lips and hands were gross to deal with it. What, moreover, in the extremity of a man's want, had he not already said? They were simply shut up there with their moment, and he, at least, felt it throb and throb in the hush.

At last she turned round. "He will never, never understand that I can have been so base."

Mackern awkwardly demurred. "Base?"

"Letting you, from the first, make, to me, such a difference."

"I don't think you could help it." He was still awkward.

"How can he believe that? How can he admit it?"

She asked it too wofully to expect a reply, but the young man thought a moment. "You can't look to me to speak for him"—he said it as feeling his way and without a smile. "He should have looked out for himself."

"He trusted me. He trusted me," she repeated.

"So did I—so did I."

"Yes. Yes." She looked straight at him, as if tasting all her bitterness. "But I pity him so that it kills me!"

"And only him?"—and Philip Mackern came nearer. "It's perfectly simple," he went on. "I'll abide by that measure. It shall be the one you pity most."

She kept her eyes on him till she burst into tears. "Pity *me*—pity *me*!"

He drew her to him and held her close and long, and even at that high moment it was perhaps the deepest thing in his gratitude that he did pity her.

"Europe"

"OUR FEELING is, you know, that Becky *should* go."

That earnest little remark comes back to me, even after long years, as the first note of something that began, for my observation, the day I went with my sister-in-law to take leave of her good friends. It is a memory of the American time, which revives so at present—under some touch that doesn't signify—that it rounds itself off as an anecdote. That walk to say good-bye was the beginning; and the end, so far as I was concerned with it, was not till long after; yet even the end also appears to me now as of the old days. I went, in those days, on occasion, to see my sister-in-law, in whose affairs, on my brother's death, I had had to take a helpful hand. I continued to go, indeed, after these little matters were straightened out, for the pleasure, periodically, of the impression—the change to the almost pastoral sweetness of the good Boston suburb from the loud, longitudinal New York. It was another world, with other manners, a different tone, a different taste; a savour nowhere so mild, yet so distinct, as in the square white house—with the pair of elms, like gigantic wheat-sheaves in front, the rustic orchard not far behind, the old-fashioned door-lights, the big blue and white jars in the porch, the straight, bricked walk from the high gate—that enshrined the extraordinary merit of Mrs. Rimmle and her three daughters.

These ladies were so much of the place and the place so much of themselves that, from the first of their being revealed to me, I felt that nothing else at Brookbridge much mattered. They were what, for me, at any rate, Brookbridge had most to give: I mean in the way of what it was naturally strongest in, the thing that we called in New York the New England expression, the air of Puritanism reclaimed and refined. The Rimmles had brought this down to a wonderful delicacy. They struck me even then—all four almost equally—as very ancient and very earnest, and I think theirs must have been the house, in all the world, in which "culture" first came to the aid of morning calls. The head of the family was the widow of a great public character—as public characters were understood at Brookbridge—whose speeches on anniversaries formed a part of the body of national eloquence spouted in the New England schools by little boys covetous of the most marked, though perhaps the easiest, distinction. He was reported to have been celebrated, and in such fine declamatory connections that he seemed to gesticulate even from the tomb. He was understood to have made, in his wife's company, the tour of Europe at a date not immensely removed from that of the battle of Waterloo. What was the age, then, of the bland, firm, antique Mrs. Rimmle at the period of her being first revealed to me? That is a point I am not in a position to determine— I remember mainly that I was young enough to regard her as having reached the limit. And yet the limit for Mrs. Rimmle must have been prodigiously extended; the scale of its extension is, in fact, the very moral of this reminiscence. She was old, and her daughters were old, but I was destined to know them all as older. It was only by comparison and habit that— however much I recede—Rebecca, Maria, and Jane were the "young ladies."

I think it was felt that, though their mother's life, after thirty years of widowhood, had had a grand backward stretch, her blandness and firmness—and this in spite of her extreme physical frailty—would be proof against any surrender not overwhelmingly justified by time. It had appeared, years before, at a crisis of which the waves had not even yet quite subsided, a surrender not justified by anything that she should go, with her daughters, to Europe for her health. Her health was supposed to require constant support; but when it had at that period tried conclusions with the idea of Europe, it was not the idea of Europe that had been insidious enough to prevail. She had not gone, and Becky, Maria, and Jane had not gone, and this was long ago. They still merely floated in the air of the visit achieved, with such introductions and such acclamations, in the early part of the century; they still, with fond glances at the sunny parlour-walls, only referred, in conversation, to divers pictorial and other reminders of it. The Miss Rimmles had quite been brought up on it, but Becky, as the most literary, had most mastered the subject. There were framed letters—tributes to their eminent father—suspended among the mementoes, and of two or three of these, the most foreign and complimentary, Becky had executed translations that figured beside the text. She knew already, through this and other illumination, so much about Europe that it was hard to believe, for her, in that limit of adventure which consisted only of her having been twice to Philadelphia. The others had not been to Philadelphia, but there was a legend that Jane had been to Saratoga. Becky was a short, stout, fair person with round, serious eyes, a high forehead, the sweetest, neatest enunciation, and a miniature of her father—"done in Rome"—worn as a breastpin. She had written the life, she had edited the speeches, of the original of this ornament, and now at last, beyond the seas, she was really to tread in his footsteps.

Fine old Mrs. Rimmle, in the sunny parlour and with a certain austerity of cap and chair—though with a gay new "front" that looked like rusty brown plush—had had so unusually good a winter that the question of her sparing two members of her family for an absence had been threshed as fine, I could feel, as even under that Puritan roof any case of conscience had ever been threshed. They were to make their dash while the coast, as it were, was clear, and each of the daughters had tried—heroically, angelically, and for the sake of each of her sisters—not to be one of the two. What I encountered that first time was an opportunity to concur with enthusiasm in the general idea that Becky's wonderful preparation would be wasted if she were the one to stay with their mother. They talked of Becky's preparation—they had a sly, old-maidish humour that was as mild as milk—as if it were some mixture, for application somewhere, that she kept in a precious bottle. It had been settled, at all events, that, armed with this concoction and borne aloft by their introductions, she and Jane were to start. They were wonderful on their introductions, which proceeded naturally from their mother and were addressed to the charming families that, in vague generations, had so admired vague Mr. Rimmle. Jane, I found at Brookbridge, had to be described, for want of other description, as the pretty one, but it would not have served to identify her unless you had seen the others. *Her* preparation was only this figment of her prettiness—only, that is, unless one took into account something that, on the spot, I silently divined: the lifelong, secret, passionate ache of her little rebellious desire. They were all growing old in the yearning to go, but Jane's yearning was the sharpest. She struggled with it as people at Brookbridge mostly struggled with what they liked, but fate, by threatening to prevent what she *dis*liked, and what was therefore duty—which was to stay at home instead of Maria—had bewildered her, I judged, not a little. It was she who, in the words I have quoted, mentioned to me Becky's case and Becky's affinity as the clearest of all. Her mother, moreover, on the general subject, had still more to say.

"I positively desire, I really quite insist that they shall go," the old lady explained to us from her stiff chair. "We've talked about it so often, and they've had from me so clear an account—I've amused them again and again with it—of what is to be seen and enjoyed. If they've had hitherto too many duties to leave, the time seems to have come to recognise that there are also many duties to *seek*. Wherever we go we find them—I always remind the girls of that. There's a duty that calls them to those wonderful countries, just as it called, at the right time, their father and myself—if it be only that of laying up for the years to come the same store of remarkable impressions, the same wealth of knowledge and food for conversation as, since my return, I have found myself so happy to possess." Mrs. Rimmle spoke of her return as of something of the year before last, but the future of her daughters was, somehow, by a different law, to be on the scale of great vistas, of endless aftertastes. I think that, without my being quite ready to say it, even this first impression of her was somewhat upsetting; there was a large, placid perversity, a grim secrecy of intention, in her estimate of the ages.

"Well, I'm so glad you don't delay it longer," I said to Miss Becky before we withdrew. "And whoever should go," I continued in the spirit of the sympathy with which the good sisters had already inspired me, "I quite feel, with your family, you know, that *you* should. But of course I hold that every one should." I suppose I wished to attenuate my solemnity; there was something in it, however, that I couldn't help. It must have been a faint foreknowledge.

"Have you been a great deal yourself?" Miss Jane, I remember, inquired.

"Not so much but that I hope to go a good deal more. So perhaps we shall meet," I encouragingly suggested.

I recall something—something in the nature of susceptibility to encouragement—that this brought into the more expressive brown eyes to which Miss Jane mainly owed it that she was the pretty one. "Where, do you think?"

I tried to think. "Well, on the Italian lakes—Como, Bellagio, Lugano." I liked to say the names to them.

" 'Sublime, but neither bleak nor bare—nor misty are the mountains there!' " Miss Jane softly breathed, while her sister looked at her as if her familiarity with the poetry of the subject made her the most interesting feature of the scene she evoked.

But Miss Becky presently turned to me. "Do you know everything——?"

"Everything?"

"In Europe."

"Oh, yes," I laughed, "and one or two things even in America."

The sisters seemed to me furtively to look at each other. "Well, you'll have to be quick—to meet *us*," Miss Jane resumed.

"But surely when you're once there you'll stay on."

"Stay on?"—they murmured it simultaneously and with the oddest vibration of dread as well as of desire. It was as if they had been in the presence of a danger and yet wished me, who "knew everything," to torment them with still more of it.

Well, I did my best. "I mean it will never do to cut it short."

"No, that's just what I keep saying," said brilliant Jane. "It would be better, in that case, not to go."

"Oh, don't talk about not going—at this time!" It was none of my business, but I felt shocked and impatient.

"No, not at *this* time!" broke in Miss Maria, who, very red in the face, had joined us. Poor Miss Maria was known as the flushed one; but she was not flushed—she only had an unfortunate surface. The third day after this was to see them embark.

Miss Becky, however, desired as little as any one to be in any way extravagant. "It's only the thought of our mother," she explained.

I looked a moment at the old lady, with whom my sister-in-law was engaged. "Well—your mother's magnificent."

"*Isn't* she magnificent?"—they eagerly took it up.

She *was*—I could reiterate it with sincerity, though I perhaps mentally drew the line when Miss Maria again risked, as a fresh ejaculation: "I think she's better than Europe!"

"Maria!" they both, at this, exclaimed with a strange emphasis; it was as if they feared she had suddenly turned cynical over the deep domestic drama of their casting of lots. The innocent laugh with which she answered them gave the measure of her cynicism.

We separated at last, and my eyes met Mrs. Rimmle's as I held for an instant her aged hand. It was doubtless only my fancy that her calm, cold look quietly accused me of something. Of what *could* it accuse me? Only, I thought, of thinking.

II

I left Brookbridge the next day, and for some time after that had no occasion to hear from my kinswoman; but when she finally wrote there was a passage in her letter that affected me more than all the rest. "Do you know the poor Rimmles never, after all, 'went'? The old lady, at the eleventh hour, broke down; everything broke down, and all of *them* on top of it, so that the dear things are with us still. Mrs. Rimmle, the night after our call, had, in the most unexpected manner, a turn for the worse—something in the nature (though they're rather mysterious about it) of a seizure; Becky and Jane felt it—dear, devoted, stupid angels that they are—heartless to leave her at such a moment, and Europe's indefinitely postponed. However, they think they're still going—or *think* they think it—when she's better. They also think—or think they think—that she *will* be better. I certainly pray she may." So did I—quite fervently. I was conscious of a real pang—I didn't know how much they had made me care.

Late that winter my sister-in-law spent a week in New York; when almost my first inquiry on meeting her was about the health of Mrs. Rimmle.

"Oh, she's rather bad—she really is, you know. It's not surprising that at her age she should be infirm."

"Then what the deuce *is* her age?"

"I can't tell you to a year—but she's immensely old."

"That of course I saw," I replied—"unless you literally mean so old that the records have been lost."

My sister-in-law thought. "Well, I believe she wasn't positively young when she married. She lost three or four children before these women were born."

We surveyed together a little, on this, the "dark backward." "And they were born, I gather, *after* the famous tour? Well, then, as the famous tour was in a manner to celebrate—wasn't it?—the restoration of the Bourbons——" I considered, I gasped. "My dear child, what on earth do you make her out?"

My relative, with her Brookbridge habit, transferred her share of the question to the moral plane—turned it forth to wander, by implication at least, in the sandy desert of responsibility. "Well, you know, we all immensely admire her."

"You can't admire her more than I do. She's awful."

My interlocutress looked at me with a certain fear. "She's *really* ill."

"Too ill to get better?"

"Oh, no—we hope not. Because then they'll be able to go."

"And *will* they go, if she should?"

"Oh, the moment they should be quite satisfied. I mean *really*," she added.

I'm afraid I laughed at her—the Brookbridge "really" was a thing so by itself. "But if she shouldn't get better?" I went on.

"Oh, don't speak of it! They want so to go."

"It's a pity they're so infernally good," I mused.

"No—don't say that. It's what keeps them up."

"Yes, but isn't it what keeps *her* up too?"

My visitor looked grave. "Would you like them to kill her?"

I don't know that I was then prepared to say I should—though I believe I came very near it. But later on I burst all bounds, for the subject grew and grew. I went again before the good sisters ever did—I mean I went to Europe. I think I went twice, with a brief interval, before my fate again brought round for me a couple of days at Brookbridge. I had been there repeatedly, in the previous time, without making the acquaintance of the Rimmles; but now that I had had the revelation I couldn't have it too much, and the first request I preferred was to be taken again to see them. I remember well indeed the scruple I felt—the real delicacy—about betraying that *I* had, in the pride of my power, since our other meeting, stood, as their phrase went, among romantic scenes; but they were themselves the first to speak of it, and what, moreover, came home to me was that the coming and going of their friends in general—Brookbridge itself having even at that period one foot in Europe—was such as to place constantly before them the pleasure that was only postponed. They were thrown back, after all, on what the situation, under a final analysis, had most to give—the sense that, as every one kindly said to them and they kindly said to every one, Europe would keep. Every one felt for them so deeply that their own kindness in alleviating every one's feeling was really what came out most. Mrs. Rimmle was still in her stiff chair and in the sunny parlour, but if *she* made no scruple of introducing the Italian lakes my heart sank to observe that she dealt with them, as a topic, not in the least in the leave-taking manner in which Falstaff babbled of green fields.

I am not sure that, after this, my pretexts for a day or two with my sister-in-law were not apt to be a mere cover for another glimpse of these particulars: I at any rate never went to Brookbridge without an irrepressible eagerness for our customary call. A long time seems to me thus to have passed, with glimpses and lapses, considerable impatience and still more pity. Our visits indeed grew shorter, for, as my companion said, they were more and more of a strain. It finally struck me that the good sisters even shrank from me a little, as from one who penetrated their consciousness in spite of himself. It was as if they knew where I thought they ought to be, and were moved to deprecate at last, by a systematic silence on the subject of that hemisphere, the criminality I fain would fix on them. They were full instead—as with the instinct of throwing dust in my eyes—of little pathetic hypocrisies about Brookbridge interests and delights. I dare say that as time went on my deeper sense of their situation came practically to rest on my companion's report of it. I think I recollect, at all events, every word we ever exchanged about them, even if I have lost the thread of the special occasions. The impression they made on me after each interval always broke out with extravagance as I walked away with her.

"*She* may be as old as she likes—I don't care. It's the fearful age the 'girls' are reaching that constitutes the scandal. One shouldn't pry into such matters, I know; but the years and the chances are really going. They're all growing old together—it will presently be too late; and their mother meanwhile perches over them like a vulture—what shall I call it?—calculating. Is she waiting for them successively to drop off? She'll survive them each and all. There's something too remorseless in it."

"Yes; but what do you want her to do? If the poor thing *can't* die, she can't. Do you want her to take poison or to open a blood-vessel? I dare say she would prefer to go."

"I beg your pardon," I must have replied; "you daren't say anything of the sort. If she would prefer to go she *would* go. She would feel the propriety, the decency, the necessity of going. She just prefers *not* to go. She prefers to stay and keep up the tension, and her calling them 'girls' and talking of the good time they'll still have is the mere conscious mischief of a subtle old witch. They won't have *any* time—there isn't any time to have! I mean there's, on her own part, no real loss of measure or of perspective in it. She *knows* she's a hundred and ten, and she takes a cruel pride in it."

My sister-in-law differed with me about this; she held that the old woman's attitude was an honest one and that her magnificent vitality, so great in spite of her infirmities, made it inevitable she should attribute youth to persons who had come into the world so much later. "Then suppose she should die?"—so my fellow-student of the case always put it to me.

"Do you mean while her daughters are away? There's not the least fear of that—not even if at the very moment of their departure she should be *in extremis*. They would find her all right on their return."

"But think how they would feel not to have been with her!"

"That's only, I repeat, on the unsound assumption. If they would only go to-morrow—literally make a good rush for it—they'll be with her when they come back. That will give them plenty of time." I'm afraid I even heartlessly added that if she *should*, against every probability, pass away in their absence, they wouldn't have to come back at all—which would be just the compensation proper to their long privation. And then Maria would come out to join the two others, and they would be—though but for the too scanty remnant of their career—as merry as the day is long.

I remained ready, somehow, pending the fulfilment of that vision, to sacrifice Maria; it was only over the urgency of the case for the others respectively that I found myself balancing. Sometimes it was for Becky I thought the tragedy deepest—sometimes, and in quite a different manner, I thought it most dire for Jane. It was Jane, after all, who had most sense of life. I seemed in fact dimly to descry in Jane a sense—as yet undescried by herself or by any one—of all sorts of queer things. Why didn't *she* go? I used desperately to ask; why didn't she make a bold personal dash for it, strike up a partnership with some one or other of the travelling spinsters in whom Brookbridge more and more abounded? Well, there came a flash for me at a particular point of the grey middle desert: my correspondent was able to let me know that poor Jane at last *had* sailed. She had gone of a sudden—I liked my sister-in-law's view of suddenness—with the kind Hathaways, who had made an irresistible grab at her and lifted her off her feet. They were going for the summer and for Mr. Hathaway's health, so that the opportunity was perfect and it was impossible not to be glad that something very like physical force had finally prevailed. This was the general feeling at Brookbridge, and I might imagine what Brookbridge had been brought to from the fact that, at the very moment she was hustled off, the doctor, called to her mother at the peep of dawn, had considered that *he* at least must stay. There had been real alarm—greater than ever before; it actually did seem as if this time the end had come. But it was Becky, strange to say, who, though fully recognizing the nature of the crisis, had kept the situation in hand and insisted upon action. This, I remember, brought back to me a discomfort with which I had been familiar from the first. One of the two had sailed, and I was sorry it was not the other. But if it had been the other I should have been equally sorry.

I saw with my eyes, that very autumn, what a fool Jane would have been if she had again backed out. Her mother had of course survived the peril of which I had heard, profiting by it indeed as she had profited by every other; she was sufficiently better again to have come down stairs. It was there that, as usual, I found her, but with a difference of effect produced somehow by the absence of one of the girls. It was as if, for the others, though they had not gone to Europe, Europe had come to them: Jane's letters had been so frequent and so beyond even what could have been hoped. It was the first time, however, that I perceived on the old woman's part a certain failure of lucidity. Jane's flight was, clearly, the great fact with her, but she spoke of it as if the fruit had now been plucked and the parenthesis closed. I don't know what sinking sense of still further physical duration I gathered, as a menace, from this first hint of her confusion of mind.

"My daughter has been; my daughter has been——" She kept saying it, but didn't say where; that seemed unnecessary, and she only repeated the words to her visitors with a face that was all puckers and yet now, save in so far as it expressed an ineffaceable complacency, all blankness. I think she wanted us a little to know that she had not stood in the way. It added to something—I scarce knew what—that I found myself desiring to extract privately from Becky. As our visit was to be of the shortest my opportunity—for one of the young ladies always came to the door with us—was at hand. Mrs. Rimmle, as we took leave, again sounded her phrase, but she added this time: "I'm so glad she's going to have always——"

I knew so well what she meant that, as she again dropped, looking at me queerly and becoming momentarily dim, I could help her out. "Going to have what *you* have?"

"Yes, yes—my privilege. Wonderful experience," she mumbled. She bowed to me a little as if I would understand. "She has things to tell."

I turned, slightly at a loss, to Becky. "She has then already arrived?"

Becky was at that moment looking a little strangely at her mother, who answered my question. "She reached New York this morning—she comes on to-day."

"Oh, then——!" But I let the matter pass as I met Becky's eye—I saw there was a hitch somewhere. It was not she but Maria who came out with us; on which I cleared up the question of their sister's reappearance.

"Oh, no, not to-night," Maria smiled; "that's only the way mother puts it. We shall see her about the end of November— the Hathaways are so indulgent. They kindly extend their tour."

"For *her* sake? How sweet of them!" my sister-in-law exclaimed.

I can see our friend's plain, mild old face take on a deeper mildness, even though a higher colour, in the light of the open door. "Yes, it's for Jane they prolong it. And do you know what they write?" She gave us time, but it was too great a responsibility to guess. "Why, that it has brought her out."

"Oh, I knew it *would*!" my companion sympathetically sighed.

Maria put it more strongly still. "They say we wouldn't know her."

This sounded a little awful, but it was, after all, what I had expected.

III

My correspondent in Brookbridge came to me that Christmas, with my niece, to spend a week; and the arrangement had of course been prefaced by an exchange of letters, the first of which from my sister-in-law scarce took space for acceptance of my invitation before going on to say: "The Hathaways are back—but without Miss Jane!" She presented in a few words the situation thus created at Brookbridge, but was not yet, I gathered, fully in possession of the other one—the situation created in "Europe" by the presence there of that lady. The two together, at any rate, demanded, I quickly felt, all my attention, and perhaps my impatience to receive my relative was a little sharpened by my desire for the whole story. I had it at last, by the Christmas fire, and I may say without reserve that it gave me all I could have hoped for. I listened eagerly, after which I produced the comment: "Then she simply refused——"

"To budge from Florence? Simply. She had it out there with the poor Hathaways, who felt responsible for her safety, pledged to restore her to her mother's, to her sisters' hands, and showed herself in a light, they mention under their breath, that made their dear old hair stand on end. Do you know what, when they first got back, they said of her—at least it was *his* phrase—to two or three people?"

I thought a moment. "That she had 'tasted blood'?"

My visitor fairly admired me. "How clever of you to guess! It's exactly what he did say. She appeared—she continues to appear, it seems—in a new character."

I wondered a little. "But that's exactly—don't you remember?—what Miss Maria reported to us from them; that we 'wouldn't know her.'"

My sister-in-law perfectly remembered. "Oh, yes—she broke out from the first. But when they left her she was worse."

"Worse?"

"Well, different—different from anything she ever *had* been, or—for that matter—had had a chance to be." My interlocutress hung fire a moment, but presently faced me. "Rather strange and free and obstreperous."

"Obstreperous?" I wondered again.

"Peculiarly so, I inferred, on the question of not coming away. She wouldn't hear of it, and, when they spoke of her mother, said she had given her mother up. She had thought she should like Europe, but didn't know she should like it so much. They had been fools to bring her if they expected to take her away. She was going to see what she could—she hadn't yet seen half. The end of it was, at any rate, that they had to leave her alone."

I seemed to see it all—to see even the scared Hathaways. "So she *is* alone?"

"She told them, poor thing, it appears, and in a tone they'll never forget, that she was, at all events, quite old enough to be. She cried—she quite went on—over not having come sooner. That's why the only way for her," my companion mused, "*is*, I suppose, to stay. They wanted to put her with some people or other—to find some American family. But she says she's on her own feet."

"And she's still in Florence?"

"No—I believe she was to travel. She's bent on the East."

I burst out laughing. "Magnificent Jane! It's most interesting. Only I feel that I distinctly *should* 'know' her. To my sense, always, I must tell you, she had it in her."

My relative was silent a little. "So it now appears Becky always felt."

"And yet pushed her off? Magnificent Becky!"

My companion met my eyes a moment. "You don't know the queerest part. I mean the way it has *most* brought her out."

I turned it over; I felt I should like to know—to that degree indeed that, oddly enough, I jocosely disguised my eagerness. "You don't mean she has taken to drink?"

My visitor hesitated. "She has taken to flirting."

I expressed disappointment. "Oh, she took to *that* long ago. Yes," I declared at my kinswoman's stare, "she positively flirted—with *me*!"

The stare perhaps sharpened. "Then you flirted with *her*?"

"How else could I have been as sure as I wanted to be? But has she means?"

"Means to flirt?"—my friend looked an instant as if she spoke literally. "I don't understand about the means—though of course they have something. But I have my impression," she went on. "I think that Becky——" It seemed almost too grave to say.

But *I* had no doubts. "That Becky's backing her?"

She brought it out. "Financing her."

"Stupendous Becky! So that morally then——"

"Becky's quite in sympathy. But isn't it too odd?" my sister-in-law asked.

"Not in the least. Didn't we know, as regards Jane, that Europe was to bring her out? Well, it has also brought out Rebecca."

"It has indeed!" my companion indulgently sighed. "So what would it do if she were there?"

"I should like immensely to see. And we *shall* see."

"Why, do you believe she'll still go?"

"Certainly. She *must*."

But my friend shook it off. "She won't."

"She shall!" I retorted with a laugh. But the next moment I said: "And what does the old woman say?"

"To Jane's behaviour? Not a word—never speaks of it. She talks now much less than she used—only seems to wait. But it's my belief she thinks."

"And—do you mean—knows?"

"Yes, knows that she's abandoned. In her silence there she takes it in."

"It's her way of making Jane pay?" At this, somehow, I felt more serious. "Oh, dear, dear—she'll disinherit her!"

When, in the following June, I went on to return my sister-in-law's visit the first object that met my eyes in her little white parlour was a figure that, to my stupefaction, presented itself for the moment as that of Mrs. Rimmle. I had gone to my room after arriving, and, on dressing, had come down: the apparition I speak of had arisen in the interval. Its ambiguous character lasted, however, but a second or two—I had taken Becky for her mother because I knew no one but her mother of that extreme age. Becky's age was quite startling; it had made a great stride, though, strangely enough, irrecoverably seated as she now was in it, she had a wizened brightness that I had scarcely yet seen in her. I remember indulging on this occasion in two silent observations: one to the effect that I had not hitherto been conscious of her full resemblance to the old lady, and the other to the effect that, as I had said to my sister-in-law at Christmas, "Europe," even as reaching her only through Jane's sensibilities, had really at last brought her out. She was in fact "out" in a manner of which this encounter offered to my eyes a unique example: it was the single hour, often as I had been at Brookbridge, of my meeting her elsewhere than in her mother's drawing-room. I surmise that, besides being adjusted to her more marked time of life, the garments she wore abroad, and in particular her little plain bonnet, presented points of resemblance to the close sable sheath and the quaint old headgear that, in the white house behind the elms, I had from far back associated with the eternal image in the stiff chair. Of course I immediately spoke of Jane, showing an interest and asking for news; on which she answered me with a smile, but not at all as I had expected.

"*Those* are not really the things you want to know—where she is, whom she's with, how she manages and where she's going next—oh, no!" And the admirable woman gave a laugh that was somehow both light and sad—sad, in particular, with a strange, long weariness. "What you do want to know is when she's coming back."

I shook my head very kindly, but out of a wealth of experience that, I flattered myself, was equal to Miss Becky's. "I do know it. Never."

Miss Becky, at this, exchanged with me a long, deep look. "Never."

We had, in silence, a little luminous talk about it, in the course of which she seemed to tell me the most interesting things. "And how's your mother?" I then inquired.

She hesitated, but finally spoke with the same serenity. "My mother's all right. You see, she's not alive."

"Oh, Becky!" my sister-in-law pleadingly interjected.

But Becky only addressed herself to me. "Come and see if she is. *I* think she isn't—but Maria perhaps isn't so clear. Come, at all events, and judge and tell me."

It was a new note, and I was a little bewildered. "Ah, but I'm not a doctor!"

"No, thank God—you're not. That's why I ask you." And now she said good-bye.

I kept her hand a moment. "*You're* more alive than ever!"

"I'm very tired." She took it with the same smile, but for Becky it was much to say.

IV

"Not alive," the next day, was certainly what Mrs. Rimmle looked when, coming in according to my promise, I found her, with Miss Maria, in her usual place. Though shrunken and diminished she still occupied her high-backed chair with a visible theory of erectness, and her intensely aged face—combined with something dauntless that belonged to her very presence and that was effective even in this extremity—might have been that of some centenarian sovereign, of indistinguishable sex, brought forth to be shown to the people as a disproof of the rumour of extinction. Mummified and openeyed she looked at me, but I had no impression that she made me out. I had come this time without my sister-in-law, who had frankly pleaded to me—which also, for a daughter of Brookbridge, was saying much—that the house had grown too painful. Poor Miss Maria excused Miss Becky on the score of her not being well—and that, it struck me, was saying most of all. The absence of the others gave the occasion a different note; but I talked with Miss Maria for five minutes and perceived that—save for her saying, of her own movement, anything about Jane—she now spoke as if her mother had lost hearing or sense, or both, alluding freely and distinctly, though indeed favourably, to her condition. "She has expected your visit and she much enjoys it," my interlocutress said, while the old woman, soundless and motionless, simply fixed me without expression. Of course there was little to keep me; but I became aware, as I rose to go, that there was more than I had supposed. On my approaching her to take leave Mrs. Rimmle gave signs of consciousness.

"Have you heard about Jane?"

I hesitated, feeling a responsibility, and appealed for direction to Maria's face. But Maria's face was troubled, was turned altogether to her mother's. "About her life in Europe?" I then rather helplessly asked.

The old woman fronted me, on this, in a manner that made me feel silly. "Her life?"—and her voice, with this second effort, came out stronger. "Her death, if you please."

"Her death?" I echoed, before I could stop myself, with the accent of deprecation.

Miss Maria uttered a vague sound of pain, and I felt her turn away, but the marvel of her mother's little unquenched spark still held me. "Jane's dead. We've heard," said Mrs. Rimmle. "We've heard from—where is it we've heard from?" She had quite revived—she appealed to her daughter.

The poor old girl, crimson, rallied to her duty. "From Europe."

Mrs. Rimmle made at us both a little grim inclination of the head. "From Europe." I responded, in silence, with a deflection from every rigour, and, still holding me, she went on: "And now Rebecca's going."

She had gathered by this time such emphasis to say it that again, before I could help myself, I vibrated in reply. "To Europe—now?" It was as if for an instant she had made me believe it.

She only stared at me, however, from her wizened mask; then her eyes followed my companion. "Has she gone?"

"Not yet, mother." Maria tried to treat it as a joke, but her smile was embarrassed and dim.

"Then where is she?"

"She's lying down."

The old woman kept up her hard, queer gaze, but directing it, after a minute, to me. "She's going."

"Oh, some day!" I foolishly laughed; and on this I got to the door, where I separated from my younger hostess, who came no further. Only, as I held the door open, she said to me under cover of it and very quietly:

"It's poor mother's idea."

I saw—it was her idea. Mine was—for some time after this, even after I had returned to New York and to my usual occupations—that I should never again see Becky. I had seen her for the last time, I believed, under my sister-in-law's roof, and in the autumn it was given to me to hear from that fellow-admirer that she had succumbed at last to the situation. The day of the call I have just described had been a date in the process of her slow shrinkage—it was literally the first time she had, as they said at Brookbridge, given up. She had been ill for years, but the other state of health in the contemplation of which she had spent so much of her life had left her, till too late, no margin for meeting it. The encounter, at last, came simply in the form of the discovery that it *was* too late; on which, naturally, she had given up more and more. I had heard indeed, all summer, by letter, how Brookbridge had watched her do so; whereby the end found me in a manner prepared. Yet in spite of my preparation there remained with me a soreness, and when I was next—it was some six months later—on the scene of her martyrdom I replied, I fear, with an almost rabid negative to the question put to me in due course by my kinswoman. "Call on them? Never again!"

I went, none the less, the very next day. Everything was the same in the sunny parlour—everything that most mattered, I mean: the immemorial mummy in the high chair and the tributes, in the little frames on the walls, to the celebrity of its late husband. Only Maria Rimmle was different: if Becky, on my last seeing her, had looked as old as her mother, Maria—save that she moved about—looked older. I remember that she moved about, but I scarce remember what she said; and indeed what was there to say? When I risked a question, however, she had a reply.

"But *now* at least——?" I tried to put it to her suggestively.

At first she was vague. " 'Now?' "

"Won't Miss Jane come back?"

Oh, the headshake she gave me! "Never." It positively pictured to me, for the instant, a well-preserved woman, a sort of rich, ripe *seconde jeunesse* by the Arno.

"Then that's only to make more sure of your finally joining her."

Maria Rimmle repeated her headshake. "Never."

We stood so, a moment, bleakly face to face; I could think of no attenuation that would be particularly happy. But while I tried I heard a hoarse gasp that, fortunately, relieved me—a signal strange and at first formless from the occupant of the high-backed chair. "Mother wants to speak to you," Maria then said.

So it appeared from the drop of the old woman's jaw, the expression of her mouth opened as if for the emission of sound. It was difficult to me, somehow, to seem to sympathize without hypocrisy, but, so far as a step nearer could do so, I invited communication. "Have you heard where Becky's gone?" the wonderful witch's white lips then extraordinarily asked.

It drew from Maria, as on my previous visit, an uncontrollable groan, and this, in turn, made me take time to consider. As I considered, however, I had an inspiration. "To Europe?"

I must have adorned it with a strange grimace, but my inspiration had been right. "To Europe," said Mrs. Rimmle.

The Great Condition

"Ah there, confound it!" said Bertram Braddle when he had once more frowned, so far as he could frown, over his telegram. "I *must* catch the train if I'm to have my morning clear in town. And it's a most abominable nuisance!"

"Do you mean on account of—a—*her*?" asked, after a minute's silent sympathy, the friend to whom—in the hall of the hotel, still bestrewn with the appurtenances of the newly disembarked—he had thus querulously addressed himself.

He looked hard for an instant at Henry Chilver, but the hardness was not all produced by Chilver's question. His annoyance at not being able to spend his night at Liverpool was visibly the greatest that such a privation can be conceived as producing, and might have seemed indeed to transcend the limits of its occasion. "I promised her the second day out that, no matter at what hour we should get in, I would see her up to London and save her having to take a step by herself."

"And you piled up the assurance"—Chilver somewhat irrelevantly laughed—"with each successive day!"

"Naturally—for what is there to do between New York and Queenstown but pile up? And now, with this pistol at my head"—crumpling the telegram with an angry fist, he tossed it into the wide public chimney-place—"I leave her to scramble through to-morrow as she can. She has to go on to Brighton and she doesn't know——" And Braddle's quickened sense of the perversity of things dropped to a moment's helpless communion with the aggravating face of his watch.

"She doesn't know——?" his friend conscientiously echoed.

"Oh, she doesn't know anything! Should you say it's too late to ask for a word with her?"

Chilver, with his eyes on the big hotel-clock, wondered. "Lateish—isn't it?—when she must have been gone this quarter of an hour to her room."

"Yes, I'm bound to say she *has* managed *that* for herself!" and Braddle stuck back his watch. "So that, as I haven't time to write, there's nothing for me but to wire her—ever so apol-ogetically—the first thing in the morning from town."

"Surely—as for the steamer special there are now only about five minutes left."

"Good then—I join you," said Braddle with a sigh of sub-mission. "But where's the brute who took my things? Yours went straight to the station?"

"No—they're still out there on the cab from which I set you down. And there's your chap with your stuff"—Chilver's eye had just caught the man—"he's ramming it into the lift. Collar him before it goes up." Bertram Braddle, on this, sprang forward in time; then while at an office-window that opened into an inner sanctuary he explained his case to a neatly fitted priestess whose cold eyes looked straight through nonsense, putting it before her that he should after all not require the room he had telegraphed for, his companion only turned uneasily about at a distance and made no approach to the arrested four-wheeler that, at the dock, had received both the gentlemen and their effects. "I join you—I join you," Braddle repeated as he brought back his larger share of these.

Chilver appeared meanwhile to have found freedom of mind for a decision. "But, my dear fellow, shall I too then go?"

Braddle stared. "Why, I thought you so eminently *had* to."

"Not if I can be of any use to you. I mean by stopping over and offering my—I admit very inferior—aid——"

"To Mrs. Damerel?" Braddle took in his friend's sudden and—as it presented itself—singularly obliging change of plan. "Ah, you want to be of use to *her*?"

"Only if it will take her off your mind till you see her again. I don't mind telling you now," Chilver courageously contin-ued, "that I'm not positively in such a hurry. I said I'd catch the train because I thought you wanted to be alone with her."

The young men stood there now a trifle rigidly, but very expressively, face to face: Bertram Braddle, the younger but much the taller, smooth, handsome and heavy, with the com-position of his dress so elaborately informal, his pleasant mo-nocular scowl so religiously fixed, his hat so despairingly tilted, and his usual air—innocent enough, however—of looking down from some height still greater—as every one knew about the rich, the bloated Braddles—than that of his fine stature; Chilver, slight and comparatively colourless, rather sharp than bright, but with—in spite of a happy brown moustache, scantily professional, but envied by the man whose large, empty, sunny face needed, as some one had said, a little planting—no particular "looks" save those that dwelt in his intelligent eyes. "And what then did you think I wanted to do?"

"Exactly what you say. To present yourself in a taking light—to deepen the impression you've been at so much trouble to make. But if you don't care for my stopping——!" And tossing away the end of his cigarette with a gesture of good-humoured renouncement, Chilver moved across the marble slabs to the draughty portal that kept swinging from the street.

There were porters, travellers, other impediments in his way, and this gave Braddle an appreciable time to watch his receding back before it disappeared; the prompt consequence of which was an "I say, Chilver!" launched after him sharply enough to make him turn round before passing out. The speaker had not otherwise stirred, and the interval of space doubtless took something from the straightness of their further mute communication. This interval, the next minute, as Chilver failed to return, Braddle diminished by gaining the door in company with a porter whose arm he had seized on the way. "Take this gentleman's things off the cab and put on mine." Then as he turned to his friend: "Go and tell the young woman there that you'll have the room I've given up."

Chilver laid upon him a hand still interrogative enough not to be too grateful. "Are you very sure it's all right?"

Braddle's face simply followed for a moment, in the outer lamplight, the progress of the operation he had decreed. "Do you think I'm going to allow you to make out that I'm afraid?"

"Well, my dear chap, why shouldn't you be?" Henry Chilver, with this retort, did nothing; he only, with his hands in his pockets, let the porter and the cabman bestir themselves. "I simply wanted to be civil."

"Oh, I'll risk it!" said the younger man with a free enough laugh. "Be awfully attentive, you know."

"Of course it won't be anything like the same thing to *her*," Chilver went on.

"Of course not, but explain. Tell her I'm wiring, writing. Do everything, in short. Good-bye."

"Good-bye, good-bye, old man." And Chilver went down with him to the rearranged cab. "So many thanks."

"Thanks?" said the other as he got in.

"I mean because I'm—hang it!—just tired enough to be glad to go to bed."

"Oh!" came rather dryly from Braddle out of the window of the cab.

"Shan't I go with you to the station?" his companion asked.

"Dear no—much obliged!"

"Well, you shall have my report!" Chilver continued.

"Ah, I shall have Mrs. Damerel's!" Braddle answered as the cab drove away.

II

The fatigue of which Chilver had spoken sought relief for the time in a good deal of rather pointless activity, and it was not for an hour after he had taken possession of his room that he lay down to close his eyes. He moved, before this, in his narrow limits, up and down and to and fro; he left his smaller portmanteau gaping but unpacked; he fumbled in his dressing-bag for a book and dropped with it into a chair. But when in this position he let his attention very soon wander and his lids finally droop, it was not at all that sleep had overcome him. Something had overcome him, on the contrary, that, a quarter of an hour later, made him jump up and consult the watch he had transferred from his pocket to his bedside as his only step toward undressing. He quickly restored it to its receptacle and, catching up his hat, left the room and took his course down stairs. Here, for another quarter of an hour, he wandered, waited, looked about. He had been rather positive to his comrade on the question of Mrs. Damerel's possible, impossible, reappearance; but his movements, for some time, could have been explained only by an unquenched imagination that, late though the hour, she might "nip" down—so in fact he mentally phrased it: well, for what? To indulge—it was conceivable—an appetite unappeased by the five and twenty meals (Braddle had seen them all served to her on deck) of the rapid voyage. He kept glancing into the irresponsive coffee-room and peeping through the glass door of a smaller blank, bright apartment in which a lonely, ugly lady, hatted and coated and hugging a bundle of shawls, sat glaring into space with an anxiety of her own. When at last he returned to his room, however, it was quite with the recognition that such a person as Mrs. Damerel wouldn't at all at that hour be knocking about the hotel. On the other hand—his vigil still encouraged the reflection—what appeared less like her than her giving them the slip, on their all leaving the dock, so unceremoniously; making her independent dash for a good room at the inn the very moment the Customs people had passed her luggage? It was perhaps the fatiguing futility of this question that at last sent Henry Chilver to bed and to sleep.

That restorative proved the next morning to have considerably cleared and settled his consciousness. He found himself immediately aware of being in no position to say what was or was not "like" Mrs. Damerel. He knew as little about her as Braddle knew, and it was his conviction that Braddle's ignorance had kept regular step with all the rest of the conditions. These conditions were, to begin with, that, seated next her at table for the very first repast, Bertram had struck up with her a friendship of which the leaps and bounds were, in the social, the sentimental sphere, not less remarkable than those with which the great hurrying ship took its way through the sea. They were, further, that, unlike all the other women, so numerous and, in the fine weather, so "chatty," she had succeeded in incurring the acquaintance of nobody in the immense company but themselves. Three or four men had more or less made up to her, but with none of the ladies had she found it inevitable to exchange, to his observation—and oh, his attention, at least, had been deep!—three words. The great fact above all had been—as it now glimmered back to him—that he had studied her not so much in her own demonstrations, which had been few and passive, as in those of his absolutely alienated companion. He had been reduced to contemplation resignedly remote, since Braddle now monopolised her, and had thus seen her largely through his surprise

at the constancy of Braddle's interest. The affinities hitherto—
in other cases—recognised by his friend he had generally made
out as of an order much less fine. There were lots of women
on the ship who might easily have been supposed to be a good
deal more his affair. Not one of them had, however, by any
perversity corresponding with that of the connection under
his eyes, become in any degree Chilver's own. He had the
feeling, on the huge crowded boat, of making the voyage in
singular solitude, a solitude mitigated only by the amusement
of finding Braddle so "mashed" and of wondering what
would come of it. Much less, up to that moment, had come
of the general American exposure than each, on their sailing
westward for the more and more prescribed near view, had
freely foretold to the other as the least they were likely to get
off with. The near view of the big queer country had at last,
this summer, imposed itself: so many other men had got it
and were making it, in talk, not only a convenience but a good
deal of a nuisance, that it appeared to have become, defen-
sively, as necessary as the electric light in the flat one might
wish to let; as to which the two friends, after their ten bustling
weeks, had now in fact grown to feel that they could press
the American button with the best.

But they had been on the whole—Chilver at least had
been—disappointed in the celebrated (and were they not *all*,
in the United States, celebrated?) native women. He didn't
quite know what he had expected: something or other, at any
rate, that had not taken place. He felt as if he had carried over
in his portmanteau a court-suit or a wedding-garment and
were bringing it back untouched, unfolded, in creases un-
relieved and almost painfully aware of themselves. They had
taken lots of letters—most of them, some fellow who knew
had told them, awfully good ones; they had been to Washington and Boston and Newport and Mount Desert, walking
round and round the vociferous whirlpool, but neither tumbling in nor feeling at any moment, as it appeared, at all dangerously dizzy; so that here—in relation to Mrs. Damerel—
was the oddity of an impression vertiginous only after everything might have been supposed to be well over. This lady
was the first female American they had met, of almost any age,
who was not celebrated; yet she was the one who suggested

most to Chilver something he now imagined himself originally
to have gone forth expecting to feel. She was a person to
whom they couldn't possibly have had a letter; she had never
in her life been to Newport; she was on her way to England
for the first time; she was, in short, most inconsistently,
though indeed quite unblushingly, obscure. She was only
charming in a new way. It was newer, somehow, than any of
the others that were so fresh. Yet what should he call it if he
were trying—in a foolish flight of analysis to somebody else—
to describe it? When he asked himself this he was verily
brought, from one thing to another, to recognising that it
was probably in fact as old as the hills. All that was new in it
was that he was in love with her; and moreover without in
the least knowing her, so completely, so heroically, from the
point of honour, had he, for all the six days, left her to poor
Braddle. Well, if he should now take her up to town he would
be a little less ignorant. He liked, naturally, to think he should
be of use to her, but he flattered himself he kept the point of
honour well in view. To Braddle—given Braddle's uneasi-
ness—he should be equally of use.

III

This last appearance was in a short time abundantly confirmed; not only when, in London, after the discharge of his
mission, he submitted to his friend a detailed account of that
happy transaction, but ten days later, on Braddle's own return
from Brighton, where he had promptly put in a week—a week
of which, visibly, the sole and irresistible motive was Mrs.
Damerel, established there as a sequel to Chilver's attendance
on her from Liverpool to Euston and from Euston, within the
hour—so immediately that she got off before her other friend
had had time to turn up at either station—to Victoria. This
other friend passed in London, while at Brighton, the inside
of a day, rapping with a familiar stick—at an hour supposedly
not dedicated, in those grey courts, to profane speculation—
the door of the dingy Temple chambers in which, after the
most extravagant holiday of his life, Henry Chilver had found
it salutary to sit and imagine himself "reading." But Braddle
had always been, portentously, a person of free mornings—

his nominal occupation that of looking after his father's "interests," and his actual that of spending, though quite without scandal, this personage's money, of which, luckily, there seemed an abundance. What came from him on this occasion connected itself with something that had passed between them on their previous meeting, the one immediately following the incident at Liverpool. Chilver had at that time been rather surprised to hear his friend suddenly bring out: "You don't then think there's anything 'off' about her?"

"Off?" Chilver could at least be perfectly vague. "Off what?"

"What's the beastly phrase? 'Off colour.' I mean do you think she's all right?"

"Are you in love with her?" Chilver after a moment demanded.

"Damn it, of course I'm in love with her!" Braddle joylessly articulated.

"Well then, doesn't that give you——?"

"Give me what?" he asked with impatience at his companion's pause.

"Well, a sort of searching light——"

"For reading her clear?" Braddle broke in. "How can you ask—as a man of the world—anything so idiotic? Where did you ever discover that being in love makes a searching light, makes anything but a most damnable and demoralising darkness? One has been in love with creatures such that one's condition has lighted nothing in the world but one's asininity. *I* have at any rate. And so have you!"

"No, I've never been really in love at all," said Chilver good-humouredly.

"The less credit to you then to have—in two or three cases I recall—made such a fool of yourself. I, at all events—I don't mind your knowing," Braddle went on—"am harder hit, far and away, than I've ever been. But I don't in the least pretend to place her or to have a free judgment about her. I've already—since we landed—had two letters from her, and I go down to-morrow to see her. That *may* assist me—it ought to—to make her out a little better. But I've a gruesome feeling that it won't!"

"Then how can I help you?" Chilver inquired with just irritation enough to make him, the next moment—though his interlocutor, interestingly worried but really most inexpert, had no answer for the question—sorry to have shown it. "If you've heard from her," he continued, "did she send me a message?"

"None whatever."

"Nor say anything about me?"

"Not a word."

"Ah!" said Henry Chilver while their eyes again met with some insistence. He somehow liked Mrs. Damerel's silence after the hours he had spent with her; but his state of mind was again predominantly of not wanting Braddle to see in him any emotion. "A woman may surely be called all right, it seems to me, when she's pretty and clever and good."

" 'Good'?" Braddle echoed. "How do you know she's good?"

"Why, confound you, she's such a lady."

"*Isn't* she?"—Braddle took it up with equal promptitude and inconsequence. Then he recovered himself. "All the same, one has known ladies——!"

"Yes, one has. But she's quite the best thing that, in the whole time, we've come across."

"Oh, by a long shot. Think of those women on the ship. It's only that she's so poor," Braddle added.

Chilver hesitated. "Is she so awfully?"

"She has evidently to count her shillings."

"Well, if she had been bad she'd be rich," Chilver returned after another silence. "So what more do you want?"

"Nothing. Nothing," Braddle repeated.

"Good-bye, then."

"Good-bye."

On which the elder man had taken leave; so that what was inevitably to follow had to wait for their next meeting. Mrs. Damerel's victim betrayed on this second occasion still more markedly the state of a worried man, and his friend measured his unrest by his obvious need of a patient ear, a need with which Chilver's own nature, this interlocutor felt, would not in the same conditions have been acquainted. Even while he wondered, however, at the freedom his visitor used, Chilver recognised that had it been a case of more or less fatuous happiness Braddle would probably have kept the matter to himself. His host made the reflection that *he*, on the other hand, might have babbled about a confidence, but would never have opened his mouth about a fear. Braddle's fear, like many fears, had a considerable queerness, and Chilver, in presence of it and even before a full glimpse, had begun to describe it to himself as a fixed idea. It was as if according to Braddle, there had been something in Mrs. Damerel's history that she ought really to have told a fellow before letting him in so far.

"But how far?"

"Why, hang it, I'd marry her to-morrow."

Chilver waited a moment. "Is what you mean that she'd marry *you*?"

"Yes, blest if I don't believe she certainly would."

"You mean if you'd let her off——?"

"Yes," Braddle concurred; "the obligation of letting me know the particular thing that, whatever it is, right or wrong, I've somehow got it so tormentingly into my head that she keeps back."

"When you say 'keeps back,' do you mean that you've questioned her?"

"Oh, not about *that*!" said Braddle with beautiful simplicity.

"Then do you expect her to volunteer information——"

"That may damage her so awfully with me?" Braddle had taken it up intelligently, but appeared sufficiently at a loss as to what he expected. "I'm sure she knows well enough I want to know."

"I don't think I understand what you're talking about," Chilver replied after a longish stare at the fire.

"Well, about something or other in her life; some awkward passage, some beastly episode or accident; the things that do happen, that often *have* happened, to women you might think perfectly straight—come now! and that they very often quite successfully hide. You know what I'm driving at: some chapter in the book difficult to read aloud—some unlucky page she'd like to tear out. God forgive me, some slip."

Chilver, quitting the fire, had taken a turn round the room. "Is it your idea," he presently inquired, "that there may have been only *one*? I mean one 'slip.' " He pulled up long enough in front of them to give his visitor's eyes time to show a guess at possible derision, then he went on in another manner. "No, no; I really don't understand. You seem to me to see her as a column of figures each in itself highly satisfactory, but which, when you add them up, make only a total of doubt."

"That's exactly it!" Braddle spoke almost with admiration of this neat formula. "She hasn't really *any* references."

"But, my dear man, it's not as if you were engaging a housemaid."

Braddle was arrested but a moment. "It's much worse. For any one else I shouldn't mind——!"

"What I don't grasp," his companion broke in, "is your liking her so much as to 'mind' so much, without by the same stroke liking her enough not to mind at all."

Braddle took in without confusion this approach to subtlety. "But suppose it should be something rather awful?"

It was his confidant, rather, who was a trifle disconcerted. "Isn't it just as easy—besides being much more comfortable— to suppose there's nothing?"

"No. If it had been, don't you see that I *would* have supposed it? There's something. I don't know what there is; but there's something."

"Then ask her."

Braddle wondered. "Would *you*?"

"Oh dear, no!"

"Then *I* won't!" Braddle returned with an odd air of defiance that made his host break into a laugh. "Suppose," he continued, "she should swear there's nothing."

"The chance of that is just why it strikes me you might ask her."

"I 'might'? I thought you said one shouldn't."

"*I* shouldn't. But I haven't your ideas."

"Ah, but you don't know her."

Chilver hesitated. "Precisely. And what you mean is that, even if she should swear there's nothing, you wouldn't believe her?"

Braddle appeared to give a silent and even somewhat diffident assent. "There's nothing I should hate like that. I should hate it still more than being as I am. If you had seen more of her," he pursued, "you would know what I mean by her having no references. Her whole life has been so extraordinarily—so conveniently, as one might say—away from everything."

"I see—so conveniently for *her*. Beyond verification."

"Exactly; the record's inaccessible. It's all the 'great West.' We saw something of the great West, and I thought it rather *too* great. She appears to have put in a lot of California and the Sandwich Islands. I may be too particular, but I don't fancy a Sandwich Islands past. Even for her husband and for her little girl—for their having lived as little as for their having died—she has nothing to show. She hasn't so much as a photograph, a lock of hair or an announcement in a newspaper."

Chilver thought. "But perhaps she wouldn't naturally leave such things about the sitting-room of a Brighton lodging."

"I dare say not. But it isn't only such things. It's tremendously odd her never having even by mere chance knocked against anything or any one that one has ever heard of or could—if one should want to—get at."

Again Henry Chilver reflected. "Well, that's what struck me as especially nice, or rather as very remarkable in her—her being, with all her attraction, one of the obscure seventy millions; a mere little almost nameless tossed-up flower out of the huge mixed lap of the great American people. I mean for the charming person she is. I doubt if, after all, any other huge mixed lap——"

"Yes, if she were English, on those lines," Braddle sagaciously interrupted, "one wouldn't look at her, would one? I say, fancy her English!"

Chilver was silent a little. "What you don't like is her music."

His visitor met his eyes. "Why, it's awfully good."

"Is it? I mean her having, as you told me on the boat, given lessons."

"That certainly is not what I most like her to have done—I mean on account of some of the persons she may have given them *to*; but when her voice broke down she had to do something. She had sung in public—though only in concerts; but that's another thing. She lost her voice after an illness. I don't know what the illness was. It was after her husband's death. She plays quite wonderfully—better, she says, really, than she sang; so she has that resource. She gave the lessons in the Sandwich Islands. She admits that, fighting for her own hand, as she says, she has kept some queer company. I've asked her for details, but she only says she'll tell me 'some day.' Well, *what* day, don't you know? Finally she inherited a little money—she says from a distant cousin. I don't call *that* distant—setting her up. It isn't much, but it made the difference, and there she is. She says she's afraid of London; but I don't quite see in what sense. She heard about her place at Brighton from some 'Western friends.' But how can I go and ask them?"

"The Western friends?" said Chilver.

"No, the people of the house—about the other people. The place is rather beastly, but it seems all right. At any rate she likes it. If there's an awful hole on earth it's Brighton, but she thinks it 'perfectly fascinating.' Now isn't that a rum note? She's the most extraordinary mixture."

Chilver had listened with an air of strained delicacy to this broken trickle of anguish, speaking to the point only when it appeared altogether to have ceased. "Well, my dear man, what is it, may I ask in all sympathy, you would like me, in the circumstances, to do? Do you want me to sound her for you?"

"Don't be *too* excruciatingly funny," Braddle after a moment replied.

"Well then, clear the thing up."

"But how?"

"By making her let you know the worst."

"And by what means—if I don't ask her?"

"Simply by proposing."

"Marriage?"

"Marriage, naturally."

"You consider," Braddle inquired, "that that will infallibly make her speak?"

"Not infallibly, but probably."

Braddle looked all round the room. "But if it shouldn't?"

His friend took another turn about. "Well—risk it!"

IV

Henry Chilver remained for a much longer time than he would have expected in ignorance of the effect of that admonition; two full months elapsed without bringing him news. Something, he meanwhile reasoned, he *should* know— ought to know: it was due to him assuredly that Bertram Braddle shouldn't—quite apart from the distance travelled in the company of Mrs. Damerel—go so far even with *him* without recognising the propriety of going further. But at last, as the weeks passed, he arrived at his own estimate of a situation which had clearly nothing more to give him. It was a situation that had simply ceased to be one. Braddle was afraid and had remained afraid, just as he was ashamed and had remained ashamed. He had bolted, in his embarrassment, to Australia or the Cape; unless indeed he had dashed off once more to America, this time perhaps in quest of his so invidious "references." Was he looking for tracks in the great West or listening to twaddle in the Sandwich Islands? In any case Mrs. Damerel would be alone, and the point of honour, for Chilver himself, would have had its day. The sharpest thing in his life at present was the desire to see her again, and he considered that every hour without information made a difference for the question of avoiding her from delicacy. Finally, one morning, with the first faint winter light, it became vivid to him that the dictate of delicacy was positively the other way—was that, on the basis of Braddle's disappearance, he should make her some sign of recollection. He had not forgotten the address observed on one of her luggage-labels the day he had seen her up from Liverpool. Mightn't he, for instance, run down to her place that very morning? Braddle couldn't expect——! What Braddle couldn't expect, however, was lost in the suppressed sound with which, on passing into his sitting-room and taking up his fresh letters, he greeted the superscription of the last of the half-dozen just placed on his table. The envelope bore the postmark of Brighton, and if he had languished for information the very first lines—the note was only of a page—were charged with it. Braddle announced his engagement to Mrs. Damerel, spoke briefly, but with emphasis, of their great happiness and their early nuptials, and hoped

very much his correspondent would be able to come down
and see them for a day.

Henry Chilver, it may be stated, had, for reasons of feeling—he felt somehow so deeply refuted—to wait a certain
time to answer. What had Mrs. Damerel's lover, he wondered,
succeeded at last in extracting from her? She had made up her
mind as to what she could safely do—she had let him know
the worst and he had swallowed it down? What *was* it, the
queer suppressed chapter; what was the awkward page they
had agreed to tear out together? Chilver found himself envy-
ing his friend the romance of having been sustained in the
special effort, the extreme sacrifice, involved in such an understanding. But he had for many days, on the whole vision,
odd impatiences that were followed by odder recoveries. One
of these variations was a sudden drop of the desire to be in
presence of the woman for the sight of whom he had all winter consistently been yearning. What was most marked, however, was the shake he had vigorously to give himself on
perceiving his thoughts again and again take the direction that
poor Braddle had too successfully imparted to them. His curiosity about the concession she might have made to Braddle's
was an assumption—without Braddle's excuses—that she had
really had something to conceal till she was sure of her man.
This was idiotic, because the idea was one that never would
have originated with himself.

He did at last fix a day, none the less, and went down; but
there, on the spot, his imagination was, to his surprise, freshly
excited by the very fact that there were no apparent signs of
a drama. It was as if he could see, after all, even face to face
with her, what had stirred within the man she had for a time
only imperfectly subdued. Why should she have tried to be so
simple—too simple? She overdid it, she ignored too much.
Clear, soft, sweet, yet not a bit silly, she might well strike a
fellow as having had more history than she—what should one
call it?—owned up to. There were moments when Chilver
thought he got hold of it in saying to himself that she was
too clever to be merely what she was. There was something
in her that, more than anything ever in any one, gratified his
taste and seemed to him to testify to the happiest exercise of
her own; and such things brought up the puzzle of how so

much taste could have landed her simply where she was. Where she was—well, was doubtless where she would find comfort, for the man she had accepted was now visibly at peace, even though he had not yet, as appeared, introduced her to his people. The fact of which Chilver was at last as at first most conscious was the way she succeeded in withholding from his own penetration every trace of the great question she had had out with her intended, who yet couldn't have failed— one would quite have defied him—to give it to her somehow that he had on two occasions allowed his tongue to betray him to the other person he most trusted. Braddle, whose taste was not his strong point, had probably mentioned this indiscretion to her as a drollery; or else she had simply questioned him, got it out of him. This made their guest a participant, but there was something beautiful and final in the curtain that, on her side, she had dropped. It never gave, all day, the faintest stir. That affected Chilver as the mark of what there might be behind.

Yet when in the evening his friend went with him to the station—for the visitor had declined to sleep and was taking the last train back—he had, after they had walked two or three times up and down the platform, the greatest mystification of all. They were smoking; there were ten minutes to spare, and they moved to and fro in silence. They had been talking all day—mainly in Mrs. Damerel's company, but the circumstance that neither spoke at present was not the less marked. Yet if Chilver was waiting for something on his host's part he could scarcely have said for what. He was aware now that if Mrs. Damerel had, as he privately phrased it, "spoken," it was scarcely to be expected that the man with a standpoint altered by a definite engagement would—at the present stage at least—repeat to him her words. He felt, however, as the fruitless moments ebbed, a trifle wronged, at all events disappointed: since he had been dragged into the business, as he always for himself expressed it, it would only have been fair to throw a sop to his conjecture. What, moreover, was Braddle himself so perversely and persistently mum for—without an allusion that should even serve as a penance—unless to draw out some advance which might help him to revert with an approach to grace? Chilver nevertheless made no advance, and at last as, ceasing to stroll, they stood at the open door of an empty compartment, the train was almost immediately to start. At this moment they exchanged a long, queer stare.

"Well, good-bye," said the elder man.

"Good-bye." Chilver still waited before entering the carriage, but just as he was about to give up his companion added: "You see I followed your advice. I took the risk."

"Oh—about the question we discussed?" Chilver broke now, on the instant, into friendly response. "See then how right I was."

Braddle looked up and down the train. "I don't know."

"You're not satisfied?"

"Satisfied?" Still Braddle looked away.

"With what she has told you."

Braddle faced him again. "She has told me nothing."

"Nothing?"

"Nothing. She has accepted me—that's all. Not a bit else. So you see you *weren't* so right."

"Oh—oh!" exclaimed Chilver protestingly. The guard at this moment interposing with a "Take your seats, please!" and sharply, on his entering the carriage, shutting the door on him, he continued the conversation from the window, on which he rested his elbows. During the movement his protest had changed to something else. "Ah, but won't she yet——?"

"Let me have it? I'm sure I don't know. All I can say is that nothing has come from her."

"Then it's because there *is* nothing."

"I hope so," said Braddle from the platform.

"So you see," Chilver called out as the train moved, "I *was* right!" And he leaned forth as the distance grew and Braddle stood motionless and grave, gaily insisting and taking leave with his waving hand. But when he drew in his head and dropped into a seat he rather collapsed, tossing his hat across the compartment and sinking back into a corner and an attitude from which, staring before him and not even lighting another cigarette, he never budged till he reached Victoria.

A fortnight later the footfall of Mrs. Damerel's intended was loud on the old staircase in the Temple and the knob of his stick louder still on the old door. "It's only that it has rather stuck in my crop," he presently explained, "that I let you leave Brighton the other day with the pretension that you had been 'right,' as you called it, about the risk—attending the particular step—that I took. I can't help it if I want you to know—for it bores me that you're so pleased—that you weren't in the least right. You were most uncommonly wrong."

"Wrong?"

"Wrong."

Chilver looked vaguely about as if suddenly in search of something, then moved with an odd general inconsequence to the window. "As the day's so fine, do you mind our getting out of this beastly stuffy place into the Gardens? We can talk there." His hat was apparently what he had been looking for, and he took it up, and with it some cigarettes. Braddle, though seemingly disconcerted by what threatened to be practically a change of subject, replied that he didn't care a hang; so that, leaving the room, they passed together down to the court and through other battered courts and crooked ways. The dim London sunshine in the great surrounded garden had a kindness, and the hum of the town was as hindered and yet as present as the faint sense of spring. The two men stopped together before a bench, but neither for the moment sat down. "Do you mean she *has* told you?" Chilver at last brought out.

"No—it's just what she hasn't done."

"Then how the deuce am I wrong?"

"She has admitted that there *is* something."

Chilver markedly wondered. "Something? What?"

"That's just what I want to know."

"Then you *have* asked her?"

Braddle hesitated. "I couldn't resist my curiosity, my anxiety —call it what you will. I've been too worried. I put it to her the day after you were down there."

"And how did you put it?"

"Oh, just simply, brutally, disgustingly. I said: 'Isn't there something about yourself—something or other that has happened to you—that you're keeping back?'"

Chilver was attentive, but not solemn. "Well?"

"Oh, she admitted it."

"And in what terms?"

" 'Well, since you really drive me to the wall, there *is* something.' "

Chilver continued to consider. "And is that all she says?"

"No—she says she *will* tell me."

"Ah well, then!" And Chilver spoke with a curious—in fact, a slightly ambiguous—little renewed sound of superiority.

"Yes," his friend ruefully returned, "but not, you see, for six months."

"Oh, I see! I see!" Chilver thoughtfully repeated. "So you've got to wait—which I admit perfectly that you must find rather a bore. Yet if *she's* willing," he went on with more cheer and as if still seeking a justification of his original judgment—"if *she's* willing, you see, I wasn't so much out."

Bertram Braddle demurred. "But she isn't willing."

His interlocutor stared. "I thought you said she proposed it."

"Proposed what?"

"Why, the six months' wait—to make sure of you."

"Ah, but she'll *be* sure of me, after she has married me. The delay she asks for is not for our marriage," Braddle explained, "but only—from the date of our marriage—for the information."

"A-ah!" Chilver murmured, as if only now with a full view. "She means she'll speak when you *are* married."

"When we are. And then only on a great condition."

"How great?"

"Well, that if after the six months I still want it very much. She argues, you know, that I *sha'n't* want it."

"You won't then—you won't!" cried Chilver with a laugh at the odd word and passing his arm into his friend's to make him walk again. They talked and they talked; Chilver kept his companion's arm and they quite had the matter out.

"What's that, you know," Braddle asked, "but a way to get off altogether?"

"You mean for you to get off from knowing?"

"Ah no, for *her*——"

"To get off from telling? It *is* that, rather, of course," Chilver conceded. "But why shouldn't she get off—if you should be ready to let her?"

"Oh, but if I shouldn't be?" Braddle broke in.

"Why then, if she promises, she'll tell you."

"Yes, but by that time the knot will be tight."

"And what difference will that make if you don't mind? She argues, as you say, that after that amount of marriage, of experience of her, you won't care——!"

"What she does tell me may *be*?" Braddle smoked a moment in silence. "But suppose it should be one of those things——" He dropped again.

"Well, what things?"

"That a man can't like in *any* state of satisfaction."

"I don't know what things you mean."

"Come, I say—you do! Suppose it should be something really awful."

"Well, her calculation is that, awful or not," Chilver said, "she'll have sufficiently attached you to make you willing either totally to forego her disclosure or else easily to bear it."

"Oh, I know her calculation—which is very charming as well as very clever and very brave. But my danger——"

"Oh, you think too much of your danger!"

Braddle stopped short. "*You* don't!"

Chilver, however, who had coloured, spent much of the rest of the time they remained together in assuring him that he allowed this element all its weight. Only he came back at the last to what, practically, he had come back to in their other talks. "I don't quite see why she doesn't strike you as worth almost *any* risk."

"Do you mean that that's the way she strikes you?"

"Oh, I've not to tell you at this time of day," said Chilver, "how well I think of her."

His companion was now seated on a bench from which he himself had shortly before risen. "Ah, but I don't suppose you pretend to know her."

"No—certainly not, I admit. But I don't see how *you* should either, if you come to that."

"I don't; but it's exactly what I'm trying for, confound it! Besides," Braddle pursued, "she doesn't put you the great condition."

Chilver took a few steps away; then as he came back, "No; she doesn't!"

"Wait till some woman does," Braddle went on. "Then you'll see how you feel under it—then you can talk. If I wasn't so infernally fond of her," he gloomily added, "I wouldn't mind."

"Wouldn't mind what?"

"Why, what she has been. What she has done."

"Oh!" Chilver vaguely ejaculated.

"And I only mind now to the extent of wanting to know." On which Braddle rose from his seat with a heavy sigh. "Hang it, I've got to know, you know!" he declared as they walked on together.

V

Henry Chilver learned, however, in the course of time that he had won no victory on this, after all, rather reasonable ground—learned it from Mrs. Damerel herself, who came up to town in the spring and established herself, in the neighbourhood of Kensington Square, in modest but decent quarters, where her late suitor's best friend went to pay her his respects. The great condition had, as each party saw it, been fruitlessly maintained, for neither had, under whatever pressure, found a way to give in. The most remarkable thing of all was that Chilver should so rapidly have become aware of owing his acquaintance with these facts directly to Mrs. Damerel. He had, for that matter, on the occasion of his very first call, an impression strangely new to him—the consciousness that they had already touched each other much more than any contact between them explained. They met in the air of a common knowledge, so that when, for instance, almost immediately, without precautions or approaches, she said of Bertram Braddle: "He has gone off—heaven knows where!—to find out about me," he was not in the least struck with the length of the jump. He was instantly sensible, on the contrary, of the greatest pleasure in showing by his reply that he needed no explanation. "And do you think he'll succeed?"

"I don't know. He's so clever."

This, it seemed to Henry Chilver, was a wonderful speech, and he sat there and candidly admired her for it. There were all sorts of things in it—faint, gentle ironies and humilities, and above all the fact that the description was by no means exact. Poor Braddle was not, for such a measure as hers, clever, or markedly wouldn't be for such an undertaking. The words completely, on the part of the woman who might be supposed to have had a kindness for him, gave him away; but surely that was, in the face of his attitude, a mild revenge. It seemed to Chilver that until in her little makeshift suburban drawing-room he found himself alone with Mrs. Damerel he himself had not effectively judged this position. He saw it now sharply, supremely, as the only one that had been possible to his friend, but finer still was the general state of perception, quickened to a liberal intensity, that made him so see it. He couldn't have expressed the case otherwise than by saying that poor Braddle had had to be right to be so ridiculously wrong. There might well have been, it appeared, in Mrs. Damerel's past a missing link or two; but what was the very office of such a fact—when taken with other facts not a bit less vivid— but to give one a splendid chance to show a confidence? Not the confidence that, as one could only put it to one's self, there had not been anything, but the confidence that, what-ever there had been, one wouldn't find that one couldn't— for the sake of the rest—swallow it.

This was at bottom the great result of the first stages of Chilver's now independent, as he felt it to be, acquaintance with Mrs. Damerel—a sudden view of any, of every, dim pas-sage, that was more than a tender acceptance of the particular obscurity, that partook really of the nature of affirmation and insistence. It all made her, with everything that for her ad-vantage happened to help it on, extraordinarily touching to him, clothed her in the beauty of her general admission and her general appeal. Were not this admission and this appeal enough, and could anything be imagined more ponderously clumsy, more tactless and even truculent, than to want to gouge out the bleeding details? The charming woman was, to Chilver's view, about of his own age—not altogether so young, therefore, as Braddle, which was doubtless a note, too, in the latter's embarrassment—and that evidently did give time for a certain quantity of more or less trying, of really complicating experience. There it practically was, this experi-ence, in the character of her delicacy, in her kindly, witty, sensitive face, worn fine, too fine perhaps, but only to its increase of expression. She was neither a young fool nor an old one, assuredly; but if the intenser acquaintance with life had made the object of one's affection neither false nor hard, how could one, on the whole, since the story might be so interesting, wish it away? Mrs. Damerel's admission was so much evidence of her truth and her appeal so much evidence of her softness. She might easily have hated them both for guessing. She was at all events just faded enough to match the small assortment of Chilver's fatigued illusions—those that he had still, for occasions, in somewhat sceptical use, but that had lost their original violence of colour.

The second time he saw her alone he came back to what she had told him of Bertram Braddle. "If he should succeed—as to what you spoke of, wherever he has gone—would your engagement come on again?"

Mrs. Damerel hesitated, but she smiled. "Do you mean whether he'll be likely to wish it?"

"No," said Chilver, with something of a blush; "I mean whether you'll be."

She still smiled. "Dear, no. I consider, you know, that I gave him his chance."

"That you seem to me certainly to have done. Everything between you, then, as I understand it, is at an end?"

"It's very good of you," said Mrs. Damerel, "to desire so much to understand it. But I never give," she laughed, "but one chance!"

Chilver met her as he could. "You evidently can't have given any one very many!"

"Oh, you know," she replied, "I don't in the least regard it as a matter of course that, many or few, they should be eagerly seized. Mr. Braddle has only behaved as almost any man in his situation would have done."

Chilver at first, on this, only lost himself a while. "Yes, almost any man. I don't consider that the smallest blame attaches to him."

"It would be too monstrous."

Again he was briefly silent, but he had his inspiration. "Yes, let us speak of him gently." Then he added: "You've answered me enough. You're free."

"Free indeed is what I feel," she replied with her light irony, "when I talk to you with this extraordinary frankness."

"Ah, the frankness is mine! It comes from the fact that from the first, through Braddle, I knew. And you knew I knew. And I knew that too. It has made something between us."

"It might have made something rather different from this," said Mrs. Damerel.

He wondered an instant. "Different from my sitting here so intimately with you?"

"I mightn't have been able to bear that. I might have hated the sight of you."

"Ah, that would have been only," said Chilver, "if you had really liked me!"

She matched quickly enough the spirit of this. "Oh, but it wasn't so easy to like you little enough!"

"Little enough to endure me? Well, thank heaven, at any rate, we've found a sort of way!" Then he went on with real sincerity: "I feel as if our friend had tremendously helped me. Oh, how easily I want to let him down! There it is."

She breathed, after a moment, her assent in a sigh. "There it is!"

There indeed it was for several days during which this sigh frequently came back to him as a note of patience, of dignity in helpless submission, penetrating beyond any that had ever reached him. She had been put completely in his power, her good name handed over to him, by no act of her own, and in all her manner in presence of the awkward fact there was something that blinked it as little as it braved it. He wondered so hard, with this, why, even after the talk I have just reported, they were each not more embarrassed, that it could only take him a tolerably short time to discover the reason. If there was something between them it had been between them, in silence and distance, from the first, from even before the moment when his friend, on the ship, by the favour of better opportunity, had tumbled in deep and temporarily blocked, as it were, the passage. Braddle was good-looking, good-humoured, well-connected, rich; and how could she have known of the impression of the man in the background any more than the man in the background could have known of hers? If she had accepted Braddle hadn't it been just to build out, in her situation, at a stroke, the worry of an alternative that was impossible? Of himself she had seen nothing but that he was out of the question, and she had agreed for conscience, for prudence, as a safeguard and a provision, to throw in her lot with a charming, fortunate fellow who was extremely in love. Chilver had, in his meditations, no sooner read these things clear than he had another flash that completed the vision. Hadn't she then, however, having done so much for reason, stood out, with her intended, on the item of the great condition—made great precisely by the insistence of each—exactly because, after all, that left the door open to her imagination, her dream, her hope? Hadn't her idea been to make for Bertram—troubled herself and wavering for the result—a calculated difficulty, a real test? Oh, if there was a test, how *he* was ready to meet it! Henry Chilver's insistence would take a different line from that of his predecessor. He stood at the threshold of the door, left open indeed, so that he had only to walk over. By the end of the week he had proposed.

VI

It was at his club, one day of the following year, that he next came upon his old friend, whom he had believed, turning the matter often round, he should—in time, though the time might be long—inevitably meet again on some ground socially workable. That the time might be long had been indicated by a circumstance that came up again as soon as, fairly face to face, they fell, in spite of everything, to talking together. "Ah, you *will* speak to me then," said Chilver, "though you don't answer my letters!"

Braddle showed a strange countenance, partly accounted for by the fact that he was brown, seasoned, a trifle battered and had almost grown thin. But he had still his good monocular scowl, on the strength of which—it was really so much less a threat than a positive appeal from a supersubtle world— any old friend, recognising it again, would take almost anything from him. Yes indeed, quite anything, Chilver felt after they had been a few minutes together: he had become so quickly conscious of pity, of all sorts of allowances, and this had already operated as such a quickener of his private happiness. He had immediately proposed that they should look for a quiet corner, and they had found one in the smoking-room, always empty in the middle of the afternoon. Here it seemed to him that Braddle showed him what he himself had escaped. He had escaped being as *he* was—that was it: "as *he* was" was a state that covered now, to Chilver's sense, such vast spaces of exclusion and privation. It wasn't exactly that he was haggard or ill; his case was perhaps even not wholly clear to him, and he had still all the rest of his resources; but he was miserably afloat, and he could only be for Chilver the big, sore, stupid monument of his irretrievable mistake. "Did you write me more than once?" he finally asked.

"No—but once. But I thought it, I'm bound to say, an awfully good letter, and you took no notice of it, you know, whatever. You never returned me a word."

"I know," said Braddle, smoking hard and looking away; "it reached me at Hawaii. It *was*, I dare say, as good a letter as such a letter could be. I remember—I remember: all right; thanks. But I couldn't answer it. I didn't like it, and yet I couldn't trust myself to tell you so in the right way. So I let it alone."

"And we've therefore known nothing whatever about you."

Braddle sat jogging his long foot. "What is it you've wanted to know?"

The question made Chilver feel a little foolish. What *was* it, after all? "Well, what had become of you, and that sort of thing. I supposed," he added, "that you might be feeling as you say, and there was a lot, in connection with you, of course I myself felt, for me to think about. I even hesitated a good deal to write to you at all, and I waited, you remember, don't you? till after my marriage. I don't know what your state of mind may be to-day, but you'll never, my dear chap, get a 'rise' out of me. I bear you no grudge."

His companion, at this, looked at him again. "Do you mean for what I said——?"

"What you said——?"

"About *her*."

"Oh no—I mean for the way you've treated us."

"How do you know how I've treated you?" Braddle asked.

"Ah, I only pretend to speak of what I *do* know! Your not coming near us. You've been in the Sandwich Islands?" Chilver went on after a pause.

"Oh yes."

"And in California?"

"Yes—all over the place."

"All the while you've been gone?"

"No, after a time I gave it up. I've been round the world—in extraordinary holes."

"And have you come back to England," Chilver asked, "to stay a while?"

"I don't know—I don't know!" his friend replied with some impatience.

They kept it up, but with pauses—pauses during which, as they listened, in the big, stale, empty room, always dreary in the absence of talk and the silence of the billiard-balls just beyond—the loud tick of the clock gave their position almost as much an air of awkward penance as if they had had "lines" to do or were staying after school. Chilver wondered if it would after all practically fail, his desire that they should remain friends. His wife—beautiful creature!—would give every help, so that it would really depend on Braddle himself. It might indeed have been as an issue to the ponderation of some such question on his own part that poor Bertram suddenly exclaimed: "I see you're happy—I can make *that* out!"

He had said it in a way suggesting that it might make with him a difference for the worse, but Chilver answered none the less good-humouredly. "I'm afraid I can't pretend that I'm in the least miserable. But is it impossible you should come and see us?—come and judge, as it were, for yourself?"

Braddle looked graver than ever. "Would it suit your wife?"

"Oh, she's not afraid, I think!" his companion laughed. "You spoke just now," he after a moment continued, "of something that in your absence, in your travels, you 'gave up.' Let me ask you frankly if you meant that you had undertaken inquiries——"

"Yes; I 'nosed round,' as they say out there; I looked about and tried to pick something." Braddle spoke on a drop of his interlocutor, checked evidently by a certain hardness of defiance in his good eyes; but he couldn't know that Chilver wished to draw him out only to be more sorry for him, hesitating simply because of the desire not to put his proceeding to him otherwise than gracefully. "Awfully low-minded, as well as idiotic, I dare say you'll think it—but I'm not prepared to allow that it was not quite my own affair."

"Oh, *she* knew!" said Chilver comfortably enough.

"Knew I shouldn't find out anything? Well, I didn't. So she was right."

Thus they sat for a moment and seemed to smoke at her infallibility. "Do you mean anything objectionable?" Chilver presently inquired.

"Anything at all. Not a scrap. Not a trace of her passage— not an echo of her name. That, however—that I wouldn't, that I couldn't," Braddle added, "you'll have known for yourself."

"No, I wasn't sure."

"Then *she* was."

"Perhaps," said Chilver. "But she didn't tell me."

His friend hesitated. "Then what *has* she told you?"

"She has told me nothing."

"Nothing?"

"Nothing," said Henry Chilver, smiling as with the enjoyment of his companion's surprise. "But do come and see us," he pursued as Braddle abruptly rose and stood—now with a gravity that was almost portentous—looking down at him.

"I'm horribly nervous. Excuse me. You make me so," the younger man declared after a pause.

Chilver, who with this had got up soothingly and still laughingly, laid a reassuring hand upon him. "Dear old man— take it easy!"

"Thanks about coming to see you," Braddle went on. "I must think of it. Give me time."

"Time? Haven't you had months?"

Braddle turned it over. "Yes; but not on seeing you this way. I'm abominably nervous, at all events. There have been things—my silence among them—which I haven't known how you'd take."

"Well, you see how."

Braddle's stare was after all rather sightless. "I see—but I don't understand. I'll tell you what you might do—you might come to *me*."

"Oh, delighted. The old place?"

"The old place." Braddle had taken out his eyeglass to wipe it, and he cocked it characteristically back. "*Our* relation's rather rum, you know."

"Yours and my wife's? Oh, most unconventional; you may depend on it she feels that herself."

Braddle kept fixing him. "Then does *she* want to crow over me?"

"To crow?" Chilver was vague. "About what?"

His interlocutor hesitated. "About having at least got *you*."

"Oh, she's naturally pleased at that; but her satisfaction's after all a thing she can keep within bounds; and to see you again can only, I think, remind her more than anything else of what she did lose and now misses: your general situation, your personal advantages, your connections, expectations, magnificence."

Braddle, on this, after a lingering frown, turned away, looking at his watch and moving for a minute to the window. "When will you come? To-night?"

Chilver thought. "Rather late—yes. With pleasure."

His friend presently came back with an expression rather changed. "What I meant just now was what it all makes of my relation and yours—the way we go into it."

"Ah, well, that was extraordinary—the way we went into it—from the first. It was you, permit me to remark," Chilver pleasantly said, "who originally *began* going into it. Since you broke the ice I don't in the least mind its remaining broken."

"Ah, but at that time," Braddle returned, "I didn't know in the least what you were up to."

"And do I now know any more what *you* are? However," Chilver went on, "if you imply that I haven't acted with most scrupulous fairness, we *shall*, my dear fellow, quarrel as much as you please. I pressed you hard for your own interest."

"Oh, my 'interest'!" his companion threw off with another move to some distance; coming back, however, as quickly and before Chilver had time to take this up. "It's all right—I've nothing to say. Your letter was very clever and very handsome." Then, "I'm not 'up to' anything," Braddle added with simplicity.

The simplicity just renewed his interlocutor's mirth. "In that case why shouldn't we manage?"

"Manage?"

"To make the best, all round, of the situation."

"I've no difficulty whatever," said Braddle, "in doing that. If I'm nervous I'm still much less so than I was before I went away. And as to my having broken off, I feel more and more how impossible it was I should have done anything else."

"I'm sure of it—so we *will* manage."

It was as if this prospect, none the less, was still not clear to Braddle. "Then as you've so much confidence I can ask you why—if what you said just now of me is true—she shouldn't have paid for me a price that she was going, after all, to find herself ready to pay for *you*."

"A price? What price?"

"Why, the one we've been talking about. That of waiving her great condition." On which, as Chilver was, a moment—though without embarrassment—silent for this explanation, his interlocutor pursued: "The condition of your waiting—"

"Ah," said Chilver, "it remained. She didn't waive it."

Oh, how Braddle looked at him! "You accepted it?"

Chilver gave a laugh at his friend's stare. "Why are you so surprised when all my urgency to *you* was to accept it and when I thought you were going to?" Bertram had flushed, and he was really astonished. "Hadn't you then known?"

"Your letter didn't say that."

"Oh, I didn't go into our terms."

"No," said Braddle with some severity, "you slurred them over. I know what you urged on me and what you thought I was going to do. *I* thought I was going to do it too. But at the scratch I couldn't."

"So you believed *I* wouldn't?"

Poor Braddle was, after all, candid enough. "At the scratch, yes; when it came—the question—to yourself, and in spite of your extraordinary preaching. I think I took for granted that she must have done for you what she didn't do for me—that, liking you all for yourself, don't you see? and therefore so much better, she must have come round."

"For myself, better or worse, I grant you, was the only way she could like me," Chilver replied. "But she didn't come round."

"You married her *with* it?"

This was a question, however—it was in particular an emphasis—as to the interpretation of which he showed a certain reserve. "With what?"

"Why, damn it, with the condition."

"Oh, yes—with the condition." It sounded, on Chilver's lips, positively gay.

"You waited?"

"I waited."

This answer produced between them for the time—and, as might be said, by its visible effect on the recipient—a hush during which poor Bertram did two or three pointless things: took up an ash-tray that was near them and vaguely examined it, then looked at the clock and at his watch, then again restlessly moved off a few steps and came back. At his watch he gave a second glare. "I say, after all—*don't* come to-night."

"You can't stand me?"

"Well, I don't mind telling you you've rather upset me. It's my abject nerves; but they'll settle down in a few days, and then I'll make you a sign. Good-bye."

"Good-bye." Chilver held a minute the hand he had put out. "Don't be too long. My secondary effect on you may perhaps be better."

"Oh, it isn't really you. I mean it's *her*."

"Talking about her? Then we'll talk of something else. You'll give me the account——"

"Oh, as I told you, there *was* no account!" Braddle quite artlessly broke in. Chilver laughed out again at this, and his interlocutor went on: "What's the matter is that, though it's none of my business, I can't resist a brutal curiosity—a kind of suspense."

"Suspense?" Chilver echoed with good-humoured deprecation.

"Of course I do see you're thoroughly happy."

"Thoroughly."

Braddle still waited. "Then it isn't anything——?"

"Anything?"

"To make a row about. I mean what you know."

"But I *don't* know."

"Not yet? She hasn't told you?"

"I haven't asked."

Braddle wondered. "But it's six months."

"It's seven. I've let it pass."

"Pass?" Braddle repeated with a strange sound.

"So would *you* in my place."

"Oh, no, I beg your pardon!" Braddle almost exultantly declared. "But I give you a year."

"That's what *I've* given," said Chilver serenely.

His companion had a gasp. "Given *her*?"

"I bettered even, in accepting it, the great condition. I allowed her double the time."

Braddle wondered till he turned almost pale. "Then it's because you're afraid."

"To spoil my happiness?"

"Yes—and hers."

"Well, my dear boy," said Chilver cheerfully, "it may be that."

"Unless," his friend went on, "you're—in the interest of every one, if you'll permit me the expression?—magnificently lying." Chilver's slow, good-humoured headshake was so clearly, however, the next moment, a sufficient answer to this that the younger man could only add as dryly as he might: "You'll know when you want to."

"I shall know, doubtless, when I ask. But I feel at present that I shall never ask."

"Never?"

"Never."

Braddle waited a moment. "Then how the devil shall *I* know?"

Something in the tone of it renewed his companion's laughter. "Have you supposed I'd tell you?"

"Well, you ought to, you know. And—yes—I've believed it."

"But, my good man, I can't ask for *you*."

Braddle turned it over. "Why not, when one thinks of it? You know you owe me something."

"But—good heavens!—what?"

"Well, some kindness. You know you've all the fun of being awfully sorry for me."

"My dear chap!" Chilver murmured, patting his shoulder. "Well, give me time!" he easily added.

"To the end of your year? I'll come back *then*," said Braddle, going off.

VII

He came back punctually enough, and one of the results of it was a talk that, a few weeks later, he had one Sunday afternoon with Mrs. Chilver, whom, till this occasion—though it was not his first visit to the house—he had not yet seen alone. It took him then but ten minutes—ten minutes of a marked but subsiding want of ease—to break out with a strong appeal to her on the question of the danger of the possible arrival of somebody else. "*Would* you mind—of course I know it's an immense deal for me to ask—having it just said at the door that you're not at home? I do so want really to get *at* you."

"Oh, you needn't be afraid of an interruption." Mrs. Chilver seemed only amused. "No one comes to us. You see what our life is. Whom have you yet met here?"

He appeared struck with this. "Yes. Of course your living at Hammersmith——"

"We have to live where we can live for tenpence a year." He was silent at this touch, with a silence that, like an exclamation, betrayed a kind of helplessness, and she went on explaining as if positively to assist him. "Besides, we haven't the want. And so few people know us. We're our own company."

"Yes—that's just it. I never saw such a pair. It's as if you did it on purpose. But it was to show you how I feel at last the luxury of seeing you without Chilver."

"Ah, but I can't forbid *him* the door!" she laughed.

He kept his eyes for a minute on that of the room. "Do you mean he *will* come in?"

"Oh, if he does it won't be to hurt you. He's not jealous."

"Well, *I* am," said the visitor frankly, "and I verily believe it's his not being—and showing it so—that partly has to do with that. If he cared I believe I shouldn't. Besides, what does it matter——?" He threshed about in his place uncomfortably.

She sat there—with all her effaced anxieties—patient and pretty. "What does what matter?"

"Why, *how* it happens—since it does happen—that he's always here."

"But you see he isn't!"

He made an eager movement. "Do you mean then we *can* talk?"

She just visibly hesitated. "He and I only want to be kind to you."

"That's just what's awful!" He fell back again. "It's the way he has kept me on and on. I mean without——" But he had another drop.

"Without what?"

Poor Braddle at last sprang up. "Do you mind my being in a horrible fidget and floundering about the room?"

She demurred, but without gravity. "Not if you don't again knock over the lamp. Do you remember the day you did that at Brighton?"

With his ambiguous frown at her he stopped short. "Yes, and how even that didn't move you."

"Well, don't presume on it again!" she laughed.

"You mean it might move you this time?" he went on.

"No; I mean that as I've now got better lamps——!"

He roamed there among her decent frugalities and, as regarded other matters as well as lamps, noted once more—as he had done on other occasions—the extreme moderation of the improvement. He had rather imagined on Chilver's part more margin. Then at last suddenly, with an effect of irrelevance: "Why *don't* people, as you say, come to you?"

"That's the kind of thing," she smiled, "you *used* to ask so much."

"Oh, too much, of course, and it's absurd my still wanting to know. It's none of my business; but, you know, nothing is if you come to that. It's your extraordinary kindness—the way you give me my head—that puts me up to things. Only you're trying the impossible—you can't keep me on. I mean without—well, what I spoke of just now. Do you mind my bringing it bang out like a brute?" he continued, stopping before her again. "Isn't it a question of either really taking me in or quite leaving me out?" As she had nothing, however, at first, for this inquiry but silence, and as her face made her silence charming, his appeal suddenly changed. "Do you mind my going on like this?"

"I don't mind anything. You want, I judge, some help. What help can I give you?"

He dropped, at this, straight into his chair again. "There you are! You pitied me even from the first—regularly beforehand. You're so confoundedly superior"—he almost sufficiently joked. "Of course I know all our relations are most extraordinary, but I think yours and mine is the strangest—unless it be yours and Chilver's."

"Let us say it's his and *yours*, and have done with it," she smiled.

"Do you know what I came back then for?—I mean the second time, *this* time?"

"Why, to see *me*, I've all these days supposed."

"Well," said Braddle with a slight hesitation, "it was, to that extent, to show my confidence."

But she also hesitated. "Your confidence in what?"

He had still another impatience, with the force of which he again changed his place. "Am I giving him away? How much do you know?"

In the air of his deep unrest her soft stillness—lending itself, but only by growing softer—had little by little taken on a beauty. "I'm trying to follow you—to understand. I know of your meeting with Henry last year at a club."

"Ah then, if he gave me away——!"

"I gathered rather, I seem to remember, from what he mentioned to me, that he must rather have given me too. But I don't in the least mind."

"Well, what passed between us then," said Braddle, "is why I came back. He made me, if I should wait, a sort of promise——"

"Oh"—she took him up—"I don't think he was conscious of anything like a promise. He said at least nothing to me of that." With which, as Braddle's face had exceedingly fallen, "But I know what you then wanted and what you still want to know," she added.

On this, for a time, they sat there with a long look. "I would rather have had it from *him*," he said at last.

"It would certainly have been more natural," she intelligently returned. "But he has given you no chance to press him again?"

"None—and with an evident intention: seeing me only with you."

"Well, at the present moment he doesn't see you at all. Nor me either!" Mrs. Chilver added as if to cover something in the accent of her former phrase. "But if he has avoided close quarters with you it has been not to disappoint you."

"He won't, after all, tell me?"

"He can't. He has nothing to tell."

Poor Braddle showed at this what his disappointment could be. "He has not even yet asked you?"

"Not even yet—after fifteen months. But don't be hard on him," she pleaded. "*You* wouldn't."

"For all this time?" Braddle spoke almost with indignation at the charge. "My dear lady—rather!"

"No, no," she gently insisted, "not even to tell *him*."

"He told you then," Braddle demanded, "that I thought he ought, if on no other grounds, to ask just *in order* to tell me?"

"Oh dear, no. He only told me he had met you, and where you had been. We don't speak of his 'asking,' " she explained.

"Don't you?" Her visitor stared.

"Never."

"Then how have you known——?"

"What you want so much? Why, by having seen it in you before—and just *how* much—and seeing it now. I've been feeling all along," she said, "how you must have argued."

"Oh, we didn't argue!"

"I think *you* did."

He had slowly got up—now less actively but not less intensely nervous—and stood there heedless of this and rather differently looking at her. "He never talks with you of his asking?"

"Never," she repeated.

"And you still stick to it that *I* wouldn't?"

She hesitated. "Have talked of it?"

"Have asked."

She was beautiful as she smiled up at him. "It would have been a little different. *You* would have talked."

He remained there a little in silence; what he might have done seemed so both to separate them and to hold them together. "And Chilver, you feel, will now never ask?"

"Never now."

He seemed to linger for conviction. "If he was going to, you mean, he would have done it——"

"Yes"—she was prompt—"the moment his time was up."

"I see"—and, turning away, he moved slowly about. "So you're safe?"

"Safe."

"And I'm just where I was!" he oddly threw off.

"I'm amazed again," Mrs. Chilver said, "at your so clinging to it that you would have had the benefit of his information."

It was a remark that pulled him up as if something like a finer embarrassment had now come to him. "I've only in mind his information as to the fact that he had made you speak."

"And what good would *that* have done you?"

"Without the details?"—he was indeed thinking.

"I like your expressions!" said Mrs. Chilver.

"Yes—aren't they hideous?" He had jerked out his glass and, with a returning flush, appeared to affect to smile over it. But the drop of his glass showed something in each of his eyes that, though it might have come from the rage, came evidently—to his companion's vision at least—from the more pardonable pain, of his uncertainty. "But there we are!"

The manner in which these last words reached her had clearly to do with her finally leaving her place, watching him meanwhile as he wiped his glass. "Yes—there we are. He did tell me," she went on, "that you had told him where you had been and that you could pick up nothing——"

"Against you?" he broke in. "Not a beggarly word."

"And you tried hard?"

"I worked like a nigger. It was no use."

"But say you had succeeded—what," she asked, "was your idea?"

"Why, not to have had the thing any longer between us."

He brought this out with such simplicity that she stared. "But if it had been——?"

"Yes?"—the way she hung fire made him eager.

"Well—something you would have loathed."

"*Is* it?"—he almost sprang at her. "For pity's sake, *what* is it?" he broke out in a key that now filled the room supremely with the strange soreness of his yearning for his justification.

She kept him waiting, after she had taken this in, but another instant. "You would rather, you say, have had it from *him*——"

"But I must take it as I can get it? Oh, anyhow!" he fairly panted.

"Then with a condition."

It threw him back into a wail that was positively droll. "Another?"

"This one," she dimly smiled, "is comparatively easy. You must promise me with the last solemnity——"

"Yes!"

"On the sacred honour of a gentleman——"

"Yes!"

"To repeat to no one whatever what you now have from me."

Thus completely expressed, the condition checked him but a moment. "Very well!"

"You promise?"

"On the sacred honour of a gentleman."

"Then I invite you to make the inference most directly suggested by the vanity of your researches."

He looked about him. "The inference?"

"As to what a fault may have been that it's impossible to find out."

He got hold as he could. "It may have been hidden."

"Then anything hidden, from so much labour, so well——"

"May not have existed?" he stammered after she had given him time to take something from her deep eyes. He glared round and round with it—seemed to have it on his hands before the world. "Then what did you mean——?"

"Ah, sir, what did *you?* You invented my past."

"Do you mean you *hadn't* one?" cried Bertram Braddle.

"None I would have mentioned to you. It was *you* who brought it up."

He appealed, in his stupefaction, to the immensity of the vacancy itself. "There's *nothing*?"

She made no answer for a moment, only looking, while he dropped hard on her sofa, so far away that her eyes might have been fixed on the blue Pacific. "There's the upshot of your inquiry."

He followed her, while she moved before him, from his place. "What did you then so intensely keep back?"

"What did *you*," she asked as she paused, "so intensely put forward? I kept back what you have from me now."

"*This*," he gasped from the depths of his collapse, "is what you would have told me?"

"If, as my loyal husband, you had brought it up again. But you wouldn't!" she once more declared.

"And I should have gone on thinking——"

"Yes," she interrupted—"that you were, for *not* bringing it up, the most delicate and most generous of men."

It seemed all to roll over him and sweep him down, but he gave, in his swift passage, a last clutch. "You consent to let *him* think you——?"

"He thinks me what he finds me!" said Mrs. Chilver.

Braddle got up from the sofa, looking about for his hat and stick; but by the time he had reached the door with them he rose again to the surface. "I, too, then am to leave him his idea——?"

"Well, of what?" she demanded as he faltered.

"Of your—whatever you called it."

"I called it nothing. You relieved me of the question of the name."

He gloomily shook his head. "You see to what end! Chilver, at any rate," he said, "has his view, and to that extent has a name for it."

"Only to the extent of having the one you gave him."

"Well, what I gave him he took!" Braddle, with returning spirit, declared. "What I suggested—God forgive me!—he believed."

"Yes—that he might make his sacrifice. You speak," said Mrs. Chilver, "of his idea. His sacrifice is his idea. And his idea," she added, "is his happiness."

"His sacrifice of your reputation?"

"Well—to whom?"

"To *me*," said Bertram Braddle. "Do you expect me now to permit that?"

Mrs. Chilver serenely enough considered. "I shall protect his happiness, which is above all his vision of his own attitude, and I don't see how you can prevent this save by breaking your oath."

"Oh, my oath!" And he prolonged the groan of his resentment.

It evidently—what he felt—made her sorry for him, and she spoke in all kindness. "It's only your punishment!" she sighed after him as he departed.

The Real Right Thing

WHEN, after the death of Ashton Doyne—but three months after—George Withermore was approached, as the phrase is, on the subject of a "volume," the communication came straight from his publishers, who had been, and indeed much more, Doyne's own; but he was not surprised to learn, on the occurrence of the interview they next suggested, that a certain pressure as to the early issue of a Life had been brought to bear upon them by their late client's widow. Doyne's relations with his wife had been, to Withermore's knowledge, a very special chapter—which would present itself, by the way, as a delicate one for the biographer; but a sense of what she had lost, and even of what she had lacked, had betrayed itself, on the poor woman's part, from the first days of her bereavement, sufficiently to prepare an observer at all initiated for some attitude of reparation, some espousal even exaggerated of the interests of a distinguished name. George Withermore was, as he felt, initiated; yet what he had not expected was to hear that she had mentioned him as the person in whose hands she would most promptly place the materials for a book.

These materials—diaries, letters, memoranda, notes, documents of many sorts—were her property, and wholly in her control, no conditions at all attaching to any portion of her heritage; so that she was free at present to do as she liked—free, in particular, to do nothing. What Doyne would have arranged had he had time to arrange could be but supposition and guess. Death had taken him too soon and too suddenly, and there was all the pity that the only wishes he was known to have expressed were wishes that put it positively out of account. He had broken short off—that was the way of it; and the end was ragged and needed trimming. Withermore was conscious, abundantly, how close he had stood to him, but he was not less aware of his comparative obscurity. He was young, a journalist, a critic, a hand-to-mouth character, with little, as yet, as was vulgarly said, to show. His writings were few and small, his relations scant and vague. Doyne, on the other hand, had lived long enough—above all had had talent enough—to become great, and among his many friends gilded also with greatness were several to whom his wife would have struck those who knew her as much more likely to appeal.

The preference she had, at all events, uttered—and uttered in a roundabout, considerate way that left him a measure of freedom—made our young man feel that he must at least see her and that there would be in any case a good deal to talk about. He immediately wrote to her, she as promptly named an hour, and they had it out. But he came away with his particular idea immensely strengthened. She was a strange woman, and he had never thought her an agreeable one; only there was something that touched him now in her bustling, blundering impatience. She wanted the book to make up, and the individual whom, of her husband's set, she probably believed she might most manipulate was in every way to help it to make up. She had not taken Doyne seriously enough in life, but the biography should be a solid reply to every imputation on herself. She had scantly known how such books were constructed, but she had been looking and had learned something. It alarmed Withermore a little from the first to see that she would wish to go in for quantity. She talked of "volumes"—but he had his notion of that.

"My thought went straight to *you*, as his own would have done," she had said almost as soon as she rose before him there in her large array of mourning—with her big black eyes, her big black wig, her big black fan and gloves, her general gaunt, ugly, tragic, but striking and, as might have been thought from a certain point of view, "elegant" presence. "You're the one he liked most; oh, *much*!"—and it had been quite enough to turn Withermore's head. It little mattered that he could afterward wonder if she had known Doyne enough, when it came to that, to be sure. He would have said for himself indeed that her testimony on such a point would scarcely have counted. Still, there was no smoke without fire; she knew at least what she meant, and he was not a person she could have an interest in flattering. They went up together, without delay, to the great man's vacant study, which was at the back of the house and looked over the large green garden—a beautiful and inspiring scene, to poor Withermore's view—common to the expensive row.

"You can perfectly work here, you know," said Mrs. Doyne: "you shall have the place quite to yourself—I'll give it all up to you; so that in the evenings, in particular, don't you see? for quiet and privacy, it will be perfection."

Perfection indeed, the young man felt as he looked about—having explained that, as his actual occupation was an evening paper and his earlier hours, for a long time yet, regularly taken up, he would have to come always at night. The place was full of their lost friend; everything in it had belonged to him; everything they touched had been part of his life. It was for the moment too much for Withermore—too great an honour and even too great a care; memories still recent came back to him, and, while his heart beat faster and his eyes filled with tears, the pressure of his loyalty seemed almost more than he could carry. At the sight of his tears Mrs. Doyne's own rose to her lids, and the two, for a minute, only looked at each other. He half expected her to break out: "Oh, help me to feel as I know you know I want to feel!" And after a little one of them said, with the other's deep assent—it didn't matter which: "It's here that we're *with* him." But it was definitely the young man who put it, before they left the room, that it was there he was with *them*.

The young man began to come as soon as he could arrange it, and then it was, on the spot, in the charmed stillness, between the lamp and the fire and with the curtains drawn, that a certain intenser consciousness crept over him. He turned in out of the black London November; he passed through the large, hushed house and up the red-carpeted staircase where he only found in his path the whisk of a soundless, trained maid, or the reach, out of a doorway, of Mrs. Doyne's queenly weeds and approving tragic face; and then, by a mere touch of the well-made door that gave so sharp and pleasant a click, shut himself in for three or four warm hours with the spirit—as he had always distinctly declared it—of his master. He was not a little frightened when, even the first night, it came over him that he had really been most affected, in the whole matter, by the prospect, the privilege and the luxury, of this sensation. He had not, he could now reflect, definitely considered the question of the book—as to which there was here, even already, much to consider: he had simply let his affection and admiration—to say nothing of his gratified pride—meet, to the full, the temptation Mrs. Doyne had offered them.

How did he know, without more thought, he might begin to ask himself, that the book was, on the whole, to be desired? What warrant had he ever received from Ashton Doyne himself for so direct and, as it were, so familiar an approach? Great was the art of biography, but there were lives and lives, there were subjects and subjects. He confusedly recalled, so far as that went, old words dropped by Doyne over contemporary compilations, suggestions of how he himself discriminated as to other heroes and other panoramas. He even remembered how his friend, at moments, would have seemed to show himself as holding that the "literary" career might—save in the case of a Johnson and a Scott, with a Boswell and a Lockhart to help—best content itself to be represented. The artist was what he *did*—he was nothing else. Yet how, on the other hand, was not *he*, George Withermore, poor devil, to have jumped at the chance of spending his winter in an intimacy so rich? It had been simply dazzling—that was the fact. It hadn't been the "terms," from the publishers—though these were, as they said at the office, all right; it had been Doyne himself, his company and contact and presence—it had been just what it was turning out, the possibility of an intercourse closer than that of life. Strange that death, of the two things, should have the fewer mysteries and secrets! The first night our young man was alone in the room it seemed to him that his master and he were really for the first time together.

II

Mrs. Doyne had for the most part let him expressively alone, but she had on two or three occasions looked in to see if his needs had been met, and he had had the opportunity of thanking her on the spot for the judgment and zeal with which she had smoothed his way. She had to some extent herself been looking things over and had been able already to muster several groups of letters; all the keys of drawers and cabinets she had, moreover, from the first placed in his hands, with helpful information as to the apparent whereabouts of different matters. She had put him, in a word, in the fullest possible possession, and whether or no her husband had trusted her, she at least, it was clear, trusted her husband's friend. There grew upon Withermore, nevertheless, the impression that, in spite of all these offices, she was not yet at peace, and that a certain unappeasable anxiety continued even to keep step with her confidence. Though she was full of consideration, she was at the same time perceptibly *there*: he felt her, through a supersubtle sixth sense that the whole connection had already brought into play, hover, in the still hours, at the top of landings and on the other side of doors, gathered from the soundless brush of her skirts the hint of her watchings and waitings. One evening when, at his friend's table, he had lost himself in the depths of correspondence, he was made to start and turn by the suggestion that some one was behind him. Mrs. Doyne had come in without his hearing the door, and she gave a strained smile as he sprang to his feet. "I hope," she said, "I haven't frightened you."

"Just a little—I was so absorbed. It was as if, for the instant," the young man explained, "it had been himself."

The oddity of her face increased in her wonder. "Ashton?"

"He does seem so near," said Withermore.

"To you too?"

This naturally struck him. "He does then to you?"

She hesitated, not moving from the spot where she had first stood, but looking round the room as if to penetrate its duskier angles. She had a way of raising to the level of her nose the big black fan which she apparently never laid aside and with which she thus covered the lower half of her face, her rather hard eyes, above it, becoming the more ambiguous. "Sometimes."

"Here," Withermore went on, "it's as if he might at any moment come in. That's why I jumped just now. The time is so short since he really used to—it only *was* yesterday. I sit in his chair, I turn his books, I use his pens, I stir his fire, exactly as if, learning he would presently be back from a walk, I had come up here contentedly to wait. It's delightful—but it's strange."

Mrs. Doyne, still with her fan up, listened with interest. "Does it worry you?"

"No—I like it."

She hesitated again. "Do you ever feel as if he were—a—quite—a—personally in the room?"

"Well, as I said just now," her companion laughed, "on hearing you behind me I seemed to take it so. What do we want, after all," he asked, "but that he shall be with us?"

"Yes, as you said he would be—that first time." She stared in full assent. "He *is* with us."

She was rather portentous, but Withermore took it smiling. "Then we must keep him. We must do only what he would like."

"Oh, only that, of course—only. But if he *is* here——?" And her sombre eyes seemed to throw it out, in vague distress, over her fan.

"It shows that he's pleased and wants only to help? Yes, surely; it must show that."

She gave a light gasp and looked again round the room. "Well," she said as she took leave of him, "remember that I too want only to help." On which, when she had gone, he felt sufficiently—that she had come in simply to see he was all right.

He was all right more and more, it struck him after this, for as he began to get into his work he moved, as it appeared to him, but the closer to the idea of Doyne's personal presence. When once this fancy had begun to hang about him he welcomed it, persuaded it, encouraged it, quite cherished it, looking forward all day to feeling it renew itself in the evening, and waiting for the evening very much as one of a pair of lovers might wait for the hour of their appointment. The smallest accidents humoured and confirmed it, and by the end of three or four weeks he had come quite to regard it as the consecration of his enterprise. Wasn't it what settled the question of what Doyne would have thought of what they were doing? What they were doing was what he wanted done, and they could go on, from step to step, without scruple or doubt. Withermore rejoiced indeed at moments to feel this certitude: there were times of dipping deep into some of Doyne's secrets when it was particularly pleasant to be able to hold that

Doyne desired him, as it were, to know them. He was learning
many things that he had not suspected, drawing many curtains, forcing many doors, reading many riddles, going, in
general, as they said, behind almost everything. It was at an
occasional sharp turn of some of the duskier of these wanderings "behind" that he really, of a sudden, most felt himself,
in the intimate, sensible way, face to face with his friend; so
that he could scarcely have told, for the instant, if their meeting occurred in the narrow passage and tight squeeze of the
past, or at the hour and in the place that actually held him.
Was it '67, or was it but the other side of the table?

Happily, at any rate, even in the vulgarest light publicity
could ever shed, there would be the great fact of the way
Doyne was "coming out." He was coming out too beautifully—better yet than such a partisan as Withermore could
have supposed. Yet, all the while, as well, how would this
partisan have represented to any one else the special state of
his own consciousness? It wasn't a thing to talk about—it was
only a thing to feel. There were moments, for instance, when,
as he bent over his papers, the light breath of his dead host
was as distinctly in his hair as his own elbows were on the
table before him. There were moments when, had he been
able to look up, the other side of the table would have shown
him this companion as vividly as the shaded lamplight showed
him his page. That he couldn't at such a juncture look up was
his own affair, for the situation was ruled—that was but natural—by deep delicacies and fine timidities, the dread of too
sudden or too rude an advance. What was intensely in the air
was that if Doyne *was* there it was not nearly so much for
himself as for the young priest of his altar. He hovered and
lingered, he came and went, he might almost have been,
among the books and the papers, a hushed, discreet librarian,
doing the particular things, rendering the quiet aid, liked by
men of letters.

Withermore himself, meanwhile, came and went, changed
his place, wandered on quests either definite or vague; and
more than once, when, taking a book down from a shelf and
finding in it marks of Doyne's pencil, he got drawn on and
lost, he had heard documents on the table behind him gently
shifted and stirred, had literally, on his return, found some

letter he had mislaid pushed again into view, some wilderness cleared by the opening of an old journal at the very date he wanted. How should he have gone so, on occasion, to the special box or drawer, out of fifty receptacles, that would help him, had not his mystic assistant happened, in fine prevision, to tilt its lid, or to pull it half open, in just the manner that would catch his eye?—in spite, after all, of the fact of lapses and intervals in which, *could* one have really looked, one would have seen somebody standing before the fire a trifle detached and over-erect—somebody fixing one the least bit harder than in life.

III

That this auspicious relation had in fact existed, had continued, for two or three weeks, was sufficiently proved by the dawn of the distress with which our young man found himself aware that he had, for some reason, from a certain evening, begun to miss it. The sign of that was an abrupt, surprised sense—on the occasion of his mislaying a marvellous unpublished page which, hunt where he would, remained stupidly, irrecoverably lost—that his protected state was, after all, exposed to some confusion and even to some depression. If, for the joy of the business, Doyne and he had, from the start, been together, the situation had, within a few days of his first new suspicion of it, suffered the odd change of their ceasing to be so. That was what was the matter, he said to himself, from the moment an impression of mere mass and quantity struck him as taking, in his happy outlook at his material, the place of his pleasant assumption of a clear course and a lively pace. For five nights he struggled; then, never at his table, wandering about the room, taking up his references only to lay them down, looking out of the window, poking the fire, thinking strange thoughts and listening for signs and sounds not as he suspected or imagined, but as he vainly desired and invoked them, he made up his mind that he was, for the time at least, forsaken.

The extraordinary thing thus became that it made him not only sad not to feel Doyne's presence, but in a high degree uneasy. It was stranger, somehow, that he shouldn't be there than it had ever been that he *was*—so strange indeed at last that Withermore's nerves found themselves quite inconsequently affected. They had taken kindly enough to what was of an order impossible to explain, perversely reserving their sharpest state for the return to the normal, the supersession of the false. They were remarkably beyond control when, finally, one night, after resisting an hour or two, he simply edged out of the room. It had only now, for the first time, become impossible to him to remain there. Without design, but panting a little and positively as a man scared, he passed along his usual corridor and reached the top of the staircase. From this point he saw Mrs. Doyne looking up at him from the bottom quite as if she had known he would come; and the most singular thing of all was that, though he had been conscious of no notion to resort to her, had only been prompted to relieve himself by escape, the sight of her position made him recognize it as just, quickly feel it as a part of some monstrous oppression that was closing over both of them. It was wonderful how, in the mere modern London hall, between the Tottenham Court Road rugs and the electric light, it came up to him from the tall black lady, and went again from him down to her, that he knew what she meant by looking as if he would know. He descended straight, she turned into her own little lower room, and there, the next thing, with the door shut, they were, still in silence and with queer faces, confronted over confessions that had taken sudden life from these two or three movements. Withermore gasped as it came to him why he had lost his friend. "He has been with *you*?"

With this it was all out—out so far that neither had to explain and that, when "What do you suppose is the matter?" quickly passed between them, one appeared to have said it as much as the other. Withermore looked about at the small, bright room in which, night after night, she had been living her life as he had been living his own upstairs. It was pretty, cosy, rosy; but she had by turns felt in it what he had felt and heard in it what he had heard. Her effect there—fantastic black, plumed and extravagant, upon deep pink—was that of some "decadent" coloured print, some poster of the newest school. "You understood he had left me?" he asked.

She markedly wished to make it clear. "This evening—yes. I've made things out."

"You knew—before—that he was with me?"

She hesitated again. "I felt he wasn't with *me*. But on the stairs——"

"Yes?"

"Well—he passed, more than once. He was in the house. And at your door——"

"Well?" he went on as she once more faltered.

"If I stopped I could sometimes tell. And from your face," she added, "to-night, at any rate, I knew your state."

"And that was why you came out?"

"I thought you'd come to me."

He put out to her, on this, his hand, and they thus, for a minute, in silence, held each other clasped. There was no peculiar presence for either, now—nothing more peculiar than that of each for the other. But the place had suddenly become as if consecrated, and Withermore turned over it again his anxiety. "What *is* then the matter?"

"I only want to do the real right thing," she replied after a moment.

"And are we not doing it?"

"I wonder. Are *you* not?"

He wondered too. "To the best of my belief. But we must think."

"We must think," she echoed. And they did think— thought, with intensity, the rest of that evening together, and thought, independently—Withermore at least could answer for himself—during many days that followed. He intermitted for a little his visits and his work, trying, in meditation, to catch himself in the act of some mistake that might have accounted for their disturbance. Had he taken, on some important point—or looked as if he might take—some wrong line or wrong view? had he somewhere benightedly falsified or inadequately insisted? He went back at last with the idea of having guessed two or three questions he might have been on the way to muddle; after which he had, above stairs, another period of agitation, presently followed by another interview, below, with Mrs. Doyne, who was still troubled and flushed.

"He's there?"

"He's there."

"I knew it!" she returned in an odd gloom of triumph. Then as to make it clear: "He has not been again with *me*."

"Nor with me again to help," said Withermore.

She considered. "Not to help?"

"I can't make it out—I'm at sea. Do what I will, I feel I'm wrong."

She covered him a moment with her pompous pain. "How do you feel it?"

"Why, by things that happen. The strangest things. I can't describe them—and you wouldn't believe them."

"Oh yes, I would!" Mrs. Doyne murmured.

"Well, he intervenes." Withermore tried to explain. "However I turn, I find him."

She earnestly followed. " 'Find' him?"

"I meet him. He seems to rise there before me."

Mrs. Doyne, staring, waited a little. "Do you mean you see him?"

"I feel as if at any moment I may. I'm baffled. I'm checked." Then he added: "I'm afraid."

"Of *him*?" asked Mrs. Doyne.

He thought. "Well—of what I'm doing."

"Then what, that's so awful, *are* you doing?"

"What you proposed to me. Going into his life."

She showed, in her gravity, now, a new alarm. "And don't you *like* that?"

"Doesn't *he*? That's the question. We lay him bare. We serve him up. What is it called? We give him to the world."

Poor Mrs. Doyne, as if on a menace to her hard atonement, glared at this for an instant in deeper gloom. "And why shouldn't we?"

"Because we don't know. There are natures, there are lives, that shrink. He mayn't wish it," said Withermore. "We never asked him."

"How *could* we?"

He was silent a little. "Well, we ask him now. That's, after all, what our start has, so far, represented. We've put it to him."

"Then—if he has been with us—we've had his answer."

Withermore spoke now as if he knew what to believe. "He hasn't been 'with' us—he has been against us."

"Then why did you think——"

"What I *did* think, at first—that what he wishes to make us feel is his sympathy? Because, in my original simplicity, I was mistaken. I was—I don't know what to call it—so excited and charmed that I didn't understand. But I understand at last. He only wanted to communicate. He strains forward out of his darkness; he reaches toward us out of his mystery; he makes us dim signs out of his horror."

" 'Horror'?" Mrs. Doyne gasped with her fan up to her mouth.

"At what we're doing." He could by this time piece it all together. "I see now that at first——"

"Well, what?"

"One had simply to feel he was there, and therefore not indifferent. And the beauty of that misled me. But he's there as a protest."

"Against *my* Life?" Mrs. Doyne wailed.

"Against *any* Life. He's there to *save* his Life. He's there to be let alone."

"So you give up?" she almost shrieked.

He could only meet her. "He's there as a warning."

For a moment, on this, they looked at each other deep. "You *are* afraid!" she at last brought out.

It affected him, but he insisted. "He's there as a curse!"

With that they parted, but only for two or three days; her last word to him continuing to sound so in his ears that, between his need really to satisfy her and another need presently to be noted, he felt that he might not yet take up his stake. He finally went back at his usual hour and found her in her usual place. "Yes, I *am* afraid," he announced as if he had turned that well over and knew now all it meant. "But I gather that you're not."

She faltered, reserving her word. "What is it you fear?"

"Well, that if I go on I *shall* see him."

"And then——?"

"Oh, then," said George Withermore, "I *should* give up!"

She weighed it with her lofty but earnest air. "I think, you know, we must have a clear sign."

"You wish me to try again?"

She hesitated. "You see what it means—for me—to give up."

"Ah, but *you* needn't," Withermore said.

She seemed to wonder, but in a moment she went on. "It would mean that he won't take from me——" But she dropped for despair.

"Well, what?"

"Anything," said poor Mrs. Doyne.

He faced her a moment more. "I've thought myself of the clear sign. I'll try again."

As he was leaving her, however, she remembered. "I'm only afraid that to-night there's nothing ready—no lamp and no fire."

"Never mind," he said from the foot of the stairs; "I'll find things."

To which she answered that the door of the room would probably, at any rate, be open; and retired again as if to wait for him. She had not long to wait; though, with her own door wide and her attention fixed, she may not have taken the time quite as it appeared to her visitor. She heard him, after an interval, on the stair, and he presently stood at her entrance, where, if he had not been precipitate, but rather, as to step and sound, backward and vague, he showed at least as livid and blank.

"I give up."

"Then you've seen him?"

"On the threshold—guarding it."

"Guarding it?" She glowed over her fan. "Distinct?"

"Immense. But dim. Dark. Dreadful," said poor George Withermore.

She continued to wonder. "You didn't go in?"

The young man turned away. "He forbids!"

"You say *I* needn't," she went on after a moment. "Well then, need I?"

"See him?" George Withermore asked.

She waited an instant. "Give up."

"You must decide." For himself he could at last but drop upon the sofa with his bent face in his hands. He was not quite to know afterwards how long he had sat so; it was enough that what he did next know was that he was alone among her favourite objects. Just as he gained his feet, however, with this sense and that of the door standing open to the hall, he found himself afresh confronted, in the light, the warmth, the rosy space, with her big black perfumed presence. He saw at a glance, as she offered him a huger, bleaker stare over the mask of her fan, that she had been above; and so it was that, for the last time, they faced together their strange question. "You've seen him?" Withermore asked.

He was to infer later on from the extraordinary way she closed her eyes and, as if to steady herself, held them tight and long, in silence, that beside the unutterable vision of Ashton Doyne's wife his own might rank as an escape. He knew before she spoke that all was over. "I give up."

Paste

"I'VE FOUND a lot more things," her cousin said to her the day after the second funeral; "they're up in her room—but they're things I wish *you'd* look at."

The pair of mourners, sufficiently stricken, were in the garden of the vicarage together, before luncheon, waiting to be summoned to that meal, and Arthur Prime had still in his face the intention, she was moved to call it rather than the expression, of feeling something or other. Some such appearance was in itself of course natural within a week of his stepmother's death, within three of his father's; but what was most present to the girl, herself sensitive and shrewd, was that he seemed somehow to brood without sorrow, to suffer without what she in her own case would have called pain. He turned away from her after this last speech—it was a good deal his habit to drop an observation and leave her to pick it up without assistance. If the vicar's widow, now in her turn finally translated, had not really belonged to him it was not for want of her giving herself, so far as he ever would take her; and she had lain for three days all alone at the end of the passage, in the great cold chamber of hospitality, the dampish, greenish room where visitors slept and where several of the ladies of the parish had, without effect, offered, in pairs and successions, piously to watch with her. His personal connection with the parish was now slighter than ever, and he had really not waited for this opportunity to show the ladies what he thought of them. She felt that she herself had, during her doleful month's leave from Bleet, where she was governess, rather taken her place in the same snubbed order; but it was presently, none the less, with a better little hope of coming in for some remembrance, some relic, that she went up to look at the things he had spoken of, the identity of which, as a confused cluster of bright objects on a table in the darkened room, shimmered at her as soon as she had opened the door.

They met her eyes for the first time, but in a moment, before touching them, she knew them as things of the theatre, as very much too fine to have been, with any verisimilitude,

135

things of the vicarage. They were too dreadfully good to be true, for her aunt had had no jewels to speak of, and these were coronets and girdles, diamonds, rubies and sapphires. Flagrant tinsel and glass, they looked strangely vulgar, but if, after the first queer shock of them, she found herself taking them up, it was for the very proof, never yet so distinct to her, of a far-off faded story. An honest widowed cleric with a small son and a large sense of Shakspeare had, on a brave latitude of habit as well as of taste—since it implied his having in very fact dropped deep into the "pit"—conceived for an obscure actress, several years older than himself, an admiration of which the prompt offer of his reverend name and hortatory hand was the sufficiently candid sign. The response had perhaps, in those dim years, in the way of eccentricity, even bettered the proposal, and Charlotte, turning the tale over, had long since drawn from it a measure of the career renounced by the undistinguished *comédienne*—doubtless also tragic, or perhaps pantomimic, at a pinch—of her late uncle's dreams. This career could not have been eminent and must much more probably have been comfortless.

"You see what it is—old stuff of the time she never liked to mention."

Our young woman gave a start; her companion had, after all, rejoined her and had apparently watched a moment her slightly scared recognition. "So I said to myself," she replied. Then, to show intelligence, yet keep clear of twaddle: "How peculiar they look!"

"They look awful," said Arthur Prime. "Cheap gilt, diamonds as big as potatoes. These are trappings of a ruder age than ours. Actors do themselves better now."

"Oh now," said Charlotte, not to be less knowing, "actresses have real diamonds."

"Some of them." Arthur spoke drily.

"I mean the bad ones—the nobodies too."

"Oh, some of the nobodies have the biggest. But mamma wasn't of that sort."

"A nobody?" Charlotte risked.

"Not a nobody to whom somebody—well, not a nobody with diamonds. It isn't all worth, this trash, five pounds."

There was something in the old gewgaws that spoke to her, and she continued to turn them over. "They're relics. I think they have their melancholy and even their dignity."

Arthur observed another pause. "Do you care for them?" he then asked. "I mean," he promptly added, "as a souvenir."

"Of you?" Charlotte threw off.

"Of me? What have I to do with it? Of your poor dead aunt who was so kind to you," he said with virtuous sternness.

"Well, I would rather have them than nothing."

"Then please take them," he returned in a tone of relief which expressed somehow more of the eager than of the gracious.

"Thank you." Charlotte lifted two or three objects up and set them down again. Though they were lighter than the materials they imitated they were so much more extravagant that they struck her in truth as rather an awkward heritage, to which she might have preferred even a matchbox or a penwiper. They were indeed shameless pinchbeck. "Had you any idea she had kept them?"

"I don't at all believe she *had* kept them or knew they were there, and I'm very sure my father didn't. They had quite equally worked off any tenderness for the connection. These odds and ends, which she thought had been given away or destroyed, had simply got thrust into a dark corner and been forgotten."

Charlotte wondered. "Where then did you find them?"

"In that old tin box"—and the young man pointed to the receptacle from which he had dislodged them and which stood on a neighbouring chair. "It's rather a good box still, but I'm afraid I can't give you *that*."

The girl gave the box no look; she continued only to look at the trinkets. "What corner had she found?"

"She hadn't 'found' it," her companion sharply insisted; "she had simply lost it. The whole thing had passed from her mind. The box was on the top shelf of the old schoolroom closet, which, until one put one's head into it from a stepladder, looked, from below, quite cleared out. The door is narrow and the part of the closet to the left goes well into the wall. The box had stuck there for years."

Charlotte was conscious of a mind divided and a vision vaguely troubled, and once more she took up two or three of the subjects of this revelation; a big bracelet in the form of a gilt serpent with many twists and beady eyes, a brazen belt studded with emeralds and rubies, a chain, of flamboyant architecture, to which, at the Theatre Royal Little Peddlington, Hamlet's mother had probably been careful to attach the portrait of the successor to Hamlet's father. "Are you very sure they're not really worth something? Their mere weight alone——!" she vaguely observed, balancing a moment a royal diadem that might have crowned one of the creations of the famous Mrs. Jarley.

But Arthur Prime, it was clear, had already thought the question over and found the answer easy. "If they had been worth anything to speak of she would long ago have sold them. My father and she had unfortunately never been in a position to keep any considerable value locked up." And while his companion took in the obvious force of this he went on with a flourish just marked enough not to escape her: "If they're worth anything at all—why, you're only the more welcome to them."

Charlotte had now in her hand a small bag of faded, figured silk—one of those antique conveniences that speak to us, in the terms of evaporated camphor and lavender, of the part they have played in some personal history; but, though she had for the first time drawn the string, she looked much more at the young man than at the questionable treasure it appeared to contain. "I shall like them. They're all I have."

"All you have——?"

"That belonged to her."

He swelled a little, then looked about him as if to appeal—as against her avidity—to the whole poor place. "Well, what else do you want?"

"Nothing. Thank you very much." With which she bent her eyes on the article wrapped, and now only exposed, in her superannuated satchel—a necklace of large pearls, such as might once have graced the neck of a provincial Ophelia and borne company to a flaxen wig. "This perhaps *is* worth something. Feel it." And she passed him the necklace, the weight of which she had gathered for a moment into her hand.

He measured it in the same way with his own, but remained quite detached. "Worth at most thirty shillings."

"Not more?"

"Surely not if it's paste?"

"But *is* it paste?"

He gave a small sniff of impatience. "Pearls nearly as big as filberts?"

"But they're heavy," Charlotte declared.

"No heavier than anything else." And he gave them back with an allowance for her simplicity. "Do you imagine for a moment they're real?"

She studied them a little, feeling them, turning them round. "Mightn't they possibly be?"

"Of that size—stuck away with that trash?"

"I admit it isn't likely," Charlotte presently said. "And pearls are so easily imitated."

"That's just what—to a person who knows—they're not. These have no lustre, no play."

"No—they *are* dull. They're opaque."

"Besides," he lucidly inquired, "how could she ever have come by them?"

"Mightn't they have been a present?"

Arthur stared at the question as if it were almost improper. "Because actresses are exposed——?" He pulled up, however, not saying to what, and before she could supply the deficiency had, with the sharp ejaculation of "No, they mightn't!" turned his back on her and walked away. His manner made her feel that she had probably been wanting in tact, and before he returned to the subject, the last thing that evening, she had satisfied herself of the ground of his resentment. They had been talking of her departure the next morning, the hour of her train and the fly that would come for her, and it was precisely these things that gave him his effective chance. "I really can't allow you to leave the house under the impression that my stepmother was at *any* time of her life the sort of person to allow herself to be approached——"

"With pearl necklaces and that sort of thing?" Arthur had made for her somehow the difficulty that she couldn't show him she understood him without seeming pert.

It at any rate only added to his own gravity. "That sort of thing, exactly."

"I didn't think when I spoke this morning—but I see what you mean."

"I mean that she was beyond reproach," said Arthur Prime.

"A hundred times yes."

"Therefore if she couldn't, out of her slender gains, ever have paid for a row of pearls——"

"She couldn't, in that atmosphere, ever properly have had one? Of course she couldn't. I've seen perfectly since our talk," Charlotte went on, "that that string of beads isn't even, as an imitation, very good. The little clasp itself doesn't seem even gold. With false pearls, I suppose," the girl mused, "it naturally wouldn't be."

"The whole thing's rotten paste," her companion returned as if to have done with it. "If it were *not*, and she had kept it all these years hidden——"

"Yes?" Charlotte sounded as he paused.

"Why, I shouldn't know what to think!"

"Oh, I see." She had met him with a certain blankness, but adequately enough, it seemed, for him to regard the subject as dismissed; and there was no reversion to it between them before, on the morrow, when she had with difficulty made a place for them in her trunk, she carried off these florid survivals.

At Bleet she found small occasion to revert to them and, in an air charged with such quite other references, even felt, after she had laid them away, much enshrouded, beneath various piles of clothing, as if they formed a collection not wholly without its note of the ridiculous. Yet she was never, for the joke, tempted to show them to her pupils, though Gwendolen and Blanche, in particular, always wanted, on her return, to know what she had brought back; so that without an accident by which the case was quite changed they might have appeared to enter on a new phase of interment. The essence of the accident was the sudden illness, at the last moment, of Lady Bobby, whose advent had been so much counted on to spice the five days' feast laid out for the coming of age of the eldest son of the house; and its equally marked effect was the despatch of a pressing message, in quite another direction, to

Mrs. Guy, who, could she by a miracle be secured—she was always engaged ten parties deep—might be trusted to supply, it was believed, an element of exuberance scarcely less active. Mrs. Guy was already known to several of the visitors already on the scene, but she was not yet known to our young lady, who found her, after many wires and counterwires had at last determined the triumph of her arrival, a strange, charming little red-haired, black-dressed woman, with the face of a baby and the authority of a commodore. She took on the spot the discreet, the exceptional young governess into the confidence of her designs and, still more, of her doubts; intimating that it was a policy she almost always promptly pursued.

"To-morrow and Thursday are all right," she said frankly to Charlotte on the second day, "but I'm not half satisfied with Friday."

"What improvement then do you suggest?"

"Well, my strong point, you know, is *tableaux vivants*."

"Charming. And what is your favourite character?"

"Boss!" said Mrs. Guy with decision; and it was very markedly under that ensign that she had, within a few hours, completely planned her campaign and recruited her troop. Every word she uttered was to the point, but none more so than, after a general survey of their equipment, her final inquiry of Charlotte. She had been looking about, but half appeased, at the muster of decoration and drapery. "We shall be dull. We shall want more colour. You've nothing else?"

Charlotte had a thought. "No—I've *some* things."

"Then why don't you bring them?"

The girl hesitated. "Would you come to my room?"

"No," said Mrs. Guy—"bring them to-night to mine."

So Charlotte, at the evening's end, after candlesticks had flickered through brown old passages bedward, arrived at her friend's door with the burden of her aunt's relics. But she promptly expressed a fear. "Are they too garish?"

When she had poured them out on the sofa Mrs. Guy was but a minute, before the glass, in clapping on the diadem. "Awfully jolly—we can do Ivanhoe!"

"But they're only glass and tin."

"Larger than life they are, *rather!*—which is exactly what, for tableaux, is wanted. *Our* jewels, for historic scenes, don't tell—the real thing falls short. Rowena must have rubies as big as eggs. Leave them with me," Mrs. Guy continued—"they'll inspire me. Good-night."

The next morning she was in fact—yet very strangely—inspired. "Yes, *I'll* do Rowena. But I don't, my dear, understand."

"Understand what?"

Mrs. Guy gave a very lighted stare. "How you come to have such things."

Poor Charlotte smiled. "By inheritance."

"Family jewels?"

"They belonged to my aunt, who died some months ago. She was on the stage a few years in early life, and these are a part of her trappings."

"She left them to you?"

"No; my cousin, her stepson, who naturally has no use for them, gave them to me for remembrance of her. She was a dear kind thing, always so nice to me, and I was fond of her."

Mrs. Guy had listened with visible interest. "But it's *he* who must be a dear kind thing!"

Charlotte wondered. "You think so?"

"Is *he*," her friend went on, "also 'always so nice' to you?"

The girl, at this, face to face there with the brilliant visitor in the deserted breakfast-room, took a deeper sounding. "What is it?"

"Don't you know?"

Something came over her. "The pearls——?" But the question fainted on her lips.

"Doesn't *he* know?"

Charlotte found herself flushing. "They're *not* paste?"

"Haven't you looked at them?"

She was conscious of two kinds of embarrassment. "*You* have?"

"Very carefully."

"And they're real?"

Mrs. Guy became slightly mystifying and returned for all answer: "Come again, when you've done with the children, to my room."

Our young woman found she had done with the children, that morning, with a promptitude that was a new joy to them, and when she reappeared before Mrs. Guy this lady had already encircled a plump white throat with the only ornament, surely, in all the late Mrs. Prime's—the effaced Miss Bradshaw's—collection, in the least qualified to raise a question. If Charlotte had never yet once, before the glass, tied the string of pearls about her own neck, this was because she had been capable of no such condescension to approved "imitation"; but she had now only to look at Mrs. Guy to see that, so disposed, the ambiguous objects might have passed for frank originals. "What in the world have you done to them?"

"Only handled them, understood them, admired them and put them on. That's what pearls want; they want to be worn—it wakes them up. They're alive, don't you see? How *have* these been treated? They must have been buried, ignored, despised. They were half dead. Don't you *know* about pearls?" Mrs. Guy threw off as she fondly fingered the necklace.

"How *should* I? Do *you*?"

"Everything. These were simply asleep, and from the moment I really touched them—well," said their wearer lovingly, "it only took one's eye!"

"It took more than mine—though I did just wonder; and than Arthur's," Charlotte brooded. She found herself almost panting. "Then their value——?"

"Oh, their value's excellent."

The girl, for a deep moment, took another plunge into the wonder, the beauty and mystery, of them. "Are you *sure*?"

Her companion wheeled round for impatience. "Sure? For what kind of an idiot, my dear, do you take me?"

It was beyond Charlotte Prime to say. "For the same kind as Arthur—and as myself," she could only suggest. "But my cousin didn't know. He thinks they're worthless."

"Because of the rest of the lot? Then your cousin's an ass. But what—if, as I understood you, he gave them to you—has he to do with it?"

"Why, if he gave them to me as worthless and they turn out precious——"

"You must give them back? I don't see that—if he was such a fool. He took the risk."

Charlotte fed, in fancy, on the pearls, which, decidedly, were exquisite, but which at the present moment somehow presented themselves much more as Mrs. Guy's than either as Arthur's or as her own. "Yes—he did take it; even after I had distinctly hinted to him that they looked to me different from the other pieces."

"Well, then!" said Mrs. Guy with something more than triumph—with a positive odd relief.

But it had the effect of making our young woman think with more intensity. "Ah, you see he thought they couldn't be different, because—so peculiarly—they shouldn't be."

"Shouldn't? I don't understand."

"Why, how would she have got them?"—so Charlotte candidly put it.

"She? Who?" There was a capacity in Mrs. Guy's tone for a sinking of persons—!

"Why, the person I told you of: his stepmother, my uncle's wife—among whose poor old things, extraordinarily thrust away and out of sight, he happened to find them."

Mrs. Guy came a step nearer to the effaced Miss Bradshaw. "Do you mean she may have stolen them?"

"No. But she had been an actress."

"Oh, well then," cried Mrs. Guy, "wouldn't that be just how?"

"Yes, except that she wasn't at all a brilliant one, nor in receipt of large pay." The girl even threw off a nervous joke. "I'm afraid she couldn't have been our Rowena."

Mrs. Guy took it up. "Was she very ugly?"

"No. She may very well, when young, have looked rather nice."

"Well, then!" was Mrs. Guy's sharp comment and fresh triumph.

"You mean it was a present? That's just what he so dislikes the idea of her having received—a present from an admirer capable of going such lengths."

"Because she wouldn't have taken it for nothing? *Speriamo*—that she wasn't a brute. The 'length' her admirer went was the length of a whole row. Let us hope she was just a little kind!"

"Well," Charlotte went on, "that she was 'kind' might seem to be shown by the fact that neither her husband, nor his son, nor I, his niece, knew or dreamed of her possessing anything so precious; by her having kept the gift all the rest of her life beyond discovery—out of sight and protected from suspicion."

"As if, you mean"—Mrs. Guy was quick—"she had been wedded to it and yet was ashamed of it? Fancy," she laughed while she manipulated the rare beads, "being ashamed of *these*!"

"But you see she had married a clergyman."

"Yes, she must have been 'rum.' But at any rate he had married *her*. What did he suppose?"

"Why, that she had never been of the sort by whom such offerings are encouraged."

"Ah, my dear, the sort by whom they are *not*——!" But Mrs. Guy caught herself up. "And her stepson thought the same?"

"Overwhelmingly."

"Was he, then, if only her stepson——"

"So fond of her as that comes to? Yes; he had never known, consciously, his real mother, and, without children of her own, she was very patient and nice with him. And *I* liked her so," the girl pursued, "that at the end of ten years, in so strange a manner, to 'give her away'——"

"Is impossible to you? Then don't!" said Mrs. Guy with decision.

"Ah, but if they're real I can't keep them!" Charlotte, with her eyes on them, moaned in her impatience. "It's too difficult."

"Where's the difficulty, if he has such sentiments that he would rather sacrifice the necklace than admit it, with the presumption it carries with it, to be genuine? You've only to be silent."

"And keep it? How can *I* ever wear it?"

"You'd have to hide it, like your aunt?" Mrs. Guy was amused. "You can easily sell it."

Her companion walked round her for a look at the affair from behind. The clasp was certainly, doubtless intentionally, misleading, but everything else was indeed lovely. "Well, I must think. Why didn't *she* sell them?" Charlotte broke out in her trouble.

Mrs. Guy had an instant answer. "Doesn't that prove what they secretly recalled to her? You've only to be silent!" she ardently repeated.

"I must think—I must think!"

Mrs. Guy stood with her hands attached but motionless. "Then you want them back?"

As if with the dread of touching them Charlotte retreated to the door. "I'll tell you to-night."

"But may I wear them?"

"Meanwhile?"

"This evening—at dinner."

It was the sharp, selfish pressure of this that really, on the spot, determined the girl; but for the moment, before closing the door on the question, she only said: "As you like!"

They were busy much of the day with preparation and re-hearsal, and at dinner, that evening, the concourse of guests was such that a place among them for Miss Prime failed to find itself marked. At the time the company rose she was therefore alone in the schoolroom, where, towards eleven o'clock, she received a visit from Mrs. Guy. This lady's white shoulders heaved, under the pearls, with an emotion that the very red lips which formed, as if for the full effect, the happiest opposition of colour, were not slow to translate. "My dear, you should have seen the sensation—they've had a success!"

Charlotte, dumb a moment, took it all in. "It *is* as if they knew it—they're more and more alive. But so much the worse for both of us! I can't," she brought out with an effort, "be silent."

"You mean to return them?"

"If I don't I'm a thief."

Mrs. Guy gave her a long, hard look: what was decidedly not of the baby in Mrs. Guy's face was a certain air of estab-lished habit in the eyes. Then, with a sharp little jerk of her head and a backward reach of her bare beautiful arms, she undid the clasp and, taking off the necklace, laid it on the table. "If you do, you're a goose."

"Well, of the two——!" said our young lady, gathering it up with a sigh. And as if to get it, for the pang it gave, out of sight as soon as possible, she shut it up, clicking the lock, in the drawer of her own little table; after which, when she turned again, her companion, without it, looked naked and plain. "But what will you say?" it then occurred to her to demand.

"Downstairs—to explain?" Mrs. Guy was, after all, trying at least to keep her temper. "Oh, I'll put on something else and say that clasp is broken. And you won't of course name *me* to him," she added.

"As having undeceived me? No—I'll say that, looking at the thing more carefully, it's my own private idea."

"And does he know how little you really know?"

"As an expert—surely. And he has much, always, the conceit of his own opinion."

"Then he won't believe you—as he so hates to. He'll stick to his judgment and maintain his gift, and we shall have the darlings back!" With which reviving assurance Mrs. Guy kissed for good-night.

She was not, however, to be gratified or justified by any prompt event, for, whether or no paste entered into the composition of the ornament in question, Charlotte shrank from the temerity of despatching it to town by post. Mrs. Guy was thus disappointed of the hope of seeing the business settled— "by return," she had seemed to expect—before the end of the revels. The revels, moreover, rising to a frantic pitch, pressed for all her attention, and it was at last only in the general confusion of leave-taking that she made, parenthetically, a dash at her young friend.

"Come, what will you take for them?"

"The pearls? Ah, you'll have to treat with my cousin."

Mrs. Guy, with quick intensity, lent herself. "Where then does he live?"

"In chambers in the Temple. You can find him."

"But what's the use, if *you* do neither one thing nor the other?"

"Oh, I *shall* do the 'other,'" Charlotte said: "I'm only waiting till I go up. You want them so awfully?" She curiously, solemnly again, sounded her.

"I'm dying for them. There's a special charm in them—I don't know what it is: they tell so their history."

"But what do you know of that?"

"Just what they themselves say. It's all *in* them—and it comes out. They breathe a tenderness—they have the white glow of it. My dear," hissed Mrs. Guy in supreme confidence and as she buttoned her glove—"they're things of love!"

"Oh!" our young woman vaguely exclaimed.

"They're things of passion!"

"Mercy!" she gasped, turning short off. But these words remained, though indeed their help was scarce needed, Charlotte being in private face to face with a new light, as she by this time felt she must call it, on the dear dead, kind, colourless lady whose career had turned so sharp a corner in the middle. The pearls had quite taken their place as a revelation. She might have received them for nothing—admit that; but she couldn't have kept them so long and so unprofitably hidden, couldn't have enjoyed them only in secret, for nothing; and she had mixed them, in her reliquary, with false things, in order to put curiosity and detection off the scent. Over this strange fact poor Charlotte interminably mused: it became more touching, more attaching for her than she could now confide to any ear. How bad, or how happy—in the sophisticated sense of Mrs. Guy and the young man at the Temple—the effaced Miss Bradshaw must have been to have had to be so mute! The little governess at Bleet put on the necklace now in secret sessions; she wore it sometimes under her dress; she came to feel, verily, a haunting passion for it. Yet in her penniless state she would have parted with it for money; she gave herself also to dreams of what in this direction it would do for her. The sophistry of her so often saying to herself that Arthur had after all definitely pronounced her welcome to any gain from his gift that might accrue—this trick remained innocent, as she perfectly knew it for what it was. Then there was always the possibility of his—as she could only picture it—rising to the occasion. Mightn't he have a grand magnanimous moment?—mightn't he just say: "Oh, of course I couldn't have afforded to let you have it if I had known; but since you *have* got it, and have made out the truth by

your own wit, I really can't screw myself down to the shabbiness of taking it back"?

She had, as it proved, to wait a long time—to wait till, at
the end of several months, the great house of Bleet had, with
due deliberation, for the season, transferred itself to town;
after which, however, she fairly snatched at her first freedom
to knock, dressed in her best and armed with her disclosure,
at the door of her doubting kinsman. It was still with doubt
and not quite with the face she had hoped that he listened to
her story. He had turned pale, she thought, as she produced
the necklace, and he appeared, above all, disagreeably affected.
Well, perhaps there was reason, she more than ever remembered; but what on earth was one, in close touch with the
fact, to do? She had laid the pearls on his table, where, without his having at first put so much as a finger to them, they
met his hard, cold stare.

"I don't believe in them," he simply said at last.

"That's exactly then," she returned with some spirit, "what
I wanted to hear!"

She fancied that at this his colour changed; it was indeed
vivid to her afterwards—for she was to have a long recall of
the scene—that she had made him quite angrily flush. "It's a
beastly unpleasant imputation, you know!"—and he walked
away from her as he had always walked at the vicarage.

"It's none of *my* making, I'm sure," said Charlotte Prime.
"If you're afraid to believe they're real——"

"Well?"—and he turned, across the room, sharp round
at her.

"Why, it's not my fault."

He said nothing more, for a moment, on this; he only came
back to the table. "They're what I originally said they were.
They're rotten paste."

"Then I may keep them?"

"No. I want a better opinion."

"Than your own?"

"Than *your* own." He dropped on the pearls another queer
stare, then, after a moment, bringing himself to touch them,
did exactly what she had herself done in the presence of Mrs.
Guy at Bleet—gathered them together, marched off with
them to a drawer, put them in and clicked the key. "You say

I'm afraid," he went on as he again met her; "but I shan't be afraid to take them to Bond Street."

"And if the people say they're real———?"

He hesitated—then had his strangest manner. "They won't say it! They shan't!"

There was something in the way he brought it out that deprived poor Charlotte, as she was perfectly aware, of any manner at all. "Oh!" she simply sounded, as she had sounded for her last word to Mrs. Guy; and, within a minute, without more conversation, she had taken her departure.

A fortnight later she received a communication from him, and towards the end of the season one of the entertainments in Eaton Square was graced by the presence of Mrs. Guy. Charlotte was not at dinner, but she came down afterwards, and this guest, on seeing her, abandoned a very beautiful young man on purpose to cross and speak to her. The guest had on a lovely necklace and had apparently not lost her habit of overflowing with the pride of such ornaments.

"Do you see?" She was in high joy.

They were indeed splendid pearls—so far as poor Charlotte could feel that she knew, after what had come and gone, about such mysteries. Charlotte had a sickly smile. "They're almost as fine as Arthur's."

"Almost? Where, my dear, are your eyes? They *are* 'Arthur's!'" After which, to meet the flood of crimson that accompanied her young friend's start: "I tracked them—after your folly, and, by miraculous luck, recognised them in the Bond Street window to which he had disposed of them."

"*Disposed* of them?" the girl gasped. "He wrote me that I had insulted his mother and that the people had shown him he was right—had pronounced them utter paste."

Mrs. Guy gave a stare. "Ah, I told you he wouldn't bear it! No. But I had, I assure you," she wound up, "to drive my bargain!"

Charlotte scarce heard or saw; she was full of her private wrong. "He wrote me," she panted, "that he had smashed them."

Mrs. Guy could only wonder and pity. "He's really mor-bid!" But it was not quite clear which of the pair she pitied; though Charlotte felt really morbid too after they had separated and she found herself full of thought. She even went the length of asking herself what sort of a bargain Mrs. Guy had driven and whether the marvel of the recognition in Bond Street had been a veracious account of the matter. Hadn't she perhaps in truth dealt with Arthur directly? It came back to Charlotte almost luridly that she had had his address.

The Great Good Place

GEORGE DANE had waked up to a bright new day, the face of nature well washed by last night's downpour and shining as with high spirits, good resolutions, lively intentions—the great glare of recommencement, in short, fixed in his patch of sky. He had sat up late to finish work—arrears overwhelming; then at last had gone to bed with the pile but little reduced. He was now to return to it after the pause of the night; but he could only look at it, for the time, over the bristling hedge of letters planted by the early postman an hour before and already, on the customary table by the chimney-piece, formally rounded and squared by his systematic servant. It was something too merciless, the domestic perfection of Brown. There were newspapers on another table, ranged with the same rigour of custom, newspapers too many—what could any creature want of so much news?—and each with its hand on the neck of the other, so that the row of their bodiless heads was like a series of decapitations. Other journals, other periodicals of every sort, folded and in wrappers, made a huddled mound that had been growing for several days and of which he had been wearily, helplessly aware. There were new books, also in wrappers as well as disenveloped and dropped again—books from publishers, books from authors, books from friends, books from enemies, books from his own bookseller, who took, it sometimes struck him, inconceivable things for granted. He touched nothing, approached nothing, only turned a heavy eye over the work, as it were, of the night—the fact, in his high, wide-windowed room, where the hard light of duty could penetrate every corner, of the unashamed admonition of the day. It was the old rising tide, and it rose and rose even under a minute's watching. It had been up to his shoulders last night—it was up to his chin now.

Nothing had passed while he slept—everything had stayed; nothing, that he could yet feel, had died—many things had been born. To let them alone, these things, the new things, let them utterly alone and see if that, by chance, wouldn't somehow prove the best way to deal with them: this fancy brushed his face for a moment as a possible solution, just giving it, as many a time before, a cool wave of air. Then he knew again as well as ever that leaving was difficult, leaving impossible—that the only remedy, the true, soft, effacing sponge, would be to *be* left, to be forgotten. There was no footing on which a man who had ever liked life—liked it, at any rate, as *he* had—could now escape from it. He must reap as he had sown. It was a thing of meshes; he had simply gone to sleep under the net and had simply waked up there. The net was too fine; the cords crossed each other at spots so near together, making at each a little tight, hard knot that tired fingers, this morning, were too limp and too tender to touch. Our poor friend's touched nothing—only stole significantly into his pockets as he wandered over to the window and faintly gasped at the energy of nature. What was most overwhelming was that she herself was so ready. She had soothed him rather, the night before, in the small hours by the lamp. From behind the drawn curtain of his study the rain had been audible and in a manner merciful; washing the window in a steady flood, it had seemed the right thing, the retarding, interrupting thing, the thing that, if it would only last, might clear the ground by floating out to a boundless sea the innumerable objects among which his feet stumbled and strayed. He had positively laid down his pen as on a sense of friendly pressure from it. The kind, full swash had been on the glass when he turned out his lamp; he had left his phrase unfinished and his papers lying quite as if for the flood to bear them away on its bosom. But there still, on the table, were the bare bones of the sentence—and not all of those; the single thing borne away and that he could never recover was the missing half that might have paired with it and begotten a figure.

Yet he could at last only turn back from the window; the world was everywhere, without and within, and, with the great staring egotism of its health and strength, was not to be trusted for tact or delicacy. He faced about precisely to meet his servant and the absurd solemnity of two telegrams on a tray. Brown ought to have kicked them into the room—then he himself might have kicked them out.

"And you told me to remind you, sir——"

George Dane was at last angry. "Remind me of nothing!"

"But you insisted, sir, that I was to insist!"

He turned away in despair, speaking with a pathetic quaver at absurd variance with his words: "If you insist, Brown, I'll kill you!" He found himself anew at the window, whence, looking down from his fourth floor, he could see the vast neighbourhood, under the trumpet-blare of the sky, beginning to rush about. There was a silence, but he knew Brown had not left him—knew exactly how straight and serious and stupid and faithful he stood there. After a minute he heard him again.

"It's only because, sir, you know, sir, you can't remember——"

At this Dane did flash round; it was more than at such a moment he could bear. "Can't remember, Brown? I can't forget. That's what's the matter with me."

Brown looked at him with the advantage of eighteen years of consistency. "I'm afraid you're not well, sir."

Brown's master thought. "It's a shocking thing to say, but I wish to heaven I weren't! It would be perhaps an excuse."

Brown's blankness spread like the desert. "To put them off?"

"Ah!" The sound was a groan; the plural pronoun, *any* pronoun, so mistimed. "Who is it?"

"Those ladies you spoke of—to lunch."

"Oh!" The poor man dropped into the nearest chair and stared a while at the carpet. It was very complicated.

"How many will there be, sir?" Brown asked.

"Fifty!"

"Fifty, sir?"

Our friend, from his chair, looked vaguely about; under his hand were the telegrams, still unopened, one of which he now tore asunder. "'Do hope you sweetly won't mind, to-day, 1.30, my bringing poor dear Lady Mullet, who is so awfully bent,'" he read to his companion.

His companion weighed it. "How many does *she* make, sir?"

"Poor dear Lady Mullet? I haven't the least idea."

"Is she—a—deformed, sir?" Brown inquired, as if in this case she might make more.

His master wondered, then saw he figured some personal curvature. "No; she's only bent on coming!" Dane opened the other telegram and again read out: " 'So sorry it's at eleventh hour impossible, and count on you here, as very greatest favour, at two sharp instead.' "

"How many does *that* make?" Brown imperturbably continued.

Dane crumpled up the two missives and walked with them to the waste-paper basket, into which he thoughtfully dropped them. "I can't say. You must do it all yourself. I shan't be there."

It was only on this that Brown showed an expression. "You'll go instead——"

"I'll go instead!" Dane raved.

Brown, however, had had occasion to show before that *he* would never desert their post. "Isn't that rather sacrificing the three?" Between respect and reproach he paused.

"*Are* there three?"

"I lay for four in all."

His master had, at any rate, caught his thought. "Sacrificing the three to the one, you mean? Oh, I'm not going to *her*!"

Brown's famous "thoroughness"—his great virtue—had never been so dreadful. "Then where *are* you going?"

Dane sat down to his table and stared at his ragged phrase. " 'There is a happy land—far, far away!' " He chanted it like a sick child and knew that for a minute Brown never moved. During this minute he felt between his shoulders the gimlet of criticism.

"Are you quite sure you're all right?"

"It's my certainty that overwhelms me, Brown. Look about you and judge. Could anything be more 'right,' in the view of the envious world, than everything that surrounds us here; that immense array of letters, notes, circulars; that pile of printers' proofs, magazines and books; these perpetual telegrams, these impending guests; this retarded, unfinished and interminable work? What could a man want more?"

"Do you mean there's too much, sir?"—Brown had sometimes these flashes.

"There's too much. There's too much. But *you* can't help it, Brown."

"No, sir," Brown assented. "Can't *you?*"

"I'm thinking—I must see. There are hours——!" Yes, there were hours, and this was one of them: he jerked himself up for another turn in his labyrinth, but still not touching, not even again meeting, his interlocutor's eye. If he was a genius for any one he was a genius for Brown; but it was terrible what that meant, being a genius for Brown. There had been times when he had done full justice to the way it kept him up; now, however, it was almost the worst of the avalanche. "Don't trouble about me," he went on insincerely and looking askance through his window again at the bright and beautiful world. "Perhaps it will rain—that *may* not be over. I do love the rain," he weakly pursued. "Perhaps, better still, it will snow."

Brown now had indeed a perceptible expression, and the expression was fear. "Snow, sir—the end of May?" Without pressing this point he looked at his watch. "You'll feel better when you've had breakfast."

"I dare say," said Dane, whom breakfast struck in fact as a pleasant alternative to opening letters. "I'll come in immediately."

"But without waiting——?"

"Waiting for what?"

Brown had at last, under his apprehension, his first lapse from logic, which he betrayed by hesitating in the evident hope that his companion would, by a flash of remembrance, relieve him of an invidious duty. But the only flashes now were the good man's own. "You say you can't forget, sir; but you do forget——"

"Is it anything very horrible?" Dane broke in.

Brown hung fire. "Only the gentleman you told me you had asked——"

Dane again took him up; horrible or not, it came back—indeed its mere coming back classed it. "To breakfast to-day? It *was* to-day; I see." It came back, yes, came back; the appointment with the young man—he supposed him young—and whose letter, the letter about—what was it?—had struck him. "Yes, yes; wait, wait."

"Perhaps he'll do you good, sir," Brown suggested.

"Sure to—sure to. All right!" Whatever he might do, he would at least prevent some other doing: that was present to our friend as, on the vibration of the electric bell at the door of the flat, Brown moved away. Two things, in the short interval that followed, were present to Dane: his having utterly forgotten the connection, the whence, whither and why of his guest; and his continued disposition not to touch—no, not with the finger. Ah, if he might *never* again touch! All the unbroken seals and neglected appeals lay there while, for a pause that he couldn't measure, he stood before the chimney-piece with his hands still in his pockets. He heard a brief exchange of words in the hall, but never afterward recovered the time taken by Brown to reappear, to precede and announce another person—a person whose name, somehow, failed to reach Dane's ear. Brown went off again to serve breakfast, leaving host and guest confronted. The duration of this first stage also, later on, defied measurement; but that little mattered, for in the train of what happened came promptly the second, the third, the fourth, the rich succession of the others. Yet what happened was but that Dane took his hand from his pocket, held it straight out and felt it taken. Thus indeed, if he had wanted never again to touch, it was already done.

II

He might have been a week in the place—the scene of his new consciousness—before he spoke at all. The occasion of it then was that one of the quiet figures he had been idly watching drew at last nearer and showed him a face that was the highest expression—to his pleased but as yet slightly confused perception—of the general charm. What *was* the general charm? He couldn't, for that matter, easily have phrased it; it was such an abyss of negatives, such an absence of everything. The oddity was that, after a minute, he was struck as by the reflection of his own very image in this first interlocutor seated with him, on the easy bench, under the high, clear portico and above the wide, far-reaching garden, where the things that most showed in the greenness were the surface of still water and the white note of old statues. The absence of everything was, in the aspect of the Brother who had thus informally joined him—a man of his own age, tired, distinguished, modest, kind—really, as he could soon see, but the absence of what he didn't want. He didn't want, for the time, anything but just to *be* there, to stay in the bath. He was in the bath yet, the broad, deep bath of stillness. They sat in it together now, with the water up to their chins. He had not had to talk, he had not had to think, he had scarce even had to feel. He had been sunk that way before, sunk—when and where?—in another flood; only a flood of rushing waters, in which bumping and gasping were all. This was a current so slow and so tepid that one floated practically without motion and without chill. The break of silence was not immediate, though Dane seemed indeed to feel it begin before a sound passed. It could pass quite sufficiently without words that he and his mate were Brothers, and what that meant.

Dane wondered, but with no want of ease—for want of ease was impossible—if his friend found in *him* the same likeness, the proof of peace, the gage of what the place could do. The long afternoon crept to its end; the shadows fell further and the sky glowed deeper; but nothing changed—nothing *could* change—in the element itself. It was a conscious security. It was wonderful! Dane had lived into it, but he was still immensely aware. He would have been sorry to lose that, for just this fact, as yet, the blessed fact of consciousness, seemed the greatest thing of all. Its only fault was that, being in itself such an occupation, so fine an unrest in the heart of gratitude, the life of the day all went to it. But what even then was the harm? He had come only to come, to take what he found. This was the part where the great cloister, inclosed externally on three sides and probably the largest, lightest, fairest effect, to his charmed sense, that human hands could ever have expressed in dimensions of length and breadth, opened to the south its splendid fourth quarter, turned to the great view an outer gallery that combined with the rest of the portico to form a high, dry loggia, such as he a little pretended to himself he had, in Italy, in old days, seen in old cities, old convents, old villas. This recall of the disposition of some great abode of an Order, some mild Monte Cassino, some Grande Chartreuse more accessible, was his main term of comparison; but he knew he had really never anywhere beheld anything at once so calculated and so generous.

Three impressions in particular had been with him all the week, and he could only recognise in silence their happy effect on his nerves. How it was all managed he couldn't have told—he had been content moreover till now with his ignorance of cause and pretext; but whenever he chose to listen with a certain intentness he made out, as from a distance, the sound of slow, sweet bells. How could they be so far and yet so audible? How could they be so near and yet so faint? How, above all, could they, in such an arrest of life, be, to *time* things, so frequent? The very essence of the bliss of Dane's whole change had been precisely that there was nothing now to time. It was the same with the slow footsteps that always, within earshot, to the vague attention, marked the space and the leisure, seemed, in long, cool arcades, lightly to fall and perpetually to recede. This was the second impression, and it melted into the third, as, for that matter, every form of softness, in the great good place, was but a further turn, without jerk or gap, of the endless roll of serenity. The quiet footsteps were quiet figures; the quiet figures that, to the eye, kept the picture human and brought its perfection within reach. This perfection, he felt on the bench by his friend, was now more in reach than ever. His friend at last turned to him a look different from the looks of friends in London clubs.

"The thing was to find it out!"

It was extraordinary how this remark fitted into his thought. "Ah, wasn't it? And when I think," said Dane, "of all the people who haven't and who never will!" He sighed over these unfortunates with a tenderness that, in its degree, was practically new to him, feeling, too, how well his companion would know the people he meant. He only meant some, but they were all who would want it; though of these, no doubt—well, for reasons, for things that, in the world, he had observed—there would never be too many. Not all perhaps who wanted would really find; but none at least would find who didn't really want. And then what the need would have to have been first! What it at first had to be for himself! He felt afresh, in the light of his companion's face, what it

might still be even when deeply satisfied, as well as what communication was established by the mere mutual knowledge
of it.

"Every man must arrive by himself and on his own feet—
isn't that so? We're brothers here for the time, as in a great
monastery, and we immediately think of each other and recognise each other as such; but we must have first got here as
we can, and we meet after long journeys by complicated ways.
Moreover we meet—don't we?—with closed eyes."

"Ah, don't speak as if we were dead!" Dane laughed.

"I shan't mind death if it's like this," his friend replied.

It was too obvious, as Dane gazed before him, that one
wouldn't; but after a moment he asked, with the first articu-
lation, as yet, of his most elementary wonder: "Where is it?"

"I shouldn't be surprised if it were much nearer than one
ever suspected."

"Nearer town, do you mean?"

"Nearer everything—nearer every one."

George Dane thought. "Somewhere, for instance, down in
Surrey?"

His Brother met him on this with a shade of reluctance.
"Why should we call it names? It must have a climate,
you see."

"Yes," Dane happily mused; "without that——!" All it so
securely did have overwhelmed him again, and he couldn't
help breaking out: "*What* is it?"

"Oh, it's positively a part of our ease and our rest and our
change, I think, that we don't at all know and that we may
really call it, for that matter, anything in the world we like—
the thing, for instance, we love it most for being."

"I know what *I* call it," said Dane after a moment. Then
as his friend listened with interest: "Just simply 'The Great
Good Place.'"

"I see—what can you say more? I've put it to myself perhaps a little differently." They sat there as innocently as small
boys confiding to each other the names of toy animals. "The
Great Want Met."

"Ah, yes, that's it!"

"Isn't it enough for us that it's a place carried on, for our
benefit, so admirably that we strain our ears in vain for a creak

of the machinery? Isn't it enough for us that it's simply a thorough hit?"

"Ah, a hit!" Dane benignantly murmured.

"It does for us what it pretends to do," his companion went on; "the mystery isn't deeper than that. The thing is probably simple enough in fact, and on a thoroughly practical basis; only it has had its origin in a splendid thought, in a real stroke of genius."

"Yes," Dane exclaimed, "in a sense—on somebody or other's part—so exquisitely personal!"

"Precisely—it rests, like all good things, on experience. The 'great want' comes home—that's the great thing it does! On the day it came home to the right mind this dear place was constituted. It always, moreover, in the long run, *has* been met—it always must be. How can it not require to be, more and more, as pressure of every sort grows?"

Dane, with his hands folded in his lap, took in these words of wisdom. "Pressure of every sort *is* growing!" he placidly observed.

"I see well enough what that fact has done to *you*," his Brother returned.

Dane smiled. "I couldn't have borne it longer. I don't know what would have become of me."

"I know what would have become of *me*."

"Well, it's the same thing."

"Yes," said Dane's companion, "it's doubtless the same thing." On which they sat in silence a little, seeming pleasantly to follow, in the view of the green garden, the vague movements of the monster—madness, surrender, collapse—they had escaped. Their bench was like a box at the opera. "And I may perfectly, you know," the Brother pursued, "have seen you before. I may even have known you well. We don't know."

They looked at each other again serenely enough, and at last Dane said: "No, we don't know."

"That's what I meant by our coming with our eyes closed. Yes—there's something out. There's a gap—a link missing, the great hiatus!" the Brother laughed. "It's as simple a story as the old, old rupture—the break that lucky Catholics have always been able to make, that they are still, with their in-

numerable religious houses, able to make, by going into 'retreat.' I don't speak of the pious exercises; I speak only of the
material simplification. I don't speak of the putting off of
one's self; I speak only—if one has a self worth sixpence—of
the getting it back. The place, the time, the way were, for
those of the old persuasion, always there—are indeed practically there for them as much as ever. They can always get off—
the blessed houses receive. So it was high time that we—we
of the great Protestant peoples, still more, if possible, in the
sensitive individual case, overscored and overwhelmed, still
more congested with mere quantity and prostituted, through
our 'enterprise,' to mere profanity—should learn how to get
off, should find somewhere *our* retreat and remedy. There was
such a huge chance for it!"

Dane laid his hand on his companion's arm. "It's charming,
how, when we speak for ourselves, we speak for each other.
That was exactly what I said!" He had fallen to recalling from
over the gulf the last occasion.

The Brother, as if it would do them both good, only desired
to draw him out. "What you said——?"

"To *him*—that morning." Dane caught a far bell again and
heard a slow footstep. A quiet figure passed somewhere—neither of them turned to look. What was, little by little, more
present to him was the perfect taste. It was supreme—it was
everywhere. "I just dropped my burden—and he received it."

"And was it very great?"

"Oh, such a load!" Dane laughed.

"Trouble, sorrow, doubt?"

"Oh, no; worse than that!"

"Worse?"

" 'Success'—the vulgarest kind!" And Dane laughed again.

"Ah, I know that, too! No one in future, as things are
going, will be able to face success."

"Without something of this sort—never. The better it is
the worse—the greater the deadlier. But my one pain here,"
Dane continued, "is in thinking of my poor friend."

"The person to whom you've already alluded?"

"My substitute in the world. Such an unutterable benefactor. He turned up that morning when everything had somehow got on my nerves, when the whole great globe indeed,

nerves, or no nerves, seemed to have squeezed itself into my study. It wasn't a question of nerves, it was a mere question of the displacement of everything—of submersion by our eternal too much. I didn't know *où donner de la tête*—I couldn't have gone a step further."

The intelligence with which the Brother listened kept them as children feeding from the same bowl. "And then you got the tip?"

"I got the tip!" Dane happily sighed.

"Well, we all get it. But I dare say differently."

"Then how did *you*——?"

The Brother hesitated, smiling. "You tell me first."

III

"Well," said George Dane, "it was a young man I had never seen—a man, at any rate, much younger than myself—who had written to me and sent me some article, some book. I read the stuff, was much struck with it, told him so and thanked him—on which, of course, I heard from him again. He asked me things—his questions were interesting; but to save time and writing I said to him: 'Come to see me—we can talk a little; but all I can give you is half an hour at breakfast.' He turned up at the hour on a day when, more than ever in my life before, I seemed, as it happened, in the endless press and stress, to have lost possession of my soul and to be surrounded only with the affairs of other people and the irrelevant, destructive, brutalising sides of life. It made me literally ill—made me feel as I had never felt that if I should once really, for an hour, lose hold of the thing itself, the thing I was trying for, I should never recover it again. The wild waters would close over me, and I should drop straight to the bottom where the vanquished dead lie."

"I follow you every step of your way," said the friendly Brother. "The wild waters, you mean, of our horrible time."

"Of our horrible time—precisely. Not, of course—as we sometimes dream—of any other."

"Yes, any other is only a dream. We really know none but our own."

"No, thank God—that's enough," Dane said. "Well, my young man turned up, and I hadn't been a minute in his presence before making out that practically it would be in him somehow or other to help me. He came to me with envy, envy extravagant—really passionate. I was, heaven save us, the great 'success' for him; he himself was broken and beaten. How can I say what passed between us?—it was so strange, so swift, so much a matter, from one to the other, of instant perception and agreement. He was so clever and haggard and hungry!"

"Hungry?" the Brother asked.

"I don't mean for bread, though he had none too much, I think, even of that. I mean for—well, what *I* had and what I was a monument of to him as I stood there up to my neck in preposterous evidence. He, poor chap, had been for ten years serenading closed windows and had never yet caused a shutter to show that it stirred. My dim blind was the first to be raised an inch; my reading of his book, my impression of it, my note and my invitation, formed literally the only response ever dropped into his dark street. He saw in my littered room, my shattered day, my bored face and spoiled temper— it's embarrassing, but I must tell you—the very blaze of my glory. And he saw in the blaze of my glory—deluded innocent!—what he had yearned for in vain."

"What he had yearned for was to *be* you," said the Brother. Then he added: "I see where you're coming out."

"At my saying to him by the end of five minutes: 'My dear fellow, I wish you'd just try it—wish you'd, for a while, just *be* me!' You go straight to the mark, and that was exactly what occurred—extraordinary though it was that we should both have understood. I saw what he could give, and he did too. He saw moreover what I could take; in fact what he saw was wonderful."

"He must be very remarkable!" the Brother laughed.

"There's no doubt of it whatever—far more remarkable than I. That's just the reason why what I put to him in joke—with a fantastic, desperate irony—became, on his hands, with his vision of his chance, the blessed guarantee of my sitting on this spot in your company. 'Oh, if I could just shift it all—make it straight over for an hour to other shoulders! If there only *were* a pair!'—that's the way I put it to him. And then at something in his face, 'Would *you*, by a miracle, undertake it?' I asked. I let him know all it meant—how it meant that he should at that very moment step in. It meant that he should finish my work and open my letters and keep my engagements and be subject, for better or worse, to my contacts and complications. It meant that he should live with my life, and think with my brain, and write with my hand, and speak with my voice. It meant, above all, that I should get off. He accepted with magnificence—rose to it like a hero. Only he said: 'What will become of *you*?' "

"There was the hitch!" the Brother admitted.

"Ah, but only for a minute. He came to my help again," Dane pursued, "when he saw I couldn't quite meet that, could at least only say that I wanted to think, wanted to cease, wanted to do the thing itself—the thing I was trying for, miserable me, and that thing only—and therefore wanted first of all really to *see* it again, planted out, crowded out, frozen out as it now so long had been. 'I know what you want,' he after a moment quietly remarked to me. 'Ah, what I want doesn't exist!' 'I know what you want,' he repeated. At that I began to believe him."

"Had you any idea yourself?" the Brother asked.

"Oh, yes," said Dane, "and it was just my idea that made me despair. There it was as sharp as possible in my imagination and my longing—there it was so utterly *not* in fact. We were sitting together on my sofa as we waited for breakfast. He presently laid his hand on my knee—showed me a face that the sudden great light in it had made, for me, indescribably beautiful. "It exists—it exists," he at last said. And so, I remember, we sat a while and looked at each other, with the final effect of my finding that I absolutely believed him. I remember we weren't at all solemn—we smiled with the joy of discoverers. He was as glad as I—he was tremendously glad. That came out in the whole manner of his reply to the appeal that broke from me: 'Where is it, then, in God's name? Tell me without delay where it is!' "

The Brother had attended with a sympathy! "He gave you the address?"

"He was thinking it out—feeling for it, catching it. He has a wonderful head of his own and must be making of the whole thing, while we sit here gossiping, something much better than ever *I* did. The mere sight of his face, the sense of his hand on my knee, made me, after a little, feel that he not only knew what I wanted, but was getting nearer to it than I could have got in ten years. He suddenly sprang up and went over to my study-table—sat straight down there as if to write me my passport. Then it was—at the mere sight of his back, which was turned to me—that I felt the spell work. I simply sat and watched him with the queerest, deepest, sweetest sense in the world—the sense of an ache that had stopped. All life was lifted; I myself at least was somehow off the ground. He was already where I had been."

"And where were you?" the Brother amusedly inquired.

"Just on the sofa always, leaning back on the cushion and feeling a delicious ease. He was already me."

"And who were you?" the Brother continued.

"Nobody. That was the fun."

"That *is* the fun," said the Brother, with a sigh like soft music.

Dane echoed the sigh, and, as nobody talking with nobody, they sat there together still and watched the sweet wide picture darken into tepid night.

IV

At the end of three weeks—so far as time was distinct—Dane began to feel there was something he had recovered. It was the thing they never named—partly for want of the need and partly for lack of the word; for what indeed was the description that would cover it all? The only real need was to know it, to see it, in silence. Dane had a private, practical sign for it, which, however, he had appropriated by theft—"the vision and the faculty divine." That, doubtless, was a flattering phrase for his idea of his genius; the genius, at all events, was what he had been in danger of losing and had at last held by a thread that might at any moment have broken. The change was that, little by little, his hold had grown firmer, so that he drew in the line—more and more each day—with a pull that he was delighted to find it would bear. The mere dream-sweetness of the place was superseded; it was more and more a world of reason and order, of sensible, visible arrangement. It ceased to be strange—it was high, triumphant clearness. He cultivated, however, but vaguely, the question of where he was, finding it near enough the mark to be almost sure that if he was not in Kent he was probably in Hampshire. He paid for everything but that—that wasn't one of the items. Payment, he had soon learned, was definite; it consisted of sovereigns and shillings—just like those of the world he had left, only parted with more ecstatically—that he put, in his room, in a designated place and that were taken away in his absence by one of the unobtrusive, effaced agents—shadows projected on the hours like the noiseless march of the sundial— that were always at work. The institution had sides that had their recalls, and a pleased, resigned perception of these things was at once the effect and the cause of its grace.

Dane picked out of his dim past a dozen halting similes. The sacred, silent convent was one; another was the bright country-house. He did the place no outrage to liken it to an hotel; he permitted himself on occasion to trace its resemblance to a club. Such images, however, but flickered and went out—they lasted only long enough to light up the difference. An hotel without noise, a club without newspapers— when he turned his face to what it was "without" the view opened wide. The only approach to a real analogy was in himself and his companions. They were brothers, guests, members; they were even, if one liked—and they didn't in the least mind what they were called—"regular boarders." It was not they who made the conditions, it was the conditions that made them. These conditions found themselves accepted, clearly, with an appreciation, with a rapture, it was rather to be called, that had to do—as the very air that pervaded them and the force that sustained—with their quiet and noble assurance. They combined to form the large, simple idea of a general refuge—an image of embracing arms, of liberal accommodation. What was the effect, really, but the poetisation by perfect taste of a type common enough? There was no daily miracle; the perfect taste, with the aid of space, did the trick.

What underlay and overhung it all, better yet, Dane mused, was some original inspiration, but confirmed, unquenched, some happy thought of an individual breast. It had been born somehow and somewhere—it had had to insist on being—the blessed conception. The author might remain in the obscure, for that was part of the perfection: personal service so hushed and regulated that you scarce caught it in the act and only knew it by its results. Yet the wise mind was everywhere—the whole thing, infallibly, centred, at the core, in a consciousness. And what a consciousness it had been, Dane thought, a consciousness how like his own! The wise mind had felt, the wise mind had suffered; then, for all the worried company of minds, the wise mind had seen a chance. Of the creation thus arrived at you could none the less never have said if it were the last echo of the old or the sharpest note of the modern.

Dane again and again, among the far bells and the soft footfalls, in cool cloister and warm garden, found himself wanting not to know more and yet liking not to know less. It was part of the general beauty that there was no personal publicity, much less any personal success. Those things were in the world—in what he had left; there was no vulgarity here of credit or claim or fame. The real exquisite was to be without the complication of an identity, and the greatest boon of all, doubtless, the solid security, the clear confidence one could feel in the keeping of the contract. That was what had been most in the wise mind—the importance of the absolute sense, on the part of its beneficiaries, that what was offered was guaranteed. They had no concern but to pay—the wise mind knew what they paid for. It was present to Dane each hour that he could never be overcharged. Oh, the deep, deep bath, the soft, cool plash in the stillness!—this, time after time, as if under regular treatment, a sublimated German "cure," was the vivid name for his luxury. The inner life woke up again, and it was the inner life, for people of his generation, victims of the modern madness, mere maniacal extension and motion, that was returning health. He had talked of independence and written of it, but what a cold, flat word it had been! This was the wordless fact itself—the uncontested possession of the long, sweet, stupid day. The fragrance of flowers just wandered through the void, and the quiet recurrence of delicate, plain fare in a high, clean refectory where the soundless, simple service was the triumph of art. That, as he analysed, remained the constant explanation: all the sweetness and serenity were created, calculated things. He analysed, however, but in a desultory way and with a positive delight in the residuum of mystery that made for the great artist in the background the innermost shrine of the idol of a temple; there were odd moments for it, mild meditations when, in the broad cloister of peace or some garden-nook where the air was light, a special glimpse of beauty or reminder of felicity seemed, in passing, to hover and linger. In the mere ecstasy of change that had at first possessed him he had not discriminated—had only let himself sink, as I have mentioned, down to hushed depths. Then had come the slow, soft stages of intelligence and notation, more marked and more fruitful perhaps after that long talk with his mild mate in the twilight, and seeming to wind up the process by putting the key into his hand. This key, pure gold, was simply the cancelled list. Slowly and blissfully he read into the general wealth of his comfort all the particular absences of which it was composed. One by one he touched, as it were, all the things it was such rapture to be without.

It was the paradise of his own room that was most indebted to them—a great square, fair chamber, all beautified with omissions, from which, high up, he looked over a long valley to a far horizon, and in which he was vaguely and pleasantly reminded of some old Italian picture, some Carpaccio or some early Tuscan, the representation of a world without newspapers and letters, without telegrams and photographs, without the dreadful, fatal too much. There, for a blessing, he *could* read and write; there, above all, he could do nothing— he could live. And there were all sorts of freedoms—always, for the occasion, the particular right one. He could bring a book from the library—he could bring two, he could bring three. An effect produced by the charming place was that, for some reason, he never wanted to bring more. The library was a benediction—high and clear and plain, like everything else, but with something, in all its arched amplitude, unconfused and brave and gay. He should never forget, he knew, the throb of immediate perception with which he first stood there, a single glance round sufficing so to show him that it would give him what for years he had desired. He had not had detachment, but there was detachment here—the sense of a great silver bowl from which he could ladle up the melted hours. He strolled about from wall to wall, too pleasantly in tune on that occasion to sit down punctually or to choose; only recognising from shelf to shelf every dear old book that he had had to put off or never returned to; every deep, distinct voice of another time that, in the hubbub of the world, he had had to take for lost and unheard. He came back, of course, soon, came back every day; enjoyed there, of all the rare, strange moments, those that were at once most quickened and most caught—moments in which every apprehension counted double and every act of the mind was a lover's embrace. It was the quarter he perhaps, as the days went on, liked best; though indeed it only shared with the rest of the place, with every aspect to which his face happened to be turned, the power to remind him of the masterly general control.

There were times when he looked up from his book to lose himself in the mere tone of the picture that never failed at any moment or at any angle. The picture was always there, yet was made up of things common enough. It was in the way an open window in a broad recess let in the pleasant morning; in the way the dry air pricked into faint freshness the gilt of old bindings; in the way an empty chair beside a table unlittered showed a volume just laid down; in the way a happy Brother—as detached as oneself and with his innocent back presented—lingered before a shelf with the slow sound of turned pages. It was a part of the whole impression that, by some extraordinary law, one's vision seemed less from the facts than the facts from one's vision; that the elements were determined at the moment by the moment's need or the moment's sympathy. What most prompted this reflection was the degree in which, after a while, Dane had a consciousness of company. After that talk with the good Brother on the bench there were other good Brothers in other places—always in cloister or garden some figure that stopped if he himself stopped and with which a greeting became, in the easiest way in the world, a sign of the diffused amenity. Always, always, however, in all contacts, was the balm of a happy ignorance. What he had felt the first time recurred: the friend was always new and yet at the same time—it was amusing, not disturbing—suggested the possibility that he might be but an old one altered. That was only delightful—as positively delightful in the particular, the actual conditions as it might have been the reverse in the conditions abolished. These others, the abolished, came back to Dane at last so easily that he could exactly measure each difference, but with what he had finally been hustled on to hate in them robbed of its terror in consequence of something that had happened. What had happened was that in tranquil walks and talks the deep spell had worked and he had got his soul again. He had drawn in by this time, with his lightened hand, the whole of the long line, and that fact just dangled at the end. He could put his other hand on it, he could unhook it, he was once more in possession. This, as it befell, was exactly what he supposed he must have said to a comrade beside whom, one afternoon in the cloister, he found himself measuring steps.

"Oh, it comes—comes of itself, doesn't it, thank goodness?—just by the simple fact of finding room and time!"

The comrade was possibly a novice or in a different stage from his own; there was at any rate a vague envy in the recognition that shone out of the fatigued, yet freshened face. "It has come to *you* then?—you've got what you wanted?" That was the gossip and interchange that could pass to and fro. Dane, years before, had gone in for three months of hydropathy, and there was a droll echo, in this scene, of the old questions of the water-cure, the questions asked in the periodical pursuit of the "reaction"—the ailment, the progress of each, the action of the skin and the state of the appetite. Such memories worked in now—all familiar reference, all easy play of mind; and among them our friends, round and round, fraternised ever so softly, until, suddenly stopping short, Dane, with a hand on his companion's arm, broke into the happiest laugh he had yet sounded.

V

"Why, it's raining!" And he stood and looked at the splash of the shower and the shine of the wet leaves. It was one of the summer sprinkles that bring out sweet smells.

"Yes—but why not?" his mate demanded.

"Well—because it's so charming. It's so exactly right."

"But everything *is*. Isn't that just why we're here?"

"Just exactly," Dane said; "only I've been living in the beguiled supposition that we've somehow or other a climate."

"So have I; so, I dare say, has every one. Isn't that the blessed moral?—that we live in beguiled suppositions. They come so easily here, and nothing contradicts them." The good Brother looked placidly forth—Dane could identify his phase. "A climate doesn't consist in its never raining, does it?"

"No, I dare say not. But somehow the good I've got has been half the great, easy absence of all that friction of which the question of weather mostly forms a part—has been indeed largely the great, easy, perpetual air-bath."

"Ah, yes—that's not a delusion; but perhaps the sense comes a little from our breathing an emptier medium. There are fewer things *in* it! Leave people alone, at all events, and the air is what they take to. Into the closed and the stuffy they have to be driven. I've had, too—I think we must all have—a fond sense of the south."

"But imagine it," said Dane, laughing, "in the beloved British islands and so near as we are to Bradford!"

His friend was ready enough to imagine. "To Bradford?" he asked, quite unperturbed. "How near?"

Dane's gaiety grew. "Oh, it doesn't matter!"

His friend, quite unmystified, accepted it. "There are things to puzzle out—otherwise it would be dull. It seems to me one can puzzle them."

"It's because we're so well disposed," Dane said.

"Precisely—we find good in everything."

"In everything," Dane went on. "The conditions settle that—they determine us."

They resumed their stroll, which evidently represented on the good Brother's part infinite agreement. "Aren't they probably in fact very simple?" he presently inquired. "Isn't simplification the secret?"

"Yes, but applied with a tact!"

"There it is. The thing's so perfect that it's open to as many interpretations as any other great work—a poem of Goethe, a dialogue of Plato, a symphony of Beethoven."

"It simply stands quiet, you mean," said Dane, "and lets us call it names?"

"Yes, but all such loving ones. We're 'staying' with some one—some delicious host or hostess who never shows."

"It's liberty-hall—absolutely," Dane assented.

"Yes—or a convalescent home."

To this, however, Dane demurred. "Ah, that, it seems to me, scarcely puts it. You weren't *ill*—were you? I'm very sure *I* really wasn't. I was only, as the world goes, too 'beastly well'!"

The good Brother wondered. "But if we couldn't keep it up——?"

"We couldn't keep it *down*—that was all the matter!"

"I see—I see." The good Brother sighed contentedly; after which he brought out again with kindly humour: "It's a sort of kindergarten!"

"The next thing you'll be saying that we're babes at the breast!"

"Of some great mild, invisible mother who stretches away into space and whose lap is the whole valley——?"

"And her bosom"—Dane completed the figure—"the noble eminence of our hill? That will do; anything will do that covers the essential fact."

"And what do you call the essential fact?"

"Why, that—as in old days on Swiss lake-sides—we're *en pension*."

The good Brother took this gently up. "I remember—I remember: seven francs a day without wine! But, alas, it's more than seven francs here."

"Yes, it's considerably more," Dane had to confess. "Perhaps it isn't particularly cheap."

"Yet should you call it particularly dear?" his friend after a moment inquired.

George Dane had to think. "How do I know, after all?

What practice has one ever had in estimating the inestimable? Particular cheapness certainly isn't the note that we feel struck all round; but don't we fall naturally into the view that there *must* be a price to anything so awfully sane?"

The good Brother in his turn reflected. "We fall into the view that it must pay—that it does pay."

"Oh, yes; it does pay!" Dane eagerly echoed. "If it didn't it wouldn't last. It has *got* to last, of course!" he declared.

"So that we can come back?"

"Yes—think of knowing that we shall be able to!"

They pulled up again at this and, facing each other, thought of it, or at any rate pretended to; for what was really in their eyes was the dread of a loss of the clue. "Oh, when we want it again we shall find it," said the good Brother. "If the place really pays, it will keep on."

"Yes, that's the beauty; that it isn't, thank heaven, carried on only for love."

"No doubt, no doubt; and yet, thank heaven, there's love in it too." They had lingered as if, in the mild, moist air, they were charmed with the patter of the rain and the way the garden drank it. After a little, however, it did look rather as if they were trying to talk each other out of a faint, small fear. They saw the increasing rage of life and the recurrent need, and they wondered proportionately whether to return to the front when their hour should sharply strike would be the end of the dream. Was this a threshold perhaps, after all, that could only be crossed one way? They must return to the front sooner or later—that was certain: for each his hour would strike. The flower would have been gathered and the trick played—the sands, in short, would have run.

There, in its place, *was* life—with all its rage; the vague unrest of the need for action knew it again, the stir of the faculty that had been refreshed and reconsecrated. They seemed each, thus confronted, to close their eyes a moment for dizziness; then they were again at peace, and the Brother's confidence rang out. "Oh, we shall meet!"

"Here, do you mean?"

"Yes—and I dare say in the world too."

"But we shan't recognise or know," said Dane.

"In the world, do you mean?"

"Neither in the world nor here."

"Not a bit—not the least little bit, you think?"

Dane turned it over. "Well, so it is that it seems to me all best to hang together. But we shall see."

His friend happily concurred. "We shall see." And at this, for farewell, the Brother held out his hand.

"You're going?" Dane asked.

"No, but I thought *you* were."

It was odd, but at this Dane's hour seemed to strike—his consciousness to crystallise. "Well, I am. I've got it. You stay?" he went on.

"A little longer."

Dane hesitated. "You haven't yet got it?"

"Not altogether—but I think it's coming."

"Good!" Dane kept his hand, giving it a final shake, and at that moment the sun glimmered again through the shower, but with the rain still falling on the hither side of it and seeming to patter even more in the brightness. "Hallo—how charming!"

The Brother looked a moment from under the high arch—then again turned his face to our friend. He gave this time his longest, happiest sigh. "Oh, it's all right!"

But why was it, Dane after a moment found himself wondering, that in the act of separation his own hand was so long retained? Why but through a queer phenomenon of change, on the spot, in his companion's face—change that gave it another, but an increasing and above all a much more familiar identity, an identity not beautiful, but more and more distinct, an identity with that of his servant, with the most conspicuous, the physiognomic seat of the public propriety of Brown? To this anomaly his eyes slowly opened; it was not his good Brother, it was verily Brown who possessed his hand. If his eyes had to open, it was because they had been closed and because Brown appeared to think he had better wake up. So much as this Dane took in, but the effect of his taking it was a relapse into darkness, a recontraction of the lids just prolonged enough to give Brown time, on a second thought, to withdraw his touch and move softly away. Dane's next consciousness was that of the desire to make sure he *was* away, and this desire had somehow the result of dissipating the obscurity. The obscurity was completely gone by the time he had made out that the back of a person writing at his study-table was presented to him. He recognised a portion of a figure that he had somewhere described to some-body—the intent shoulders of the unsuccessful young man who had come that bad morning to breakfast. It was strange, he at last reflected, but the young man was still there. How long had he stayed—days, weeks, months? He was exactly in the position in which Dane had last seen him. Everything—stranger still—was exactly in that posi-tion; everything, at least, but the light of the window, which came in from another quarter and showed a differ-ent hour. It wasn't after breakfast now; it was after—well, what? He suppressed a gasp—it was after everything. And yet—quite literally—there were but two other differences. One of these was that if he was still on the sofa he was now lying down; the other was the patter on the glass that showed him how the rain—the great rain of the night—had come back. It was the rain of the night, yet when had he last heard it? But two minutes before? Then how many were there before the young man at the table, who seemed intensely occupied, found a moment to look round at him and, on meeting his open eyes, get up and draw near?

"You've slept all day," said the young man.

"All day?"

The young man looked at his watch. "From ten to six. You were extraordinarily tired. I just, after a bit, let you alone, and you were soon off." Yes, that was it; he had been "off"—off, off, off. He began to fit it together; while he had been off the young man had been on. But there were still some few con-fusions; Dane lay looking up. "Everything's done," the young man continued.

"Everything?"

"Everything."

Dane tried to take it all in, but was embarrassed and could only say weakly and quite apart from the matter: "I've been so happy!"

"So have I," said the young man. He positively looked so; seeing which George Dane wondered afresh, and then, in his wonder, read it indeed quite as another face, quite, in a puz-

zling way, as another person's. Every one was a little some
one else. While he asked himself who else then the young man
was, this benefactor, struck by his appealing stare, broke again
into perfect cheer. "It's all right!" That answered Dane's
question; the face was the face turned to him by the good
Brother there in the portico while they listened together to
the rustle of the shower. It was all queer, but all pleasant and
all distinct, so distinct that the last words in his ear—the same
from both quarters—appeared the effect of a single voice.
Dane rose and looked about his room, which seemed disen-
cumbered, different, twice as large. It *was* all right.

Maud-Evelyn

O N SOME allusion to a lady who, though unknown to myself, was known to two or three of the company, it was asked by one of these if we had heard the odd circumstance of what she had just "come in for"—the piece of luck suddenly overtaking, in the grey afternoon of her career, so obscure and lonely a personage. We were at first, in our ignorance, mainly reduced to crude envy; but old Lady Emma, who for a while had said nothing, scarcely even appearing to listen and letting the chatter, which was indeed plainly beside the mark, subside of itself, came back from a mental absence to observe that if what had happened to Lavinia was wonderful, certainly, what had for years gone before it, led up to it, had likewise not been without some singular features. From this we perceived that Lady Emma had a story—a story moreover out of the ken even of those of her listeners acquainted with the quiet person who was the subject of it. Almost the oddest thing—as came out afterwards—was that such a situation should, for the world, have remained so in the background of this person's life. By "afterwards" I mean simply before we separated; for what came out came on the spot, under encouragement and pressure, our common, eager solicitation. Lady Emma, who always reminded me of a fine old instrument that has first to be tuned, agreed, after a few of our scrapings and fingerings, that, having said so much, she couldn't, without wantonly tormenting us, forbear to say all. She had known Lavinia, whom she mentioned throughout only by that name, from far away, and she had also known—— But what she had known I must give as nearly as possible as she herself gave it. She talked to us from her corner of the sofa, and the flicker of the firelight in her face was like the glow of memory, the play of fancy, from within.

I

"Then why on earth don't you take him?" I asked. I think that was the way that, one day when she was about twenty—

before some of you perhaps were born—the affair, for me, must have begun. I put the question because I knew she had had a chance, though I didn't know how great a mistake her failure to embrace it was to prove. I took an interest because I liked them both—you see how I like young people still—and because, as they had originally met at my house, I had in a manner to answer to each for the other. I'm afraid I'm thrown baldly back on the fact that if the girl was the daughter of my earliest, almost my only governess, to whom I had remained much attached and who, after leaving me, had married—for a governess—"well," Marmaduke (it isn't *his* real name!) was the son of one of the clever men who had—I was charming then, I assure you I was—wanted, years before, and this one as a widower, to marry me. I hadn't cared, somehow, for widowers, but even after I had taken somebody else I was conscious of a pleasant link with the boy whose stepmother it had been open to me to become and to whom it was perhaps a little a matter of vanity with me to show that I should have been for him one of the kindest. This was what the woman his father eventually did marry was not, and that threw him upon me the more.

Lavinia was one of nine, and her brothers and sisters, who have never done anything for her, help, actually, in different countries and on something, I believe, of that same scale, to people the globe. There were mixed in her then, in a puzzling way, two qualities that mostly exclude each other—an extreme timidity and, as the smallest fault that could qualify a harmless creature for a world of wickedness, a self-complacency hard in tiny, unexpected spots, for which I used sometimes to take her up, but which, I subsequently saw, would have done something for the flatness of her life had they not evaporated with everything else. She was at any rate one of those persons as to whom you don't know whether they might have been attractive if they had been happy, or might have been happy if they had been attractive. If I was a trifle vexed at her not jumping at Marmaduke, it was probably rather less because I expected wonders of him than because I thought she took her own prospect too much for granted. She had made a mistake and, before long, admitted it; yet I remember that when she expressed to me a conviction that he would ask her again, I also thought this highly probable, for in the meantime I had spoken to him. "She does care for you," I declared; and I can see at this moment, long ago though it be, his handsome empty young face look, on the words, as if, in spite of itself for a little, it really thought. I didn't press the matter, for he had, after all, no great things to offer; yet my conscience was easier, later on, for having not said less. He had three hundred and fifty a year from his mother, and one of his uncles had promised him something—I don't mean an allowance, but a place, if I recollect, in a business. He assured me that he loved as a man loves—a man of twenty-two!—but once. He said it, at all events, as a man says it but once.

"Well, then," I replied, "your course is clear."

"To speak to her again, you mean?"

"Yes—try it."

He seemed to try it a moment in imagination; after which, a little to my surprise, he asked: "Would it be very awful if she should speak to *me*?"

I stared. "Do you mean pursue you—overtake you? Ah, if you're running away——"

"I'm not running away!"—he was positive as to that. "But when a fellow has gone so far——"

"He can't go any further? Perhaps," I replied dryly. "But in that case he shouldn't talk of 'caring.'"

"Oh, but I do, I do."

I shook my head. "Not if you're too proud!" On which I turned away, looking round at him again, however, after he had surprised me by a silence that seemed to accept my judgment. Then I saw he had not accepted it; I perceived it indeed to be essentially absurd. He expressed more, on this, than I had yet seen him do—had the queerest, frankest, and, for a young man of his conditions, saddest smile.

"I'm *not* proud. It isn't *in* me. If you're not, you're not, you know. I don't think I'm proud enough."

It came over me that this was, after all, probable; yet somehow I didn't at the moment like him the less for it, though I spoke with some sharpness. "Then what's the matter with you?"

He took a turn or two about the room, as if what he had just said had made him a little happier. "Well, how can a man say more?" Then, just as I was on the point of assuring him that I didn't know what he had said, he went on: "I swore to her that I would never marry. Oughtn't that to be enough?"

"To make her come after you?"

"No—I suppose scarcely that; but to make her feel sure of me—to make her wait."

"Wait for what?"

"Well, till I come back."

"Back from where?"

"From Switzerland—haven't I told you? I go there next month with my aunt and my cousin."

He was quite right about not being proud—this was an alternative distinctly humble.

II

And yet see what it brought forth—the beginning of which was something that, early in the autumn, I learned from poor Lavinia. He had written to her, they were still such friends; and thus it was that she knew his aunt and his cousin to have come back without him. He had stayed on—stayed much longer and travelled much further: he had been to the Italian lakes and to Venice; he was now in Paris. At this I vaguely wondered, knowing that he was always short of funds and that he must, by his uncle's beneficence, have started on the journey on a basis of expenses paid. "Then whom has he picked up?" I asked; but feeling sorry, as soon as I had spoken, to have made Lavinia blush. It was almost as if he had picked up some improper lady, though in this case he wouldn't have told her, and it wouldn't have saved him money.

"Oh, he makes acquaintance so quickly, knows people in two minutes," the girl said. "And every one always wants to be nice to him."

This was perfectly true, and I saw what she saw in it. "Ah, my dear, he will have an immense circle ready for you!"

"Well," she replied, "if they do run after us I'm not likely to suppose it will ever be for me. It will be for *him*, and they may do to me what they like. My pleasure will be—but you'll see." I already saw—saw at least what she supposed she herself saw: her drawing-room crowded with female fashion and her attitude angelic. "Do you know what he said to me again before he went?" she continued.

I wondered; he *had* then spoken to her. "That he will never, never marry——"

"Any one but *me*!" She ingenuously took me up. "Then you knew?"

It might be. "I guessed."

"And don't you believe it?"

Again I hesitated. "Yes." Yet all this didn't tell me why she had changed colour. "Is it a secret—whom he's with?"

"Oh no, they seem so nice. I was only struck with the way you know him—your seeing immediately that it must be a new friendship that has kept him over. It's the devotion of the Dedricks," Lavinia said. "He's travelling with them."

Once more I wondered. "Do you mean they're taking him about?"

"Yes—they've invited him."

No, indeed, I reflected—he wasn't proud. But what I said was: "Who in the world are the Dedricks?"

"Kind, good people whom, last month, he accidentally met. He was walking some Swiss pass—a long, rather stupid one, I believe, without his aunt and his cousin, who had gone round some other way and were to meet him somewhere. It came on to rain in torrents, and while he was huddling under a shelter he was overtaken by some people in a carriage, who kindly made him get in. They drove him, I gather, for several hours; it began an intimacy, and they've continued to be charming to him."

I thought a moment. "Are they ladies?"

Her own imagination meanwhile had also strayed a little. "I think about forty."

"Forty ladies?"

She quickly came back. "Oh no; I mean Mrs. Dedrick is."

"About forty? Then Miss Dedrick——"

"There isn't any Miss Dedrick."

"No daughter?"

"Not with them, at any rate. No one but the husband."

I thought again. "And how old is *he*?"

Lavinia followed my example. "Well, about forty, too."

"About forty-two?" We laughed, but "That's all right!" I said; and so, for the time, it seemed.

He continued absent, none the less, and I saw Lavinia repeatedly, and we always talked of him, though this represented a greater concern with his affairs than I had really supposed myself committed to. I had never sought the acquaintance of his father's people, nor seen either his aunt or his cousin, so that the account given by these relatives of the circumstances of their separation reached me at last only through the girl, to whom, also—for she knew them as little—it had circuitously come. They considered, it appeared, the poor ladies he had started with, that he had treated them ill and thrown them over, sacrificing them selfishly to company picked up on the road—a reproach deeply resented by Lavinia, though about the company too I could see she was not much more at her ease. "How can he help it if he's so taking?" she asked; and to be properly indignant in one quarter she had to pretend to be delighted in the other. Marmaduke *was* "taking"; yet it also came out between us at last that the Dedricks must certainly be extraordinary. We had scant added evidence, for his letters stopped, and that naturally was one of our signs. I had meanwhile leisure to reflect—it was a sort of study of the human scene I always liked—on what to be taking consisted of. The upshot of my meditations, which experience has only confirmed, was that it consisted simply of itself. It was a quality implying no others. Marmaduke *had* no others. What indeed was his need of any?

III

He at last, however, turned up; but then it happened that if, on his coming to see me, his immediate picture of his charming new friends quickened even more than I had expected my sense of the variety of the human species, my curiosity about them failed to make me respond when he suggested I should go to see them. It's a difficult thing to explain, and I don't pretend to put it successfully, but doesn't it often happen that one may think well enough of a person without being inflamed with the desire to meet—on the ground of any such sentiment—other persons who think still better? Somehow—

little harm as there was in Marmaduke—it was but half a
recommendation of the Dedricks that they were crazy about
him. I didn't say this—I was careful to say little; which didn't
prevent his presently asking if he mightn't then bring them to
me. "If not, why not?" he laughed. He laughed about everything.

"Why not? Because it strikes me that your surrender doesn't
require any backing. Since you've done it you must take care
of yourself."

"Oh, but they're as safe," he returned, "as the Bank of
England. They're wonderful—for respectability and goodness."

"Those are precisely qualities to which my poor intercourse
can contribute nothing." He hadn't, I observed, gone so far
as to tell me they would be "fun," and he *had*, on the other
hand, promptly mentioned that they lived in Westbourne Terrace. They were not forty—they were forty-five; but Mr. Dedrick had already, on considerable gains, retired from some
primitive profession. They were the simplest, kindest, yet most
original and unusual people, and nothing could exceed,
frankly, the fancy they had taken to him. Marmaduke spoke
of it with a placidity of resignation that was almost irritating.
I suppose I should have despised him if, after benefits accepted, he had said they bored him; yet their not boring him
vexed me even more than it puzzled. "Whom do they know?"

"No one but me. There are people in London like that."

"Who know no one but you?"

"No—I mean no one at all. There are extraordinary people
in London, and awfully nice. You haven't an idea. You people
don't know every one. They lead their lives—they go their
way. One finds—what do you call it?—refinement, books,
cleverness, don't you know, and music, and pictures, and
religion, and an excellent table—all sorts of pleasant things.
You only come across them by chance; but it's all perpetually
going on."

I assented to this: the world was very wonderful, and one
must certainly see what one could. In my own quarter too I
found wonders enough. "But are you," I asked, "as fond of
them——"

"As they are of *me*?" He took me up promptly, and his eyes were quite unclouded. "I'm quite sure I shall become so."

"Then are you taking Lavinia——?"

"Not to see them—no." I saw, myself, the next minute, of course, that I had made a mistake. "On what footing *can* I?"

I bethought myself. "I keep forgetting you're not engaged."

"Well," he said after a moment, "I shall never marry another."

It somehow, repeated again, gave on my nerves. "Ah, but what good will that do her, or me either, if you don't marry *her*?"

He made no answer to this—only turned away to look at something in the room; after which, when he next faced me, he had a heightened colour. "She ought to have taken me that day," he said gravely and gently; fixing me also as if he wished to say more.

I remember that his very mildness irritated me; some show of resentment would have been a promise that the case might still be righted. But I dropped it, the silly case, without letting him say more, and, coming back to Mr. and Mrs. Dedrick, asked him how in the world, without either occupation or society, they passed so much of their time. My question appeared for a moment to leave him at a loss, but he presently found light; which, at the same time, I saw on my side, really suited him better than further talk about Lavinia. "Oh, they live for Maud-Evelyn."

"And who's Maud-Evelyn?"

"Why, their daughter."

"Their daughter?" I had supposed them childless.

He partly explained. "Unfortunately they've lost her."

"Lost her?" I required more.

He hesitated again. "I mean that a great many people would take it that way. But *they* don't—they won't."

I speculated. "Do you mean other people would have given her up?"

"Yes—perhaps even tried to forget her. But the Dedricks can't."

I wondered what she had done: had it been anything very bad? However, it was none of my business, and I only said: "They communicate with her?"

"Oh, all the while."

"Then why isn't she with them?"

Marmaduke thought. "She *is*—now."

"'Now'? Since when?"

"Well, this last year."

"Then why do you say they've lost her?"

"Ah," he said, smiling sadly, "*I* should call it that. I, at any rate," he went on, "don't see her."

Still more I wondered. "They keep her apart?"

He thought again. "No, it's not that. As I say, they live for her."

"But they don't want *you* to—is that it?"

At this he looked at me for the first time, as I thought, a little strangely. "How *can* I?"

He put it to me as if it were bad of him, somehow, that he shouldn't; but I made, to the best of my ability, a quick end of that. "You can't. Why in the world *should* you? Live for *my* girl. Live for Lavinia."

IV

I had unfortunately run the risk of boring him again with that idea, and, though he had not repudiated it at the time, I felt in my having returned to it the reason why he never reappeared for weeks. I saw "my girl," as I had called her, in the interval, but we avoided with much intensity the subject of Marmaduke. It was just this that gave me my perspective for finding her constantly full of him. It determined me, in all the circumstances, not to rectify her mistake about the childlessness of the Dedricks. But whatever I left unsaid, her naming the young man was only a question of time, for at the end of a month she told me he had been twice to her mother's and that she had seen him on each of these occasions.

"Well then?"

"Well then, he's very happy."

"And still taken up——"

"As much as ever, yes, with those people. He didn't tell me so, but I could see it."

I could too, and her own view of it. "What, in that case, did he tell you?"

"Nothing—but I think there's something he wants to. Only not what *you* think," she added.

I wondered then if it were what I had had from him the last time. "Well, what prevents him?" I asked.

"From bringing it out? I don't know."

It was in the tone of this that she struck, to my ear, the first note of an acceptance so deep and a patience so strange that they gave me, at the end, even more food for wonderment than the rest of the business. "If he can't speak, why does he come?"

She almost smiled. "Well, I think I *shall* know."

I looked at her; I remember that I kissed her. "You're admirable; but it's very ugly."

"Ah," she replied, "he only wants to be kind!"

"To *them*? Then he should let others alone. But what I call ugly is his being content to be so 'beholden'——"

"To Mr. and Mrs. Dedrick?" She considered as if there might be many sides to it. "But mayn't he do them some good?"

The idea failed to appeal to me. "What good can Marmaduke do? There's one thing," I went on, "in case he should want you to know them. Will you promise me to refuse?"

She only looked helpless and blank. "Making their acquaintance?"

"Seeing them, going near them—ever, ever."

Again she brooded. "Do you mean *you* won't?"

"Never, never."

"Well, then, I don't think I want to."

"Ah, but that's not a promise." I kept her up to it. "I want your word."

She demurred a little. "But why?"

"So that at least he shan't make use of you," I said with energy.

My energy overbore her, though I saw how she would really have given herself. "I promise, but it's only because it's something I know he will never ask."

I differed from her at the time, believing the proposal in question to have been exactly the subject she had supposed him to be wishing to broach; but on our very next meeting I heard from her of quite another matter, upon which, as soon as she came in, I saw her to be much excited.

"You know then about the daughter without having told me? He called again yesterday," she explained as she met my stare at her unconnected plunge, "and now I know that he *has* wanted to speak to me. He at last brought it out."

I continued to stare. "Brought what?"

"Why, everything." She looked surprised at my face. "Didn't he tell you about Maud-Evelyn?"

I perfectly recollected, but I momentarily wondered. "He spoke of there being a daughter, but only to say that there's something the matter with her. What is it?"

The girl echoed my words. "What 'is' it?—you dear, strange thing! The matter with her is simply that she's dead."

"Dead?" I was naturally mystified. "When then did she die?"

"Why, years and years ago—fifteen, I believe. As a little girl. Didn't you understand it so?"

"How *should* I?—when he spoke of her as 'with' them and said that they lived for her!"

"Well," my young friend explained, "that's just what he meant—they live for her memory. She *is* with them in the sense that they think of nothing else."

I found matter for surprise in this correction, but also, at first, matter for relief. At the same time it left, as I turned it over, a fresh ambiguity. "If they think of nothing else, how can they think so much of Marmaduke?"

The difficulty struck her, though she gave me even then a dim impression of being already, as it were, rather on Marmaduke's side, or, at any rate—almost as against herself—in sympathy with the Dedricks. But her answer was prompt: "Why, that's just their reason—that they can talk to him so much about her."

"I see." Yet still I wondered. "But what's *his* interest——?"

"In being drawn into it?" Again Lavinia met her difficulty. "Well, that she was so interesting! It appears she was lovely."

I doubtless fairly gaped. "A little girl in a pinafore?"

"She was out of pinafores; she was, I believe, when she died, about fourteen. Unless it was sixteen! She was at all events wonderful for beauty."

"That's the rule. But what good does it do him if he has never seen her?"

She thought a moment, but this time she had no answer. "Well, you must ask him!"

I determined without delay to do so; but I had before me meanwhile other contradictions. "Hadn't I better ask him on the same occasion what he means by their 'communicating'?"

Oh, this was simple. "They go in for 'mediums,' don't you know, and raps, and sittings. They began a year or two ago."

"Ah, the idiots!" I remember, at this, narrow-mindedly exclaiming. "Do they want to drag *him* in——?"

"Not in the least; they don't desire it, and he has nothing to do with it."

"Then where does his fun come in?"

Lavinia turned away; again she seemed at a loss. At last she brought out: "Make him show you her little photograph."

But I remained unenlightened. "Is her little photograph his fun?"

Once more she coloured for him. "Well, it represents a young loveliness!"

"That he goes about showing?"

She hesitated. "I think he has only shown it to *me*."

"Ah, you're just the last one!" I permitted myself to observe.

"Why so, if I'm also struck?"

There was something about her that began to escape me, and I must have looked at her hard. "It's very good of you to be struck!"

"I don't only mean by the beauty of the face," she went on; "I mean by the whole thing—by that also of the attitude of the parents, their extraordinary fidelity and the way that, as he says, they have made of her memory a real religion. That was what, above all, he came to tell me about."

I turned away from her now, and she soon afterwards left me; but I couldn't help its dropping from me before we parted that I had never supposed him to be *that* sort of fool.

V

If I were really the perfect cynic you probably think me I should frankly say that the main interest of the rest of this matter lay for me in fixing the sort of fool I *did* suppose him. But I'm afraid, after all, that my anecdote amounts mainly to a presentation of my own folly. I shouldn't be so in possession of the whole spectacle had I not ended by accepting it, and I shouldn't have accepted it had it not, for my imagination, been saved somehow from grotesqueness. Let me say at once, however, that grotesqueness, and even indeed something worse, did at first appear to me strongly to season it. After that talk with Lavinia I immediately addressed to our friend a request that he would come to see me; when I took the liberty of challenging him outright on everything she had told me. There was one point in particular that I desired to clear up and that seemed to me much more important even than the colour of Maud-Evelyn's hair or the length of her pinafores: the question, I of course mean, of my young man's good faith. Was he altogether silly or was he only altogether mercenary? I felt my choice restricted for the moment to these alternatives.

After he had said to me "It's as ridiculous as you please, but they've simply adopted me" I had it out with him, on the spot, on the issue of common honesty, the question of what he was conscious, so that his self-respect should be saved, of being able to give such benefactors in return for such bounty. I'm obliged to say that to a person so inclined at the start to quarrel with him his amiability could yet prove persuasive. His contention was that the equivalent he represented was something for his friends alone to measure. He didn't for a moment pretend to sound deeper than the fancy they had taken to him. He had not, from the first, made up to them in any way: it was all their own doing, their own insistence, their own eccentricity, no doubt, and even, if I liked, their own insanity. Wasn't it enough that he was ready to declare to me, looking me straight in the eye, that he was "really and truly" fond of them and that they didn't bore him a mite? I had evidently— didn't I see?—an ideal for him that he wasn't at all, if I didn't mind, the fellow to live up to. It was he himself who put it so, and it drew from me the pronouncement that there *was* something irresistible in the refinement of his impudence. "I don't go near Mrs. Jex," he said—Mrs. Jex was their favourite medium: "I do find *her* ugly and vulgar and tiresome, and I hate that part of the business. Besides," he added in words that I afterwards remembered, "I don't require it: I do beautifully without it. But my friends themselves," he pursued, "though they're of a type you've never come within miles of, are not ugly, are not vulgar, are not in any degree whatever any sort of a 'dose.' They're, on the contrary, in their own unconventional way, the very best company. They're endlessly amusing. They're delightfully queer and quaint and kind— they're like people in some old story or of some old time. It's at any rate our own affair—mine and theirs—and I beg you to believe that I should make short work of a remonstrance on the subject from any one but you."

I remember saying to him three months later: "You've never yet told me what they really want of you"; but I'm afraid this was a form of criticism that occurred to me precisely because I had already begun to guess. By that time indeed I had had great initiations, and poor Lavinia had had them as well—hers in fact throughout went further than mine—and we had shared them together, and I had settled down to a tolerably exact sense of what I was to see. It was what Lavinia added to it that really made the picture. The portrait of the little dead girl had evoked something attractive, though one had not lived so long in the world without hearing of plenty of little dead girls; and the day came when I felt as if I had actually sat with Marmaduke in each of the rooms converted by her parents—with the aid not only of the few small, cherished relics, but that of the fondest figments and fictions, ingenious imaginary mementoes and tokens, the unexposed make-believes of the sorrow that broods and the passion that clings—into a temple of grief and worship. The child, incontestably beautiful, had evidently been passionately loved, and in the absence from their lives—I suppose originally a mere accident—of such other elements, either new pleasures or new pains, as abound for most people, their feeling had drawn to itself their whole consciousness: it had become mildly maniacal. The idea was fixed, and it kept others out. The world, for the most part, allows no leisure for such a ritual, but the world had consistently neglected this plain, shy couple, who were sensitive to the wrong things and whose sincerity and fidelity, as well as their tameness and twaddle, were of a rigid, antique pattern.

I must not represent that either of these objects of interest, or my care for their concerns, took up all my leisure; for I had many claims to meet and many complications to handle, a hundred preoccupations and much deeper anxieties. My young woman, on her side, had other contacts and contingencies—other troubles too, poor girl; and there were stretches of time in which I neither saw Marmaduke nor heard a word of the Dedricks. Once, only once, abroad, in Germany at a railway-station, I met him in their company. They were colourless, commonplace, elderly Britons, of the kind you identify by the livery of their footman or the labels of their luggage, and the mere sight of them justified me to my conscience in having avoided, from the first, the stiff problem of conversation with them. Marmaduke saw me on the spot and came over to me. There was no doubt whatever of *his* vivid bloom. He had grown fat—or almost, but not with grossness—and might perfectly have passed for the handsome, happy, full-blown son of doting parents who couldn't let him out of view and to whom he was a model of respect and solicitude. They followed him with placid, pleased eyes when he joined me, but asking nothing at all for themselves and quite fitting into his own manner of saying nothing about them. It had its charm, I confess, the way he could be natural and easy, and yet intensely conscious too, on such a basis. What he was conscious of was that there were things I by this time knew; just as, while we stood there and good-humouredly sounded each other's faces—for, having accepted everything at last, I was only a little curious—I knew that he measured my insight. When he returned again to his doting parents I had to admit that, doting as they were, I felt him not to have been spoiled. It was incongruous in such a career, but he was rather more of a man. There came back to me with a shade of regret after I had got on this occasion into my train, which was not theirs, a memory of some words that, a couple of years before, I had uttered to poor Lavinia. She had said to me, speaking in reference to what was then our frequent topic and on some fresh evidence that I have forgotten: "He feels now, you know, about Maud-Evelyn quite as the old people themselves do."

"Well," I had replied, "it's only a pity he's paid for it!"

"Paid?" She had looked very blank.

"By all the luxuries and conveniences," I had explained, "that he comes in for through living with them. For that's what he practically does."

At present I saw how wrong I had been. He was paid, but paid differently, and the mastered wonder of that was really what had been between us in the waiting-room of the station. Step by step, after this, I followed.

VI

I can see Lavinia for instance in her ugly new mourning immediately after her mother's death. There had been long anxieties connected with this event, and she was already faded, already almost old. But Marmaduke, on her bereavement, had been to her, and she came straightway to me.

"Do you know what he thinks now?" she soon began. "He thinks he knew her."

"Knew the child?" It came to me as if I had half expected it.

"He speaks of her now as if she hadn't been a child." My visitor gave me the strangest fixed smile. "It appears that she wasn't so young—it appears she had grown up."

I stared. "How can it 'appear'? They *know*, at least! There were the facts."

"Yes," said Lavinia, "but they seem to have come to take a different view of them. He talked to me a long time, and all about *her*. He told me things."

"What kind of things? Not trumpery stuff, I hope, about 'communicating'—about his seeing or hearing her?"

"Oh no, he doesn't go in for that; he leaves it to the old couple, who, I believe, cling to their mediums, keep up their sittings and their rappings and find in it all a comfort, an amusement, that he doesn't grudge them and that he regards as harmless. I mean anecdotes—memories of his own. I mean things she said to him and that they did together—places they went to. His mind is full of them."

I turned it over. "Do you think he's decidedly mad?"

She shook her head with her bleached patience. "Oh no, it's too beautiful!"

"Then are *you* taking it up? I mean the preposterous theory——"

"It *is* a theory," she broke in, "but it isn't necessarily preposterous. Any theory has to suppose something," she sagely pursued, "and it depends at any rate on what it's a theory *of*. It's wonderful to see this one work."

"Wonderful always to see the growth of a legend!" I laughed. "This is a rare chance to watch one in formation. They're all three in good faith building it up. Isn't that what you made out from him?"

Her tired face fairly lighted. "Yes—you understand it; and you put it better than I. It's the gradual effect of brooding over the past; the past, that way, grows and grows. They make it and make it. They've persuaded each other—the parents— of so many things that they've at last also persuaded *him*. It has been contagious."

"It's you who put it well," I returned. "It's the oddest thing I ever heard of, but it is, in its way, a reality. Only we mustn't speak of it to others."

She quite accepted that precaution. "No—to nobody. *He* doesn't. He keeps it only for me."

"Conferring on you thus," I again laughed, "such a precious privilege!"

She was silent a moment, looking away from me. "Well, he has kept his vow."

"You mean of not marrying? Are you very sure?" I asked. "Didn't he perhaps——?" But I faltered at the boldness of my joke.

The next moment I saw I needn't. "He *was* in love with her," Lavinia brought out.

I broke now into a peal which, however provoked, struck even my own ear at the moment as rude almost to profanity. "He literally tells you outright that he's making believe?"

She met me effectively enough. "I don't think he *knows* he is. He's just completely in the current."

"The current of the old people's twaddle?"

Again my companion hesitated; but she knew what she thought. "Well, whatever we call it, I like it. It isn't so common, as the world goes, for any one—let alone for two or three—to feel and to care for the dead as much as that. It's self-deception, no doubt, but it comes from something that—well," she faltered again, "is beautiful when one does hear of it. They make her out older, so as to imagine they had her longer; and they make out that certain things really happened to her, so that she shall have had more life. They've invented a whole experience for her, and Marmaduke has become a part of it. There's one thing, above all, they want her to have had." My young friend's face, as she analysed the mystery, fairly grew bright with her vision. It came to me with a faint dawn of awe that the attitude of the Dedricks *was* contagious. "And she did have it!" Lavinia declared.

I positively admired her, and if I could yet perfectly be rational without being ridiculous, it was really, more than anything else, to draw from her the whole image. "She had the bliss of knowing Marmaduke? Let us agree to it, then, since she's not here to contradict us. But what I don't get over is the scant material for *him*!" It may easily be conceived how little, for the moment, I could get over it. It was the last time my impatience was to be too much for me, but I remember how it broke out. "A man who might have had *you*!"

For an instant I feared I had upset her—thought I saw in her face the tremor of a wild wail. But poor Lavinia was magnificent. "It wasn't that he might have had 'me'—that's nothing: it was, at the most, that I might have had *him*. Well, isn't that just what has happened? He's mine from the moment no one else has him. I give up the past, but don't you see what it does for the rest of life? I'm surer than ever that he won't marry."

"Of course, he won't—to quarrel, with those people!"

For a minute she answered nothing; then, "Well, for whatever reason!" she simply said. Now, however, I had gouged out of her a couple of still tears, and I pushed away the whole obscure comedy.

VII

I might push it away, but I couldn't really get rid of it; nor, on the whole, doubtless, did I want to, for to have in one's life, year after year, a particular question or two that one couldn't comfortably and imposingly make up one's mind about was just the sort of thing to keep one from turning stupid. There had been little need of my enjoining reserve upon Lavinia: she obeyed, in respect to impenetrable silence save with myself, an instinct, an interest of her own. We never therefore gave poor Marmaduke, as you call it, "away"; we were much too tender, let alone that she was also too proud; and, for himself, evidently, there was not, to the end, in London, another person in his confidence. No echo of the queer part he played ever came back to us; and I can't tell you how this fact, just by itself, brought home to me little by little a sense of the charm he was under. I met him "out" at long intervals—met him usually at dinner. He had grown like a person with a position and a history. Rosy and rich-looking, fat, moreover, distinctly fat at last, there was almost in him something of the bland—yet not too bland—young head of an hereditary business. If the Dedricks had been bankers he might have constituted the future of the house. There was none the less a long middle stretch during which, though we were all so much in London, he dropped out of my talks with Lavinia. We were conscious, she and I, of his absence from them; but we clearly felt in each quarter that there are things after all unspeakable, and the fact, in any case, had nothing to do with her seeing or not seeing our friend. I was sure, as it happened, that she did see him. But there were moments that for myself still stand out.

One of these was a certain Sunday afternoon when it was so dismally wet that, taking for granted I should have no visitors, I had drawn up to the fire with a book—a successful novel of the day—that I promised myself comfortably to finish. Suddenly, in my absorption, I heard a firm rat-tat-tat; on which I remember giving a groan of inhospitality. But my visitor proved in due course Marmaduke, and Marmaduke proved—in a manner even less, at the point we had reached, to have been counted on—still more attaching than my novel. I think it was only an accident that he became so; it would have been the turn of a hair either way. He hadn't come to speak—he had only come to talk, to show once more that we could continue good old friends without his speaking. But somehow there were the circumstances: the insidious fireside, the things in the room, with their reminders of his younger time; perhaps even too the open face of my book, looking at him from where I had laid it down for him and giving him a chance to feel that he could supersede Wilkie Collins. There was at all events a promise of intimacy, of opportunity for him in the cold lash of the windows by the storm. We should be alone; it was cosy; it was safe.

The action of these impressions was the more marked that what was touched by them, I afterwards saw, was not at all a desire for an effect—was just simply a spirit of happiness that needed to overflow. It had finally become too much for him. His past, rolling up year after year, had grown too interesting. But he was, all the same, directly stupefying. I forget what turn of our preliminary gossip brought it out, but it came, in explanation of something or other, as it had not yet come: "When a man has had for a few months what *I* had, you know!" The moral appeared to be that nothing in the way of human experience of the exquisite could again particularly matter. He saw, however, that I failed immediately to fit his reflection to a definite case, and he went on with the frankest smile: "You look as bewildered as if you suspected me of alluding to some sort of thing that isn't usually spoken of; but I assure you I mean nothing more reprehensible than our blessed engagement itself."

"Your blessed engagement?" I couldn't help the tone in which I took him up; but the way he disposed of that was something of which I feel to this hour the influence. It was only a look, but it put an end to my tone for ever. It made me, on my side, after an instant, look at the fire—look hard and even turn a little red. During this moment I saw my alternatives and I chose; so that when I met his eyes again I was fairly ready. "You still feel," I asked with sympathy, "how much it did for you?"

I had no sooner spoken than I saw that that would be from that moment the right way. It instantly made all the difference. The main question would be whether I could keep it up.

I remember that only a few minutes later, for instance, this question gave a flare. His reply had been abundant and imperturbable—had included some glance at the way death brings into relief even the faintest things that have preceded it; on which I felt myself suddenly as restless as if I had grown afraid of him. I got up to ring for tea; he went on talking—talking about Maud-Evelyn and what she had been for him; and when the servant had come up I prolonged, nervously, on purpose, the order I had wished to give. It made time, and I could speak to the footman sufficiently without thinking: what I thought of really was the risk of turning right round with a little outbreak. The temptation was strong; the same influences that had worked for my companion just worked, in their way, during that minute or two, for me. *Should* I, taking him unaware, flash at him a plain "I say, just settle it for me once for all. *Are* you the boldest and basest of fortune-hunters, or have you only, more innocently and perhaps more pleasantly, suffered your brain slightly to soften?" But I missed the chance—which I didn't in fact afterwards regret. My servant went out, and I faced again to my visitor, who continued to converse. I met his eyes once more, and their effect was repeated. If anything had happened to his brain this effect was perhaps the domination of the madman's stare. Well, he was the easiest and gentlest of madmen. By the time the footman came back with tea I was in for it; I was in for everything. By "everything" I mean my whole subsequent treatment of the case. It *was*—the case was—really beautiful. So, like all the rest, the hour comes back to me: the sound of the wind and the rain; the look of the empty, ugly, cabless square and of the stormy spring light; the way that, uninterrupted and absorbed, we had tea together by my fire. So it was that he found me receptive and that I found myself able to look merely grave and kind when he said, for example: "Her father and mother, you know, really, that first day—the day they picked me up on the Splügen—recognised me as the proper one."

"The proper one?"

"To make their son-in-law. They wanted her so," he went on, "to have had, don't you know, just everything."

"Well, if she did have it"—I tried to be cheerful—"isn't the whole thing then all right?"

"Oh, it's all right *now*," he replied—"now that we've got it all there before us. You see, they couldn't like me so much"—he wished me thoroughly to understand—"without wanting me to have been the man."

"I see—that was natural."

"Well," said Marmaduke, "it prevented the possibility of any one else."

"Ah, that would never have done!" I laughed.

His own pleasure at it was impenetrable, splendid. "You see, they couldn't do much, the old people—and they can do still less now—with the future; so they had to do what they could with the past."

"And they seem to have done," I concurred, "remarkably much."

"Everything, simply. Everything," he repeated. Then he had an idea, though without insistence or importunity—I noticed it just flicker in his face. "If you *were* to come to Westbourne Terrace——"

"Oh, don't speak of that!" I broke in. "It wouldn't be decent now. I should have come, if at all, ten years ago."

But he saw, with his good humour, further than this. "I see what you mean. But there's much more in the place now than then."

"I dare say. People get new things. All the same——!" I was at bottom but resisting my curiosity.

Marmaduke didn't press me, but he wanted me to know. "There are our rooms—the whole set; and I don't believe you ever saw anything more charming, for *her* taste was extraordinary. I'm afraid too that I myself have had much to say to them." Then as he made out that I was again a little at sea, "I'm talking," he went on, "of the suite prepared for her marriage." He "talked" like a crown prince. "They were ready, to the last touch—there was nothing more to be done. And they're just as they were—not an object moved, not an arrangement altered, not a person but ourselves coming in: they're only exquisitely kept. All our presents are there—I should have liked you to see them."

It had become a torment by this time—I saw that I had made a mistake. But I carried it off. "Oh, I couldn't have borne it!"

"They're not sad," he smiled—"they're too lovely to be sad. They're happy. And the things——!" He seemed, in the excitement of our talk, to have them before him.

"They're so very wonderful?"

"Oh, selected with a patience that makes them almost price-less. It's really a museum. There was nothing they thought too good for her."

I had lost the museum, but I reflected that it could contain no object so rare as my visitor. "Well, you've helped them—you could do *that*."

He quite eagerly assented. "I could do that, thank God—I could do that! I felt it from the first, and it's what I *have* done." Then as if the connection were direct: "All *my* things are there."

I thought a moment. "Your presents?"

"Those I made her. She loved each one, and I remember about each the particular thing she said. Though I do say it," he continued, "none of the others, as a matter of fact, come near mine. I look at them every day, and I assure you I'm not ashamed." Evidently, in short, he had spared nothing, and he talked on and on. He really quite swaggered.

VIII

In relation to times and intervals I can only recall that if this visit of his to me had been in the early spring it was one day in the late autumn—a day, which couldn't have been in the same year, with the difference of hazy, drowsy sunshine and brown and yellow leaves—that, taking a short cut across Ken-sington Gardens, I came, among the untrodden ways, upon a couple occupying chairs under a tree, who immediately rose at the sight of me. I had been behind them at recognition, the fact that Marmaduke was in deep mourning having per-haps, so far as I had observed it, misled me. In my desire both not to look flustered at meeting them and to spare their own confusion I bade them again be seated and asked leave, as a third chair was at hand, to share a little their rest. Thus it befell that after a minute Lavinia and I had sat down, while our friend, who had looked at his watch, stood before us among the fallen foliage and remarked that he was sorry to have to leave us. Lavinia said nothing, but I expressed regret; I couldn't, however, as it struck me, without a false or a vulgar note speak as if I had interrupted a tender passage or separated a pair of lovers. But I could look him up and down, take in his deep mourning. He had not made, for going off, any other pretext than that his time was up and that he was due at home. "Home," with him now, had but one meaning: I knew him to be completely quartered in Westbourne Terrace. "I hope nothing has happened," I said—"that you've lost no one whom *I* know."

Marmaduke looked at my companion, and she looked at Marmaduke. "He has lost his wife," she then observed.

Oh, this time, I fear, I had a small quaver of brutality; but it was at him I directed it. "Your wife? I didn't know you had *had* a wife!"

"Well," he replied, positively gay in his black suit, his black gloves, his high hatband, "the more we live in the past, the more things we find in it. That's a literal fact. You would see the truth of it if your life had taken such a turn."

"*I* live in the past," Lavinia put in gently and as if to help us both.

"But with the result, my dear," I returned, "of not making, I hope, such extraordinary discoveries!" It seemed absurd to be afraid to be light.

"May none of her discoveries be more fatal than mine!" Marmaduke wasn't uproarious, but his treatment of the matter had the good taste of simplicity. "They've wanted it so for her," he continued to me wonderfully, "that we've at last seen our way to it—I mean to what Lavinia has mentioned." He hesitated but three seconds—he brought it brightly out. "Maud-Evelyn had *all* her young happiness."

I stared, but Lavinia was, in her peculiar manner, as brilliant. "The marriage *did* take place," she quietly, stupendously explained to me.

Well, I was determined not to be left. "So you're a widower," I gravely asked, "and these are the signs?"

"Yes; I shall wear them always now."

"But isn't it late to have begun?"

My question had been stupid, I felt the next instant; but it didn't matter—he was quite equal to the occasion. "Oh, I had to wait, you know, till all the facts about my marriage had given me the right." And he looked at his watch again. "Excuse me—I *am* due. Good-bye, good-bye." He shook hands with each of us, and as we sat there together watching him walk away I was struck with his admirable manner of looking the character. I felt indeed as our eyes followed him that we were at one on this, and I said nothing till he was out of sight. Then by the same impulse we turned to each other.

"I thought he was never to marry!" I exclaimed to my friend.

Her fine wasted face met me gravely. "He isn't—ever. He'll be still more faithful."

"Faithful this time to whom?"

"Why, to Maud-Evelyn." I said nothing—I only checked an ejaculation; but I put out a hand and took one of hers, and for a minute we kept silence. "Of course it's only an idea," she began again at last, "but it seems to me a beautiful one." Then she continued resignedly and remarkably: "And now *they* can die."

"Mr. and Mrs. Dedrick?" I pricked up my ears. "Are they dying?"

"Not quite, but the old lady, it appears, is failing, steadily weakening; less, as I understand it, from any definite ailment than because she just feels her work done and her little sum of passion, as Marmaduke calls it, spent. Fancy, with her convictions, all her reasons for wanting to die! And if she goes, he says, Mr. Dedrick won't long linger. It will be quite 'John Anderson my jo.'"

"Keeping her company down the hill, to lie beside her at the foot?"

"Yes, having settled all things."

I turned these things over as we walked away, and how they had settled them—for Maud-Evelyn's dignity and Marmaduke's high advantage; and before we parted that afternoon—we had taken a cab in the Bayswater Road and she had come home with me—I remember saying to her: "Well then, when they die won't he be free?"

She seemed scarce to understand. "Free?"

"To do what he likes."

She wondered. "But he does what he likes now."

"Well then, what *you* like!"

"Oh, you know what *I* like——!"

Ah, I closed her mouth! "You like to tell horrid fibs—yes, I know it!"

What she had then put before me, however, came in time to pass: I heard in the course of the next year of Mrs. Dedrick's extinction, and some months later, without, during the interval, having seen a sign of Marmaduke, wholly taken up with his bereaved patron, learned that her husband had touchingly followed her. I was out of England at the time; we had had to put into practice great economies and let our little place; so that, spending three winters successively in Italy, I devoted the periods between, at home, altogether to visits among people, mainly relatives, to whom these friends of mine were not known. Lavinia of course wrote to me—wrote, among many things, that Marmaduke was ill and had not seemed at all himself since the loss of his "family," and this in spite of the circumstance, which she had already promptly communicated, that they had left him, by will, "almost everything." I knew before I came back to remain that she now saw him often and, to the extent of the change that had overtaken his strength and his spirits, greatly ministered to him. As soon as we at last met I asked for news of him; to which she replied: "He's gradually going." Then on my surprise: "He has had his life."

"You mean that, as he said of Mrs. Dedrick, his sum of passion is spent?"

At this she turned away. "You've never understood."

I *had*, I conceived; and when I went subsequently to see him I was moreover sure. But I only said to Lavinia on this first occasion that I would immediately go; which was precisely what brought out the climax, as I feel it to be, of my story. "He's not now, you know," she turned round to admonish me, "in Westbourne Terrace. He has taken a little old house in Kensington."

"Then he hasn't kept the things?"

"He has kept everything." She looked at me still more as if I had never understood.

"You mean he has moved them?"

She was patient with me. "He has moved nothing. Every-thing is as it was, and kept with the same perfection."

I wondered. "But if he doesn't live there?"

"It's just what he does."

"Then how can he be in Kensington?"

She hesitated, but she had still more than her old grasp of it. "He's in Kensington—without living."

"You mean that at the other place——?"

"Yes, he spends most of his time. He's driven over there every day—he remains there for hours. He keeps it for that."

"I see—it's still the museum."

"It's still the temple!" Lavinia replied with positive aus-terity.

"Then why did he move?"

"Because, you see, there"—she faltered again—"I could come to him. And he wants me," she said with admirable simplicity.

Little by little I took it in. "After the death of the parents, even, you never went?"

"Never."

"So you haven't seen anything?"

"Anything of hers? Nothing."

I understood, oh perfectly; but I won't deny that I was disappointed: I had hoped for an account of his wonders and I immediately felt that it wouldn't be for me to take a step that she had declined. When, a short time later, I saw them together in Kensington Square—there were certain hours of the day that she regularly spent with him—I observed that everything about him was new, handsome and simple. They were, in their strange, final union—if union it could be called—very natural and very touching; but he was visibly stricken—he had his ailment in his eyes. She moved about him like a sister of charity—at all events like a sister. He was neither robust nor rosy now, nor was his attention visibly very present, and I privately and fancifully asked myself where it wandered and waited. But poor Marmaduke was a gentleman to the end—he wasted away with an excellent manner. He died twelve days ago; the will was opened; and last week, having meanwhile heard from her of its contents, I saw Lavinia. He leaves her everything that he himself had inherited. But she spoke of it all in a way that caused me to say in surprise: "You haven't yet been to the house?"

"Not yet. I've only seen the solicitors, who tell me there will be no complications."

There was something in her tone that made me ask more. "Then you're not curious to see what's there?"

She looked at me with a troubled—almost a pleading—sense, which I understood; and presently she said: "Will you go with me?"

"Some day, with pleasure—but not the first time. You must go alone then. The 'relics' that you'll find there," I added—for I had read her look—"you must think of now not as hers——"

"But as his?"

"Isn't that what his death—with his so close relation to them—has made them for you?"

Her face lighted—I saw it was a view she could thank me for putting into words. "I see—I see. They *are* his. I'll go."

She went, and three days ago she came to me. They're really marvels, it appears, treasures extraordinary, and she has them all. Next week I go with her—I shall see them at last. Tell *you* about them, you say? My dear man, everything.

Miss Gunton of Poughkeepsie

"IT'S ASTONISHING what you take for granted!" Lady Champer had exclaimed to her young friend at an early stage; and this might have served as a sign that even then the little plot had begun to thicken. The reflection was uttered at the time the outlook of the charming American girl in whom she found herself so interested was still much in the rough. They had often met, with pleasure to each, during a winter spent in Rome; and Lily had come to her in London towards the end of May with further news of a situation the dawn of which, in March and April, by the Tiber, the Arno and the Seine, had considerably engaged her attention. The Prince had followed Miss Gunton to Florence and then with almost equal promptitude to Paris, where it was both clear and comical for Lady Champer that the rigour of his uncertainty as to parental commands and remittances now detained him. This shrewd woman promised herself not a little amusement from her view of the possibilities of the case. Lily was on the whole showing a wonder; therefore the drama would lose nothing from her character, her temper, her tone. She was waiting—this was the truth she had imparted to her clever protectress—to see if her Roman captive would find himself drawn to London. Should he really turn up there she would the next thing start for America, putting him to the test of that wider range and declining to place her confidence till he should have arrived in New York at her heels. If he remained in Paris or returned to Rome she would stay in London and, as she phrased it, have a good time by herself. Did he expect her to go back to Paris for him? Why not in that case just as well go back to Rome at once? The first thing for her, Lily intimated to her London adviser, was to show what, in her position, *she* expected.

Her position meanwhile was one that Lady Champer, try as she would, had as yet succeeded neither in understanding nor in resigning herself not to understand. It was that of being extraordinarily pretty, amazingly free and perplexingly good, and of presenting these advantages in a positively golden light. How was one to estimate a girl whose nearest approach to a drawback—that is to an encumbrance—appeared to be a grandfather carrying on a business in an American city her ladyship had never otherwise heard of, with whom communication was all by cable and on the subject of "drawing"? Expression was on the old man's part moreover as concise as it was expensive, consisting as it inveterately did of but the single word "Draw." Lily drew, on every occasion in life, and it at least could not be said of the pair—when the "family idea," as embodied in America, was exposed to criticism—that they were not in touch. Mr. Gunton had given her further Mrs. Brine, to come out with her, and with this provision and the perpetual pecuniary he plainly figured—to Lily's own mind—as solicitous to the point of anxiety. Mrs. Brine's scheme of relations seemed in truth to be simpler still. There was a transatlantic "Mr. Brine," of whom she often spoke— and never in any other way; but she wrote for newspapers; she prowled in catacombs, visiting more than once even those of Paris; she haunted hotels; she picked up compatriots; she spoke above all a language that often baffled comprehension. She mattered, however, but little; she was mainly so occupied in having what Lily had likewise independently glanced at—a good time by herself. It was difficult enough indeed to Lady Champer to see the wonderful girl reduced to that, yet she was a little person who kept one somehow in presence of the incalculable. Old measures and familiar rules were of no use at all with her—she had so broken the moulds and so mixed the marks. What was confounding was her disparities—the juxtaposition in her of beautiful sun-flushed heights and deep dark holes. She had none of the things that the other things implied. She dangled in the air in a manner that made one dizzy; though one took comfort, at the worst, in feeling that one was there to catch her if she fell. Falling, at the same time, appeared scarce one of her properties, and it was positive for Lady Champer at moments that if one held out one's arms one might be, after all, much more likely to be pulled up. That was really a part of the excitement of the acquaintance.

"Well," said this friend and critic on one of the first of the London days, "say he does, on your return to your own country, go after you: how do you read, on that occurrence, the course of events?"

"Why, if he comes after me I'll have him."

"And do you think it so easy to 'have' him?"

Lily appeared, lovely and candid—and it was an air and a way she often had—to wonder what she thought. "I don't know that I think it any easier than he seems to think it to have *me*. I know moreover that, though he wants awfully to see the country, he wouldn't just now come to America unless to marry me; and if I take him at all," she pursued, "I want first to be able to show him to the girls."

"Why 'first'?" Lady Champer asked. "Wouldn't it do as well last?"

"Oh, I should want them to see me in Rome too," said Lily. "But, dear me, I'm afraid I want a good many things! What I most want of course is that he should show me unmistakably what *he* wants. Unless he wants me more than anything else in the world I don't want him. Besides, I hope he doesn't think I'm going to be married anywhere but in my own place."

"I see," said Lady Champer. "It's for your wedding you want the girls. And it's for the girls you want the Prince."

"Well, we're all bound by that promise. And of course *you'll* come!"

"Ah, my dear child——!" Lady Champer gasped.

"You can come with the old Princess. You'll be just the right company for her."

The elder friend considered afresh, with depth, the younger's beauty and serenity. "You *are*, love, beyond everything!"

The beauty and serenity took on for a moment a graver cast. "Why do you so often say that to me?"

"Because you so often make it the only thing to say. But you'll some day find out why," Lady Champer added with an intention of encouragement.

Lily Gunton, however, was a young person to whom encouragement looked queer; she had grown up without need of it, and it seemed indeed scarce required in her situation. "Do you mean you believe his mother won't come?"

"Over mountains and seas to see you married?—and to be seen also of the girls? If she does, *I* will. But we had perhaps better," Lady Champer wound up, "not count our chickens before they're hatched." To which, with one of the easy

returns of gaiety that were irresistible in her, Lily made answer that neither of the ladies in question struck her quite as
chickens.

The Prince at all events presented himself in London with
a promptitude that contributed to make the warning gratui-
tous. Nothing could have exceeded, by this time, Lady Champer's appreciation of her young friend, whose merits "town"
at the beginning of June threw into renewed relief; but she
had the imagination of greatness and, though she believed she
tactfully kept it to herself, she thought what the young man
had thus done a great deal for a Roman prince to do. Take
him as he was, with the circumstances—and they were certainly peculiar, and he was charming—it was a far cry for him
from Piazza Colonna to Clarges Street. If Lady Champer had
the imagination of greatness, which the Prince in all sorts of
ways gratified, Miss Gunton of Poughkeepsie—it was vain to
pretend the contrary—was not great in any particular save
one. She was great when she "drew." It was true that at the
beginning of June she did draw with unprecedented energy
and in a manner that, though Mrs. Brine's remarkable nerve
apparently could stand it, fairly made a poor baronet's widow,
little as it was her business, hold her breath. It was none of
her business at all, yet she talked of it even with the Prince
himself—to whom it was indeed a favourite subject and whose
greatness, oddly enough, never appeared to shrink in the effect it produced upon him. The line they took together was
that of wondering if the scale of Lily's drafts made really most
for the presumption that the capital at her disposal was rapidly
dwindling, or for that of its being practically infinite. "Many
a fellow," the young man smiled, "would marry her to pull
her up." He was in any case of the opinion that it was an
occasion for deciding—one way or the other—quickly. Well,
he did decide—so quickly that within the week Lily communicated to her friend that he had offered her his hand, his
heart, his fortune and all his titles, grandeurs and appurtenances. She had given him his answer, and he was in bliss;
though nothing, as yet, was settled but that.

Tall, fair, active, educated, amiable, simple, carrying so naturally his great name and pronouncing so kindly Lily's small
one, the happy youth, if he was one of the most ancient of

princes, was one of the most modern of Romans. This second character it was his special aim and pride to cultivate. He would have been pained at feeling himself an hour behind his age; and he had a way—both touching and amusing to some observers—of constantly comparing his watch with the dial of the day's news. It was in fact easy to see that in deciding to ally himself with a young alien of vague origin, whose striking beauty was reinforced only by her presumptive money, he had even put forward a little the fine hands of his timepiece. No one else, however—not even Lady Champer, and least of all Lily herself—had quite taken the measure, in this connection, of his merit. The quick decision he had spoken of was really a flying leap. He desired incontestably to rescue Miss Gunton's remainder; but to rescue it he had to take it for granted, and taking it for granted was nothing less than—at whatever angle considered—a risk. He never, naturally, used the word to her, but he distinctly faced a peril. The sense of what he had staked on a vague return gave him, at the height of the London season, bad nights, or rather bad mornings—for he danced with his intended, as a usual thing, conspicuously, till dawn—besides obliging him to take, in the form of long explanatory, argumentative and persuasive letters to his mother and sisters, his uncles, aunts, cousins and preferred confidants, large measures of justification at home. The family sense was strong in his huge old house, just as the family array was numerous; he was dutifully conscious of the trust reposed in him, and moved from morning till night, he perfectly knew, as the observed of a phalanx of observers; whereby he the more admired himself for his passion, precipitation and courage. He had only a probability to go upon, but he was—and by the romantic tradition of his race—so in love that he should surely not be taken in.

His private agitation of course deepened when, to do honour to her engagement and as if she would have been ashamed to do less, Lily "drew" again most gloriously; but he managed to smile beautifully on her asking him if he didn't want her to be splendid, and at his worst hours he went no further than to wish that he might be married on the morrow. Unless it were the next day, or at most the next month, it really at moments seemed best that it should never be at all. On the most favourable view—with the solidity of the residuum fully assumed—there were still minor questions and dangers. A vast America, arching over his nuptials, bristling with expectant bridesmaids and underlaying their feet with expensive flowers, stared him in the face and prompted him to the reflection that if she dipped so deep into the mere remote overflow her dive into the fount itself would verily be a header. If she drew at such a rate in London how wouldn't she draw at Poughkeepsie? he asked himself, and practically asked Lady Champer; yet bore the strain of the question, without an answer, so nobly that when, with small delay, Poughkeepsie seemed simply to heave with reassurances, he regarded the ground as firm and his tact as rewarded. "And now at last, dearest," he said, "since everything's so satisfactory, you *will* write?" He put it appealingly, endearingly, yet as if he could scarce doubt.

"Write, love? Why," she replied, "I've done nothing *but* write! I've written ninety letters."

"But not to mamma," he smiled.

"Mamma?"—she stared. "My dear boy, I've not at this time of day to remind you that I've the misfortune to have no mother. I lost mamma, you know, as you lost your father, in childhood. You may be sure," said Lily Gunton, "that I wouldn't otherwise have waited for you to prompt me."

There came into his face a kind of amiable convulsion. "Of course, darling, I remember—your beautiful mother (she *must* have been beautiful!) whom I should have been so glad to know. I was thinking of *my* mamma—who'll be so delighted to hear from you." The Prince spoke English in perfection— had lived in it from the cradle and appeared, particularly when alluding to his home and family, to matters familiar and of fact, or to those of dress and sport, of general recreation, to draw such a comfort from it as made the girl think of him as scarce more a foreigner than a pleasant, auburn, slightly awkward, slightly slangy and extremely well-tailored young Briton would have been. He sounded "mamma" like a rosy English schoolboy; yet just then, for the first time, the things with which he was connected struck her as in a manner strange and far-off. Everything in him, none the less—face and voice and tact, above all his deep desire—laboured to bring them near and make them natural. This was intensely the case as he went on: "Such a little letter as you *might* send would really be awfully jolly."

"My dear child," Lily replied on quick reflection, "I'll write to her with joy the minute I hear from her. Won't she write to *me*?"

The Prince just visibly flushed. "In a moment if you'll only——"

"Write to her first?"

"Just pay her a little—no matter how little—your respects."

His attenuation of the degree showed perhaps a sense of a weakness of position; yet it was no perception of this that made the girl immediately say: "Oh, *caro*, I don't think I can begin. If you feel that *she* won't—as you evidently do—is it because you've asked her and she has refused?" The next moment, "I see you *have*!" she exclaimed. His rejoinder to this was to catch her in his arms, to press his cheek to hers, to murmur a flood of tender words in which contradiction, confession, supplication and remonstrance were oddly confounded; but after he had sufficiently disengaged her to allow her to speak again his effusion was checked by what came. "Do you really mean you can't induce her?" It renewed itself on the first return of ease; or it, more correctly perhaps, in order to renew itself, took this return—a trifle too soon—for granted. Singular, for the hour, was the quickness with which ease could leave them—so blissfully at one as they were; and, to be brief, it had not come back even when Lily spoke of the matter to Lady Champer. It is true that she waited but little to do so. She then went straight to the point. "What would you do if his mother doesn't write?"

"The old Princess—to *you*?" Her ladyship had not had time to mount guard in advance over the tone of this, which was doubtless (as she instantly, for that matter, herself became aware) a little too much that of "Have you really expected she would?" What Lily had expected found itself therefore not unassisted to come out—and came out indeed to such a tune that with all kindness, but with a melancholy deeper than any she had ever yet in the general connection used, Lady Champer was moved to remark that the situation might have been found more possible had a little more historic sense been brought to it. "You're the dearest thing in the world, and I can't imagine a girl's carrying herself in any way, in a difficult position, better than you do; only I'm bound to say I think you ought to remember that you're entering a very great house, of tremendous antiquity, fairly groaning under the weight of ancient honours, the heads of which—through the tradition of the great part they've played in the world—are accustomed to a great deal of deference. The old Princess, my dear, you see"—her ladyship gathered confidence a little as she went—"is a most prodigious personage."

"Why, Lady Champer, of course she is, and that's just what I like her for!" said Lily Gunton.

"She has never in her whole life made an advance, any more than any one has ever dreamed of expecting it of her. It's a pity that while you were there you didn't see her, for I think it would have helped you to understand. However, as you did see his sisters, the two Duchesses and dear little Donna Claudia, you know how charming they all *can* be. They only want to be nice, I know, and I dare say that on the smallest opportunity you'll hear from the Duchesses."

The plural had a sound of splendour, but Lily quite kept her head. "What do you call an opportunity? Am I not giving them, by accepting their son and brother, the best—and in fact the only—opportunity they could desire?"

"I like the way, darling," Lady Champer smiled, "you talk about 'accepting'!"

Lily thought of this—she thought of everything. "Well, say it would have been a better one still for them if I had refused him."

Her friend caught her up. "But you haven't."

"Then they must make the most of the occasion as it is." Lily was very sweet, but very lucid. "The Duchesses may write or not, as they like; but I'm afraid the Princess simply *must*." She hesitated, but after a moment went on: "He oughtn't to be willing moreover that I shouldn't expect to be welcomed."

"He isn't!" Lady Champer blurted out.

Lily jumped at it. "Then he has told you? It's her attitude?"

She had spoken without passion, but her friend was scarce the less frightened. "My poor child, what can he do?"

Lily saw perfectly. "He can make her."

Lady Champer turned it over, but her fears were what was clearest. "And if he doesn't?"

"If he 'doesn't'?" The girl ambiguously echoed it.

"I mean if he can't."

Well, Lily, more cheerfully, declined, for the hour, to consider this. He would certainly do for her what was right; so that after all, though she had herself put the question, she disclaimed the idea that an answer was urgent. There was time, she conveyed—which Lady Champer only desired to believe; a faith moreover somewhat shaken in the latter when the Prince entered her room the next day with the information that there was none—none at least to leave everything in the air. Lady Champer had not yet made up her mind as to which of these young persons she liked most to draw into confidence, nor as to whether she most inclined to take the Roman side with the American or the American side with the Roman. But now in truth she was settled; she gave proof of it in the increased lucidity with which she spoke for Lily.

"Wouldn't the Princess depart—a—from her usual attitude for such a great occasion?"

The difficulty was a little that the young man so well understood his mother. "The devil of it is, you see, that it's for Lily herself, so much more, she thinks the occasion great."

Lady Champer mused. "If you hadn't her consent I could understand it. But from the moment she thinks the girl good enough for you to marry——"

"Ah, she doesn't!" the Prince gloomily interposed. "However," he explained, "she accepts her because there are reasons—my own feeling, now so my very life, don't you see? But it isn't quite open arms. All the same, as I tell Lily, the arms *would* open."

"If she'd make the first step? Hum!" said Lady Champer, not without the note of grimness. "She'll be obstinate."

The young man, with a melancholy eye, quite coincided. "She'll be obstinate."

"So that I strongly recommend you to manage it," his friend went on after a pause. "It strikes me that if the Princess can't do it for Lily she might at least do it for you. Any girl you marry becomes thereby somebody."

"Of course—doesn't she? She certainly ought to do it for *me*. I'm after all the head of the house."

"Well then, make her!" said Lady Champer a little impatiently.

"I will. Mamma adores me, and I adore *her*."

"And you adore Lily, and Lily adores you—therefore everybody adores everybody, especially as I adore you both. With so much adoration all round, therefore, things ought to march."

"They shall!" the young man declared with spirit. "I adore you too—you don't mention that; for you help me immensely. But what do you suppose she'll do if she doesn't?"

The agitation already visible in him ministered a little to vagueness; but his friend after an instant disembroiled it. "What do I suppose Lily will do if your mother remains stiff?" Lady Champer faltered, but she let him have it. "She'll break."

His wondering eyes became strange. "Just for that?"

"You may certainly say it isn't much—when people love as you do."

"Ah, I'm afraid then Lily doesn't!"—and he turned away in his trouble.

She watched him while he moved, not speaking for a minute. "My dear young man, are you afraid of your mamma?"

He faced short about again. "I'm afraid of this—that if she does do it she won't forgive her. She *will* do it—yes. But Lily will be for her, in consequence, ever after, the person who has made her submit herself. She'll hate her for that—and then she'll hate me for being concerned in it." The Prince presented it all with clearness—almost with charm. "What do you say to that?"

His friend had to think. "Well, only, I fear, that we belong, Lily and I, to a race unaccustomed to counting with such passions. Let her hate!" she, however, a trifle inconsistently wound up.

"But I love her so!"

"Which?" Lady Champer asked it almost ungraciously; in such a tone at any rate that, seated on the sofa with his elbows on his knees, his much-ringed hands nervously locked together and his eyes of distress wide open, he met her with visible surprise. What she met *him* with is perhaps best noted by the fact that after a minute of it his hands covered his bent face and she became aware she had drawn tears. This produced such regret in her that before they parted she did what she could to attenuate and explain—making a great point, at all events, of her rule, with Lily, of putting only his own side of the case. "I insist awfully, you know, on your greatness!"

He jumped up, wincing. "Oh, that's horrid."

"I don't know. Whose fault is it then, at any rate, if trying to help you may have that side?" This was a question that, with the tangle he had already to unwind, only added a twist; yet she went on as if positively to add another. "Why on earth don't you, all of you, leave them alone?"

"Leave them——?"

"All your Americans."

"Don't you like them then—the women?"

She hesitated. "No. Yes. They're an interest. But they're a nuisance. It's a question, very certainly, if they're worth the trouble they give."

This at least it seemed he could take in. "You mean that one should be quite sure first what they *are* worth?"

He made her laugh now. "It would appear that you never *can* be. But also really that you can't keep your hands off."

He fixed the social scene an instant with his heavy eye. "Yes. Doesn't it?"

"However," she pursued as if he again a little irritated her, "Lily's position is quite simple."

"Quite. She just loves me."

"I mean simple for herself. She really makes no differences. It's only we—you and I—who make them all."

The Prince wondered. "But she tells me she delights in us; has, that is, such a sense of what we are supposed to 'represent.'"

"Oh, she *thinks* she has. Americans think they have all sorts of things; but they haven't. That's just *it*"—Lady Champer was philosophic. "Nothing but their Americanism. If you marry anything you marry that; and if your mother accepts anything that's what she accepts." Then, though the young man followed the demonstration with an apprehension almost pathetic, she gave him without mercy the whole of it. "Lily's rigidly logical. A girl—as *she* knows girls—is 'welcomed,' on her engagement, before anything else can happen, by the family of her young man; and the motherless girl, alone in the world, more punctually than any other. His mother—if she's a 'lady'—takes it upon herself. Then the girl goes and stays with them. But she does nothing before. *Tirez-vous de là.*"

The young man sought on the spot to obey this last injunction, and his effort presently produced a flash. "Oh, if she'll come and *stay* with us"—all would, easily, be well! The flash went out, however, when Lady Champer returned: "Then let the Princess invite her."

Lily a fortnight later simply said to her, from one hour to the other, "I'm going home," and took her breath away by sailing on the morrow with the Bransbys. The tense cord had somehow snapped; the proof was in the fact that the Prince, dashing off to his good friend at this crisis an obscure, an ambiguous note, started the same night for Rome. Lady Champer, for the time, sat in darkness, but during the summer many things occurred; and one day in the autumn, quite unheralded and with the signs of some of them in his face, the Prince appeared again before her. He was not long in telling her his story, which was simply that he had come to her, all the way from Rome, for news of Lily and to talk of Lily. She was prepared, as it happened, to meet his impatience; yet her preparation was but little older than his arrival and was deficient moreover in an important particular. She was not prepared to knock him down, and she made him talk to gain time. She had however, to understand, put a primary question: "She never wrote then?"

"Mamma? Oh yes—when she at last got frightened at Miss Gunton's having become so silent. She wrote in August; but Lily's own decisive letter—letter to me, I mean—crossed with it. It was too late—that put an end."

"A *real* end?"

Everything in the young man showed how real. "On the ground of her being willing no longer to keep up, by the stand she had taken, such a relation between mamma and *me*. But her rupture," he wailed, "keeps it up more than anything else."

"And is it very bad?"

"Awful, I assure you. I've become for my mother a person who has made her make, all for nothing, an unprecedented advance, a humble submission; and she's so disgusted, all round, that it's no longer the same old charming thing for us to be together. It makes it worse for her that I'm still madly in love."

"Well," said Lady Champer after a moment, "if you're still madly in love I can only be sorry for you."

"You can *do* nothing for me?—don't advise me to go over?"

She had to take a longer pause. "You don't at all know then what has happened?—that old Mr. Gunton has died and left her everything?"

All his vacancy and curiosity came out in a wild echo. " 'Everything'?"

"She writes me that it's a great deal of money."

"You've just heard from her then?"

"This morning. I seem to make out," said Lady Champer, "an extraordinary number of dollars."

"Oh, I was sure it was!" the young man moaned.

"And she's engaged," his friend went on, "to Mr. Bransby."

He bounded, rising before her. "Mr. Bransby?"

" 'Adam P.'—the gentleman with whose mother and sisters she went home. *They*, she writes, have beautifully welcomed her."

"*Dio mio!*" The Prince stared; he had flushed with the blow, and the tears had come into his eyes. "And I believed she loved me!"

"*I* didn't!" said Lady Champer with some curtness.

He gazed about; he almost rocked; and, unconscious of her words, he appealed, inarticulate and stricken. At last, however, he found his voice. "What on earth then shall I do? I can less than ever go back to mamma!"

She got up for him, she thought for him, pushing a better chair into her circle. "Stay here with me, and I'll ring for tea. Sit there nearer the fire—you're cold."

"Awfully!" he confessed as he sank. "And I believed she loved me!" he repeated as he stared at the fire.

"*I* didn't!" Lady Champer once more declared. This time, visibly, he heard her, and she immediately met his wonder. "No—it was all the rest; your great historic position, the glamour of your name and your past. Otherwise what she stood out for wouldn't be excusable. But she has the sense of such things, and *they* were what she loved." So, by the fire, his hostess explained it, while he wondered the more.

"I thought that last summer you told me just the contrary."

It seemed, to do her justice, to strike her. "Did I? Oh, well, how does one know? With Americans one is lost!"

The Tree of Knowledge

IT WAS one of the secret opinions, such as we all have, of Peter Brench that his main success in life would have consisted in his never having committed himself about the work, as it was called, of his friend, Morgan Mallow. This was a subject on which it was, to the best of his belief, impossible, with veracity, to quote him, and it was nowhere on record that he had, in the connection, on any occasion and in any embarrassment, either lied or spoken the truth. Such a triumph had its honour even for a man of other triumphs—a man who had reached fifty, who had escaped marriage, who had lived within his means, who had been in love with Mrs. Mallow for years without breathing it, and who, last not least, had judged himself once for all. He had so judged himself in fact that he felt an extreme and general humility to be his proper portion; yet there was nothing that made him think so well of his parts as the course he had steered so often through the shallows just mentioned. It became thus a real wonder that the friends in whom he had most confidence were just those with whom he had most reserves. He couldn't tell Mrs. Mallow—or at least he supposed, excellent man, he couldn't—that she was the one beautiful reason he had never married; any more than he could tell her husband that the sight of the multiplied marbles in that gentleman's studio was an affliction of which even time had never blunted the edge. His victory, however, as I have intimated, in regard to these productions, was not simply in his not having let it out that he deplored them; it was, remarkably, in his not having kept it in by anything else.

The whole situation, among these good people, was verily a marvel, and there was probably not such another for a long way from the spot that engages us—the point at which the soft declivity of Hampstead began at that time to confess in broken accents to St. John's Wood. He despised Mallow's statues and adored Mallow's wife, and yet was distinctly fond of Mallow, to whom, in turn, he was equally dear. Mrs. Mallow rejoiced in the statues—though she preferred, when

pressed, the busts; and if she was visibly attached to Peter
Brench it was because of his affection for Morgan. Each loved
the other, moreover, for the love borne in each case to Lan-
celot, whom the Mallows respectively cherished as their only
child and whom the friend of their fireside identified as the
third—but decidedly the handsomest—of his godsons. Already in the old years it had come to that—that no one, for
such a relation, could possibly have occurred to any of them,
even to the baby itself, but Peter. There was luckily a certain
independence, of the pecuniary sort, all round: the Master
could never otherwise have spent his solemn *Wanderjahre* in
Florence and Rome and continued, by the Thames as well as
by the Arno and the Tiber, to add unpurchased group to
group and model, for what was too apt to prove in the event
mere love, fancy-heads of celebrities either too busy or too
buried—too much of the age or too little of it—to sit. Neither
could Peter, lounging in almost daily, have found time to keep
the whole complicated tradition so alive by his presence. He
was massive, but mild, the depositary of these mysteries—large
and loose and ruddy and curly, with deep tones, deep eyes,
deep pockets, to say nothing of the habit of long pipes, soft
hats and brownish, greyish, weather-faded clothes, apparently
always the same.

He had "written," it was known, but had never spoken—
never spoken, in particular, of that; and he had the air (since,
as was believed, he continued to write) of keeping it up in
order to have something more—as if he had not, at the worst,
enough—to be silent about. Whatever his air, at any rate,
Peter's occasional unmentioned prose and verse were quite
truly the result of an impulse to maintain the purity of his
taste by establishing still more firmly the right relation of fame
to feebleness. The little green door of his domain was in a
garden-wall on which the stucco was cracked and stained, and
in the small detached villa behind it everything was old, the
furniture, the servants, the books, the prints, the habits and
the new improvements. The Mallows, at Carrara Lodge, were
within ten minutes, and the studio there was on their little
land, to which they had added, in their happy faith, to build
it. This was the good fortune, if it was not the ill, of her
having brought him, in marriage, a portion that put them in

a manner at their ease and enabled them thus, on their side, to keep it up. And they did keep it up—they always had—the infatuated sculptor and his wife, for whom nature had refined on the impossible by relieving them of the sense of the difficult. Morgan had, at all events, everything of the sculptor but the spirit of Phidias—the brown velvet, the becoming *beretto*, the "plastic" presence, the fine fingers, the beautiful accent in Italian and the old Italian factotum. He seemed to make up for everything when he addressed Egidio with the "tu" and waved him to turn one of the rotary pedestals of which the place was full. They were tremendous Italians at Carrara Lodge, and the secret of the part played by this fact in Peter's life was, in a large degree, that it gave him, sturdy Briton that he was, just the amount of "going abroad" he could bear. The Mallows were all his Italy, but it was in a measure for Italy he liked them. His one worry was that Lance—to which they had shortened his godson—was, in spite of a public school, perhaps a shade too Italian. Morgan, meanwhile, looked like somebody's flattering idea of somebody's own person as expressed in the great room provided at the Uffizzi museum for Portraits of Artists by Themselves. The Master's sole regret that he had not been born rather to the brush than to the chisel sprang from his wish that he might have contributed to that collection.

It appeared, with time, at any rate, to be to the brush that Lance had been born; for Mrs. Mallow, one day when the boy was turning twenty, broke it to their friend, who shared, to the last delicate morsel, their problems and pains, that it seemed as if nothing would really do but that he should embrace the career. It had been impossible longer to remain blind to the fact that he gained no glory at Cambridge, where Brench's own college had, for a year, tempered its tone to him as for Brench's own sake. Therefore why renew the vain form of preparing him for the impossible? The impossible—it had become clear—was that he should be anything but an artist.

"Oh dear, dear!" said poor Peter.

"Don't you believe in it?" asked Mrs. Mallow, who still, at more than forty, had her violet velvet eyes, her creamy satin skin and her silken chestnut hair.

"Believe in what?"

"Why, in Lance's passion."

"I don't know what you mean by 'believing in it.' I've never been unaware, certainly, of his disposition, from his earliest time, to daub and draw; but I confess I've hoped it would burn out."

"But why should it," she sweetly smiled, "with his wonderful heredity? Passion is passion—though of course, indeed, you, dear Peter, know nothing of that. Has the Master's ever burned out?"

Peter looked off a little and, in his familiar, formless way, kept up for a moment a sound between a smothered whistle and a subdued hum. "Do you think he's going to be another Master?"

She seemed scarce prepared to go that length, yet she had, on the whole, a most marvellous trust. "I know what you mean by that. Will it be a career to incur the jealousies and provoke the machinations that have been at times almost too much for his father? Well—say it may be, since nothing but clap-trap, in these dreadful days, *can*, it would seem, make its way, and since, with the curse of refinement and distinction, one may easily find one's self begging one's bread. Put it at the worst—say he *has* the misfortune to wing his flight further than the vulgar taste of his stupid countrymen can follow. Think, all the same, of the happiness—the same that the Master has had. He'll *know*."

Peter looked rueful. "Ah, but *what* will he know?"

"Quiet joy!" cried Mrs. Mallow, quite impatient and turning away.

II

He had of course, before long, to meet the boy himself on it and to hear that, practically, everything was settled. Lance was not to go up again, but to go instead to Paris where, since the die was cast, he would find the best advantages. Peter had always felt that he must be taken as he was, but had never perhaps found him so much as he was as on this occasion. "You chuck Cambridge then altogether? Doesn't that seem rather a pity?"

Lance would have been like his father, to his friend's sense, had he had less humour, and like his mother had he had more beauty. Yet it was a good middle way, for Peter, that, in the modern manner, he was, to the eye, rather the young stock-broker than the young artist. The youth reasoned that it was a question of time—there was such a mill to go through, such an awful lot to learn. He had talked with fellows and had judged. "One has got, to-day," he said, "don't you see? to know."

His interlocutor, at this, gave a groan. "Oh, hang it, *don't* know!"

Lance wondered. " 'Don't'? Then what's the use——?"

"The use of what?"

"Why, of anything. Don't you think I've talent?"

Peter smoked away, for a little, in silence; then went on: "It isn't knowledge, it's ignorance that—as we've been beautifully told—is bliss."

"Don't you think I've talent?" Lance repeated.

Peter, with his trick of queer, kind demonstrations, passed his arm round his godson and held him a moment. "How do I know?"

"Oh," said the boy, "if it's your own ignorance you're defending——!"

Again, for a pause, on the sofa, his godfather smoked. "It isn't. I've the misfortune to be omniscient."

"Oh, well," Lance laughed again, "if you know *too* much——!"

"That's what I do, and why I'm so wretched."

Lance's gaiety grew. "Wretched? Come, I say!"

"But I forgot," his companion went on—"you're not to know about that. It would indeed, for you too, make the too much. Only I'll tell you what I'll do." And Peter got up from the sofa. "If you'll go up again, I'll pay your way at Cambridge."

Lance stared, a little rueful in spite of being still more amused. "Oh, Peter! You disapprove so of Paris?"

"Well, I'm afraid of it."

"Ah, I see."

"No, you don't see—yet. But you will—that is you would. And you mustn't."

The young man thought more gravely. "But one's innocence, already——"

"Is considerably damaged? Ah, that won't matter," Peter persisted—"we'll patch it up here."

"Here? Then you want me to stay at home?"

Peter almost confessed to it. "Well, we're so right—we four together—just as we are. We're so safe. Come, don't spoil it."

The boy, who had turned to gravity, turned from this, on the real pressure in his friend's tone, to consternation. "Then what's a fellow to be?"

"My particular care. Come, old man"—and Peter now fairly pleaded—"*I'll* look out for you."

Lance, who had remained on the sofa with his legs out and his hands in his pockets, watched him with eyes that showed suspicion. Then he got up. "You think there's something the matter with me—that I can't make a success."

"Well, what do you call a success?"

Lance thought again. "Why, the best sort, I suppose, is to please one's self. Isn't that the sort that, in spite of cabals and things, is—in his own peculiar line—the Master's?"

There were so much too many things in this question to be answered at once that they practically checked the discussion, which became particularly difficult in the light of such renewed proof that, though the young man's innocence might, in the course of his studies, as he contended, somewhat have shrunken, the finer essence of it still remained. That was indeed exactly what Peter had assumed and what, above all, he desired; yet, perversely enough, it gave him a chill. The boy believed in the cabals and things, believed in the peculiar line, believed, in short, in the Master. What happened a month or two later was not that he went up again at the expense of his godfather, but that a fortnight after he had got settled in Paris this personage sent him fifty pounds.

He had meanwhile, at home, this personage, made up his mind to the worst; and what it might be had never yet grown quite so vivid to him as when, on his presenting himself one Sunday night, as he never failed to do, for supper, the mistress of Carrara Lodge met him with an appeal as to—of all things in the world—the wealth of the Canadians. She was earnest, she was even excited. "Are many of them *really* rich?"

He had to confess that he knew nothing about them, but he often thought afterwards of that evening. The room in which they sat was adorned with sundry specimens of the Master's genius, which had the merit of being, as Mrs. Mallow herself frequently suggested, of an unusually convenient size. They were indeed of dimensions not customary in the products of the chisel and had the singularity that, if the objects and features intended to be small looked too large, the objects and features intended to be large looked too small. The Master's intention, whether in respect to this matter or to any other, had, in almost any case, even after years, remained undiscoverable to Peter Brench. The creations that so failed to reveal it stood about on pedestals and brackets, on tables and shelves, a little staring white population, heroic, idyllic, allegoric, mythic, symbolic, in which "scale" had so strayed and lost itself that the public square and the chimney-piece seemed to have changed places, the monumental being all diminutive and the diminutive all monumental; branches, at any rate, markedly, of a family in which stature was rather oddly irrespective of function, age and sex. They formed, like the Mallows themselves, poor Brench's own family—having at least, to such a degree, the note of familiarity. The occasion was one of those he had long ago learnt to know and to name—short flickers of the faint flame, soft gusts of a kinder air. Twice a year, regularly, the Master believed in his fortune, in addition to believing all the year round in his genius. This time it was to be made by a bereaved couple from Toronto, who had given him the handsomest order for a tomb to three lost children, each of whom they desired to be, in the composition, emblematically and characteristically represented.

Such was naturally the moral of Mrs. Mallow's question: if their wealth was to be assumed, it was clear, from the nature of their admiration, as well as from mysterious hints thrown out (they were a little odd!) as to other possibilities of the same mortuary sort, that their further patronage might be; and not less evident that, should the Master become at all known in those climes, nothing would be more inevitable than a run of Canadian custom. Peter had been present before at runs of custom, colonial and domestic— present at each of those of which the aggregation had left so few gaps in the marble company round him; but it was his habit never, at these junctures, to prick the bubble in advance. The fond illusion, while it lasted, eased the wound of elections never won, the long ache of medals and diplomas carried off, on every chance, by every one but the Master; it lighted the lamp, moreover, that would glimmer through the next eclipse. They lived, however, after all—as it was always beautiful to see—at a height scarce susceptible of ups and downs. They strained a point, at times, charmingly, to admit that the public was, here and there, not too bad to buy; but they would have been nowhere without their attitude that the Master was always too good to sell. They were, at all events, deliciously formed, Peter often said to himself, for their fate; the Master had a vanity, his wife had a loyalty, of which success, depriving these things of innocence, would have diminished the merit and the grace. Any one could be charming under a charm, and, as he looked about him at a world of prosperity more void of proportion even than the Master's museum, he wondered if he knew another pair that so completely escaped vulgarity.

"What a pity Lance isn't with us to rejoice!" Mrs. Mallow on this occasion sighed at supper.

"We'll drink to the health of the absent," her husband replied, filling his friend's glass and his own and giving a drop to their companion; "but we must hope that he's preparing himself for a happiness much less like this of ours this evening—excusable as I grant it to be!—than like the comfort we have always—whatever has happened or has not happened—been able to trust ourselves to enjoy. The comfort," the Master explained, leaning back in the pleasant lamplight and firelight, holding up his glass and looking round at his marble family, quartered more or less, a monstrous brood, in every room—"the comfort of art in itself!"

Peter looked a little shyly at his wine. "Well—I don't care what you may call it when a fellow doesn't—but Lance must learn to *sell*, you know. I drink to his acquisition of the secret of a base popularity!"

"Oh yes, *he* must sell," the boy's mother, who was still more, however, this seemed to give out, the Master's wife, rather artlessly conceded.

"Oh," the sculptor, after a moment, confidently pronounced, "Lance *will*. Don't be afraid. He will have learnt."

"Which is exactly what Peter," Mrs. Mallow gaily returned—"why in the world were you so perverse, Peter?—wouldn't, when he told him, hear of."

Peter, when this lady looked at him with accusatory affection—a grace, on her part, not infrequent—could never find a word; but the Master, who was always all amenity and tact, helped him out now as he had often helped him before. "That's his old idea, you know—on which we've so often differed: his theory that the artist should be all impulse and instinct. *I* go in, of course, for a certain amount of school. Not too much—but a due proportion. There's where his protest came in," he continued to explain to his wife, "as against what *might*, don't you see? be in question for Lance."

"Ah, well"—and Mrs. Mallow turned the violet eyes across the table at the subject of this discourse—"he's sure to have meant, of course, nothing but good; but that wouldn't have prevented him, if Lance *had* taken his advice, from being, in effect, horribly cruel."

They had a sociable way of talking of him to his face as if he had been in the clay or—at most—in the plaster, and the Master was unfailingly generous. He might have been waving Egidio to make him revolve. "Ah, but poor Peter was not so wrong as to what it may, after all, come to that he *will* learn."

"Oh, but nothing artistically bad," she urged—still, for poor Peter, arch and dewy.

"Why, just the little French tricks," said the Master: on which their friend had to pretend to admit, when pressed by Mrs. Mallow, that these aesthetic vices had been the objects of his dread.

III

"I know now," Lance said to him the next year, "why you were so much against it." He had come back, supposedly for a mere interval, and was looking about him at Carrara Lodge, where indeed he had already, on two or three occasions, since his expatriation, briefly appeared. This had the air of a longer holiday. "Something rather awful has happened to me. It *isn't* so very good to know."

"I'm bound to say high spirits don't show in your face," Peter was rather ruefully forced to confess. "Still, are you very sure you do know?"

"Well, I at least know about as much as I can bear." These remarks were exchanged in Peter's den, and the young man, smoking cigarettes, stood before the fire with his back against the mantel. Something of his bloom seemed really to have left him.

Poor Peter wondered. "You're clear then as to what in particular I wanted you not to go for?"

"In particular?" Lance thought. "It seems to me that, in particular, there can have been but one thing."

They stood for a little sounding each other. "Are you quite sure?"

"Quite sure I'm a beastly duffer? Quite—by this time."

"Oh!"—and Peter turned away as if almost with relief.

"It's *that* that isn't pleasant to find out."

"Oh, I don't care for 'that,' " said Peter, presently coming round again. "I mean I personally don't."

"Yet I hope you can understand a little that I myself should!"

"Well, what do you mean by it?" Peter sceptically asked.

And on this Lance had to explain—how the upshot of his studies in Paris had inexorably proved a mere deep doubt of his means. These studies had waked him up, and a new light was in his eyes; but what the new light did was really to show him too much. "Do you know what's the matter with me? I'm too horribly intelligent. Paris was really the last place for me. I've learnt what I can't do."

Poor Peter stared—it was a staggerer; but even after they had had, on the subject, a longish talk in which the boy brought out to the full the hard truth of his lesson, his friend betrayed less pleasure than usually breaks into a face to the happy tune of "I told you so!" Poor Peter himself made now indeed so little a point of having told him so that Lance broke ground in a different place a day or two after. "What was it then that—before I went—you were afraid I should find out?" This, however, Peter refused to tell him—on the ground that if he hadn't yet guessed perhaps he never would, and that nothing at all, for either of them, in any case, was to be gained by giving the thing a name. Lance eyed him, on this, an instant, with the bold curiosity of youth—with the air indeed of having in his mind two or three names, of which one or other would be right. Peter, nevertheless, turning his back again, offered no encouragement, and when they parted afresh it was with some show of impatience on the side of the boy. Accordingly, at their next encounter, Peter saw at a glance that he had now, in the interval, divined and that, to sound his note, he was only waiting till they should find themselves alone. This he had soon arranged, and he then broke straight out. "Do you know your conundrum has been keeping me awake? But in the watches of the night the answer came over me—so that, upon my honour, I quite laughed out. Had you been supposing I had to go to Paris to learn *that*?" Even now, to see him still so sublimely on his guard, Peter's young friend had to laugh afresh. "You won't give a sign till you're sure? Beautiful old Peter!" But Lance at last produced it. "Why, hang it, the truth about the Master."

It made between them, for some minutes, a lively passage, full of wonder, for each, at the wonder of the other. "Then how long have you understood——"

"The true value of his work? I understood it," Lance recalled, "as soon as I began to understand anything. But I didn't begin fully to do that, I admit, till I got *là-bas*."

"Dear, dear!"—Peter gasped with retrospective dread.

"But for what have you taken me? I'm a hopeless muff—that I *had* to have rubbed in. But I'm not such a muff as the Master!" Lance declared.

"Then why did you never tell me——?"

"That I hadn't, after all"—the boy took him up—"remained such an idiot? Just because I never dreamed *you* knew. But I beg your pardon. I only wanted to spare you. And what I don't now understand is how the deuce then, for so long, you've managed to keep bottled."

Peter produced his explanation, but only after some delay and with a gravity not void of embarrassment. "It was for your mother."

"Oh!" said Lance.

"And that's the great thing now—since the murder *is* out. I want a promise from you. I mean"—and Peter almost feverishly followed it up—"a vow from you, solemn and such as you owe me, here on the spot, that you'll sacrifice anything rather than let her ever guess——"

"That *I've* guessed?"—Lance took it in. "I see." He evidently, after a moment, had taken in much. "But what is it you have in mind that I may have a chance to sacrifice?"

"Oh, one has always something."

Lance looked at him hard. "Do you mean that *you've* had——?" The look he received back, however, so put the question by that he found soon enough another. "Are you really sure my mother doesn't know?"

Peter, after renewed reflection, was really sure. "If she does, she's too wonderful."

"But aren't we all too wonderful?"

"Yes," Peter granted—"but in different ways. The thing's so desperately important because your father's little public consists only, as you know then," Peter developed—"well, of how many?"

"First of all," the Master's son risked, "of himself. And last of all too. I don't quite see of whom else."

Peter had an approach to impatience. "Of your mother, I say—*always*."

Lance cast it all up. "You absolutely feel that?"

"Absolutely."

"Well then, with yourself, that makes three."

"Oh, *me!*"—and Peter, with a wag of his kind old head, modestly excused himself. "The number is, at any rate, small enough for any individual dropping out to be too dreadfully missed. Therefore, to put it in a nutshell, take care, my boy—that's all—that *you're* not!"

"I've got to keep on humbugging?" Lance sighed.

"It's just to warn you of the danger of your failing of that that I've seized this opportunity."

"And what do you regard in particular," the young man asked, "as the danger?"

"Why, this certainty: that the moment your mother, who feels so strongly, should suspect your secret—well," said Peter desperately, "the fat would be on the fire."

Lance, for a moment, seemed to stare at the blaze. "She'd throw me over?"

"She'd throw *him* over."

"And come round to us?"

Peter, before he answered, turned away. "Come round to *you*." But he had said enough to indicate—and, as he evidently trusted, to avert—the horrid contingency.

IV

Within six months again, however, his fear was, on more occasions than one, all before him. Lance had returned to Paris, to another trial; then had reappeared at home and had had, with his father, for the first time in his life, one of the scenes that strike sparks. He described it with much expression to Peter, as to whom—since they had never done so before—it was a sign of a new reserve on the part of the pair at Carrara Lodge that they at present failed, on a matter of intimate interest, to open themselves—if not in joy, then in sorrow—to their good friend. This produced perhaps, practically, between the parties, a shade of alienation and a slight intermission of commerce—marked mainly indeed by the fact that, to talk at his ease with his old playmate, Lance had, in general, to come to see him. The closest, if not quite the gayest relation they had yet known together was thus ushered in. The difficulty for poor Lance was a tension at home, begotten by the fact that his father wished him to be, at least, the sort of success he himself had been. He hadn't "chucked" Paris—though nothing appeared more vivid to him than that Paris had chucked him; he would go back again because of the fascination in trying, in seeing, in sounding the depths—in learning one's lesson, in fine, even if the lesson were simply that of one's impotence in the presence of one's larger vision. But what did the Master, all aloft in his senseless fluency, know of impotence, and what vision—to be called such—had he, in all his blind life, ever had? Lance, heated and indignant, frankly appealed to his godparent on this score.

His father, it appeared, had come down on him for having, after so long, nothing to show, and hoped that, on his next return, this deficiency would be repaired. *The* thing, the Master complacently set forth was—for any artist, however inferior to himself—at least to "do" something. "What can you do? That's all I ask!" *He* had certainly done enough, and there was no mistake about what he had to show. Lance had tears in his eyes when it came thus to letting his old friend know how great the strain might be on the "sacrifice" asked of him. It wasn't so easy to continue humbugging—as from son to parent—after feeling one's self despised for not grovelling in mediocrity. Yet a noble duplicity was what, as they intimately faced the situation, Peter went on requiring; and it was still, for a time, what his young friend, bitter and sore, managed loyally to comfort him with. Fifty pounds, more than once again, it was true, rewarded, both in London and in Paris, the young friend's loyalty; none the less sensibly, doubtless, at the moment, that the money was a direct advance on a decent sum for which Peter had long since privately prearranged an ultimate function. Whether by these arts or others, at all events, Lance's just resentment was kept for a season—but only for a season—at bay. The day arrived when he warned his companion that he could hold out—or hold in—no longer. Carrara Lodge had had to listen to another lecture delivered from a great height—an infliction really heavier, at last, than, without striking back or in some way letting the Master have the truth, flesh and blood could bear.

"And what I don't see is," Lance observed with a certain irritated eye for what was, after all, if it came to that, due to himself too—"What I don't see is, upon my honour, how *you*, as things are going, can keep the game up."

"Oh, the game for me is only to hold my tongue," said placid Peter. "And I have my reason."

"Still my mother?"

Peter showed, as he had often shown it before—that is by turning it straight away—a queer face. "What will you have? I haven't ceased to like her."

"She's beautiful—she's a dear, of course," Lance granted; "but what is she to you, after all, and what is it to you that, as to anything whatever, she should or she shouldn't?"

Peter, who had turned red, hung fire a little. "Well—it's all, simply, what I make of it."

There was now, however, in his young friend, a strange, an adopted, insistence. "What are you, after all, to *her*?"

"Oh, nothing. But that's another matter."

"She cares only for my father," said Lance the Parisian.

"Naturally—and that's just why."

"Why you've wished to spare her?"

"Because she cares so tremendously much."

Lance took a turn about the room, but with his eyes still on his host. "How awfully—always—you must have liked her!"

"Awfully. Always," said Peter Brench.

The young man continued for a moment to muse—then stopped again in front of him. "Do you know how much she cares?" Their eyes met on it, but Peter, as if his own found something new in Lance's, appeared to hesitate, for the first time for so long, to say he did know. "*I've* only just found out," said Lance. "She came to my room last night, after being present, in silence and only with her eyes on me, at what I had had to take from him; she came—and she was with me an extraordinary hour."

He had paused again, and they had again for a while sounded each other. Then something—and it made him suddenly turn pale—came to Peter. "She *does* know?"

"She does know. She let it all out to me—so as to demand of me no more than that, as she said, of which she herself had been capable. She has always, always known," said Lance without pity.

Peter was silent a long time; during which his companion might have heard him gently breathe and, on touching him, might have felt within him the vibration of a long, low sound suppressed. By the time he spoke, at last, he had taken everything in. "Then I do see how tremendously much."

"Isn't it wonderful?" Lance asked.

"Wonderful," Peter mused.

"So that if your original effort to keep me from Paris was to keep me from knowledge——!" Lance exclaimed as if with a sufficient indication of this futility.

It might have been at the futility that Peter appeared for a little to gaze. "I think it must have been—without my quite at the time knowing it—to keep *me*!" he replied at last as he turned away.

The Abasement of the Northmores

WHEN Lord Northmore died public reference to the event took for the most part rather a ponderous and embarrassed form. A great political figure had passed away. A great light of our time had been quenched in mid-career. A great usefulness had somewhat anticipated its term, though a great part, none the less, had been signally played. The note of greatness, all along the line, kept sounding, in short, by a force of its own, and the image of the departed evidently lent itself with ease to figures and flourishes, the poetry of the daily press. The newspapers and their purchasers equally did their duty by it—arranged it neatly and impressively, though perhaps with a hand a little violently expeditious, upon the funeral car, saw the conveyance properly down the avenue, and then, finding the subject suddenly quite exhausted, proceeded to the next item on their list. His lordship had been a person, in fact, in connection with whom there was almost nothing but the fine monotony of his success to mention. This success had been his profession, his means as well as his end; so that his career admitted of no other description and demanded, indeed suffered, no further analysis. He had made politics, he had made literature, he had made land, he had made a bad manner and a great many mistakes, he had made a gaunt, foolish wife, two extravagant sons and four awkward daughters —he had made everything, as he *could* have made almost anything, thoroughly pay. There had been something deep down in him that did it, and his old friend Warren Hope, the person knowing him earliest and probably, on the whole, best, had never, even to the last, for curiosity, quite made out what it was. The secret was one that this distinctly distanced competitor had in fact mastered as little for intellectual relief as for emulous use; and there was quite a kind of tribute to it in the way that, the night before the obsequies and addressing himself to his wife, he said after some silent thought: "Hang it, you know, I must see the old boy through. I must go to the grave."

Mrs. Hope looked at her husband at first in anxious silence. "I've no patience with you. You're much more ill than *he* ever was."

"Ah, but if that qualifies me but for the funerals of others——!"

"It qualifies you to break my heart by your exaggerated chivalry, your renewed refusal to consider your interests. You sacrificed them to him, for thirty years, again and again, and from this supreme sacrifice—possibly that of your life—you might, in your condition, I think, be absolved." She indeed lost patience. "To the grave—in this weather—after his treatment of you!"

"My dear girl," Hope replied, "his treatment of me is a figment of your ingenious mind—your too-passionate, your beautiful loyalty. Loyalty, I mean, to *me*."

"I certainly leave it to you," she declared, "to have any to *him*!"

"Well, he was, after all, one's oldest, one's earliest friend. I'm not in such bad case—I do go out; and I want to do the decent thing. The fact remains that we never broke—we always kept together."

"Yes indeed," she laughed in her bitterness, "he always took care of that! He never recognised you, but he never let you go. You kept him up, and he kept you down. He used you, to the last drop he could squeeze, and left you the only one to wonder, in your incredible idealism and your incorrigible modesty, how on earth such an idiot made his way. He made his way on your back. You put it candidly to others—'What in the world was his gift?' And others are such gaping idiots that they too haven't the least idea. *You* were his gift!"

"And you're mine, my dear!" her husband, pressing her to him, more resignedly laughed. He went down the next day by "special" to the interment, which took place on the great man's own property, in the great man's own church. But he went alone—that is in a numerous and distinguished party, the flower of the unanimous, gregarious demonstration; his wife had no wish to accompany him, though she was anxious while he was absent. She passed the time uneasily, watching the weather and fearing the cold; she roamed from room to room, pausing vaguely at dull windows, and before he came back she had thought of many things. It was as if, while he saw the great man buried, she also, by herself, in the contracted home of their later years, stood before an open grave. She lowered into it, with her weak hands, the heavy past and all their common dead dreams and accumulated ashes. The pomp surrounding Lord Northmore's extinction made her feel more than ever that it was not Warren who had made anything pay. He had been always what he was still, the cleverest man and the hardest worker she knew; but what was there, at fifty-seven, as the vulgar said, to "show" for it all but his wasted genius, his ruined health and his paltry pension? It was the term of comparison conveniently given her by his happy rival's now foreshortened splendour that fixed these things in her eye. It was as happy rivals to their own flat union that she always had thought of the Northmore pair; the two men, at least, having started together, after the University, shoulder to shoulder and with—superficially speaking—much the same outfit of preparation, ambition and opportunity. They had begun at the same point and wanting the same things—only wanting them in such different ways. Well, the dead man had wanted them in the way that got them; had got too, in his peerage, for instance, those Warren had never wanted: there was nothing else to be said. There was nothing else, and yet, in her sombre, her strangely apprehensive solitude at this hour, she said much more than I can tell. It all came to this—that there had been, somewhere and somehow, a wrong. Warren was the one who should have succeeded. But she was the one person who knew it now, the single other person having descended, with *his* knowledge, to the tomb.

She sat there, she roamed there, in the waiting greyness of her small London house, with a deepened sense of the several odd knowledges that had flourished in their company of three. Warren had always known everything and, with his easy power—in nothing so high as for indifference—had never cared. John Northmore had known, for he had, years and years before, told her so; and thus had had a reason the more—in addition to not believing her stupid—for guessing at her view. She lived back; she lived it over; she had it all there in her hand. John Northmore had known her first, and how he had wanted to marry her the fat little bundle of his love-letters still survived to tell. He had introduced Warren Hope to her—quite by accident and because, at the time they had chambers together, he couldn't help it: that was the one thing he *had* done for them. Thinking of it now, she perhaps saw how much he might conscientiously have considered that it disburdened him of more. Six months later she had accepted Warren, and for just the reason the absence of which had determined her treatment of his friend. She had believed in his future. She held that John Northmore had never afterwards remitted the effort to ascertain the degree in which she felt herself "sold." But, thank God, she had never shown him.

Her husband came home with a chill, and she put him straight to bed. For a week, as she hovered near him, they only looked deep things at each other; the point was too quickly passed at which she could bearably have said "I told you so!" That his late patron should never have had difficulty in making *him* pay was certainly no marvel. But it was indeed a little too much, after all, that he should have made him pay with his life. This was what it had come to—she was sure, now, from the first. Congestion of the lungs, that night, declared itself, and on the morrow, sickeningly, she was face to face with pneumonia. It was more than—with all that had gone before—they could meet. Warren Hope ten days later succumbed. Tenderly, divinely as he loved her, she felt his surrender, through all the anguish, as an unspeakable part of the sublimity of indifference into which his hapless history had finally flowered. "His easy power, his easy power!"—her passion had never yet found such relief in that simple, secret phrase for him. He was so proud, so fine and so flexible, that to fail a little had been as bad for him as to fail much; therefore he had opened the flood-gates wide—had thrown, as the saying was, the helve after the hatchet. He had amused himself with seeing what the devouring world would take. Well, it had taken all.

II

But it was after he had gone that his name showed as written in water. What had he left? He had only left *her* and her grey desolation, her lonely piety and her sore, unresting rebellion.

Sometimes, when a man died, it did something for him that life had not done; people, after a little, on one side or the other, discovered and named him, annexing him to their flag. But the sense of having lost Warren Hope appeared not in the least to have quickened the world's wit; the sharper pang for his widow indeed sprang just from the commonplace way in which he was spoken of as known. She received letters enough, when it came to that, for of course, personally, he had been liked; the newspapers were fairly copious and perfectly stupid; the three or four societies, "learned" and other, to which he had belonged, passed resolutions of regret and condolence, and the three or four colleagues about whom he himself used to be most amusing stammered eulogies; but almost anything, really, would have been better for her than the general understanding that the occasion had been met. Two or three solemn noodles in "administrative circles" wrote her that she must have been gratified at the unanimity of regret, the implication being clearly that she was ridiculous if she were not. Meanwhile what she felt was that she could have borne well enough his not being noticed at all; what she couldn't bear was this treatment of him as a minor celebrity. He was, in economics, in the higher politics, in philosophic history, a splendid unestimated genius, or he was nothing. He wasn't, at any rate—heaven forbid!—a "notable figure." The waters, none the less, closed over him as over Lord Northmore; which was precisely, as time went on, the fact she found it hardest to accept. That personage, the week after his death, without an hour of reprieve, the place swept as clean of him as a hall, lent for a charity, of the tables and booths of a three-days' bazaar—that personage had gone straight to the bottom, dropped like a crumpled circular into the waste-basket. Where then was the difference?—if the end *was* the end for each alike? For Warren it should have been properly the beginning.

During the first six months she wondered what she could herself do, and had much of the time the sense of walking by some swift stream on which an object dear to her was floating out to sea. All her instinct was to keep up with it, not to lose sight of it, to hurry along the bank and reach in advance some point from which she could stretch forth and catch and save it. Alas, it only floated and floated; she held it in sight, for the stream was long, but no convenient projection offered itself to the rescue. She ran, she watched, she lived with her great fear; and all the while, as the distance to the sea diminished, the current visibly increased. At the last, to do anything, she must hurry. She went into his papers, she ransacked his drawers; something of that sort, at least, she might do. But there were difficulties, the case was special; she lost herself in the labyrinth, and her competence was questioned; two or three friends to whose judgment she appealed struck her as tepid, even as cold, and publishers, when sounded—most of all in fact the house through which his three or four important volumes had been given to the world—showed an absence of eagerness for a collection of literary remains. It was only now that she fully understood how remarkably little the three or four important volumes had "done." He had successfully kept that from her, as he had kept other things she might have ached at: to handle his notes and memoranda was to come at every turn, in the wilderness, the wide desert, upon the footsteps of his scrupulous soul. But she had at last to accept the truth that it was only for herself, her own relief, she must follow him. His work, unencouraged and interrupted, failed of a final form: there would have been nothing to offer but fragments of fragments. She felt, all the same, in recognising this, that she abandoned him; he died for her at that hour over again.

The hour moreover happened to coincide with another hour, so that the two mingled their bitterness. She received a note from Lady Northmore, announcing a desire to gather in and publish his late lordship's letters, so numerous and so interesting, and inviting Mrs. Hope, as a more than probable depositary, to be so good as to contribute to the project those addressed to her husband. This gave her a start of more kinds than one. The long comedy of his late lordship's greatness was *not* then over? The monument was to be built to him that she had but now schooled herself to regard as impossible for his defeated friend? Everything was to break out afresh, the comparisons, the contrasts, the conclusions so invidiously in his favour?—the business all cleverly managed to place him in the light and keep every one else in the shade? Letters?—had

John Northmore indited three lines that could, at that time of day, be of the smallest consequence? Whose idea was such a publication, and what infatuated editorial patronage could the family have secured? She of course didn't know, but she should be surprised if there were material. Then it came to her, on reflection, that editors and publishers must of course have flocked—his star would still rule. Why shouldn't he make his letters pay in death as he had made them pay in life? Such as they were they *had* paid. They would be a tremendous success. She thought again of her husband's rich, confused relics—thought of the loose blocks of marble that could only lie now where they had fallen; after which, with one of her deep and frequent sighs, she took up anew Lady Northmore's communication.

His letters to Warren, kept or not kept, had never so much as occurred to her. Those to herself were buried and safe—she knew where her hand would find them; but those to herself her correspondent had carefully not asked for and was probably unaware of the existence of. They belonged moreover to that phase of the great man's career that was distinctly—as it could only be called—previous: previous to the greatness, to the proper subject of the volume, and, in especial, to Lady Northmore. The faded fat packet lurked still where it had lurked for years; but she could no more to-day have said why she had kept it than why—though he knew of the early episode—she had never mentioned her preservation of it to Warren. This last circumstance certainly absolved her from mentioning it to Lady Northmore, who, no doubt, knew of the episode too. The odd part of the matter was, at any rate, that her retention of these documents had not been an accident. She had obeyed a dim instinct or a vague calculation. A calculation of what? She couldn't have told: it had operated, at the back of her head, simply as a sense that, not destroyed, the complete little collection made for safety. But for whose, just heaven? Perhaps she should still see; though nothing, she trusted, would occur requiring her to touch the things or to read them over. She wouldn't have touched them or read them over for the world.

She had not as yet, at all events, overhauled those receptacles in which the letters Warren kept would have accumulated; and she had her doubts of their containing any of Lord Northmore's. Why should he have kept any? Even she herself had had more reasons. Was his lordship's later epistolary manner supposed to be good, or of the kind that, on any grounds, prohibited the waste-basket or the fire? Warren had lived in a deluge of documents, but these perhaps he might have regarded as contributions to contemporary history. None the less, surely, he wouldn't have stored up many. She began to look, in cupboards, boxes, drawers yet unvisited, and she had her surprises both as to what he had kept and as to what he hadn't. Every word of her own was there—every note that, in occasional absence, he had ever had from her. Well, that matched happily enough her knowing just where to put her finger on every note that, on such occasions, she herself had received. *Their* correspondence at least was complete. But so, in fine, on one side, it gradually appeared, was Lord Northmore's. The superabundance of these missives had not been sacrificed by her husband, evidently, to any passing convenience; she judged more and more that he had preserved every scrap; and she was unable to conceal from herself that she was—she scarce knew why—a trifle disappointed. She had not quite unhopefully, even though vaguely, seen herself writing to Lady Northmore that, to her great regret and after an exhausting search, she could find nothing at all.

She found, alas, in fact, everything. She was conscientious and she hunted to the end, by which time one of the tables quite groaned with the fruits of her quest. The letters appeared moreover to have been cared for and roughly classified—she should be able to consign them to the family in excellent order. She made sure, at the last, that she had overlooked nothing, and then, fatigued and distinctly irritated, she prepared to answer in a sense so different from the answer she had, as might have been said, planned. Face to face with her note, however, she found she couldn't write it; and, not to be alone longer with the pile on the table, she presently went out of the room. Late in the evening—just before going to bed— she came back, almost as if she hoped there might have been since the afternoon some pleasant intervention in the interest of her distaste. Mightn't it have magically happened that her discovery was a mistake?—that the letters were either not there or were, after all, somebody's else? Ah, they *were* there, and as she raised her lighted candle in the dusk the pile on the table squared itself with insolence. On this, poor lady, she had for an hour her temptation.

It was obscure, it was absurd; all that could be said of it was that it was, for the moment, extreme. She saw herself, as she circled round the table, writing with perfect impunity: "Dear Lady Northmore, I have hunted high and low and have found nothing whatever. My husband evidently, before his death, destroyed everything. I'm *so* sorry—I should have liked so much to help you. Yours most truly." She should have only, on the morrow, privately and resolutely to annihilate the heap, and those words would remain an account of the matter that nobody was in a position to challenge. What good it would do her?—was *that* the question? It would do her the good that it would make poor Warren seem to have been just a little less used and duped. This, in her mood, would ease her off. Well, the temptation was real; but so, she after a while felt, were other things. She sat down at midnight to her note. "Dear Lady Northmore, I am happy to say I have found a great deal—my husband appears to have been so careful to keep everything. I have a mass at your disposition if you can conveniently send. So glad to be able to help your work. Yours most truly." She stepped out as she was and dropped the letter into the nearest pillar-box. By noon the next day the table had, to her relief, been cleared. Her ladyship sent a responsible servant—her butler, in a four-wheeler, with a large japanned box.

III

After this, for a twelvemonth, there were frequent announcements and allusions. They came to her from every side, and there were hours at which the air, to her imagination, contained almost nothing else. There had been, at an early stage, immediately after Lady Northmore's communication to her, an official appeal, a circular *urbi et orbi*, reproduced, applauded, commented in every newspaper, desiring all possessors of letters to remit them without delay to the family. The family, to do it justice, rewarded the sacrifice freely—so far as it was a reward to keep the world informed of the rapid prog-ress of the work. Material had shown itself more copious than was to have been conceived. Interesting as the imminent vol-umes had naturally been expected to prove, those who had been favoured with a glimpse of their contents already felt warranted in promising the public an unprecedented treat. They would throw upon certain sides of the writer's mind and career lights hitherto unsuspected. Lady Northmore, deeply indebted for favours received, begged to renew her solicita-tion; gratifying as the response had been, it was believed that, particularly in connection with several dates, which were given, a residuum of buried treasure might still be looked for.

Mrs. Hope saw, she felt, as time went on, fewer and fewer people; yet her circle was even now not too narrow for her to hear it blown about that Thompson and Johnson had "been asked." Conversation in the London world struck her for a time as almost confined to such questions and such answers. "Have *you* been asked?" "Oh yes—rather. Months ago. And you?" The whole place was under contribution, and the strik-ing thing was that being asked had been clearly accompanied, in every case, with the ability to respond. The spring had but to be touched—millions of letters flew out. Ten volumes, at such a rate, Mrs. Hope mused, would not exhaust the supply. She mused a great deal—did nothing but muse; and, strange as this may at first appear, it was inevitable that one of the final results of her musing should be a principle of doubt. It could only seem possible, in view of such unanimity, that she should, after all, have been mistaken. It *was* then, to the gen-eral sense, the great departed's, a reputation sound and safe. It wasn't he who had been at fault—it was her silly self, still burdened with the fallibility of Being. He had been a giant then, and the letters would triumphantly show it. She had looked only at the envelopes of those she had surrendered, but she was prepared for anything. There was the fact, not to be blinked, of Warren's own marked testimony. The attitude of others was but *his* attitude; and she sighed as she perceived him in this case, for the only time in his life, on the side of the chattering crowd.

She was perfectly aware that her obsession had run away with her, but as Lady Northmore's publication really loomed

into view—it was now definitely announced for March, and
they were in January—her pulses quickened so that she found
herself, in the long nights, mostly lying awake. It was in one
of these vigils that, suddenly, in the cold darkness, she felt the
brush of almost the only thought that, for many a month, had
not made her wince; the effect of which was that she bounded
out of bed with a new felicity. Her impatience flashed, on the
spot, up to its maximum—she could scarce wait for day to
give herself to action. Her idea was neither more nor less than
immediately to collect and put forth the letters of *her* hero.
She would publish her husband's own—glory be to God!—
and she even wasted none of her time in wondering why she
had waited. She *had* waited—all too long; yet it was perhaps
no more than natural that, for eyes sealed with tears and a
heart heavy with injustice, there should not have been an instant vision of where her remedy lay. She thought of it already
as her remedy—though she would probably have found an
awkwardness in giving a name, publicly, to her wrong. It was
a wrong to feel, but not, doubtless, to talk about. And lo,
straightway, the balm had begun to drop: the balance would
so soon be even. She spent all that day in reading over her
own old letters, too intimate and too sacred—oh, unluckily!—
to figure in her project, but pouring wind, nevertheless, into
its sails and adding magnificence to her presumption. She had
of course, with separation, all their years, never frequent and
never prolonged, known her husband as a correspondent
much less than others; still, these relics constituted a property—she was surprised at their number—and testified hugely
to his inimitable gift.

He was a letter-writer if you liked—natural, witty, various,
vivid, playing, with the idlest, lightest hand, up and down the
whole scale. His easy power—his easy power: everything that
brought him back brought back that. The most numerous
were of course the earlier, and the series of those during their
engagement, witnesses of their long probation, which were
rich and unbroken; so full indeed and so wonderful that she
fairly groaned at having to defer to the common measure of
married modesty. There was discretion, there was usage, there
was taste; but she would fain have flown in their face. If there
were pages too intimate to publish, there were too many

others too rare to suppress. Perhaps after her death——! It not only pulled her up, the happy thought of that liberation alike for herself and for her treasure, making her promise herself straightway to arrange: it quickened extremely her impatience for the term of her mortality, which would leave a free field to the justice she invoked. Her great resource, however, clearly, would be the friends, the colleagues, the private admirers to whom he had written for years, to whom she had known him to write, and many of whose own letters, by no means remarkable, she had come upon in her recent sortings and siftings. She drew up a list of these persons and immediately wrote to them or, in cases in which they had passed away, to their widows, children, representatives; reminding herself in the process not disagreeably, in fact quite inspiringly, of Lady Northmore. It had struck her that Lady Northmore took, somehow, a good deal for granted; but this idea failed, oddly enough, to occur to her in regard to Mrs. Hope. It was indeed with her ladyship she began, addressing her exactly in the terms of this personage's own appeal, every word of which she remembered.

Then she waited, but she had not, in connection with that quarter, to wait long. "Dear Mrs. Hope, I have hunted high and low and have found nothing whatever. My husband evidently, before his death, destroyed everything. I'm so sorry— I should have liked so much to help you. Yours most truly." This was all Lady Northmore wrote, without the grace of an allusion to the assistance she herself had received; though even in the first flush of amazement and resentment our friend recognised the odd identity of form between her note and another that had never been written. She was answered as she had, in the like case, in her one evil hour, dreamed of answering. But the answer was not over with this—it had still to flow in, day after day, from every other source reached by her question. And day after day, while amazement and resentment deepened, it consisted simply of three lines of regret. Everybody had looked, and everybody had looked in vain. Everybody would have been so glad, but everybody was reduced to being, like Lady Northmore, so sorry. Nobody could find anything, and nothing, it was therefore to be gathered, had been kept. Some of these informants were more prompt than others, but all replied in time, and the business went on for a month, at the end of which the poor woman, stricken, chilled to the heart, accepted perforce her situation and turned her face to the wall. In this position, as it were, she remained for days, taking heed of nothing and only feeling and nursing her wound. It was a wound the more cruel for having found her so unguarded. From the moment her remedy had been whispered to her, she had not had an hour of doubt, and the beautiful side of it had seemed that it was, above all, so easy. The strangeness of the issue was even greater than the pain. Truly it was a world *pour rire*, the world in which John Northmore's letters were classed and labelled for posterity and Warren Hope's kindled fires. All sense, all measure of anything, could only leave one—leave one indifferent and dumb. There was nothing to be done—the show was upside-down. John Northmore was immortal and Warren Hope was damned. And for herself, she was finished. She was beaten. She leaned thus, motionless, muffled, for a time of which, as I say, she took no account; then at last she was reached by a great sound that made her turn her veiled head. It was the report of the appearance of Lady Northmore's volumes.

IV

This was a great noise indeed, and all the papers, that day, were particularly loud with it. It met the reader on the threshold, and the work was everywhere the subject of a "leader" as well as of a review. The reviews moreover, she saw at a glance, overflowed with quotation; it was enough to look at two or three sheets to judge of the enthusiasm. Mrs. Hope looked at the two or three that, for confirmation of the single one she habitually received, she caused, while at breakfast, to be purchased; but her attention failed to penetrate further; she couldn't, she found, face the contrast between the pride of the Northmores on such a morning and her own humiliation. The papers brought it too sharply home; she pushed them away and, to get rid of them, not to feel their presence, left the house early. She found pretexts for remaining out; it was as if there had been a cup prescribed for her to drain, yet she could put off the hour of the ordeal. She filled the time as she might; bought things, in shops, for which she had no use, and called on friends for whom she had no taste. Most of her friends, at present, were reduced to that category, and she had to choose, for visits, the houses guiltless, as she might have said, of her husband's blood. She couldn't speak to the people who had answered in such dreadful terms her late circular; on the other hand the people out of its range were such as would also be stolidly unconscious of Lady Northmore's publication and from whom the sop of sympathy could be but circuitously extracted. As she had lunched at a pastrycook's, so she stopped out to tea, and the March dusk had fallen when she got home. The first thing she then saw in her lighted hall was a large neat package on the table; whereupon she knew before approaching it that Lady Northmore had sent her the book. It had arrived, she learned, just after her going out; so that, had she not done this, she might have spent the day with it. She now quite understood her prompt instinct of flight. Well, flight had helped her, and the touch of the great indifferent general life. She would at last face the music.

She faced it, after dinner, in her little closed drawing-room, unwrapping the two volumes—*The Public and Private Correspondence of the Right Honourable &c., &c.*—and looking well, first, at the great escutcheon on the purple cover and at the various portraits within, so numerous that wherever she opened she came on one. It had not been present to her before that he was so perpetually "sitting," but he figured in every phase and in every style, and the gallery was enriched with views of his successive residences, each one a little grander than the last. She had ever, in general, found that, in portraits, whether of the known or the unknown, the eyes seemed to seek and to meet her own; but John Northmore everywhere looked straight away from her, quite as if he had been in the room and were unconscious of acquaintance. The effect of this was, oddly enough, so sharp that at the end of ten minutes she found herself sinking into his text as if she had been a stranger and beholden, vulgarly and accidentally, to one of the libraries.

She had been afraid to plunge, but from the moment she got in she was—to do every one, all round, justice—thoroughly held. She sat there late, and she made so many reflections and discoveries that—as the only way to put it—she passed from mystification to stupefaction. Her own contribution had been almost exhaustively used; she had counted Warren's letters before sending them and perceived now that scarce a dozen were not all there—a circumstance explaining to her Lady Northmore's present. It was to these pages she had turned first, and it was as she hung over them that her stupefaction dawned. It took, in truth, at the outset, a particular form—the form of a sharpened wonder at Warren's unnatural piety. Her original surprise had been keen—when she had tried to take reasons for granted; but her original surprise was as nothing to her actual bewilderment. The letters to Warren had been practically, she judged, for the family, the great card; yet if the great card made only that figure, what on earth was one to think of the rest of the pack?

She pressed on, at random, with a sense of rising fever; she trembled, almost panting, not to be sure too soon; but wherever she turned she found the prodigy spread. The letters to Warren were an abyss of inanity; the others followed suit as they could; the book was surely then a sandy desert, the publication a theme for mirth. She so lost herself, as her perception of the scale of the mistake deepened, in uplifting visions, that when her parlour-maid, at eleven o'clock, opened the door she almost gave the start of guilt surprised. The girl, withdrawing for the night, had come but to say so, and her mistress, supremely wide-awake and with remembrance kindled, appealed to her, after a blank stare, with intensity. "What have you done with the papers?"

"The papers, ma'am?"

"All those of this morning—don't tell me you've destroyed them! Quick, quick—bring them back." The young woman, by a rare chance, had not destroyed them; she presently reappeared with them, neatly folded; and Mrs. Hope, dismissing her with benedictions, had at last, in a few minutes, taken the time of day. She saw her impression portentously reflected in the public prints. It was not then the illusion of her jealousy—it was the triumph, unhoped for, of her justice. The reviewers observed a decorum, but, frankly, when one came to look, their stupefaction matched her own. What she had taken in the morning for enthusiasm proved mere perfunctory attention, unwarned in advance and seeking an issue for its mystification. The question was, if one liked, asked civilly, but it was asked, none the less, all round: "What *could* have made Lord Northmore's family take him for a letter-writer?" Pompous and ponderous, yet loose and obscure, he managed, by a trick of his own, to be both slipshod and stiff. Who, in such a case, had been primarily responsible, and under what strangely belated advice had a group of persons destitute of wit themselves been thus deplorably led thus astray? With fewer accomplices in the preparation, it might almost have been assumed that they had been dealt with by practical jokers.

They had at all events committed an error of which the most merciful thing to say was that, as founded on loyalty, it was touching. These things, in the welcome offered, lay perhaps not quite on the face, but they peeped between the lines and would force their way through on the morrow. The long quotations given were quotations marked Why?— "Why," in other words, as interpreted by Mrs. Hope, "drag to light such helplessness of expression? why give the text of his dulness and the proof of his fatuity?" The victim of the error had certainly been, in his way and day, a useful and remarkable person, but almost any other evidence of the fact might more happily have been adduced. It rolled over her, as she paced her room in the small hours, that the wheel had come full circle. There was after all a rough justice. The monument that had over-darkened her was reared, but it would be within a week the opportunity of every humourist, the derision of intelligent London. Her husband's strange share in it continued, that night, between dreams and vigils, to puzzle her, but light broke with her final waking, which was comfortably late. She opened her eyes to it, and, as it stared straight into them, she greeted it with the first laugh that had for a long time passed her lips. How could she, idiotically, not have guessed? Warren, playing insidiously the part of a guardian, had done what he had done on purpose! He had acted to an end long foretasted, and the end—the full taste—had come.

V

It was after this, none the less—after the other organs of criticism, including the smoking-rooms of the clubs, the lobbies of the House and the dinner-tables of everywhere, had duly embodied their reserves and vented their irreverence, and the unfortunate two volumes had ranged themselves, beyond appeal, as a novelty insufficiently curious and prematurely stale— it was when this had come to pass that Mrs. Hope really felt how beautiful her own chance would now have been and how sweet her revenge. The success of *her* volumes, for the inevitability of which nobody had had an instinct, would have been as great as the failure of Lady Northmore's, for the inevitability of which everybody had had one. She read over and over her letters and asked herself afresh if the confidence that had preserved *them* might not, at such a crisis, in spite of everything, justify itself. Did not the discredit to English wit, as it were, proceeding from the uncorrected attribution to an established public character of such mediocrity of thought and form, really demand, for that matter, some such redemptive stroke as the appearance of a collection of masterpieces gathered from a similar walk? To have such a collection under one's hand and yet sit and see one's self not use it was a torment through which she might well have feared to break down.

But there was another thing she might do, not redemptive indeed, but perhaps, after all, as matters were going, apposite. She fished out of their nook, after long years, the packet of John Northmore's epistles to herself, and, reading them over in the light of his later style, judged them to contain to the full the promise of that inimitability; felt that they would deepen the impression and that, in the way of the *inédit*, they constituted her supreme treasure. There was accordingly a terrible week for her in which she itched to put them forth. She composed mentally the preface, brief, sweet, ironic, representing her as prompted by an anxious sense of duty to a great reputation and acting upon the sight of laurels so lately gathered. There would naturally be difficulties; the documents were her own, but the family, bewildered, scared, suspicious, figured to her fancy as a dog with a dust-pan tied to its tail and ready for any dash to cover at the sound of the clatter of tin. They would have, she surmised, to be consulted, or, if not consulted, would put in an injunction; yet of the two courses, that of scandal braved for the man she had rejected drew her on, while the charm of this vision worked, still further than that of delicacy over-ridden for the man she had married.

The vision closed round her and she lingered on the idea—fed, as she handled again her faded fat packet, by re-perusals more richly convinced. She even took opinions as to the interference open to her old friend's relatives; took, in fact, from this time on, many opinions; went out anew, picked up old threads, repaired old ruptures, resumed, as it was called, her place in society. She had not been for years so seen of men as during the few weeks that followed the abasement of the Northmores. She called, in particular, on every one she had cast out after the failure of her appeal. Many of these persons figured as Lady Northmore's contributors, the unwitting agents of the unprecedented exposure; they having, it was sufficiently clear, acted in dense good faith. Warren, foreseeing and calculating, might have the benefit of such subtlety, but it was not for any one else. With every one else—for they did, on facing her, as she said to herself, look like fools—she made inordinately free; putting right and left the question of what, in the past years, they, or their progenitors, could have been thinking of. "What on earth had you in mind, and where, among you, were the rudiments of intelligence, when you burnt up my husband's priceless letters and clung as if for salvation to Lord Northmore's? You see how you have been saved!" The weak explanations, the imbecility, as she judged it, of the reasons given, were so much balm to her wound. The great balm, however, she kept to the last: she would go to see Lady Northmore only when she had exhausted all other comfort. That resource would be as supreme as the treasure of the fat packet. She finally went and, by a happy chance, if chance could ever be happy in such a house, was received. She remained half an hour—there were other persons present, and, on rising to go, felt that she was satisfied. She had taken in what she desired, had sounded what she saw; only, unexpectedly, something had overtaken her more absolute than the hard need she had obeyed or the vindictive advantage she had cherished. She had counted on herself for almost anything but for pity of these people, yet it was in pity that, at the end of ten minutes, she felt everything else dissolve.

They were suddenly, on the spot, transformed for her by the depth of their misfortune, and she saw them, the great Northmores, as—of all things—consciously weak and flat. She neither made nor encountered an allusion to volumes published or frustrated; and so let her arranged inquiry die away that when, on separation, she kissed her wan sister in widowhood, it was not with the kiss of Judas. She had meant to ask lightly if she mightn't have *her* turn at editing; but the renunciation with which she re-entered her house had formed itself before she left the room. When she got home indeed she at first only wept—wept for the commonness of failure and the strangeness of life. Her tears perhaps brought her a sense of philosophy; it was all as broad as it was long. When they were spent, at all events, she took out for the last time the faded fat packet. Sitting down by a receptacle daily emptied for the benefit of the dustman, she destroyed, one by one, the gems of the collection in which each piece had been a gem. She tore up, to the last scrap, Lord Northmore's letters. It would never be known now, as regards this series, either that they had been hoarded or that they had been sacrificed. And she was content so to let it rest. On the following day she began another task. She took out her husband's and attacked the business of transcription. She copied them piously, tenderly, and, for the purpose to which she now found herself settled, judged almost no omissions imperative. By the time they should be published——! She shook her head, both knowingly and resignedly, as to criticism so remote. When her transcript was finished she sent it to a printer to set up, and then, after receiving and correcting proof, and with every precaution for secrecy, had a single copy struck off and the type, under her eyes, dispersed. Her last act but one—or rather perhaps but two—was to put these sheets, which, she was pleased to find, would form a volume of three hundred pages,

carefully away. Her next was to add to her testamentary instrument a definite provision for the issue, after her death, of
such a volume. Her last was to hope that death would come
in time.

The Third Person

WHEN, a few years since, two good ladies, previously not intimate nor indeed more than slightly acquainted, found themselves domiciled together in the small but ancient town of Marr, it was as a result, naturally, of special considerations. They bore the same name and were second cousins; but their paths had not hitherto crossed; there had not been coincidence of age to draw them together; and Miss Frush, the more mature, had spent much of her life abroad. She was a bland, shy, sketching person, whom fate had condemned to a monotony—triumphing over variety—of Swiss and Italian *pensions*, in any one of which, with her well-fastened hat, her gauntlets and her stout boots, her camp-stool, her sketch-book, her Tauchnitz novel, she would have served with peculiar propriety as a frontispiece to the natural history of the English old maid. She would have struck you indeed, poor Miss Frush, as so happy an instance of the type that you would perhaps scarce have been able to equip her with the dignity of the individual. This was what she enjoyed, however, for those brought nearer—a very insistent identity, once even of prettiness, but which now, blanched and bony, timid and inordinately queer, with its utterance all vague interjection and its aspect all eyeglass and teeth, might be acknowledged without inconvenience and deplored without reserve. Miss Amy, her kinswoman, who, ten years her junior, showed a different figure—such as, oddly enough, though formed almost wholly in English air, might have appeared much more to betray a foreign influence—Miss Amy was brown, brisk and expressive: when really young she had even been pronounced showy. She had an innocent vanity on the subject of her foot, a member which she somehow regarded as a guarantee of her wit, or at least of her good taste. Even had it not been pretty she flattered herself it would have been shod: she would never—no, never, like Susan—have given it up. Her bright brown eye was comparatively bold, and she had accepted Susan once for all as a frump. She even thought her, and silently deplored her as, a goose. But she was none the less herself a lamb.

255

They had benefited, this innocuous pair, under the will of an old aunt, a prodigiously ancient gentlewoman, of whom, in her later time, it had been given them, mainly by the office of others, to see almost nothing; so that the little property they came in for had the happy effect of a windfall. Each, at least, pretended to the other that she had never dreamed—as in truth there had been small encouragement for dreams in the sad character of what they now spoke of as the late lady's "dreadful *entourage*." Terrorised and deceived, as they considered, by her own people, Mrs. Frush was scantily enough to have been counted on for an act of almost inspired justice. The good luck of her husband's nieces was that she had really outlived, for the most part, their ill-wishers and so, at the very last, had died without the blame of diverting fine Frush property from fine Frush use. Property quite of her own she had done as she liked with; but she had pitied poor expatriated Susan and had remembered poor unhusbanded Amy, though lumping them together perhaps a little roughly in her final provision. Her will directed that, should no other arrangement be more convenient to her executors, the old house at Marr might be sold for their joint advantage. What befell, however, in the event, was that the two legatees, advised in due course, took an early occasion—and quite without concert—to judge their prospects on the spot. They arrived at Marr, each on her own side, and they were so pleased with Marr that they remained. So it was that they met: Miss Amy, accompanied by the office-boy of the local solicitor, presented herself at the door of the house to ask admittance of the caretaker. But when the door opened it offered to sight not the caretaker, but an unexpected, unexpecting lady in a very old waterproof, who held a long-handled eyeglass very much as a child holds a rattle. Miss Susan, already in the field, roaming, prying, meditating in the absence on an errand of the woman in charge, offered herself in this manner as in settled possession; and it was on that idea that, through the eyeglass, the cousins viewed each other with some penetration even before Amy came in. Then at last when Amy did come in it was not, any more than Susan, to go out again.

It would take us too far to imagine what might have happened had Mrs. Frush made it a condition of her benevolence that the subjects of it should inhabit, should live at peace together, under the roof she left them; but certain it is that as they stood there they had at the same moment the same unprompted thought. Each became aware on the spot that the dear old house itself was exactly what she, and exactly what the other, wanted; it met in perfection their longing for a quiet harbour and an assured future; each, in short, was willing to take the other in order to get the house. It was therefore not sold; it was made, instead, their own, as it stood, with the dead lady's extremely "good" old appurtenances not only undisturbed and undivided, but piously reconstructed and infinitely admired, the agents of her testamentary purpose rejoicing meanwhile to see the business so simplified. They might have had their private doubts—or their wives might have; might cynically have predicted the sharpest of quarrels, before three months were out, between the deluded yokefellows, and the dissolution of the partnership with every circumstance of recrimination. All that need be said is that such prophets would have prophesied vulgarly. The Misses Frush were not vulgar; they had drunk deep of the cup of singleness and found it prevailingly bitter; they were not unacquainted with solitude and sadness, and they recognised with due humility the supreme opportunity of their lives. By the end of three months, moreover, each knew the worst about the other. Miss Amy took her evening nap before dinner, an hour at which Miss Susan could never sleep—it was so odd; whereby Miss Susan took hers after that meal, just at the hour when Miss Amy was keenest for talk. Miss Susan, erect and unsupported, had feelings as to the way in which, in almost any posture that could pass for a seated one, Miss Amy managed to find a place in the small of her back for two out of the three sofa-cushions—a smaller place, obviously, than they had ever been intended to fit.

But when this was said all was said; they continued to have, on either side, the pleasant consciousness of a personal soil, not devoid of fragmentary ruins, to dig in. They had a theory that their lives had been immensely different, and each appeared now to the other to have conducted her career so perversely only that she should have an unfamiliar range of anecdote for her companion's ear. Miss Susan, at foreign *pen-*

sions, had met the Russian, the Polish, the Danish, and even
an occasional flower of the English, nobility, as well as many
of the most extraordinary Americans, who, as she said, had
made everything of her and with whom she had remained,
often, in correspondence; while Miss Amy, after all less conventional, at the end of long years of London, abounded in
reminiscences of literary, artistic and even—Miss Susan heard
it with bated breath—theatrical society, under the influence of
which she had written—there, it came out!—a novel that had
been anonymously published and a play that had been strikingly type-copied. Not the least charm, clearly, of this picturesque outlook at Marr would be the support that might be
drawn from it for getting back, as she hinted, with "general
society" bravely sacrificed, to "real work." She had in her
head hundreds of plots—with which the future, accordingly,
seemed to bristle for Miss Susan. The latter, on her side, was
only waiting for the wind to go down to take up again her
sketching. The wind at Marr was often high, as was natural
in a little old huddled, red-roofed, historic south-coast town
which had once been in a manner mistress, as the cousins
reminded each other, of the "Channel," and from which, high
and dry on its hilltop though it might be, the sea had not so
far receded as not to give, constantly, a taste of temper. Miss
Susan came back to English scenery with a small sigh of fondness to which the consciousness of Alps and Apennines only
gave more of a quaver; she had picked out her subjects and,
with her head on one side and a sense that they were easier
abroad, sat sucking her water-colour brush and nervously—
perhaps even a little inconsistently—waiting and hesitating.
What had happened was that they had, each for herself, re-
discovered the country; only Miss Amy, emergent from
Bloomsbury lodgings, spoke of it as primroses and sunsets,
and Miss Susan, rebounding from the Arno and the Reuss,
called it, with a shy, synthetic pride, simply England.

   The country was at any rate in the house with them as well
as in the little green girdle and in the big blue belt. It was in
the objects and relics that they handled together and wondered over, finding in them a ground for much inferred importance and invoked romance, stuffing large stories into very
small openings and pulling every faded bell-rope that might

jingle rustily into the past. They were still here in the presence, at all events, of their common ancestors, as to whom, more than ever before, they took only the best for granted. Was not the best, for that matter—the best, that is, of little melancholy, middling, disinherited Marr—seated in every stiff chair of the decent old house and stitched into the patchwork of every quaint old counterpane? Two hundred years of it squared themselves in the brown, panelled parlour, creaked patiently on the wide staircase and bloomed herbaceously in the red-walled garden. There was nothing any one had ever done or been at Marr that a Frush hadn't done it or been it. Yet they wanted more of a picture and talked themselves into the fancy of it; there were portraits—half a dozen, comparatively recent (they called 1800 comparatively recent,) and something of a trial to a descendant who had copied Titian at the Pitti; but they were curious of detail and would have liked to people a little more thickly their backward space, to set it up behind their chairs as a screen embossed with figures. They threw off theories and small imaginations, and almost conceived themselves engaged in researches; all of which made for pomp and circumstance. Their desire was to discover something, and, emboldened by the broader sweep of wing of her companion, Miss Susan herself was not afraid of discovering something bad. Miss Amy it was who had first remarked, as a warning, that this was what it might all lead to. It was she, moreover, to whom they owed the formula that, had anything *very* bad ever happened at Marr, they should be sorry if a Frush hadn't been in it. This was the moment at which Miss Susan's spirit had reached its highest point: she had declared, with her odd, breathless laugh, a prolonged, an alarmed or alarming gasp, that she should really be quite ashamed. And so they rested a while; not saying quite how far they were prepared to go in crime—not giving the matter a name. But there would have been little doubt for an observer that each supposed the other to mean that she not only didn't draw the line at murder, but stretched it so as to take in—well, gay deception. If Miss Susan could conceivably have asked whether Don Juan had ever touched at that port, Miss Amy would, to a certainty, have wanted to know by way of answer at what port he had *not* touched. It was only unfortunately true that no one of the portraits of gentlemen looked at all like him and no one of those of ladies suggested one of his victims.

At last, none the less, the cousins had a find, came upon a box of old odds and ends, mainly documentary; partly printed matter, newspapers and pamphlets yellow and grey with time, and, for the rest, epistolary—several packets of letters, faded, scarce decipherable, but clearly sorted for preservation and tied, with sprigged ribbon of a far-away fashion, into little groups. Marr, below ground, is solidly founded—underlaid with great straddling cellars, sound and dry, that are like the groined crypts of churches and that present themselves to the meagre modern conception as the treasure-chambers of stout merchants and bankers in the old bustling days. A recess in the thickness of one of the walls had yielded up, on resolute investigation—that of the local youth employed for odd jobs and who had happened to explore in this direction on his own account—a collection of rusty superfluities among which the small chest in question had been dragged to light. It produced of course an instant impression and figured as a discovery; though indeed as rather a deceptive one on its having, when forced open, nothing better to show, at the best, than a quantity of rather illegible correspondence. The good ladies had naturally had for the moment a fluttered hope of old golden guineas—a miser's hoard; perhaps even of a hatful of those foreign coins of old-fashioned romance, ducats, doubloons, pieces of eight, as are sometimes found to have come to hiding, from over seas, in ancient ports. But they had to accept their disappointment—which they sought to do by making the best of the papers, by agreeing, in other words, to regard them as wonderful. Well, they *were*, doubtless, wonderful; which didn't prevent them, however, from appearing to be, on superficial inspection, also rather a weary labyrinth. Baffling, at any rate, to Miss Susan's unpractised eyes, the little pale-ribboned packets were, for several evenings, round the fire, while she luxuriously dozed, taken in hand by Miss Amy; with the result that on a certain occasion when, toward nine o'clock, Miss Susan woke up, she found her fellow-labourer fast asleep. A slightly irritated confession of ignorance of the Gothic character was the further consequence, and the upshot of this, in turn, was the idea of appeal to Mr. Patten. Mr.

Patten was the vicar and was known to interest himself, as such, in the ancient annals of Marr; in addition to which—and to its being even held a little that his sense of the affairs of the hour was sometimes sacrificed to such inquiries—he was a gentleman with a humour of his own, a flushed face, a bushy eyebrow and a black wide-awake worn sociably askew. "He will tell us," said Amy Frush, "if there's anything in them."

"Yet if it should be," Susan suggested, "anything we mayn't like?"

"Well, that's just what I'm thinking of," returned Miss Amy in her offhand way. "If it's anything we shouldn't know——"

"We've only to tell him not to tell us? Oh, certainly," said mild Miss Susan. She took upon herself even to give him that warning when, on the invitation of our friends, Mr. Patten came to tea and to talk things over; Miss Amy sitting by and raising no protest, but distinctly promising herself that, whatever there might be to be known, and however objectionable, she would privately get it out of their initiator. She found herself already hoping that it *would* be something too bad for her cousin—too bad for any one else at all—to know, and that it most properly might remain between them. Mr. Patten, at sight of the papers, exclaimed, perhaps a trifle ambiguously, and by no means clerically, "My eye, what a lark!" and retired, after three cups of tea, in an overcoat bulging with his spoil.

II

At ten o'clock that evening the pair separated, as usual, on the upper landing, outside their respective doors, for the night; but Miss Amy had hardly set down her candle on her dressing-table before she was startled by an extraordinary sound, which appeared to proceed not only from her companion's room, but from her companion's throat. It was something she would have described, had she ever described it, as between a gurgle and a shriek, and it brought Amy Frush, after an interval of stricken stillness that gave her just time to say to herself "Some one under her bed!" breathlessly and bravely back to the landing. She had not reached it, however, before her neighbour, bursting in, met her and stayed her.

"There's some one in my room!"

They held each other. "But who?"

"A man."

"Under the bed?"

"No—just standing there."

They continued to hold each other, but they rocked. "Standing? Where? How?"

"Why, right in the middle—before my dressing-glass."

Amy's blanched face by this time matched her mate's, but its terror was enhanced by speculation. "To look at himself?"

"No—with his back to it. To look at *me*," poor Susan just audibly breathed. "To keep me off," she quavered. "In strange clothes—of another age; with his head on one side."

Amy wondered. "On one side?"

"Awfully!" the refugee declared while, clinging together, they sounded each other.

This, somehow, for Miss Amy, was the convincing touch; and on it, after a moment, she was capable of the effort of darting back to close her own door. "You'll remain then with me."

"Oh!" Miss Susan wailed with deep assent; quite, as if, had she been a slangy person, she would have ejaculated "Rather!" So they spent the night together; with the assumption thus marked, from the first, both that it would have been vain to confront their visitor as they didn't even pretend to each other that they would have confronted a housebreaker; and that by leaving the place at his mercy nothing worse could happen than had already happened. It was Miss Amy's approaching the door again as with intent ear and after a hush that had represented between them a deep and extraordinary inter-change—it was this that put them promptly face to face with the real character of the occurrence. "Ah," Miss Susan, still under her breath, portentously exclaimed, "it isn't any one——!"

"No"—her partner was already able magnificently to take her up. "It isn't any one——"

"Who can really hurt us"—Miss Susan completed her thought. And Miss Amy, as it proved, had been so indescrib-ably prepared that this thought, before morning, had, in the strangest, finest way, made for itself an admirable place with them. The person the elder of our pair had seen in her room was not—well, just simply was not any one in from outside. He was a different thing altogether. Miss Amy had felt it as soon as she heard her friend's cry and become aware of her commotion; as soon, at all events, as she saw Miss Susan's face. That was all—and there it was. There had been something hitherto wanting, they felt, to their small state and importance; it was present now, and they were as handsomely conscious of it as if they had previously missed it. The element in question, then, was a third person in their association, a hovering presence for the dark hours, a figure that with its head very much—too much—on one side, could be trusted to look at them out of unnatural places; yet only, it doubtless might be assumed, to look at them. They had it at last—had what was to be had in an old house where many, too many, things had happened, where the very walls they touched and floors they trod could have told secrets and named names, where every surface was a blurred mirror of life and death, of the endured, the remembered, the forgotten. Yes; the place was h—— but they stopped at sounding the word. And by morning, wonderful to say, they were used to it—had quite lived into it.

Not only this indeed, but they had their prompt theory. There was a connection between the finding of the box in the vault and the appearance in Miss Susan's room. The heavy air of the past had been stirred by the bringing to light of what had so long been hidden. The communication of the papers to Mr. Patten had had its effect. They faced each other in the morning at breakfast over the certainty that their queer roused inmate was the sign of the violated secret of these relics. No matter; for the sake of the secret they would put up with his attention; and—this, in them, was most beautiful of all—they must, though he was such an addition to their grandeur, keep him quite to themselves. Other people might hear of what was in the letters, but they should never hear of *him*. They were not afraid that either of the maids should see him— he was not a matter for maids. The question indeed was whether—should he keep it up long—they themselves would find that they could really live with him. Yet perhaps his keeping it up would be just what would make them indifferent.

They turned these things over, but spent the next nights together; and on the third day, in the course of their afternoon walk, descried at a distance the vicar, who, as soon as he saw them, waved his arms violently—either as a warning or as a joke—and came more than half-way to meet them. It was in the middle—or what passed for such—of the big, bleak, blank, melancholy square of Marr; a public place, as it were, of such an absurd capacity for a crowd; with the great ivy-mantled choir and stopped transept of the nobly-planned church telling of how many centuries ago it had, for its part, given up growing.

"Why, my dear ladies," cried Mr. Patten as he approached, "do you know what, of all things in the world, I seem to make out for you from your funny old letters?" Then as they waited, extremely on their guard now: "Neither more nor less, if you please, than that one of your ancestors in the last century— Mr. Cuthbert Frush, it would seem, by name—was hanged."

They never knew afterwards which of the two had first found composure—found even dignity—to respond. "And pray, Mr. Patten, for what?"

"Ah, that's just what I don't yet get hold of. But if you don't mind my digging away"—and the vicar's bushy, jolly brows turned from one of the ladies to the other—"I think I can run it to earth. They hanged, in those days, you know," he added as if he had seen something in their faces, "for almost any trifle!"

"Oh, I hope it wasn't for a trifle!" Miss Susan strangely tittered.

"Yes, of course one would like that, while he was about it— well, it had been, as they say," Mr. Patten laughed, "rather for a sheep than for a lamb!"

"Did they hang at that time for a sheep?" Miss Amy wonderingly asked.

It made their friend laugh again. "The question's whether *he* did! But we'll find out. Upon my word, you know, I quite want to myself. I'm awfully busy, but I think I can promise you that you shall hear. You *don't* mind?" he insisted.

"I think we could bear *anything*," said Miss Amy.

Miss Susan gazed at her, on this, as for reference and appeal. "And what is he, after all, at this time of day, *to* us?"

Her kinswoman, meeting the eyeglass fixedly, spoke with gravity. "Oh, an ancestor's always an ancestor."

"Well said and well felt, dear lady!" the vicar declared. "Whatever they may have done——"

"It isn't every one," Miss Amy replied, "that has them to be ashamed of."

"And we're not ashamed *yet*!" Miss Frush jerked out.

"Let me promise you then that you shan't be. Only, for I am busy," said Mr. Patten, "give me time."

"Ah, but we want the truth!" they cried with high emphasis as he quitted them. They were much excited now.

He answered by pulling up and turning round as short as if his professional character had been challenged. "Isn't it just in the truth—and the truth only—that I deal?"

This they recognised as much as his love of a joke, and so they were left there together in the pleasant, if slightly over-done, void of the square, which wore at moments the air of a conscious demonstration, intended as an appeal, of the shrink-age of the population of Marr to a solitary cat. They walked on after a little, but they waited till the vicar was ever so far away before they spoke again; all the more that their doing so must bring them once more to a pause. Then they had a long look. "Hanged!" said Miss Amy—yet almost exultantly.

This was, however, because it was not she who had seen. "That's why his head——" but Miss Susan faltered.

Her companion took it in. "Oh, has such a dreadful twist?"

"It *is* dreadful!" Miss Susan at last dropped, speaking as if she had been present at twenty executions.

There would have been no saying, at any rate, what it didn't evoke from Miss Amy. "It breaks their neck," she contributed after a moment.

Miss Susan looked away. "That's why, I suppose, the head turns so fearfully awry. It's a most peculiar effect."

So peculiar, it might have seemed, that it made them silent afresh. "Well then, I hope he killed some one!" Miss Amy broke out at last.

Her companion thought. "Wouldn't it depend on whom——?"

"No!" she returned with her characteristic briskness—a briskness that set them again into motion.

That Mr. Patten was tremendously busy was evident indeed, as even by the end of the week he had nothing more to impart. The whole thing meanwhile came up again—on the Sunday afternoon; as the younger Miss Frush had been quite confident that, from one day to the other, it must. They went inveterately to evening church, to the close of which supper was postponed; and Miss Susan, on this occasion, ready the first, patiently awaited her mate at the foot of the stairs. Miss Amy at last came down, buttoning a glove, rustling the tail of a frock and looking, as her kinswoman always thought, conspicuously young and smart. There was no one at Marr, she held, who dressed like her; and Miss Amy, it must be owned, had also settled to this view of Miss Susan, though taking it in a different spirit. Dusk had gathered, but our frugal pair were always tardy lighters, and the grey close of day, in which the elder lady, on a high-backed hall chair, sat with hands patiently folded, had for all cheer the subdued glow—always subdued—of the small fire in the drawing-room, visible through a door that stood open. Into the drawing-room Miss Amy passed in search of the prayer-book she had laid down there after morning church, and from it, after a minute, without this volume, she returned to her companion. There was something in her movement that spoke—spoke for a moment so largely that nothing more was said till, with a quick unanimity, they had got themselves straight out of the house. There, before the door, in the cold, still twilight of the winter's end, while the church bells rang and the windows of the great choir showed across the empty square faintly red, they had it out again. But it was Miss Susan herself, this time, who had to bring it.

"He's there?"

"Before the fire—with his back to it."

"Well, now you see!" Miss Susan exclaimed with elation and as if her friend had hitherto doubted her.

"Yes, I see—and what you mean." Miss Amy was deeply thoughtful.

"About his head?"

"It *is* on one side," Miss Amy went on. "It makes him——" she considered. But she faltered as if still in his presence.

"It makes him awful!" Miss Susan murmured. "The way," she softly moaned, "he looks at you!"

Miss Amy, with a glance, met this recognition. "Yes—doesn't he?" Then her eyes attached themselves to the red windows of the church. "But it means something."

"The Lord knows what it means!" her associate gloomily sighed. Then, after an instant, "Did he move?" Miss Susan asked.

"No—and *I* didn't."

"Oh, I did!" Miss Susan declared, recalling to her more precipitous retreat.

"I mean I took my time. I waited."

"To see him fade?"

Miss Amy for a moment said nothing. "He doesn't fade. That's *it*."

"Oh, then you did move!" her relative rejoined.

Again for a little she was silent. "One *has* to. But I don't know what really happened. Of course I came back to you. What I mean is that I took him thoroughly in. He's young," she added.

"But he's *bad*!" said Miss Susan.

"He's handsome!" Miss Amy brought out after a moment. And she showed herself even prepared to continue: "Splendidly."

" 'Splendidly'!—with his neck broken and with that terrible look?"

"It's just the look that makes him so. It's the wonderful eyes. They mean something," Amy Frush brooded.

She spoke with a decision of which Susan presently betrayed the effect. "And what do they mean?"

Her friend had stared again at the glimmering windows of St. Thomas of Canterbury. "That it's time we should get to church."

III

The curate that evening did duty alone; but on the morrow the vicar called and, as soon as he got into the room, let them again have it. "He was hanged for smuggling!"

They stood there before him almost cold in their surprise and diffusing an air in which, somehow, this misdemeanour sounded out as the coarsest of all. *"Smuggling?"* Miss Susan disappointedly echoed—as if it presented itself to the first chill of their apprehension that he had then only been vulgar.

"Ah, but they hanged for it freely, you know, and I was an idiot for not having taken it, in his case, for granted. If a man swung, hereabouts, it *was* mostly for that. Don't you know it's on that we stand here to-day, such as we are—on the fact of what our bold, bad forefathers were not afraid of? It's in the floors we walk on and under the roofs that cover us. They smuggled so hard that they never had time to do anything else; and if they broke a head not their own it was only in the awkwardness of landing their brandy-kegs. I mean, dear ladies," good Mr. Patten wound up, "no disrespect to *your* forefathers when I tell you that—as I've rather been supposing that, like all the rest of us, you were aware—they conveniently lived by it."

Miss Susan wondered—visibly almost doubted. "Gentle-folks?"

"It was the gentlefolks who were the worst."

"They must have been the bravest!" Miss Amy interjected. She had listened to their visitor's free explanation with a rapid return of colour. "And since if they lived by it they also died for it——"

"There's nothing at all to be said against them? I quite agree with you," the vicar laughed, "for all my cloth; and I even go so far as to say, shocking as you may think me, that we owe them, in our shabby little shrunken present, the sense of a bustling background, a sort of undertone of romance. They give us"—he humorously kept it up, verging perilously near, for his cloth, upon positive paradox—"our little handful of legend and our small possibility of ghosts." He paused an instant, with his lighter pulpit manner, but the ladies exchanged no look. They were in fact already, with an immense revulsion, carried quite as far away. "Every penny in the place, really, that hasn't been earned by subtler —not nobler—arts in our own virtuous time, and though it's a pity there are not more of 'em: every penny in the place was picked up, somehow, by a clever trick, and at the risk of your neck, when the backs of the king's officers were turned. It's shocking, you know, what I'm saying to you, and I wouldn't say it to every one, but I think of some of the shabby old things about us, that represent such pickings, with a sort of sneaking kindness—as of relics of our heroic age. What are we now? We were at any rate devils of fellows then!"

Susan Frush considered it all solemnly, struggling with the spell of this evocation. "But must we forget that they were wicked?"

"Never!" Mr. Patten laughed. "Thank you, dear friend, for reminding me. Only I'm worse than they!"

"But would you do it?"

"Murder a coastguard——?" The vicar scratched his head.

"I hope," said Miss Amy rather surprisingly, "you'd defend yourself." And she gave Miss Susan a superior glance. "*I* would!" she distinctly added.

Her companion anxiously took it up. "Would you defraud the revenue?"

Miss Amy hesitated but a moment; then with a strange laugh, which she covered, however, by turning instantly away, "Yes!" she remarkably declared.

Their visitor, at this, amused and amusing, eagerly seized her arm. "Then may I count on you on the stroke of midnight to help me——?"

"To help you——?"

"To land the last new Tauchnitz."

She met the proposal as one whose fancy had kindled, while her cousin watched them as if they had suddenly improvised a drawing-room charade. "A service of danger?"

"Under the cliff—when you see the lugger stand in!"

"Armed to the teeth?"

"Yes—but invisibly. Your old waterproof——!"

"Mine is new. I'll take Susan's!"

This good lady, however, had her reserves. "Mayn't one of them, all the same—here and there—have been sorry?"

Mr. Patten wondered. "For the jobs he muffed?"

"For the wrong—as it *was* wrong—he did."

" 'One' of them?" She had gone too far, for the vicar suddenly looked as if he divined in the question a reference.

They became, however, as promptly unanimous in meeting this danger, as to which Miss Susan in particular showed an inspired presence of mind. "Two of them!" she sweetly smiled. "May not Amy and I——?"

"Vicariously repent?" said Mr. Patten. "That depends—for the true honour of Marr—on how you show it."

"Oh, we *sha'n't* show it!" Miss Amy cried.

"Ah, then," Mr. Patten returned, "though atonements, to be efficient, are supposed to be public, you may do penance in secret as much as you please!"

"Well, *I* shall do it," said Susan Frush.

Again, by something in her tone, the vicar's attention appeared to be caught. "Have you then in view a particular form——?"

"Of atonement?" She coloured now, glaring rather helplessly, in spite of herself, at her companion. "Oh, if you're sincere you'll always find one."

Amy came to her assistance. "The way she often treats me has made her—though there's after all no harm in her—familiar with remorse. Mayn't we, at any rate," the younger lady continued, "now have our letters back?" And the vicar left them with the assurance that they should receive the bundle on the morrow.

They were indeed so at one as to shrouding their mystery that no explicit agreement, no exchange of vows, needed to pass between them; they only settled down, from this moment, to an unshared possession of their secret, an economy in the use and, as may even be said, the enjoyment of it, that was part of their general instinct and habit of thrift. It had been the disposition, the practice, the necessity of each to keep, fairly indeed to clutch, everything that, as they often phrased it, came their way; and this was not the first time such an influence had determined for them an affirmation of property in objects to which ridicule, suspicion, or some other inconvenience, might attach. It was their simple philosophy that one never knew of what service an odd object might *not* be; and there were days now on which they felt themselves to have made a better bargain with their aunt's executors than

was witnessed in those law-papers which they had at first tim-
orously regarded as the record of advantages taken of them
in matters of detail. They had got, in short, more than was
vulgarly, more than was even shrewdly supposed—such an
indescribable unearned increment as might scarce more be
divulged as a dread than as a delight. They drew together,
old-maidishly, in a suspicious, invidious grasp of the idea that
a dread of their very own—and blissfully not, of course, that
of a failure of any essential supply—might, on nearer acquaintance, positively turn to a delight.

Upon some such attempted consideration of it, at all events,
they found themselves embarking after their last interview
with Mr. Patten, an understanding conveyed between them in
no redundancy of discussion, no flippant repetitions nor profane recurrences, yet resting on a sense of added margin, of
appropriated history, of liberties taken with time and space,
that would leave them prepared both for the worst and for
the best. The best would be that something that would turn
out to their advantage might prove to be hidden about the
place; the worst would be that they might find themselves
growing to depend only too much on excitement. They found
themselves amazingly reconciled, on Mr. Patten's information,
to the particular character thus fixed on their visitor; they
knew by tradition and fiction that even the highwaymen of
the same picturesque age were often gallant gentlemen; therefore a smuggler, by such a measure, fairly belonged to the
aristocracy of crime. When their packet of documents came
back from the vicarage Miss Amy, to whom her associate continued to leave them, took them once more in hand; but with
an effect, afresh, of discouragement and languor—a headachy
sense of faded ink, of strange spelling and crabbed characters,
of allusions she couldn't follow and parts she couldn't match.
She placed the tattered papers piously together, wrapping
them tenderly in a piece of old figured silken stuff; then, as
solemnly as if they had been archives or statutes or title-deeds,
laid them away in one of the several small cupboards lodged
in the thickness of the wainscoted walls. What really most
sustained our friends in all ways was their consciousness of
having, after all—and so contrariwise to what appeared—a
man in the house. It removed them from that category of the

manless into which no lady really lapses till every issue is
closed. Their visitor was an issue—at least to the imagination,
and they arrived finally, under provocation, at intensities of
flutter in which they felt themselves so compromised by his
hoverings that they could only consider with relief the fact of
nobody's knowing.

The real complication indeed at first was that for some
weeks after their talks with Mr. Patten the hoverings quite
ceased; a circumstance that brought home to them in some
degree a sense of indiscretion and indelicacy. They hadn't
mentioned him, no; but they had come perilously near it, and
they had doubtless, at any rate, too recklessly let in the light
on old buried and sheltered things, old sorrows and shames.
They roamed about the house themselves at times, fitfully and
singly, when each supposed the other out or engaged; they
paused and lingered, like soundless apparitions, in corners,
doorways, passages, and sometimes suddenly met, in these experiments, with a suppressed start and a mute confession.
They talked of him practically never; but each knew how the
other thought—all the more that it was (oh yes, unmistakably!) in a manner different from her own. They were together, none the less, in feeling, while, week after week, he
failed again to show, as if they had been guilty of blowing,
with an effect of sacrilege, on old gathered silvery ashes. It
frankly came out for them that, possessed as they so strangely,
yet so ridiculously were, they should be able to settle to nothing till their consciousness was yet again confirmed. Whatever
the subject of it might have for them of fear or favour, profit
or loss, he had taken the taste from everything else. He had
converted *them* into wandering ghosts. At last, one day, with
nothing they could afterwards perceive to have determined it,
the change came—came, as the previous splash in their stillness had come, by the pale testimony of Miss Susan.

She waited till after breakfast to speak of it—or Miss Amy,
rather, waited to hear her; for she showed during the meal
the face of controlled commotion that her comrade already
knew and that must, with the game loyally played, serve as
preface to a disclosure. The younger of the friends really
watched the elder, over their tea and toast, as if seeing her for
the first time as possibly tortuous, suspecting in her some in-

tention of keeping back what had happened. What had happened was that the image of the hanged man had reappeared in the night; yet only after they had moved together to the drawing-room did Miss Amy learn the facts.

"I was beside the bed—in that low chair; about"—since Miss Amy must know—"to take off my right shoe. I had noticed nothing before, and had had time partly to undress—had got into my wrapper. So, suddenly—as I happened to look—there he was. And there," said Susan Frush, "he stayed."

"But where do you mean?"

"In the high-backed chair, the old flowered chintz 'ear-chair' beside the chimney."

"All night?—and you in your wrapper?" Then as if this image almost challenged her credulity, "Why didn't you go to bed?" Miss Amy inquired.

"With a—a person in the room?" her friend wonderfully asked; adding after an instant as with positive pride: "I never broke the spell!"

"And didn't freeze to death?"

"Yes, almost. To say nothing of not having slept, I can assure you, one wink. I shut my eyes for long stretches, but whenever I opened them he was still there, and I never for a moment lost consciousness."

Miss Amy gave a groan of conscientious sympathy. "So that you're feeling now of course half dead."

Her companion turned to the chimney-glass a wan, glazed eye. "I dare say I *am* looking impossible."

Miss Amy, after an instant, found herself still conscientious. "You are." Her own eyes strayed to the glass, lingering there while she lost herself in thought. "Really," she reflected with a certain dryness, "if that's the kind of thing it's to be——!" there would seem, in a word, to be no withstanding it for either. Why, she afterwards asked herself in secret, should the restless spirit of a dead adventurer have addressed itself, in its trouble, to such a person as her queer, quaint, inefficient housemate? It was in *her*, she dumbly and somewhat sorely argued, that an unappeased soul of the old race should show a confidence. To this conviction she was the more directed by the sense that Susan had, in relation to the preference shown, vain and foolish complacencies. She had her idea of what, in their prodigious predicament, should be, as she called it, "done," and that was a question that Amy from this time began to nurse the small aggression of not so much as discussing with her. She had certainly, poor Miss Frush, a new, an obscure reticence, and since she wouldn't speak first she should have silence to her fill. Miss Amy, however, peopled the silence with conjectural visions of her kinswoman's secret communion. Miss Susan, it was true, showed nothing, on any particular occasion, more than usual; but this was just a part of the very felicity that had begun to harden and uplift her. Days and nights hereupon elapsed without bringing felicity of any order to Amy Frush. If she had no emotions it was, she suspected, because Susan had them all; and—it would have been preposterous had it not been pathetic—she proceeded rapidly to hug the opinion that Susan was selfish and even something of a sneak. Politeness, between them, still reigned, but confidence had flown, and its place was taken by open ceremonies and confessed precautions. Miss Susan looked blank but resigned; which maintained again, unfortunately, her superior air and the presumption of her duplicity. Her manner was of not knowing where her friend's shoe pinched; but it might have been taken by a jaundiced eye for surprise at the challenge of her monopoly. The unexpected resistance of her nerves was indeed a wonder: was that then the result, even for a shaky old woman, of shocks sufficiently repeated? Miss Amy brooded on the rich inference that, if the first of them didn't prostrate and the rest didn't undermine, one might keep them up as easily as—well, say an unavowed acquaintance or a private commerce of letters. She was startled at the comparison into which she fell—but what was this but an intrigue like another? And fancy Susan carrying one on! That history of the long night hours of the pair in the two chairs kept before her—for it was always present—the extraordinary measure. Was the situation it involved only grotesque—or was it quite grimly grand? It struck her as both; but that was the case with all their situations. Would it be in herself, at any rate, to show such a front? She put herself such questions till she was tired of them. A few good moments of her own would have cleared the air. Luckily they were to come.

IV

It was on a Sunday morning in April, a day brimming over with the turn of the season. She had gone into the garden before church; they cherished alike, with pottering intimacies and opposed theories and a wonderful apparatus of old gloves and trowels and spuds and little botanical cards on sticks, this feature of their establishment, where they could still differ without fear and agree without diplomacy, and which now, with its vernal promise, threw beauty and gloom and light and space, a great good-natured ease, into their wavering scales. She was dressed for church; but when Susan, who had, from a window, seen her wandering, stooping, examining, touching, appeared in the doorway to signify a like readiness, she suddenly felt her intention checked. "Thank you," she said, drawing near; "I think that, though I've dressed, I won't, after all, go. Please therefore, proceed without me."

Miss Susan fixed her. "You're not well?"

"Not particularly. I shall be better—the morning's so perfect—here."

"Are you really ill?"

"Indisposed; but not enough so, thank you, for you to stay with me."

"Then it has come on but just now?"

"No—I felt not quite fit when I dressed. But it won't do."

"Yet you'll stay out here?"

Miss Amy looked about. "It will depend!"

Her friend paused long enough to have asked what it would depend on, but abruptly, after this contemplation, turned instead and, merely throwing over her shoulder an "At least take care of yourself!" went rustling, in her stiffest Sunday fashion, about her business. Miss Amy, left alone, as she clearly desired to be, lingered a while in the garden, where the sense of things was somehow made still more delicious by the sweet, vain sounds from the church tower; but by the end of ten minutes she had returned to the house. The sense of things was not delicious there, for what it had at last come to was that, as they thought of each other what they couldn't say, all their contacts were hard and false. The real wrong was in what Susan thought—as to which she was much too proud and too sore to undeceive her. Miss Amy went vaguely to the drawing-room.

They sat as usual, after church, at their early Sunday dinner, face to face; but little passed between them save that Miss Amy felt better, that the curate had preached, that nobody else had stayed away, and that everybody had asked why Amy had. Amy, hereupon, satisfied everybody by feeling well enough to go in the afternoon; on which occasion, on the other hand— and for reasons even less luminous than those that had operated with her mate in the morning—Miss Susan remained within. Her comrade came back late, having, after church, paid visits; and found her, as daylight faded, seated in the drawing-room, placid and dressed, but without so much as a Sunday book—the place contained whole shelves of such reading—in her hand. She looked so as if a visitor had just left her that Amy put the question: "Has any one called?"

"Dear, no; I've been quite alone."

This again was indirect, and it instantly determined for Miss Amy a conviction—a conviction that, on her also sitting down just as she was and in a silence that prolonged itself, promoted in its turn another determination. The April dusk gathered, and still, without further speech, the companions sat there. But at last Miss Amy said in a tone not quite her commonest: "This morning he came—while you were at church. I suppose it must have been really—though of course I couldn't know it—what I was moved to stay at home for." She spoke now— out of her contentment—as if to oblige with explanations.

But it was strange how Miss Susan met her. "You stay at home for him? *I* don't!" She fairly laughed at the triviality of the idea.

Miss Amy was naturally struck by it and after an instant even nettled. "Then why did you do so this afternoon?"

"Oh, it wasn't for *that*!" Miss Susan lightly quavered. She made her distinction. "I *really* wasn't well."

At this her cousin brought it out. "But he has been with you?"

"My dear child," said Susan, launched unexpectedly even to herself, "he's with me so often that if I put myself out for him——!" But as if at sight of something that showed, through the twilight, in her friend's face, she pulled herself up.

Amy, however, spoke with studied stillness. "You've ceased then to put yourself out? You gave me, you remember, an instance of how you once did!" And she tried, on her side, a laugh.

"Oh yes—that was at first. But I've seen such a lot of him since. Do you mean *you* hadn't?" Susan asked. Then as her companion only sat looking at her: "Has this been really the first time for you—since we last talked?"

Miss Amy for a minute said nothing. "You've actually believed me——"

"To be enjoying on your own account what *I* enjoy? How couldn't I, at the very least," Miss Susan cried—"so grand and strange as you must allow me to say you've struck me?"

Amy hesitated. "I hope I've sometimes struck you as decent!"

But it was a touch that, in her friend's almost amused preoccupation with the simple fact, happily fell short. "You've only been waiting for what didn't come?"

Miss Amy coloured in the dusk. "It came, as I tell you, to-day."

"Better late than never!" And Miss Susan got up.

Amy Frush sat looking. "It's because you thought you had ground for jealousy that *you've* been extraordinary?"

Poor Susan, at this, quite bounced about. "Jealousy?"

It was a tone—never heard from her before—that brought Amy Frush to her feet; so that for a minute, in the unlighted room where, in honour of the spring, there had been no fire and the evening chill had gathered, they stood as enemies. It lasted, fortunately, even long enough to give one of them time suddenly to find it horrible. "But why should we quarrel *now*?" Amy broke out in a different voice.

Susan was not too alienated quickly enough to meet it. "It *is* rather wretched."

"Now when we're equal," Amy went on.

"Yes—I suppose we are." Then, however, as if just to attenuate the admission, Susan had her last lapse from grace.

"They say, you know, that when women do quarrel it's usually about a man."

Amy recognised it, but also with a reserve. "Well then, let there first *be* one!"

"And don't you call *him*——?"

"No!" Amy declared and turned away, while her companion showed her a vain wonder for what she could in that case have expected. Their identity of privilege was thus established, but it is not certain that the air with which she indicated that the subject had better drop didn't press down for an instant her side of the balance. She knew that she knew most about men.

The subject did drop for the time, it being agreed between them that neither should from that hour expect from the other any confession or report. They would treat all occurrences now as not worth mentioning—a course easy to pursue from the moment the suspicion of jealousy had, on each side, been so completely laid to rest. They led their life a month or two on the smooth ground of taking everything for granted; by the end of which time, however, try as they would, they had set up no question that—while they met as a pair of gentlewomen living together only must meet—could successfully pretend to take the place of that of Cuthbert Frush. The spring softened and deepened, reached out its tender arms and scattered its shy graces; the earth broke, the air stirred, with emanations that were as touches and voices of the past; our friends bent their backs in their garden and their noses over its symptoms; they opened their windows to the mildness and tracked it in the lanes and by the hedges; yet the plant of conversation between them markedly failed to renew itself with the rest. It was not indeed that the mildness was not within them as well as without; all asperity, at least, had melted away; they were more than ever pleased with their general acquisition, which, at the winter's end, seemed to give out more of its old secrets, to hum, however faintly, with more of its old echoes, to creak, here and there, with the expiring throb of old aches. The deepest sweetness of the spring at Marr was just in its being in this way an attestation of age and rest. The place never seemed to have lived and lingered so long as when kind nature, like a maiden blessing a crone, laid rosy hands on its grizzled head. Then the new season was a light held up to show all the dignity of the years, but also all the wrinkles and scars. The good ladies in whom we are interested changed, at any rate, with the happy days, and it finally came out not only that the invidious note had dropped, but that it had positively turned to music. The whole tone of the time made so for tenderness that it really seemed as if at moments they were sad for each other. They had their grounds at last: each found them in her own consciousness; but it was as if each waited, on the other hand, to be sure she could speak without offence. Fortunately, at last, the tense cord snapped.

The old churchyard at Marr is still liberal; it does its immemorial utmost to people, with names and dates and memories and eulogies, with generations fore-shortened and confounded, the high empty table at which the grand old cripple of the church looks down over the low wall. It serves as an easy thoroughfare, and the stranger finds himself pausing in it with a sense of respect and compassion for the great maimed, ivied shoulders—as the image strikes him—of stone. Miss Susan and Miss Amy were strangers enough still to have sunk down one May morning on the sun-warmed tablet of an ancient tomb and to have remained looking about them in a sort of anxious peace. Their walks were all pointless now, as if they always stopped and turned, for an unconfessed want of interest, before reaching their object. That object presented itself at every start as the same to each, but they had come back too often without having got near it. This morning, strangely, on the return and almost in sight of their door, they were more in presence of it than they had ever been, and they seemed fairly to touch it when Susan said at last, quite in the air and with no traceable reference: "I hope you don't mind, dearest, if I'm awfully sorry for you."

"Oh, I know it," Amy returned—"I've felt it. But what does it do for us?" she asked.

Then Susan saw, with wonder and pity, how little resentment for penetration or patronage she had had to fear and out of what a depth of sentiment similar to her own her companion helplessly spoke. "You're sorry for *me*?"

Amy at first only looked at her with tired eyes, putting out a hand that remained a while on her arm. "Dear old girl! You might have told me before," she went on as she took everything in; "though, after all, haven't we each really known it?"

"Well," said Susan, "we've waited. We could only wait."

"Then if we've waited together," her friend returned, "that *has* helped us."

"Yes—to keep him in his place. Who would ever believe in him?" Miss Susan wearily wondered. "If it wasn't for you and for me——"

"Not doubting of each other?"—her companion took her up: "yes, there wouldn't be a creature. It's lucky for us," said Miss Amy, "that we *don't* doubt."

"Oh, if we did we shouldn't be sorry."

"No—except, selfishly, for ourselves. I am, I assure you, for *my* self—it has made me older. But, luckily, at any rate, we trust each other."

"We do," said Miss Susan.

"We do," Miss Amy repeated—they lingered a little on that. "But except making one feel older, what has it done for one?"

"There it is!"

"And though we've kept him in his place," Miss Amy continued, "he has also kept us in ours. We've lived with it," she declared in melancholy justice. "And we wondered at first if we could!" she ironically added. "Well, isn't just what we feel now that we can't any longer?"

"No—it must stop. And I've my idea," said Susan Frush.

"Oh, I assure you I've mine!" her cousin responded.

"Then if you want to act, don't mind me."

"Because you certainly won't *me*? No, I suppose not. Well!" Amy sighed, as if, merely from this, relief had at last come. Her comrade echoed it; they remained side by side; and nothing could have had more oddity than what was assumed alike in what they had said and in what they still kept back. There would have been this at least in their favour for a questioner of their case, that each, charged dejectedly with her own experience, took, on the part of the other, the extraordinary—the ineffable, in fact—all for granted. They never named it again—as indeed it was not easy to name; the whole matter shrouded itself in personal discriminations and privacies; the comparison of notes had become a thing impossible. What was definite was that they had lived into their queer story, passed through it as through an observed, a studied, eclipse of the usual, a period of reclusion, a financial, social or moral crisis, and only desired now to live out of it again. The questioner we have been supposing might even have fancied that each, on her side, had hoped for something from it that she finally perceived it was never to give, which would have been exactly, moreover, the core of her secret and the explanation of her reserve. They at least, as the business stood, put each other to no test, and, if they were in fact disillusioned and disappointed, came together, after their long blight, solidly on that. It fully appeared between them that they felt a great deal older. When they got up from their sun-warmed slab, however, reminding each other of luncheon, it was with a visible increase of ease and with Miss Susan's hand drawn, for the walk home, into Miss Amy's arm. Thus the "idea" of each had continued unspoken and ungrudged. It was as if each wished the other to try her own first; from which it might have been gathered that they alike presented difficulty and even entailed expense. The great questions remained. What then did he mean? what then did he want? Absolution, peace, rest, his final reprieve—merely to say *that* saw them no further on the way than they had already come. What were they at last to do for him? What could they give him that he would take? The ideas they respectively nursed still bore no fruit, and at the end of another month Miss Susan was frankly anxious about Miss Amy. Miss Amy as freely admitted that people *must* have begun to notice strange marks in them and to look for reasons. They were changed—they must change back.

V

Yet it was not till one morning at midsummer, on their meeting for breakfast, that the elder lady fairly attacked the younger's last entrenchment. "Poor, poor Susan!" Miss Amy had said to herself as her cousin came into the room; and a moment later she brought out, for very pity, her appeal. "What then *is* yours?"

"My idea?" It was clearly, at last, a vague comfort to Miss Susan to be asked. Yet her answer was desolate. "Oh, it's no use!"

"But how do you know?"

"Why, I tried it—ten days ago, and I thought at first it had answered. But it hasn't."

"He's back again?"

Wan, tired, Miss Susan gave it up. "Back again."

Miss Amy, after one of the long, odd looks that had now become their most frequent form of intercourse, thought it over. "And just the same?"

"Worse."

"Dear!" said Miss Amy, clearly knowing what that meant. "Then what did you do?"

Her friend brought it roundly out. "I made my sacrifice."

Miss Amy, though still more deeply interrogative, hesitated. "But of what?"

"Why, of my little all—or almost."

The "almost" seemed to puzzle Miss Amy, who, moreover, had plainly no clue to the property or attribute so described. "Your 'little all'?"

"Twenty pounds."

"Money?" Miss Amy gasped.

Her tone produced on her companion's part a wonder as great as her own. "What then is it yours to give?"

"My idea? It's not to *give*!" cried Amy Frush.

At the finer pride that broke out in this poor Susan's blankness flushed. "What then is it to do?"

But Miss Amy's bewilderment outlasted her reproach. "Do you mean he takes money?"

"The Chancellor of the Exchequer does—for 'conscience.'"

Her friend's exploit shone larger. "Conscience-money? You sent it to Government?" Then while, as the effect of her surprise, her mate looked too much a fool, Amy melted to kindness. "Why, you secretive old thing!"

Miss Susan presently pulled herself more together. "When your ancestor has robbed the revenue and his spirit walks for remorse——"

"You pay to get rid of him? I see—and it becomes what the vicar called his atonement by deputy. But what if it isn't remorse?" Miss Amy shrewdly asked.

"But it *is*—or it seemed to me so."

"Never to me," said Miss Amy.

Again they searched each other. "Then, evidently, with you he's different."

Miss Amy looked away. "I dare say!"

"So what *is* your idea?"

Miss Amy thought. "I'll tell you only if it works."

"Then, for God's sake, try it!"

Miss Amy, still with averted eyes and now looking easily wise, continued to think. "To try it I shall have to leave you. That's why I've waited so long." Then she fully turned, and with expression: "Can you face three days alone?"

"Oh—'alone!' I wish I ever were!"

At this her friend, as for very compassion, kissed her; for it seemed really to have come out at last—and welcome!—that poor Susan was the worse beset. "I'll do it! But I must go up to town. Ask me no questions. All I can tell you now is——"

"Well?" Susan appealed while Amy impressively fixed her.

"It's no more remorse than *I'm* a smuggler."

"What is it then?"

"It's bravado."

An "Oh!" more shocked and scared than any that, in the whole business, had yet dropped from her, wound up poor Susan's share in this agreement, appearing as it did to represent for her a somewhat lurid inference. Amy, clearly, had lights of her own. It was by their aid, accordingly, that she immediately prepared for the first separation they had had yet to suffer; of which the consequence, two days later, was that Miss Susan, bowed and anxious, crept singly, on the return from their parting, up the steep hill that leads from the station of Marr and passed ruefully under the ruined town-gate, one of the old defences, that arches over it.

But the full sequel was not for a month—one hot August night when, under the dim stars, they sat together in their little walled garden. Though they had by this time, in general, found again—as women only can find—the secret of easy speech, nothing, for the half-hour, had passed between them: Susan had only sat waiting for her comrade to wake up. Miss Amy had taken of late to interminable dozing—as if with forfeits and arrears to recover; she might have been a convalescent from fever repairing tissue and getting through time. Susan Frush watched her in the warm dimness, and the question between them was fortunately at last so simple that she had freedom to think her pretty in slumber and to fear that she herself, so unguarded, presented an appearance less graceful. She was impatient, for her need had at last come, but she waited, and while she waited she thought. She had already often done so, but the mystery deepened to-night in the story told, as it seemed to her, by her companion's frequent relapses. What had been, three weeks before, the effort intense enough to leave behind such a trail of fatigue? The marks, sure enough, had shown in the poor girl that morning of the termination of the arranged absence for which not three days, but ten, without word or sign, were to prove no more than sufficient. It was at an unnatural hour that Amy had turned up, dusty, dishevelled, inscrutable, confessing for the time to nothing more than a long night-journey. Miss Susan prided herself on having played the game and respected, however tormenting, the conditions. She had her conviction that her friend had been out of the country, and she marvelled, thinking of her own old wanderings and her present settled fears, at the spirit with which a person who, whatever she had previously done, had not travelled, could carry off such a flight. The hour had come at last for this person to name her remedy. What determined it was that, as Susan Frush sat there, she took home the fact that the remedy was by this time not to be questioned. It had acted as her own had not, and Amy, to all appearance, had only waited for her to admit it. Well, she was ready when Amy woke—woke immediately to meet her eyes and to show, after a moment, in doing so, a vision of what was in her mind. "What *was* it now?" Susan finally said.

"My idea? Is it possible you've not guessed?"

"Oh, you're deeper, much deeper," Susan sighed, "than I."

Amy didn't contradict that—seemed indeed, placidly enough, to take it for truth; but she presently spoke as if the difference, after all, didn't matter now. "Happily for us to-day—isn't it so?—our case is the same. I can speak, at any rate, for myself. He has left me."

"Thank God then!" Miss Susan devoutly murmured. "For he has left *me*."

"Are you sure?"

"Oh, I think so."

"But how?"

"Well," said Miss Susan after an hesitation, "how are *you*?"

Amy, for a little, matched her pause. "Ah, that's what I can't tell you. I can only answer for it that he's gone."

"Then allow me also to prefer not to explain. The sense of relief has for some reason grown strong in me during the last half-hour. That's such a comfort that it's enough, isn't it?"

"Oh, plenty!" The garden-side of their old house, a window or two dimly lighted, massed itself darkly in the summer night, and, with a common impulse, they gave it, across the little lawn, a long, fond look. Yes, they could be sure. "Plenty!" Amy repeated. "He's gone."

Susan's elder eyes hovered, in the same way, through her elegant glass, at his purified haunt. "He's gone. And how," she insisted, "*did* you do it?"

"Why, you dear goose"—Miss Amy spoke a little strangely—"I went to Paris."

"To Paris?"

"To see what I could bring back—that I mightn't, that I shouldn't. To do a stroke with!" Miss Amy brought out.

But it left her friend still vague. "A stroke——?"

"To get through the Customs—under their nose."

It was only with this that, for Miss Susan, a pale light dawned. "You wanted to smuggle? *That* was your idea?"

"It was *his*," said Miss Amy. "He wanted no 'conscience money' spent for him," she now more bravely laughed: "it was quite the other way about—he wanted some bold deed done, of the old wild kind; he wanted some big risk taken. And I took it." She sprang up, rebounding, in her triumph.

Her companion, gasping, gazed at her. "Might they have hanged you too?"

Miss Amy looked up at the dim stars. "If I had defended myself. But luckily it didn't come to that. What I brought in I brought"—she rang out, more and more lucid, now, as she talked—"triumphantly. To appease him—I braved them. I chanced it, at Dover, and they never knew."

"Then you hid it——?"

"About my person."

With the shiver of this Miss Susan got up, and they stood there duskily together. "It was so small?" the elder lady wonderingly murmured.

"It was big enough to have satisfied him," her mate replied with just a shade of sharpness. "I chose it, with much thought, from the forbidden list."

The forbidden list hung a moment in Miss Susan's eyes, suggesting to her, however, but a pale conjecture. "A Tauchnitz?"

Miss Amy communed again with the August stars. "It was the *spirit* of the deed that told."

"A Tauchnitz?" her friend insisted.

Then at last her eyes again dropped, and the Misses Frush moved together to the house. "Well, he's satisfied."

"Yes, and"—Miss Susan mused a little ruefully as they went—"you got at last your week in Paris!"

The Special Type

I NOTE it as a wonderful case of its kind—the finest of all perhaps, in fact, that I have ever chanced to encounter. The kind, moreover, is the greatest kind, the roll recruited, for our high esteem and emulation, from history and fiction, legend and song. In the way of service and sacrifice for love I've really known nothing go beyond it. However, you can judge. My own sense of it happens just now to be remarkably rounded off by the sequel—more or less looked for on her part—of the legal step taken by Mrs. Brivet. I hear from America that, a decent interval being held to have elapsed since her gain of her divorce, she is about to marry again—an event that will, it would seem, put an end to any question of the disclosure of the real story. It's this that's the real story, or will be, with nothing wanting, as soon as I shall have heard that her husband (who, on his side, has only been waiting for her to move first) has sanctified his union with Mrs. Cavenham.

I

She was, of course, often in and out, Mrs. Cavenham, three years ago, when I was painting her portrait; and the more so that I found her, I remember, one of those comparatively rare sitters who present themselves at odd hours, turn up without an appointment. The thing is to get most women to keep those they do make; but she used to pop in, as she called it, on the chance, letting me know that if I had a moment free she was quite at my service. When I hadn't the moment free she liked to stay to chatter, and she more than once expressed to me, I recollect, her theory that an artist really, for the time, could never see too much of his model. I must have shown her rather frankly that I understood her as meaning that a model could never see too much of her artist. I understood in fact everything, and especially that she was, in Brivet's absence, so unoccupied and restless that she didn't know what to do with herself. I was conscious in short that it was he who would pay for the picture, and that gives, I think, the measure of my enlightenment. If I took such pains and bore so with her folly, it was fundamentally for Brivet.

I was often at that time, as I had often been before, occupied—for various "subjects"—with Mrs. Dundene, in connection with which a certain occasion comes back to me as the first slide in the lantern. If I had invented my story I couldn't have made it begin better than with Mrs. Cavenham's irruption during the presence one morning of that lady. My door, by some chance, had been unguarded, and she was upon us without a warning. This was the sort of thing my model hated—the one, I mean, who, after all, sat mainly to oblige; but I remember how well she behaved. She was not dressed for company, though indeed a dress was never strictly necessary to her best effect. I recall that I had a moment of uncertainty, but I must have dropped the name of each for the other, as it was Mrs. Cavenham's line always, later on, that I had made them acquainted; and inevitably, though I wished her not to stay and got rid of her as soon as possible, the two women, of such different places in the scale, but of such almost equal beauty, were face to face for some minutes, of which I was not even at the moment unaware that they made an extraordinary use for mutual inspection. It was sufficient; they from that instant knew each other.

"Isn't she lovely?" I remember asking—and quite without the spirit of mischief—when I came back from restoring my visitor to her cab.

"Yes, awfully pretty. But I hate her."

"Oh," I laughed, "she's not so bad as that."

"Not so handsome as I, you mean?" And my sitter protested. "It isn't fair of you to speak as if I were one of those who can't bear even at the worst—or the best—another woman's looks. I should hate her even if she were ugly."

"But what have you to do with her?"

She hesitated; then with characteristic looseness: "What have I to do with anyone?"

"Well, there's no one else I know of that you do hate."

"That shows," she replied, "how good a reason there must be, even if I don't know it yet."

She knew it in the course of time, but I have never seen a

reason, I must say, operate so little for relief. As a history of the hatred of Alice Dundene my anecdote becomes wondrous indeed. Meanwhile, at any rate, I had Mrs. Cavenham again with me for her regular sitting, and quite as curious as I had expected her to be about the person of the previous time.

"Do you mean she isn't, so to speak, a lady?" she asked after I had, for reasons of my own, fenced a little. "Then if she's not 'professional' either, what is she?"

"Well," I returned as I got at work, "she escapes, to my mind, any classification save as one of the most beautiful and good-natured of women."

"I see her beauty," Mrs. Cavenham said. "It's immense. Do you mean that her good-nature's as great?"

I had to think a little. "On the whole, yes."

"Then I understand. That represents a greater quantity than *I*, I think, should ever have occasion for."

"Oh, the great thing's to be sure to have enough," I growled.

But she laughed it off. "Enough, certainly, is as good as a feast!"

It was—I forget how long, some months—after this that Frank Brivet, whom I had not seen for two years, knocked again at my door. I didn't at all object to him at my other work as I did to Mrs. Cavenham, but it was not till he had been in and out several times that Alice—which is what most people still really call her—chanced to see him and received in such an extraordinary way the impression that was to be of such advantage to him. She had been obliged to leave me that day before he went—though he stayed but a few minutes later; and it was not till the next time we were alone together that I was struck with her sudden interest, which became frankly pressing. I had met her, to begin with, expansively enough.

"An American? But what *sort*—don't you know? There are so many."

I didn't mean it as an offence, but in the matter of men, and though her acquaintance with them is so large, I always simplify with her. "*The* sort. He's rich."

"And how rich?"

"Why, *as* an American. Disgustingly."

I told her on this occasion more about him, but it was on that fact, I remember, that, after a short silence, she brought out with a sigh: "Well, I'm sorry. I should have liked to love him for himself."

II

Quite apart from having been at school with him, I'm conscious—though at times he so puts me out—that I've a taste for Frank Brivet. I'm quite aware, by the same token—and even if when a man's so rich it's difficult to tell—that he's not everyone's affinity. I was struck, at all events, from the first of the affair, with the way he clung to me and seemed inclined to haunt my studio. He's fond of art, though he has some awful pictures, and more or less understands mine; but it wasn't this that brought him. Accustomed as I was to notice what his wealth everywhere does for him, I was rather struck with his being so much thrown upon me and not giving London—the big fish that rises so to the hook baited with gold—more of a chance to perform to him. I very soon, however, understood. He had his reasons for wishing not to be seen much with Mrs. Cavenham, and, as he was in love with her, felt the want of some machinery for keeping temporarily away from her. I was his machinery, and, when once I perceived this, was willing enough to turn his wheel. His situation, moreover, became interesting from the moment I fairly grasped it, which he soon enabled me to do. His old reserve on the subject of Mrs. Brivet went to the winds, and it's not my fault if I let him see how little I was shocked by his confidence. His marriage had originally seemed to me to require much more explanation than anyone could give, and indeed in the matter of women in general, I confess, I've never seized his point of view. His inclinations are strange, and strange, too, perhaps, his indifferences. Still, I can enter into some of his aversions, and I agreed with him that his wife was odious.

"She has hitherto, since we began practically to live apart," he said, "mortally hated the idea of doing anything so pleasant for me as to divorce me. But I've reason to believe she has now changed her mind. She'd like to get clear."

I waited a moment. "For a man?"

"Oh, such a jolly good one! Remson Sturch."

I wondered. "Do you call *him* good?"

"Good for *her*. If she only can be got to be—which it oughtn't to be difficult to make her—fool enough to marry him, he'll give her the real size of his foot, and I shall be avenged in a manner positively ideal."

"Then will she institute proceedings?"

"She can't, as things stand. She has nothing to go upon. I've been," said poor Brivet, "I positively have, so blameless." I thought of Mrs. Cavenham, and, though I said nothing, he went on after an instant as if he knew it. "They can't put a finger. I've been so d——d particular."

I hesitated. "And your idea is now not to be particular any more?"

"Oh, about *her*," he eagerly replied, "always!" On which I laughed out and he coloured. "But my idea is nevertheless, at present," he went on, "to pave the way; that is, I mean, if I can keep the person you're thinking of so totally out of it that not a breath in the whole business can possibly touch her."

"I see," I reflected. "She isn't willing?"

He stared. "To be compromised? Why the devil *should* she be?"

"Why shouldn't she—for *you?* Doesn't she love you?"

"Yes, and it's because she does, dearly, that I don't feel the right way to repay her is by spattering her over."

"Yet if she stands," I argued, "straight in the splash——!"

"She doesn't!" he interrupted me, with some curtness. "She stands a thousand miles out of it; she stands on a pinnacle; she stands as she stands in your charming portrait—lovely, lonely, untouched. And so she must remain."

"It's beautiful, it's doubtless inevitable," I returned after a little, "that you should feel so. Only, if your wife doesn't divorce you for a woman you love, I don't quite see how she can do it for the woman you don't."

"Nothing is more simple," he declared; on which I saw he had figured it out rather more than I thought. "It will be quite enough if she *believes* I love her."

"If the lady in question does—or Mrs. Brivet?"

"Mrs. Brivet—confound her! If she believes I love somebody else. I must have the appearance, and the appearance must of course be complete. All I've got to do is to take up——"

"To take up——?" I asked, as he paused.

"Well, publicly, with someone or other; someone who could easily be squared. One would undertake, after all, to produce the impression."

"On your wife naturally, you mean?"

"On my wife, and on the person concerned."

I turned it over and did justice to his ingenuity. "But what impression would you undertake to produce on——?"

"Well?" he inquired as I just faltered.

"On the person *not* concerned. How would the lady you just accused me of having in mind be affected toward such a proceeding?"

He had to think a little, but he thought with success. "Oh, I'd answer for her."

"To the other lady?" I laughed.

He remained quite grave. "To myself. She'd leave us alone. As it would be for her good, she'd understand."

I was sorry for him, but he struck me as artless. "Understand, in that interest, the 'spattering' of another person?"

He coloured again, but he was sturdy. "It must of course be exactly the right person—a special type. Someone who, in the first place," he explained, "wouldn't mind, and of whom, in the second, she wouldn't be jealous."

I followed perfectly, but it struck me as important all round that we should be clear. "But wouldn't the danger be great that any woman who shouldn't have that effect—the effect of jealousy—upon her wouldn't have it either on your wife?"

"Ah," he acutely returned, "my wife wouldn't be warned. She wouldn't be 'in the know.' "

"I see." I quite caught up. "The two other ladies distinctly would."

But he seemed for an instant at a loss. "Wouldn't it be indispensable only as regards one?"

"Then the other would be simply sacrificed?"

"She would be," Brivet splendidly put it, "remunerated."

I was pleased even with the sense of financial power betrayed by the way he said it, and I at any rate so took the measure of his intention of generosity and his characteristically big view of the matter that this quickly suggested to me what at least might be his exposure. "But suppose that, in spite of 'remuneration,' this secondary personage should perversely like you? She would have to be indeed, as you say, a special type, but even special types may have general feelings. Suppose she should like you too much."

It had pulled him up a little. "What do you mean by 'too much'?"

"Well, more than enough to leave the case quite as simple as you'd require it."

"Oh, money always simplifies. Besides, I should make a point of being a brute." And on my laughing at this: "I should pay her enough to keep her down, to make her easy. But the thing," he went on with a drop back to the less mitigated real—"the thing, hang it! is first to find her."

"Surely," I concurred; "for she should have to lack, you see, no requirement whatever for plausibility. She must be, for instance, not only 'squareable,' but—before anything else even—awfully handsome."

"Oh, 'awfully'!" He could make light of *that*, which was what Mrs. Cavenham was.

"It wouldn't do for her, at all events," I maintained, "to be a bit less attractive than——"

"Well, than who?" he broke in, not only with a comic effect of disputing my point, but also as if he knew whom I was thinking of.

Before I could answer him, however, the door opened, and we were interrupted by a visitor—a visitor who, on the spot, in a flash, primed me with a reply. But I had of course for the moment to keep it to myself. "Than Mrs. Dundene!"

III

I had nothing more than that to do with it, but before I could turn round it was done; by which I mean that Brivet, whose previous impression of her had, for some sufficient reason, failed of sharpness, now jumped straight to the perception that here to his hand for the solution of his problem was the missing quantity and the appointed aid. They were in presence on this occasion, for the first time, half an hour, during which he sufficiently showed me that he felt himself to have found the special type. He was certainly to that extent right that nobody could—in those days in particular—without a rapid sense that she was indeed "special," spend any such time in the company of our extraordinary friend. I couldn't quarrel with his recognising so quickly what I had myself instantly recognised, yet if it did in truth appear almost at a glance that she would, through the particular facts of situation, history, aspect, tone, temper, beautifully "do," I felt from the first so affected by the business that I desired to wash my hands of it. There was something I wished to say to him before it went further, but after that I cared only to be out of it. I may as well say at once, however, that I never *was* out of it; for a man habitually ridden by the twin demons of imagination and observation is never—enough for his peace—out of anything. But I wanted to be able to apply to either, should anything happen, " 'Thou canst not say *I* did it!' " What might in particular happen was represented by what I said to Brivet the first time he gave me a chance. It was what I had wished before the affair went further, but it had then already gone so far that he had been twice—as he immediately let me know—to see her at home. He clearly desired me to keep up with him, which I was eager to declare impossible; but he came again to see me only after he had called. Then I instantly made my point, which was that she was really, hang it! too good for his fell purpose.

"But, my dear man, my purpose is a sacred one. And if, moreover, she herself doesn't think she's too good——"

"Ah," said I, "she's in love with you, and so it isn't fair."

He wondered. "Fair to *me*?"

"Oh, I don't care a button for you! What I'm thinking of is her risk."

"And what do you mean by her risk?"

"Why, her finding, of course, before you've done with her, that she can't do without you."

He met me as if he had quite thought of that. "Isn't it much more *my* risk?"

"Ah, but you take it deliberately, walk into it with your eyes open. What I want to be sure of, liking her as I do, is that she fully understands."

He had been moving about my place with his hands in his pockets, and at this he stopped short. "How much do you like her?"

"Oh, ten times more than she likes me; so *that* needn't trouble you. Does she understand that it can be only to help somebody else?"

"Why, my dear chap, she's as sharp as a steam-whistle."

"So that she also already knows who the other person is?"

He took a turn again, then brought out, "There's no other person for her but me. Of course, as yet, there are things one doesn't say; I haven't set straight to work to dot all my i's, and the beauty of her, as she's really charming—and would be charming in *any* relation—is just exactly that I don't expect to have to. We'll work it out all right, I think, so that what I most wanted just to make sure of from you was what you've been good enough to tell me. I mean that you don't object—for yourself."

I could with philosophic mirth allay that scruple, but what I couldn't do was to let him see what really most worried me. It stuck, as they say, in my crop that a woman like—yes, when all was said and done—Alice Dundene should simply minister to the convenience of a woman like Rose Cavenham. "But there's one thing more." This was as far as I could go. "I may take from you then that she not only knows it's for your divorce and remarriage, but can fit the shoe on the very person?"

He waited a moment. "Well, you may take from me that I find her no more of a fool than, as I seem to see, many other fellows have found her."

I too was silent a little, but with a superior sense of being able to think it all out further than he. "She's magnificent!"

"Well, so am I!" said Brivet. And for months afterward there was much—in fact everything—in the whole picture to justify his claim. I remember how it struck me as a lively sign of this that Mrs. Cavenham, at an early day, gave up her pretty house in Wilton Street and withdrew for a time to America. That was palpable design and diplomacy, but I'm afraid that I quite as much, and doubtless very vulgarly, read into it that she had had money from Brivet to go. I even promised my-self, I confess, the entertainment of finally making out that, whether or no the marriage should come off, she would not have been the person to find the episode least lucrative.

She left the others, at all events, completely together, and so, as the plot, with this, might be said definitely to thicken, it came to me in all sorts of ways that the curtain had gone up on the drama. It came to me, I hasten to add, much less from the two actors themselves than from other quarters—the usual sources, which never fail, of chatter; for after my friends' direction was fairly taken they had the good taste on either side to handle it, in talk, with gloves, not to expose it to what I should have called the danger of definition. I even seemed to divine that, allowing for needful preliminaries, they dealt even with each other on this same unformulated plane, and that it well might be that no relation in London at that moment, between a remarkable man and a beautiful woman, had more of the general air of good manners. I saw for a long time, directly, but little of them, for they were naturally much taken up, and Mrs. Dundene in particular intermitted, as she had never yet done in any complication of her chequered career, her calls at my studio. As the months went by I couldn't but feel—partly, perhaps, for this very reason—that their undertaking announced itself as likely not to fall short of its aim. I gathered from the voices of the air that nothing whatever was neglected that could make it a success, and just this vision it was that made me privately project wonders into it, caused anxiety and curiosity often again to revisit me, and led me in fine to say to myself that so rich an effect could be arrived at on either side only by a great deal of heroism. As the omens markedly developed I supposed the heroism had likewise done so, and that the march of the matter was logical I inferred from the fact that even though the ordeal, all round, was more protracted than might have been feared, Mrs. Cavenham made no fresh appearance. This I took as a sign that she knew she was safe—took indeed as the feature not the least striking of the situation constituted in her interest. I held my tongue, naturally, about her interest, but I watched it from a distance with an attention that, had I been caught in the act, might have led to a mistake about the direction of my sympathy. I had to make it my proper secret that, while I lost as little as possible of what was being done for her, I felt more and more that I myself could never have begun to do it.

IV

She came back at last, however, and one of the first things she did on her arrival was to knock at my door and let me know immediately, to smooth the way, that she was there on particular business. I was not to be surprised—though even if I were she shouldn't mind—to hear that she wished to bespeak from me, on the smallest possible delay, a portrait, full-length for preference, of our delightful friend Mr. Brivet. She brought this out with a light perfection of assurance of which the first effect—I couldn't help it—was to make me show myself almost too much amused for good manners. She first stared at my laughter, then wonderfully joined in it, looking meanwhile extraordinarily pretty and elegant—more completely handsome in fact, as well as more completely happy, than I had ever yet seen her. She was distinctly the better, I quickly saw, for what was being done for her, and it was an odd spectacle indeed that while, out of her sight and to the exclusion of her very name, the good work went on, it put roses in her cheeks and rings on her fingers and the sense of success in her heart. What had made me laugh, at all events, was the number of other ideas suddenly evoked by her request, two of which, the next moment, had disengaged themselves with particular brightness. She wanted, for all her confidence, to omit no precaution, to close up every issue, and she had acutely conceived that the possession of Brivet's picture—full-length, above all!—would constitute for her the strongest possible appearance of holding his supreme pledge. If that had been her foremost thought her second then had been that if I should paint him he would have to sit, and that in order to sit he would have to return. He had been at this time, as I knew, for many weeks in foreign cities—which helped moreover to explain to me that Mrs. Cavenham had thought it compatible with her safety to reopen her London house. Everything accordingly seemed to make for a victory, but there *was* such a thing, her proceeding implied, as one's—

at least as *her*—susceptibility and her nerves. This question of his return I of course immediately put to her; on which she immediately answered that it was expressed in her very proposal, inasmuch as this proposal was nothing but the offer that Brivet had himself made her. The thing was to be his gift; she had only, he had assured her, to choose her artist and arrange the time; and she had amiably chosen me—chosen me for the dates, as she called them, immediately before us. I doubtless— but I don't care—give the measure of my native cynicism in confessing that I didn't the least avoid showing her that I saw through her game. "Well, I'll do him," I said, "if he'll come himself and ask me."

She wanted to know, at this, of course, if I impugned her veracity. "You don't believe what I tell you? You're afraid for your money?"

I took it in high good-humour. "For my money not a bit."

"For what then?"

I had to think first how much I could say, which seemed to me, naturally, as yet but little. "I know perfectly that whatever happens Brivet always pays. But let him come; then we'll talk."

"Ah, well," she returned, "you'll see if he doesn't come." And come he did in fact—though without a word from myself directly—at the end of ten days; on which we immediately got to work, an idea highly favourable to it having meanwhile shaped itself in my own breast. Meanwhile too, however, before his arrival, Mrs. Cavenham had been again to see me, and this it was precisely, I think, that determined my idea. My present explanation of what afresh passed between us is that she really felt the need to build up her security a little higher by borrowing from my own vision of what had been happening. I had not, she saw, been very near to that, but I had been at least, during her time in America, nearer than she. And I had doubtless somehow "aggravated" her by appearing to disbelieve in the guarantee she had come in such pride to parade to me. It had in any case befallen that, on the occasion of her second visit, what I least expected or desired—her avowal of being "in the know"—suddenly went too far to stop. When she did speak she spoke with elation. "Mrs. Brivet has filed her petition."

"For getting rid of him?"

"Yes, in order to marry again; which is exactly what he wants her to do. It's wonderful—and, in a manner, I think, quite splendid—the way he has made it easy for her. He has met her wishes handsomely—obliged her in every particular."

As she preferred, subtly enough, to put it all as if it were for the sole benefit of his wife, I was quite ready for this tone; but I privately defied her to keep it up. "Well, then, he hasn't laboured in vain."

"Oh, it *couldn't* have been in vain. What has happened has been the sort of thing that she couldn't possibly fail to act upon."

"Too great a scandal, eh?"

She but just paused at it. "Nothing neglected, certainly, or omitted. He was not the man to undertake it——"

"And not put it through? No, I should say he wasn't the man. In any case he apparently hasn't been. But he must have found the job——"

"Rather a bore?" she asked as I had hesitated.

"Well, not so much a bore as a delicate matter."

She seemed to demur. "Delicate?"

"Why, your sex likes him so."

"But isn't just that what has made it easy?"

"Easy for *him*—yes," I after a moment admitted.

But it wasn't what she meant. "And not difficult, also, for *them*."

This was the nearest approach I was to have heard her make, since the day of the meeting of the two women at my studio, to naming Mrs. Dundene. She never, to the end of the affair, came any closer to her in speech than by the collective and promiscuous plural pronoun. There might have been a dozen of them, and she took cognizance, in respect to them, only of quantity. It was as if it had been a way of showing how little of anything else she imputed. Quality, as distinguished from quantity, was what *she* had. "Oh, I think," I said, "that we can scarcely speak for them."

"Why not? They must certainly have had the most beautiful time. Operas, theatres, suppers, dinners, diamonds, carriages, journeys hither and yon with him, poor dear, telegrams sent by each from everywhere to everywhere and always lying

about, elaborate arrivals and departures at stations for everyone to see, and, in fact, quite a crowd usually collected—as
many witnesses as you like. Then," she wound up, "his
brougham standing always—half the day and half the night—
at their doors. He has had to keep a brougham, and the
proper sort of man, just for that alone. In other words unlimited publicity."

"I see. What more can they have wanted? Yes," I pon-
dered, "they like, for the most part, we suppose, a studied,
outrageous *affichage*, and they must have thoroughly enjoyed
it."

"Ah, but it was only that."

I wondered. "Only what?"

"Only *affiché*. Only outrageous. Only the *form* of—well, of
what would definitely serve. He never saw them alone."

I wondered—or at least appeared to—still more. "Never?"

"Never. Never once." She had a wonderful air of answering
for it. "I know."

I saw that, after all, she really believed she knew, and I had
indeed, for that matter, to recognise that I myself believed her
knowledge to be sound. Only there went with it a complacency, an enjoyment of having really made me see what could
be done for her, so little to my taste that for a minute or two
I could scarce trust myself to speak: she looked somehow, as
she sat there, so lovely, and yet, in spite of her loveliness—or
perhaps even just because of it—so smugly selfish; she put it
to me with so small a consciousness of anything but her personal triumph that, while she had kept her skirts clear, her
name unuttered and her reputation untouched, "they" had
been in it even more than her success required. It was their
skirts, their name and their reputation that, in the proceedings
at hand, would bear the brunt. It was only after waiting a
while that I could at last say: "You're perfectly sure then of
Mrs. Brivet's intention?"

"Oh, we've had formal notice."

"And he's himself satisfied of the sufficiency——?"

"Of the sufficiency——?"

"Of what he has done."

She rectified. "Of what he has *appeared* to do."

"That *is* then enough?"

"Enough," she laughed, "to send him to the gallows!" To which I could only reply that all was well that ended well.

V

All for me, however, as it proved, had not ended yet. Brivet, as I have mentioned, duly reappeared to sit for me, and Mrs. Cavenham, on his arrival, as consistently went abroad. He confirmed to me that lady's news of how he had "fetched," as he called it, his wife—let me know, as decently owing to me after what had passed, on the subject, between us, that the forces set in motion had logically operated; but he made no other allusion to his late accomplice—for I now took for granted the close of the connection—than was conveyed in this intimation. He spoke—and the effect was almost droll—as if he had had, since our previous meeting, a busy and responsible year and wound up an affair (as he was accustomed to wind up affairs) involving a mass of detail; he even dropped into occasional reminiscence of what he had seen and enjoyed and disliked during a recent period of rather far-reaching adventure; but he stopped just as short as Mrs. Cavenham had done—and, indeed, much shorter than she—of introducing Mrs. Dundene by name into our talk. And what was singular in this, I soon saw, was—apart from a general discretion—that he abstained not at all because his mind was troubled, but just because, on the contrary, it was so much at ease. It was perhaps even more singular still, meanwhile, that, though I had scarce been able to bear Mrs. Cavenham's manner in this particular, I found I could put up perfectly with that of her friend. She had annoyed me, but he didn't—I give the inconsistency for what it is worth. The obvious state of his conscience had always been a strong point in him and one that exactly irritated some people as much as it charmed others; so that if, in general, it was positively, and in fact quite aggressively approving, this monitor, it had never held its head so high as at the juncture of which I speak. I took all this in with eagerness, for I saw how it would play into my work. Seeking as I always do, instinctively, to represent sitters in the light of the thing, whatever it may be, that facially, least wittingly or responsibly, gives the pitch of their aspect, I felt immediately that I should have the clue for making a capital thing of Brivet were I to succeed in showing him in just this freshness of his cheer. His cheer was that of his being able to say to himself that he had got all he wanted precisely *as* he wanted: without having harmed a fly. He had arrived so neatly where most men arrive besmirched, and what he seemed to cry out as he stood before my canvas—wishing everyone well all round—was: "See how clever and pleasant and practicable, how jolly and lucky and rich I've been!" I determined, at all events, that I would make some such characteristic words as these cross, at any cost, the footlights, as it were, of my frame.

Well, I can't but feel to this hour that I really hit my nail— that the man *is* fairly painted in the light and that the work remains as yet my high-water mark. He himself was delighted with it—and all the more, I think, that before it was finished he received from America the news of his liberation. He had not defended the suit—as to which judgment, therefore, had been expeditiously rendered; and he was accordingly free as air and with the added sweetness of every augmented appearance that his wife was herself blindly preparing to seek chastisement at the hands of destiny. There being at last no obstacle to his open association with Mrs. Cavenham, he called her directly back to London to admire my achievement, over which, from the very first glance, she as amiably let herself go. It was the very view of him she had desired to possess; it was the dear man in his intimate essence for those who knew him; and for any one who should ever be deprived of him it would be the next best thing to the sound of his voice. We of course by no means lingered, however, on the contingency of privation, which was promptly swept away in the rush of Mrs. Cavenham's vision of how straight also, above and beyond, I had, as she called it, attacked. I couldn't quite myself, I fear, tell how straight, but Mrs. Cavenham perfectly could, and did, for everybody: she had at her fingers' ends all the reasons why the thing would be a treasure even for those who had never seen "Frank."

I had finished the picture, but was, according to my practice, keeping it near me a little, for afterthoughts, when I received from Mrs. Dundene the first visit she had paid me for many a month. "I've come," she immediately said, "to ask you a favour"; and she turned her eyes, for a minute, as if contentedly full of her thought, round the large workroom she already knew so well and in which her beauty had really rendered more services than could ever be repaid. There were studies of her yet on the walls; there were others thrust away in corners; others still had gone forth from where she stood and carried to far-away places the reach of her lingering look. I had greatly, almost inconveniently missed her, and I don't know why it was that she struck me now as more beautiful than ever. She had always, for that matter, had a way of seeming each time a little different and a little better. Dressed very simply in black materials, feathers and lace, that gave the impression of being light and fine, she had indeed the air of a special type, but quite as some great lady might have had it. She looked like a princess in Court mourning. Oh, she had been a case for the petitioner—was everything the other side wanted! "Mr. Brivet," she went on to say, "has kindly offered me a present. I'm to ask of him whatever in the world I most desire."

I knew in an instant, on this, what was coming, but I was at first wholly taken up with the simplicity of her allusion to her late connection. Had I supposed that, like Brivet, she wouldn't allude to it at all? or had I stupidly assumed that if she did it would be with ribaldry and rancour? I hardly know; I only know that I suddenly found myself charmed to receive from her thus the key of my own freedom. There was something I wanted to say to her, and she had thus given me leave. But for the moment I only repeated as with amused interest: "Whatever in the world——?"

"Whatever in all the world."

"But that's immense, and in what way can poor *I* help——?"

"By painting him for me. I want a portrait of him."

I looked at her a moment in silence. She was lovely. "That's what—'in all the world'—you've chosen?"

"Yes—thinking it over: full-length. I want it for remembrance, and I want it as you will do it. It's the only thing I do want."

"Nothing else?"

"Oh, it's enough." I turned about—she was wonderful. I had whisked out of sight for a month the picture I had produced for Mrs. Cavenham, and it was now completely covered with a large piece of stuff. I stood there a little, thinking of it, and she went on as if she feared I might be unwilling. "*Can't* you do it?"

It showed me that she had not heard from him of my having painted him, and this, further, was an indication that, his purpose effected, he had ceased to see her. "I suppose you know," I presently said, "what you've done for him?"

"Oh yes; it was what I wanted."

"It was what *he* wanted!" I laughed.

"Well, I want what he wants."

"Even to his marrying Mrs. Cavenham?"

She hesitated. "As well her as anyone, from the moment he couldn't marry *me*."

"It was beautiful of you to be so sure of that," I returned.

"How could I be anything else but sure? He doesn't so much as *know* me!" said Alice Dundene.

"No," I declared, "I verily believe he doesn't. There's your picture," I added, unveiling my work.

She was amazed and delighted. "I may have *that*?"

"So far as I'm concerned—absolutely."

"Then he had himself the beautiful thought of sitting for me?"

I faltered but an instant. "Yes."

Her pleasure in what I had done was a joy to me. "Why, it's of a truth——! It's perfection."

"I think it is."

"It's the whole story. It's life."

"That's what I tried for," I said; and I added to myself: "Why the deuce *do* we?"

"It will be *him* for me," she meanwhile went on. "I shall *live* with it, keep it all to myself, and—do you know what it will do?—it will seem to make up."

"To make up?"

"I never saw him alone," said Mrs. Dundene.

I am still keeping the thing to send to her, punctually, on the day he's married; but I had of course, on my understanding with her, a tremendous bout with Mrs. Cavenham, who protested with indignation against my "base treachery" and made to Brivet an appeal for redress which, enlightened, face

to face with the magnificent humility of his other friend's selection, he couldn't, for shame, entertain. All he was able to
do was to suggest to me that I might for one or other of the
ladies, at my choice, do him again; but I had no difficulty in
replying that my best was my best and that what was done
was done. He assented with the awkwardness of a man in
dispute between women, and Mrs. Cavenham remained furi-
ous. "Can't 'they'—of *all* possible things, think!—take something else?"

"Oh, they want *him*!"

"Him?" It was monstrous.

"To live with," I explained—"to make up."

"To make up for what?"

"Why, you know, they never saw him alone."

The Tone of Time

I WAS too pleased with what it struck me that, as an old, old friend, I had done for her, not to go to her that very afternoon with the news. I knew she worked late, as in general I also did; but I sacrificed for her sake a good hour of the February daylight. She was in her studio, as I had believed she would be, where her card ("Mary J. Tredick"—not Mary Jane, but Mary Juliana) was manfully on the door; a little tired, a little old and a good deal spotted, but with her ugly spectacles taken off, as soon as I appeared, to greet me. She kept on, while she scraped her palette and wiped her brushes, the big stained apron that covered her from head to foot and that I have often enough before seen her retain in conditions giving the measure of her renunciation of her desire to dazzle. Every fresh reminder of this brought home to me that she had given up everything but her work, and that there had been in her history some reason. But I was as far from the reason as ever. She had given up too much; this was just why one wanted to lend her a hand. I told her, at any rate, that I had a lovely job for her.

"To copy something I do like?"

Her complaint, I knew, was that people only gave orders, if they gave them at all, for things she did not like. But this wasn't a case of copying—not at all, at least, in the common sense. "It's for a portrait—quite in the air."

"Ah, you do portraits yourself!"

"Yes, and you know how. My trick won't serve for this. What's wanted is a pretty picture."

"Then of whom?"

"Of nobody. That is of anybody. Anybody you like."

She naturally wondered. "Do you mean I'm myself to choose my sitter?"

"Well, the oddity is that there is to *be* no sitter."

"Whom then is the picture to represent?"

"Why, a handsome, distinguished, agreeable man, of not more than forty, clean-shaven, thoroughly well-dressed, and a perfect gentleman."

She continued to stare. "And I'm to find him myself?"

I laughed at the term she used. "Yes, as you 'find' the canvas, the colours and the frame." After which I immediately explained. "I've just had the 'rummest' visit, the effect of which was to make me think of you. A lady, unknown to me and unintroduced, turned up at my place at three o'clock. She had come straight, she let me know, without preliminaries, on account of one's high reputation—the usual thing—and of her having admired one's work. Of course I instantly saw—I mean I saw it as soon as she named her affair—that she hadn't understood my work at all. What am I good for in the world but just the impression of the given, the presented case? I can do but the face I see."

"And do you think I can do the face I don't?"

"No, but you see so many more. You see them in fancy and memory, and they come out, for you, from all the museums you've haunted and all the great things you've studied. I *know* you'll be able to see the one my visitor wants and to give it—what's the *crux* of the business—the tone of time."

She turned the question over. "What does she want it for?"

"Just *for* that—for the tone of time. And, except that it's to hang over her chimney, she didn't tell me. I've only my idea that it's to represent, to symbolise, as it were, her husband, who's not alive and who perhaps never was. This is exactly what will give you a free hand."

"With nothing to go by—no photographs or other portraits?"

"Nothing."

"She only proposes to describe him?"

"Not even; she wants the picture itself to do that. Her only condition is that he be a *très-bel homme*."

She had begun at last, a little thoughtfully, to remove her apron. "Is she French?"

"I don't know. I give it up. She calls herself Mrs. Bridgenorth."

Mary wondered. "*Connais pas!* I never heard of her."

"You wouldn't."

"You mean it's not her real name?"

I hesitated. "I mean that she's a very downright fact, full of the implication that she'll pay a downright price. It's clear to me that you can ask what you like; and it's therefore a chance that I can't consent to your missing." My friend gave no sign either way, and I told my story. "She's a woman of fifty, perhaps of more, who has been pretty, and who still presents herself, with her grey hair a good deal powdered, as I judge, to carry it off, extraordinarily well. She was a little frightened and a little free; the latter because of the former. But she did uncommonly well, I thought, considering the oddity of her wish. This oddity she quite admits; she began indeed by insisting on it so in advance that I found myself expecting I didn't know what. She broke at moments into French, which was perfect, but no better than her English, which isn't vulgar; not more at least than that of everybody else. The things people *do* say, and the way they say them, to artists! She wanted immensely, I could see, not to fail of her errand, not to be treated as absurd; and she was extremely grateful to me for meeting her so far as I did. She was beautifully dressed and she came in a brougham."

My listener took it in; then, very quietly, "Is she respectable?" she inquired.

"Ah, there you are!" I laughed; "and how you always pick the point right out, even when one has endeavoured to diffuse a specious glamour! She's extraordinary," I pursued after an instant; "and just what she wants of the picture, I think, is to make her a little less so."

"Who is she, then? What is she?" my companion simply went on.

It threw me straightway back on one of my hobbies. "Ah, my dear, what is so interesting as life? What is, above all, so stupendous as London? There's everything in it, everything in the world, and nothing too amazing not some day to pop out at you. What is a woman, faded, preserved, pretty, powdered, vague, odd, dropping on one without credentials, but with a carriage and very good lace? What is such a person but a person who *may* have had adventures, and have made them, in one way or another, pay? They're, however, none of one's business; it's scarcely on the cards that one should ask her. I should like, with Mrs. Bridgenorth, to see a fellow ask! She goes in for propriety, the real thing. If I suspect her of being the creation of her own talents, she has clearly, on the

other hand, seen a lot of life. Will you meet her?" I next
demanded.

My hostess waited. "No."

"Then you won't try?"

"Need I meet her to try?" And the question made me guess
that, so far as she had understood, she began to feel herself a
little taken. "It seems strange," she none the less mused, "to
attempt to please her on such a basis. To attempt," she presently added, "to please her at all. It's your idea that she's not
married?" she, with this, a trifle inconsequently asked.

"Well," I replied, "I've only had an hour to think of it, but
I somehow already see the scene. Not immediately, not the
day after, or even perhaps the year after the thing she desires
is set up there, but in due process of time and on convenient
opportunity, the transfiguration will occur. 'Who is that awfully handsome man?' 'That? Oh, that's an old sketch of my
dear dead husband.' Because I told her—insidiously sounding
her—that she would want it to look old, and that the tone of
time is exactly what you're full of."

"I believe I am," Mary sighed at last.

"Then put on your hat." I had proposed to her on my
arrival to come out to tea with me, and it was when left alone
in the studio while she went to her room that I began to feel
sure of the success of my errand. The vision that had an hour
before determined me grew deeper and brighter for her while
I moved about and looked at her things. There were more of
them there on her hands than one liked to see; but at least
they sharpened my confidence, which was pleasant for me in
view of that of my visitor, who had accepted without reserve
my plea for Miss Tredick. Four or five of her copies of famous
portraits—ornaments of great public and private collections—
were on the walls, and to see them again together was to feel
at ease about my guarantee. The mellow manner of them was
what I had had in my mind in saying, to excuse myself to Mrs.
Bridgenorth, "Oh, my things, you know, look as if they had
been painted to-morrow!" It made no difference that Mary's
Vandykes and Gainsboroughs were reproductions and rep-
licas, for I had known her more than once to amuse herself
with doing the thing quite, as she called it, off her own bat.
She had copied so bravely so many brave things that she had

at the end of her brush an extraordinary bag of tricks. She had always replied to me that such things were mere clever humbug, but mere clever humbug was what our client happened to want. The thing was to let her have it—one could trust her for the rest. And at the same time that I mused in this way I observed to myself that there was already something more than, as the phrase is, met the eye in such response as I felt my friend had made. I had touched, without intention, more than one spring; I had set in motion more than one impulse. I found myself indeed quite certain of this after she had come back in her hat and her jacket. She was different— her idea had flowered; and she smiled at me from under her tense veil, while she drew over her firm, narrow hands a pair of fresh gloves, with a light distinctly new. "Please tell your friend that I'm greatly obliged to both of you and that I take the order."

"Good. And to give him all his good looks?"

"It's just to do *that* that I accept. I shall make him supremely beautiful—and supremely base."

"Base?" I just demurred.

"The finest gentleman you'll ever have seen, and the worst friend."

I wondered, as I was startled; but after an instant I laughed for joy. "Ah well, so long as he's not mine! I see we *shall* have him," I said as we went, for truly I had touched a spring. In fact I had touched *the* spring.

It rang, more or less, I was presently to find, all over the place. I went, as I had promised, to report to Mrs. Bridgenorth on my mission, and though she declared herself much gratified at the success of it I could see she a little resented the apparent absence of any desire on Miss Tredick's part for a preliminary conference. "I only thought she might have liked just to see me, and have imagined I might like to see *her*."

But I was full of comfort. "You'll see her when it's finished. You'll see her in time to thank her."

"And to pay her, I suppose," my hostess laughed, with an asperity that was, after all, not excessive. "Will she take very long?"

I thought. "She's so full of it that my impression would be that she'll do it off at a heat."

"She *is* full of it then?" she asked; and on hearing to what tune, though I told her but half, she broke out with admiration. "You artists are the most extraordinary people!" It was almost with a bad conscience that I confessed we indeed were, and while she said that what she meant was that we seemed to understand everything, and I rejoined that this was also what *I* meant, she took me into another room to see the place for the picture—a proceeding of which the effect was singularly to confirm the truth in question. The place for the picture—in her own room, as she called it, a boudoir at the back, overlooking the general garden of the approved modern row and, as she said, only just wanting that touch—proved exactly the place (the space of a large panel in the white woodwork over the mantel) that I had spoken of to my friend. She put it quite candidly, "Don't you see what it will do?" and looked at me, wonderfully, as for a sign that I could sympathetically take from her what she didn't literally say. She said it, poor woman, so very nearly that I had no difficulty whatever. The portrait, tastefully enshrined there, of the finest gentleman one should ever have seen, would do even more for herself than it would do for the room.

I may as well mention at once that my observation of Mrs. Bridgenorth was not in the least of a nature to unseat me from the hobby I have already named. In the light of the impression she made on me life seemed quite as prodigious and London quite as amazing as I had ever contended, and nothing could have been more in the key of that experience than the manner in which everything was vivid between us and nothing expressed. We remained on the surface with the tenacity of shipwrecked persons clinging to a plank. Our plank was our concentrated gaze at Mrs. Bridgenorth's mere present. We allowed her past to exist for us only in the form of the prettiness that she had gallantly rescued from it and to which a few scraps of its identity still adhered. She was amiable, gentle, consistently proper. She gave me more than anything else the sense, simply, of waiting. She was like a house so freshly and successfully "done up" that you were surprised it wasn't oc-

cupied. She was waiting for something to happen—for somebody to come. She was waiting, above all, for Mary Tredick's
work. She clearly counted that it would help her.

I had foreseen the fact—the picture was produced at a heat;
rapidly, directly, at all events, for the sort of thing it proved
to be. I left my friend alone at first, left the ferment to work,
troubling her with no questions and asking her for no news;
two or three weeks passed, and I never went near her. Then
at last, one afternoon as the light was failing, I looked in. She
immediately knew what I wanted. "Oh yes, I'm doing him."

"Well," I said, "I've respected your intensity, but I *have* felt
curious."

I may not perhaps say that she was never so sad as when
she laughed, but it's certain that she always laughed when she
was sad. When, however, poor dear, for that matter, was she,
secretly, not? Her little gasps of mirth were the mark of her
worst moments. But why should she have one of these just
now? "Oh, I know your curiosity!" she replied to me; and
the small chill of her amusement scarcely met it. "He's coming out, but I can't show him to you yet. I must muddle it
through in my own way. It has insisted on being, after all, a
'likeness,' " she added. "But nobody will ever know."

"Nobody?"

"Nobody *she* sees."

"Ah, she doesn't, poor thing," I returned, "seem to see
anybody!"

"So much the better. I'll risk it." On which I felt I should
have to wait, though I had suddenly grown impatient. But I
still hung about, and while I did so she explained. "If what
I've done is really a portrait, the conditions itself prescribed
it. If I was to do the most beautiful man in the world I could
do but one."

We looked at each other; then I laughed. "It can scarcely
be *me*! But you're getting," I asked, "the great thing?"

"The infamy? Oh yes, please God."

It took away my breath a little, and I even for the moment
scarce felt at liberty to press. But one could always be cheerful.
"What I meant is the tone of time."

"Getting it, my dear man? Didn't I get it long ago? Don't
I *show* it—the tone of time?" she suddenly, strangely sighed

at me, with something in her face I had never yet seen. "I can't give it to him more than—for all these years—he was to have given it to *me*."

I scarce knew what smothered passion, what remembered wrong, what mixture of joy and pain my words had accidentally quickened. Such an effect of them could only become, for me, an instant pity, which, however, I brought out but indirectly. "It's the tone," I smiled, "in which you're speaking now."

This served, unfortunately, as something of a check. "I didn't mean to speak now." Then with her eyes on the picture, "I've said everything there. Come back," she added, "in three days. He'll be all right."

He was indeed when at last I saw him. She had produced an extraordinary thing—a thing wonderful, ideal, for the part it was to play. My only reserve, from the first, was that it was too fine for its part, that something much less "sincere" would equally have served Mrs. Bridgenorth's purpose, and that relegation to that lady's "own room"—whatever charm it was to work there—might only mean for it cruel obscurity. The picture is before me now, so that I could describe it if description availed. It represents a man of about five-and-thirty, seen only as to the head and shoulders, but dressed, the observer gathers, in a fashion now almost antique and which was far from contemporaneous with the date of the work. His high, slightly narrow face, which would be perhaps too aquiline but for the beauty of the forehead and the sweetness of the mouth, has a charm that even, after all these years, still stirs my imagination. His type has altogether a distinction that you feel to have been firmly caught and yet not vulgarly emphasised. The eyes are just too near together, but they are, in a wondrous way, both careless and intense, while lip, cheek, and chin, smooth and clear, are admirably drawn. Youth is still, you see, in all his presence, the joy and pride of life, the perfection of a high spirit and the expectation of a great fortune, which he takes for granted with unconscious insolence. Nothing has ever happened to humiliate or disappoint him, and if my fancy doesn't run away with me the whole presentation of him is a guarantee that he will die without having suffered. He is so handsome, in short, that you can scarcely say what he means, and so happy that you can scarcely guess what he feels.

It is of course, I hasten to add, an appreciably feminine rendering, light, delicate, vague, imperfectly synthetic—insistent and evasive, above all, in the wrong places; but the composition, none the less, is beautiful and the suggestion infinite. The grandest air of the thing struck me in fact, when first I saw it, as coming from the high artistic impertinence with which it offered itself as painted about 1850. It would have been a rare flower of refinement for that dark day. The "tone"—that of such a past as it pretended to—was there almost to excess, a brown bloom into which the image seemed mysteriously to retreat. The subject of it looks at me now across more years and more knowledge, but what I felt at the moment was that he managed to be at once a triumphant trick and a plausible evocation. He hushed me, I remember, with so many kinds of awe that I shouldn't have dreamt of asking who he was. All I said, after my first incoherences of wonder at my friend's practised skill, was: "And you've arrived at this truth without documents?"

"It depends on what you call documents."

"Without notes, sketches, studies?"

"I destroyed them years ago."

"Then you once had them?"

She just hung fire. "I once had everything."

It told me both more and less then I had asked; enough at all events to make my next question, as I uttered it, sound even to myself a little foolish. "So that it's all memory?"

From where she stood she looked once more at her work; after which she jerked away and, taking several steps, came back to me with something new—whatever it was I had already seen—in her air and answer. "It's all *hate*!" she threw at me, and then went out of the room. It was not till she had gone that I quite understood why. Extremely affected by the impression visibly made on me, she had burst into tears but had wished me not to see them. She left me alone for some time with her wonderful subject, and I again, in her absence, made things out. He was dead—he had been dead for years; the sole humiliation, as I have called it, that he was to know had come to him in that form. The canvas held and cherished

him, in any case, as it only holds the dead. She had suffered
from him, it came to me, the worst that a woman can suffer,
and the wound he had dealt her, though hidden, had never
effectually healed. It had bled again while she worked. Yet
when she at last reappeared there was but one thing to say.
"The beauty, heaven knows, I see. But I don't see what you
call the infamy."

She gave him a last look—again she turned away. "Oh, he
was like that."

"Well, whatever he was like," I remember replying, "I wonder you can bear to part with him. Isn't it better to let her
see the picture first here?"

As to this she doubted. "I don't think I want her to come."

I wondered. "You continue to object so to meet her?"

"What good will it do? It's quite impossible I should alter
him for her."

"Oh, she won't want *that*!" I laughed. "She'll adore him
as he is."

"Are you quite sure of your idea?"

"That he's to figure as Mr. Bridgenorth? Well, if I hadn't
been from the first, my dear lady, I should be now. Fancy,
with the chance, her *not* jumping at him! Yes, he'll figure as
Mr. Bridgenorth."

"Mr. Bridgenorth!" she echoed, making the sound, with
her small, cold laugh, grotesquely poor for him. He might
really have been a prince, and I wondered if he hadn't been.
She had, at all events, a new notion. "Do you mind my having
it taken to your place and letting her come to see it there?"
Which—as I immediately embraced her proposal, deferring
to her reasons, whatever they were—was what was speedily
arranged.

II

The next day therefore I had the picture in charge, and on
the following Mrs. Bridgenorth, whom I had notified, arrived.
I had placed it, framed and on an easel, well in evidence, and
I have never forgotten the look and the cry that, as she became aware of it, leaped into her face and from her lips. It
was an extraordinary moment, all the more that it found me

quite unprepared—so extraordinary that I scarce knew at first what had happened. By the time I really perceived, moreover, more things had happened than one, so that when I pulled myself together it was to face the situation as a whole. She had recognised on the instant the subject; that came first and was irrepressibly vivid in her. Her recognition had, for the length of a flash, lighted for her the possibility that the stroke had been directed. That came second, and she flushed with it as with a blow in the face. What came third—and it was what was really most wondrous—was the quick instinct of getting both her strange recognition and her blind suspicion well in hand. She couldn't control, however, poor woman, the strong colour in her face and the quick tears in her eyes. She could only glare at the canvas, gasping, grimacing, and try to gain time. Whether in surprise or in resentment she intensely reflected, feeling more than anything else how little she might prudently show; and I was conscious even at the moment that nothing of its kind could have been finer than her effort to swallow her shock in ten seconds.

How many seconds she took I didn't measure; enough, assuredly, for me also to profit. I gained more time than she, and the greatest oddity doubtless was my own private manœuvre—the quickest calculation that, acting from a mere confused instinct, I had ever made. If she had known the great gentleman represented there and yet had determined on the spot to carry herself as ignorant, all my loyalty to Mary Tredick came to the surface in a prompt counter-move. What gave me opportunity was the red in her cheek. "Why, you've known him!"

I saw her ask herself for an instant if she mightn't successfully make her startled state pass as the mere glow of pleasure —her natural greeting to her acquisition. She was pathetically, yet at the same time almost comically, divided. Her line was so to cover her tracks that every avowal of a past connection was a danger; but it also concerned her safety to learn, in the light of our astounding coincidence, how far she already stood exposed. She meanwhile begged the question. She smiled through her tears. "He's too magnificent!"

But I gave her, as I say, all too little time. "Who is he? Who *was* he?"

It must have been my look still more than my words that determined her. She wavered but an instant longer, panted, laughed, cried again, and then, dropping into the nearest seat, gave herself up so completely that I was almost ashamed. "Do you think I'd tell you his *name*?" The burden of the backward years—all the effaced and ignored—lived again, almost like an accent unlearned but freshly breaking out at a touch, in the very sound of the words. These perceptions she, however, the next thing showed me, were a game at which two could play. She had to look at me but an instant. "Why, you really *don't* know it!"

I judged best to be frank. "I don't know it."

"Then how does *she*?"

"How do you?" I laughed. "I'm a different matter."

She sat a minute turning things round, staring at the picture. "The likeness, the likeness!" It was almost too much.

"It's so true?"

"Beyond everything."

I considered. "But a resemblance to a known individual— that wasn't what you wanted."

She sprang up at this in eager protest. "Ah, no one else would see it."

I showed again, I fear, my amusement. "No one but you and she?"

"It's her doing *him*!" She was held by her wonder. "Doesn't she, on your honour, know?"

"That his is the very head you would have liked if you had dared? Not a bit. How *should* she? She knows nothing—on my honour."

Mrs. Bridgenorth continued to marvel. "She just painted him for the kind of face——?"

"That corresponds with my description of what you wished? Precisely."

"But *how*—after so long? From memory? As a friend?"

"As a reminiscence—yes. Visual memory, you see, in our uncanny race, is wonderful. As the ideal thing, simply, for your purpose. You *are* then suited?" I after an instant added.

She had again been gazing, and at this turned her eyes on me; but I saw she couldn't speak, couldn't do more at least than sound, unutterably, "Suited!" so that I was positively not surprised when suddenly—just as Mary had done, the power to produce this effect seeming a property of the model—she burst into tears. I feel no harsher in relating it, however I may appear, than I did at the moment, but it is a fact that while she just wept I literally had a fresh inspiration on behalf of Miss Tredick's interests. I knew exactly, moreover, before my companion had recovered herself, what she would next ask me; and I consciously brought this appeal on in order to have it over. I explained that I had not the least idea of the identity of our artist's sitter, to which she had given me no clue. I had nothing but my impression that she had known him—known him well; and, from whatever material she had worked, the fact of his having also been known to Mrs. Bridgenorth was a coincidence pure and simple. It partook of the nature of prodigy, but such prodigies did occur. My visitor listened with avidity and credulity. She was so far reassured. Then I saw her question come. "Well, if she doesn't dream he was ever any-thing to me—or what he will be now—I'm going to ask you, as a very particular favour, never to tell her. She will want to know of course exactly how I've been struck. You'll naturally say that I'm delighted, but may I exact from you that you say nothing else?"

There was supplication in her face, but I had to think. "There are conditions I must put to you first, and one of them is also a question, only more frank than yours. Was this mysterious personage—frustrated by death—to have married you?"

She met it bravely. "Certainly, if he had lived."

I was only amused at an artlessness in her "certainly." "Very good. But why do you wish the coincidence——"

"Kept from her?" She knew exactly why. "Because if she suspects it she won't let me have the picture. Therefore," she added with decision, "you must let me pay for it on the spot."

"What do you mean by on the spot?"

"I'll send you a cheque as soon as I get home."

"Oh," I laughed, "let us understand. Why do you consider she won't let you have the picture?"

She made me wait a little for this, but when it came it was perfectly lucid. "Because she'll then see how much more I must want it."

"How much less—wouldn't it be rather, since the bargain was, as the more convenient thing, not for a likeness?"

"Oh," said Mrs. Bridgenorth with impatience, "the likeness will take care of itself. She'll put this and that together." Then she brought out her real apprehension. "She'll be jealous."

"Oh!" I laughed. But I was startled.

"She'll hate me!"

I wondered. "But I don't think she liked him."

"Don't think?" She stared at me, with her echo, over all that might be in it, then seemed to find little enough. "I *say!*"

It was almost comically the old Mrs. Bridgenorth. "But I gather from her that he was bad."

"Then what was *she?*"

I barely hesitated. "What were *you?*"

"That's my own business." And she turned again to the picture. "He was good enough for her to do *that* of him."

I took it in once more. "Artistically speaking, for the way it's done, it's one of the most curious things I've ever seen."

"It's a grand treat!" said poor Mrs. Bridgenorth more simply.

It was, it *is* really; which is exactly what made the case so interesting. "Yet I feel somehow that, as I say, it wasn't done with love."

It was wonderful how she understood. "It was done with rage."

"Then what have you to fear?"

She knew again perfectly. "What happened when he made *me* jealous. So much," she declared, "that if you'll give me your word for silence——"

"Well?"

"Why, I'll double the money."

"Oh," I replied, taking a turn about in the excitement of our concurrence, "that's exactly what—to do a still better stroke for her—it had just come to *me* to propose!"

"It's understood then, on your oath as a gentleman?" She was so eager that practically this settled it, though I moved to and fro a little while she watched me in suspense. It vibrated all round us that she had gone out to the thing in a stifled flare, that a whole close relation had in the few minutes revived. We know it of the truly amiable person that he will strain a point for another that he wouldn't strain for himself. The stroke to put in for Mary was positively prescribed. The work represented really much more than had been covenanted, and if the purchaser chose so to value it this was her own affair. I decided. "If it's understood also on *your* word."

We were so at one that we shook hands on it. "And when may I send?"

"Well, I shall see her this evening. Say early to-morrow."

"Early to-morrow." And I went with her to her brougham, into which, I remember, as she took leave, she expressed regret that she mightn't then and there have introduced the canvas for removal. I consoled her with remarking that she couldn't have got it in—which was not quite true.

I saw Mary Tredick before dinner, and though I was not quite ideally sure of my present ground with her I instantly brought out my news. "She's so delighted that I felt I must in conscience do something still better for you. She's not to have it on the original terms. I've put up the price."

Mary wondered. "But to what?"

"Well, to four hundred. If you say so I'll try even for five."

"Oh, she'll never give that."

"I beg your pardon."

"After the agreement?" She looked grave. "I don't like such leaps and bounds."

"But, my dear child, they're yours. You contracted for a decorative trifle and you've produced a breathing masterpiece."

She thought. "Is that what she calls it?" Then, as having to think too, I hesitated, "What does she know?" she pursued.

"She knows she wants it."

"So much as that?"

At this I had to brace myself a little. "So much that she'll send me the cheque this afternoon, and that you'll have mine by the first post in the morning."

"Before she has even received the picture?"

"Oh, she'll send for it to-morrow." And as I was dining out and had still to dress, my time was up. Mary came with me to the door, where I repeated my assurance. "You shall receive my cheque by the first post." To which I added: "If it's little enough for a lady so much in need to pay for *any* husband, it isn't worth mentioning as the price of such a one as you've given her!"

I was in a hurry, but she held me. "Then you've felt your idea confirmed?"

"My idea?"

"That that's what I *have* given her?"

I suddenly fancied I had perhaps gone too far; but I had kept my cab and was already in it. "Well, put it," I called with excess of humour over the front, "that you've, at any rate, given *him* a wife!"

When on my return from dinner that night I let myself in, my first care, in my dusky studio, was to make light for another look at Mary's subject. I felt the impulse to bid him good night, but, to my astonishment, he was no longer there. His place was a void—he had already disappeared. I saw, however, after my first surprise, what had happened—saw it moreover, frankly, with some relief. As my servants were in bed I could ask no questions, but it was clear that Mrs. Bridgenorth, whose note, containing its cheque, lay on my table, had been after all unable to wait. The note, I found, mentioned nothing but the enclosure; but it had come by hand, and it was her silence that told the tale. Her messenger had been instructed to "act"; he had come with a vehicle, he had transferred to it canvas and frame. The prize was now therefore landed and the incident closed. I didn't altogether, the next morning, know why, but I had slept the better for the sense of these things, and as soon as my attendant came in I asked for details. It was on this that his answer surprised me. "No, sir, there was no man; she came herself. She had only a four-wheeler, but I helped her, and we got it in. It was a squeeze, sir, but she *would* take it."

I wondered. "She had a four-wheeler? and not her servant?"

"No, no, sir. She came, as you may say, single-handed."

"And not even in her brougham, which would have been larger?"

My man, with his habit, weighed it. "But *have* she a brougham, sir?"

"Why, the one she was here in yesterday."

Then light broke. "Oh, *that* lady! It wasn't her, sir. It was Miss Tredick."

Light broke, but darkness a little followed it—a darkness that, after breakfast, guided my steps back to my friend. There, in its own first place, I met her creation; but I saw it would be a different thing meeting *her*. She immediately put down on a table, as if she had expected me, the cheque I had sent her overnight. "Yes, I've brought it away. And I can't take the money."

I found myself in despair. "You want to keep him?"

"I don't understand what has happened."

"You just back out?"

"I don't understand," she repeated, "what has happened." But what I had already perceived was, on the contrary, that she very nearly, that she in fact quite remarkably, did understand. It was as if in my zeal I had given away my case, and I felt that my test was coming. She had been thinking all night with intensity, and Mrs. Bridgenorth's generosity, coupled with Mrs. Bridgenorth's promptitude, had kept her awake. Thence, for a woman nervous and critical, imaginations, visions, questions. "Why, in writing me last night, did you take for granted it was *she* who had swooped down? Why," asked Mary Tredick, "should she swoop?"

Well, if I could drive a bargain for Mary I felt I could *a fortiori* lie for her. "Because it's her way. She does swoop. She's impatient and uncontrolled. And it's affectation for you to pretend," I said with diplomacy, "that you see no reason for her falling in love——"

"Falling in love?" She took me straight up.

"With that gentleman. Certainly. What woman wouldn't? What woman didn't? I really don't see, you know, your right to back out."

"I won't back out," she presently returned, "if you'll answer me a question. Does she know the man represented?" Then as I hung fire: "It has come to me that she must. It would account for so much. For the strange way I feel," she went on, "and for the extraordinary sum you've been able to extract from her."

It was a pity, and I flushed with it, besides wincing at the word she used. But Mrs. Bridgenorth and I, between us, had clearly made the figure too high. "You think that, if she *had* guessed, I would naturally work it to 'extract' more?"

She turned away from me on this and, looking blank in her trouble, moved vaguely about. Then she stopped. "I see him set up there. I hear her say it. What you said she would make him pass for."

I believe I foolishly tried—though only for an instant—to look as if I didn't remember what I had said. "Her husband?"

"He wasn't."

The next minute I had risked it. "Was he yours?"

I don't know what I had expected, but I found myself surprised at her mere pacific head-shake. "No."

"Then why mayn't he have been——?"

"Another woman's? Because he died, to my absolute knowledge, unmarried." She spoke as quietly. "He had known many women, and there was one in particular with whom he became—and too long remained—ruinously intimate. She tried to make him marry her, and he was very near it. Death, however, saved him. But she was the reason——"

"Yes?" I feared again from her a wave of pain, and I went on while she kept it back. "Did you know her?"

"She was one I wouldn't." Then she brought it out. "She was the reason he failed me." Her successful detachment somehow said all, reduced me to a flat, kind "Oh!" that marked my sense of her telling me, against my expectation, more than I knew what to do with. But it was just while I wondered how to turn her confidence that she repeated, in a changed voice, her challenge of a moment before. "Does she know the man represented?"

"I haven't the least idea." And having so acquitted myself I added, with what strikes me now as futility: "She certainly—yesterday—didn't name him."

"Only recognised him?"

"If she did she brilliantly concealed it."

"So that you got nothing from her?"

It was a question that offered me a certain advantage. "I thought you accused me of getting too much."

She gave me a long look, and I now saw everything in her face. "It's very nice—what you're doing for me, and you do it handsomely. It's beautiful—beautiful, and I thank you with all my heart. But I know."

"And what do you know?"

She went about now preparing her usual work. "What he must have been to her."

"You mean she was the person?"

"Well," she said, putting on her old spectacles, "she was one of them."

"And you accept so easily the astounding coincidence——?"

"Of my finding myself, after years, in so extraordinary a relation with her? What do you call easily? I've passed a night of torment."

"But what put it into your head——?"

"That I had so blindly and strangely given him back to her? *You* put it—yesterday."

"And how?"

"I can't tell you. You didn't in the least mean to—on the contrary. But you dropped the seed. The plant, after you had gone," she said with a business-like pull at her easel, "the plant began to grow. I *saw* them there—in your studio—face to face."

"You were jealous?" I laughed.

She gave me through her glasses another look, and they seemed, from this moment, in their queerness, to have placed her quite on the other side of the gulf of time. She was firm there; she was settled; I couldn't get at her now. "I see she told you I *would* be." I doubtless kept down too little my start at it, and she immediately pursued. "You say I accept the coincidence, which is of course prodigious. But such things happen. Why shouldn't I accept it if you do?"

"*Do* I?" I smiled.

She began her work in silence, but she presently exclaimed: "I'm glad I didn't meet her!"

"I don't yet see why you wouldn't."

"Neither do I. It was an instinct."

"Your instincts"—I tried to be ironic—"are miraculous."

"They *have* to be, to meet such accidents. I must ask you kindly to tell her, when you return her gift, that now I have done the picture I find I must after all keep it for myself."

"Giving no reason?"

She painted away. "She'll know the reason."

Well, by this time I knew it too; I knew so many things that I fear my resistance was weak. If our wonderful client hadn't been his wife in fact, she was not to be helped to become his wife in fiction. I knew almost more than I can say, more at any rate than I could then betray. He had been bound in common mercy to stand by my friend, and he had basely forsaken her. This indeed brought up the obscure, into which I shyly gazed. "Why, even granting your theory, should you grudge her the portrait? It was painted in bitterness."

"Yes. Without that——!"

"It wouldn't have come? Precisely. Is it in bitterness, then, you'll keep it?"

She looked up from her canvas. "In what would *you* keep it?"

It made me jump. "Do you mean I *may*?" Then I had my idea. "I'd give you her price for it!"

Her smile through her glasses was beautiful. "And afterwards make it over to her? You shall have it when I die." With which she came away from her easel, and I saw that I was staying her work and should properly go. So I put out my hand to her. "It took—whatever you will!—to paint it," she said, "but I shall keep it in joy." I could answer nothing now—had to cease to pretend; the thing was in her hands. For a moment we stood there, and I had again the sense, melancholy and final, of her being, as it were, remotely glazed and fixed into what she had done. "He's taken from me, and for all those years he's kept. Then she herself, by a prodigy——!" She lost herself again in the wonder of it.

"Unwittingly gives him back?"

She fairly, for an instant over the marvel, closed her eyes. "Gives him back."

Then it was I saw how he would be kept! But it was the end of my vision. I could only write, ruefully enough, to Mrs. Bridgenorth, whom I never met again, but of whose death—preceding by a couple of years Mary Tredick's—I happened to hear. This is an old man's tale. I have inherited the picture, in the deep beauty of which, however, darkness still lurks. No one, strange to say, has ever recognised the model, but everyone asks his name. I don't even know it.

Broken Wings

Conscious as he was of what was between them, though perhaps less conscious than ever of why there should at that time of day be anything, he would yet scarce have supposed they could be so long in a house together without some word or some look. It had been since the Saturday afternoon and that made twenty-four hours. The party—five-and-thirty people, and some of them great—was one in which words and looks might more or less have gone astray. The effect, none the less, he judged, would have been, for her quite as for himself, that no sound and no sign from the other had been picked up by either. They had happened, both at dinner and at luncheon, to be so placed as not to have to glare—or to grin—across; and for the rest they could each, in such a crowd, as freely help the general ease to keep them apart as assist it to bring them together. One chance there was, of course, that might be beyond their control. He had been the night before half surprised at not finding her his "fate" when the long procession to the dining-room solemnly hooked itself together. He would have said in advance—recognising it as one of the sharp "notes" of Mundham—that, should the gathering contain a literary lady, the literary lady would, for congruity, be apportioned to the arm, when there was a question of arms, of the gentleman present who represented the nearest thing to literature. Poor Straith represented "art" and that, no doubt, would have been near enough had not the party offered for choice a slight excess of men. The representative of art had been of the two or three who went in alone, whereas Mrs. Harvey had gone in with one of the representatives of banking.

It was certain, however, that she would not again be consigned to Lord Belgrove, and it was just possible that he himself should not be again alone. She would be, on the whole, the most probable remedy to that state, on his part, of disgrace; and this precisely was the great interest of their situation—they were the only persons present without some advantage over somebody else. They hadn't a single advan-

326

tage; they could be named for nothing but their cleverness; they were at the bottom of the social ladder. The social ladder, even at Mundham, had—as they might properly have been told, as indeed practically they *were* told—to end somewhere; which is no more than to say that, as he strolled about and thought of many things, Stuart Straith had, after all, a good deal the sense of helping to hold it up. Another of the things he thought of was the special oddity—for it was nothing else—of his being there at all, and being there in particular so out of his order and his turn. He couldn't answer for Mrs. Harvey's turn. It might well be that she was *in* hers; but these Saturday-to-Monday occasions had hitherto mostly struck him as great gilded cages as to which care was taken that the birds should be birds of a feather.

There had been a wonderful walk in the afternoon, within the limits of the place, to a far-away tea-house; and, in spite of the combinations and changes of this episode, he had still escaped the necessity of putting either his old friend or himself to the test. Also it had been all, he flattered himself, without the pusillanimity of his avoiding her. Life was, indeed, well understood in these great conditions; the conditions constituted in their greatness a kind of fundamental facility, provided a general exemption, bathed the hour, whatever it was, in a universal blandness, that were all a happy solvent for awkward relations. It was beautiful, for instance, that if their failure to meet amid so much meeting had been of Mrs. Harvey's own contrivance he couldn't be in the least vulgarly sure of it. There were places in which he would have had no doubt, places different enough from Mundham. He felt all the same and without anguish that these were much more *his* places—even if she didn't feel that they were much more hers. The day had been warm and splendid, and this moment of its wane—with dinner in sight, but as across a field of polished pink marble which seemed to say that wherever in such a house there was space there was also, benignantly, time—formed, of the whole procession of the hours, the one dearest to our friend, who on such occasions interposed it, whenever he could, between the set of impressions that ended and the set that began with "dressing." The great terraces and gardens were almost void; people had scattered, though not altogether even yet to dress. The air of the place, with the immense house all seated aloft in strength, robed with summer and crowned with success, was such as to contribute something of its own to the poetry of early evening. This visitor, at any rate, saw and felt it all through one of those fine hazes of August that remind you—at least, they reminded *him*—of the artful gauze stretched across the stage of a theatre when an effect of mystery or some particular pantomimic ravishment is desired.

Should he, in fact, have to pair with Mrs. Harvey for dinner it would be a shame to him not to have addressed her sooner; and should she, on the contrary, be put with someone else the loss of so much of the time would have but the greater ugliness. Didn't he meanwhile make out that there were ladies in the lower garden, from which the sound of voices, faint, but, as always in the upper air of Mundham, exceedingly sweet, was just now borne to him? She might be among them, and if he should find her he would let her know he had sought her. He would treat it frankly as an occasion for declaring that what had happened between them—or rather what had *not* happened—was too absurd. What at present occurred, however, was that in his quest of her he suddenly, at the turn of an alley, perceived her, not far off, seated in a sort of bower with the Ambassador. With this he pulled up, going another way and pretending not to see them. Three times already that afternoon he had observed her in different situations with the Ambassador. He was the more struck accordingly when, upward of an hour later, again alone and with his state unremedied, he saw her placed for dinner next his Excellency. It was not at all what would have been at Mundham her right seat, so that it could only be explained by his Excellency's direct request. She *was* a success! This time Straith was well in her view and could see that in the candlelight of the wonderful room, where the lustres were, like the table, all crystal and silver, she was as handsome as anyone, taking the women of her age, and also as "smart" as the evening before, and as true as any of the others to the law of a marked difference in her smartness. If the beautiful way she held herself—for decidedly it *was* beautiful—came in a great measure from the good thing she professionally made of it all, our observer could reflect that the poor thing *he* professionally made of it probably affected his attitude in just the opposite way; but they communicated neither in the glare nor in the grin that he had dreaded. Still, their eyes did now meet, and then it seemed to him that her own were strange.

II

She, on her side, had her private consciousness, and quite as full a one, doubtless, as he, but with the advantage that, when the company separated for the night, she was not, like her friend, reduced to a vigil unalloyed. Lady Claude, at the top of the stairs, had said, "May I look in—in five minutes—if you don't mind?" and then had arrived in due course and in a wonderful new beribboned gown, the thing just launched for such occasions. Lady Claude was young and earnest and delightfully bewildered and bewildering, and however interesting she might, through certain elements in her situation, have seemed to a literary lady, her own admirations and curiosities were such as from the first promised to rule the hour. She had already expressed to Mrs. Harvey a really informed enthusiasm. She not only delighted in her numerous books, which was a tribute the author had not infrequently met, but she even appeared to have read them—an appearance with which her interlocutress was much less acquainted. The great thing was that she also yearned to write, and that she had turned up in her fresh furbelows not only to reveal this secret and to ask for direction and comfort, but literally to make a stranger confidence, for which the mystery of midnight seemed propitious. Midnight was, indeed, as the situation developed, well over before her confidence was spent, for it had ended by gathering such a current as floated forth, with everything in Lady Claude's own life, many things more in that of her adviser. Mrs. Harvey was, at all events, amused, touched, and effectually kept awake; and at the end of half an hour they had quite got what might have been called their second wind of frankness and were using it for a discussion of the people in the house. Their primary communion had been simply on the question of the pecuniary profits of literature as the producer of so many admired volumes was prepared to present them to an aspirant. Lady Claude was in financial difficulties and desired the literary issue. This was the breathless revelation she had rustled over a mile of crimson velvet corridor to make.

"Nothing?" she had three minutes later incredulously gasped. "I can make nothing at all?" But the gasp was slight compared with the stupefaction produced in her by a brief further parley, in the course of which Mrs. Harvey had, after a hesitation, taken her own plunge. "*You* make so little—wonderful *you*!" And then, as the producer of the admired volumes simply sat there in her dressing-gown, with the saddest of slow head-shakes, looking suddenly too wan even to care that it was at last all out: "What, in that case, is the use of success and celebrity and genius? You *have* no success?" She had looked almost awestruck at this further confession of her friend. They were face to face in a poor human crudity, which transformed itself quickly into an effusive embrace. "You've had it and lost it? Then when it has been as great as yours one *can* lose it?"

"More easily than one can get it."

Lady Claude continued to marvel. "But you do so much—and it's so beautiful!" On which Mrs. Harvey simply smiled again in her handsome despair, and after a moment found herself again in the arms of her visitor. The younger woman had remained for a little a good deal arrested and hushed, and had, at any rate, sensitive and charming, immediately dropped, in the presence of this almost august unveiling, the question of her own thin troubles. But there are short cuts at that hour of night that morning scarce knows, and it took but little more of the breath of the real to suggest to Lady Claude more questions in such a connection than she could answer for herself. "How, then, if you haven't private means, do you get on?"

"Ah! I don't get on."

Lady Claude looked about. There were objects scattered in the fine old French room. "You have lovely things."

"Two."

"Two?"

"Two frocks. I couldn't stay another day."

"Ah, what is *that*? I couldn't either," said Lady Claude soothingly. "And you have," she continued, in the same spirit, "your nice maid——"

"Who's indeed a charming woman, but my cook in disguise!" Mrs. Harvey dropped.

"Ah, you *are* clever!" her friend cried, with a laugh that was as a climax of reassurance.

"Extraordinarily. But don't think," Mrs. Harvey hastened to add, "that I mean that that's why I'm here."

Her companion candidly thought. "Then why are you?"

"I haven't the least idea. I've been wondering all the while, as I've wondered so often before on such occasions, and without arriving at any other reason than that London is so wild."

Lady Claude wondered. "Wild?"

"Wild!" said her friend, with some impatience. "That's the way London strikes."

"But do you call such an invitation a blow?"

"Yes—crushing. No one else, at all events, either," Mrs. Harvey added, "could tell you why I'm here."

Lady Claude's power to receive—and it was perhaps her most attaching quality—was greater still, when she felt strongly, than her power to protest. "Why, how can you say that when you've only to see how everyone likes and admires you? Just look at the Ambassador," she had earnestly insisted. And this was what had precisely, as I have mentioned, carried the stream of their talk a good deal away from its source. It had therefore not much further to go before setting in motion the name of Stuart Straith, as to whom Lady Claude confessed to an interest—good-looking, distinguished, "sympathetic," as he was—that she could really almost hate him for having done nothing whatever to encourage. He had not spoken to her once.

"But, my dear, if he hasn't spoken to *me*!"

Lady Claude appeared to regret this not too much for a hint that, after all, there might be a difference. "Oh, but *could* he?"

"Without my having spoken to him first?" Mrs. Harvey turned it over. "Perhaps not; but I couldn't have done that."

Then, to explain, and not only because Lady Claude was naturally vague, but because what was still visibly most vivid to her was her independent right to have been "made up" to: "And yet not because we're not acquainted."

"You know him, then?"

"But too well."

"You mean you don't like him?"

"On the contrary, I like him—to distraction."

"Then what's the matter?" Lady Claude asked with some impatience.

Her friend hesitated but a moment. "Well, he wouldn't have me."

" 'Have' you?"

"Ten years ago, after Mr. Harvey's death, when, if he had lifted a finger, I would have married him."

"But he didn't lift it?"

"He was too grand. I was too small—by *his* measure. He wanted to keep himself; he saw his future."

Lady Claude earnestly followed. "His present position?"

"Yes—everything that was to come to him; his steady rise in value."

"Has it been so great?"

"Surely—his situation and name. Don't you know his lovely work and what's thought of it?"

"Oh yes, I know. That's why——" But Lady Claude stopped. After which: "But if he's still keeping himself?"

"Oh, it's not for me," said Mrs. Harvey.

"And evidently not for *me*. Whom then," her visitor asked, "does he think good enough?"

"Oh, these great people!" Mrs. Harvey smiled.

"But *we're* great people—you and I!" And Lady Claude kissed her good night.

"You mustn't, all the same," the elder woman said, "betray the secret of *my* greatness, which I've told you, please remember, only in the deepest confidence."

Her tone had a quiet purity of bitterness that for a moment longer held her friend, after which Lady Claude had the happy inspiration of meeting it with graceful gaiety. "It's quite for the best, I'm sure, that Mr. Straith wouldn't have you. You've kept yourself too; you'll marry yet—an ambassador!" And with another good night she reached the door. "You say you don't get on, but you do."

"Ah!" said Mrs. Harvey with vague attenuation.

"Oh yes, you do," Lady Claude insisted, while the door emphasised it with a little clap that sounded through the still house.

III

The first night of *The New Girl* occurred, as everyone remembers, three years ago, and the play is running yet, a fact that may render strange the failure to be widely conscious of which two persons in the audience were guilty. It was not till afterward present either to Mrs. Harvey or to Stuart Straith that *The New Girl* was one of the greatest successes of modern times. Indeed if the question had been put to them on the spot they might have appeared much at sea. But this, I may as well immediately say, was the result of their having found themselves side by side in the stalls and thereby given most of their attention to their own predicament. Straith showed that he felt the importance of meeting it promptly, for he turned to his neighbour, who was already in her place, as soon as her identity had come distinct through his own arrival and subsidence. "I don't quite see how you can help speaking to me now."

Her face could only show him how long she had been aware of his approach. "The sound of your voice, coming to me straight, makes it indeed as easy for me as I could possibly desire."

He looked about at the serried rows, the loaded galleries and the stuffed boxes, with recognitions and nods; and this made between them another pause, during which, while the music seemed perfunctory and the bustle that, in a London audience, represents concentration increased, they felt how effectually, in the thick, preoccupied medium, how extraordinarily, they were together.

"Well, that second afternoon at Mundham, just before dinner, I was very near forcing your hand. But something put me off. You're really too grand."

"Oh!" she murmured.

"Ambassadors," said Stuart Straith.

"Oh!" she again sounded. And before anything more could pass the curtain was up. It came down in due course and achieved, after various intervals, the rest of its movements without interrupting, for our friends, the sense of an evening of talk. They said when it was down almost nothing about the play, and when one of them toward the end put to the other, vaguely, "Is—a—this thing going?" the question had scarce the effect of being even relevant. What was clearest to them was that the people about were somehow enough taken up to leave them at their ease—but what taken up with they but half made out. Mrs. Harvey had, none the less, mentioned early that her presence had a reason and that she ought to attend, and her companion had asked her what she thought of a certain picture made at a given moment by the stage, in the reception of which he was so interested that it was really what had brought him. These were glances, however, that quickly strayed—strayed, for instance (as this could carry them far), in its coming to one of them to say that, whatever the piece might be, the real thing, as they had seen it at Mundham, was more than a match for any piece. For it was Mundham that *was*, theatrically, the real thing; better for scenery, dresses, music, pretty women, bare shoulders, everything—even incoherent dialogue; a much bigger and braver show, and got up as it were, infinitely more "regardless." By Mundham they were held long enough to find themselves, though with an equal surprise, quite at one as to the special oddity of their having caught each other in such a plight. Straith said that he supposed what his friend meant was that it was odd *he* should have been there; to which she returned that she had been imputing to him exactly that judgment of her own presence.

"But why shouldn't *you* be?" he asked. "Isn't that just what you *are*? Aren't you, in your way—like those people—a child of fortune and fashion?"

He got no more answer to this for some time than if he had fairly wounded her; he indeed that evening got no answer at all that was direct. But in the next interval she brought out with abruptness, taking no account of some other matter he had just touched, "Don't you really know——?"

She had paused.

"Know what?"

Again she went on without heeding. "A place like Mundham is, for me, a survival, though poor Mundham in particular won't, for me, have survived that visit—for which it's to be pitied, isn't it? It was a glittering ghost—since laid!—of my old time."

Straith at this almost gave a start. "Have *you* got a new time?"

"Do you mean that you have?"

"Well," said Straith, "mine may now be called middle-aged. It seems so long, I mean, since I set my watch to it."

"Oh, I haven't even a watch!" she returned with a laugh. "I'm beyond watches." After which she added: "We *might* have met more—or, I should say perhaps, have got more out of it when we *have* met."

"Yes, it has been too little. But I've always explained it by our living in such different worlds."

Mrs. Harvey had an occasional incoherence. "Are you unhappy?"

He gave her a singular smile. "You said just now that you're beyond watches. I'm beyond unhappiness."

She turned from him and presently brought out: "I ought absolutely to take away *something* of the play."

"By all means. There's certainly something *I* shall take."

"Ah, then you must help me—give it me."

"With all my heart," said Straith, "if it *can* help you. It's my feeling of our renewal."

She had one of the sad, slow head-shakes that at Mundham had been impressive to Lady Claude. "That won't help me."

"Then you must let me put to you now what I should have tried to get near enough to you there to put if I hadn't been so afraid of the Ambassador. What has it been so long—our impossibility?"

"Well, I can only answer for my own vision of it, which is—which always was—that you were sorry for me, but felt a sort of scruple of showing me that you had nothing better than pity to give."

"May I come to see you?" Straith asked some minutes after this.

Her words, for which he had also awhile to wait, had, in truth, as little as his own the appearance of a reply. "*Are* you unhappy—really? Haven't you everything?"

"You're beautiful!" he said for all answer. "Mayn't I come?"

She hesitated.

"Where is your studio?"

"Oh, not too far to reach from it. Don't be anxious; I can walk, or even take the bus."

Mrs. Harvey once more delayed. Then she answered: "Mayn't I rather come there?"

"I shall be but too delighted."

It was said with promptness, even precipitation; yet the understanding, shortly after, appeared to have left between them a certain awkwardness, and it was almost as if to change the subject and relieve them equally that she suddenly reminded him of something he had spoken earlier. "You were to tell me why in particular you had to be here."

"Oh yes. To see my dresses."

"Yours!" She wondered.

"The second act. I made them out for them—drew them."

Before she could check it her tone escaped. "You?"

"I." He looked straight before him. "For the fee. And we didn't even notice them."

"*I* didn't," she confessed. But it offered the fact as a sign of her kindness for him, and this kindness was traceably what inspired something she said in the draughty porch, after the performance, while the footman of the friend, a fat, rich, immensely pleased lady, who had given her a lift and then rejoined her from a seat in the balcony, went off to make sure of the brougham. "May I do something about your things?"

" 'Do something'?"

"When I've paid you my visit. Write something—about your pictures. I do a correspondence," said Mrs. Harvey.

He wondered as she had done in the stalls. "For a paper?"

"The *Blackport Banner*. A 'London Letter.' The new books, the new plays, the new twaddle of any sort—a little music, a little gossip, a little 'art.' You'll help me—I need it awfully—with the art. I do three a month."

"*You*—wonderful you?" He spoke as Lady Claude had done, and could no more help it again than Mrs. Harvey had been able to help it in the stalls.

"Oh, as you say, for the fee!" On which, as the footman signalled, her old lady began to plunge through the crowd.

IV

At the studio, where she came to him within the week, her first movement had been to exclaim on the splendid abundance of his work. She had looked round charmed—so struck as to be, as she called it, crushed. "You've such a wonderful lot to show."

"Indeed I have!" said Stuart Straith.

"That's where you beat *us*."

"I think it may very well be," he went on, "where I beat almost everyone."

"And is much of it new?"

He looked about with her. "Some of it is pretty old. But my things have a way, I admit, of growing old extraordinarily fast. They seem to me in fact, nowadays, quite 'born old.' "

She had the manner, after a little, of coming back to something. "You *are* unhappy. You're *not* beyond it. You're just nicely, just fairly and squarely, in the middle of it."

"Well," said Straith, "if it surrounds me like a desert, so that I'm lost in it, that comes to the same thing. But I want you to tell me about yourself."

She had continued at first to move about, and had taken out a pocket-book, which she held up at him. "This time I shall insist on notes. You made my mind a blank about that play, which is the sort of thing we can't afford. If it hadn't been for my fat old lady and the next day's papers!" She kept looking, going up to things, saying, "How wonderful!" and "Oh, your *way*!" and then stopping for a general impression, something in the whole charm. The place, high, handsome, neat, with two or three pale tapestries and several rare old pieces of furniture, showed a perfection of order, an absence of loose objects, as if it had been swept and squared for the occasion and made almost too immaculate. It was polished and cold—rather cold for the season and the weather; and

Stuart Straith himself, buttoned and brushed, as fine and as clean as his room, might at her arrival have reminded her of the master of a neat, bare ship on his deck awaiting a cargo. "May I see everything? May I 'use' everything?"

"Oh no; you mayn't by any means use everything. You mayn't use half. *Did* I spoil your 'London Letter'?" he continued after a moment.

"No one can spoil them as I spoil them myself. I can't do them—I don't know how, and don't want to. I do them wrong, and the people want such trash. Of course they'll sack me."

She was in the centre, and he had the effect of going round her, restless and vague, in large, slow circles. "Have you done them long?"

"Two or three months—this lot. But I've done others, and I know what happens. Oh, my dear, I've done strange things!"

"And is it a good job?"

She hesitated, then puffed, prettily enough, an indifferent sigh. "Three-and-ninepence. Is that good?" He had stopped before her, looking at her up and down. "What do you get," she went on, "for what you do for a play?"

"A little more, it would seem, than you. Four-and-sixpence. But I've only done, as yet, that one. Nothing else has offered."

"I see. But something *will*, eh?"

Poor Straith took a turn again. "Did you like them—for colour?" But again he pulled up. "Oh, I forgot; we didn't notice them!"

For a moment they could laugh about it. "I noticed them, I assure you, in the *Banner*. 'The costumes in the second act are of the most marvellous beauty.' That's what I said."

"Oh, that will fetch the managers!" But before her again he seemed to take her in from head to foot. "You speak of 'using' things. If you'd only use yourself—for my enlightenment. Tell me all."

"You look at me," said Mrs. Harvey, "as with the wonder of who designs *my* costumes. How I dress on it, how I do even what I still do on it, is *that* what you want to know?"

"What has happened to you?" Straith asked.

"How do I keep it up?" she continued, as if she had not heard him. "But I *don't* keep it up. *You* do," she declared as she again looked round her.

Once more it set him off, but for a pause once more almost as quick. "How long have you been——?"

"Been what?" she asked as he faltered.

"Unhappy."

She smiled at him from a depth of indulgence. "As long as you've been ignorant—that what I've been *wanting* is your pity. Ah, to have to know, as I believed I did, that you supposed it would wound me, and not to have been able to make you see that it was the one thing left to me that would help me! Give me your pity now. It's all I want. I don't care for anything else. But give me that."

He had, as it happened at the moment, to do a smaller and a usual thing before he could do one so great and so strange. The youth whom he kept for service arrived with a tea-tray, in arranging a place for which, with the sequel of serving Mrs. Harvey, seating her and seeing the youth again out of the room, some minutes passed.

"What pity could I dream of for you," he demanded as he at last dropped near her, "when I was myself so miserably sore?"

"Sore?" she wondered. "But you were happy—then."

"Happy not to have struck you as good enough? For I didn't, you know," he insisted. "You had your success, which was so immense. You had your high value, your future, your big possibilities; and I perfectly understood that, given those things, and given also my very much smaller situation, you should wish to keep yourself."

"Oh, oh!" She gasped as if hurt.

"I understand it; but how could it really make me 'happy'?" he asked.

She turned at him as with her hand on the old scar she could now carry. "You mean that all these years you've really not known——?"

"But not known what?"

His voice was so blank that at the sound of it, and at something that looked out from him, she only found another "Oh, oh!" which became the next instant a burst of tears.

V

She had appeared at first unwilling to receive him at home; but he understood it after she had left him, turning over more and more everything their meeting had shaken to the surface, and piecing together memories that at last, however darkly, made a sense. He was to call on her, it was finally agreed, but not till the end of the week, when she should have finished "moving"—she had but just changed quarters; and meanwhile, as he came and went, mainly in the cold chamber of his own past endeavour, which looked even to himself as studios look when artists are dead and the public, in the arranged place, are admitted to stare, he had plenty to think about. What had come out—he could see it now—was that each, ten years before, had miserably misunderstood and then had turned for relief from pain to a perversity of pride. But it was himself above all that he now sharply judged, since women, he felt, have to get on as they can, and for the mistake of this woman there were reasons he had, with a sore heart, to acknowledge. She had really found in the pomp of his early success, at the time they used to meet, and to care to, exactly the ground for her sense of failure with him that he had found in the vision of her gross popularity for his conviction that she judged him as comparatively small. Each had blundered, as sensitive souls of the "artistic temperament" blunder, into a conception not only of the other's attitude, but of the other's material situation at the moment, that had thrown them back on stupid secrecy, where their estrangement had grown like an evil plant in the shade. He had positively believed her to have gone on all the while making the five thousand a year that the first eight or ten of her so supremely happy novels had brought her in, just as she, on her side, had read into the felicity of his first new hits, his pictures "of the year" at three or four Academies, the absurdest theory of the sort of career that, thanks to big dealers and intelligent buyers, his gains would have built up for him. It looked vulgar enough now, but it had been grave enough then. His long, detached delusion about her "prices," at any rate, appeared to have been more than matched by the strange stories oc-

casionally floated to her—and all to make her but draw more
closely in—on the subject of his own.

It was with each equally that everything had changed—
everything but the stiff consciousness in either of the need to
conceal changes from the other. If she had cherished for long
years the soreness of her not being "good" enough, so this
was what had counted most in her sustained effort to appear
at least as good as he. London, meanwhile, was big; London
was blind and benighted; and nothing had ever occurred to
undermine for him the fiction of her prosperity. Before his
eyes there, while she sat with him, she had pulled off one by
one those vain coverings of her state that she confessed she
had hitherto done her best—and so always with an eye on
himself—deceptively to draw about it. He had felt frozen, as
he listened, at such likenesses to things he knew. He recognised as she talked, and he groaned as he understood. He
understood—oh, at last, whatever he had not done before!
And yet he could well have smiled, out of their common
abyss, at such odd identities and recurrences. Truly the arts
were sisters, as was so often said; for what apparently could
be more like the experience of one than the experience of
another? And she spared him things with it all. He felt that
too, just as, even while showing her how he followed, he had
bethought himself of closing his lips for the hour, none too
soon, on his own stale story. There had been a beautiful intelligence, for that matter, in her having asked him nothing
more. She had overflowed because shaken by not finding him
happy, and her surrender had somehow offered itself to him
as her way—the first that sprang up—of considering his trouble. She had left him, at all events, in full possession of all the
phases through which in "literary circles" acclaimed states
may pass on their regular march to eclipse and extinction. One
had but one's hour, and if one had it soon—it was really almost a case of choice—one didn't have it late. It might, moreover, never even remotely have approached, at its best, things
ridiculously rumoured. Straith felt, on the whole, how little
he had known of literary circles or of any mystery but his own,
indeed; on which, up to actual impending collapse, he had
mounted such anxious guard.

It was when he went on the Friday to see her that he took

in the latest of the phases in question, which might very well be almost the final one; there was at least that comfort in it. She had just settled in a small flat, where he recognised in the steady disposal, for the best, of various objects she had not yet parted with, her reason for having made him wait. Here they had together—these two worn and baffled workers—a wonderful hour of gladness in their lost battle and of freshness in their lost youth; for it was not till Stuart Straith had also raised the heavy mask and laid it beside her own on the table, that they began really to feel themselves recover something of that possibility of each other they had so wearily wasted. Only she couldn't get over it that he was like herself, and that what she had shrunken to in her three or four simplified rooms had its perfect image in the hollow show of his ordered studio and his accumulated work. He told her everything now, kept as little back as she had kept at their previous meeting, while she repeated over and over, "You—wonderful you?" as if the knowledge made a deeper darkness of fate, as if the pain of his having come down at all almost quenched the joy of his having come so much nearer. When she learned that he had not for three years sold a picture—"You, beautiful you?"—it seemed a new cold breath out of the dusk of her own outlook. Disappointment and despair were in such relations contagious, and there was clearly as much less again left to her as the little that was left to him. He showed her, laughing at the long queerness of it, how awfully little, as they called it, this was. He let it all come, but with more mirth than misery, and with a final abandonment of pride that was like changing at the end of a dreadful day from tight boots to slippers. There were moments when they might have resembled a couple united by some misdeed and meeting to decide on some desperate course; they gave themselves so to the great irony—the vision of the comic in contrasts—that precedes surrenders and extinctions.

They went over the whole thing, remounted the dwindling stream, reconstructed, explained, understood—recognised, in short, the particular example they gave, and how, without mutual suspicion, they had been giving it side by side. "We're simply the case," Straith familiarly put it, "of having been had enough of. No case is perhaps more common, save that, for you and for me, each in our line, it did look in the good time—didn't it?—as if nobody *could* have enough." With which they counted backward, gruesome as it was, the symptoms of satiety up to the first dawn, and lived again together the unforgettable hours—distant now—out of which it had begun to glimmer that the truth had to be faced and the right names given to the wrong facts. They laughed at their original explanations and the minor scale, even, of their early fears; compared notes on the fallibility of remedies and hopes, and, more and more united in the identity of their lesson, made out perfectly that, though there appeared to be many kinds of success, there was only one kind of failure. And yet what had been hardest had not been to have to shrink, but—the long game of bluff, as Straith called it—to have to keep up. It fairly swept them away at present, however, the hugeness of the relief of no longer keeping up as against each other. This gave them all the measure of the motive their courage, on either side, in silence and gloom, had forced into its service.

"Only what shall we do now for a motive?" Straith went on.

She thought. "A motive for courage?"

"Yes—to keep up."

"And go again, for instance, do you mean, to Mundham? We shall, thank heaven, never go again to Mundham. The Mundhams are over."

> "Nous n'irons plus au bois;
> Les lauriers sont coupés,"

sang Straith. "It does cost."

"As everything costs that one does for the rich. It's not our poor relations who make us pay."

"No; one must have means to acknowledge the others. We can't afford the opulent. But it isn't only the money they take."

"It's the imagination," said Mrs. Harvey. "As they have none themselves——"

"It's an article we have to supply? We have certainly to use a lot to protect ourselves," Straith agreed. "And the strange thing is that they like us."

She thought again. "That's what makes it easy to cut them. They forgive."

"Yes," her companion laughed; "once they really don't know you enough——!"

"They treat you as old friends. But what do we want now of courage?" she went on.

He wondered. "Yes, after all, what?"

"To keep up, I mean. Why *should* we keep up?"

It seemed to strike him. "I see. After all, why? The courage *not* to keep up——"

"We have *that*, at least," she declared, "haven't we?" Standing there at her little high-perched window, which overhung grey housetops, they let the consideration of this pass between them in a deep look, as well as in a hush of which the intensity had something commensurate. "If we're beaten!" she then continued.

"Let us at least be beaten together!" He took her in his arms; she let herself go, and he held her long and close for the compact. But when they had recovered themselves enough to handle their agreement more responsibly, the words in which they confirmed it broke in sweetness as well as sadness from both together: "And now to work!"

The Two Faces

THE SERVANT, who, in spite of his sealed, stamped look, appeared to have his reasons, stood there for instruction, in a manner not quite usual, after announcing the name. Mrs. Grantham, however, took it up—"Lord Gwyther?"—with a quick surprise that for an instant justified him even to the small scintilla in the glance she gave her companion, which might have had exactly the sense of the butler's hesitation. This companion, a shortish, fairish, youngish man, clean-shaven and keen-eyed, had, with a promptitude that would have struck an observer—which the butler indeed was—sprung to his feet and moved to the chimney-piece, though his hostess herself, meanwhile, managed not otherwise to stir. "Well?" she said, as for the visitor to advance; which she immediately followed with a sharper "He's not there?"

"Shall I show him up, ma'am?"

"But of course!" The point of his doubt made her at last rise for impatience, and Bates, before leaving the room, might still have caught the achieved irony of her appeal to the gentleman into whose communion with her he had broken. "Why in the world not——? What a way——!" she exclaimed, as Sutton felt beside his cheek the passage of her eyes to the glass behind him.

"He wasn't sure you'd see anyone."

"I don't see 'anyone,' but I see individuals."

"That's just it; and sometimes you don't see them."

"Do you mean ever because of *you*?" she asked as she touched into place a tendril of hair. "That's just his impertinence, as to which I shall speak to him."

"Don't," said Shirley Sutton. "Never notice anything."

"That's nice advice from you," she laughed, "who notice everything!"

"Ah, but I speak of nothing."

She looked at him a moment. "You're still more impertinent than Bates. You'll please not budge," she went on.

"Really? I must sit him out?" he continued as, after a minute, she had not again spoken—only glancing about, while

345

she changed her place, partly for another look at the glass and partly to see if she could improve her seat. What she felt was rather more than, clever and charming though she was, she could hide. "If you're wondering how you seem, I can tell you. Awfully cool and easy."

She gave him another stare. She was beautiful and conscious. "And if you're wondering how *you* seem——"

"Oh, I'm not!" he laughed from before the fire; "I always perfectly know."

"How you seem," she retorted, "is as if you didn't!"

Once more for a little he watched her. "You're looking lovely for him—extraordinarily lovely, within the marked limits of your range. But that's enough. Don't be clever."

"Then who *will* be?"

"There you are!" he sighed with amusement.

"Do you know him?" she asked as, through the door left open by Bates, they heard steps on the landing.

Sutton had to think an instant, and produced a "No" just as Lord Gwyther was again announced, which gave an unexpectedness to the greeting offered him a moment later by this personage—a young man, stout and smooth and fresh, but not at all shy, who, after the happiest rapid passage with Mrs. Grantham, put out a hand with a frank, pleasant "How d'ye do?"

"Mr. Shirley Sutton," Mrs. Grantham explained.

"Oh yes," said her second visitor, quite as if he knew; which, as he couldn't have known, had for her first the interest of confirming a perception that his lordship would be—no, not at all, in general, embarrassed, only was now exceptionally and especially agitated. As it is, for that matter, with Sutton's total impression that we are particularly and almost exclusively concerned, it may be further mentioned that he was not not less clear as to the really handsome way in which the young man kept himself together and little by little—though with all proper aid indeed—finally found his feet. All sorts of things, for the twenty minutes, occurred to Sutton, though one of them was certainly not that it would, after all, be better he should go. One of them was that their hostess was doing it in perfection—simply, easily, kindly, yet with something the least bit queer in her wonderful eyes; another was that if he had been recognised without the least ground it was through a tension of nerves on the part of his fellow-guest that produced inconsequent motions; still another was that, even had departure been indicated, he would positively have felt dissuasion in the rare promise of the scene. This was in especial after Lord Gwyther not only had announced that he was now married, but had mentioned that he wished to bring his wife to Mrs. Grantham for the benefit so certain to be derived. It was the passage immediately produced by that speech that provoked in Sutton the intensity, as it were, of his arrest. He already knew of the marriage as well as Mrs. Grantham herself, and as well also as he knew of some other things; and this gave him, doubtless, the better measure of what took place before him and the keener consciousness of the quick look that, at a marked moment—though it was not absolutely meant for him any more than for his companion—Mrs. Grantham let him catch.

She smiled, but it had a gravity. "I think, you know, you ought to have told me before."

"Do you mean when I first got engaged? Well, it all took place so far away, and we really told, at home, so few people."

Oh, there might have been reasons; but it had not been quite right. "You were married at Stuttgart? That wasn't too far for *my* interest, at least, to reach."

"Awfully kind of you—and of course one knew you *would* be kind. But it wasn't at Stuttgart; it was over there, but quite in the country. We should have managed it in England but that her mother naturally wished to be present, yet was not in health to come. So it was really, you see, a sort of little hole-and-corner German affair."

This didn't in the least check Mrs. Grantham's claim, but it started a slight anxiety. "Will she be—a, then, German?"

Sutton knew her to know perfectly what Lady Gwyther would "be," but he had by this time, while their friend explained, his independent interest. "Oh dear, no! My father-in-law has never parted with the proud birthright of a Briton. But his wife, you see, holds an estate in Würtemberg from *her* mother, Countess Kremnitz, on which, with the awful condition of his English property, you know, they've found it for years a tremendous saving to live. So that though Valda was luckily born at home she has practically spent her life over there."

"Oh, I see." Then, after a slight pause, "Is Valda her pretty name?" Mrs. Grantham asked.

"Well," said the young man, only wishing, in his candour, it was clear, to be drawn out—"well, she has, in the manner of her mother's people, about thirteen; but that's the one we generally use."

Mrs. Grantham hesitated but an instant. "Then may *I* generally use it?"

"It would be too charming of you; and nothing would give her—as, I assure you, nothing would give *me*, greater pleasure." Lord Gwyther quite glowed with the thought.

"Then I think that instead of coming alone you might have brought her to see me."

"It's exactly what," he instantly replied, "I came to ask your leave to do." He explained that for the moment Lady Gwyther was not in town, having as soon as she arrived gone down to Torquay to put in a few days with one of her aunts, also her godmother, to whom she was an object of great interest. She had seen no one yet, and no one—not that *that* mattered—had seen her; she knew nothing whatever of London and was awfully frightened at facing it and at what—however little—might be expected of her. "She wants some one," he said, "some one who knows the whole thing, don't you see? and who's thoroughly kind and clever, as you would be, if I may say so, to take her by the hand." It was at this point and on these words that the eyes of Lord Gwyther's two auditors inevitably and wonderfully met. But there was nothing in the way he kept it up to show that he caught the encounter. "She wants, if I may tell you so, for the great labyrinth, a real friend; and asking myself what I could do to make things ready for her, and who would be absolutely the best woman in London——"

"You thought, naturally, of *me*?" Mrs. Grantham had listened with no sign but the faint flash just noted; now, however, she gave him the full light of her expressive face—which immediately brought Shirley Sutton, looking at his watch, once more to his feet.

"She *is* the best woman in London!" He addressed himself

with a laugh to the other visitor, but offered his hand in farewell to their hostess.

"You're going?"

"I must," he said without scruple.

"Then we do meet at dinner?"

"I hope so." On which, to take leave, he returned with
interest to Lord Gwyther the friendly clutch he had a short
time before received.

II

They did meet at dinner, and if they were not, as it happened,
side by side, they made that up afterwards in the happiest
angle of a drawing-room that offered both shine and shadow
and that was positively much appreciated, in the circle in
which they moved, for the favourable "corners" created by its
shrewd mistress. Her face, charged with something produced
in it by Lord Gwyther's visit, had been with him so constantly
for the previous hours that, when she instantly challenged him
on his "treatment" of her in the afternoon, he was on the
point of naming it as his reason for not having remained with
her. Something new had quickly come into her beauty; he
couldn't as yet have said what, nor whether on the whole to
its advantage or its loss. Till he could make up his mind about
that, at any rate, he would say nothing; so that, with sufficient
presence of mind, he found a better excuse. If in short he had
in defiance of her particular request left her alone with Lord
Gwyther, it was simply because the situation had suddenly
turned so exciting that he had fairly feared the contagion of
it—the temptation of its making him, most improperly, put in
his word.

They could now talk of these things at their ease. Other
couples, ensconced and scattered, enjoyed the same privilege,
and Sutton had more and more the profit, such as it was, of
feeling that his interest in Mrs. Grantham had become—what
was the luxury of so high a social code—an acknowledged and
protected relation. He knew his London well enough to know
that he was on the way to be regarded as her main source of
consolation for the trick that, several months before, Lord

Gwyther had publicly played her. Many persons had not held that, by the high social code in question, his lordship could have "reserved the right" to turn up in that way, from one day to another, engaged. For himself London took, with its short cuts and its cheap psychology, an immense deal for granted. To his own sense he was never—could in the nature of things never be—any man's "successor." Just what had constituted the predecessorship of other men was apparently that they had been able to make up their mind. He, worse luck, was at the mercy of her face, and more than ever at the mercy of it now, which meant, moreover, not that it made a slave of him, but that it made, disconcertingly, a sceptic. It was the absolute perfection of the handsome; but things had a way of coming into it. "I felt," he said, "that you were there together at a point at which you had a right to the ease that the absence of a listener would give. I reflected that when you made me promise to stay you hadn't guessed——"

"That he could possibly have come to me on such an extraordinary errand? No, of course I hadn't guessed. Who *would*? But didn't you see how little I was upset by it?"

Sutton demurred. Then with a smile, "I think *he* saw how little."

"You yourself didn't, then?"

He again held back, but not, after all, to answer. "He was wonderful, wasn't he?"

"I think he was," she replied after a moment. To which she added: "Why did he pretend that way he knew you?"

"He didn't pretend. He felt on the spot as if we were friends." Sutton had found this afterwards, and found truth in it. "It was an effusion of cheer and hope. He was so glad to see me there, and to find you happy."

"Happy?"

"Happy. Aren't you?"

"Because of *you*?"

"Well—according to the impression he received as he came in."

"That was sudden then," she asked, "and unexpected?"

Her companion thought. "Prepared in some degree, but confirmed by the sight of us, there together, so awfully jolly and sociable over your fire."

Mrs. Grantham turned this round. "If he knew I was 'happy' then—which, by the way, is none of his business, nor of yours either—why in the world did he come?"

"Well, for good manners, and for his idea," said Sutton.

She took it in, appearing to have no hardness of rancour that could bar discussion. "Do you mean by his idea his proposal that I should grandmother his wife? And, if you do, is the proposal your reason for calling him wonderful?"

Sutton laughed. "Pray, what's yours?" As this was a question, however, that she took her time to answer or not to answer—only appearing interested for a moment in a combination that had formed itself on the other side of the room—he presently went on. "What's *his*?—that would seem to be the point. His, I mean, for having decided on the extraordinary step of throwing his little wife, bound hands and feet, into your arms. Intelligent as you are, and with these three or four hours to have thought it over, I yet don't see how that can fail still to mystify you."

She continued to watch their opposite neighbours. " 'Little,' you call her. Is she so very small?"

"Tiny, tiny—she *must* be; as different as possible in every way—of necessity—from you. They always *are* the opposite pole, you know," said Shirley Sutton.

She glanced at him now. "You strike me as of an impudence——!"

"No, no. I only like to make it out with you."

She looked away again and, after a little, went on. "I'm sure she's charming, and only hope one isn't to gather that he's already tired of her."

"Not a bit! He's tremendously in love, and he'll remain so."

"So much the better. And if it's a question," said Mrs. Grantham, "of one's doing what one can for her, he has only, as I told him when you had gone, to give me the chance."

"Good! So he *is* to commit her to you?"

"You use extraordinary expressions, but it's settled that he brings her."

"And you'll really and truly help her?"

"Really and truly?" said Mrs. Grantham, with her eyes again upon him. "Why not? For what do you take me?"

"Ah, isn't that just what I still have the discomfort, every day I live, of asking myself?"

She had made, as she spoke, a movement to rise, which, as if she was tired of his tone, his last words appeared to determine. But, also getting up, he held her, when they were on their feet, long enough to hear the rest of what he had to say. "If you do help her, you know, you'll show him that you've understood."

"Understood what?"

"Why, his idea—the deep, acute train of reasoning that has led him to take, as one may say, the bull by the horns; to reflect that as you might, as you probably *would*, in any case, get at her, he plays the wise game, as well as the bold one, by assuming your generosity and placing himself publicly under an obligation to you."

Mrs. Grantham showed not only that she had listened, but that she had for an instant considered. "What is it you elegantly describe as my getting 'at' her?"

"He takes his risk, but puts you, you see, on your honour."

She thought a moment more. "What profundities indeed then over the simplest of matters! And if your idea is," she went on, "that if I do help her I shall show him I've understood them, so it will be that if I don't——"

"You'll show him"—Sutton took her up—"that you haven't? Precisely. But in spite of not wanting to appear to have understood *too* much——"

"I may still be depended on to do what I can? Quite certainly. You'll see what I may still be depended on to do." And she moved away.

III

It was not, doubtless, that there had been anything in their rather sharp separation at that moment to sustain or prolong the interruption; yet it definitely befell that, circumstances aiding, they practically failed to meet again before the great party at Burbeck. This occasion was to gather in some thirty persons from a certain Friday to the following Monday, and it was on the Friday that Sutton went down. He had known in advance that Mrs. Grantham was to be there, and this perhaps, during the interval of hindrance, had helped him a little to be patient. He had before him the certitude of a real full cup—two days brimming over with the sight of her. He found, however, on his arrival that she was not yet in the field, and presently learned that her place would be in a small contingent that was to join the party on the morrow. This knowledge he extracted from Miss Banker, who was always the first to present herself at any gathering that was to enjoy her, and whom, more-over—partly on that very account—the wary not less than the speculative were apt to hold themselves well-advised to engage with at as early as possible a stage of the business. She was stout, red, rich, mature, universal—a massive, much-fingered volume, alphabetical, wonderful, indexed, that opened of itself at the right place. She opened for Sutton instinctively at G——, which happened to be remarkably convenient. "What she's really waiting over for is to bring down Lady Gwyther."

"Ah, the Gwythers are coming?"

"Yes; caught, through Mrs. Grantham, just in time. *She'll* be the feature—everyone wants to see her."

Speculation and wariness met and combined at this moment in Shirley Sutton. "Do you mean—a—Mrs. Grantham?"

"Dear no! Poor little Lady Gwyther, who, but just arrived in England, appears now literally for the first time in her life in any society whatever, and whom (don't you know the ex-traordinary story? you ought to—*you*!) she, of all people, has so wonderfully taken up. It will be quite—here—as if she were 'presenting' her."

Sutton, of course, took in more things than even appeared. "I never know what I ought to know; I only know, inveter-ately, what I oughtn't. So what *is* the extraordinary story?"

"You really haven't heard——?"

"Really!" he replied without winking.

"It happened, indeed, but the other day," said Miss Banker, "yet everyone is already wondering. Gwyther has thrown his wife on her mercy—but I won't believe you if you pretend to me you don't know why he shouldn't."

Sutton asked himself then what he *could* pretend. "Do you mean because she's merciless?"

She hesitated. "If you don't know, perhaps I oughtn't to tell you."

He liked Miss Banker, and found just the right tone to plead. "*Do* tell me."

"Well," she sighed, "it will be your own fault——! They had been such friends that there could have been but one name for the crudity of his original *procédé*. When I was a girl we used to call it throwing over. They call it in French to *lâcher*. But I refer not so much to the act itself as to the manner of it, though you may say indeed, of course, that there is in such cases, after all, only one manner. Least said, soonest mended."

Sutton seemed to wonder. "Oh, he said too much?"

"He said nothing. That was it."

Sutton kept it up. "But was *what*?"

"Why, what she must, like any woman in her shoes, have felt to be his perfidy. He simply went and *did* it—took to himself this child, that is, without the preliminary of a scandal or a rupture—before she could turn round."

"I follow you. But it would appear from what you say that she *has* turned round now."

"Well," Miss Banker laughed, "we shall see for ourselves how far. It will be what everyone will try to see."

"Oh, then we've work cut out!" And Sutton certainly felt that he himself had—an impression that lost nothing from a further talk with Miss Banker in the course of a short stroll in the grounds with her the next day. He spoke as one who had now considered many things.

"Did I understand from you yesterday that Lady Gwyther's a 'child'?"

"Nobody knows. It's prodigious the way she has managed."

"The way Lady Gwyther has——?"

"No; the way May Grantham has kept her till this hour in her pocket."

He was quick at his watch. "Do you mean by 'this hour' that they're due now?"

"Not till tea. All the others arrive together in time for that." Miss Banker had clearly, since the previous day, filled in gaps and become, as it were, revised and enlarged. "She'll have kept a cat from seeing her, so as to produce her entirely herself."

"Well," Sutton mused, "that will have been a very noble sort of return——"

"For Gwyther's behaviour? Very. Yet I feel creepy."

"Creepy?"

"Because so much depends for the girl—in the way of the right start or the wrong start—on the signs and omens of this first appearance. It's a great house and a great occasion, and we're assembled here, it strikes me, very much as the Roman mob at the circus used to be to see the next Christian maiden brought out to the tigers."

"Oh, if she *is* a Christian maiden——!" Sutton murmured. But he stopped at what his imagination called up.

It perhaps fed that faculty a little that Miss Banker had the effect of making out that Mrs. Grantham might individually be, in any case, something of a Roman matron. "She has kept her in the dark so that we may only take her from her hand. She will have formed her for us."

"In so few days?"

"Well, she will have prepared her—decked her for the sacrifice with ribbons and flowers."

"Ah, if you only mean that she will have taken her to her dressmaker——!" And it came to Sutton, at once as a new light and as a check, almost, to anxiety, that this was all poor Gwyther, mistrustful probably of a taste formed by Stuttgart, might have desired of their friend.

There were usually at Burbeck many things taking place at once; so that wherever else, on such occasions, tea might be served, it went forward with matchless pomp, weather permitting, on a shaded stretch of one of the terraces and in presence of one of the prospects. Shirley Sutton, moving, as the afternoon waned, more restlessly about and mingling in dispersed groups only to find they had nothing to keep him quiet, came upon it as he turned a corner of the house—saw it seated there in all its state. It might be said that at Burbeck it was, like everything else, made the most of. It constituted immediately, with multiplied tables and glittering plate, with rugs and cushions and ices and fruit and wonderful porcelain and beautiful women, a scene of splendour, almost an incident of grand opera. One of the beautiful women might quite have been expected to rise with a gold cup and a celebrated song.

One of them did rise, as it happened, while Sutton drew near, and he found himself a moment later seeing nothing and nobody but Mrs. Grantham. They met on the terrace, just away from the others, and the movement in which he had the effect of arresting her might have been that of withdrawal. He quickly saw, however, that if she had been about to pass into the house it was only on some errand—to get something or to call someone—that would immediately have restored her to the public. It somehow struck him on the spot—and more than ever yet, though the impression was not wholly new to him—that she felt herself a figure for the forefront of the stage and indeed would have been recognised by anyone at a glance as the *prima donna assoluta*. She caused, in fact, during the few minutes he stood talking to her, an extraordinary series of waves to roll extraordinarily fast over his sense, not the least mark of the matter being that the appearance with which it ended was again the one with which it had begun. "The face—the face," as he kept dumbly repeating; that was at last, as at first, all he could clearly see. She had a perfection resplendent, but what in the world had it done, this perfection, to her beauty? It was her beauty, doubtless, that looked out at him, but it was into something else that, as their eyes met, he strangely found himself looking.

It was as if something had happened in consequence of which she had changed, and there was that in this swift perception that made him glance eagerly about for Lady Gwyther. But as he took in the recruited group—identities of the hour added to those of the previous twenty-four—he saw, among his recognitions, one of which was the husband of the person missing, that Lady Gwyther was not there. Nothing in the whole business was more singular than his consciousness that, as he came back to his interlocutress after the nods and smiles and hand-waves he had launched, she knew what had been his thought. She knew for whom he had looked without success; but why should this knowledge visibly have hardened and sharpened her, and precisely at a moment when she was unprecedentedly magnificent? The indefinable apprehension that had somewhat sunk after his second talk with Miss Banker and then had perversely risen again—this nameless anxiety now produced on him, with a sudden sharper pinch, the effect of a great suspense. The action of that, in turn, was to show him that he had not yet fully known how much he had at stake on a final view. It was revealed to him for the first time that he "really cared" whether Mrs. Grantham were a safe nature. It was too ridiculous by what a thread it hung, but something was certainly in the air that would definitely tell him.

What was in the air descended the next moment to earth. He turned round as he caught the expression with which her eyes attached themselves to something that approached. A little person, very young and very much dressed, had come out of the house, and the expression in Mrs. Grantham's eyes was that of the artist confronted with her work and interested, even to impatience, in the judgment of others. The little person drew nearer, and though Sutton's companion, without looking at him now, gave it a name and met it, he had jumped for himself at certitude. He saw many things—too many, and they appeared to be feathers, frills, excrescences of silk and lace—massed together and conflicting, and after a moment also saw struggling out of them a small face that struck him as either scared or sick. Then, with his eyes again returning to Mrs. Grantham, he saw another.

He had no more talk with Miss Banker till late that evening—an evening during which he had felt himself too noticeably silent; but something had passed between this pair, across dinner-table and drawing-room, without speech, and when they at last found words it was in the needed ease of a quiet end of the long, lighted gallery, where she opened again at the very paragraph.

"You were right—that *was* it. She did the only thing that, at such short notice, she *could* do. She took her to her dressmaker."

Sutton, with his back to the reach of the gallery, had, as if to banish a vision, buried his eyes for a minute in his hands. "And oh, the face—the face!"

"Which?" Miss Banker asked.

"Whichever one looks at."

"But May Grantham's glorious. She has turned herself out——"

"With a splendour of taste and a sense of effect, eh? Yes." Sutton showed he saw far.

"She *has* the sense of effect. The sense of effect as exhibited in Lady Gwyther's clothes——!" was something Miss Banker failed of words to express. "Everybody's overwhelmed. Here, you know, that sort of thing's grave. The poor creature's lost."

"Lost?"

"Since on the first impression, as we said, so much depends. The first impression's made—oh, made! I defy her now ever to unmake it. Her husband, who's proud, won't like her the better for it. And I don't see," Miss Banker went on, "that her prettiness *was* enough—a mere little feverish, frightened freshness; what *did* he see in her?—to be so blasted. It has been done with an atrocity of art——"

"That supposes the dressmaker then also a devil?"

"Oh, your London women and their dressmakers!" Miss Banker laughed.

"But the face—the face!" Sutton woefully repeated.

"May's?"

"The little girl's. It's exquisite."

"Exquisite?"

"For unimaginable pathos."

"Oh!" Miss Banker dropped.

"She has at last begun to see." Sutton showed again how far *he* saw. "It glimmers upon her innocence, she makes it dimly out—what has been done with her. She's even worse this evening—the way, my eye, she looked at dinner!—than when she came. Yes"—he was confident—"it has dawned (how couldn't it, out of all of you?) and she knows."

"She ought to have known before!" Miss Banker intelligently sighed.

"No; she wouldn't in that case have been so beautiful."

"Beautiful?" cried Miss Banker; "overloaded like a monkey in a show!"

"The face, yes; which goes to the heart. It's that that makes it," said Shirley Sutton. "And it's that"—he thought it out—"that makes the other."

"I see. Conscious?"

"Horrible!"

"You take it hard," said Miss Banker.

Lord Gwyther, just before she spoke, had come in sight and now was near them. Sutton on this, appearing to wish to avoid him, reached, before answering his companion's observation, a door that opened close at hand. "So hard," he replied from that point, "that I shall be off to-morrow morning."

"And not see the rest?" she called after him.

But he had already gone, and Lord Gwyther, arriving, amiably took up her question. "The rest of what?"

Miss Banker looked him well in the eyes. "Of Mrs. Grantham's clothes."

Mrs. Medwin

"WELL, we *are* a pair!" the poor lady's visitor broke out to her, at the end of her explanation, in a manner disconcerting enough. The poor lady was Miss Cutter, who lived in South Audley Street, where she had an "upper half" so concise that it had to pass, boldly, for convenient; and her visitor was her half-brother, whom she had not seen for three years. She was remarkable for a maturity of which every symptom might have been observed to be admirably controlled, had not a tendency to stoutness just affirmed its independence. Her present, no doubt, insisted too much on her past, but with the excuse, sufficiently valid, that she must certainly once have been prettier. She was clearly not contented with once—she wished to be prettier again. She neglected nothing that could produce that illusion, and, being both fair and fat, dressed almost wholly in black. When she added a little colour it was not, at any rate, to her drapery. Her small rooms had the peculiarity that everything they contained appeared to testify with vividness to her position in society, quite as if they had been furnished by the bounty of admiring friends. They were adorned indeed almost exclusively with objects that nobody buys, as had more than once been remarked by spectators of her own sex, for herself, and would have been luxurious if luxury consisted mainly in photographic portraits slashed across with signatures, in baskets of flowers beribboned with the cards of passing compatriots, and in a neat collection of red volumes, blue volumes, alphabetical volumes, aids to London lucidity, of every sort, devoted to addresses and engagements. To be in Miss Cutter's tiny drawing-room, in short, even with Miss Cutter alone—should you by any chance have found her so—was somehow to be in the world and in a crowd. It was like an agency—it bristled with particulars.

This was what the tall, lean, loose gentleman lounging there before her might have appeared to read in the suggestive scene over which, while she talked to him, his eyes moved without haste and without rest. "Oh, come, Mamie!" he occasionally threw off; and the words were evidently connected with the impression thus absorbed. His comparative youth spoke of waste even as her positive—her too positive—spoke of economy. There was only one thing, that is, to make up in him for everything he had lost, though it was distinct enough indeed that this thing might sometimes serve. It consisted in the perfection of an indifference, an indifference at the present moment directed to the plea—a plea of inability, of pure destitution—with which his sister had met him. Yet it had even now a wider embrace, took in quite sufficiently all consequences of queerness, confessed in advance to the false note that, in such a setting, he almost excruciatingly constituted. He cared as little that he looked at moments all his impudence as that he looked all his shabbiness, all his cleverness, all his history. These different things were written in him—in his premature baldness, his seamed, strained face, the lapse from bravery of his long tawny moustache; above all, in his easy, friendly, universally acquainted eye, so much too sociable for mere conversation. What possible relation with him could be natural enough to meet it? He wore a scant, rough Inverness cape and a pair of black trousers, wanting in substance and marked with the sheen of time, that had presumably once served for evening use. He spoke with the slowness helplessly permitted to Americans—as something too slow to be stopped—and he repeated that he found himself associated with Miss Cutter in a harmony worthy of wonder. She had been telling him not only that she couldn't possibly give him ten pounds, but that his unexpected arrival, should he insist on being much in view, might seriously interfere with arrangements necessary to her own maintenance; on which he had begun by replying that he of course knew she had long ago spent her money, but that he looked to her now exactly because she had, without the aid of that convenience, mastered the art of life.

"I'd really go away with a fiver, my dear, if you'd only tell me how you do it. It's no use saying only, as you've always said, that 'people are very kind to you.' What the devil are they kind to you *for*?"

"Well, one reason is precisely that no particular inconvenience has hitherto been supposed to attach to me. I'm just what I am," said Mamie Cutter; "nothing less and nothing more. It's awkward to have to explain to you, which, moreover, I really needn't in the least. I'm clever and amusing and charming." She was uneasy and even frightened, but she kept her temper and met him with a grace of her own. "I don't think you ought to ask me more questions than I ask you."

"Ah, my dear," said the odd young man, "*I've* no mysteries. Why in the world, since it was what you came out for and have devoted so much of your time to, haven't you pulled it off? Why haven't you married?"

"Why haven't *you*?" she retorted. "Do you think that if I had it would have been better for you?—that my husband would for a moment have put up with you? Do you mind my asking you if you'll kindly go *now*?" she went on after a glance at the clock. "I'm expecting a friend, whom I must see alone, on a matter of great importance——"

"And my being seen with you may compromise your respectability or undermine your nerve?" He sprawled imperturbably in his place, crossing again, in another sense, his long black legs and showing, above his low shoes, an absurd reach of parti-coloured sock. "I take your point well enough, but mayn't you be after all quite wrong? If you can't do anything for me couldn't you at least do something *with* me? If it comes to that, I'm clever and amusing and charming too! I've been such an ass that you don't appreciate me. But people like me—I assure you they do. They usually don't know what an ass I've been; they only see the surface, which"—and he stretched himself afresh as she looked him up and down— "you *can* imagine them, can't you, rather taken with? *I'm* 'what I am' too; nothing less and nothing more. That's true of us as a family, you see. We *are* a crew!" He delivered himself serenely. His voice was soft and flat, his pleasant eyes, his simple tones tending to the solemn, achieved at moments that effect of quaintness which is, in certain connections, socially so known and enjoyed. "English people have quite a weakness for me—more than any others. I get on with them beautifully. I've always been with them abroad. They think me," the young man explained, "diabolically American."

"You!" Such stupidity drew from her a sigh of compassion.

Her companion apparently quite understood it. "Are you homesick, Mamie?" he asked, with wondering irrelevance.

The manner of the question made her for some reason, in spite of her preoccupations, break into a laugh. A shade of indulgence, a sense of other things, came back to her. "You *are* funny, Scott!"

"Well," remarked Scott, "that's just what I claim. But *are* you so homesick?" he spaciously inquired, not as if to a practical end, but from an easy play of intelligence.

"I'm just dying of it!" said Mamie Cutter.

"Why, so am I!" Her visitor had a sweetness of concurrence.

"We're the only decent people," Miss Cutter declared. "And I know. *You* don't—you can't; and I can't explain. Come in," she continued with a return of her impatience and an increase of her decision, "at seven sharp."

She had quitted her seat some time before, and now, to get him into motion, hovered before him while, still motionless, he looked up at her. Something intimate, in the silence, appeared to pass between them—a community of fatigue and failure and, after all, of intelligence. There was a final, cynical humour in it. It determined him, at any rate, at last, and he slowly rose, taking in again as he stood there the testimony of the room. He might have been counting the photographs, but he looked at the flowers with detachment. "Who's coming?"

"Mrs. Medwin."

"American?"

"Dear no!"

"Then what are you doing for her?"

"I work for everyone," she promptly returned.

"For everyone who pays? So I suppose. Yet isn't it only we who do pay?"

There was a drollery, not lost on her, in the way his queer presence lent itself to his emphasised plural. "Do you consider that *you* do?"

At this, with his deliberation, he came back to his charming idea. "Only try me, and see if I can't be *made* to. Work me in." On her sharply presenting her back he stared a little at the clock. "If I come at seven may I stay to dinner?"

It brought her round again. "Impossible. I'm dining out."

"With whom?"

She had to think. "With Lord Considine."

"Oh, my eye!" Scott exclaimed.

She looked at him gloomily. "Is *that* sort of tone what makes you pay? I think you might understand," she went on, "that if you're to sponge on me successfully you mustn't ruin me. I must have *some* remote resemblance to a lady."

"Yes? But why must *I?*" Her exasperated silence was full of answers, of which, however, his inimitable manner took no account. "You don't understand my real strength; I doubt if you even understand your own. You're clever, Mamie, but you're not so clever as I supposed. However," he pursued, "it's out of Mrs. Medwin that you'll get it."

"Get what?"

"Why, the cheque that will enable you to assist me."

On this, for a moment, she met his eyes. "If you'll come back at seven sharp—not a minute before, and not a minute after, I'll give you two five-pound notes."

He thought it over. "Whom are you expecting a minute after?"

It sent her to the window with a groan almost of anguish, and she answered nothing till she had looked at the street. "If you injure me, you know, Scott, you'll be sorry."

"I wouldn't injure you for the world. What I want to do in fact is really to help you, and I promise you that I won't leave you—by which I mean won't leave London—till I've effected something really pleasant for you. I like you, Mamie, because I like pluck; I like you much more than you like me. I like you very, *very* much." He had at last with this reached the door and opened it, but he remained with his hand on the latch. "What does Mrs. Medwin want of you?" he thus brought out.

She had come round to see him disappear, and in the relief of this prospect she again just indulged him. "The impossible."

He waited another minute. "And you're going to do it?"

"I'm going to do it," said Mamie Cutter.

"Well, then, that ought to be a haul. Call it *three* fivers!" he laughed. "At seven sharp." And at last he left her alone.

II

Miss Cutter waited till she heard the house-door close; after which, in a sightless, mechanical way, she moved about the room, readjusting various objects that he had not touched. It was as if his mere voice and accent had spoiled her form. But she was not left too long to reckon with these things, for Mrs. Medwin was promptly announced. This lady was not, more than her hostess, in the first flush of her youth; her appearance—the scattered remains of beauty manipulated by taste—resembled one of the light repasts in which the fragments of yesterday's dinner figure with a conscious ease that makes up for the want of presence. She was perhaps of an effect still too immediate to be called interesting, but she was candid, gentle and surprised—not fatiguingly surprised, only just in the right degree; and her white face—it was too white—with the fixed eyes, the somewhat touzled hair and the Louis Seize hat, might at the end of the very long neck have suggested the head of a princess carried, in a revolution, on a pike. She immediately took up the business that had brought her, with the air, however, of drawing from the omens then discernible less confidence than she had hoped. The complication lay in the fact that if it was Mamie's part to present the omens, that lady yet had so to colour them as to make her own service large. She perhaps over-coloured, for her friend gave way to momentary despair.

"What you mean is then that it's simply impossible?"

"Oh no," said Mamie, with a qualified emphasis. "It's *possible*."

"But disgustingly difficult?"

"As difficult as you like."

"Then what can I do that I haven't done?"

"You can only wait a little longer."

"But that's just what I *have* done. I've done nothing else. I'm always waiting a little longer!"

Miss Cutter retained, in spite of this pathos, her grasp of the subject. "*The* thing, as I've told you, is for you first to be seen."

"But if people won't look at me?"

"They will."

"They *will*?" Mrs. Medwin was eager.

"They shall," her hostess went on. "It's their only having heard—without having seen."

"But if they stare straight the other way?" Mrs. Medwin continued to object. "You can't simply go up to them and twist their heads about."

"It's just what I can," said Mamie Cutter.

But her charming visitor, heedless for the moment of this attenuation, had found the way to put it. "It's the old story. You can't go into the water till you swim, and you can't swim till you go into the water. I can't be spoken to till I'm seen, but I can't be seen till I'm spoken to."

She met this lucidity, Miss Cutter, with but an instant's lapse. "You say I can't twist their heads about. But I *have* twisted them."

It had been quietly produced, but it gave her companion a jerk. "They say 'Yes'?"

She summed it up. "All but one. *She* says 'No.'"

Mrs. Medwin thought; then jumped. "Lady Wantridge?"

Miss Cutter, as more delicate, only bowed admission. "I shall see her either this afternoon or late to-morrow. But she has written."

Her visitor wondered again. "May I see her letter?"

"No." She spoke with decision. "But I shall square her."

"Then how?"

"Well"—and Miss Cutter, as if looking upward for inspiration, fixed her eyes awhile on the ceiling—"well, it will come to me."

Mrs. Medwin watched her—it was impressive. "And will *they* come to you—the others?" This question drew out the fact that they would—so far, at least, as they consisted of Lady Edward, Lady Bellhouse and Mrs. Pouncer, who had engaged to muster, at the signal of tea, on the 14th—prepared, as it were, for the worst. There was of course always the chance that Lady Wantridge might take the field in such force as to paralyse them, though that danger, at the same time, seemed inconsistent with her being squared. It didn't perhaps all quite ideally hang together; but what it sufficiently came to was that if she was the one who could do most *for* a person in Mrs. Medwin's position she was also the one who could do most against. It would therefore be distinctly what our friend familiarly spoke of as "collar-work." The effect of these mixed considerations was at any rate that Mamie eventually acquiesced in the idea, handsomely thrown out by her client, that she should have an "advance" to go on with. Miss Cutter confessed that it seemed at times as if one scarce *could* go on; but the advance was, in spite of this delicacy, still more delicately made—made in the form of a banknote, several sovereigns, some loose silver and two coppers, the whole contents of her purse, neatly disposed by Mrs. Medwin on one of the tiny tables. It seemed to clear the air for deeper intimacies, the fruit of which was that Mamie, lonely, after all, in her crowd, and always more helpful than helped, eventually brought out that the way Scott had been going on was what seemed momentarily to overshadow her own power to do so.

"I've had a descent from him." But she had to explain. "My half-brother—Scott Homer. A wretch."

"What kind of a wretch?"

"Every kind. I lose sight of him at times—he disappears abroad. But he always turns up again, worse than ever."

"Violent?"

"No."

"Maudlin?"

"No."

"Only unpleasant?"

"No. Rather pleasant. Awfully clever—awfully travelled and easy."

"Then what's the matter with him?"

Mamie mused, hesitated—seemed to see a wide past. "I don't know."

"Something in the background?" Then as her friend was silent, "Something queer about cards?" Mrs. Medwin threw off.

"I don't know—and I don't want to!"

"Ah well, I'm sure *I* don't," Mrs. Medwin returned with spirit. The note of sharpness was perhaps also a little in the observation she made as she gathered herself to go. "Do you mind my saying something?"

Mamie took her eyes quickly from the money on the little stand. "You may say what you like."

"I only mean that anything awkward you may have to keep out of the way does seem to make more wonderful, doesn't it, that you should have got just where you are? I allude, you know, to your position."

"I see." Miss Cutter somewhat coldly smiled. "To my power."

"So awfully remarkable in an American."

"Ah, you like us so."

Mrs. Medwin candidly considered. "But we don't, dearest."

Her companion's smile brightened. "Then why do you come to me?"

"Oh, I like *you!*" Mrs. Medwin made out.

"Then that's it. There are no 'Americans.' It's always 'you.'"

"Me?" Mrs. Medwin looked lovely, but a little muddled.

"Me!" Mamie Cutter laughed. "But if you like me, you dear thing, you can judge if I like *you.*" She gave her a kiss to dismiss her. "I'll see you again when I've seen her."

"Lady Wantridge? I hope so, indeed. I'll turn up late to-morrow, if you don't catch me first. Has it come to you yet?" the visitor, now at the door, went on.

"No; but it will. There's time."

"Oh, a little less every day!"

Miss Cutter had approached the table and glanced again at the gold and silver and the note, not indeed absolutely overlooked the two coppers. "The balance," she put it, "the day after?"

"That very night, if you like."

"Then count on me."

"Oh, if I didn't——!" But the door closed on the dark idea. Yearningly then, and only when it had done so, Miss Cutter took up the money.

She went out with it ten minutes later, and, the calls on her time being many, remained out so long that at half-past six she had not come back. At that hour, on the other hand, Scott Homer knocked at her door, where her maid, who opened it with a weak pretence of holding it firm, ventured to announce to him, as a lesson well learnt, that he had not been expected till seven. No lesson, none the less, could prevail against his native art. He pleaded fatigue, her, the maid's, dreadful depressing London, and the need to curl up somewhere. If she would just leave him quiet half an hour that old sofa upstairs would do for it, of which he took quickly such effectual possession that when, five minutes later, she peeped, nervous for her broken vow, into the drawing-room, the faithless young woman found him extended at his length and peacefully asleep.

III

The situation before Miss Cutter's return developed in other directions still, and when that event took place, at a few minutes past seven, these circumstances were, by the foot of the stair, between mistress and maid, the subject of some interrogative gasps and scared admissions. Lady Wantridge had arrived shortly after the interloper, and wishing, as she said, to wait, had gone straight up in spite of being told he was lying down.

"She distinctly understood he was there?"

"Oh yes, ma'am; I thought it right to mention."

"And what did you call him?"

"Well, ma'am, I thought it unfair to *you* to call him anything but a gentleman."

Mamie took it all in, though there might well be more of it than one could quickly embrace. "But if she has had time," she flashed, "to find out he isn't one?"

"Oh, ma'am, she had a quarter of an hour."

"Then she isn't with him still?"

"No, ma'am; she came down again at last. She rang, and I saw her here, and she said she wouldn't wait longer."

Miss Cutter darkly mused. "Yet had already waited——?"

"Quite a quarter."

"Mercy on us!" She began to mount. Before reaching the top, however, she had reflected that quite a quarter was long if Lady Wantridge had only been shocked. On the other hand, it was short if she had only been pleased. But how *could* she have been pleased? The very essence of their actual crisis was just that there was no pleasing her. Mamie had but to open the drawing-room door indeed to perceive that this was not true at least of Scott Homer, who was horribly cheerful.

Miss Cutter expressed to her brother without reserve her sense of the constitutional, the brutal selfishness that had determined his mistimed return. It had taken place, in violation of their agreement, exactly at the moment when it was most cruel to her that he should be there, and if she must now completely wash her hands of him he had only himself to thank. She had come in flushed with resentment and for a moment had been voluble; but it would have been striking that, though the way he received her might have seemed but to aggravate, it presently justified him by causing their relation really to take a stride. He had the art of confounding those who would quarrel with him by reducing them to the humiliation of an irritated curiosity.

"What *could* she have made of you?" Mamie demanded.

"My dear girl, she's not a woman who's eager to make too much of anything—anything, I mean, that will prevent her from doing as she likes, what she takes into her head. Of course," he continued to explain, "if it's something she doesn't want to do, she'll make as much as Moses."

Mamie wondered if that was the way he talked to her visitor, but felt obliged to own to his acuteness. It was an exact description of Lady Wantridge, and she was conscious of tucking it away for future use in a corner of her miscellaneous little mind. She withheld, however, all present acknowledgment, only addressing him another question. "Did you really get on with her?"

"Have you still to learn, darling—I can't help again putting it to you—that I get on with everybody? That's just what I don't seem able to drive into you. Only see how I get on with *you*."

She almost stood corrected. "What I mean is, of course, whether——"

"Whether she made love to me? Shyly, yet—or because—shamefully? She would certainly have liked awfully to stay."

"Then why didn't she?"

"Because, on account of some other matter—and I could see it was true—she hadn't time. Twenty minutes—she was here less—were all she came to give you. So don't be afraid I've frightened her away. She'll come back."

Mamie thought it over. "Yet you didn't go with her to the door?"

"She wouldn't let me, and I know when to do what I'm told—quite as much as what I'm not told. She wanted to find out about me. I mean from your little creature; a pearl of fidelity, by the way."

"But what on earth did she come up for?" Mamie again found herself appealing, and, just by that fact, showing her need of help.

"Because she always goes up." Then, as, in the presence of this rapid generalisation, to say nothing of that of such a relative altogether, Miss Cutter could only show as comparatively blank: "I mean she knows when to go up and when to come down. She has instincts; she didn't know whom you might have up here. It's a kind of compliment to you anyway. Why, Mamie," Scott pursued, "you don't know the curiosity we any of us inspire. You wouldn't believe what I've seen. The bigger bugs they are the more they're on the look-out."

Mamie still followed, but at a distance. "The look-out for what?"

"Why, for anything that will help them to live. You've been here all this time without making out then, about them, what I've had to pick out as I can? They're dead, don't you see? And *we're* alive."

"You? Oh!"—Mamie almost laughed about it.

"Well, they're a worn-out old lot, anyhow; they've used up their resources. They do look out; and I'll do them the justice to say they're not afraid—not even of me!" he continued as his sister again showed something of the same irony. "Lady Wantridge, at any rate, wasn't; that's what I mean by her having made love to me. She does what she likes. Mind it, you know." He was by this time fairly teaching her to know one of her best friends, and when, after it, he had come back to the great point of his lesson—that of her failure, through feminine inferiority, practically to grasp the truth that their being just as they were, he and she, was the real card for them to play—when he had renewed that reminder he left her absolutely in a state of dependence. Her impulse to press him on the subject of Lady Wantridge dropped; it was as if she had felt that, whatever had taken place, something would somehow come of it. She was to be, in a manner, disappointed, but the impression helped to keep her over to the next morning, when, as Scott had foretold, his new acquaintance did reappear, explaining to Miss Cutter that she had acted the day before to gain time and that she even now sought to gain it by not waiting longer. What, she promptly intimated she had asked herself, could that friend be thinking of? She must show where she stood before things had gone too far. If she had brought her answer without more delay she wished to make it sharp. Mrs. Medwin? Never! "No, my dear—not I. *There* I stop."

Mamie had known it would be "collar-work," but somehow now, at the beginning, she felt her heart sink. It was not that she had expected to carry the position with a rush, but that, as always after an interval, her visitor's defences really loomed—and quite, as it were, to the material vision—too large. She was always planted with them, voluminous, in the very centre of the passage; was like a person accommodated with a chair in some unlawful place at the theatre. She wouldn't move and you couldn't get round. Mamie's calculation indeed had not been on getting round; she was obliged to recognise that, too foolishly and fondly, she had dreamed of producing a surrender. Her dream had been the fruit of her need; but, conscious that she was even yet unequipped for pressure, she felt, almost for the first time in her life, superficial and crude. She was to be paid—but with what was she, to that end, to pay? She had engaged to find an answer to this question, but the answer had not, according to her promise, "come." And Lady Wantridge meanwhile massed herself, and there was no view of her that didn't show her as verily, by some process too obscure to be traced, the hard depository of the social law. She was no younger, no fresher, no stronger, really, than any of them; she was only, with a kind of haggard fineness, a sharpened taste for life, and, with all sorts of things behind and beneath her, more abysmal and more immoral, more secure and more impertinent. The points she made were two in number. One was that she absolutely declined; the other was that she quite doubted if Mamie herself had measured the job. The thing couldn't be done. But say it *could* be; was Mamie quite the person to do it? To this Miss Cutter, with a sweet smile, replied that she quite understood how little she might seem so. "I'm only one of the persons to whom it has appeared that *you* are."

"Then who are the others?"

"Well, to begin with, Lady Edward, Lady Bellhouse and Mrs. Pouncer."

"Do you mean that they'll come to meet her?"

"I've seen them, and they've promised."

"To come, of course," Lady Wantridge said, "if *I* come."

Her hostess hesitated. "Oh, of course, you could prevent them. But I should take it as awfully kind of you not to. *Won't* you do this for me?" Mamie pleaded.

Her friend looked about the room very much as Scott had done. "Do they really understand what it's *for*?"

"Perfectly. So that she may call."

"And what good will that do her?"

Miss Cutter faltered, but she presently brought it out. "Of course what one hopes is that you'll ask her."

"Ask her to call?"

"Ask her to dine. Ask her, if you'd be so *truly* sweet, for a Sunday, or something of that sort, and even if only in one of your *most* mixed parties, to Catchmore."

Miss Cutter felt the less hopeful after this effort in that her companion only showed a strange good nature. And it was not the amiability of irony; yet it *was* amusement. "Take Mrs. Medwin into my family?"

"Some day, when you're taking forty others."

"Ah, but what I don't see is what it does for *you*. You're already so welcome among us that you can scarcely improve your position even by forming for us the most delightful relation."

"Well, I know how dear you are," Mamie Cutter replied; "but one has, after all, more than one side, and more than one sympathy. I like her, you know." And even at this Lady Wantridge was not shocked; she showed that ease and blandness which were her way, unfortunately, of being most impossible. She remarked that *she* might listen to such things, because she was clever enough for them not to matter; only Mamie should take care how she went about saying them at

large. When she became definite, however, in a minute, on
the subject of the public facts, Miss Cutter soon found herself
ready to make her own concession. Of course, she didn't dispute *them*: there they were; they were unfortunately on record, and nothing was to be done about them but to—Mamie
found it, in truth, at this point, a little difficult.

"Well, what? Pretend already to have forgotten them?"

"Why not, when you've done it in so many other cases?"

"There *are* no other cases so bad. One meets them, at any
rate, as they come. Some you can manage, others you can't.
It's no use, you must give them up. They're past patching;
there's nothing to be done with them. There's nothing, accordingly, to be done with Mrs. Medwin but to put her off."
And Lady Wantridge rose to her height.

"Well, you know, I *do* do things," Mamie quavered with a
smile so strained that it partook of exaltation.

"You help people? Oh yes, I've known you to do wonders.
But stick," said Lady Wantridge with strong and cheerful emphasis, "to your Americans!"

Miss Cutter, gazing, got up. "You don't do justice, Lady
Wantridge, to your own compatriots. Some of them are really
charming. Besides," said Mamie, "working for mine often
strikes me, so far as the interest—the inspiration and excitement, don't you know?—go, as rather too easy. You all, as I
constantly have occasion to say, like us so!"

Her companion frankly weighed it. "Yes; it takes that to
account for your position. I've always thought of you, nevertheless, as keeping, for their benefit, a regular working agency.
They come to you, and you place them. There remains, I
confess," her ladyship went on in the same free spirit, "the
great wonder——"

"Of how I first placed my poor little self? Yes," Mamie
bravely conceded, "when *I* began there was no agency. I just
worked my passage. I didn't even come to *you*, did I? You
never noticed me till, as Mrs. Short Stokes says, 'I was 'way,
'way up!' Mrs. Medwin," she threw in, "can't get over it."
Then, as her friend looked vague: "Over my social situation."

"Well, it's no great flattery to you to say," Lady Wantridge
good-humouredly returned, "that she certainly can't hope for

one resembling it." Yet it really seemed to spread there before them. "You simply *made* Mrs. Short Stokes."

"In spite of her name!" Mamie smiled.

"Oh, your names——! In spite of everything."

"Ah, I'm something of an artist." With which, and a relapse marked by her wistful eyes into the gravity of the matter, she supremely fixed her friend. She felt how little she minded betraying at last the extremity of her need, and it was out of this extremity that her appeal proceeded. "Have I really had your last word? It means so much to me."

Lady Wantridge came straight to the point. "You mean you depend on it?"

"Awfully!"

"Is it all you have?"

"All. Now."

"But Mrs. Short Stokes and the others—'rolling,' aren't they? Don't they pay up?"

"Ah," sighed Mamie, "if it wasn't for them——!"

Lady Wantridge perceived. "You've had so much?"

"I couldn't have gone on."

"Then what do you do with it all?"

"Oh, most of it goes back to them. There are all sorts, and it's all help. Some of them have nothing."

"Oh, if you feed the hungry," Lady Wantridge laughed, "you're indeed in a great way of business. Is Mrs. Medwin"—her transition was immediate—"really rich?"

"Really. He left her everything."

"So that if I do say 'yes'——"

"It will quite set me up."

"I see—and how much more responsible it makes one! But I'd rather myself give you the money."

"Oh!" Mamie coldly murmured.

"You mean I mayn't suspect your prices? Well, I daresay I don't! But I'd rather give you ten pounds."

"Oh!" Mamie repeated in a tone that sufficiently covered her prices. The question was in every way larger. "Do you *never* forgive?" she reproachfully inquired. The door opened, however, at the moment she spoke, and Scott Homer presented himself.

IV

Scott Homer wore exactly, to his sister's eyes, the aspect he had worn the day before, and it also formed, to her sense, the great feature of his impartial greeting.

"How d'ye do, Mamie? How d'ye do, Lady Wantridge?"

"How d'ye do again?" Lady Wantridge replied with an equanimity striking to her hostess. It was as if Scott's own had been contagious; it was almost indeed as if she had seen him before. *Had* she ever so seen him—before the previous day? While Miss Cutter put to herself this question her visitor, at all events, met the one she had previously uttered.

"Ever 'forgive'?" this personage echoed in a tone that made as little account as possible of the interruption. "Dear, yes! The people I *have* forgiven!" She laughed—perhaps a little nervously; and she was now looking at Scott. The way she looked at him was precisely what had already had its effect for his sister. "The people I can!"

"Can you forgive *me*?" asked Scott Homer.

She took it so easily. "But—what?"

Mamie interposed; she turned directly to her brother. "Don't try her. Leave it so." She had had an inspiration; it was the most extraordinary thing in the world. "Don't try *him*"—she had turned to their companion. She looked grave, sad, strange. "Leave it so." Yes, it was a distinct inspiration, which she couldn't have explained, but which had come, prompted by something she had caught—the extent of the recognition expressed—in Lady Wantridge's face. It had come absolutely of a sudden, straight out of the opposition of the two figures before her—quite as if a concussion had struck a light. The light was helped by her quickened sense that her friend's silence on the incident of the day before showed some sort of consciousness. She looked surprised. "Do you know my brother?"

"*Do* I know you?" Lady Wantridge asked of him.

"No, Lady Wantridge," Scott pleasantly confessed, "not one little mite!"

'Well, then, if you *must* go——!' and Mamie offered her a hand. "But I'll go down with you. Not *you*!" she launched at her brother, who immediately effaced himself. His way of doing so—and he had already done so, as for Lady Wantridge, in respect to their previous encounter—struck her even at the moment as an instinctive, if slightly blind, tribute to her possession of an idea; and as such, in its celerity, made her so admire him, and their common wit, that, on the spot, she more than forgave him his queerness. He was right. He could be as queer as he liked! The queerer the better! It was at the foot of the stairs, when she had got her guest down, that what she had assured Mrs. Medwin would come did indeed come. "*Did* you meet him here yesterday?"

"Dear, yes. Isn't he too funny?"

"Yes," said Mamie gloomily. "He *is* funny. But had you ever met him before?"

"Dear, no!"

"Oh!"—and Mamie's tone might have meant many things.

Lady Wantridge, however, after all, easily overlooked it. "I only knew he was one of your odd Americans. That's why, when I heard yesterday, here, that he was up there awaiting your return, I didn't let that prevent me. I thought he might be. He certainly," her ladyship laughed, "*is.*"

"Yes, he's very American," Mamie went on in the same way.

"As you say, we *are* fond of you! Good-bye," said Lady Wantridge.

But Mamie had not half done with her. She felt more and more—or she hoped at least—that she looked strange. She *was*, no doubt, if it came to that, strange. "Lady Wantridge," she almost convulsively broke out, "I don't know whether you'll understand me, but I seem to feel that I must act with you—I don't know what to call it!—responsibly. He *is* my brother."

"Surely—and why not?" Lady Wantridge stared. "He's the image of you!"

"Thank you!"—and Mamie was stranger than ever.

"Oh, he's good-looking. He's handsome, my dear. Oddly—but distinctly!" Her ladyship was for treating it much as a joke.

But Mamie, all sombre, would have none of this. She boldly gave him up. "I think he's awful."

"He is indeed—delightfully. And where *do* you get your ways of saying things? It isn't anything—and the things aren't anything. But it's so droll."

"Don't let yourself, all the same," Mamie consistently pursued, "be carried away by it. The thing can't be done—simply."

Lady Wantridge wondered. " 'Done simply'?"

"Done at all."

"But what can't be?"

"Why, what you might think—from his pleasantness. What he spoke of your doing for him."

Lady Wantridge recalled. "Forgiving him?"

"He asked you if you couldn't. But you can't. It's too dreadful for me, as so near a relation, to have, loyally—loyally to *you*—to say it. But he's impossible."

It was so portentously produced that her ladyship had somehow to meet it. "What's the matter with him?"

"I don't know."

"Then what's the matter with *you*?" Lady Wantridge inquired.

"It's because I *won't* know," Mamie—not without dignity—explained.

"Then *I* won't either!"

"Precisely. Don't. It's something," Mamie pursued, with some inconsequence, "that—somewhere or other, at some time or other—he appears to have done; something that has made a difference in his life."

" 'Something'?" Lady Wantridge echoed again. "What kind of thing?"

Mamie looked up at the light above the door, through which the London sky was doubly dim. "I haven't the least idea."

"Then what kind of difference?"

Mamie's gaze was still at the light. "The difference you see."

Lady Wantridge, rather obligingly, seemed to ask herself what she saw. "But I don't see any! It seems, at least," she added, "such an amusing one! And he has such nice eyes."

"Oh, *dear* eyes!" Mamie conceded; but with too much sadness, for the moment, about the connections of the subject, to say more.

It almost forced her companion, after an instant, to proceed. "Do you mean he can't go home?"

She weighed her responsibility. "I only make out—more's the pity!—that he doesn't."

"Is it then something too terrible——?"

She thought again. "I don't know what—for men—*is* too terrible."

"Well then, as you don't know what 'is' for women either—good-bye!" her visitor laughed.

It practically wound up the interview; which, however, terminating thus on a considerable stir of the air, was to give Miss Cutter, the next few days, the sense of being much blown about. The degree to which, to begin with, she had been drawn—or perhaps rather pushed—closer to Scott was marked in the brief colloquy that, on her friend's departure, she had with him. He had immediately said it. "You'll see if she doesn't ask me down!"

"So soon?"

"Oh, I've known them at places—at Cannes, at Pau, at Shanghai—to do it sooner still. I always know when they will. You *can't* make out they don't love me!" He spoke almost plaintively, as if he wished she could.

"Then I don't see why it hasn't done you more good."

"Why, Mamie," he patiently reasoned, "what more good *could* it? As I tell you," he explained, "it has just been my life."

"Then why do you come to me for money?"

"Oh, they don't give me *that*!" Scott returned.

"So that it only means then, after all, that I, at the best, must keep you up?"

He fixed on her the nice eyes that Lady Wantridge admired. "Do you mean to tell me that already—at this very moment—I am not distinctly keeping *you*?"

She gave him back his look. "Wait till she *has* asked you, and then," Mamie added, "decline."

Scott, not too grossly, wondered. "As acting for *you*?"

Mamie's next injunction was answer enough. "But *before*—yes—call."

He took it in. "Call—but decline. Good."

"The rest," she said, "I leave to you." And she left it, in fact, with such confidence that for a couple of days she was not only conscious of no need to give Mrs. Medwin another turn of the screw, but positively evaded, in her fortitude, the reappearance of that lady. It was not till the third day that she waited upon her, finding her, as she had expected, tense.

"Lady Wantridge *will*——?"

"Yes, though she says she won't."

"She says she won't? O—oh!" Mrs. Medwin moaned.

"Sit tight all the same. I *have* her!"

"But how?"

"Through Scott—whom she wants."

"Your bad brother!" Mrs. Medwin stared. "What does she want of him?"

"To amuse them at Catchmore. Anything for that. And he *would*. But he sha'n't!" Mamie declared. "He sha'n't go unless she comes. She must meet you first—you're my condition."

"O—o—oh!" Mrs. Medwin's tone was a wonder of hope and fear. "But doesn't he want to go?"

"He wants what *I* want. She draws the line at *you*. I draw the line at *him*."

"But *she*—doesn't she mind that he's bad?"

It was so artless that Mamie laughed. "No; it doesn't touch her. Besides, perhaps he isn't. It isn't as for *you*—people seem not to know. He has settled everything, at all events, by going to see her. It's before her that he's the thing she will have to have."

"Have to?"

"For Sundays in the country. A feature—*the* feature."

"So she has asked him?"

"Yes; and he has declined."

"For *me*?" Mrs. Medwin panted.

"For me," said Mamie, on the doorstep. "But I don't leave him for long." Her hansom had waited. "She'll come."

Lady Wantridge did come. She met in South Audley Street, on the fourteenth, at tea, the ladies whom Mamie had named to her, together with three or four others, and it was rather a master-stroke for Miss Cutter that, if Mrs. Medwin was modestly present, Scott Homer was as markedly not. This occasion, however, is a medal that would take rare casting, as would also, for that matter, even the minor light and shade, the lower relief, of the pecuniary transaction that Mrs. Medwin's flushed gratitude scarce awaited the dispersal of the company munificently to complete. A new understanding indeed on the spot rebounded from it, the conception of which, in Mamie's mind, had promptly bloomed. "He sha'n't go *now* unless he takes you." Then, as her fancy always moved quicker for her client than her client's own—"Down with him to Catchmore! When he goes to amuse them, *you*," she comfortably declared, "shall amuse them too." Mrs. Medwin's response was again rather oddly divided, but she was sufficiently intelligible when it came to meeting the intimation that this latter would be an opportunity involving a separate fee. "Say," Mamie had suggested, "the same."

"Very well; the same."

The knowledge that it was to be the same had perhaps something to do, also, with the obliging spirit in which Scott eventually went. It was all, at the last, rather hurried—a party rapidly got together for the Grand Duke, who was in England but for the hour, who had good-naturedly proposed himself, and who liked his parties small, intimate and funny. This one was of the smallest, and it was finally judged to conform neither too little nor too much to the other conditions—after a brief whirlwind of wires and counterwires, and an iterated waiting of hansoms at various doors—to include Mrs. Medwin. It was from Catchmore itself that, snatching a moment on the wondrous Sunday afternoon, this lady had the harmonious thought of sending the new cheque. She was in bliss enough, but her scribble none the less intimated that it was Scott who amused them most. He *was* the feature.

The Beldonald Holbein

M**RS. MUNDEN** had not yet been to my studio on so good a pretext as when she first put it to me that it would be quite open to me—should I only care, as she called it, to throw the handkerchief—to paint her beautiful sister-in-law. I needn't go here, more than is essential, into the question of Mrs. Munden, who would really, by the way, be a story in herself. She has a manner of her own of putting things, and some of those she has put to me——! Her implication was that Lady Beldonald had not only seen and admired certain examples of my work, but had literally been prepossessed in favour of the painter's "personality." Had I been struck with this sketch I might easily have imagined that Lady Beldonald was throwing *me* the handkerchief. "She hasn't done," my visitor said, "what she ought."

"Do you mean she has done what she oughtn't?"

"Nothing horrid—oh dear, no." And something in Mrs. Munden's tone, with the way she appeared to muse a moment, even suggested to me that what she "oughtn't" was perhaps what Lady Beldonald had too much neglected. "She hasn't got on."

"What's the matter with her?"

"Well, to begin with, she's American."

"But I thought that was the way of ways to get on."

"It's one of them. But it's one of the ways of being awfully out of it too. There are so many!"

"So many Americans?" I asked.

"Yes, plenty of *them*," Mrs. Munden sighed. "So many ways, I mean, of being one."

"But if your sister-in-law's way is to be beautiful——?"

"Oh, there are different ways of that too."

"And she hasn't taken the right way?"

"Well," my friend returned, as if it were rather difficult to express, "she hasn't done with it——"

"I see," I laughed; "what she oughtn't!"

Mrs. Munden in a manner corrected me, but it *was* difficult to express. "My brother, at all events, was certainly selfish.

Till he died she was almost never in London; they wintered, year after year, for what he supposed to be his health—which it didn't help, since he was so much too soon to meet his end—in the south of France and in the dullest holes he could pick out, and when they came back to England he always kept her in the country. I must say for her that she always behaved beautifully. Since his death she has been more in London, but on a stupidly unsuccessful footing. I don't think she quite understands. She hasn't what *I* should call a life. It may be, of course, that she doesn't want one. That's just what I can't exactly find out. I can't make out how much she knows."

"I can easily make out," I returned with hilarity, "how much *you* do!"

"Well, you're very horrid. Perhaps she's too old."

"Too old for what?" I persisted.

"For anything. Of course she's no longer even a little young; only preserved—oh, but preserved, like bottled fruit, in syrup! I want to help her, if only because she gets on my nerves, and I really think the way of it would be just the right thing of yours at the Academy and on the line."

"But suppose," I threw out, "she should give on *my* nerves?"

"Oh, she will. But isn't that all in the day's work, and don't great beauties always——?"

"*You* don't," I interrupted; but I at any rate saw Lady Beldonald later on—the day came when her kinswoman brought her, and then I understood that her life had its centre in her own idea of her appearance. Nothing else about her mattered—one knew her all when one knew that. She is indeed in one particular, I think, sole of her kind—a person whom vanity has had the odd effect of keeping positively safe and sound. This passion is supposed surely, for the most part, to be a principle of perversion and injury, leading astray those who listen to it and landing them, sooner or later, in this or that complication; but it has landed her ladyship nowhere whatever—it has kept her from the first moment of full consciousness, one feels, exactly in the same place. It has protected her from every danger, has made her absolutely proper and prim. If she is "preserved," as Mrs. Munden originally described her to me, it is her vanity that has beautifully done it—putting her years ago in a plate-glass case and closing up the receptacle against every breath of air. How shouldn't she be preserved, when you might smash your knuckles on this transparency before you could crack it? And she *is*—oh, amazingly! Preservation is scarce the word for the rare condition of her surface. She looks *naturally* new, as if she took out every night her large, lovely, varnished eyes and put them in water. The thing was to paint her, I perceived, *in* the glass case—a most tempting, attaching feat; render to the full the shining, interposing plate and the general show-window effect.

It was agreed, though it was not quite arranged, that she should sit to me. If it was not quite arranged, this was because, as I was made to understand from an early stage, the conditions for our start must be such as should exclude all elements of disturbance, such, in a word, as she herself should judge absolutely favourable. And it seemed that these conditions were easily imperilled. Suddenly, for instance, at a moment when I was expecting her to meet an appointment—the first—that I had proposed, I received a hurried visit from Mrs. Munden, who came on her behalf to let me know that the season happened just not to be propitious and that our friend couldn't be quite sure, to the hour, when it would again become so. Nothing, she felt, would make it so but a total absence of worry.

"Oh, a 'total absence,' " I said, "is a large order! We live in a worrying world."

"Yes; and she feels exactly that—more than you'd think. It's in fact just why she mustn't have, as she has now, a particular distress on at the very moment. She wants to look, of course, her best, and such things tell on her appearance."

I shook my head. "Nothing tells on her appearance. Nothing reaches it in any way; nothing gets *at* it. However, I can understand her anxiety. But what's her particular distress?"

"Why, the illness of Miss Dadd."

"And who in the world's Miss Dadd?"

"Her most intimate friend and constant companion—the lady who was with us here that first day."

"Oh, the little round, black woman who gurgled with admiration?"

"None other. But she was taken ill last week, and it may very well be that she'll gurgle no more. She was very bad yesterday and is no better to-day, and Nina is much upset. If anything happens to Miss Dadd she'll have to get another, and, though she has had two or three before, that won't be so easy."

"Two or three Miss Dadds? Is it possible? And still wanting another!" I recalled the poor lady completely now. "No; I shouldn't indeed think it would be easy to get another. But why is a succession of them necessary to Lady Beldonald's existence?"

"Can't you guess?" Mrs. Munden looked deep, yet impatient. "They help."

"Help what? Help whom?"

"Why, every one. You and me for instance. To do what? Why, to think Nina beautiful. She has them for that purpose; they serve as foils, as accents serve on syllables, as terms of comparison. They make her 'stand out.' It's an effect of contrast that must be familiar to you artists; it's what a woman does when she puts a band of black velvet under a pearl ornament that may require, as she thinks, a little showing off."

I wondered. "Do you mean she always has them black?"

"Dear no; I've seen them blue, green, yellow. They may be what they like, so long as they're always one other thing."

"Hideous?"

Mrs. Munden hesitated. "Hideous is too much to say; she doesn't really require them as bad as that. But consistently, cheerfully, loyally plain. It's really a most happy relation. She loves them for it."

"And for what do they love *her*?"

"Why, just for the amiability that they produce in her. Then, also, for their 'home.' It's a career for them."

"I see. But if that's the case," I asked, "why are they so difficult to find?"

"Oh, they must be safe; it's all in that: her being able to depend on them to keep to the terms of the bargain and never have moments of rising—as even the ugliest woman will now and then (say when she's in love)—superior to themselves."

I turned it over. "Then if they can't inspire passions the poor things mayn't even at least feel them?"

"She distinctly deprecates it. That's why such a man as you may be, after all, a complication."

I continued to muse. "You're very sure Miss Dadd's ailment isn't an affection that, being smothered, has struck in?" My joke, however, was not well timed, for I afterwards learned that the unfortunate lady's state had been, even while I spoke, such as to forbid all hope. The worst symptoms had appeared; she was not destined to recover; and a week later I heard from Mrs. Munden that she would in fact "gurgle" no more.

II

All this, for Lady Beldonald, had been an agitation so great that access to her apartment was denied for a time even to her sister-in-law. It was much more out of the question, of course, that she should unveil her face to a person of my special business with it; so that the question of the portrait was, by common consent, postponed to that of the installation of a successor to her late companion. Such a successor, I gathered from Mrs. Munden, widowed, childless, and lonely, as well as inapt for the minor offices, she had absolutely to have; a more or less humble *alter ego* to deal with the servants, keep the accounts, make the tea and arrange the light. Nothing seemed more natural than that she should marry again, and obviously that might come; yet the predecessors of Miss Dadd had been contemporaneous with a first husband, and others formed in her image might be contemporaneous with a second. I was much occupied in those months, at any rate, so that these questions and their ramifications lost themselves for a while to my view, and I was only brought back to them by Mrs. Munden's coming to me one day with the news that we were all right again—her sister-in-law was once more "suited." A certain Mrs. Brash, an American relative whom she had not seen for years, but with whom she had continued to communicate, was to come out to her immediately; and this person, it appeared, could be quite trusted to meet the conditions. She was ugly—ugly enough, without abuse of it, and she was unlimitedly good. The position offered her by Lady Beldonald was, moreover, exactly what she needed; widowed also, after many troubles and reverses, with her fortune of the smallest and her various children either buried or placed about, she had never had time or means to come to England, and would really be grateful in her declining years for the new experience and the pleasant light work involved in her cousin's hospitality. They had been much together early in life, and Lady Beldonald was immensely fond of her—would have in fact tried to get hold of her before had not Mrs. Brash been always in bondage to family duties, to the variety of her tribulations. I dare say I laughed at my friend's use of the term "position"—the position, one might call it, of a candlestick or a sign-post, and I dare say I must have asked if the special service the poor lady was to render had been made clear to her. Mrs. Munden left me, at all events, with the rather droll image of her faring forth, across the sea, quite consciously and resignedly to perform it.

The point of the communication had, however, been that my sitter was again looking up and would doubtless, on the arrival and due initiation of Mrs. Brash, be in form really to wait on me. The situation must, further, to my knowledge, have developed happily, for I arranged with Mrs. Munden that our friend, now all ready to begin, but wanting first just to see the things I had most recently done, should come once more, as a final preliminary, to my studio. A good foreign friend of mine, a French painter, Paul Outreau, was at the moment in London, and I had proposed, as he was much interested in types, to get together for his amusement a small afternoon party. Everyone came, my big room was full, there was music and a modest spread; and I have not forgotten the light of admiration in Outreau's expressive face as, at the end of half an hour, he came up to me in his enthusiasm.

"*Bonté divine, mon cher—que cette vieille est donc belle!*"

I had tried to collect all the beauty I could, and also all the youth, so that for a moment I was at a loss. I had talked to many people and provided for the music, and there were figures in the crowd that were still lost to me. "What old woman do you mean?"

"I don't know her name—she was over by the door a moment ago. I asked somebody and was told, I think, that she's American."

I looked about and saw one of my guests attach a pair of fine eyes to Outreau very much as if she knew he must be talking of her. "Oh, Lady Beldonald! Yes, she's handsome; but the great point about her is that she has been 'put up,' to keep, and that she wouldn't be flattered if she knew you spoke of her as old. A box of sardines is only 'old' after it has been opened. Lady Beldonald never has yet been—but I'm going to do it." I joked, but I was somehow disappointed. It was a type that, with his unerring sense for the *banal*, I shouldn't have expected Outreau to pick out.

"You're going to paint her? But, my dear man, she *is* painted—and as neither you nor I can do it. *Où est-elle donc?*" He had lost her, and I saw I had made a mistake. "She's the greatest of all the great Holbeins."

I was relieved. "Ah, then, not Lady Beldonald! But do I possess a Holbein, of *any* price, unawares?"

"There she is—there she is! Dear, dear, dear, what a head!" And I saw whom he meant—and what: a small old lady in a black dress and a black bonnet, both relieved with a little white, who had evidently just changed her place to reach a corner from which more of the room and of the scene was presented to her. She appeared unnoticed and un-known, and I immediately recognised that some other guest must have brought her and, for want of opportunity, had as yet to call my attention to her. But two things, simultane-ously with this and with each other, struck me with force; one of them the truth of Outreau's description of her, the other the fact that the person bringing her could only have been Lady Beldonald. She *was* a Holbein—of the first water; yet she was also Mrs. Brash, the imported "foil," the in-dispensable "accent," the successor to the dreary Miss Dadd! By the time I had put these things together—Ou-treau's "American" having helped me—I was in just such full possession of her face as I had found myself, on the other first occasion, of that of her patroness. Only with so different a consequence. I couldn't look at her enough, and I stared and stared till I became aware she might have fan-cied me challenging her as a person unpresented. "All the same," Outreau went on, equally held, "*c'est une tête à faire*. If I were only staying long enough for a crack at her!

But I tell you what"—and he seized my arm—"bring her over!"

"Over?"

"To Paris. She'd have a *succès fou.*"

"Ah, thanks, my dear fellow," I was now quite in a position to say; "she's the handsomest thing in London, and"—for what I might do with her was already before me with intensity—"I propose to keep her to myself." It was before me with intensity, in the light of Mrs. Brash's distant perfection of a little white old face, in which every wrinkle was the touch of a master; but something else, I suddenly felt, was not less so, for Lady Beldonald, in the other quarter, and though she couldn't have made out the subject of our notice, continued to fix us, and her eyes had the challenge of those of the woman of consequence who has missed something. A moment later I was close to her, apologising first for not having been more on the spot at her arrival, but saying in the next breath uncontrollably, "Why, my dear lady, it's a Holbein!"

"A Holbein? What?"

"Why, the wonderful sharp old face—so extraordinarily, consummately drawn—in the frame of black velvet. That of Mrs. Brash, I mean—isn't it her name?—your companion."

This was the beginning of a most odd matter—the essence of my anecdote; and I think the very first note of the oddity must have sounded for me in the tone in which her ladyship spoke after giving me a silent look. It seemed to come to me out of a distance immeasurably removed from Holbein. "Mrs. Brash is not my 'companion' in the sense you appear to mean. She's my rather near relation and a very dear old friend. I *love* her—and you must know her."

"Know her? Rather! Why, to see her is to want, on the spot, to 'go' for her. She also must sit for me."

"*She?* Louisa Brash?" If Lady Beldonald had the theory that her beauty directly showed it when things were not well with her, this impression, which the fixed sweetness of her serenity had hitherto struck me by no means as justifying, gave me now my first glimpse of its grounds. It was as if I had never before seen her face invaded by anything I should have called an expression. This expression, moreover, was of the faintest— was like the effect produced on a surface by an agitation both deep within and as yet much confused. "Have you told her so?" she then quickly asked, as if to soften the sound of her surprise.

"Dear no, I've but just noticed her—Outreau a moment ago put me on her. But we're both so taken, and he also wants——"

"To *paint* her?" Lady Beldonald uncontrollably murmured.

"Don't be afraid we shall fight for her," I returned with a laugh for this tone. Mrs. Brash was still where I could see her without appearing to stare, and she mightn't have seen I was looking at her, though her protectress, I am afraid, could scarce have failed of this perception. "We must each take our turn, and at any rate she's a wonderful thing, so that, if you'll take her to Paris, Outreau promises her there——"

"There?" my companion gasped.

"A career bigger still than among *us*, as he considers that we haven't half their eye. He guarantees her a *succès fou*."

She couldn't get over it. "Louisa Brash? In Paris?"

"They do see," I exclaimed, "more than we; and they live extraordinarily, don't you know, *in* that. But she'll do something here too."

"And what will she do?"

If, frankly, now, I couldn't help giving Mrs. Brash a longer look, so after it I could as little resist sounding my interlocutress. "You'll see. Only give her time."

She said nothing during the moment in which she met my eyes; but then: "Time, it seems to me, is exactly what you and your friend want. If you haven't talked with her——"

"We haven't seen her? Oh, we see bang off—with a click like a steel spring. It's our trade; it's our life; and we should be donkeys if we made mistakes. That's the way I saw you yourself, my lady, if I may say so; that's the way, with a long pin straight through your body, I've got you. And just so I've got *her*."

All this, for reasons, had brought my guest to her feet; but her eyes, while we talked, had never once followed the direction of mine. "You call her a Holbein?"

"Outreau did, and I of course immediately recognised it. Don't *you*? She brings the old boy to life! It's just as I should call you a Titian. You bring *him* to life."

She couldn't be said to relax, because she couldn't be said to have hardened; but something at any rate on this took place in her—something indeed quite disconnected from what I would have called her. "Don't you understand that she has always been supposed——?" It had the ring of impatience; nevertheless, on a scruple, it stopped short.

I knew what it was, however, well enough to say it for her if she preferred. "To be nothing whatever to look at? To be unfortunately plain—or even if you like repulsively ugly? Oh yes, I understand it perfectly, just as I understand—I have to as a part of my trade—many other forms of stupidity. It's nothing new to one that ninety-nine people out of a hundred have no eyes, no sense, no taste. There are whole communities impenetrably sealed. I don't say your friend is a person to make the men turn round in Regent Street. But it adds to the joy of the few who do see that they have it so much to themselves. Where in the world can she have lived? You must tell me all about that—or rather, if she'll be so good, *she* must."

"You mean then to speak to her——?"

I wondered as she pulled up again. "Of her beauty?"

"Her beauty!" cried Lady Beldonald so loud that two or three persons looked round.

"Ah, with every precaution of respect!" I declared in a much lower tone. But her back was by this time turned to me, and in the movement, as it were, one of the strangest little dramas I have ever known was well launched.

III

It was a drama of small, smothered intensely private things, and I knew of but one other person in the secret; yet that person and I found it exquisitely susceptible of notation, followed it with an interest the mutual communication of which did much for our enjoyment, and were present with emotion at its touching catastrophe. The small case—for so small a case—had made a great stride even before my little party separated, and in fact within the next ten minutes.

In that space of time two things had happened; one of which was that I made the acquaintance of Mrs. Brash, and the other that Mrs. Munden reached me, cleaving the crowd, with one of her usual pieces of news. What she had to impart was that, on her having just before asked Nina if the conditions of our sitting had been arranged with me, Nina had replied, with something like perversity, that she didn't propose to arrange them, that the whole affair was "off" again, and that she preferred not to be, for the present, further pressed. The question for Mrs. Munden was naturally what had happened and whether I understood. Oh, I understood perfectly, and what I at first most understood was that even when I had brought in the name of Mrs. Brash intelligence was not yet in Mrs. Munden. She was quite as surprised as Lady Beldonald had been on hearing of the esteem in which I held Mrs. Brash's appearance. She was stupefied at learning that I had just in my ardour proposed to the possessor of it to sit to me. Only she came round promptly—which Lady Beldonald really never did. Mrs. Munden was in fact wonderful; for when I had given her quickly "Why, she's a Holbein, you know," she took it up, after a first fine vacancy, with an immediate abysmal "Oh, *is* she?" that, as a piece of social gymnastics, did her the greatest honour; and she was in fact the first in London to spread the tidings. For a face-about it was magnificent. But she was also the first, I must add, to see what would really happen—though this she put before me only a week or two later.

"It will kill her, my dear—that's what it will do!"

She meant neither more nor less than that it would kill Lady Beldonald if I were to paint Mrs. Brash; for at this lurid light had we arrived in so short a space of time. It was for me to decide whether my æsthetic need of giving life to my idea was such as to justify me in destroying it in a woman after all, in most eyes, so beautiful. The situation was, after all, sufficiently queer; for it remained to be seen what I should positively gain by giving up Mrs. Brash. I appeared to have in any case lost Lady Beldonald, now too "upset"—it was always Mrs. Munden's word about her and, as I inferred, her own about herself—to meet me again on our previous footing. The only thing, I of course soon saw, was to temporise—to drop the whole question for the present and yet so far as possible keep each of the pair in view. I may as well say at once that this plan and this process gave their principal interest to the next several months. Mrs. Brash had turned up, if I remember, early in the new year, and her little wonderful career was in our particular circle one of the features of the following season. It was at all events for myself the most attaching; it is not my fault if I am so put together as often to find more life in situations obscure and subject to interpretation than in the gross rattle of the foreground. And there were all sorts of things, things touching, amusing, mystifying—and above all such an instance as I had never yet met—in this funny little fortune of the useful American cousin. Mrs. Munden was promptly at one with me as to the rarity and, to a near and human view, the beauty and interest of the position. We had neither of us ever before seen that degree and that special sort of personal success come to a woman for the first time so late in life. I found it an example of poetic, of absolutely retributive, justice; so that my desire grew great to work it, as we say, on those lines. I had seen it all from the original moment at my studio; the poor lady had never known an hour's appreciation—which, moreover, in perfect good faith, she had never missed. The very first thing I did after producing so unintentionally the resentful retreat of her protectress had been to go straight over to her and say almost without preliminaries that I should hold myself immeasurably obliged if she would give me a few sittings. What I thus came face to face with was, on the instant, her whole unenlightened past, and the full, if foreshortened, revelation of what among us all was now unfailingly in store for her. To turn the handle and start that tune came to me on the spot as a temptation. Here was a poor lady who had waited for the approach of old age to find out what she was worth. Here was a benighted being to whom it was to be disclosed in her fifty-seventh year (I was to make that out) that she had something that might pass for a face. She looked much more than her age, and was fairly frightened—as if I had been trying on her some possibly heartless London trick—when she had taken in my appeal. That showed me in what an air she had lived and—as I should have been tempted to put it had I spoken out—among what children of darkness. Later on I did them more justice; saw more that her wonderful points must have been points largely the fruit of time, and even that possibly she might never in all her life have looked so well as at this particular moment. It might have been that if her hour had struck I just happened to be present at the striking. What had occurred, all the same, was at the worst a sufficient comedy.

The famous "irony of fate" takes many forms, but I had never yet seen it take quite this one. She had been "had over" on an understanding, and she was not playing fair. She had broken the law of her ugliness and had turned beautiful on the hands of her employer. More interesting even perhaps than a view of the conscious triumph that this might prepare for her, and of which, had I doubted of my own judgment, I could still take Outreau's fine start as the full guarantee— more interesting was the question of the process by which such a history could get itself enacted. The curious thing was that, all the while, the reasons of her having passed for plain— the reasons for Lady Beldonald's fond calculation, which they quite justified—were written large in her face, so large that it was easy to understand them as the only ones she herself had ever read. What was it, then, that actually made the old stale sentence mean something so different?—into what new combinations, what extraordinary language, unknown but understood at a glance, had time and life translated it? The only thing to be said was that time and life were artists who beat us all, working with recipes and secrets that we could never find out. I really ought to have, like a lecturer or a showman, a chart or a blackboard to present properly the relation, in the wonderful old tender, battered, blanched face, between the original elements and the exquisite final "style." I could do it with chalks, but I can scarcely do it thus. However, the thing was, for any artist who respected himself, to *feel* it—which I abundantly did; and then not to conceal from *her* that I felt it—which I neglected as little. But she was really, to do her complete justice, the last to understand; and I am not sure that, to the end—for there was an end—she quite made it all out or knew where she was. When you have been brought up for fifty years on black, it must be hard to adjust your organism, at a day's notice, to gold-colour. Her whole nature had been pitched in the key of her supposed plainness. She had known how to be ugly—it was the only thing she had learnt save, if possible, how not to mind it. Being beautiful, at any rate, took a new set of muscles. It was on the prior theory, literally, that she had developed her admirable dress, instinctively felicitous, always either black or white, and a matter of rather severe squareness and studied line. She was magnificently neat; everything she showed had a way of looking both old and fresh; and there was on every occasion the same picture in her draped head—draped in low-falling black—and the fine white plaits (of a painter's white, somehow) disposed on her chest. What had happened was that these arrangements, determined by certain considerations, lent themselves in effect much better to certain others. Adopted as a kind of refuge, they had really only deepened her accent. It was singular, moreover, that, so constituted, there was nothing in her aspect of the ascetic or the nun. She was a good, hard, sixteenth-century figure, not withered with innocence, bleached rather by life in the open. She was, in short, just what we had made of her, a Holbein for a great museum; and our position, Mrs. Munden's and mine, rapidly became that of persons having such a treasure to dispose of. The world—I speak of course mainly of the art-world—flocked to see it.

IV

"But has she any idea herself, poor thing?" was the way I had put it to Mrs. Munden on our next meeting after the incident at my studio; with the effect, however, only of leaving my friend at first to take me as alluding to Mrs. Brash's possible prevision of the chatter she might create. I had my own sense of that—this prevision had been *nil*; the question was of her consciousness of the office for which Lady Beldonald had counted on her and for which we were so promptly proceeding to spoil her altogether.

"Oh, I think she arrived with a goodish notion," Mrs. Munden had replied when I had explained; "for she's clever too, you know, as well as good-looking, and I don't see how, if she ever really *knew* Nina, she could have supposed for a moment that she was not wanted for whatever she might have left to give up. Hasn't she moreover always been made to feel that she's ugly enough for anything?" It was even at this point already wonderful how my friend had mastered the case, and

what lights, alike for its past and its future, she was prepared
to throw on it. "If she has seen herself as ugly enough for
anything, she has seen herself—and that was the only way—
as ugly enough for Nina; and she has had her own manner of
showing that she understands without making Nina commit
herself to anything vulgar. Women are never without ways for
doing such things—both for communicating and receiving
knowledge—that I can't explain to you, and that you wouldn't
understand if I could, as you must *be* a woman even to do
that. I dare say they've expressed it all to each other simply
in the language of kisses. But doesn't it, at any rate, make
something rather beautiful of the relation between them as
affected by our discovery?"

I had a laugh for her plural possessive. "The point is, of
course, that if there was a conscious bargain, and our action
on Mrs. Brash is to deprive her of the sense of keeping her
side of it, various things may happen that won't be good
either for her or for ourselves. She may conscientiously throw
up the position."

"Yes," my companion mused—"for she *is* conscientious.
Or Nina, without waiting for that, may cast her forth."

I faced it all. "Then *we* should have to keep her."

"As a regular model?" Mrs. Munden was ready for anything. "Oh, that would be lovely!"

But I further worked it out. "The difficulty is that she's *not*
a model, hang it—that she's too good for one, that she's the
very thing herself. When Outreau and I have each had our
go, that will be all; there'll be nothing left for anyone else.
Therefore it behoves us quite to understand that our attitude's
a responsibility. If we can't do for her positively more than
Nina does——"

"We must let her alone?" My companion continued to
muse. "I see!"

"Yet don't," I returned, "see too much. We *can* do more."

"Than Nina?" She was again on the spot. "It wouldn't,
after all, be difficult. We only want the directly opposite
thing—and which is the only one the poor dear can give.
Unless, indeed," she suggested, "we simply retract—we
back out."

I turned it over. "It's too late for that. Whether Mrs. Brash's peace is gone, I can't say. But Nina's is."

"Yes, and there's no way to bring it back that won't sacrifice her friend. We can't turn round and say Mrs. Brash *is* ugly, can we? But fancy Nina's not having *seen!*" Mrs. Munden exclaimed.

"She doesn't see now," I answered. "She can't, I'm certain, make out what we mean. The woman, for *her* still, is just what she always was. But she has, nevertheless, had her stroke, and her blindness, while she wavers and gropes in the dark, only adds to her discomfort. Her blow was to see the attention of the world deviate."

"All the same, I don't think, you know," my interlocutress said, "that Nina will have made her a scene, or that, whatever we do, she'll ever make her one. That isn't the way it will happen, for she's exactly as conscientious as Mrs. Brash."

"Then what *is* the way?" I asked.

"It will just happen in silence."

"And what will 'it,' as you call it, be?"

"Isn't that what we want really to see?"

"Well," I replied after a turn or two about, "whether we want it or not, it's exactly what we *shall* see; which is a reason the more for fancying, between the pair there—in the quiet, exquisite house, and full of superiorities and suppressions as they both are—the extraordinary situation. If I said just now that it's too late to do anything but accept, it's because I've taken the full measure of what happened at my studio. It took but a few moments—but she tasted of the tree."

My companion wondered. "Nina?"

"Mrs. Brash." And to have to put it so ministered, while I took yet another turn, to a sort of agitation. Our attitude *was* a responsibility.

But I had suggested something else to my friend, who appeared for a moment detached. "Should you say she'll hate her worse if she *doesn't* see?"

"Lady Beldonald? Doesn't see what *we* see, you mean, than if she does? Ah, I give *that* up!" I laughed. "But what I can tell you is why I hold that, as I said just now, we can do most. We can do this: we can give to a harmless and sensitive crea-

ture hitherto practically disinherited—and give with an unexpectedness that will immensely add to its price—the pure
joy of a deep draught of the very pride of life, of an acclaimed
personal triumph in our superior, sophisticated world."

Mrs. Munden had a glow of response for my sudden eloquence. "Oh, it will be beautiful!"

V

Well, that is what, on the whole, and in spite of everything,
it really was. It has dropped into my memory a rich little
gallery of pictures, a regular panorama of those occasions that
were the proof of the privilege that had made me for a moment—in the words I have just recorded—lyrical. I see Mrs.
Brash on each of these occasions practically enthroned and
surrounded and more or less mobbed; see the hurrying and
the nudging and the pressing and the staring; see the people
"making up" and introduced, and catch the word when they
have had their turn; hear it above all, the great one—"Ah yes,
the famous Holbein!"—passed about with that perfection of
promptitude that makes the motions of the London mind so
happy a mixture of those of the parrot and the sheep. Nothing
would be easier, of course, than to tell the whole little tale
with an eye only for that silly side of it. Great was the silliness,
but great also as to this case of poor Mrs. Brash, I will say for
it, the good nature. Of course, furthermore, it took in particular "our set," with its positive child-terror of the *banal*, to
be either so foolish or so wise; though indeed I've never quite
known where our set begins and ends, and have had to content myself on this score with the indication once given me
by a lady next whom I was placed at dinner: "Oh, it's
bounded on the north by Ibsen and on the south by Sargent!"
Mrs. Brash never sat to me; she absolutely declined; and when
she declared that it was quite enough for her that I had with
that fine precipitation invited her, I quite took this as she
meant it, for before we had gone very far our understanding,
hers and mine, was complete. Her attitude was as happy as
her success was prodigious. The sacrifice of the portrait was a
sacrifice to the true inwardness of Lady Beldonald, and did
much, for the time, I divined, toward muffling their domestic

tension. All that was thus in her power to say—and I heard of a few cases of her having said it—was that she was sure I would have painted her beautifully if she hadn't prevented me. She couldn't even tell the truth, which was that I certainly would have done so if Lady Beldonald hadn't; and she never could mention the subject at all before that personage. I can only describe the affair, naturally, from the outside, and heaven forbid indeed that I should try too closely to reconstruct the possible strange intercourse of these good friends at home.

My anecdote, however, would lose half such point as it may possess were I to omit all mention of the charming turn that her ladyship appeared gradually to have found herself able to give to her deportment. She had made it impossible I should myself bring up our old, our original question, but there was real distinction in her manner of now accepting certain other possibilities. Let me do her that justice; her effort at magnanimity must have been immense. There couldn't fail, of course, to be ways in which poor Mrs. Brash paid for it. How much she had to pay we were, in fact, soon enough to see; and it is my intimate conviction that, as a climax, her life at last was the price. But while she lived, at least—and it was with an intensity, for those wondrous weeks, of which she had never dreamed—Lady Beldonald herself faced the music. This is what I mean by the possibilities, by the sharp actualities indeed, that she accepted. She took our friend out, she showed her at home, never attempted to hide or to betray her, played her no trick whatever so long as the ordeal lasted. She drank deep, on *her* side too, of the cup—the cup that for her own lips could only be bitterness. There was, I think, scarce a special success of her companion's at which she was not personally present. Mrs. Munden's theory of the silence in which all this would be muffled for them was, none the less, and in abundance, confirmed by our observations. The whole thing was to be the death of one or the other of them, but they never spoke of it at tea. I remember even that Nina went so far as to say to me once, looking me full in the eyes, quite sublimely, "I've made out what you mean—she *is* a picture." The beauty of this, moreover, was that, as I am persuaded, she hadn't really made it out at all—the words were the mere hypocrisy of her reflective endeavour for virtue. She couldn't possibly have made it out; her friend was as much as ever "dreadfully plain" to her; she must have wondered to the last what on earth possessed us. Wouldn't it in fact have been, after all, just this failure of vision, this supreme stupidity in short, that kept the catastrophe so long at bay? There was a certain sense of greatness for her in seeing so many of us so absurdly mistaken; and I recall that on various occasions, and in particular when she uttered the words just quoted, this high serenity, as a sign of the relief of her soreness, if not of the effort of her conscience, did something quite visible to my eyes, and also quite unprecedented, for the beauty of her face. She got a real lift from it—such a momentary discernible sublimity that I recollect coming out on the spot with a queer, crude, amused "Do you know I believe I could paint you *now*?"

She was a fool not to have closed with me then and there; for what has happened since has altered everything—what was to happen a little later was so much more than I could swallow. This was the disappearance of the famous Holbein from one day to the other—producing a consternation among us all as great as if the Venus of Milo had suddenly vanished from the Louvre. "She has simply shipped her straight back"—the explanation was given in that form by Mrs. Munden, who added that any cord pulled tight enough would end at last by snapping. At the snap, in any case, we mightily jumped, for the masterpiece we had for three or four months been living with had made us feel its presence as a luminous lesson and a daily need. We recognised more than ever that it had been, for high finish, the gem of our collection—we found what a blank it left on the wall. Lady Beldonald might fill up the blank, but *we* couldn't. That she did soon fill it up—and, heaven help us, *how*?—was put before me after an interval of no great length, but during which I had not seen her. I dined on the Christmas of last year at Mrs. Munden's, and Nina, with a "scratch lot," as our hostess said, was there, and, the preliminary wait being longish, approached me very sweetly. "I'll come to you to-morrow if you like," she said; and the effect of it, after a first stare at her, was to make me look all round. I took in, in these two motions, two things; one of which was that, though now again so satisfied herself of her high state, she could give me nothing comparable to what I should have got had she taken me up at the moment of my meeting her on her distinguished concession; the other that she was "suited" afresh, and that Mrs. Brash's successor was fully installed. Mrs. Brash's successor was at the other side of the room, and I became conscious that Mrs. Munden was waiting to see my eyes seek her. I guessed the meaning of the wait; what *was* one, this time, to say? Oh, first and foremost, assuredly, that it was immensely droll, for this time, at least, there was no mistake. The lady I looked upon, and as to whom my friend, again quite at sea, appealed to me for a formula, was as little a Holbein, or a specimen of any other school, as she was, like Lady Beldonald herself, a Titian. The formula was easy to give, for the amusement was that her prettiness—yes, literally, prodigiously, her prettiness—was distinct. Lady Beldonald had been magnificent—had been almost intelligent. Miss What's-her-name continues pretty, continues even young, and doesn't matter a straw! She matters so ideally little that Lady Beldonald is practically safer, I judge, than she has ever been. There has not been a symptom of chatter about this person, and I believe her protectress is much surprised that we are not more struck.

It was, at any rate, strictly impossible to me to make an appointment for the day as to which I have just recorded Nina's proposal; and the turn of events since then has not quickened my eagerness. Mrs. Munden remained in correspondence with Mrs. Brash—to the extent, that is, of three letters, each of which she showed me. They so told, to our imagination, her terrible little story that we were quite prepared—or thought we were—for her going out like a snuffed candle. She resisted, on her return to her original conditions, less than a year; the taste of the tree, as I had called it, had been fatal to her; what she had contentedly enough lived without before for half a century she couldn't now live without for a day. I know nothing of her original conditions—some minor American city—save that for her to have gone back to them was clearly to have stepped out of her frame. We performed, Mrs. Munden and I, a small funeral service for her by talking it all over and making it all out. It wasn't—the minor American city—a market for Holbeins, and what had occurred was that the poor old picture, banished from its museum and refreshed by the rise of no new movement to hang it, was capable of the miracle of a silent revolution, of itself turning, in its dire dishonour, its face to the wall. So it stood, without the intervention of the ghost of a critic, till they happened to pull it round again and find it mere dead paint. Well, it had had, if that is anything, its season of fame, its name on a thousand tongues and printed in capitals in the catalogue. *We* had not been at fault. I haven't, all the same, the least note of her—not a scratch. And I did her so in intention! Mrs. Munden continues to remind me, however, that this is not the sort of rendering with which, on the other side, after all, Lady Beldonald proposes to content herself. She has come back to the question of her own portrait. Let me settle it then at last. Since she *will* have the real thing—well, hang it, she shall!

The Story in It

THE WEATHER had turned so much worse that the rest of the day was certainly lost. The wind had risen and the storm gathered force; they gave from time to time a thump at the firm windows and dashed even against those protected by the verandah their vicious splotches of rain. Beyond the lawn, beyond the cliff, the great wet brush of the sky dipped deep into the sea. But the lawn, already vivid with the touch of May, showed a violence of watered green; the budding shrubs and trees repeated the note as they tossed their thick masses, and the cold, troubled light, filling the pretty drawing-room, marked the spring afternoon as sufficiently young. The two ladies seated there in silence could pursue without difficulty—as well as, clearly, without interruption—their respective tasks; a confidence expressed, when the noise of the wind allowed it to be heard, by the sharp scratch of Mrs. Dyott's pen at the table where she was busy with letters.

Her visitor, settled on a small sofa that, with a palm-tree, a screen, a stool, a stand, a bowl of flowers and three photographs in silver frames, had been arranged near the light wood-fire as a choice "corner"—Maud Blessingbourne, her guest, turned audibly, though at intervals neither brief nor regular, the leaves of a book covered in lemon-coloured paper and not yet despoiled of a certain fresh crispness. This effect of the volume, for the eye, would have made it, as presumably the newest French novel—and evidently, from the attitude of the reader, "good"—consort happily with the special tone of the room, a consistent air of selection and suppression, one of the finer æsthetic evolutions. If Mrs. Dyott was fond of ancient French furniture, and distinctly difficult about it, her inmates could be fond—with whatever critical cocks of charming dark-braided heads over slender sloping shoulders—of modern French authors. Nothing had passed for half an hour—nothing, at least, to be exact, but that each of the companions occasionally and covertly intermitted her pursuit in such a manner as to ascertain the degree of absorption of the other without turning round.

What their silence was charged with, therefore, was not only a sense of the weather, but a sense, so to speak, of its own nature. Maud Blessingbourne, when she lowered her book into her lap, closed her eyes with a conscious patience that seemed to say she waited; but it was nevertheless she who at last made the movement representing a snap of their tension. She got up and stood by the fire, into which she looked a minute; then came round and approached the window as if to see what was really going on. At this Mrs. Dyott wrote with refreshed intensity. Her little pile of letters had grown, and if a look of determination was compatible with her fair and slightly faded beauty, the habit of attending to her business could always keep pace with any excursion of her thought. Yet she was the first who spoke.

"I trust your book has been interesting."

"Well enough; a little mild."

A louder throb of the tempest had blurred the sound of the words. "A little wild?"

"Dear, no—timid and tame; unless I've quite lost my sense."

"Perhaps you have," Mrs. Dyott placidly suggested—"reading so many."

Her companion made a motion of feigned despair. "Ah, you take away my courage for going to my room, as I was just meaning to, for another."

"Another French one?"

"I'm afraid."

"Do you carry them by the dozen——"

"Into innocent British homes?" Maud tried to remember. "I believe I brought three—seeing them in a shop window as I passed through town. It never rains but it pours! But I've already read two."

"And are they the only ones you do read?"

"French ones?" Maud considered. "Oh, no. D'Annunzio."

"And what's that?" Mrs. Dyott asked as she affixed a stamp.

"Oh, you dear thing!" Her friend was amused, yet almost showed pity. "I know you don't read," Maud went on; "but why should you? *You* live!"

"Yes—wretchedly enough," Mrs. Dyott returned, getting her letters together. She left her place, holding them as a neat, achieved handful, and came over to the fire, while Mrs. Blessingbourne turned once more to the window, where she was met by another flurry.

Maud spoke then as if moved only by the elements. "Do you expect him through all this?"

Mrs. Dyott just waited, and it had the effect, indescribably, of making everything that had gone before seem to have led up to the question. This effect was even deepened by the way she then said, "Whom do you mean?"

"Why, I thought you mentioned at luncheon that Colonel Voyt was to walk over. Surely he can't."

"Do you care very much?" Mrs. Dyott asked.

Her friend now hesitated. "It depends on what you call 'much.' If you mean should I like to see him—then certainly."

"Well, my dear, I think he understands you're here."

"So that as he evidently isn't coming," Maud laughed, "it's particularly flattering! Or rather," she added, giving up the prospect again, "it would be, I think, quite extraordinarily flattering if he did. Except that, of course," she subjoined, "he might come partly for you."

" 'Partly' is charming. Thank you for 'partly.' If you *are* going upstairs, will you kindly," Mrs. Dyott pursued, "put these into the box as you pass?"

The younger woman, taking the little pile of letters, considered them with envy. "Nine! You *are* good. You're always a living reproach!"

Mrs. Dyott gave a sigh. "I don't do it on purpose. The only thing, this afternoon," she went on, reverting to the other question, "would be their not having come down."

"And as to that you don't know."

"No—I don't know." But she caught even as she spoke a rat-tat-tat of the knocker, which struck her as a sign. "Ah, there!"

"Then I go." And Maud whisked out.

Mrs. Dyott, left alone, moved with an air of selection to the window, and it was as so stationed, gazing out at the wild weather, that the visitor, whose delay to appear spoke of the wiping of boots and the disposal of drenched mackintosh and cap, finally found her. He was tall, lean, fine, with little in him, on the whole, to confirm the titular in the "Colonel

Voyt" by which he was announced. But he had left the army, and his reputation for gallantry mainly depended now on his fighting Liberalism in the House of Commons. Even these facts, however, his aspect scantly matched; partly, no doubt, because he looked, as was usually said, un-English. His black hair, cropped close, was lightly powdered with silver, and his dense glossy beard, that of an emir or a caliph, and grown for civil reasons, repeated its handsome colour and its somewhat foreign effect. His nose had a strong and shapely arch, and the dark grey of his eyes was tinted with blue. It had been said of him—in relation to these signs— that he would have struck you as a Jew had he not, in spite of his nose, struck you so much as an Irishman. Neither responsibility could in fact have been fixed upon him, and just now, at all events, he was only a pleasant, weather-washed, wind-battered Briton, who brought in from a struggle with the elements that he appeared quite to have enjoyed a certain amount of unremoved mud and an unusual quantity of easy expression. It was exactly the silence ensuing on the retreat of the servant and the closed door that marked between him and his hostess the degree of this ease. They met, as it were, twice: the first time while the servant was there and the second as soon as he was not. The difference was great between the two encounters, though we must add in justice to the second that its marks were at first mainly negative. This communion consisted only in their having drawn each other for a minute as close as possible—as possible, that is, with no help but the full clasp of hands. Thus they were mutually held, and the closeness was at any rate such that, for a little, though it took account of dangers, it did without words. When words presently came the pair were talking by the fire, and she had rung for tea. He had by this time asked if the note he had despatched to her after breakfast had been safely delivered.

"Yes, before luncheon. But I'm always in a state when— except for some extraordinary reason—you send such things by hand. I knew, without it, that you had come. It never fails. I'm sure when you're there—I'm sure when you're not."

He wiped, before the glass, his wet moustache. "I see. But this morning I had an impulse."

"It was beautiful. But they make me as uneasy, sometimes, your impulses, as if they were calculations; make me wonder what you have in reserve."

"Because when small children are too awfully good they die? Well, I *am* a small child compared to you—but I'm not dead yet. I cling to life."

He had covered her with his smile, but she continued grave. "I'm not half so much afraid when you're nasty."

"Thank you! What then did you do," he asked, "with my note?"

"You deserve that I should have spread it out on my dressing-table—or left it, better still, in Maud Blessingbourne's room."

He wondered while he laughed. "Oh, but what does *she* deserve?"

It was her gravity that continued to answer. "Yes—it would probably kill her."

"She believes so in you?"

"She believes so in *you*. So don't be *too* nice to her."

He was still looking, in the chimney-glass, at the state of his beard—brushing from it, with his handkerchief, the traces of wind and wet. "If she also then prefers me when I'm nasty, it seems to me I ought to satisfy her. Shall I now, at any rate, see her?"

"She's so like a pea on a pan over the possibility of it that she's pulling herself together in her room."

"Oh then, we must try and keep her together. But why, graceful, tender, pretty too—quite, or almost—as she is, doesn't she remarry?"

Mrs. Dyott appeared—and as if the first time—to look for the reason. "Because she likes too many men."

It kept up his spirits. "And how many *may* a lady like——?"

"In order not to like any of them too much? Ah, that, you know, I never found out—and it's too late now. When," she presently pursued, "did you last see her?"

He really had to think. "Would it have been since last November or so?—somewhere or other where we spent three days."

"Oh, at Surredge? I know all about that. I thought you also met afterwards."

He had again to recall. "So we did! Wouldn't it have been somewhere at Christmas? But it wasn't by arrangement!" he laughed, giving with his forefinger a little pleasant nick to his hostess's chin. Then as if something in the way she received this attention put him back to his question of a moment before, "Have you kept my note?"

She held him with her pretty eyes. "Do you want it back?"

"Ah, don't speak as if I did take things——!"

She dropped her gaze to the fire. "No, you don't; not even the hard things a really generous nature often would." She quitted, however, as if to forget that, the chimney-place. "I put it *there*!"

"You've burnt it? Good!" It made him easier, but he noticed the next moment on a table the lemon-coloured volume left there by Mrs. Blessingbourne, and, taking it up for a look, immediately put it down. "You might, while you were about it, have burnt that too."

"You've read it?"

"Dear, yes. And you?"

"No," said Mrs. Dyott; "it wasn't for me Maud brought it."

It pulled her visitor up. "Mrs. Blessingbourne brought it?"

"For such a day as this." But she wondered. "How you look! Is it so awful?"

"Oh, like his others." Something had occurred to him; his thought was already far. "Does she know?"

"Know what?"

"Why, anything."

But the door opened too soon for Mrs. Dyott, who could only murmur quickly—

"Take care!"

<h2 style="text-align:center">II</h2>

It was in fact Mrs. Blessingbourne, who had under her arm the book she had gone up for—a pair of covers that this time showed a pretty, a candid blue. She was followed next minute by the servant, who brought in tea, the consumption of which, with the passage of greetings, inquiries and other light civilities between the two visitors, occupied a quarter of an hour. Mrs. Dyott meanwhile, as a contribution to so much amenity, mentioned to Maud that her fellow-guest wished to scold her for the books she read—a statement met by this friend with the remark that he must first be sure about them. But as soon as he had picked up the new volume he broke out into a frank "Dear, dear!"

"Have you read that too?" Mrs. Dyott inquired. "How much you'll have to talk over together! The other one," she explained to him, "Maud speaks of as terribly tame."

"Ah, I must have that out with her! You don't feel the extraordinary force of the fellow?" Voyt went on to Mrs. Blessingbourne.

And so, round the hearth, they talked—talked soon, while they warmed their toes, with zest enough to make it seem as happy a chance as any of the quieter opportunities their imprisonment might have involved. Mrs. Blessingbourne did feel, it then appeared, the force of the fellow, but she had her reserves and reactions, in which Voyt was much interested. Mrs. Dyott rather detached herself, mainly gazing, as she leaned back, at the fire; she intervened, however, enough to relieve Maud of the sense of being listened to. That sense, with Maud, was too apt to convey that one was listened to for a fool. "Yes, when I read a novel I mostly read a French one," she had said to Voyt in answer to a question about her usual practice; "for I seem with it to get hold more of the real thing—to get more life for my money. Only I'm not so infatuated with them but that sometimes for months and months on end I don't read any fiction at all."

The two books were now together beside them. "Then when you begin again you read a mass?"

"Dear, no. I only keep up with three or four authors."

He laughed at this over the cigarette he had been allowed to light. "I like your 'keeping up,' and keeping up in particular with 'authors.'"

"One must keep up with somebody," Mrs. Dyott threw off.

"I dare say I'm ridiculous," Mrs. Blessingbourne conceded without heeding it; "but that's the way we express ourselves in my part of the country."

"I only alluded," said Voyt, "to the tremendous conscience of your sex. It's more than mine can keep up with. You take everything too hard. But if you can't read the novel of British and American manufacture, heaven knows I'm at one with you. It seems really to show our sense of life as the sense of puppies and kittens."

"Well," Maud more patiently returned, "I'm told all sorts of people are now doing wonderful things; but somehow I remain outside."

"Ah, it's *they*, it's our poor twangers and twaddlers who remain outside. They pick up a living in the street. And who indeed would want them in?"

Mrs. Blessingbourne seemed unable to say, and yet at the same time to have her idea. The subject, in truth, she evidently found, was not so easy to handle. "People lend me things, and I try; but at the end of fifty pages——"

"There you are! Yes—heaven help us!"

"But what I mean," she went on, "isn't that I don't get wofully weary of the eternal French thing. What's *their* sense of life?"

"Ah, *voilà*!" Mrs. Dyott softly sounded.

"Oh, but it *is* one; you can make it out," Voyt promptly declared. "They do what they feel, and they feel more things than we. They strike so many more notes, and with so different a hand. When it comes to any account of a relation, say, between a man and a woman—I mean an intimate or a curious or a suggestive one—where are we compared to them? They don't exhaust the subject, no doubt," he admitted; "but we don't touch it, don't even skim it. It's as if we denied its existence, its possibility. You'll doubtless tell me, however," he went on, "that as all such relations *are* for us, at the most, much simpler, we can only have all round less to say about them."

She met this imputation with the quickest amusement. "I beg your pardon. I don't think I shall tell you anything of the sort. I don't know that I even agree with your premise."

"About such relations?" He looked agreeably surprised. "You think we make them larger?—or subtler?"

Mrs. Blessingbourne leaned back, not looking, like Mrs. Dyott, at the fire, but at the ceiling. "I don't know what I think."

"It's not that she doesn't know," Mrs. Dyott remarked. "It's only that she doesn't say."

But Voyt had this time no eye for their hostess. For a moment he watched Maud. "It sticks out of you, you know, that you've yourself written something. Haven't you—and published? I've a notion I could read *you*."

"When I do publish," she said without moving, "you'll be the last one I shall tell. I *have*," she went on, "a lovely subject, but it would take an amount of treatment——!"

"Tell us then at least what it is."

At this she again met his eyes. "Oh, to tell it would be to express it, and that's just what I can't do. What I meant to say just now," she added, "was that the French, to my sense, give us only again and again, for ever and ever, the same couple. There they are once more, as one has had them to satiety, in that yellow thing, and there I shall certainly again find them in the blue."

"Then why do you keep reading about them?" Mrs. Dyott demanded.

Maud hesitated. "I don't!" she sighed. "At all events, I sha'n't any more. I give it up."

"You've been looking for something, I judge," said Colonel Voyt, "that you're not likely to find. It doesn't exist."

"What is it?" Mrs. Dyott inquired.

"I never look," Maud remarked, "for anything but an interest."

"Naturally. But your interest," Voyt replied, "is in something different from life."

"Ah, not a bit! I *love* life—in art, though I hate it anywhere else. It's the poverty of the life those people show, and the awful bounders, of both sexes, that they represent."

"Oh, now we have you!" her interlocutor laughed. "To me, when all's said and done, they seem to be—as near as art can come—in the truth of the truth. It can only take what life gives it, though it certainly may be a pity that that isn't better. Your complaint of their monotony is a complaint of their conditions. When you say we get always the same couple what do you mean but that we get always the same passion? Of course we do!" Voyt declared. "If what you're looking for is another, that's what you won't anywhere find."

Maud for a while said nothing, and Mrs. Dyott seemed

to wait. "Well, I suppose I'm looking, more than anything else, for a decent woman."

"Oh then, you mustn't look for her in pictures of passion. That's not her element nor her whereabouts."

Mrs. Blessingbourne weighed the objection. "Doesn't it depend on what you mean by passion?"

"I think one can mean only one thing: the enemy to be-haviour."

"Oh, I can imagine passions that are, on the contrary, friends to it."

Her interlocutor thought. "Doesn't it depend perhaps on what you mean by behaviour?"

"Dear, no. Behaviour is just behaviour—the most definite thing in the world."

"Then what do you mean by the 'interest' you just now spoke of? The picture of that definite thing?"

"Yes—call it that. Women aren't *always* vicious, even when they're——"

"When they're what?" Voyt asked.

"When they're unhappy. They can be unhappy and good."

"That one doesn't for a moment deny. But can they be 'good' and interesting?"

"That must be Maud's subject!" Mrs. Dyott explained. "To show a woman who *is*. I'm afraid, my dear," she continued, "you could only show yourself."

"You'd show then the most beautiful specimen conceiv-able"—and Voyt addressed himself to Maud. "But doesn't it prove that life is, against your contention, more interesting than art? Life you embellish and elevate; but art would find itself able to do nothing with you, and, on such impossible terms, would ruin you."

The colour in her faint consciousness gave beauty to her stare. " 'Ruin' me?"

"He means," Mrs. Dyott again indicated, "that you would ruin 'art.' "

"Without, on the other hand"—Voyt seemed to assent—"its giving at all a coherent impression of you."

"She wants her romance cheap!" said Mrs. Dyott.

"Oh, no—I should be willing to pay for it. I don't see

why the romance—since you give it that name—should be all, as the French inveterately make it, for the women who are bad."

"Oh, they pay for it!" said Mrs. Dyott.

"*Do* they?"

"So, at least"—Mrs. Dyott a little corrected herself—"one has gathered (for I don't read your books, you know!) that they're usually shown as doing."

Maud wondered, but looking at Voyt, "They're shown often, no doubt, as paying for their badness. But are they shown as paying for their romance?"

"My dear lady," said Voyt, "their romance *is* their badness. There isn't any other. It's a hard law, if you will, and a strange, but goodness has to go without that luxury. Isn't to *be* good just exactly, all round, to go without?" He put it before her kindly and clearly—regretfully too, as if he were sorry the truth should be so sad. He and she, his pleasant eyes seemed to say, would, had they had the making of it, have made it better. "One has heard it before—at least *I* have; one has heard your question put. But always, when put to a mind not merely muddled, for an inevitable answer. 'Why don't you, *cher monsieur*, give us the drama of virtue?' 'Because, *chère madame*, the high privilege of virtue is precisely to avoid drama.' The adventures of the honest lady? The honest lady hasn't—can't possibly have adventures."

Mrs. Blessingbourne only met his eyes at first, smiling with a certain intensity. "Doesn't it depend a little on what you call adventures?"

"My poor Maud," said Mrs. Dyott, as if in compassion for sophistry so simple, "adventures are just adventures. That's all you can make of them!"

But her friend went on, for their companion, as if without hearing. "Doesn't it depend a good deal on what you call drama?" Maud spoke as one who had already thought it out. "Doesn't it depend on what you call romance?"

Her listener gave these arguments his very best attention. "Of course you may call things anything you like—speak of them as one thing and mean quite another. But why should it depend on anything? Behind these words we use—the adventure, the novel, the drama, the romance, the situation, in short, as we most comprehensively say—behind them all stands the same sharp fact that they all, in their different ways, represent."

"Precisely!" Mrs. Dyott was full of approval.

Maud, however, was full of vagueness. "What great fact?"

"The fact of a relation. The adventure's a relation; the relation's an adventure. The romance, the novel, the drama are the picture of one. The subject the novelist treats is the rise, the formation, the development, the climax, and for the most part the decline, of one. And what is the honest lady doing on that side of the town?"

Mrs. Dyott was more pointed. "She doesn't so much as *form* a relation."

But Maud bore up. "Doesn't it depend, again, on what you call a relation?"

"Oh," said Mrs. Dyott, "if a gentleman picks up her pocket-handkerchief——"

"Ah, even that's one," their friend laughed, "if she has thrown it to him. We can only deal with one that *is* one."

"Surely," Maud replied. "But if it's an innocent one——?"

"Doesn't it depend a good deal," Mrs. Dyott asked, "on what you call innocent?"

"You mean that the adventures of innocence have so often been the material of fiction? Yes," Voyt replied; "that's exactly what the bored reader complains of. He has asked for bread and been given a stone. What is it but, with absolute directness, a question of interest, or, as people say, of the story? What's a situation undeveloped but a subject lost? If a relation stops, where's the story? If it doesn't stop, where's the innocence? It seems to me you must choose. It would be very pretty if it were otherwise, but that's how we flounder. Art is our flounderings shown."

Mrs. Blessingbourne—and with an air of deference scarce supported perhaps by its sketchiness—kept her deep eyes on this definition. "But sometimes we flounder out."

It immediately touched in Colonel Voyt the spring of a genial derision. "That's just where I expected *you* would! One always sees it come."

"He has, you notice," Mrs. Dyott parenthesised to Maud,

"seen it come so often; and he has always waited for it and met it."

"Met it, dear lady, simply enough! It's the old story, Mrs. Blessingbourne. The relation is innocent that the heroine gets out of. The book is innocent that's the story of her getting out. But what the devil—in the name of innocence—was she doing *in*?"

Mrs. Dyott promptly echoed the question. "You have to be in, you know, to *get* out. So there you are already with your relation. It's the end of your goodness."

"And the beginning," said Voyt, "of your play!"

"Aren't they all, for that matter, even the worst," Mrs. Dyott pursued, "supposed *some* time or other to get out? But if, meanwhile, they've been in, however briefly, long enough to adorn a tale——"

"They've been in long enough to point a moral. That is to point ours!" With which, and as if a sudden flush of warmer light had moved him, Colonel Voyt got up. The veil of the storm had parted over a great red sunset.

Mrs. Dyott also was on her feet, and they stood before his charming antagonist, who, with eyes lowered and a somewhat fixed smile, had not moved. "We've spoiled her subject!" the elder lady sighed.

"Well," said Voyt, "it's better to spoil an artist's subject than to spoil his reputation. I mean," he explained to Maud with his indulgent manner, "his appearance of knowing what he has got hold of, for that, in the last resort, is his happiness."

She slowly rose at this, facing him with an aspect as handsomely mild as his own. "You can't spoil my happiness."

He held her hand an instant as he took leave. "I wish I could add to it!"

III

When he had quitted them and Mrs. Dyott had candidly asked if her friend had found him rude or crude, Maud replied—though not immediately—that she had feared showing only too much that she found him charming. But if Mrs. Dyott took this, it was to weigh the sense. "How could you show it too much?"

"Because I always feel that that's my only way of showing anything. It's absurd, if you like," Mrs. Blessingbourne pursued, "but I never know, in such intense discussions, what strange impression I may give."

Her companion looked amused. "Was it intense?"

"*I* was," Maud frankly confessed.

"Then it's a pity you were so wrong. Colonel Voyt, you know, is right." Mrs. Blessingbourne at this gave one of the slow, soft, silent headshakes to which she often resorted and which, mostly accompanied by the light of cheer, had somehow, in spite of the small obstinacy that smiled in them, a special grace. With this grace, for a moment, her friend, looking her up and down, appeared impressed, yet not too much so to take, the next minute, a decision. "Oh, my dear, I'm sorry to differ from anyone so lovely—for you're awfully beautiful to-night, and your frock's the very nicest I've ever seen you wear. But he's as right as he can be."

Maud repeated her motion. "Not so right, at all events, as he thinks he is. Or perhaps I can say," she went on, after an instant, "that I'm not so wrong. I do know a little what I'm talking about."

Mrs. Dyott continued to study her. "You *are* vexed. You naturally don't like it—such destruction."

"Destruction?"

"Of your illusion."

"I *have* no illusion. If I had, moreover, it wouldn't be destroyed. I have, on the whole, I think, my little decency."

Mrs. Dyott stared. "Let us grant it for argument. What, then?"

"Well, I've also my little drama."

"An attachment?"

"An attachment."

"That you shouldn't have?"

"That I shouldn't have."

"A passion?"

"A passion."

"Shared?"

"Ah, thank goodness, no!"

Mrs. Dyott continued to gaze. "The object's unaware——?"

"Utterly."

Mrs. Dyott turned it over. "Are you sure?"

"Sure."

"That's what you call your decency? But isn't it," Mrs. Dyott asked, "rather *his*?"

"Dear, no. It's only his good fortune."

Mrs. Dyott laughed. "But yours, darling—your good fortune: where does *that* come in?"

"Why, in my sense of the romance of it."

"The romance of what? Of his not knowing?"

"Of my not wanting him to. If I did"—Maud had touchingly worked it out—"where would be my honesty?"

The inquiry, for an instant, held her friend; yet only, it seemed, for a stupefaction that was almost amusement. "Can you want or not want as you like? Where in the world, if you don't want, is your romance?"

Mrs. Blessingbourne still wore her smile, and she now, with a light gesture that matched it, just touched the region of her heart. "There!"

Her companion admiringly marvelled. "A lovely place for it, no doubt!—but not quite a place, that I can see, to make the sentiment a relation."

"Why not? What more is required for a relation for *me*?"

"Oh, all sorts of things, I should say! And many more, added to those, to make it one for the person you mention."

"Ah, that I don't pretend it either should be or *can* be. I only speak for myself."

It was said in a manner that made Mrs. Dyott, with a visible mixture of impressions, suddenly turn away. She indulged in a vague movement or two, as if to look for something; then again found herself near her friend, on whom with the same abruptness, in fact with a strange sharpness, she conferred a kiss that might have represented either her tribute to exalted consistency or her idea of a graceful close of the discussion. "You deserve that one should speak *for* you!"

Her companion looked cheerful and secure. "How *can* you, without knowing——?"

"Oh, by guessing! It's not——?"

But that was as far as Mrs. Dyott could get. "It's not," said Maud, "anyone you've ever seen."

"Ah then, I give you up!"

And Mrs. Dyott conformed, for the rest of Maud's stay, to the spirit of this speech. It was made on a Saturday night, and Mrs. Blessingbourne remained till the Wednesday following, an interval during which, as the return of fine weather was confirmed by the Sunday, the two ladies found a wider range of action. There were drives to be taken, calls made, objects of interest seen, at a distance; with the effect of much easy talk and still more easy silence. There had been a question of Colonel Voyt's probable return on the Sunday, but the whole time passed without a sign from him, and it was merely mentioned by Mrs. Dyott, in explanation, that he must have been suddenly called, as he was so liable to be, to town. That this in fact was what had happened he made clear to her on Thursday afternoon, when, walking over again late, he found her alone. The consequence of his Sunday letters had been his taking, that day, the 4.15. Mrs. Voyt had gone back on Thursday, and he now, to settle on the spot the question of a piece of work begun at his place, had rushed down for a few hours in anticipation of the usual collective move for the week's end. He was to go up again by the late train, and had to count a little—a fact accepted by his hostess with the hard pliancy of practice—his present happy moments. Too few as these were, however, he found time to make of her an inquiry or two not directly bearing on their situation. The first was a recall of the question for which Mrs. Blessingbourne's entrance on the previous Saturday had arrested her answer. Did that lady know of anything between them?

"No. I'm sure. There's one thing she does know," Mrs. Dyott went on; "but it's quite different and not so very wonderful."

"What, then, is it?"

"Well, that she's herself in love."

Voyt showed his interest. "You mean she told you?"

"I got it out of her."

He showed his amusement. "Poor thing! And with whom?"

"With you."

His surprise, if the distinction might be made, was less than his wonder. "You got that out of her too?"

"No—it remains in. Which is much the best way for it. For you to know it would be to end it."

He looked rather cheerfully at sea. "Is that then why you tell me?"

"I mean for her to know you know it. Therefore it's in your interest not to let her."

"I see," Voyt after a moment returned. "Your real calculation is that my interest will be sacrificed to my vanity—so that, if your other idea is just, the flame will in fact, and thanks to her morbid conscience, expire by her taking fright at seeing me so pleased. But I promise you," he declared, "that she sha'n't see it. So there you are!" She kept her eyes on him and had evidently to admit, after a little, that there she was. Distinct as he had made the case, however, he was not yet quite satisfied. "Why are you so sure that I'm the man?"

"From the way she denies you."

"You put it to her?"

"Straight. If you hadn't been she would, of course, have confessed to you—to keep me in the dark about the real one."

Poor Voyt laughed out again. "Oh, you dear souls!"

"Besides," his companion pursued, "I was not in want of that evidence."

"Then what other had you?"

"Her state before you came—which was what made me ask you how much you had seen her. And her state after it," Mrs. Dyott added. "And her state," she wound up, "while you were here."

"But her state while I was here was charming."

"Charming. That's just what I say."

She said it in a tone that placed the matter in its right light—a light in which they appeared kindly, quite tenderly, to watch Maud wander away into space with her lovely head bent under a theory rather too big for it. Voyt's last word, however, was that there was just enough in it—in the theory—for them to allow that she had not shown herself, on the occasion of their talk, wholly bereft of sense. Her consciousness, if they let it alone—as they of course after this mercifully must—*was*, in the last analysis, a kind of shy romance. Not a romance like their own, a thing to make the fortune of any author up to the mark—one who should have the invention or who *could* have the courage; but a small, scared, starved, subjective satisfaction that would do her no harm and nobody else any good. Who but a duffer—he stuck to his contention—would see the shadow of a "story" in it?

Flickerbridge

F RANK GRANGER had arrived from Paris to paint a portrait—an order given him, as a young compatriot with a
future, whose early work would some day have a price, by a
lady from New York, a friend of his own people and also, as
it happened, of Addie's, the young woman to whom it was
publicly both affirmed and denied that he was engaged. Other
young women in Paris—fellow-members there of the little
tight transpontine world of art-study—professed to know that
the pair had been "several times" over so closely contracted.
This, however, was their own affair; the last phase of the relation, the last time of the times, had passed into vagueness;
there was perhaps even an impression that if they were inscrutable to their friends they were not wholly crystalline to each
other and themselves. What had occurred for Granger, at all
events, in connection with the portrait was that Mrs. Bracken,
his intending model, whose return to America was at hand,
had suddenly been called to London by her husband, occupied there with pressing business, but had yet desired that her
displacement should not interrupt her sittings. The young
man, at her request, had followed her to England and profited
by all she could give him, making shift with a small studio
lent him by a London painter whom he had known and liked,
a few years before, in the French *atelier* that then cradled, and
that continued to cradle, so many of their kind.

The British capital was a strange, grey world to him, where
people walked, in more ways than one, by a dim light; but he
was happily of such a turn that the impression, just as it came,
could nowhere ever fail him, and even the worst of these
things was almost as much an occupation—putting it only at
that—as the best. Mrs. Bracken, moreover, passed him on,
and while the darkness ebbed a little in the April days he found
himself consolingly committed to a couple of fresh subjects.
This cut him out work for more than another month, but
meanwhile, as he said, he saw a lot—a lot that, with frequency
and with much expression, he wrote about to Addie. She also
wrote to her absent friend, but in briefer snatches, a meagre-

ness to her reasons for which he had long since assented. She
had other play for her pen, as well as, fortunately, other remuneration; a regular correspondence for a "prominent Boston paper," fitful connections with public sheets perhaps also,
in cases, fitful, and a mind, above all, engrossed at times, to
the exclusion of everything else, with the study of the short
story. This last was what she had mainly come out to go into,
two or three years after he had found himself engulfed in the
mystery of Carolus. She was indeed, on her own deep sea,
more engulfed than he had ever been, and he had grown to
accept the sense that, for progress too, she sailed under more
canvas. It had not been particularly present to him till now
that he had in the least got on, but the way in which Addie
had—and evidently, still more, would—was the theme, as it
were, of every tongue. She had thirty short stories out and
nine descriptive articles. His three or four portraits of fat
American ladies—they were all fat, all ladies and all American—were a poor show compared with these triumphs; especially as Addie had begun to throw out that it was about time
they should go home. It kept perpetually coming up in Paris,
in the transpontine world, that, as the phrase was, America
had grown more interesting since they left. Addie was attentive to the rumour, and, as full of conscience as she was of
taste, of patriotism as of curiosity, had often put it to him
frankly, with what he, who was of New York, recognised as her
New England emphasis: "I'm not sure, you know, that we do
real justice to our country." Granger felt he would do it on
the day—if the day ever came—he should irrevocably marry
her. No other country could possibly have produced her.

II

But meanwhile it befell, in London, that he was stricken with
influenza and with subsequent sorrow. The attack was short
but sharp—had it lasted Addie would certainly have come to
his aid; most of a blight, really, in its secondary stage. The
good ladies his sitters—the ladies with the frizzled hair, with
the diamond earrings, with the chins tending to the massive—
left for him, at the door of his lodgings, flowers, soup and
love, so that with their assistance he pulled through; but his

convalescence was slow and his weakness out of proportion to the muffled shock. He came out, but he went about lame; it tired him to paint—he felt as if he had been ill for a month. He strolled in Kensington Gardens when he should have been at work; he sat long on penny chairs and helplessly mused and mooned. Addie desired him to return to Paris, but there were chances under his hand that he felt he had just wit enough left not to relinquish. He would have gone for a week to the sea—he would have gone to Brighton; but Mrs. Bracken had to be finished—Mrs. Bracken was so soon to sail. He just managed to finish her in time—the day before the date fixed for his breaking ground on a greater business still, the circumvallation of Mrs. Dunn. Mrs. Dunn duly waited on him, and he sat down before her, feeling, however, ere he rose, that he must take a long breath before the attack. While asking himself that night, therefore, where he should best replenish his lungs, he received from Addie, who had had from Mrs. Bracken a poor report of him, a communication which, besides being of sudden and startling interest, applied directly to his case.

His friend wrote to him under the lively emotion of having from one day to another become aware of a new relative, an ancient cousin, a sequestered gentlewoman, the sole survival of "the English branch of the family," still resident, at Flickerbridge, in the "old family home," and with whom, that he might immediately betake himself to so auspicious a quarter for change of air, she had already done what was proper to place him, as she said, in touch. What came of it all, to be brief, was that Granger found himself so placed almost as he read: he was in touch with Miss Wenham of Flickerbridge, to the extent of being in correspondence with her, before twenty-four hours had sped. And on the second day he was in the train, settled for a five-hours' run to the door of this amiable woman, who had so abruptly and kindly taken him on trust and of whom but yesterday he had never so much as heard. This was an oddity—the whole incident was—of which, in the corner of his compartment, as he proceeded, he had time to take the size. But the surprise, the incongruity, as he felt, could but deepen as he went. It was a sufficiently queer note, in the light, or the absence of it, of his late experience, that so complex a product as Addie should have *any* simple insular tie; but it was a queerer note still that she should have had one so long only to remain unprofitably unconscious of it. Not to have done something with it, used it, worked it, talked about it at least, and perhaps even written—these things, at the rate she moved, represented a loss of opportunity under which, as he saw her, she was peculiarly formed to wince. She was at any rate, it was clear, doing something with it now; using it, working it, certainly, already talking—and, yes, quite possibly writing—about it. She was, in short, smartly making up what she had missed, and he could take such comfort from his own action as he had been helped to by the rest of the facts, succinctly reported from Paris on the very morning of his start.

It was the singular story of a sharp split—in a good English house—that dated now from years back. A worthy Briton, of the best middling stock, had, early in the forties, as a very young man, in Dresden, whither he had been despatched to qualify in German for a stool in an uncle's counting-house, met, admired, wooed and won an American girl, of due attractions, domiciled at that period with her parents and a sister, who was also attractive, in the Saxon capital. He had married her, taken her to England, and there, after some years of harmony and happiness, lost her. The sister in question had, after her death, come to him, and to his young child, on a visit, the effect of which, between the pair, eventually defined itself as a sentiment that was not to be resisted. The bereaved husband, yielding to a new attachment and a new response, and finding a new union thus prescribed, had yet been forced to reckon with the unaccommodating law of the land. Encompassed with frowns in his own country, however, marriages of this particular type were wreathed in smiles in his sister's-in-law, so that his remedy was not forbidden. Choosing between two allegiances he had let the one go that seemed the least close, and had, in brief, transplanted his possibilities to an easier air. The knot was tied for the couple in New York, where, to protect the legitimacy of such other children as might come to them, they settled and prospered. Children came, and one of the daughters, growing up and marrying in her turn, was, if Frank rightly followed, the mother of his own

Addie, who had been deprived of the knowledge of her indeed, in childhood, by death, and been brought up, though without undue tension, by a stepmother—a character thus, in the connection, repeated.

The breach produced in England by the invidious action, as it was there held, of the girl's grandfather, had not failed to widen—all the more that nothing had been done on the American side to close it. Frigidity had settled, and hostility had only been arrested by indifference. Darkness, therefore, had fortunately supervened, and a cousinship completely divided. On either side of the impassable gulf, of the impenetrable curtain, each branch had put forth its leaves—a foliage wanting, in the American quarter, it was distinct enough to Granger, in no sign or symptom of climate and environment. The graft in New York had taken, and Addie was a vivid, an unmistakeable flower. At Flickerbridge, or wherever, on the other hand, strange to say, the parent stem had had a fortune comparatively meagre. Fortune, it was true, in the vulgarest sense, had attended neither party. Addie's immediate belongings were as poor as they were numerous, and he gathered that Miss Wenham's pretensions to wealth were not so marked as to expose the claim of kinship to the imputation of motive. To this lady's single identity, at all events, the original stock had dwindled, and our young man was properly warned that he would find her shy and solitary. What was singular was that, in these conditions, she should desire, she should endure, to receive him. But that was all another story, lucid enough when mastered. He kept Addie's letters, exceptionally copious, in his lap; he conned them at intervals; he held the threads.

He looked out between whiles at the pleasant English land, an April *aquarelle* washed in with wondrous breadth. He knew the French thing, he knew the American, but he had known nothing of this. He saw it already as the remarkable Miss Wenham's setting. The doctor's daughter at Flickerbridge, with nippers on her nose, a palette on her thumb and innocence in her heart, had been the miraculous link. She had become aware, even there, in our world of wonders, that the current fashion for young women so equipped was to enter the Parisian lists. Addie had accordingly chanced upon her, on the slopes of Montparnasse, as one of the English girls in one of the thorough-going sets. They had met in some easy collocation and had fallen upon common ground; after which the young woman, restored to Flickerbridge for an interlude and retailing there her adventures and impressions, had mentioned to Miss Wenham, who had known and protected her from babyhood, that that lady's own name of Adelaide was, as well as the surname conjoined with it, borne, to her knowledge, in Paris, by an extraordinary American specimen. She had then recrossed the Channel with a wonderful message, a courteous challenge, to her friend's duplicate, who had in turn granted through her every satisfaction. The duplicate had, in other words, bravely let Miss Wenham know exactly who she was. Miss Wenham, in whose personal tradition the flame of resentment appeared to have been reduced by time to the palest ashes—for whom, indeed, the story of the great schism was now but a legend only needing a little less dimness to make it romantic—Miss Wenham had promptly responded by a letter fragrant with the hope that old threads might be taken up. It was a relationship that they must puzzle out together, and she had earnestly sounded the other party to it on the subject of a possible visit. Addie had met her with a definite promise; she would come soon, she would come when free, she would come in July; but meanwhile she sent her deputy. Frank asked himself by what name she had described, by what character introduced him to Flickerbridge. He felt mainly, on the whole, as if he were going there to find out if he were engaged to her. He was at sea, really, now, as to which of the various views Addie herself took of it. To Miss Wenham she must definitely have taken one, and perhaps Miss Wenham would reveal it. This expectation was really his excuse for a possible indiscretion.

III

He was indeed to learn on arrival to what he had been committed; but that was for a while so much a part of his first general impression that the fact took time to detach itself, the first general impression demanding verily all his faculties of response. He almost felt, for a day or two, the victim of a practical joke, a gross abuse of confidence. He had presented himself with the moderate amount of flutter involved in a sense of due preparation; but he had then found that, however primed with prefaces and prompted with hints, he had not been prepared at all. How *could* he be, he asked himself, for anything so foreign to his experience, so alien to his proper world, so little to be preconceived in the sharp north light of the newest impressionism, and yet so recognised, after all, really, in the event, so noted and tasted and assimilated? It was a case he would scarce have known how to describe—could doubtless have described best with a full, clean brush, supplemented by a play of gesture; for it was always his habit to see an occasion, of whatever kind, primarily as a picture, so that he might get it, as he was wont to say, so that he might keep it, well together. He had been treated of a sudden, in this adventure, to one of the sweetest, fairest, coolest impressions of his life—one, moreover, visibly, from the start, complete and homogeneous. Oh, it was *there*, if that was all one wanted of a thing! It was so "there" that, as had befallen him in Italy, in Spain, confronted at last, in dusky side-chapel or rich museum, with great things dreamed of or with greater ones unexpectedly presented, he had held his breath for fear of breaking the spell; had almost, from the quick impulse to re-spect, to prolong, lowered his voice and moved on tiptoe. Supreme beauty suddenly revealed is apt to strike us as a pos-sible illusion, playing with our desire—instant freedom with it to strike us as a possible rashness.

This fortunately, however—and the more so as his freedom for the time quite left him—didn't prevent his hostess, the evening of his advent and while the vision was new, from be-ing exactly as queer and rare and *impayable*, as improbable, as impossible, as delightful at dinner at eight (she appeared to keep these immense hours) as she had overwhelmingly been at tea at five. She was in the most natural way in the world one of the oddest apparitions, but that the particular means to such an end *could* be natural was an inference difficult to make. He failed in fact to make it for a couple of days; but then—though then only—he made it with confidence. By this time indeed he was sure of everything, including, luckily, him-self. If we compare his impression, with slight extravagance, to some of the greatest he had ever received, this is simply because the image before him was so rounded and stamped. It expressed with pure perfection, it exhausted its character. It was so absolutely and so unconsciously what it was. He had been floated by the strangest of chances out of the rushing stream into a clear, still backwater—a deep and quiet pool in which objects were sharply mirrored. He had hitherto in life known nothing that was old except a few statues and pictures; but here everything was old, was immemorial, and nothing so much so as the very freshness itself. Vaguely to have supposed there were such nooks in the world had done little enough, he now saw, to temper the glare of their opposites. It was the fine touches that counted, and these had to be seen to be believed.

Miss Wenham, fifty-five years of age, and unappeasably timid, unaccountably strange, had, on her reduced scale, an almost Gothic grotesqueness; but the final effect of one's sense of it was an amenity that accompanied one's steps like wafted gratitude. More flurried, more spasmodic, more apologetic, more completely at a loss at one moment and more precipitately abounding at another, he had never before in all his days seen any maiden lady; yet for no maiden lady he had ever seen had he so promptly conceived a private enthusiasm. Her eyes protruded, her chin receded and her nose carried on in conversation a queer little independent motion. She wore on the top of her head an upright circular cap that made her resemble a caryatid disburdened, and on other parts of her person strange combinations of colours, stuffs, shapes, of metal, mineral and plant. The tones of her voice rose and fell, her facial convulsions, whether tending—one could scarce make out—to expression or *re*pression, succeeded each other by a law of their own; she was embarrassed at nothing and at everything, frightened at everything and at nothing, and she approached objects, subjects, the simplest questions and answers and the whole material of intercourse, either with the indirectness of terror or with the violence of despair. These things, none the less, her refinements of oddity and intensities of custom, her suggestion at once of conventions and simplicities, of ease and of agony, her roundabout, retarded suggestions and perceptions, still permitted her to strike her guest as irresistibly charming. He didn't know what to call it; she

was a fruit of time. She had a queer distinction. She had been
expensively produced, and there would be a good deal more
of her to come.

The result of the whole quality of her welcome, at any rate,
was that the first evening, in his room, before going to bed,
he relieved his mind in a letter to Addie, which, if space allowed us to embody it in our text, would usefully perform
the office of a "plate." It would enable us to present ourselves
as profusely illustrated. But the process of reproduction, as we
say, costs. He wished his friend to know how grandly their
affair turned out. She had put him in the way of something
absolutely special—an old house untouched, untouchable, indescribable, an old corner such as one didn't believe existed,
and the holy calm of which made the chatter of studios, the
smell of paint, the slang of critics, the whole sense and sound
of Paris, come back as so many signs of a huge monkey-cage.
He moved about, restless, while he wrote; he lighted cigarettes and, nervous and suddenly scrupulous, put them out
again; the night was mild and one of the windows of his large
high room, which stood over the garden, was up. He lost
himself in the things about him, in the type of the room, the
last century with not a chair moved, not a point stretched.
He hung over the objects and ornaments, blissfully few and
adorably good, perfect pieces all, and never one, for a change,
French. The scene was as rare as some fine old print with the
best bits down in the corners. Old books and old pictures,
allusions remembered and aspects conjectured, reappeared to
him; he knew now what anxious islanders had been trying for
in their backward hunt for the homely. But the homely at
Flickerbridge was all style, even as style at the same time was
mere honesty. The larger, the smaller past—he scarce knew
which to call it—was at all events so hushed to sleep round
him as he wrote that he had almost a bad conscience about
having come. How one might love it, but how one might
spoil it! To look at it too hard was positively to make it conscious and to make it conscious was positively to wake it up.
Its only safety, of a truth, was to be left still to sleep—to sleep
in its large, fair chambers, and under its high, clean canopies.

He added thus restlessly a line to his letter, maundered
round the room again, noted and fingered something else,

and then, dropping on the old flowered sofa, sustained by the tight cubes of its cushions, yielded afresh to the cigarette, hesitated, stared, wrote a few words more. He wanted Addie to know, that was what he most felt, unless he perhaps felt more how much she herself would want to. Yes, what he supremely saw was all that Addie would make of it. Up to his neck in it there he fairly turned cold at the sense of suppressed opportunity, of the outrage of privation, that his correspondent would retrospectively and, as he even divined with a vague shudder, almost vindictively nurse. Well, what had happened was that the acquaintance had been kept for her, like a packet enveloped and sealed for delivery, till her attention was free. He saw her there, heard her and felt her—felt how she would feel and how she would, as she usually said, "rave." Some of her young compatriots called it "yell," and in the reference itself, alas! illustrated their meaning. She would understand the place, at any rate, down to the ground; there wasn't the slightest doubt of that. Her sense of it would be exactly like his own, and he could see, in anticipation, just the terms of recognition and rapture in which she would abound. He knew just what she would call quaint, just what she would call bland, just what she would call weird, just what she would call wild. She would take it all in with an intelligence much more fitted than his own, in fact, to deal with what he supposed he must regard as its literary relations. She would have read the obsolete, long-winded memoirs and novels that both the figures and the setting ought clearly to remind one of; she would know about the past generations—the lumbering county magnates and their turbaned wives and round-eyed daughters, who, in other days, had treated the ruddy, sturdy, tradeless town, the solid square houses and wide, walled gardens, the streets to-day all grass and gossip, as the scene of a local "season." She would have warrant for the assemblies, dinners, deep potations; for the smoked sconces in the dusky parlours; for the long, muddy century of family coaches, "holsters," highwaymen. She would put a finger, in short, just as he had done, on the vital spot—the rich humility of the whole thing, the fact that neither Flickerbridge in general nor Miss Wenham in particular, nor anything nor anyone concerned, had a suspicion of their character and their merit. Addie and he would have to come to let in light.

He let it in then, little by little, before going to bed, through the eight or ten pages he addressed to her; assured her that it was the happiest case in the world, a little picture—yet full of "style" too—absolutely composed and transmitted, with tradition, and tradition only, in every stroke, tradition still noiselessly breathing and visibly flushing, marking strange hours in the tall mahogany clocks that were never wound up and that yet audibly ticked on. All the elements, he was sure he should see, would hang together with a charm, presenting his hostess—a strange iridescent fish for the glazed exposure of an aquarium—as floating in her native medium. He left his letter open on the table, but, looking it over next morning, felt of a sudden indisposed to send it. He would keep it to add more, for there would be more to know; yet when three days had elapsed he had still not sent it. He sent instead, after delay, a much briefer report, which he was moved to make different and, for some reason, less vivid. Meanwhile he learned from Miss Wenham how Addie had introduced him. It took time to arrive with her at that point, but after the Rubicon was crossed they went far afield.

IV

"Oh yes, she said you were engaged. That was why—since I *had* broken out so—she thought I would like to see you; as I assure you I've been so delighted to. But *aren't* you?" the good lady asked as if she saw in his face some ground for doubt.

"Assuredly—if she says so. It may seem very odd to you, but I haven't known, and yet I've felt that, being nothing whatever to you directly, I need some warrant for consenting thus to be thrust on you. We *were*," the young man explained, "engaged a year ago; but since then (if you don't mind my telling you such things; I feel now as if I could tell you anything!) I haven't quite known how I stand. It hasn't seemed that we were in a position to marry. Things are better now, but I haven't quite known how she would see them. They were so bad six months ago that I understood her, I thought, as breaking off. I haven't broken; I've only accepted, for the time—because men must be easy with women—being treated as 'the best of friends.' Well, I try to be. I wouldn't have come here if I hadn't been. I thought it would be charming for her to know you—when I heard from her the extraordinary way you had dawned upon her, and charming therefore if I could help her to it. And if I'm helping you to know *her*," he went on, "isn't that charming too?"

"Oh, I so want to!" Miss Wenham murmured, in her unpractical, impersonal way. "You're so different!" she wistfully declared.

"It's *you*, if I may respectfully, ecstatically say so, who are different. That's the point of it all. I'm not sure that anything so terrible really ought to happen to you as to know us."

"Well," said Miss Wenham, "I do know you a little, by this time, don't I? And I don't find it terrible. It's a delightful change for me."

"Oh, I'm not sure you ought to have a delightful change!"

"Why not—if you do?"

"Ah, I can bear it. I'm not sure that you can. I'm too bad to spoil—I *am* spoiled. I'm nobody, in short; I'm nothing. I've no type. You're *all* type. It has taken long, delicious years of security and monotony to produce you. You fit your frame with a perfection only equalled by the perfection with which your frame fits you. So this admirable old house, all time-softened white within and time-faded red without, so everything that surrounds you here and that has, by some extraordinary mercy, escaped the inevitable fate of exploitation: so it all, I say, is the sort of thing that, if it were the least bit to fall to pieces, could never, ah, never more, be put together again. I have, dear Miss Wenham," Granger went on, happy himself in his extravagance, which was yet all sincere, and happier still in her deep, but altogether pleased, mystification—"I've found, do you know, just the thing one has ever heard of that you most resemble. You're the Sleeping Beauty in the wood."

He still had no compunction when he heard her bewilderedly sigh: "Oh, you're too delightfully droll!"

"No, I only put things just as they are, and as I've also learned a little, thank heaven, to see them—which isn't, I quite agree with you, at all what anyone does. You're in the deep doze of the spell that has held you for long years, and it would be a shame, a crime, to wake you up. Indeed I already feel, with a thousand scruples, that I'm giving you the fatal shake. I say it even though it makes me sound a little as if I thought myself the fairy prince."

She gazed at him with her queerest, kindest look, which he was getting used to, in spite of a faint fear, at the back of his head, of the strange things that sometimes occurred when lonely ladies, however mature, began to look at interesting young men from over the seas as if the young men desired to flirt. "It's so wonderful," she said, "that you should be so very odd and yet so very good-natured." Well, it all came to the same thing—it was so wonderful that *she* should be so simple and yet so little of a bore. He accepted with gratitude the theory of his languor—which moreover was real enough and partly perhaps why he was so sensitive; he let himself go as a convalescent, let her insist on the weakness that always remained after fever. It helped him to gain time, to preserve the spell even while he talked of breaking it; saw him through slow strolls and soft sessions, long gossips, fitful, hopeless questions—there was so much more to tell than, by any contortion, she *could*—and explanations addressed gallantly and patiently to her understanding, but not, by good fortune, really reaching it. They were perfectly at cross-purposes, and it was all the better, and they wandered together in the silver haze with all communication blurred.

When they sat in the sun in her formal garden he was quite aware that the tenderest consideration failed to disguise his treating her as the most exquisite of curiosities. The term of comparison most present to him was that of some obsolete musical instrument. The old-time order of her mind and her air had the stillness of a painted spinet that was duly dusted, gently rubbed, but never tuned nor played on. Her opinions were like dried roseleaves; her attitudes like British sculpture; her voice was what he imagined of the possible tone of the old gilded, silver-stringed harp in one of the corners of the drawing-room. The lonely little decencies and modest dignities of her life, the fine grain of its conservatism, the innocence of its ignorance, all its monotony of stupidity and salubrity, its cold dulness and dim brightness, were there before him.

Meanwhile, within him, strange things took place. It was literally true that his impression began again, after a lull, to make
him nervous and anxious, and for reasons peculiarly confused,
almost grotesquely mingled, or at least comically sharp. He
was distinctly an agitation and a new taste—that he could see;
and he saw quite as much therefore the excitement she already
drew from the vision of Addie, an image intensified by the
sense of closer kinship and presented to her, clearly, with various erratic enhancements, by her friend the doctor's daughter. At the end of a few days he said to her: "Do you know
she wants to come without waiting any longer? She wants to
come while I'm here. I received this morning her letter proposing it, but I've been thinking it over and have waited to
speak to you. The thing is, you see, that if she writes to *you*
proposing it——"

"Oh, I shall be so particularly glad!"

V

They were, as usual, in the garden, and it had not yet been
so present to him that if he were only a happy cad there would
be a good way to protect her. As she wouldn't hear of his
being yet beyond precautions she had gone into the house for
a particular shawl that was just the thing for his knees, and,
blinking in the watery sunshine, had come back with it across
the fine little lawn. He was neither fatuous nor asinine, but
he had almost to put it to himself as a small task to resist the
sense of his absurd advantage with her. It filled him with
horror and awkwardness, made him think of he didn't know
what, recalled something of Maupassant's—the smitten "Miss
Harriet" and her tragic fate. There was a preposterous possibility—yes, he held the strings quite in his hands—of keeping the treasure for himself. That was the art of life—what the
real artist would consistently do. He would close the door on
his impression, treat it as a private museum. He would see
that he could lounge and linger there, live with wonderful
things there, lie up there to rest and refit. For himself he was
sure that after a little he should be able to paint there—do
things in a key he had never thought of before. When she
brought him the rug he took it from her and made her sit

down on the bench and resume her knitting; then, passing
behind her with a laugh, he placed it over her own shoulders;
after which he moved to and fro before her, his hands in his
pockets and his cigarette in his teeth. He was ashamed of the
cigarette—a villainous false note; but she allowed, liked,
begged him to smoke, and what he said to her on it, in one
of the pleasantries she benevolently missed, was that he did
so for fear of doing worse. That only showed that the end was
really in sight. "I dare say it will strike you as quite awful,
what I'm going to say to you, but I can't help it. I speak out
of the depths of my respect for you. It will seem to you horrid
disloyalty to poor Addie. Yes—there we are; there *I* am, at
least, in my naked monstrosity." He stopped and looked at
her till she might have been almost frightened. "Don't let
her come. Tell her not to. I've tried to prevent it, but she
suspects."

The poor woman wondered. "Suspects?"

"Well, I drew it, in writing to her, on reflection, as mild as
I could—having been visited, in the watches of the night, by
the instinct of what might happen. Something told me to keep
back my first letter—in which, under the first impression, I
myself rashly 'raved'; and I concocted instead of it an insincere
and guarded report. But guarded as I was I clearly didn't keep
you 'down,' as we say, enough. The wonder of your colour—
daub you over with grey as I might—must have come through
and told the tale. She scents battle from afar—by which I
mean she scents 'quaintness.' But keep her off. It's hideous,
what I'm saying—but I owe it to you. I owe it to the world.
She'll kill you."

"You mean I shan't get on with her?"

"Oh, fatally! See how *I* have. She's intelligent, remarkably
pretty, remarkably good. And she'll adore you."

"Well then?"

"Why, that will be just how she'll do for you."

"Oh, I can hold my own!" said Miss Wenham with the headshake of a horse making his sleigh-bells rattle in frosty air.

"Ah, but you can't hold hers! She'll rave about you. She'll
write about you. You're Niagara before the first white traveller—and you know, or rather you can't know, what Niagara
became *after* that gentleman. Addie will have discovered

Niagara. She will understand you in perfection; she will feel you down to the ground; not a delicate shade of you will she lose or let anyone else lose. You'll be too weird for words, but the words will nevertheless come. You'll be too exactly the real thing and to be left too utterly just as you are, and all Addie's friends and all Addie's editors and contributors and readers will cross the Atlantic and flock to Flickerbridge, so, unanimously, universally, vociferously, to leave you. You'll be in the magazines with illustrations; you'll be in the papers with headings; you'll be everywhere with everything. You don't understand—you think you do, but you don't. Heaven forbid you *should* understand! That's just your beauty—your 'sleeping' beauty. But you needn't. You can take me on trust. Don't have her. Say, as a pretext, as a reason, anything in the world you like. Lie to her— scare her away. I'll go away and give you up—I'll sacrifice everything myself." Granger pursued his exhortation, convincing himself more and more. "If I saw my way out, my way completely through, *I* would pile up some fabric of fiction for her—I would only want to be sure of its not tumbling down. One would have, you see, to keep the thing up. But I would throw dust in her eyes. I would tell her that you don't do at all—that you're not, in fact, a desirable acquaintance. I'd tell her you're vulgar, improper, scandalous; I'd tell her you're mercenary, designing, dangerous; I'd tell her the only safe course is immediately to let you drop. I would thus surround you with an impenetrable legend of conscientious misrepresentation, a circle of pious fraud, and all the while privately keep you for myself."

She had listened to him as if he were a band of music and she a small shy garden-party. "I shouldn't like you to go away. I shouldn't in the least like you not to come again."

"Ah, there it is!" he replied. "How can I come again if Addie ruins you?"

"But how will she ruin me—even if she does what you say? I know I'm too old to change and really much too queer to please in any of the extraordinary ways you speak of. If it's a question of quizzing me I don't think my cousin, or anyone else, will have quite the hand for it that *you* seem to have. So that if *you* haven't ruined me——!"

"But I *have*—that's just the point!" Granger insisted. "I've undermined you at least. I've left, after all, terribly little for Addie to do."

She laughed in clear tones. "Well, then, we'll admit that you've done everything but frighten me."

He looked at her with surpassing gloom. "No—that again is one of the most dreadful features. You'll positively like it— what's to come. You'll be caught up in a chariot of fire like the prophet—wasn't there, was there, one?—of old. That's exactly why—if one could but have done it—you would have been to be kept ignorant and helpless. There's something or other in Latin that says that it's the finest things that change the most easily for the worse. You already enjoy your dishonour and revel in your shame. It's too late—you're lost!"

VI

All this was as pleasant a manner of passing the time as any other, for it didn't prevent his old-world corner from closing round him more entirely, nor stand in the way of his making out, from day to day, some new source, as well as some new effect, of its virtue. He was really scared at moments at some of the liberties he took in talk—at finding himself so familiar; for the great note of the place was just that a certain modern ease had never crossed its threshold, that quick intimacies and quick oblivions were a stranger to its air. It had known, in all its days, no rude, no loud invasion. Serenely unconscious of most contemporary things, it had been so of nothing so much as of the diffused social practice of running in and out. Granger held his breath, on occasions, to think how Addie would run. There were moments when, for some reason, more than at others, he heard her step on the staircase and her cry in the hall. If he played freely, none the less, with the idea with which we have shown him as occupied, it was not that in every measurable way he didn't sacrifice, to the utmost, to stillness. He only hovered, ever so lightly, to take up again his thread. She wouldn't hear of his leaving her, of his being in the least fit again, as she said, to travel. She spoke of the journey to London—which was in fact a matter of many hours—as an experiment fraught with lurking complications.

He added then day to day, yet only hereby, as he reminded her, giving other complications a larger chance to multiply. He kept it before her, when there was nothing else to do, that she must consider; after which he had his times of fear that she perhaps really would make for him this sacrifice.

He knew that she had written again to Paris, and knew that he must himself again write—a situation abounding for each in the elements of a quandary. If he stayed so long, why then he wasn't better, and if he wasn't better Addie might take it into her head——! They must make it clear that he *was* better, so that, suspicious, alarmed at what was kept from her, she shouldn't suddenly present herself to nurse him. If he was better, however, why did he stay so long? If he stayed only for the attraction the sense of the attraction might be contagious. This was what finally grew clearest for him, so that he had for his mild disciple hours of still sharper prophecy. It consorted with his fancy to represent to her that their young friend had been by this time unsparingly warned; but nothing could be plainer than that this was ineffectual so long as he himself resisted the ordeal. To plead that he remained because he was too weak to move was only to throw themselves back on the other horn of their dilemma. If he was too weak to move Addie would bring him her strength—of which, when she got there, she would give them specimens enough. One morning he broke out at breakfast with an intimate conviction. They would see that she was actually starting—they would receive a wire by noon. They didn't receive it, but by his theory the portent was only the stronger. It had, moreover, its grave as well as its gay side, for Granger's paradox and pleasantry were only the most convenient way for him of saying what he felt. He literally heard the knell sound, and in expressing this to Miss Wenham with the conversational freedom that seemed best to pay his way he the more vividly faced the contingency. He could never return, and though he announced it with a despair that did what might be to make it pass as a joke, he saw that, whether or no she at last understood, she quite at last believed him. On this, to his knowledge, she wrote again to Addie, and the contents of her letter excited his curiosity. But that sentiment, though not assuaged, quite dropped when, the day after, in the evening, she let him know that she had had, an hour before, a telegram.

"She comes Thursday."

He showed not the least surprise. It was the deep calm of the fatalist. It *had* to be. "I must leave you then to-morrow."

She looked, on this, as he had never seen her; it would have been hard to say whether what was in her face was the last failure to follow or the first effort to meet. "And really not to come back?"

"Never, never, dear lady. Why should I come back? You can never be again what you *have* been. I shall have seen the last of you."

"Oh!" she touchingly urged.

"Yes, for I should next find you simply brought to self-consciousness. You'll be exactly what you are, I charitably admit—nothing more or less, nothing different. But you'll be it all in a different way. We live in an age of prodigious machinery, all organised to a single end. That end is publicity—a publicity as ferocious as the appetite of a cannibal. The thing therefore is not to have any illusions—fondly to flatter yourself, in a muddled moment, that the cannibal will spare you. He spares nobody. He spares nothing. It will be all right. You'll have a lovely time. You'll be only just a public character—blown about the world for all you are and proclaimed for all you are on the housetops. It will be for *that*, mind, I quite recognise—because Addie is superior—as well as for all you aren't. So good-bye."

He remained, however, till the next day, and noted at intervals the different stages of their friend's journey; the hour, this time, she would really have started, the hour she would reach Dover, the hour she would get to town, where she would alight at Mrs. Dunn's. Perhaps she would bring Mrs. Dunn, for Mrs. Dunn would swell the chorus. At the last, on the morrow, as if in anticipation of this, stillness settled between them; he became as silent as his hostess. But before he went she brought out, shyly and anxiously, as an appeal, the question that, for hours, had clearly been giving her thought. "Do you meet her then to-night in London?"

"Dear, no. In what position am I, alas! to do that? When can I *ever* meet her again?" He had turned it all over. "If I could meet Addie after this, you know, I could meet *you*. And if I do meet Addie," he lucidly pursued, "what will happen, by the same stroke, is that I *shall* meet you. And that's just what I've explained to you that I dread."

"You mean that she and I will be inseparable?"

He hesitated. "I mean that she'll tell me all about you. I can hear her, and her ravings, now."

She gave again—and it was infinitely sad—her little whinnying laugh. "Oh, but if what you say is true, you'll know."

"Ah, but Addie won't! Won't, I mean, know that *I* know— or at least won't believe it. Won't believe that anyone knows. Such," he added, with a strange, smothered sigh, "*is* Addie. Do you know," he wound up, "that what, after all, has most definitely happened is that you've made me see her as I've never done before?"

She blinked and gasped, she wondered and despaired. "Oh, no, it will be *you*. I've had nothing to do with it. Everything's *all* you!"

But for all it mattered now! "You'll see," he said, "that she's charming. I shall go, for to-night, to Oxford. I shall almost cross her on the way."

"Then, if she's charming, what am I to tell her from you in explanation of such strange behaviour as your flying away just as she arrives?"

"Ah, you needn't mind about that—you needn't tell her anything."

She fixed him as if as never again. "It's none of my business, of course I feel; but isn't it a little cruel if you're engaged?"

Granger gave a laugh almost as odd as one of her own. "Oh, you've cost me that!" and he put out his hand to her.

She wondered while she took it. "Cost you——?"

"We're not engaged. Good-bye."

The Birthplace

IT SEEMED to them at first, the offer, too good to be true, and their friend's letter, addressed to them to feel, as he said, the ground, to sound them as to inclinations and possibilities, had almost the effect of a brave joke at their expense. Their friend, Mr. Grant-Jackson, a highly preponderant, pushing person, great in discussion and arrangement, abrupt in overture, unexpected, if not perverse, in attitude, and almost equally acclaimed and objected to in the wide midland region to which he had taught, as the phrase was, the size of his foot—their friend had launched his bolt quite out of the blue and had thereby so shaken them as to make them fear almost more than hope. The place had fallen vacant by the death of one of the two ladies, mother and daughter, who had discharged its duties for fifteen years; the daughter was staying on alone, to accommodate, but had found, though extremely mature, an opportunity of marriage that involved retirement, and the question of the new incumbents was not a little pressing. The want thus determined was of a united couple of some sort, of the right sort, a pair of educated and competent sisters possibly preferred, but a married pair having its advantages if other qualifications were marked. Applicants, candidates, besiegers of the door of everyone supposed to have a voice in the matter, were already beyond counting, and Mr. Grant-Jackson, who was in his way diplomatic and whose voice, though not perhaps of the loudest, possessed notes of insistence, had found his preference fixing itself on some person or brace of persons who had been decent and dumb. The Gedges appeared to have struck him as waiting in silence—though absolutely, as happened, no busybody had brought them, far away in the north, a hint either of bliss or of danger; and the happy spell, for the rest, had obviously been wrought in him by a remembrance which, though now scarcely fresh, had never before borne any such fruit.

Morris Gedge had for a few years, as a young man, carried on a small private school of the order known as preparatory, and had happened then to receive under his roof the small son of the great man, who was not at that time so great. The little boy, during an absence of his parents from England, had been dangerously ill, so dangerously that they had been recalled in haste, though with inevitable delays, from a far country—they had gone to America, with the whole continent and the great sea to cross again—and had got back to find the child saved, but saved, as couldn't help coming to light, by the extreme devotion and perfect judgment of Mrs. Gedge. Without children of her own, she had particularly attached herself to this tiniest and tenderest of her husband's pupils, and they had both dreaded as a dire disaster the injury to their little enterprise that would be caused by their losing him. Nervous, anxious, sensitive persons, with a pride—as they were for that matter well aware—above their position, never, at the best, to be anything but dingy, they had nursed him in terror and had brought him through in exhaustion. Exhaustion, as befell, had thus overtaken them early and had for one reason and another managed to assert itself as their permanent portion. The little boy's death would, as they said, have done for them, yet his recovery hadn't saved them; with which it was doubtless also part of a shy but stiff candour in them that they didn't regard themselves as having in a more indirect manner laid up treasure. Treasure was not to be, in any form whatever, of their dreams or of their waking sense; and the years that followed had limped under their weight, had now and then rather grievously stumbled, had even barely escaped laying them in the dust. The school had not prospered, had but dwindled to a close. Gedge's health had failed, and, still more, every sign in him of a capacity to publish himself as practical. He had tried several things, he had tried many, but the final appearance was of their having tried him not less. They mostly, at the time I speak of, were trying his successors, while he found himself, with an effect of dull felicity that had come in this case from the mere postponement of change, in charge of the grey town-library of Blackport-on-Dwindle, all granite, fog and female fiction. This was a situation in which his general intelligence—acknowledged as his strong point—was doubtless conceived, around him, as feeling less of a strain than that mastery of particulars in which he was recognised as weak.

It was at Blackport-on-Dwindle that the silver shaft reached and pierced him; it was as an alternative to dispensing dog's-eared volumes the very titles of which, on the lips of innumerable glib girls, were a challenge to his temper, that the wardenship of so different a temple presented itself. The stipend named differed little from the slim wage at present paid him, but even had it been less the interest and the honour would have struck him as determinant. The shrine at which he was to preside—though he had always lacked occasion to approach it—figured to him as the most sacred known to the steps of men, the early home of the supreme poet, the Mecca of the English-speaking race. The tears came into his eyes sooner still than into his wife's while he looked about with her at their actual narrow prison, so grim with enlightenment, so ugly with industry, so turned away from any dream, so intolerable to any taste. He felt as if a window had opened into a great green woodland, a woodland that had a name, glorious, immortal, that was peopled with vivid figures, each of them renowned, and that gave out a murmur, deep as the sound of the sea, which was the rustle in forest shade of all the poetry, the beauty, the colour of life. It would be prodigious that of this transfigured world *he* should keep the key. No—he couldn't believe it, not even when Isabel, at sight of his face, came and helpfully kissed him. He shook his head with a strange smile. "We shan't get it. Why should we? It's perfect."

"If we don't he'll simply have been cruel; which is impossible when he has waited all this time to be kind." Mrs. Gedge did believe—she *would*; since the wide doors of the world of poetry had suddenly pushed back for them it was in the form of poetic justice that they were first to know it. She had her faith in their patron; it was sudden, but it was now complete. "He remembers—that's all; and that's our strength."

"And what's *his*?" Gedge asked. "He may *want* to put us through, but that's a different thing from being able. What are our special advantages?"

"Well, that we're just the thing." Her knowledge of the needs of the case was, as yet, thanks to scant information, of the vaguest, and she had never, more than her husband, stood on the sacred spot; but she saw herself waving a nicely-gloved hand over a collection of remarkable objects and saying to a compact crowd of gaping, awe-struck persons: "And now, please, *this* way." She even heard herself meeting with promptness and decision an occasional inquiry from a visitor in whom audacity had prevailed over awe. She had been once, with a cousin, years before, to a great northern castle, and that was the way the housekeeper had taken them round. And it was not moreover, either, that she thought of herself as a housekeeper: she was well above that, and the wave of her hand wouldn't fail to be such as to show it. This, and much else, she summed up as she answered her mate. "Our special advantages are that you're a gentleman."

"Oh!" said Gedge, as if he had never thought of it, and yet as if too it were scarce worth thinking of.

"I see it all," she went on; "they've *had* the vulgar—they find they don't do. We're poor and we're modest, but anyone can see what we are."

Gedge wondered. "Do you mean——?" More modest than she, he didn't know quite what she meant.

"We're refined. We know how to speak."

"Do we?"—he still, suddenly, wondered.

But she was, from the first, surer of everything than he; so that when a few weeks more had elapsed and the shade of uncertainty—though it was only a shade—had grown almost to sicken him, her triumph was to come with the news that they were fairly named. "We're on poor pay, though we manage"—she had on the present occasion insisted on her point. "But we're highly cultivated, and for them to get *that*, don't you see? without getting too much with it in the way of pretensions and demands, must be precisely their dream. We've no social position, but we don't *mind* that we haven't, do we? a bit; which is because we know the difference between realities and shams. We hold to reality, and that gives us common sense, which the vulgar have less than anything, and which yet must be wanted there, after all, as well as anywhere else."

Her companion followed her, but musingly, as if his horizon had within a few moments grown so great that he was almost lost in it and required a new orientation. The shining spaces surrounded him; the association alone gave a nobler arch to the sky. "Allow that we hold also a little to the romance. It seems to me that that's the beauty. We've missed it all our life, and now it's come. We shall be at head-quarters for it. We shall have our fill of it."

She looked at his face, at the effect in it of these prospects, and her own lighted as if he had suddenly grown handsome. "Certainly—we shall live as in a fairy-tale. But what I mean is that we shall give, in a way—and so gladly—quite as much as we get. With all the rest of it we're, for instance, neat." Their letter had come to them at breakfast, and she picked a fly out of the butter-dish. "It's the way we'll *keep* the place"— with which she removed from the sofa to the top of the cottage-piano a tin of biscuits that had refused to squeeze into the cupboard. At Blackport they were in lodgings—of the lowest description, she had been known, with a freedom felt by Blackport to be slightly invidious, to declare. The Birthplace—and that itself, after such a life, was exaltation— wouldn't be lodgings, since a house close beside it was set apart for the warden, a house joining on to it as a sweet old parsonage is often annexed to a quaint old church. It would all together be their home, and such a home as would make a little world that they would never want to leave. She dwelt on the gain, for that matter, to their income; as, obviously, though the salary was not a change for the better, the house, given them, would make all the difference. He assented to this, but absently, and she was almost impatient at the range of his thoughts. It was as if something, for him—the very swarm of them—veiled the view; and he presently, of himself, showed what it was.

"What I can't get over is its being such a man——!" He almost, from inward emotion, broke down.

"Such a man——?"

"Him, *him*, HIM——!" It was too much.

"Grant-Jackson? Yes, it's a surprise, but one sees how he has been meaning, all the while, the right thing by us."

"I mean *Him*," Gedge returned more coldly; "our becoming familiar and intimate—for that's what it will come to. We shall just live with Him."

"Of course—it *is* the beauty." And she added quite gaily: "The more we do the more we shall love Him."

"No doubt—but it's rather awful. The more we *know* Him," Gedge reflected, "the more we shall love Him. We don't as yet, you see, know Him so very tremendously."

"We do so quite as well, I imagine, as the sort of people they've had. And that probably isn't—unless you care, as we do—so awfully necessary. For there are the facts."

"Yes—there are the facts."

"I mean the principal ones. They're all that the people—the people who come—want."

"Yes—they must be all *they* want."

"So that they're all that those who've been in charge have needed to know."

"Ah," he said as if it were a question of honour, "*we* must know everything."

She cheerfully acceded: she had the merit, he felt, of keeping the case within bounds. "Everything. But about him personally," she added, "there isn't, is there? so very, very much."

"More, I believe, than there used to be. They've made discoveries."

It was a grand thought. "Perhaps *we* shall make some!"

"Oh, I shall be content to be a little better up in what has been done." And his eyes rested on a shelf of books, half of which, little worn but much faded, were of the florid "gift" order and belonged to the house. Of those among them that were his own most were common specimens of the reference sort, not excluding an old Bradshaw and a catalogue of the town-library. "We've not even a Set of our own. Of the Works," he explained in quick repudiation of the sense, perhaps more obvious, in which she might have taken it.

As a proof of their scant range of possessions this sounded almost abject, till the painful flush with which they met on the admission melted presently into a different glow. It was just for that kind of poorness that their new situation was, by its intrinsic charm, to console them. And Mrs. Gedge had a happy thought. "Wouldn't the Library more or less have them?"

"Oh no, we've nothing of that sort: for what do you take us?" This, however, was but the play of Gedge's high spirits: the form both depression and exhilaration most frequently took with him being a bitterness on the subject of the literary taste of Blackport. No one was so deeply acquainted with it. It acted with him in fact as so lurid a sign of the future that the charm of the thought of removal was sharply enhanced by the prospect of escape from it. The institution he served didn't of course deserve the particular reproach into which his irony had flowered; and indeed if the several Sets in which the Works were present were a trifle dusty, the dust was a little his own fault. To make up for that now he had the vision of immediately giving his time to the study of them; he saw himself indeed, inflamed with a new passion, earnestly commenting and collating. Mrs. Gedge, who had suggested that they ought, till their move should come, to read Him regularly of an evening—certain as they were to do it still more when in closer quarters with Him—Mrs. Gedge felt also, in her degree, the spell; so that the very happiest time of their anxious life was perhaps to have been the series of lamplight hours, after supper, in which, alternately taking the book, they declaimed, they almost performed, their beneficent author. He became speedily more than their author—their personal friend, their universal light, their final authority and divinity. Where in the world, they were already asking themselves, would they have been without him? By the time their appointment arrived in form their relation to him had immensely developed. It was amusing to Morris Gedge that he had so lately blushed for his ignorance, and he made this remark to his wife during the last hour they were able to give to their study, before proceeding, across half the country, to the scene of their romantic future. It was as if, in deep, close throbs, in cool after-waves that broke of a sudden and bathed his mind, all possession and comprehension and sympathy, all the truth and the life and the story, had come to him, and come, as the newspapers said, to stay. "It's absurd," he didn't hesitate to say, "to talk of our not 'knowing.' So far as we don't it's because we're donkeys. He's *in* the thing, over His ears, and the more we get into it the more we're with Him. I seem to myself at any rate," he declared, "to *see* Him in it as if He were painted on the wall."

"Oh, *doesn't* one rather, the dear thing? And don't you feel where it is?" Mrs. Gedge finely asked. "We see Him because

we love Him—that's what we do. How can we not, the old
darling—with what He's doing for us? There's no light"—she
had a sententious turn—"like true affection."

"Yes, I suppose that's it. And yet," her husband mused, "I
see, confound me, the faults."

"That's because you're so critical. You see them, but you
don't mind them. You see them, but you forgive them. You
mustn't mention them *there*. We shan't, you know, be there
for *that*."

"Dear no!" he laughed: "we'll chuck out anyone who hints
at them."

II

If the sweetness of the preliminary months had been great,
great too, though almost excessive as agitation, was the wonder of fairly being housed with Him, of treading day and night
in the footsteps He had worn, of touching the objects, or at
all events the surfaces, the substances, over which His hands
had played, which his arms, his shoulders had rubbed, of
breathing the air—or something not too unlike it—in which
His voice had sounded. They had had a little at first their
bewilderments, their disconcertedness; the place was both
humbler and grander than they had exactly prefigured, more
at once of a cottage and of a museum, a little more archaically
bare and yet a little more richly official. But the sense was
strong with them that the point of view, for the inevitable ease
of the connection, patiently, indulgently awaited them; in addition to which, from the first evening, after closing-hour,
when the last blank pilgrim had gone, the mere spell, the
mystic presence—as if they had had it quite to themselves—
were all they could have desired. They had received, by Grant-
Jackson's care and in addition to a table of instructions and
admonitions by the number, and in some particulars by the
nature, of which they found themselves slightly depressed,
various little guides, handbooks, travellers' tributes, literary
memorials and other catch-penny publications, which, however, were to be for the moment swallowed up in the interesting episode of the induction or initiation appointed for
them in advance at the hands of several persons whose con-

nection with the establishment was, as superior to their own, still more official, and at those in especial of one of the ladies who had for so many years borne the brunt. About the instructions from above, about the shilling books and the well-known facts and the full-blown legend, the supervision, the subjection, the submission, the view as of a cage in which he should circulate and a groove in which he should slide, Gedge had preserved a certain play of mind; but all power of reaction appeared suddenly to desert him in the presence of his so visibly competent predecessor and as an effect of her good offices. He had not the resource, enjoyed by his wife, of seeing himself, with impatience, attired in black silk of a make characterised by just the right shade of austerity; so that this firm, smooth, expert and consummately respectable middle-aged person had him somehow, on the whole ground, completely at her mercy.

It was evidently something of a rueful moment when, as a lesson—she being for the day or two still in the field—he accepted Miss Putchin's suggestion of "going round" with her and with the successive squads of visitors she was there to deal with. He appreciated her method—he saw there had to *be* one; he admired her as succinct and definite; for there were the facts, as his wife had said at Blackport, and they were to be disposed of in the time; yet he felt like a very little boy as he dangled, more than once, with Mrs. Gedge, at the tail of the human comet. The idea had been that they should, by this attendance, more fully embrace the possible accidents and incidents, as it were, of the relation to the great public in which they were to find themselves; and the poor man's excited perception of the great public rapidly became such as to resist any diversion meaner than that of the admirable manner of their guide. It wandered from his gaping companions to that of the priestess in black silk, whom he kept asking himself if either he or Isabel could hope by any possibility ever remotely to resemble; then it bounded restlessly back to the numerous persons who revealed to him, as it had never yet been revealed, the happy power of the simple to hang upon the lips of the wise. The great thing seemed to be—and quite surprisingly—that the business was easy and the strain, which as a strain they had feared, moderate; so that he might have been puzzled, had he fairly caught himself in the act, by his recognising as the last effect of the impression an odd absence of the ability to rest in it, an agitation deep within him that vaguely threatened to grow. "It isn't, you see, so very complicated," the black silk lady seemed to throw off, with everything else, in her neat, crisp, cheerful way; in spite of which he already, the very first time—that is after several parties had been in and out and up and down—went so far as to wonder if there weren't more in it than she imagined. She was, so to speak, kindness itself—was all encouragement and reassurance; but it was just her slightly coarse redolence of these very things that, on repetition, before they parted, dimmed a little, as he felt, the light of his acknowledging smile. That, again, she took for a symptom of some pleading weakness in him— he could never be as brave as she; so that she wound up with a few pleasant words from the very depth of her experience. "You'll get into it, never fear—it will *come*; and then you'll feel as if you had never done anything else." He was afterwards to know that, on the spot, at this moment, he must have begun to wince a little at such a menace; that he might come to feel as if he had never done anything but what Miss Putchin did loomed for him, in germ, as a penalty to pay. The support she offered, none the less, continued to strike him; she put the whole thing on so sound a basis when she said: "You see they're so nice about it—they take such an interest. And they never do a thing they shouldn't. That was always everything to mother and me." "They," Gedge had already noticed, referred constantly and hugely, in the good woman's talk, to the millions who shuffled through the house; the pronoun in question was forever on her lips, the hordes it represented filled her consciousness, the addition of their numbers ministered to her glory. Mrs. Gedge promptly met her. "It must be indeed delightful to see the effect on so many, and to feel that one may perhaps do something to make it—well, permanent." But he was kept silent by his becoming more sharply aware that this was a new view, for him, of the reference made, that he had never thought of the quality of the place as derived from Them, but from Somebody Else, and that They, in short, seemed to have got into the way of crowding out Him. He found himself even a little resenting this for Him, which perhaps had something to do with the slightly invidious cast of his next inquiry.

"And are They always, as one might say—a—stupid?"

"Stupid!" She stared, looking as if no one *could* be such a thing in such a connection. No one had ever been anything but neat and cheerful and fluent, except to be attentive and unobjectionable and, so far as was possible, American.

"What I mean is," he explained, "is there any perceptible proportion that take an interest in Him?"

His wife stepped on his toe; she deprecated irony. But his mistake fortunately was lost on their friend. "That's just why they come, that they take such an interest. I sometimes think they take more than about anything else in the world." With which Miss Putchin looked about at the place. "It *is* pretty, don't you think, the way they've got it now?" This, Gedge saw, was a different "They"; it applied to the powers that were—the people who had appointed him, the governing, visiting Body, in respect to which he was afterwards to remark to Mrs. Gedge that a fellow—it was the difficulty—didn't know "where to have her." His wife, at a loss, questioned at that moment the necessity of having her anywhere, and he said, good-humouredly, "Of course; it's all right." He was in fact content enough with the last touches their friend had given the picture. "There are many who know all about it when they come, and the Americans often are tremendously up. Mother and me really enjoyed"—it was her only slip—"the interest of the Americans. We've sometimes had ninety a day, and all wanting to see and hear everything. But you'll work them off; you'll see the way—it's all experience." She came back, for his comfort, to that. She came back also to other things: she did justice to the considerable class who arrived positive and primed. "There are those who know more about it than you do. But *that* only comes from their interest."

"Who know more about what?" Gedge inquired.

"Why, about the place. I mean they have their ideas—of what everything is, and *where* it is, and what it isn't, and where it *should* be. They do ask questions," she said, yet not so much in warning as in the complacency of being seasoned and sound; "and they're down on you when they think you go

wrong. As if you ever could! You know too much," she sagaciously smiled; "or you *will*."

"Oh, you mustn't know *too* much, must you?" And Gedge
now smiled as well. He knew, he thought, what he meant.

"Well, you must know as much as anybody else. I claim, at
any rate, that I do," Miss Putchin declared. "They never really
caught me."

"I'm very sure of *that*," Mrs. Gedge said with an elation
almost personal.

"Certainly," he added, "I don't want to be caught." She
rejoined that, in such a case, he would have *Them* down on
him, and he saw that this time she meant the powers above.
It quickened his sense of all the elements that were to reckon
with, yet he felt at the same time that the powers above were
not what he should most fear. "I'm glad," he observed, "that
they ever ask questions; but I happened to notice, you know,
that no one did to-day."

"Then you missed several—and no loss. There were three
or four put to me too silly to remember. But of course they
mostly *are* silly."

"You mean the questions?"

She laughed with all her cheer. "Yes, sir; I don't mean the
answers."

Whereupon, for a moment snubbed and silent, he felt like
one of the crowd. Then it made him slightly vicious. "I didn't
know but you meant the people in general—till I remembered
that I'm to understand from you that *they're* wise, only occasionally breaking down."

It was not really till then, he thought, that she lost patience;
and he had had, much more than he meant no doubt, a cross-
questioning air. "You'll see for yourself." Of which he was
sure enough. He was in fact so ready to take this that she
came round to full accommodation, put it frankly that every
now and then they broke out—not the silly, oh no, the intensely inquiring. "We've had quite lively discussions, don't
you know, about well-known points. They want it all *their*
way, and I know the sort that are going to as soon as I see
them. That's one of the things you do—you get to know the
sorts. And if it's what you're afraid of—their taking you up,"
she was further gracious enough to say, "you needn't mind a

bit. What *do* they know, after all, when for us it's our life? I've never moved an inch, because, you see, I shouldn't have been here if I didn't know where I was. No more will *you* be a year hence—you know what I mean, putting it impossibly—if *you* don't. I expect you do, in spite of your fancies." And she dropped once more to bed-rock. "There are the facts. Otherwise where would any of us be? That's all you've got to go upon. A person, however cheeky, can't have them *his* way just because he takes it into his head. There can only be *one* way, and," she gaily added as she took leave of them, "I'm sure it's quite enough!"

III

Gedge not only assented eagerly—one way *was* quite enough if it were the right one—but repeated it, after this conversation, at odd moments, several times over to his wife. "There can only be one way, one way," he continued to remark—though indeed much as if it were a joke; till she asked him how many more he supposed she wanted. He failed to answer this question, but resorted to another repetition, "There are the facts, the facts," which, perhaps, however, he kept a little more to himself, sounding it at intervals in different parts of the house. Mrs. Gedge was full of comment on their clever introductress, though not restrictively save in the matter of her speech, "Me and mother," and a general tone—which certainly was not their sort of thing. "I don't know," he said, "perhaps it comes with the place, since speaking in immortal verse doesn't seem to come. It must be, one seems to see, one thing or the other. I dare say that in a few months I shall also be at it—'me and the wife.' "

"Why not me and the missus at once?" Mrs. Gedge resentfully inquired. "I don't think," she observed at another time, "that I quite know what's the matter with you."

"It's only that I'm excited, awfully excited—as I don't see how one can not be. You wouldn't have a fellow drop into this berth as into an appointment at the Post Office. Here on the spot it goes to my head; how can that be helped? But we shall live into it, and perhaps," he said with an implication of the other possibility that was doubtless but part of his fine ecstasy, "we shall live through it." The place acted on his imagination—how, surely, shouldn't it? And his imagination acted on his nerves, and these things together, with the general vividness and the new and complete immersion, made rest for him almost impossible, so that he could scarce go to bed at night and even during the first week more than once rose in the small hours to move about, up and down, with his lamp, standing, sitting, listening, wondering, in the stillness, as if positively to recover some echo, to surprise some secret, of the *genius loci*. He couldn't have explained it—and didn't in fact need to explain it, at least to himself, since the impulse simply held him and shook him; but the time after closing, the time above all after the people—Them, as he felt himself on the way to think of them, predominant, insistent, all in the foreground—brought him, or ought to have brought him, he seemed to see, nearer to the enshrined Presence, enlarged the opportunity for communion and intensified the sense of it. These nightly prowls, as he called them, were disquieting to his wife, who had no disposition to share in them, speaking with decision of the whole place as just the place to be forbidding after dark. She rejoiced in the distinctness, contiguous though it was, of their own little residence, where she trimmed the lamp and stirred the fire and heard the kettle sing, repairing the while the omissions of the small domestic who slept out; she foresaw herself with some promptness, drawing rather sharply the line between her own precinct and that in which the great spirit might walk. It would be with them, the great spirit, all day—even if indeed on her making that remark, and in just that form, to her husband, he replied with a queer "But will he though?" And she vaguely imaged the development of a domestic antidote after a while, precisely, in the shape of curtains more markedly drawn and everything most modern and lively, tea, "patterns," the newspapers, the female fiction itself that they had reacted against at Blackport, quite defiantly cultivated.

These possibilities, however, were all right, as her companion said it was, all the first autumn—they had arrived at summer's end; as if he were more than content with a special set of his own that he had access to from behind, passing out of their low door for the few steps between it and the Birthplace.

With his lamp ever so carefully guarded, and his nursed keys that made him free of treasures, he crossed the dusky interval so often that she began to qualify it as a habit that "grew." She spoke of it almost as if he had taken to drink, and he humoured that view of it by confessing that the cup was strong. This had been in truth, altogether, his immediate sense of it; strange and deep for him the spell of silent sessions before familiarity and, to some small extent, disappointment had set in. The exhibitional side of the establishment had struck him, even on arrival, as qualifying too much its character; he scarce knew what he might best have looked for, but the three or four rooms bristled overmuch, in the garish light of day, with busts and relics, not even ostensibly always *His*, old prints and old editions, old objects fashioned in His likeness, furniture "of the time" and autographs of celebrated worshippers. In the quiet hours and the deep dusk, none the less, under the play of the shifted lamp and that of his own emotion, these things too recovered their advantage, ministered to the mystery, or at all events to the impression, seemed consciously to offer themselves as personal to the poet. Not one of them was really or unchallengeably so, but they had somehow, through long association, got, as Gedge always phrased it, into the secret, and it was about the secret he asked them while he restlessly wandered. It was not till months had elapsed that he found how little they had to tell him, and he was quite at his ease with them when he knew they were by no means where his sensibility had first placed them. They were as out of it as he; only, to do them justice, they had made him immensely feel. And still, too, it was not they who had done that most, since his sentiment had gradually cleared itself to deep, to deeper refinements.

The Holy of Holies of the Birthplace was the low, the sublime Chamber of Birth, sublime because, as the Americans usually said—unlike the natives they mostly found words—it was so pathetic; and pathetic because it was—well, really nothing else in the world that one could name, number or measure. It was as empty as a shell of which the kernel has withered, and contained neither busts nor prints nor early copies; it contained only the Fact—*the* Fact itself—which, as he stood sentient there at midnight, our friend, holding his breath, allowed to sink into him. He *had* to take it as the place where the spirit would most walk and where he would therefore be most to be met, with possibilities of recognition and reciprocity. He hadn't, most probably—*He* hadn't—much inhabited the room, as men weren't apt, as a rule, to convert to their later use and involve in their wider fortune the scene itself of their nativity. But as there were moments when, in the conflict of theories, the sole certainty surviving for the critic threatened to be that He had not—unlike other successful men—*not* been born, so Gedge, though little of a critic, clung to the square feet of space that connected themselves, however feebly, with the positive appearance. He was little of a critic—he was nothing of one; he hadn't pretended to the character before coming, nor come to pretend to it; also, luckily for him, he was seeing day by day how little use he could possibly have for it. It would be to him, the attitude of a high expert, distinctly a stumbling-block, and that he rejoiced, as the winter waned, in his ignorance, was one of the propositions he betook himself, in his odd manner, to enunciating to his wife. She denied it, for hadn't she, in the first place, been present, wasn't she still present, at his pious, his tireless study of everything connected with the subject? —so present that she had herself learned more about it than had ever seemed likely. Then, in the second place, he was not to proclaim on the housetops any point at which he might be weak, for who knew, if it should get abroad that they were ignorant, what effect might be produced——?

"On the attraction"—he took her up—"of the Show?"

He had fallen into the harmless habit of speaking of the place as the "Show"; but she didn't mind this so much as to be diverted by it. "No; on the attitude of the Body. You know they're pleased with us, and I don't see why you should want to spoil it. We got in by a tight squeeze—you know we've had evidence of that, and that it was about as much as our backers could manage. But we're proving a comfort to them, and it's absurd of you to question your suitability to people who were content with the Putchins."

"I don't, my dear," he returned, "question anything; but if I should do so it would be precisely because of the greater advantage constituted for the Putchins by the simplicity of their spirit. They were kept straight by the quality of their ignorance—which was denser even than mine. It was a mistake in us, from the first, to have attempted to correct or to disguise ours. We should have waited simply to become good parrots, to learn our lesson—all on the spot here, so little of it is wanted—and squawk it off."

"Ah, 'squawk,' love—what a word to use about Him!"

"It isn't about Him—nothing's about Him. None of Them care tuppence about Him. The only thing They care about is this empty shell—or rather, for it isn't empty, the extraneous, preposterous stuffing of it."

"Preposterous?"—he made her stare with this as he had not yet done.

At sight of her look, however—the gleam, as it might have been, of a queer suspicion—he bent to her kindly and tapped her cheek. "Oh, it's all right. We *must* fall back on the Putchins. Do you remember what she said?—'They've made it so pretty now.' They *have* made it pretty, and it's a first-rate show. It's a first-rate show and a first-rate billet, and He was a first-rate poet, and you're a first-rate woman—to put up so sweetly, I mean, with my nonsense."

She appreciated his domestic charm and she justified that part of his tribute which concerned herself. "I don't care how much of your nonsense you talk to me, so long as you *keep* it all for me and don't treat *Them* to it."

"The pilgrims? No," he conceded—"it isn't fair to Them. They mean well."

"What complaint have we, after all, to make of Them so long as They don't break off bits—as They used, Miss Putchin told us, so awfully—to conceal about Their Persons? She broke them at least of that."

"Yes," Gedge mused again; "I wish awfully she hadn't!"

"You would like the relics destroyed, removed? That's all that's wanted!"

"There *are* no relics."

"There won't be any soon, unless you take care." But he was already laughing, and the talk was not dropped without his having patted her once more. An impression or two, however, remained with her from it, as he saw from a question she asked him on the morrow. "What did you mean yesterday about Miss Putchin's simplicity—its keeping her 'straight'? Do you mean mentally?"

Her "mentally" was rather portentous, but he practically confessed. "Well, it kept her up. I mean," he amended, laughing, "it kept her down."

It was really as if she had been a little uneasy. "You consider there's a danger of your being affected? You know what I mean. Of its going to your head. You do know," she insisted as he said nothing. "Through your caring for him so. You'd certainly be right in that case about its having been a mistake for you to plunge so deep." And then as his listening without reply, though with his look a little sad for her, might have denoted that, allowing for extravagance of statement, he saw there was something in it: "Give up your prowls. Keep it for daylight. Keep it for *Them*."

"Ah," he smiled, "if one could! My prowls," he added, "are what I most enjoy. They're the only time, as I've told you before, that I'm really with *Him*. Then I don't see the place. He isn't the place."

"I don't care for what you 'don't' see," she replied with vivacity; "the question is of what you do see."

Well, if it was, he waited before meeting it. "Do you know what I sometimes do?" And then as she waited too: "In the Birthroom there, when I look in late, I often put out my light. That makes it better."

"Makes what——?"

"Everything."

"What is it then you see in the dark?"

"Nothing!" said Morris Gedge.

"And what's the pleasure of that?"

"Well, what the American ladies say. It's so fascinating."

IV

The autumn was brisk, as Miss Putchin had told them it would be, but business naturally fell off with the winter months and the short days. There was rarely an hour indeed without a call of some sort, and they were never allowed to forget that they kept the shop in all the world, as they might say, where custom was least fluctuating. The seasons told on it, as they tell upon travel, but no other influence, consideration or convulsion to which the population of the globe is exposed. This population, never exactly in simultaneous hordes, but in a full, swift and steady stream, passed through the smoothly-working mill and went, in its variety of degrees duly impressed and edified, on its artless way. Gedge gave himself up, with much ingenuity of spirit, to trying to keep in relation with it; having even at moments, in the early time, glimpses of the chance that the impressions gathered from so rare an opportunity for contact with the general mind might prove as interesting as anything else in the connection. Types, classes, nationalities, manners, diversities of behaviour, modes of seeing, feeling, of expression, would pass before him and become for him, after a fashion, the experience of an untravelled man. His journeys had been short and saving, but poetic justice again seemed inclined to work for him in placing him just at the point in all Europe perhaps where the confluence of races was thickest. The theory, at any rate, carried him on, operating helpfully for the term of his anxious beginnings and gilding in a manner—it was the way he characterised the case to his wife—the somewhat stodgy gingerbread of their daily routine. They had not known many people, and their visiting-list was small—which made it again poetic justice that they should be visited on such a scale. They dressed and were at home, they were under arms and received, and except for the offer of refreshment—and Gedge had his view that there would eventually be a *buffet* farmed out to a great firm—their hospitality would have made them princely if mere hospitality ever did. Thus they were launched, and it was interesting, and from having been ready to drop, originally, with fatigue, they emerged even-winded and strong in the legs, as if they had had an Alpine holiday. This experience, Gedge opined, also represented, as a gain, a like seasoning of the spirit—by which he meant a certain command of impenetrable patience.

The patience was needed for the particular feature of the ordeal that, by the time the lively season was with them again, had disengaged itself as the sharpest—the immense assumption of veracities and sanctities, of the general soundness of the legend with which everyone arrived. He was well provided, certainly, for meeting it, and he gave all he had, yet he had sometimes the sense of a vague resentment on the part of his pilgrims at his not ladling out their fare with a bigger spoon. An irritation had begun to grumble in him during the comparatively idle months of winter when a pilgrim would turn up singly. The pious individual, entertained for the half-hour, had occasionally seemed to offer him the promise of beguilement or the semblance of a personal relation; it came back again to the few pleasant calls he had received in the course of a life almost void of social amenity. Sometimes he liked the person, the face, the speech: an educated man, a gentleman, not one of the herd; a graceful woman, vague, accidental, unconscious of him, but making him wonder, while he hovered, who she was. These chances represented for him light yearnings and faint flutters; they acted indeed, within him, in a special, an extraordinary way. He would have liked to talk with such stray companions, to talk with them *really*, to talk with them as he might have talked if he had met them where he couldn't meet them—at dinner, in the "world," on a visit at a country-house. Then he could have said—and about the shrine and the idol always—things he couldn't say now. The form in which his irritation first came to him was that of his feeling obliged to say to them—to the single visitor, even when sympathetic, quite as to the gaping group—the particular things, a dreadful dozen or so, that they expected. If he had thus arrived at characterising these things as dreadful the reason touches the very point that, for a while turning everything over, he kept dodging, not facing, trying to ignore. The point was that he was on his way to become two quite different persons, the public and the private, and yet that it would somehow have to be managed that these persons should live together. He was splitting into halves, un-mistakeably—he who, whatever else he had been, had at least always been so entire and, in his way, so solid. One of the halves, or perhaps even, since the split promised to be rather unequal, one of the quarters, was the keeper, the showman, the priest of the idol; the other piece was the poor unsuc-cessful honest man he had always been.

There were moments when he recognised this primary char-acter as he had never done before; when he in fact quite shook in his shoes at the idea that it perhaps had in reserve some supreme assertion of its identity. It was honest, verily, just by reason of the possibility. It was poor and unsuccessful because here it was just on the verge of quarrelling with its bread and butter. Salvation would be of course—the salvation of the showman—rigidly to *keep* it on the verge; not to let it, in other words, overpass by an inch. He might count on this, he said to himself, if there weren't any public—if there weren't thousands of people demanding of him what he was paid for. He saw the approach of the stage at which they would affect him, the thousands of people—and perhaps even more the earnest individual—as coming really to see if he were earning his wage. Wouldn't he soon begin to fancy them in league with the Body, practically deputed by it—given, no doubt, a kindled suspicion—to look in and report observations? It was the way he broke down with the lonely pilgrim that led to his first heart-searchings—broke down as to the courage required for damping an uncritical faith. What they all most wanted was to feel that everything was "just as it was"; only the shock of having to part with that vision was greater than any individual could bear unsupported. The bad moments were upstairs in the Birthroom, for here the forces pressing on the very edge assumed a dire intensity. The mere expression of eye, all-credulous, omnivorous and fairly moistening in the act, with which many persons gazed about, might eventually make it difficult for him to remain fairly civil. Often they came in pairs—sometimes one had come before—and then they explained to each other. He never in that case corrected; he listened, for the lesson of listening: after which he would remark to his wife that there was no end to what he was learning. He saw that if he should really ever break down it would be with her he would begin. He had given her hints and digs enough, but she was so inflamed with appreciation that she either didn't feel them or pretended not to understand.

This was the greater complication that, with the return of the spring and the increase of the public, her services were more required. She took the field with him, from an early hour; she was present with the party above while he kept an eye, and still more an ear, on the party below; and how could he know, he asked himself, what she might say to them and what she might suffer *Them* to say—or in other words, poor wretches, to believe—while removed from his control? Some day or other, and before too long, he couldn't but think, he must have the matter out with her—the matter, namely, of the *morality* of their position. The morality of women was special—he was getting lights on that. Isabel's conception of her office was to cherish and enrich the legend. It was already, the legend, very taking, but what was she there for but to make it more so? She certainly wasn't there to chill any natural piety. If it was all in the air—all in their "eye," as the vulgar might say—that He *had* been born in the Birthroom, where was the value of the sixpences they took? where the equivalent they had engaged to supply? "Oh dear, yes—just about *here*"; and she must tap the place with her foot. "Altered? Oh dear, no—save in a few trifling particulars; you see the place—and isn't that just the charm of it?—quite as *He* saw it. Very poor and homely, no doubt; but that's just what's so wonderful." He didn't want to hear her, and yet he didn't want to give her her head; he didn't want to make difficulties or to snatch the bread from her mouth. But he must none the less give her a warning before they had gone *too* far. That was the way, one evening in June, he put it to her; the affluence, with the finest weather, having lately been of the largest, and the crowd, all day, fairly gorged with the story. "We mustn't, you know, go *too* far."

The odd thing was that she had now ceased to be even conscious of what troubled him—she was so launched in her own career. "Too far for what?"

"To save our immortal souls. We mustn't, love, tell too many lies."

She looked at him with dire reproach. "Ah now, are you going to begin again?"

"I never *have* begun; I haven't wanted to worry you. But, you know, we don't know anything about it." And then as she stared, flushing: "About His having been born up there. About anything, really. Not the least little scrap that would weigh, in any other connection, as evidence. So don't rub it in so."

"Rub it in how?"

"That He *was* born——" But at sight of her face he only sighed. "Oh dear, oh dear!"

"Don't you think," she replied cuttingly, "that He was born anywhere?"

He hesitated—it was such an edifice to shake. "Well, we don't know. There's very little *to* know. He covered His tracks as no other human being has ever done."

She was still in her public costume and had not taken off the gloves that she made a point of wearing as a part of that uniform; she remembered how the rustling housekeeper in the Border castle, on whom she had begun by modelling herself, had worn them. She seemed official and slightly distant. "To cover His tracks. He must have had to exist. Have we got to give *that* up?"

"No, I don't ask you to give it up *yet*. But there's very little to go upon."

"And is that what I'm to tell Them in return for everything?"

Gedge waited—he walked about. The place was doubly still after the bustle of the day, and the summer evening rested on it as a blessing, making it, in its small state and ancientry, mellow and sweet. It was good to be there, and it would be good to stay. At the same time there was something incalculable in the effect on one's nerves of the great gregarious density. That was an attitude that had nothing to do with degrees and shades, the attitude of wanting all or nothing. And you couldn't talk things over with it. You could only do this with friends, and then but in cases where you were sure the friends wouldn't betray you. "Couldn't you adopt," he replied at last, "a slightly more discreet method? What we can say is that things have been *said*; that's all *we* have to do with. 'And is this really'—when they jam their umbrellas into the floor—'the very *spot* where He was born?' 'So it has, from a long time back, been described as being.' Couldn't one meet Them, to be decent a little, in some such way as that?"

She looked at him very hard. "Is that the way *you* meet them?"

"No; I've kept on lying—without scruple, without shame."

"Then why do you haul me up?"

"Because it has seemed to me that we might, like true companions, work it out a little together."

This was not strong, he felt, as, pausing with his hands in his pockets, he stood before her; and he knew it as weaker still after she had looked at him a minute. "Morris Gedge, I propose to be *your* true companion, and I've come here to stay. That's all I've got to say." It was not, however, for "You had better try yourself and see," she presently added. "Give the place, give the story away, by so much as a look, and—well, I'd allow you about nine days. Then you'd see."

He feigned, to gain time, an innocence. "They'd take it so ill?" And then, as she said nothing: "They'd turn and rend me? They'd tear me to pieces?"

But she wouldn't make a joke of it. "They wouldn't *have* it, simply."

"No—they wouldn't. That's what I say. They won't."

"You had better," she went on, "begin with Grant-Jackson. But even that isn't necessary. It would get to him, it would get to the Body, like wildfire."

"I see," said poor Gedge. And indeed for the moment he did see, while his companion followed up what she believed her advantage.

"Do you consider it's *all* a fraud?"

"Well, I grant you there was somebody. But the details are naught. The links are missing. The evidence—in particular about that room upstairs, in itself our Casa Santa—is *nil*. It was so awfully long ago." Which he knew again sounded weak.

"Of course it was awfully long ago—that's just the beauty and the interest. Tell Them, *tell* Them," she continued, "that the evidence is *nil*, and I'll tell them something else." She spoke it with such meaning that his face seemed to show a question, to which she was on the spot of replying "I'll tell them that you're a——" She stopped, however, changing it. "I'll them exactly the opposite. And I'll find out what you say—it won't take long—to do it. If we tell different stories, *that* possibly may save us."

"I see what you mean. It would perhaps, as an oddity, have a success of curiosity. It might become a draw. Still, they but want broad masses." And he looked at her sadly. "You're no more than one of Them."

"If it's being no more than one of them to love it," she answered, "then I certainly am. And I am not ashamed of my company."

"To love *what*?" said Morris Gedge.

"To love to think He was born there."

"You think too much. It's bad for you." He turned away with his chronic moan. But it was without losing what she called after him.

"I decline to let the place down." And what was there indeed to say? They *were* there to keep it up.

V

He kept it up through the summer, but with the queerest consciousness, at times, of the want of proportion between his secret rage and the spirit of those from whom the friction came. He said to himself—so sore as his sensibility had grown—that They were gregariously ferocious at the very time he was seeing Them as individually mild. He said to himself that They were mild only because *he* was—he flattered himself that he was divinely so, considering what he might be; and that he should, as his wife had warned him, soon enough have news of it were he to deflect by a hair's breadth from the line traced for him. *That* was the collective fatuity—that it was capable of turning, on the instant, both to a general and to a particular resentment. Since the least breath of discrimination would get him the sack without mercy, it was absurd, he reflected, to speak of his discomfort as light. He was gagged, he was goaded, as in omnivorous companies he doubtless sometimes showed by a strange silent glare. They would get him the sack for that as well, if he didn't look out; therefore wasn't it in effect ferocity when you mightn't even hold your tongue? They wouldn't let you off with silence— They insisted on your committing yourself. It was the pound of flesh—They would have it; so under his coat he bled. But a wondrous peace, by exception, dropped on him one afternoon at the end of August. The pressure had, as usual, been high, but it had diminished with the fall of day, and the place was empty before the hour for closing. Then it was that, within a few minutes of this hour, there presented themselves a pair of pilgrims to whom in the ordinary course he would have remarked that they were, to his regret, too late. He was to wonder afterwards why the course had, at sight of the visitors—a gentleman and a lady, appealing and fairly young—shown for him as other than ordinary; the consequence sprang doubtless from something rather fine and unnameable, something, for instance, in the tone of the young man, or in the light of his eye, after hearing the statement on the subject of the hour. "Yes, we know it's late; but it's just, I'm afraid, *because* of that. We've had rather a notion of escaping the crowd—as, I suppose, you mostly have one now; and it was really on the chance of finding you alone——!"

These things the young man said before being quite admitted, and they were words that any one might have spoken who had not taken the trouble to be punctual or who desired, a little ingratiatingly, to force the door. Gedge even guessed at the sense that might lurk in them, the hint of a special tip if the point were stretched. There were no tips, he had often thanked his stars, at the Birthplace; there was the charged fee and nothing more; everything else was out of order, to the relief of a palm not formed by nature for a scoop. Yet in spite of everything, in spite especially of the almost audible chink of the gentleman's sovereigns, which might in another case exactly have put him out, he presently found himself, in the Birthroom, access to which he had gracefully enough granted, almost treating the visit as personal and private. The reason—well, the reason would have been, if anywhere, in something naturally persuasive on the part of the couple, unless it had been, rather, again, in the way the young man, once he was in the place, met the caretaker's expression of face, held it a moment and seemed to wish to sound it. That they were Americans was promptly clear, and Gedge could very nearly have told what kind; he had arrived at the point of distinguishing kinds, though the difficulty might have been with him now that the case before him was rare. He saw it, in fact, suddenly, in the light of the golden midland evening, which reached them through low old windows, saw it with a rush of feeling, unexpected and smothered, that made him wish for a moment to keep it before him as a case of inordinate happiness. It made him feel old, shabby, poor, but he watched it no less intensely for its doing so. They were children of fortune, of the greatest, as it might seem to Morris Gedge, and they were of course lately married; the husband, smooth-faced and soft, but resolute and fine, several years older than the wife, and the wife vaguely, delicately, irregularly, but mercilessly pretty. Somehow, the world was theirs; they gave the person who took the sixpences at the Birthplace such a sense of the high luxury of freedom as he had never had. The thing was that the world was theirs not simply because they had money—he had seen rich people enough—but because they could in a supreme degree think and feel and say what they liked. They had a nature and a culture, a tradition, a facility of some sort—and all producing in them an effect of positive beauty—that gave a light to their liberty and an ease to their tone. These things moreover suffered nothing from the fact that they happened to be in mourning; this was probably worn for some lately-deceased opulent father, or some delicate mother who would be sure to have been a part of the source of the beauty, and it affected Gedge, in the gathered twilight and at his odd crisis, as the very uniform of their distinction.

He couldn't quite have said afterwards by what steps the point had been reached, but it had become at the end of five minutes a part of their presence in the Birthroom, a part of the young man's look, a part of the charm of the moment, and a part, above all, of a strange sense within him of "Now or never!" that Gedge had suddenly, thrillingly, let himself go. He had not been definitely conscious of drifting to it; he had been, for that, too conscious merely of thinking how different, in all their range, were such a united couple from another united couple that he knew. They were everything he and his wife were not; this was more than anything else the lesson at first of their talk. Thousands of couples of whom the same was true certainly had passed before him, but none of whom it was true with just that engaging intensity. This was *because* of their transcendent freedom; that was what, at the end of five minutes, he saw it all come back to. The husband had been there at some earlier time, and he had his impression, which he wished now to make his wife share. But he already,

Gedge could see, had not concealed it from her. A pleasant irony, in fine, our friend seemed to taste in the air—he who had not yet felt free to taste his own.

"I think you weren't here four years ago"—that was what the young man had almost begun by remarking. Gedge liked his remembering it, liked his frankly speaking to him; all the more that he had given him, as it were, no opening. He had let them look about below, and then had taken them up, but without words, without the usual showman's song, of which he would have been afraid. The visitors didn't ask for it; the young man had taken the matter out of his hands by himself dropping for the benefit of the young woman a few detached remarks. What Gedge felt, oddly, was that these remarks were not inconsiderate of him; he had heard others, both of the priggish order and the crude, that might have been called so. And as the young man had not been aided to this cognition of him as new, it already began to make for them a certain common ground. The ground became immense when the visitor presently added with a smile: "There was a good lady, I recollect, who had a great deal to say."

It was the gentleman's smile that had done it; the irony *was* there. "Ah, there has been a great deal said." And Gedge's look at his interlocutor doubtless showed his sense of being sounded. It was extraordinary of course that a perfect stranger should have guessed the travail of his spirit, should have caught the gleam of his inner commentary. That probably, in spite of him, leaked out of his poor old eyes. "Much of it, in such places as this," he heard himself adding, "is of course said very irresponsibly." *Such places as this!*—he winced at the words as soon as he had uttered them.

There was no wincing, however, on the part of his pleasant companions. "Exactly so; the whole thing becomes a sort of stiff, smug convention, like a dressed-up sacred doll in a Spanish church—which you're a monster if you touch."

"A monster," said Gedge, meeting his eyes.

The young man smiled, but he thought he looked at him a little harder. "A blasphemer."

"A blasphemer."

It seemed to do his visitor good—he certainly *was* looking at him harder. Detached as he was he was interested—he was at least amused. "Then you don't claim, or at any rate you don't insist——? I mean you personally."

He had an identity for him, Gedge felt, that he couldn't have had for a Briton, and the impulse was quick in our friend to testify to this perception. "I don't insist to *you*."

The young man laughed. "It really—I assure you if I may—wouldn't do any good. I'm too awfully interested."

"Do you mean," his wife lightly inquired, "in—a—pulling it down? That is in what you've said to me."

"Has he said to you," Gedge intervened, though quaking a little, "that he would like to pull it down?"

She met, in her free sweetness, this directness with such a charm! "Oh, perhaps not quite the *house*——!"

"Good. You see we live on it—I mean *we* people."

The husband had laughed, but had now so completely ceased to look about him that there seemed nothing left for him but to talk avowedly with the caretaker. "I'm interested," he explained, "in what, I think, is *the* interesting thing—or at all events the eternally tormenting one. The fact of the abyssmally little that, in proportion, we know."

"In proportion to what?" his companion asked.

"Well, to what there must have been—to what in fact there *is*—to wonder about. That's the interest; its immense. He escapes us like a thief at night, carrying off—well, carrying off everything. And people pretend to catch Him like a flown canary, over whom you can close your hand and put Him back. He won't *go* back; he won't *come* back. He's not"—the young man laughed—"such a fool! It makes Him the happiest of all great men."

He had begun by speaking to his wife, but had ended, with his friendly, his easy, his indescribable competence, for Gedge—poor Gedge who quite held his breath and who felt, in the most unexpected way, that he had somehow never been in such good society. The young wife, who for herself meanwhile had continued to look about, sighed out, smiled out—Gedge couldn't have told which—her little answer to these remarks. "It's rather a pity, you know, that He *isn't* here. I mean as Goethe's at Weimar. For Goethe *is* at Weimar."

"Yes, my dear; that's Goethe's bad luck. There he sticks. *This* man isn't anywhere. I defy you to catch Him."

"Why not say, beautifully," the young woman laughed, "that, like the wind, He's everywhere?"

It wasn't of course the tone of discussion, it was the tone of joking, though of better joking, Gedge seemed to feel, and more within his own appreciation, than he had ever listened to; and this was precisely why the young man could go on without the effect of irritation, answering his wife but still with eyes for their companion. "I'll be hanged if He's *here!*"

It was almost as if he were taken—that is, struck and rather held—by their companion's unruffled state, which they hadn't meant to ruffle, but which suddenly presented its interest, perhaps even projected its light. The gentleman didn't know, Gedge was afterwards to say to himself, how that hypocrite was inwardly all of a tremble, how it seemed to him that his fate was being literally pulled down on his head. He was trembling for the moment certainly too much to speak; abject he might be, but he didn't want his voice to have the absurdity of a quaver. And the young woman—charming creature!—still had another word. It was for the guardian of the spot, and she made it, in her way, delightful. They had remained in the Holy of Holies, and she had been looking for a minute, with a ruefulness just marked enough to be pretty, at the queer old floor. "Then if you say it *wasn't* in this room He was born—well, what's the use?"

"What's the use of what?" her husband asked. "The use, you mean, of our coming here? Why, the place is charming in itself. And it's also interesting," he added to Gedge, "to know how you get on."

Gedge looked at him a moment in silence, but he answered the young woman first. If poor Isabel, he was thinking, could only have been like that!—not as to youth, beauty, arrangement of hair or picturesque grace of hat—these things he didn't mind; but as to sympathy, facility, light perceptive, and yet not cheap, detachment! "I don't say it wasn't—but I don't say it *was.*"

"Ah, but doesn't that," she returned, "come very much to the same thing? And don't They want also to see where He had His dinner and where He had His tea?"

"They want everything," said Morris Gedge. "They want to see where He hung up His hat and where He kept His boots and where His mother boiled her pot."

"But if you don't show them——?"

"They show *me*. It's in all their little books."

"You mean," the husband asked, "that you've only to hold your tongue?"

"I try to," said Gedge.

"Well," his visitor smiled, "I see you *can*."

Gedge hesitated. "I can't."

"Oh, well," said his friend, "what does it matter?"

"I do speak," he continued. "I can't sometimes not."

"Then how do you get on?"

Gedge looked at him more abjectly, to his own sense, than he had ever looked at anyone—even at Isabel when she frightened him. "I don't get on. I speak," he said, "since I've spoken to *you*."

"Oh, *we* shan't hurt you!" the young man reassuringly laughed.

The twilight meanwhile had sensibly thickened; the end of the visit was indicated. They turned together out of the upper room, and came down the narrow stair. The words just exchanged might have been felt as producing an awkwardness which the young woman gracefully felt the impulse to dissipate. "You must rather wonder why we've come." And it was the first note, for Gedge, of a further awkwardness—as if he had definitely heard it make the husband's hand, in a full pocket, begin to fumble.

It was even a little awkwardly that the husband still held off. "Oh, we like it as it is. There's always *something*." With which they had approached the door of egress.

"What is there, please?" asked Morris Gedge, not yet opening the door, as he would fain have kept the pair on, and conscious only for a moment after he had spoken that his question was just having, for the young man, too dreadfully wrong a sound. This personage wondered, yet feared, had evidently for some minutes been asking himself; so that, with his preoccupation, the caretaker's words had represented to him, inevitably, "What is there, please, for *me*?" Gedge already knew, with it, moreover, that he wasn't stopping him in time. He had put his question, to show he himself wasn't afraid, and he must have had in consequence, he was subsequently to reflect, a lamentable air of waiting.

The visitor's hand came out. "I hope I may take the liberty——?" What afterwards happened our friend scarcely knew, for it fell into a slight confusion, the confusion of a queer gleam of gold—a sovereign fairly thrust at him; of a quick, almost violent motion on his own part, which, to make the matter worse, might well have sent the money rolling on the floor; and then of marked blushes all round, and a sensible embarrassment; producing indeed, in turn, rather oddly, and ever so quickly, an increase of communion. It was as if the young man had offered him money to make up to him for having, as it were, led him on, and then, perceiving the mistake, but liking him the better for his refusal, had wanted to obliterate this aggravation of his original wrong. He had done so, presently, while Gedge got the door open, by saying the best thing he could, and by saying it frankly and gaily. "Luckily it doesn't at all affect the *work*!"

The small town-street, quiet and empty in the summer eventide, stretched to right and left, with a gabled and timbered house or two, and fairly seemed to have cleared itself to congruity with the historic void over which our friends, lingering an instant to converse, looked at each other. The young wife, rather, looked about a moment at all there wasn't to be seen, and then, before Gedge had found a reply to her husband's remark, uttered, evidently in the interest of conciliation, a little question of her own that she tried to make earnest. "It's our unfortunate ignorance, you mean, that doesn't?"

"Unfortunate or fortunate. I like it so," said the husband. "'The play's the thing.' Let the author alone."

Gedge, with his key on his forefinger, leaned against the doorpost, took in the stupid little street, and was sorry to see them go—they seemed so to abandon him. "That's just what They won't do—not let *me* do. It's all I want—to let the author alone. Practically"—he felt himself getting the last of his chance—"there *is* no author; that is for us to deal with. There are all the immortal people—*in* the work; but there's nobody else."

"Yes," said the young man—"that's what it comes to. There should really, to clear the matter up, be no such Person."

"As you say," Gedge returned, "it's what it comes to. There *is* no such Person."

The evening air listened, in the warm, thick midland stillness, while the wife's little cry rang out. "But *wasn't* there——?"

"There was somebody," said Gedge, against the doorpost. "But They've killed Him. And, dead as He is, They keep it up, They do it over again, They kill Him every day."

He was aware of saying this so grimly—more grimly than he wished—that his companions exchanged a glance and even perhaps looked as if they felt him extravagant. That was the way, really, Isabel had warned him all the others would be looking if he should talk to Them as he talked to *her*. He liked, however, for that matter, to hear how he should sound when pronounced incapable through deterioration of the brain. "Then if there's no author, if there's nothing to be said but that there isn't anybody," the young woman smilingly asked, "why in the world should there be a house?"

"There shouldn't," said Morris Gedge.

Decidedly, yes, he affected the young man. "Oh, I don't say, mind you, that you should pull it down!"

"Then where would you *go*?" their companion sweetly inquired.

"That's what my wife asks," Gedge replied.

"Then keep it up, keep it up!" And the husband held out his hand.

"That's what my wife says," Gedge went on as he shook it.

The young woman, charming creature, emulated the other visitor; she offered their remarkable friend her handshake. "Then mind your wife."

The poor man faced her gravely. "I would if she were such a wife as you!"

VI

It had made for him, all the same, an immense difference; it had given him an extraordinary lift, so that a certain sweet after-taste of his freedom might, a couple of months later, have been suspected of aiding to produce for him another, and

really a more considerable, adventure. It was an odd way to
think of it, but he had been, to his imagination, for twenty
minutes in good society—that being the term that best described for him the company of people to whom he hadn't to
talk, as he further phrased it, rot. It was his title to society
that he had, in his doubtless awkward way, affirmed; and the
difficulty was just that, having affirmed it, he couldn't take
back the affirmation. Few things had happened to him in life,
that is few that were agreeable, but at least *this* had, and he
wasn't so constructed that he could go on as if it hadn't. It
was going on as if it had, however, that landed him, alas! in
the situation unmistakeably marked by a visit from Grant-
Jackson, late one afternoon toward the end of October. This
had been the hour of the call of the young Americans. Every
day that hour had come round something of the deep throb
of it, the successful secret, woke up; but the two occasions
were, of a truth, related only by being so intensely opposed.
The secret had been successful in that he had said nothing of
it to Isabel, who, occupied in their own quarter while the
incident lasted, had neither heard the visitors arrive nor seen
them depart. It was on the other hand scarcely successful in
guarding itself from indirect betrayals. There were two persons in the world, at least, who felt as he did; they were persons, also, who had treated him, benignly, as feeling as *they*
did, who had been ready in fact to overflow in gifts as a sign
of it, and though they were now off in space they were still
with him sufficiently in spirit to make him play, as it were,
with the sense of their sympathy. This in turn made him, as
he was perfectly aware, more than a shade or two reckless, so
that, in his reaction from that gluttony of the public for false
facts which had from the first tormented him, he fell into the
habit of sailing, as he would have said, too near the wind, or
in other words—all in presence of the people—of washing his
hands of the legend. He had crossed the line—he knew it; he
had struck wild—They drove him to it; he had substituted,
by a succession of uncontrollable profanities, an attitude that
couldn't be understood for an attitude that but too evidently
had been.

This was of course the franker line, only he hadn't taken it,
alas! for frankness—hadn't in the least, really, *taken* it, but had

been simply himself caught up and disposed of by it, hurled by his fate against the bedizened walls of the temple, quite in the way of a priest possessed to excess of the god, or, more vulgarly, that of a blind bull in a china-shop—an animal to which he often compared himself. He had let himself fatally go, in fine, just for irritation, for rage, having, in his predicament, nothing at all to do with frankness—a luxury reserved for quite other situations. It had always been his sentiment that one lived to learn; he had learned something every hour of his life, though people mostly never knew what, in spite of its having generally been—hadn't it?—at somebody's expense. What he was at present continually learning was the sense of a form of words heretofore so vain—the famous "false position" that had so often helped out a phrase. One used names in that way without knowing what they were worth; then of a sudden, one fine day, their meaning was bitter in the mouth. This was a truth with the relish of which his fireside hours were occupied, and he was quite conscious that a man was exposed who looked so perpetually as if something had disagreed with him. The look to be worn at the Birthplace was properly the beatific, and when once it had fairly been missed by those who took it for granted, who, indeed, paid sixpence for it—like the table-wine in provincial France, it was *compris*—one would be sure to have news of the remark.

News accordingly was what Gedge had been expecting— and what he knew, above all, had been expected by his wife, who had a way of sitting at present as with an ear for a certain knock. She didn't watch him, didn't follow him about the house, at the public hours, to spy upon his treachery; and that could touch him even though her averted eyes went through him more than her fixed. Her mistrust was so perfectly expressed by her manner of showing she trusted that he never felt so nervous, never so tried to keep straight, as when she most let him alone. When the crowd thickened and they had of necessity to receive together he tried himself to get off by allowing her as much as possible the word. When people appealed to him he turned to her—and with more of ceremony than their relation warranted: he couldn't help *this* either, if it seemed ironic—as to the person most concerned or most competent. He flattered himself at these moments that no one would have guessed her being his wife; especially as, to do her justice, she met his manner with a wonderful grim bravado— grim, so to say, for himself, grim by its outrageous cheerful- ness for the simple-minded. The lore she *did* produce for them, the associations of the sacred spot that she developed, multiplied, embroidered; the things in short she said and the stupendous way she said them! She wasn't a bit ashamed; for why need virtue be ever ashamed? It *was* virtue, for it put bread into his mouth—he meanwhile, on his side, taking it out of hers. He had seen Grant-Jackson, on the October day, in the Birthplace itself—the right setting of course for such an interview; and what occurred was that, precisely, when the scene had ended and he had come back to their own sitting- room, the question she put to him for information was: "Have you settled it that I'm to starve?"

She had for a long time said nothing to him so straight— which was but a proof of her real anxiety; the straightness of Grant-Jackson's visit, following on the very slight sinuosity of a note shortly before received from him, made tension show for what it was. By this time, really, however, his decision had been taken; the minutes elapsing between his reappearance at the domestic fireside and his having, from the other threshold, seen Grant-Jackson's broad, well-fitted back, the back of a banker and a patriot, move away, had, though few, presented themselves to him as supremely critical. They formed, as it were, the hinge of his door, that door actually ajar so as to show him a possible fate beyond it, but which, with his hand, in a spasm, thus tightening on the knob, he might either open wide or close partly and altogether. He stood, in the autumn dusk, in the little museum that constituted the vestibule of the temple, and there, as with a concentrated push at the crank of a windlass, he brought himself round. The portraits on the walls seemed vaguely to watch for it; it was in their august presence—kept dimly august, for the moment, by Grant-Jackson's impressive check of his application of a match to the vulgar gas—that the great man had uttered, as if it said all, his "You know, my dear fellow, really——!" He had man- aged it with the special tact of a fat man, always, when there *was* any, very fine; he had got the most out of the time, the place, the setting, all the little massed admonitions and symbols; confronted there with his victim on the spot that he took occasion to name to him afresh as, to *his* piety and patriotism, the most sacred on earth, he had given it to be understood that in the first place he was lost in amazement and that in the second he expected a single warning now to suffice. Not to insist too much moreover on the question of gratitude, he would let his remonstrance rest, if need be, solely on the question of taste. *As* a matter of taste alone——! But he was surely not to be obliged to follow that up. Poor Gedge indeed would have been sorry to oblige him, for he saw it was precisely to the atrocious taste of unthankfulness that the allusion was made. When he said he wouldn't dwell on what the fortunate occupant of the post owed him for the stout battle originally fought on his behalf, he simply meant he *would*. That was his tact—which, with everything else that had been mentioned, in the scene, to help, really had the ground to itself. The day *had* been when Gedge couldn't have thanked him enough—though he had thanked him, he considered, almost fulsomely—and nothing, nothing that he could coherently or reputably name, had happened since then. From the moment he was pulled up, in short, he had no case, and if he exhibited, instead of one, only hot tears in his eyes, the mystic gloom of the temple either prevented his friend from seeing them or rendered it possible that they stood for remorse. He had dried them, with the pads formed by the base of his bony thumbs, before he went in to Isabel. This was the more fortunate as, in spite of her inquiry, prompt and pointed, he but moved about the room looking at her hard. Then he stood before the fire a little with his hands behind him and his coat-tails divided, quite as the person in permanent possession. It was an indication his wife appeared to take in; but she put nevertheless presently another question. "You object to telling me what he said?"

"He said 'You know, my dear fellow, really——!'"

"And is that all?"

"Practically. Except that I'm a thankless beast."

"Well!" she responded, not with dissent.

"You mean that I *am*?"

"Are those the words he used?" she asked with a scruple.

Gedge continued to think. "The words he used were that I give away the Show and that, from several sources, it has come round to Them."

"As of course a baby would have known!" And then as her husband said nothing: "Were *those* the words he used?"

"Absolutely. He couldn't have used better ones."

"Did he call it," Mrs. Gedge inquired, "the 'Show'?"

"Of course he did. The Biggest on Earth."

She winced, looking at him hard—she wondered, but only for a moment. "Well, it *is*."

"Then it's something," Gedge went on, "to have given *that* away. But," he added, "I've taken it back."

"You mean you've been convinced?"

"I mean I've been scared."

"At last, at last!" she gratefully breathed.

"Oh, it was easily done. It was only two words. But here I am."

Her face was now less hard for him. "And what two words?"

" 'You know, Mr. Gedge, that it simply won't do.' That was all. But it was the way such a man says them."

"I'm glad, then," Mrs. Gedge frankly averred, "that he *is* such a man. How did you ever think it *could* do?"

"Well, it was my critical sense. I didn't ever know I had one—till They came and (by putting me here) waked it up in me. Then I had, somehow, don't you see? to live with it; and I seemed to feel that, somehow or other, giving it time and in the long run, it might, it *ought* to, come out on top of the heap. Now that's where, he says, it simply won't do. So I must put it—I *have* put it—at the bottom."

"A very good place, then, for a critical sense!" And Isabel, more placidly now, folded her work. "*If*, that is, you can only keep it there. If it doesn't struggle up again."

"It can't struggle." He was still before the fire, looking round at the warm, low room, peaceful in the lamplight, with the hum of the kettle for the ear, with the curtain drawn over the leaded casement, a short moreen curtain artfully chosen by Isabel for the effect of the olden time, its virtue of letting the light within show ruddy to the street. "It's dead," he went on; "I killed it just now."

He spoke, really, so that she wondered. "Just now?"

"There in the other place—I strangled it, poor thing, in the dark. If you'll go out and see, there must be blood. Which, indeed," he added, "on an altar of sacrifice, is all right. But the place is forever spattered."

"I don't want to go out and see." She rested her locked hands on the needlework folded on her knee, and he knew, with her eyes on him, that a look he had seen before was in her face. "You're off your head you know, my dear, in a way." Then, however, more cheeringly: "It's a good job it hasn't been too late."

"Too late to get it under?"

"Too late for Them to give you the second chance that I thank God you accept."

"Yes, if it *had* been——!" And he looked away as through the ruddy curtain and into the chill street. Then he faced her again. "I've scarcely got over my fright yet. I mean," he went on, "for you."

"And I mean for *you*. Suppose what you had come to announce to me now were that we had *got* the sack. How should I enjoy, do you think, seeing you turn out? Yes, out *there*!" she added as his eyes again moved from their little warm circle to the night of early winter on the other side of the pane, to the rare, quick footsteps, to the closed doors, to the curtains drawn like their own, behind which the small flat town, intrinsically dull, was sitting down to supper.

He stiffened himself as he warmed his back; he held up his head, shaking himself a little as if to shake the stoop out of his shoulders, but he had to allow she was right. "What would have become of us?"

"What indeed? We should have begged our bread—or I should be taking in washing."

He was silent a little. "I'm too old. I should have begun sooner."

"Oh, God forbid!" she cried.

"The pinch," he pursued, "is that I can do nothing else."

"Nothing whatever!" she agreed with elation.

"Whereas here—if I cultivate it—I perhaps *can* still lie. But I must cultivate it."

"Oh, you old dear!" And she got up to kiss him.

"I'll do my best," he said.

VII

"Do you remember us?" the gentleman asked and smiled—with the lady beside him smiling too; speaking so much less as an earnest pilgrim or as a tiresome tourist than as an old acquaintance. It was history repeating itself as Gedge had somehow never expected, with almost everything the same except that the evening was now a mild April-end, except that the visitors had put off mourning and showed all their bravery—besides showing, as he doubtless did himself, though so differently, for a little older; except, above all, that—oh, seeing them again suddenly affected him as not a bit the thing he would have thought it. "We're in England again, and we were near; I've a brother at Oxford with whom we've been spending a day, and we thought we'd come over." So the young man pleasantly said while our friend took in the queer fact that he must himself seem to them rather coldly to gape. They had come in the same way, at the quiet close; another August had passed, and this was the second spring; the Birthplace, given the hour, was about to suspend operations till the morrow; the last lingerer had gone, and the fancy of the visitors was, once more, for a look round by themselves. This represented surely no greater presumption than the terms on which they had last parted with him seemed to warrant; so that if he did inconsequently stare it was just in fact because he was so supremely far from having forgotten them. But the sight of the pair luckily had a double effect, and the first precipitated the second—the second being really his sudden vision that everything perhaps depended for him on his recognising no complication. He must go straight on, since it was what had for more than a year now so handsomely answered; he must brazen it out consistently, since that only was what his dignity was at last reduced to. He mustn't be afraid in one way any more than he had been in another; besides which it came over him with a force that made him flush that their visit, in its essence, must have been for himself. It was good society again, and *they* were the same. It wasn't for him therefore to behave as if he couldn't meet them.

These deep vibrations, on Gedge's part, were as quick as they were deep; they came in fact all at once, so that his response, his declaration that it was all right—"Oh, *rather*; the hour doesn't matter for *you*!"—had hung fire but an instant; and when they were within and the door closed behind them, within the twilight of the temple, where, as before, the votive offerings glimmered on the walls, he drew the long breath of one who might, by a self-betrayal, have done something too dreadful. For what had brought them back was not, indubitably, the sentiment of the shrine itself—since he knew their sentiment; but their intelligent interest in the queer case of the priest. Their call was the tribute of curiosity, of sympathy, of a compassion really, as such things went, exquisite—a tribute *to* that queerness which entitled them to the frankest welcome. They had wanted, for the generous wonder of it, to see how he was getting on, how such a man in such a place *could*; and they had doubtless more than half expected to see the door opened by somebody who had succeeded him. Well, somebody *had*—only with a strange equivocation; as they would have, poor things, to make out for themselves, an embarrassment as to which he pitied them. Nothing could have been more odd, but verily it was this troubled vision of their possible bewilderment, and this compunctious view of such a return for their amenity, that practically determined for him his tone. The lapse of the months had but made their name familiar to him; they had on the other occasion inscribed it, among the thousand names, in the current public register, and he had since then, for reasons of his own, reasons of feeling, again and again turned back to it. It was nothing in itself; it told him nothing—"Mr. and Mrs. B. D. Hayes, New York"— one of those American labels that were just like every other American label and that were, precisely, the most remarkable thing about people reduced to achieving an identity in such other ways. They could be Mr. and Mrs. B. D. Hayes and yet they could be, with all presumptions missing—well, what these callers were. It had quickly enough indeed cleared the situation a little further that his friends had absolutely, the

other time, as it came back to him, warned him of his original
danger, their anxiety about which had been the last note
sounded between them. What he was afraid of, with this reminiscence, was that, finding him still safe, they would, the next
thing, definitely congratulate him and perhaps even, no less
candidly, ask him how he had managed. It was with the sense
of nipping some such inquiry in the bud that, losing no time
and holding himself with a firm grip, he began, on the spot,
downstairs, to make plain to them how he had managed. He
averted the question in short by the assurance of his answer.
"Yes, yes, I'm still here; I suppose it *is* in a manner to one's
profit that one does, such as it is, one's best." He did his best
on the present occasion, did it with the gravest face he had
ever worn and a soft serenity that was like a large damp sponge
passed over their previous meeting—over everything in it, that
is, but the fact of its pleasantness.

"We stand here, you see, in the old living-room, happily
still to be reconstructed in the mind's eye, in spite of the
havoc of time, which we have fortunately, of late years, been
able to arrest. It was of course rude and humble, but it must
have been snug and quaint, and we have at least the pleasure
of knowing that the tradition in respect to the features that
do remain is delightfully uninterrupted. Across that threshold
He habitually passed; through those low windows, in childhood, He peered out into the world that He was to make so
much happier by the gift to it of His genius; over the boards
of this floor—that is over *some* of them, for we mustn't be
carried away!—his little feet often pattered; and the beams of
this ceiling (we must really in some places take care of *our*
heads!) he endeavoured, in boyish strife, to jump up and
touch. It's not often that in the early home of genius and
renown the whole tenor of existence is laid so bare, not often
that we are able to retrace, from point to point and from step
to step, its connection with objects, with influences—to build
it round again with the little solid facts out of which it sprang.
This, therefore, I need scarcely remind you, is what makes the
small space between these walls—so modest to measurement,
so insignificant of aspect—unique on all the earth. *There is
nothing like it,*" Morris Gedge went on, insisting as solemnly
and softly, for his bewildered hearers, as over a pulpit-edge;

"there is nothing at all like it anywhere in the world. There is nothing, only reflect, for the combination of greatness, and, as we venture to say, of intimacy. You may find elsewhere perhaps absolutely fewer changes, but where shall you find a *presence* equally diffused, uncontested and undisturbed? Where in particular shall you find, on the part of the abiding spirit, an equally towering eminence? You may find elsewhere eminence of a considerable order, but where shall you find *with* it, don't you see, changes, after all, so few, and the contemporary element caught so, as it were, in the very fact?" His visitors, at first confounded, but gradually spellbound, were still gaping with the universal gape—wondering, he judged, into what strange pleasantry he had been suddenly moved to break out, and yet beginning to see in him an intention beyond a joke, so that they started, at this point, almost jumped, when, by as rapid a transition, he made, toward the old fireplace, a dash that seemed to illustrate, precisely, the act of eager catching. "It is in this old chimney corner, the quaint inglenook of our ancestors—just there in the far angle, where His little stool was placed, and where, I dare say, if we could look close enough, we should find the hearthstone scraped with His little feet—that we see the inconceivable child gazing into the blaze of the old oaken logs and making out there pictures and stories, see Him conning, with curly bent head, His well-worn hornbook, or poring over some scrap of an ancient ballad, some page of some such rudely bound volume of chronicles as lay, we may be sure, in His father's window-seat."

It was, he even himself felt at this moment, wonderfully done; no auditors, for all his thousands, had ever yet so inspired him. The odd, slightly alarmed shyness in the two faces, as if in a drawing-room, in their "good society," exactly, some act incongruous, something grazing the indecent, had abruptly been perpetrated, the painful reality of which faltered before coming home—the visible effect on his friends, in fine, wound him up as to the sense that *they* were worth the trick. It came of itself now—he had got it so by heart; but perhaps really it had never come so well, with the staleness so disguised, the interest so renewed and the clerical unction, demanded by the priestly character, so successfully distilled. Mr. Hayes of New York had more than once looked at his wife, and Mrs. Hayes of New York had more than once looked at her husband—only, up to now, with a stolen glance, with eyes it had not been easy to detach from the remarkable countenance by the aid of which their entertainer held them. At present, however, after an exchange less furtive, they ventured on a sign that they had not been appealed to in vain. "Charming, charming, Mr. Gedge!" Mr. Hayes broke out; "we feel that we've caught you in the mood."

His wife hastened to assent—it eased the tension. "It *would* be quite the way; except," she smiled, "that you'd be too dangerous. You've really a genius!"

Gedge looked at her hard, but yielding no inch, even though she touched him there at a point of consciousness that quivered. This was the prodigy for him, and had been, the year through—that he did it all, he found, easily, did it better than he had done anything else in his life; with so high and broad an effect, in truth, an inspiration so rich and free, that his poor wife now, literally, had been moved more than once to fresh fear. She had had her bad moments, he knew, after taking the measure of his new direction—moments of re-adjusted suspicion in which she wondered if he had not simply embraced another, a different perversity. There would be more than one fashion of giving away the show, and wasn't *this* perhaps a question of giving it away by excess? He could dish them by too much romance as well as by too little; she had not hitherto fairly apprehended that there might *be* too much. It was a way like another, at any rate, of reducing the place to the absurd; which reduction, if he didn't look out, would reduce *them* again to the prospect of the streets, and this time surely without an appeal. It all depended, indeed—he knew she knew that—on how much Grant-Jackson and the others, how much the Body, in a word, would take. He knew she knew what he himself held it would take—that he considered no limit could be drawn to the quantity. They simply wanted it piled up, and so did everybody else; wherefore, if no one reported him, as before, why were They to be uneasy? It was in consequence of idiots brought to reason that he had been dealt with before; but as there was now no form of idiocy that he didn't systematically flatter, goading it on really to its *own* private doom, who was ever to pull the string of the guillotine? The axe was in the air—yes; but in a world gorged to satiety there were no revolutions. And it had been vain for Isabel to ask if the other thunder-growl also hadn't come out of the blue. There was actually proof positive that the winds were now at rest. How could they be more so?—he appealed to the receipts. These were golden days—the show had never so flourished. So he had argued, so he was arguing still—and, it had to be owned, with every appearance in his favour. Yet if he inwardly winced at the tribute to his plausibility rendered by his flushed friends, this was because he felt in it the real ground of his optimism. The charming woman before him acknowledged his "genius" as he himself had had to do. He had been surprised at his facility until he had grown used to it. Whether or no he had, as a fresh menace to his future, found a new perversity, he had found a vocation much older, evidently, than he had at first been prepared to recognise. He had done himself injustice. He liked to be brave because it came so easy; he could measure it off by the yard. It was in the Birthroom, above all, that he continued to do this, having ushered up his companions without, as he was still more elated to feel, the turn of a hair. She might take it as she liked, but he had had the lucidity—all, that is, for his own safety—to meet without the grace of an answer the homage of her beautiful smile. She took it apparently, and her husband took it, but as a part of his odd humour, and they followed him aloft with faces now a little more responsive to the manner in which, on *that* spot, he would naturally come out. He came out, according to the word of his assured private receipt, "strong." He missed a little, in truth, the usual round-eyed question from them—the inveterate artless cue with which, from moment to moment, clustered troops had, for a year, obliged him. Mr. and Mrs. Hayes were from New York, but it was a little like singing, as he had heard one of his Americans once say about something, to a Boston audience. He did none the less what he could, and it was ever his practice to stop still at a certain spot in the room and, after having secured attention by look and gesture, suddenly shoot off: "Here!"

They always understood, the good people—he could fairly love them now for it; they always said, breathlessly and unanimously, "There?" and stared down at the designated point quite as if some trace of the grand event were still to be made out. This movement produced, he again looked round. "Consider it well: *the* spot of earth——!" "Oh, but it isn't *earth*!" the boldest spirit—there was always a boldest—would generally pipe out. Then the guardian of the Birthplace would be truly superior—as if the unfortunate had figured the Immortal coming up, like a potato, through the soil. "I'm not suggesting that He was born on the bare ground. He was born *here*!"—with an uncompromising dig of his heel. "There ought to be a brass, with an inscription, let in." "Into the floor?"—it always came. "Birth and burial: seedtime, summer, autumn!"—that always, with its special, right cadence, thanks to his unfailing spring, came too. "Why not as well as into the pavement of the church?—you've *seen* our grand old church?" The former of which questions nobody ever answered—abounding, on the other hand, to make up, in relation to the latter. Mr. and Mrs. Hayes even were at first left dumb by it—not indeed, to do them justice, having uttered the word that produced it. They had uttered no word while he kept the game up, and (though that made it a little more difficult) he could yet stand triumphant before them after he had finished with his flourish. Then it was only that Mr. Hayes of New York broke silence.

"Well, if we wanted to see, I think I may say we're quite satisfied. As my wife says, it *would* seem to be your line." He spoke now, visibly, with more ease, as if a light had come: though he made no joke of it, for a reason that presently appeared. They were coming down the little stair, and it was on the descent that his companion added her word.

"Do you know what we half *did* think——?" And then to her husband: "Is it dreadful to tell him?" They were in the room below, and the young woman, also relieved, expressed the feeling with gaiety. She smiled, as before, at Morris Gedge, treating him as a person with whom relations were possible, yet remaining just uncertain enough to invoke Mr. Hayes's opinion. "We *have* awfully wanted—from what we had heard." But she met her husband's graver face; he was not quite out of the wood. At this she was slightly flurried—but she cut it short. "You must know—don't you?—that, with the crowds who listen to you, we'd have heard."

He looked from one to the other, and once more again, with force, something came over him. They had kept him in mind, they were neither ashamed nor afraid to show it, and it was positively an interest, on the part of this charming creature and this keen, cautious gentleman, an interest resisting oblivion and surviving separation, that had governed their return. Their other visit had been the brightest thing that had ever happened to him, but this was the gravest; so that at the end of a minute something broke in him and his mask, of itself, fell off. He chucked, as he would have said, consistency; which, in its extinction, left the tears in his eyes. His smile was therefore queer. "Heard how I'm going it?"

The young man, though still looking at him hard, felt sure, with this, of his own ground. "Of course, you're tremendously talked about. You've gone round the world."

"You've heard of me in America?"

"Why, almost of nothing else!"

"That was what made us feel——!" Mrs. Hayes contributed.

"That you must see for yourselves?" Again he compared, poor Gedge, their faces. "Do you mean I excite—a—scandal?"

"Dear no! Admiration. You renew so," the young man observed, "the interest."

"Ah, there it is!" said Gedge with eyes of adventure that seemed to rest beyond the Atlantic.

"They listen, month after month, when they're out here, as you must have seen; and they go home and talk. But they sing your praise."

Our friend could scarce take it in. "Over *there*?"

"Over there. I think you must be even in the papers."

"Without abuse?"

"Oh, we don't abuse everyone."

Mrs. Hayes, in her beauty, it was clear, stretched the point. "They rave about you."

"Then they *don't* know?"

"Nobody knows," the young man declared; "it wasn't anyone's knowledge, at any rate, that made us uneasy."

"It was your own? I mean your own sense?"

"Well, call it that. We remembered, and we wondered what had happened. "So," Mr. Hayes now frankly laughed, "we came to see."

Gedge stared through his film of tears. "Came from America to see *me*?"

"Oh, a part of the way. But we wouldn't, in England, not have seen you."

"And now we *have*!" the young woman soothingly added.

Gedge still could only gape at the candour of the tribute. But he tried to meet them—it was what was least poor for him—in their own key. "Well, how do you like it?"

Mrs. Hayes, he thought—if their answer were important—laughed a little nervously. "Oh, you see."

Once more he looked from one to the other. "It's too beastly easy, you know."

Her husband raised his eyebrows. "You conceal your art. The emotion—yes; that must be easy; the general tone must flow. But about your facts—you've so many: how do you get *them* through?"

Gedge wondered. "You think I get too many——?"

At this they were amused together. "That's just what we came to see!"

"Well, you know, I've felt my way; I've gone step by step; you wouldn't believe how I've tried it on. *This*—where you see me—is where I've come out." After which, as they said nothing: "You hadn't thought I *could* come out?"

Again they just waited, but the husband spoke: "Are you so awfully sure you *are* out?"

Gedge drew himself up in the manner of his moments of emotion, almost conscious even that, with his sloping shoulders, his long lean neck and his nose so prominent in proportion to other matters, he looked the more like a giraffe. It was now at last that he really caught on. "I *may* be in danger again—and the danger is what has moved you? Oh!" the poor man fairly moaned. His appreciation of it quite weakened him, yet he pulled himself together. "You've your view of my danger?"

It was wondrous how, with that note definitely sounded, the air was cleared. Lucid Mr. Hayes, at the end of a minute, had put the thing in a nutshell. "I don't know what you'll think of us—for being so beastly curious."

"I think," poor Gedge grimaced, "you're only too beastly kind."

"It's all your own fault," his friend returned, "for presenting us (who are not idiots, say) with so striking a picture of a crisis. At our other visit, you remember," he smiled, "you created an anxiety for the opposite reason. Therefore if *this* should again be a crisis for you, you'd really give us the case with an ideal completeness."

"You make me wish," said Morris Gedge, "that it might be one."

"Well, don't try—for our amusement—to bring one on. I don't see, you know, how you can have much margin. Take care—take care."

Gedge took it pensively in. "Yes, that was what you said a year ago. You did me the honour to be uneasy as my wife was."

Which determined on the young woman's part an immediate question. "May I ask, then, if Mrs. Gedge is now at rest?"

"No; since you do ask. *She* fears, at least, that I go too far; *she* doesn't believe in my margin. You see, we *had* our scare after your visit. They came down."

His friends were all interest. "Ah! They came down?"

"Heavy. They brought *me* down. That's *why*——"

"Why you are down?" Mrs. Hayes sweetly demanded.

"Ah, but my dear man," her husband interposed, "you're not down; you're *up*! You're only up a different tree, but you're up at the tip-top."

"You mean I take it too high?"

"That's exactly the question," the young man answered; "and the possibility, as matching your first danger, is just what we felt we couldn't, if you didn't mind, miss the measure of."

Gedge looked at him. "I feel that I know what you at bottom *hoped*."

"We at bottom 'hope,' surely, that you're all right."

"In spite of the fool it makes of everyone?"

Mr. Hayes of New York smiled. "Say *because* of that. We only ask to believe that everyone *is* a fool!"

"Only you haven't been, without reassurance, able to imagine fools of the size that my case demands?" And Gedge had a pause, while, as if on the chance of some proof, his companion waited. "Well, I won't pretend to you that your anxiety hasn't made me, doesn't threaten to make me, a bit nervous; though I don't quite understand it if, as you say, people but rave about me."

"Oh, *that* report was from the other side; people in our country so very easily rave. You've seen small children laugh to shrieks when tickled in a new place. So there are amiable millions with us who are but small children. They perpetually present new places for the tickler. What we've seen in further lights," Mr. Hayes good-humouredly pursued, "is your people *here*—the Committee, the Board, or whatever the powers to whom you're responsible."

"Call them my friend Grant-Jackson then—my original backer, though I admit, for that reason, perhaps my most formidable critic. It's with him, practically, I deal; or rather it's by him I'm dealt with—*was* dealt with before. I stand or fall by him. But he has given me my head."

"Mayn't he then want you," Mrs. Hayes inquired, "just to show as flagrantly running away?"

"Of course—I see what you mean. I'm riding, blindly, for a fall, and They're watching (to be tender of me!) for the smash that may come of itself. It's Machiavellic—but everything's possible. And what did you just now mean," Gedge asked—"especially if you've only heard of my prosperity—by your 'further lights'?"

His friends for an instant looked embarrassed, but Mr. Hayes came to the point. "We've heard of your prosperity, but we've also, remember, within a few minutes, heard *you*."

"I was determined you *should*," said Gedge. "I'm good then—but I overdo?" His strained grin was still sceptical.

Thus challenged, at any rate, his visitor pronounced. "Well, if you don't; if at the end of six months more it's clear that you haven't overdone; then, *then*——"

"Then what?"

"Then it's great."

"But it *is* great—greater than anything of the sort ever was. I overdo, thank goodness, yes; or I would if it were a thing you *could*."

"Oh, well, if there's *proof* that you can't——!" With which, and an expressive gesture, Mr. Hayes threw up his fears.

His wife, however, for a moment, seemed unable to let them go. "Don't They want then *any* truth?—none even for the mere look of it?"

"The look of it," said Morris Gedge, "is what I give!"

It made them, the others, exchange a look of their own. Then she smiled. "Oh, well, if they think so——!"

"You at least don't? You're like my wife—which indeed, I remember," Gedge added, "is a similarity I expressed a year ago the wish for! At any rate I frighten *her*."

The young husband, with an "Ah, wives are terrible!" smoothed it over, and their visit would have failed of further excuse had not, at this instant, a movement at the other end of the room suddenly engaged them. The evening had so nearly closed in, though Gedge, in the course of their talk, had lighted the lamp nearest them, that they had not distinguished, in connection with the opening of the door of communication to the warden's lodge, the appearance of another person, an eager woman, who, in her impatience, had barely paused before advancing. Mrs. Gedge—her identity took but a few seconds to become vivid—was upon them, and she had not been too late for Mr. Hayes's last remark. Gedge saw at once that she had come with news; no need even, for that certitude, of her quick retort to the words in the air—"You may say as well, sir, that they're often, poor wives, terrified!" She knew nothing of the friends whom, at so unnatural an hour, he was showing about; but there was no livelier sign for him that this didn't matter than the possibility with which she intensely charged her "Grant-Jackson, to see you at once!"—letting it, so to speak, fly in his face.

"He has been with you?"

"Only a minute—he's there. But it's you he wants to see."

He looked at the others. "And what does he want, dear?"

"God knows! There it is. It's his horrid hour—it *was* that other time."

She had nervously turned to the others, overflowing to them, in her dismay, for all their strangeness—quite, as he said to himself, like a woman of the people. She was the bare-headed goodwife talking in the street about the row in the house, and it was in this character that he instantly introduced her: "My dear doubting wife, who will do her best to entertain you while I wait upon our friend." And he explained to her as he could his now protesting companions—"Mr. and Mrs. Hayes of New York, who have been here before." He knew, without knowing why, that her announcement chilled him; he failed at least to see why it should chill him so much. His good friends had themselves been visibly affected by it, and heaven knew that the depths of brooding fancy in him were easily stirred by contact. If they had wanted a crisis they accordingly had found one, albeit they had already asked leave to retire before it. This he wouldn't have. "Ah no, you must really see!"

"But we shan't be able to bear it, you know," said the young woman, "if it *is* to turn you out."

Her crudity attested her sincerity, and it was the latter, doubtless, that instantly held Mrs. Gedge. "It *is* to turn us out."

"Has he told you that, madam?" Mr. Hayes inquired of her—it being wondrous how the breath of doom had drawn them together.

"No, not told me; but there's something in him there—I mean in his awful manner—that matches too well with other things. We've seen," said the poor pale lady, "other things enough."

The young woman almost clutched her. "Is his manner very awful?"

"It's simply the manner," Gedge interposed, "of a very great man."

"Well, very great men," said his wife, "are very awful things."

"It's exactly," he laughed, "what we're finding out! But I mustn't keep him waiting. Our friends here," he went on, "are directly interested. You mustn't, mind you, let them go until we know."

Mr. Hayes, however, held him; he found himself stayed. "We're so directly interested that I want you to understand this. If anything happens——"

"Yes?" said Gedge, all gentle as he faltered.

"Well, *we* must set you up."

Mrs. Hayes quickly abounded. "Oh, *do* come to us!"

Again he could but look at them. They were really wonderful folk. And but Mr. and Mrs. Hayes! It affected even Isabel, through her alarm; though the balm, in a manner, seemed to foretell the wound. He had reached the threshold of his own quarters; he stood there as at the door of the chamber of judgment. But he laughed; at least he could be gallant in going up for sentence. "Very good then—I'll come to you!"

This was very well, but it didn't prevent his heart, a minute later, at the end of the passage, from thumping with beats he could count. He had paused again before going in; on the other side of this second door his poor future was to be let loose at him. It was broken, at best, and spiritless, but wasn't Grant-Jackson there, like a beast-tamer in a cage, all tights and spangles and circus attitudes, to give it a cut with the smart official whip and make it spring at him? It was during this moment that he fully measured the effect for his nerves of the impression made on his so oddly earnest friends—whose earnestness he in fact, in the spasm of this last effort, came within an ace of resenting. They had upset him by contact; he was afraid, literally, of meeting his doom on his knees; it wouldn't have taken much more, he absolutely felt, to make him approach with his forehead in the dust the great man whose wrath was to be averted. Mr. and Mrs. Hayes of New York had brought tears to his eyes; but was it to be reserved for Grant-Jackson to make him cry like a baby? He wished, yes, while he palpitated, that Mr. and Mrs. Hayes of New York hadn't had such an eccentricity of interest, for it seemed somehow to come from *them* that he was going so fast to pieces. Before he turned the knob of the door, however, he had another queer instant; making out that it had been, strictly, his case that was interesting, his funny power, however accidental, to show as in a picture the attitude of others—not his poor, dingy personality. It was this latter quantity, none the less, that was marching to execution. It is to our friend's credit that he *believed*, as he prepared to turn the knob, that he was going to be hanged; and it is certainly not less to his credit that his wife, on the chance, had his supreme thought. Here it was that—possibly with his last articulate breath—he thanked his stars, such as they were, for Mr. and Mrs. Hayes of New York. At least they would take care of her.

They were doing that certainly with some success when, ten minutes later, he returned to them. She sat between them in the beautified Birthplace, and he couldn't have been sure afterwards that each wasn't holding her hand. The three together, at any rate, had the effect of recalling to him—it was too whimsical—some picture, a sentimental print, seen and admired in his youth, a "Waiting for the Verdict," a "Counting the Hours," or something of that sort; humble respectability in suspense about humble innocence. He didn't know how he himself looked, and he didn't care; the great thing was that he wasn't crying—though he might have been; the glitter in his eyes was assuredly dry, though that there *was* a glitter, or something slightly to bewilder, the faces of the others, as they rose to meet him, sufficiently proved. His wife's eyes pierced his own, but it was Mrs. Hayes of New York who spoke. "*Was* it then for that——?"

He only looked at them at first—he felt he might now enjoy it. "Yes, it was for 'that.' I mean it was about the way I've been going on. He came to speak of it."

"And he's gone?" Mr. Hayes permitted himself to inquire.

"He's gone."

"It's over?" Isabel hoarsely asked.

"It's over."

"Then we go?"

This it was that he enjoyed. "No, my dear; we stay."

There was fairly a triple gasp; relief took time to operate. "Then why did he come?"

"In the fulness of his kind heart and of *Their* discussed and decreed satisfaction. To express Their sense——!"

Mr. Hayes broke into a laugh, but his wife wanted to know. "Of the grand work you're doing?"

"Of the way I polish it off. They're most handsome about it. The receipts, it appears, speak——"

He was nursing his effect; Isabel intently watched him, and the others hung on his lips. "Yes, speak——?"

"Well, volumes. They tell the truth."

At this Mr. Hayes laughed again. "Oh, *they* at least do?"

Near him thus, once more, Gedge knew their intelligence as one—which was so good a consciousness to get back that his tension now relaxed as by the snap of a spring and he felt his old face at ease. "So you can't say," he continued, "that we don't want it."

"I bow to it," the young man smiled. "It's what I said then. It's *great*."

"It's great," said Morris Gedge. "It couldn't be greater."

His wife still watched him; her irony hung behind. "Then we're just as we were?"

"No, not as we were."

She jumped at it. "Better?"

"Better. They give us a rise."

"Of income?"

"Of our sweet little stipend—by a vote of the Committee. That's what, as Chairman, he came to announce."

The very echoes of the Birthplace were themselves, for the instant, hushed; the warden's three companions showed, in the conscious air, a struggle for their own breath. But Isabel, with almost a shriek, was the first to recover hers. "They double us?"

"Well—call it that. 'In recognition.' There you are." Isabel uttered another sound—but this time inarticulate; partly because Mrs. Hayes of New York had already jumped at her to kiss her. Mr. Hayes meanwhile, as with too much to say, but put out his hand, which our friend took in silence. So Gedge had the last word. "And there *you* are!"

The Beast in the Jungle

WHAT determined the speech that startled him in the course of their encounter scarcely matters, being probably but some words spoken by himself quite without intention—spoken as they lingered and slowly moved together after their renewal of acquaintance. He had been conveyed by friends, an hour or two before, to the house at which she was staying; the party of visitors at the other house, of whom he was one, and thanks to whom it was his theory, as always, that he was lost in the crowd, had been invited over to luncheon. There had been after luncheon much dispersal, all in the interest of the original motive, a view of Weatherend itself and the fine things, intrinsic features, pictures, heirlooms, treasures of all the arts, that made the place almost famous; and the great rooms were so numerous that guests could wander at their will, hang back from the principal group, and, in cases where they took such matters with the last seriousness, give themselves up to mysterious appreciations and measurements. There were persons to be observed, singly or in couples, bending toward objects in out-of-the-way corners with their hands on their knees and their heads nodding quite as with the emphasis of an excited sense of smell. When they were two they either mingled their sounds of ecstasy or melted into silences of even deeper import, so that there were aspects of the occasion that gave it for Marcher much the air of the "look round," previous to a sale highly advertised, that excites or quenches, as may be, the dream of acquisition. The dream of acquisition at Weatherend would have had to be wild indeed, and John Marcher found himself, among such suggestions, disconcerted almost equally by the presence of those who knew too much and by that of those who knew nothing. The great rooms caused so much poetry and history to press upon him that he needed to wander apart to feel in a proper relation with them, though his doing so was not, as happened, like the gloating of some of his companions, to be compared to the movements of a dog sniffing a cupboard. It had an issue promptly enough in a direction that was not to have been calculated.

It led, in short, in the course of the October afternoon, to his closer meeting with May Bartram, whose face, a reminder, yet not quite a remembrance, as they sat, much separated, at a very long table, had begun merely by troubling him rather pleasantly. It affected him as the sequel of something of which he had lost the beginning. He knew it, and for the time quite welcomed it, as a continuation, but didn't know what it continued, which was an interest, or an amusement, the greater as he was also somehow aware—yet without a direct sign from her—that the young woman herself had not lost the thread. She had not lost it, but she wouldn't give it back to him, he saw, without some putting forth of his hand for it; and he not only saw that, but saw several things more, things odd enough in the light of the fact that at the moment some accident of grouping brought them face to face he was still merely fumbling with the idea that any contact between them in the past would have had no importance. If it had had no importance he scarcely knew why his actual impression of her should so seem to have so much; the answer to which, however, was that in such a life as they all appeared to be leading for the moment one could but take things as they came. He was satisfied, without in the least being able to say why, that this young lady might roughly have ranked in the house as a poor relation; satisfied also that she was not there on a brief visit, but was more or less a part of the establishment—almost a working, a remunerated part. Didn't she enjoy at periods a protection that she paid for by helping, among other services, to show the place and explain it, deal with the tiresome people, answer questions about the dates of the buildings, the styles of the furniture, the authorship of the pictures, the favourite haunts of the ghost? It wasn't that she looked as if you could have given her shillings—it was impossible to look less so. Yet when she finally drifted toward him, distinctly handsome, though ever so much older—older than when he had seen her before—it might have been as an effect of her guessing that he had, within the couple of hours, devoted more imagination to her than to all the others put together, and had thereby penetrated to a kind of truth that the others

were too stupid for. She *was* there on harder terms than anyone; she was there as a consequence of things suffered, in
one way and another, in the interval of years; and she remembered him very much as she was remembered—only a good
deal better.

By the time they at last thus came to speech they were alone
in one of the rooms—remarkable for a fine portrait over the
chimney-place—out of which their friends had passed, and the
charm of it was that even before they had spoken they had
practically arranged with each other to stay behind for talk.
The charm, happily, was in other things too; it was partly in
there being scarce a spot at Weatherend without something
to stay behind for. It was in the way the autumn day looked
into the high windows as it waned; in the way the red light,
breaking at the close from under a low, sombre sky, reached
out in a long shaft and played over old wainscots, old tapestry,
old gold, old colour. It was most of all perhaps in the way she
came to him as if, since she had been turned on to deal with
the simpler sort, he might, should he choose to keep the
whole thing down, just take her mild attention for a part of
her general business. As soon as he heard her voice, however,
the gap was filled up and the missing link supplied; the slight
irony he divined in her attitude lost its advantage. He almost
jumped at it to get there before her. "I met you years and
years ago in Rome. I remember all about it." She confessed
to disappointment—she had been so sure he didn't; and to
prove how well he did he began to pour forth the particular
recollections that popped up as he called for them. Her face
and her voice, all at his service now, worked the miracle—the
impression operating like the torch of a lamplighter who
touches into flame, one by one, a long row of gas jets.
Marcher flattered himself that the illumination was brilliant,
yet he was really still more pleased on her showing him, with
amusement, that in his haste to make everything right he had
got most things rather wrong. It hadn't been at Rome—it
had been at Naples; and it hadn't been seven years before—
it had been more nearly ten. She hadn't been either with her
uncle and aunt, but with her mother and her brother; in addition to which it was not with the Pembles that *he* had been,
but with the Boyers, coming down in their company from

Rome—a point on which she insisted, a little to his confusion, and as to which she had her evidence in hand. The Boyers she had known, but she didn't know the Pembles, though she had heard of them, and it was the people he was with who had made them acquainted. The incident of the thunderstorm that had raged round them with such violence as to drive them for refuge into an excavation—this incident had not occurred at the Palace of the Cæsars, but at Pompeii, on an occasion when they had been present there at an important find.

He accepted her amendments, he enjoyed her corrections, though the moral of them was, she pointed out, that he *really* didn't remember the least thing about her; and he only felt it as a drawback that when all was made conformable to the truth there didn't appear much of anything left. They lingered together still, she neglecting her office—for from the moment he was so clever she had no proper right to him—and both neglecting the house, just waiting as to see if a memory or two more wouldn't again breathe upon them. It had not taken them many minutes, after all, to put down on the table, like the cards of a pack, those that constituted their respective hands; only what came out was that the pack was unfortunately not perfect—that the past, invoked, invited, encouraged, could give them, naturally, no more than it had. It had made them meet—her at twenty, him at twenty-five; but nothing was so strange, they seemed to say to each other, as that, while so occupied, it hadn't done a little more for them. They looked at each other as with the feeling of an occasion missed; the present one would have been so much better if the other, in the far distance, in the foreign land, hadn't been so stupidly meagre. There weren't, apparently, all counted, more than a dozen little old things that had succeeded in coming to pass between them; trivialities of youth, simplicities of freshness, stupidities of ignorance, small possible germs, but too deeply buried—too deeply (didn't it seem?) to sprout after so many years. Marcher said to himself that he ought to have rendered her some service—saved her from a capsized boat in the Bay, or at least recovered her dressing-bag, filched from her cab, in the streets of Naples, by a lazzarone with a stiletto. Or it would have been nice if he could have been taken with fever, alone, at his hotel, and she could have come to look after him, to write to his people, to drive him out in convalescence. *Then* they would be in possession of the something or other that their actual show seemed to lack. It yet somehow presented itself, this show, as too good to be spoiled; so that they were reduced for a few minutes more to wondering a little helplessly why—since they seemed to know a certain number of the same people—their reunion had been so long averted. They didn't use that name for it, but their delay from minute to minute to join the others was a kind of confession that they didn't quite want it to be a failure. Their attempted supposition of reasons for their not having met but showed how little they knew of each other. There came in fact a moment when Marcher felt a positive pang. It was vain to pretend she was an old friend, for all the communities were wanting, in spite of which it was as an old friend that he saw she would have suited him. He had new ones enough—was surrounded with them, for instance, at that hour at the other house; as a new one he probably wouldn't have so much as noticed her. He would have liked to invent something, get her to make-believe with him that some passage of a romantic or critical kind *had* originally occurred. He was really almost reaching out in imagination—as against time—for something that would do, and saying to himself that if it didn't come this new incident would simply and rather awkwardly close. They would separate, and now for no second or for no third chance. They would have tried and not succeeded. Then it was, just at the turn, as he afterwards made it out to himself, that, everything else failing, she herself decided to take up the case and, as it were, save the situation. He felt as soon as she spoke that she had been consciously keeping back what she said and hoping to get on without it; a scruple in her that immensely touched him when, by the end of three or four minutes more, he was able to measure it. What she brought out, at any rate, quite cleared the air and supplied the link— the link it was such a mystery he should frivolously have managed to lose.

"You know you told me something that I've never forgotten and that again and again has made me think of you since; it was that tremendously hot day when we went to Sorrento, across the bay, for the breeze. What I allude to was what you said to me, on the way back, as we sat, under the awning of the boat, enjoying the cool. Have you forgotten?"

He had forgotten, and he was even more surprised than ashamed. But the great thing was that he saw it was no vulgar reminder of any "sweet" speech. The vanity of women had long memories, but she was making no claim on him of a compliment or a mistake. With another woman, a totally different one, he might have feared the recall possibly even some imbecile "offer." So, in having to say that he had indeed forgotten, he was conscious rather of a loss than of a gain; he already saw an interest in the matter of her reference. "I try to think—but I give it up. Yet I remember the Sorrento day."

"I'm not very sure you do," May Bartram after a moment said; "and I'm not very sure I ought to want you to. It's dreadful to bring a person back, at any time, to what he was ten years before. If you've lived away from it," she smiled, "so much the better."

"Ah, if *you* haven't why should I?" he asked.

"Lived away, you mean, from what I myself was?"

"From what *I* was. I was of course an ass," Marcher went on; "but I would rather know from you just the sort of ass I was than—from the moment you have something in your mind—not know anything."

Still, however, she hesitated. "But if you've completely ceased to be that sort——?"

"Why, I can then just so all the more bear to know. Besides, perhaps I haven't."

"Perhaps. Yet if you haven't," she added, "I should suppose you would remember. Not indeed that *I* in the least connect with my impression the invidious name you use. If I had only thought you foolish," she explained, "the thing I speak of wouldn't so have remained with me. It was about yourself." She waited, as if it might come to him; but as, only meeting her eyes in wonder, he gave no sign, she burnt her ships. "Has it ever happened?"

Then it was that, while he continued to stare, a light broke for him and the blood slowly came to his face, which began to burn with recognition. "Do you mean I told you——?"

But he faltered, lest what came to him shouldn't be right, lest he should only give himself away.

"It was something about yourself that it was natural one shouldn't forget—that is if one remembered you at all. That's why I ask you," she smiled, "if the thing you then spoke of has ever come to pass?"

Oh, then he saw, but he was lost in wonder and found himself embarrassed. This, he also saw, made her sorry for him, as if her allusion had been a mistake. It took him but a moment, however, to feel that it had not been, much as it had been a surprise. After the first little shock of it her knowledge on the contrary began, even if rather strangely, to taste sweet to him. She was the only other person in the world then who would have it, and she had had it all these years, while the fact of his having so breathed his secret had unaccountably faded from him. No wonder they couldn't have met as if nothing had happened. "I judge," he finally said, "that I know what you mean. Only I had strangely enough lost the consciousness of having taken you so far into my confidence."

"Is it because you've taken so many others as well?"

"I've taken nobody. Not a creature since then."

"So that I'm the only person who knows?"

"The only person in the world."

"Well," she quickly replied, "I myself have never spoken. I've never, never repeated of you what you told me." She looked at him so that he perfectly believed her. Their eyes met over it in such a way that he was without a doubt. "And I never will."

She spoke with an earnestness that, as if almost excessive, put him at ease about her possible derision. Somehow the whole question was a new luxury to him—that is, from the moment she was in possession. If she didn't take the ironic view she clearly took the sympathetic, and that was what he had had, in all the long time, from no one whomsoever. What he felt was that he couldn't at present have begun to tell her and yet could profit perhaps exquisitely by the accident of having done so of old. "Please don't then. We're just right as it is."

"Oh, I am," she laughed, "if you are!" To which she added: "Then you do still feel in the same way?"

It was impossible to him not to take to himself that she was really interested, and it all kept coming as a sort of revelation. He had thought of himself so long as abominably alone, and, lo, he wasn't alone a bit. He hadn't been, it appeared, for an hour—since those moments on the Sorrento boat. It was *she* who had been, he seemed to see as he looked at her—she who had been made so by the graceless fact of his lapse of fidelity. To tell her what he had told her—what had it been but to ask something of her? something that she had given, in her charity, without his having, by a remembrance, by a return of the spirit, failing another encounter, so much as thanked her. What he had asked of her had been simply at first not to laugh at him. She had beautifully not done so for ten years, and she was not doing so now. So he had endless gratitude to make up. Only for that he must see just how he had figured to her. "What, exactly, was the account I gave——?"

"Of the way you did feel? Well, it was very simple. You said you had had from your earliest time, as the deepest thing within you, the sense of being kept for something rare and strange, possibly prodigious and terrible, that was sooner or later to happen to you, that you had in your bones the foreboding and the conviction of, and that would perhaps overwhelm you."

"Do you call that very simple?" John Marcher asked.

She thought a moment. "It was perhaps because I seemed, as you spoke, to understand it."

"You do understand it?" he eagerly asked.

Again she kept her kind eyes on him. "You still have the belief?"

"Oh!" he exclaimed helplessly. There was too much to say.

"Whatever it is to be," she clearly made out, "it hasn't yet come."

He shook his head in complete surrender now. "It hasn't yet come. Only, you know, it isn't anything I'm to *do*, to achieve in the world, to be distinguished or admired for. I'm not such an ass as *that*. It would be much better, no doubt, if I were."

"It's to be something you're merely to suffer?"

"Well, say to wait for—to have to meet, to face, to see suddenly break out in my life; possibly destroying all further consciousness, possibly annihilating me; possibly, on the other hand, only altering everything, striking at the root of all my world and leaving me to the consequences, however they shape themselves."

She took this in, but the light in her eyes continued for him not to be that of mockery. "Isn't what you describe perhaps but the expectation—or, at any rate, the sense of danger, familiar to so many people—of falling in love?"

John Marcher thought. "Did you ask me that before?"

"No—I wasn't so free-and-easy then. But it's what strikes me now."

"Of course," he said after a moment, "it strikes you. Of course it strikes *me*. Of course what's in store for me may be no more than that. The only thing is," he went on, "that I think that if it had been that, I should by this time know."

"Do you mean because you've *been* in love?" And then as he but looked at her in silence: "You've been in love, and it hasn't meant such a cataclysm, hasn't proved the great affair?"

"Here I am, you see. It hasn't been overwhelming."

"Then it hasn't been love," said May Bartram.

"Well, I at least thought it was. I took it for that—I've taken it till now. It was agreeable, it was delightful, it was miserable," he explained. "But it wasn't strange. It wasn't what *my* affair's to be."

"You want something all to yourself—something that nobody else knows or *has* known?"

"It isn't a question of what I 'want'—God knows I don't want anything. It's only a question of the apprehension that haunts me—that I live with day by day."

He said this so lucidly and consistently that, visibly, it further imposed itself. If she had not been interested before she would have been interested now. "Is it a sense of coming violence?"

Evidently now too, again, he liked to talk of it. "I don't think of it as—when it does come—necessarily violent. I only think of it as natural and as of course, above all, unmistakeable. I think of it simply as *the* thing. *The* thing will of itself appear natural."

"Then how will it appear strange?"

Marcher bethought himself. "It won't—to *me*."

"To whom then?"

"Well," he replied, smiling at last, "say to you."

"Oh then, I'm to be present?"

"Why, you *are* present—since you know."

"I see." She turned it over. "But I mean at the catastrophe."

At this, for a minute, their lightness gave way to their gravity; it was as if the long look they exchanged held them together. "It will only depend on yourself—if you'll watch with me."

"Are you afraid?" she asked.

"Don't leave me *now*," he went on.

"Are you afraid?" she repeated.

"Do you think me simply out of my mind?" he pursued instead of answering. "Do I merely strike you as a harmless lunatic?"

"No," said May Bartram. "I understand you. I believe you."

"You mean you feel how my obsession—poor old thing!— may correspond to some possible reality?"

"To some possible reality."

"Then you *will* watch with me?"

She hesitated, then for the third time put her question. "Are you afraid?"

"Did I tell you I was—at Naples?"

"No, you said nothing about it."

"Then I don't know. And I should *like* to know," said John Marcher. "You'll tell me yourself whether you think so. If you'll watch with me you'll see."

"Very good then." They had been moving by this time across the room, and at the door, before passing out, they paused as if for the full wind-up of their understanding. "I'll watch with you," said May Bartram.

II

The fact that she "knew"—knew and yet neither chaffed him nor betrayed him—had in a short time begun to constitute between them a sensible bond, which became more marked when, within the year that followed their afternoon at Weatherend, the opportunities for meeting multiplied. The event that thus promoted these occasions was the death of the ancient lady, her great-aunt, under whose wing, since losing her mother, she had to such an extent found shelter, and who, though but the widowed mother of the new successor to the property, had succeeded—thanks to a high tone and a high temper—in not forfeiting the supreme position at the great house. The deposition of this personage arrived but with her death, which, followed by many changes, made in particular a difference for the young woman in whom Marcher's expert attention had recognised from the first a dependent with a pride that might ache though it didn't bristle. Nothing for a long time had made him easier than the thought that the aching must have been much soothed by Miss Bartram's now finding herself able to set up a small home in London. She had acquired property, to an amount that made that luxury just possible, under her aunt's extremely complicated will, and when the whole matter began to be straightened out, which indeed took time, she let him know that the happy issue was at last in view. He had seen her again before that day, both because she had more than once accompanied the ancient lady to town and because he had paid another visit to the friends who so conveniently made of Weatherend one of the charms of their own hospitality. These friends had taken him back there; he had achieved there again with Miss Bartram some quiet detachment; and he had in London succeeded in persuading her to more than one brief absence from her aunt. They went together, on these latter occasions, to the National Gallery and the South Kensington Museum, where, among vivid reminders, they talked of Italy at large—not now attempting to recover, as at first, the taste of their youth and their ignorance. That recovery, the first day at Weatherend, had served its purpose well, had given them quite enough; so that they were, to Marcher's sense, no longer hovering about the head-waters of their stream, but had felt their boat pushed sharply off and down the current.

They were literally afloat together; for our gentleman this was marked, quite as marked as that the fortunate cause of it was just the buried treasure of her knowledge. He had with his own hands dug up this little hoard, brought to light—that is to within reach of the dim day constituted by their discretions and privacies—the object of value the hiding-place of which he had, after putting it into the ground himself, so strangely, so long forgotten. The exquisite luck of having again just stumbled on the spot made him indifferent to any other question; he would doubtless have devoted more time to the odd accident of his lapse of memory if he had not been moved to devote so much to the sweetness, the comfort, as he felt, for the future, that this accident itself had helped to keep fresh. It had never entered into his plan that anyone should "know," and mainly for the reason that it was not in him to tell anyone. That would have been impossible, since nothing but the amusement of a cold world would have waited on it. Since, however, a mysterious fate had opened his mouth in youth, in spite of him, he would count that a compensation and profit by it to the utmost. That the right person *should* know tempered the asperity of his secret more even than his shyness had permitted him to imagine; and May Bartram was clearly right, because—well, because there she was. Her knowledge simply settled it; he would have been sure enough by this time had she been wrong. There was that in his situation, no doubt, that disposed him too much to see her as a mere confidant, taking all her light for him from the fact—the fact only—of her interest in his predicament, from her mercy, sympathy, seriousness, her consent not to regard him as the funniest of the funny. Aware, in fine, that her price for him was just in her giving him this constant sense of his being admirably spared, he was careful to remember that she had, after all, also a life of her own, with things that might happen to *her*, things that in friendship one should likewise take account of. Something fairly remarkable came to pass with him, for that matter, in this connection—something represented by a certain passage of his consciousness, in the suddenest way, from one extreme to the other.

He had thought himself, so long as nobody knew, the most disinterested person in the world, carrying his concentrated burden, his perpetual suspense, ever so quietly, holding his tongue about it, giving others no glimpse of it nor of its effect upon his life, asking of them no allowance and only making on his side all those that were asked. He had disturbed nobody

with the queerness of having to know a haunted man, though
he had had moments of rather special temptation on hearing
people say that they were "unsettled." If they were as unsettled as he was—he who had never been settled for an hour in
his life—they would know what it meant. Yet it wasn't, all the
same, for him to make them, and he listened to them civilly
enough. This was why he had such good—though possibly
such rather colourless—manners; this was why, above all, he
could regard himself, in a greedy world, as decently—as, in
fact, perhaps even a little sublimely—unselfish. Our point is
accordingly that he valued this character quite sufficiently to
measure his present danger of letting it lapse, against which
he promised himself to be much on his guard. He was quite
ready, none the less, to be selfish just a little, since, surely, no
more charming occasion for it had come to him. "Just a little," in a word, was just as much as Miss Bartram, taking one
day with another, would let him. He never would be in the
least coercive, and he would keep well before him the lines
on which consideration for her—the very highest—ought to
proceed. He would thoroughly establish the heads under
which her affairs, her requirements, her peculiarities—he went
so far as to give them the latitude of that name—would come
into their intercourse. All this naturally was a sign of how
much he took the intercourse itself for granted. There was
nothing more to be done about *that*. It simply existed; had
sprung into being with her first penetrating question to him
in the autumn light there at Weatherend. The real form it
should have taken on the basis that stood out large was the
form of their marrying. But the devil in this was that the very
basis itself put marrying out of the question. His conviction,
his apprehension, his obsession, in short, was not a condition
he could invite a woman to share; and that consequence of it
was precisely what was the matter with him. Something or
other lay in wait for him, amid the twists and the turns of the
months and the years, like a crouching beast in the jungle. It
signified little whether the crouching beast were destined to
slay him or to be slain. The definite point was the inevitable
spring of the creature; and the definite lesson from that was
that a man of feeling didn't cause himself to be accompanied

by a lady on a tiger-hunt. Such was the image under which he had ended by figuring his life.

They had at first, none the less, in the scattered hours spent together, made no allusion to that view of it; which was a sign he was handsomely ready to give that he didn't expect, that he in fact didn't care always to be talking about it. Such a feature in one's outlook was really like a hump on one's back. The difference it made every minute of the day existed quite independently of discussion. One discussed, of course, *like* a hunchback, for there was always, if nothing else, the hunchback face. That remained, and she was watching him; but people watched best, as a general thing, in silence, so that such would be predominantly the manner of their vigil. Yet he didn't want, at the same time, to be solemn; solemn was what he imagined he too much tended to be with other people. The thing to be, with the one person who knew, was easy and natural—to make the reference rather than be seeming to avoid it, to avoid it rather than be seeming to make it, and to keep it, in any case, familiar, facetious even, rather than pedantic and portentous. Some such consideration as the latter was doubtless in his mind, for instance, when he wrote pleasantly to Miss Bartram that perhaps the great thing he had so long felt as in the lap of the gods was no more than this circumstance, which touched him so nearly, of her acquiring a house in London. It was the first allusion they had yet again made, needing any other hitherto so little; but when she replied, after having given him the news, that she was by no means satisfied with such a trifle, as the climax to so special a suspense, she almost set him wondering if she hadn't even a larger conception of singularity for him than he had for himself. He was at all events destined to become aware little by little, as time went by, that she was all the while looking at his life, judging it, measuring it, in the light of the thing she knew, which grew to be at last, with the consecration of the years, never mentioned between them save as "the real truth" about him. That had always been his own form of reference to it, but she adopted the form so quietly that, looking back at the end of a period, he knew there was no moment at which it was traceable that she had, as he might say, got inside his condition, or exchanged the attitude of beautifully indulging for that of still more beautifully believing him.

It was always open to him to accuse her of seeing him but as the most harmless of maniacs, and this, in the long run—since it covered so much ground—was his easiest description of their friendship. He had a screw loose for her, but she liked him in spite of it, and was practically, against the rest of the world, his kind, wise keeper, unremunerated, but fairly amused and, in the absence of other near ties, not disreputably occupied. The rest of the world of course thought him queer, but she, she only, knew how, and above all why, queer; which was precisely what enabled her to dispose the concealing veil in the right folds. She took his gaiety from him—since it had to pass with them for gaiety—as she took everything else; but she certainly so far justified by her unerring touch his finer sense of the degree to which he had ended by convincing her. *She* at least never spoke of the secret of his life except as "the real truth about you," and she had in fact a wonderful way of making it seem, as such, the secret of her own life too. That was in fine how he so constantly felt her as allowing for him; he couldn't on the whole call it anything else. He allowed for himself, but she, exactly, allowed still more; partly because, better placed for a sight of the matter, she traced his unhappy perversion through portions of its course into which he could scarce follow it. He knew how he felt, but, besides knowing that, she knew how he *looked* as well; he knew each of the things of importance he was insidiously kept from doing, but she could add up the amount they made, understand how much, with a lighter weight on his spirit, he might have done, and thereby establish how, clever as he was, he fell short. Above all she was in the secret of the difference between the forms he went through—those of his little office under Government, those of caring for his modest patrimony, for his library, for his garden in the country, for the people in London whose invitations he accepted and repaid—and the detachment that reigned beneath them and that made of all behaviour, all that could in the least be called behaviour, a long act of dissimulation. What it had come to was that he wore a mask painted with the social simper, out of the eye-holes of which there looked eyes of an expression not in the least matching the other features. This the stupid world, even after years, had never more than half discovered. It was only May Bartram who had, and she achieved, by an art indescribable, the feat of at once—or perhaps it was only alternately—meeting the eyes from in front and mingling her own vision, as from over his shoulder, with their peep through the apertures.

So, while they grew older together, she did watch with him, and so she let this association give shape and colour to her own existence. Beneath *her* forms as well detachment had learned to sit, and behaviour had become for her, in the social sense, a false account of herself. There was but one account of her that would have been true all the while, and that she could give, directly, to nobody, least of all to John Marcher. Her whole attitude was a virtual statement, but the perception of that only seemed destined to take its place for him as one of the many things necessarily crowded out of his consciousness. If she had, moreover, like himself, to make sacrifices to their real truth, it was to be granted that her compensation might have affected her as more prompt and more natural. They had long periods, in this London time, during which, when they were together, a stranger might have listened to them without in the least pricking up his ears; on the other hand, the real truth was equally liable at any moment to rise to the surface, and the auditor would then have wondered indeed what they were talking about. They had from an early time made up their mind that society was, luckily, unintelligent, and the margin that this gave them had fairly become one of their commonplaces. Yet there were still moments when the situation turned almost fresh—usually under the effect of some expression drawn from herself. Her expressions doubtless repeated themselves, but her intervals were generous. "What saves us, you know, is that we answer so completely to so usual an appearance: that of the man and woman whose friendship has become such a daily habit, or almost, as to be at last indispensable." That, for instance, was a remark she had frequently enough had occasion to make, though she had given it at different times different developments. What we are especially concerned with is the turn it happened to take from her one afternoon when he had come to see her in honour of her birthday. This anniversary had fallen on a Sunday, at a season of thick fog and general outward gloom; but he had brought her his customary offering, having known her now long enough to have established a hundred little customs. It was one of his proofs to himself, the present he made her on her birthday, that he had not sunk into real selfishness. It was mostly nothing more than a small trinket, but it was always fine of its kind, and he was regularly careful to pay for it more than he thought he could afford. "Our habit saves you, at least, don't you see? because it makes you, after all, for the vulgar, indistinguishable from other men. What's the most inveterate mark of men in general? Why, the capacity to spend endless time with dull women—to spend it, I won't say without being bored, but without minding that they are, without being driven off at a tangent by it; which comes to the same thing. I'm your dull woman, a part of the daily bread for which you pray at church. That covers your tracks more than anything."

"And what covers yours?" asked Marcher, whom his dull woman could mostly to this extent amuse. "I see of course what you mean by your saving me, in one way and another, so far as other people are concerned—I've seen it all along. Only, what is it that saves *you*? I often think, you know, of that."

She looked as if she sometimes thought of that too, but in rather a different way. "Where other people, you mean, are concerned?"

"Well, you're really so in with me, you know—as a sort of result of my being so in with yourself. I mean of my having such an immense regard for you, being so tremendously grateful for all you've done for me. I sometimes ask myself if it's quite fair. Fair I mean to have so involved and—since one may say it—interested you. I almost feel as if you hadn't really had time to do anything else."

"Anything else but be interested?" she asked. "Ah, what else does one ever want to be? If I've been 'watching' with you, as we long ago agreed that I was to do, watching is always in itself an absorption."

"Oh, certainly," John Marcher said, "if you hadn't had your curiosity——! Only, doesn't it sometimes come to you, as time goes on, that your curiosity is not being particularly repaid?"

May Bartram had a pause. "Do you ask that, by any chance, because you feel at all that yours isn't? I mean because you have to wait so long."

Oh, he understood what she meant. "For the thing to happen that never does happen? For the beast to jump out? No, I'm just where I was about it. It isn't a matter as to which I can *choose*, I can decide for a change. It isn't one as to which there *can* be a change. It's in the lap of the gods. One's in the hands of one's law—there one is. As to the form the law will take, the way it will operate, that's its own affair."

"Yes," Miss Bartram replied; "of course one's fate is coming, of course it *has* come, in its own form and its own way, all the while. Only, you know, the form and the way in your case were to have been—well, something so exceptional and, as one may say, so particularly *your* own."

Something in this made him look at her with suspicion. "You say 'were to *have* been,' as if in your heart you had begun to doubt."

"Oh!" she vaguely protested.

"As if you believed," he went on, "that nothing will now take place."

She shook her head slowly, but rather inscrutably. "You're far from my thought."

He continued to look at her. "What then is the matter with you?"

"Well," she said after another wait, "the matter with me is simply that I'm more sure than ever my curiosity, as you call it, will be but too well repaid."

They were frankly grave now; he had got up from his seat, had turned once more about the little drawing-room to which, year after year, he brought his inevitable topic; in which he had, as he might have said, tasted their intimate community with every sauce, where every object was as familiar to him as the things of his own house and the very carpets were worn with his fitful walk very much as the desks in old counting-houses are worn by the elbows of generations of clerks. The generations of his nervous moods had been at work there, and the place was the written history of his whole middle life. Under the impression of what his friend had just said he knew himself, for some reason, more aware of these things, which made him, after a moment, stop again before her. "Is it, possibly, that you've grown afraid?"

"Afraid?" He thought, as she repeated the word, that his question had made her, a little, change colour; so that, lest he should have touched on a truth, he explained very kindly, "You remember that that was what you asked *me* long ago—that first day at Weatherend."

"Oh yes, and you told me you didn't know—that I was to see for myself. We've said little about it since, even in so long a time."

"Precisely," Marcher interposed—"quite as if it were too delicate a matter for us to make free with. Quite as if we might find, on pressure, that I *am* afraid. For then," he said, "we shouldn't, should we? quite know what to do."

She had for the time no answer to this question. "There have been days when I thought you were. Only, of course," she added, "there have been days when we have thought almost anything."

"Everything. Oh!" Marcher softly groaned as with a gasp, half spent, at the face, more uncovered just then than it had been for a long while, of the imagination always with them. It had always had its incalculable moments of glaring out, quite as with the very eyes of the very Beast, and, used as he was to them, they could still draw from him the tribute of a sigh that rose from the depths of his being. All that they had thought, first and last, rolled over him; the past seemed to have been reduced to mere barren speculation. This in fact was what the place had just struck him as so full of—the simplification of everything but the state of suspense. That remained only by seeming to hang in the void surrounding it. Even his original fear, if fear it had been, had lost itself in the desert. "I judge, however," he continued, "that you see I'm not afraid now."

"What I see is, as I make it out, that you've achieved something almost unprecedented in the way of getting used to danger. Living with it so long and so closely, you've lost your sense of it; you know it's there, but you're indifferent, and you cease even, as of old, to have to whistle in the dark. Considering what the danger is," May Bartram wound up, "I'm bound to say that I don't think your attitude could well be surpassed."

John Marcher faintly smiled. "It's heroic?"

"Certainly—call it that."

He considered. "I *am*, then, a man of courage?"

"That's what you were to show me."

He still, however, wondered. "But doesn't the man of courage know what he's afraid of—or *not* afraid of? I don't know *that*, you see. I don't focus it. I can't name it. I only know I'm exposed."

"Yes, but exposed—how shall I say?—so directly. So intimately. That's surely enough."

"Enough to make you feel, then—as what we may call the end of our watch—that I'm not afraid?"

"You're not afraid. But it isn't," she said, "the end of our watch. That is it isn't the end of yours. You've everything still to see."

"Then why haven't *you*?" he asked. He had had, all along, to-day, the sense of her keeping something back, and he still had it. As this was his first impression of that, it made a kind of date. The case was the more marked as she didn't at first answer; which in turn made him go on. "You know something I don't." Then his voice, for that of a man of courage, trembled a little. "You know what's to happen." Her silence, with the face she showed, was almost a confession—it made him sure. "You know, and you're afraid to tell me. It's so bad that you're afraid I'll find out."

All this might be true, for she did look as if, unexpectedly to her, he had crossed some mystic line that she had secretly drawn round her. Yet she might, after all, not have worried; and the real upshot was that he himself, at all events, needn't. "You'll never find out."

III

It was all to have made, none the less, as I have said, a date; as came out in the fact that again and again, even after long intervals, other things that passed between them wore, in relation to this hour, but the character of recalls and results. Its

immediate effect had been indeed rather to lighten insistence—almost to provoke a reaction; as if their topic had
dropped by its own weight and as if moreover, for that matter,
Marcher had been visited by one of his occasional warnings
against egotism. He had kept up, he felt, and very decently
on the whole, his consciousness of the importance of not
being selfish, and it was true that he had never sinned in that
direction without promptly enough trying to press the scales
the other way. He often repaired his fault, the season permitting, by inviting his friend to accompany him to the opera;
and it not infrequently thus happened that, to show he didn't
wish her to have but one sort of food for her mind, he was
the cause of her appearing there with him a dozen nights in
the month. It even happened that, seeing her home at such
times, he occasionally went in with her to finish, as he called
it, the evening, and, the better to make his point, sat down
to the frugal but always careful little supper that awaited his
pleasure. His point was made, he thought, by his not eternally
insisting with her on himself; made for instance, at such hours,
when it befell that, her piano at hand and each of them familiar with it, they went over passages of the opera together.
It chanced to be on one of these occasions, however, that he
reminded her of her not having answered a certain question
he had put to her during the talk that had taken place between
them on her last birthday. "What is it that saves *you*?"—saved
her, he meant, from that appearance of variation from the
usual human type. If he had practically escaped remark, as she
pretended, by doing, in the most important particular, what
most men do—find the answer to life in patching up an alliance of a sort with a woman no better than himself—how had
she escaped it, and how could the alliance, such as it was, since
they must suppose it had been more or less noticed, have
failed to make her rather positively talked about?

"I never said," May Bartram replied, "that it hadn't made
me talked about."

"Ah well then, you're not 'saved.'"

"It has not been a question for me. If you've had your
woman, I've had," she said, "my man."

"And you mean that makes you all right?"

She hesitated. "I don't know why it shouldn't make me —humanly, which is what we're speaking of—as right as it makes you."

"I see," Marcher returned. " 'Humanly,' no doubt, as showing that you're living for something. Not, that is, just for me and my secret."

May Bartram smiled. "I don't pretend it exactly shows that I'm not living for you. It's my intimacy with you that's in question."

He laughed as he saw what she meant. "Yes, but since, as you say, I'm only, so far as people make out, ordinary, you're—aren't you?—no more than ordinary either. You help me to pass for a man like another. So if I *am*, as I understand you, you're not compromised. Is that it?"

She had another hesitation, but she spoke clearly enough. "That's it. It's all that concerns me—to help you to pass for a man like another."

He was careful to acknowledge the remark handsomely. "How kind, how beautiful, you are to me! How shall I ever repay you?"

She had her last grave pause, as if there might be a choice of ways. But she chose. "By going on as you are."

It was into this going on as he was that they relapsed, and really for so long a time that the day inevitably came for a further sounding of their depths. It was as if these depths, constantly bridged over by a structure that was firm enough in spite of its lightness and of its occasional oscillation in the somewhat vertiginous air, invited on occasion, in the interest of their nerves, a dropping of the plummet and a measurement of the abyss. A difference had been made moreover, once for all, by the fact that she had, all the while, not appeared to feel the need of rebutting his charge of an idea within her that she didn't dare to express, uttered just before one of the fullest of their later discussions ended. It had come up for him then that she "knew" something and that what she knew was bad—too bad to tell him. When he had spoken of it as visibly so bad that she was afraid he might find it out, her reply had left the matter too equivocal to be let alone and yet, for Marcher's special sensibility, almost too formidable

again to touch. He circled about it at a distance that alternately narrowed and widened and that yet was not much affected by the consciousness in him that there was nothing she
could "know," after all, any better than he did. She had no
source of knowledge that he hadn't equally—except of course
that she might have finer nerves. That was what women had
where they were interested; they made out things, where people were concerned, that the people often couldn't have made
out for themselves. Their nerves, their sensibility, their imagination, were conductors and revealers, and the beauty of May
Bartram was in particular that she had given herself so to his
case. He felt in these days what, oddly enough, he had never
felt before, the growth of a dread of losing her by some catastrophe—some catastrophe that yet wouldn't at all be *the*
catastrophe: partly because she had, almost of a sudden,
begun to strike him as useful to him as never yet, and partly
by reason of an appearance of uncertainty in her health, co-
incident and equally new. It was characteristic of the inner
detachment he had hitherto so successfully cultivated and to
which our whole account of him is a reference, it was characteristic that his complications, such as they were, had never
yet seemed so as at this crisis to thicken about him, even to
the point of making him ask himself if he were, by any chance,
of a truth, within sight or sound, within touch or reach,
within the immediate jurisdiction of the thing that waited.

When the day came, as come it had to, that his friend confessed to him her fear of a deep disorder in her blood, he felt
somehow the shadow of a change and the chill of a shock.
He immediately began to imagine aggravations and disasters,
and above all to think of her peril as the direct menace for
himself of personal privation. This indeed gave him one of
those partial recoveries of equanimity that were agreeable to
him—it showed him that what was still first in his mind was
the loss she herself might suffer. "What if she should have to
die before knowing, before seeing——?" It would have been
brutal, in the early stages of her trouble, to put that question
to her; but it had immediately sounded for him to his own
concern, and the possibility was what most made him sorry
for her. If she did "know," moreover, in the sense of her
having had some—what should he think?—mystical, irresistible

light, this would make the matter not better, but worse, inasmuch as her original adoption of his own curiosity had quite
become the basis of her life. She had been living to see what
would *be* to be seen, and it would be cruel to her to have to
give up before the accomplishment of the vision. These reflections, as I say, refreshed his generosity; yet, make them as
he might, he saw himself, with the lapse of the period, more
and more disconcerted. It lapsed for him with a strange,
steady sweep, and the oddest oddity was that it gave him,
independently of the threat of much inconvenience, almost
the only positive surprise his career, if career it could be called,
had yet offered him. She kept the house as she had never
done; he had to go to her to see her—she could meet him
nowhere now, though there was scarce a corner of their loved
old London in which she had not in the past, at one time
or another, done so; and he found her always seated by her
fire in the deep, old-fashioned chair she was less and less
able to leave. He had been struck one day, after an absence
exceeding his usual measure, with her suddenly looking
much older to him than he had ever thought of her being;
then he recognised that the suddenness was all on his side—
he had just been suddenly struck. She looked older because
inevitably, after so many years, she *was* old, or almost; which
was of course true in still greater measure of her companion.
If she was old, or almost, John Marcher assuredly was, and
yet it was her showing of the lesson, not his own, that brought
the truth home to him. His surprises began here; when once
they had begun they multiplied; they came rather with a rush:
it was as if, in the oddest way in the world, they had all been
kept back, sown in a thick cluster, for the late afternoon of
life, the time at which, for people in general, the unexpected
has died out.

One of them was that he should have caught himself—for
he *had* so done—*really* wondering if the great accident would
take form now as nothing more than his being condemned to
see this charming woman, this admirable friend, pass away
from him. He had never so unreservedly qualified her as while
confronted in thought with such a possibility; in spite of
which there was small doubt for him that as an answer to his
long riddle the mere effacement of even so fine a feature of

his situation would be an abject anticlimax. It would represent, as connected with his past attitude, a drop of dignity
under the shadow of which his existence could only become
the most grotesque of failures. He had been far from holding
it a failure—long as he had waited for the appearance that was
to make it a success. He had waited for a quite other thing,
not for such a one as that. The breath of his good faith came
short, however, as he recognised how long he had waited, or
how long, at least, his companion had. That she, at all events,
might be recorded as having waited in vain—this affected him
sharply, and all the more because of his at first having done
little more than amuse himself with the idea. It grew more
grave as the gravity of her condition grew, and the state of
mind it produced in him, which he ended by watching, himself, as if it had been some definite disfigurement of his outer
person, may pass for another of his surprises. This conjoined
itself still with another, the really stupefying consciousness of
a question that he would have allowed to shape itself had he
dared. What did everything mean—what, that is, did *she*
mean, she and her vain waiting and her probable death and
the soundless admonition of it all—unless that, at this time of
day, it was simply, it was overwhelmingly too late? He had
never, at any stage of his queer consciousness, admitted the
whisper of such a correction; he had never, till within these
last few months, been so false to his conviction as not to hold
that what was to come to him had time, whether *he* struck
himself as having it or not. That at last, at last, he certainly
hadn't it, to speak of, or had it but in the scantiest measure—
such, soon enough, as things went with him, became the inference with which his old obsession had to reckon: and this
it was not helped to do by the more and more confirmed
appearance that the great vagueness casting the long shadow
in which he had lived had, to attest itself, almost no margin
left. Since it was in Time that he was to have met his fate, so
it was in Time that his fate was to have acted; and as he waked
up to the sense of no longer being young, which was exactly
the sense of being stale, just as that, in turn, was the sense of
being weak, he waked up to another matter beside. It all hung
together; they were subject, he and the great vagueness, to an
equal and indivisible law. When the possibilities themselves

had, accordingly, turned stale, when the secret of the gods had grown faint, had perhaps even quite evaporated, that, and that only, was failure. It wouldn't have been failure to be bankrupt, dishonoured, pilloried, hanged; it was failure not to be anything. And so, in the dark valley into which his path had taken its unlooked-for twist, he wondered not a little as he groped. He didn't care what awful crash might overtake him, with what ignominy or what monstrosity he might yet be associated—since he wasn't, after all, too utterly old to suffer—if it would only be decently proportionate to the posture he had kept, all his life, in the promised presence of it. He had but one desire left—that he shouldn't have been "sold."

IV

Then it was that one afternoon, while the spring of the year was young and new, she met, all in her own way, his frankest betrayal of these alarms. He had gone in late to see her, but evening had not settled, and she was presented to him in that long, fresh light of waning April days which affects us often with a sadness sharper than the greyest hours of autumn. The week had been warm, the spring was supposed to have begun early, and May Bartram sat, for the first time in the year, without a fire, a fact that, to Marcher's sense, gave the scene of which she formed part a smooth and ultimate look, an air of knowing, in its immaculate order and its cold, meaningless cheer, that it would never see a fire again. Her own aspect— he could scarce have said why—intensified this note. Almost as white as wax, with the marks and signs in her face as numerous and as fine as if they had been etched by a needle, with soft white draperies relieved by a faded green scarf, the delicate tone of which had been consecrated by the years, she was the picture of a serene, exquisite, but impenetrable sphinx, whose head, or indeed all whose person, might have been powdered with silver. She was a sphinx, yet with her white petals and green fronds she might have been a lily too—only an artificial lily, wonderfully imitated and constantly kept, without dust or stain, though not exempt from a slight droop and a complexity of faint creases, under some clear glass bell. The perfection of household care, of high polish and finish, always reigned in her rooms, but they especially looked to Marcher at present as if everything had been wound up, tucked in, put away, so that she might sit with folded hands and with nothing more to do. She was "out of it," to his vision; her work was over; she communicated with him as across some gulf, or from some island of rest that she had already reached, and it made him feel strangely abandoned. Was it—or, rather, wasn't it—that if for so long she had been watching with him the answer to their question had swum into her ken and taken on its name, so that her occupation was verily gone? He had as much as charged her with this in saying to her, many months before, that she even then knew something she was keeping from him. It was a point he had never since ventured to press, vaguely fearing, as he did, that it might become a difference, perhaps a disagreement, between them. He had in short, in this later time, turned nervous, which was what, in all the other years, he had never been; and the oddity was that his nervousness should have waited till he had begun to doubt, should have held off so long as he was sure. There was something, it seemed to him, that the wrong word would bring down on his head, something that would so at least put an end to his suspense. But he wanted not to speak the wrong word; that would make everything ugly. He wanted the knowledge he lacked to drop on him, if drop it could, by its own august weight. If she was to forsake him it was surely for her to take leave. This was why he didn't ask her again, directly, what she knew; but it was also why, approaching the matter from another side, he said to her in the course of his visit: "What do you regard as the very worst that, at this time of day, *can* happen to me?"

He had asked her that in the past often enough; they had, with the odd, irregular rhythm of their intensities and avoidances, exchanged ideas about it and then had seen the ideas washed away by cool intervals, washed like figures traced in sea-sand. It had ever been the mark of their talk that the oldest allusions in it required but a little dismissal and reaction to come out again, sounding for the hour as new. She could thus at present meet his inquiry quite freshly and patiently. "Oh yes, I've repeatedly thought, only it always seemed to me of old that I couldn't quite make up my mind. I thought of dreadful things, between which it was difficult to choose; and so must you have done."

"Rather! I feel now as if I had scarce done anything else. I appear to myself to have spent my life in thinking of nothing *but* dreadful things. A great many of them I've at different times named to you, but there were others I couldn't name."

"They were too, too dreadful?"

"Too, too dreadful—some of them."

She looked at him a minute, and there came to him as he met it an inconsequent sense that her eyes, when one got their full clearness, were still as beautiful as they had been in youth, only beautiful with a strange, cold light—a light that somehow was a part of the effect, if it wasn't rather a part of the cause, of the pale, hard sweetness of the season and the hour. "And yet," she said at last, "there are horrors we have mentioned."

It deepened the strangeness to see her, as such a figure in such a picture, talk of "horrors," but she was to do, in a few minutes, something stranger yet—though even of this he was to take the full measure but afterwards—and the note of it was already in the air. It was, for the matter of that, one of the signs that her eyes were having again such a high flicker of their prime. He had to admit, however, what she said. "Oh yes, there were times when we did go far." He caught himself in the act of speaking as if it all were over. Well, he wished it were; and the consummation depended, for him, clearly, more and more on his companion.

But she had now a soft smile. "Oh, far——!"

It was oddly ironic. "Do you mean you're prepared to go further?"

She was frail and ancient and charming as she continued to look at him, yet it was rather as if she had lost the thread. "Do you consider that we went so far?"

"Why, I thought it the point you were just making—that we *had* looked most things in the face."

"Including each other?" She still smiled. "But you're quite right. We've had together great imaginations, often great fears; but some of them have been unspoken."

"Then the worst—we haven't faced that. I *could* face it, I believe, if I knew what you think it. I feel," he explained, "as if I had lost my power to conceive such things." And he wondered if he looked as blank as he sounded. "It's spent."

"Then why do you assume," she asked, "that mine isn't?"

"Because you've given me signs to the contrary. It isn't a question for you of conceiving, imagining, comparing. It isn't a question now of choosing." At last he came out with it. "You know something that I don't. You've shown me that before."

These last words affected her, he could see in a moment, remarkably, and she spoke with firmness. "I've shown you, my dear, nothing."

He shook his head. "You can't hide it."

"Oh, oh!" May Bartram murmured over what she couldn't hide. It was almost a smothered groan.

"You admitted it months ago, when I spoke of it to you as of something you were afraid I would find out. Your answer was that I couldn't, that I wouldn't, and I don't pretend I have. But you had something therefore in mind, and I see now that it must have been, that it still is, the possibility that, of all possibilities, has settled itself for you as the worst. This," he went on, "is why I appeal to you. I'm only afraid of ignorance now—I'm not afraid of knowledge." And then as for a while she said nothing: "What makes me sure is that I see in your face and feel here, in this air and amid these appearances, that you're out of it. You've done. You've had your experience. You leave me to my fate."

Well, she listened, motionless and white in her chair, as if she had in fact a decision to make, so that her whole manner was a virtual confession, though still with a small, fine, inner stiffness, an imperfect surrender. "It *would* be the worst," she finally let herself say. "I mean the thing that I've never said."

It hushed him a moment. "More monstrous than all the monstrosities we've named?"

"More monstrous. Isn't that what you sufficiently express," she asked, "in calling it the worst?"

Marcher thought. "Assuredly—if you mean, as I do, something that includes all the loss and all the shame that are thinkable."

"It would if it *should* happen," said May Bartram. "What we're speaking of, remember, is only my idea."

"It's your belief," Marcher returned. "That's enough for me. I feel your beliefs are right. Therefore if, having this one, you give me no more light on it, you abandon me."

"No, no!" she repeated. "I'm with you—don't you see?—still." And as if to make it more vivid to him she rose from her chair—a movement she seldom made in these days—and showed herself, all draped and all soft, in her fairness and slimness. "I haven't forsaken you."

It was really, in its effort against weakness, a generous assurance, and had the success of the impulse not, happily, been great, it would have touched him to pain more than to pleasure. But the cold charm in her eyes had spread, as she hovered before him, to all the rest of her person, so that it was, for the minute, almost like a recovery of youth. He couldn't pity her for that; he could only take her as she showed—as capable still of helping him. It was as if, at the same time, her light might at any instant go out; wherefore he must make the most of it. There passed before him with intensity the three or four things he wanted most to know; but the question that came of itself to his lips really covered the others. "Then tell me if I shall consciously suffer."

She promptly shook her head. "Never!"

It confirmed the authority he imputed to her, and it produced on him an extraordinary effect. "Well, what's better than that? Do you call that the worst?"

"You think nothing is better?" she asked.

She seemed to mean something so special that he again sharply wondered, though still with the dawn of a prospect of relief. "Why not, if one doesn't *know*?" After which, as their eyes, over his question, met in a silence, the dawn deepened and something to his purpose came, prodigiously, out of her very face. His own, as he took it in, suddenly flushed to the forehead, and he gasped with the force of a perception to which, on the instant, everything fitted. The sound of his gasp filled the air; then he became articulate. "I see—if I don't suffer!"

In her own look, however, was doubt. "You see what?"

"Why, what you mean—what you've always meant."

She again shook her head. "What I mean isn't what I've always meant. It's different."

"It's something new?"

She hesitated. "Something new. It's not what you think. I see what you think."

His divination drew breath then; only her correction might be wrong. "It isn't that I *am* a donkey?" he asked between faintness and grimness. "It isn't that it's all a mistake?"

"A mistake?" she pityingly echoed. *That* possibility, for her, he saw, would be monstrous; and if she guaranteed him the immunity from pain it would accordingly not be what she had in mind. "Oh, no," she declared; "it's nothing of that sort. You've been right."

Yet he couldn't help asking himself if she weren't, thus pressed, speaking but to save him. It seemed to him he should be most lost if his history should prove all a platitude. "Are you telling me the truth, so that I sha'n't have been a bigger idiot than I can bear to know? I *haven't* lived with a vain imagination, in the most besotted illusion? I haven't waited but to see the door shut in my face?"

She shook her head again. "However the case stands *that* isn't the truth. Whatever the reality, it *is* a reality. The door isn't shut. The door's open," said May Bartram.

"Then something's to come?"

She waited once again, always with her cold, sweet eyes on him. "It's never too late." She had, with her gliding step, diminished the distance between them, and she stood nearer to him, close to him, a minute, as if still full of the unspoken. Her movement might have been for some finer emphasis of what she was at once hesitating and deciding to say. He had been standing by the chimney-piece, fireless and sparely adorned, a small, perfect old French clock and two morsels of rosy Dresden constituting all its furniture; and her hand grasped the shelf while she kept him waiting, grasped it a little as for support and encouragement. She only kept him waiting, however; that is he only waited. It had become suddenly, from her movement and attitude, beautiful and vivid to him that she had something more to give him; her wasted face delicately shone with it, and it glittered, almost as with the white lustre of silver, in her expression. She was right, incontestably, for what he saw in her face was the truth, and strangely, without consequence, while their talk of it as dreadful was still in the air, she appeared to present it as inordinately soft. This, prompting bewilderment, made him but gape the more gratefully for her revelation, so that they continued for some minutes silent, her face shining at him, her contact imponderably pressing, and his stare all kind, but all expectant. The end, none the less, was that what he had expected failed to sound. Something else took place instead, which seemed to consist at first in the mere closing of her eyes. She gave way at the same instant to a slow, fine shudder, and though he remained staring—though he stared, in fact, but the harder—she turned off and regained her chair. It was the end of what she had been intending, but it left him thinking only of that.

"Well, you don't say——?"

She had touched in her passage a bell near the chimney and had sunk back, strangely pale. "I'm afraid I'm too ill."

"Too ill to tell me?" It sprang up sharp to him, and almost to his lips, the fear that she would die without giving him light. He checked himself in time from so expressing his question, but she answered as if she had heard the words.

"Don't you know—now?"

"'Now'——?" She had spoken as if something that had made a difference had come up within the moment. But her maid, quickly obedient to her bell, was already with them. "I know nothing." And he was afterwards to say to himself that he must have spoken with odious impatience, such an impatience as to show that, supremely disconcerted, he washed his hands of the whole question.

"Oh!" said May Bartram.

"Are you in pain?" he asked, as the woman went to her.

"No," said May Bartram.

Her maid, who had put an arm round her as if to take her to her room, fixed on him eyes that appealingly contradicted her; in spite of which, however, he showed once more his mystification. "What then has happened?"

She was once more, with her companion's help, on her feet, and, feeling withdrawal imposed on him, he had found, blankly, his hat and gloves and had reached the door. Yet he waited for her answer. "What *was* to," she said.

V

He came back the next day, but she was then unable to see
him, and as it was literally the first time this had occurred in
the long stretch of their acquaintance he turned away, defeated and sore, almost angry—or feeling at least that such a
break in their custom was really the beginning of the end—
and wandered alone with his thoughts, especially with one of
them that he was unable to keep down. She was dying, and
he would lose her; she was dying, and his life would end. He
stopped in the park, into which he had passed, and stared
before him at his recurrent doubt. Away from her the doubt
pressed again; in her presence he had believed her, but as he
felt his forlornness he threw himself into the explanation that,
nearest at hand, had most of a miserable warmth for him and
least of a cold torment. She had deceived him to save him—
to put him off with something in which he should be able to
rest. What could the thing that was to happen to him be, after
all, but just this thing that had begun to happen? Her dying,
her death, his consequent solitude—*that* was what he had figured as the beast in the jungle, that was what had been in the
lap of the gods. He had had her word for it as he left her; for
what else, on earth, could she have meant? It wasn't a thing
of a monstrous order; not a fate rare and distinguished; not a
stroke of fortune that overwhelmed and immortalised; it had
only the stamp of the common doom. But poor Marcher, at
this hour, judged the common doom sufficient. It would serve
his turn, and even as the consummation of infinite waiting he
would bend his pride to accept it. He sat down on a bench
in the twilight. He hadn't been a fool. Something had *been*,
as she had said, to come. Before he rose indeed it had quite
struck him that the final fact really matched with the long
avenue through which he had had to reach it. As sharing his
suspense, and as giving herself all, giving her life, to bring it
to an end, she had come with him every step of the way. He
had lived by her aid, and to leave her behind would be cruelly,
damnably to miss her. What could be more overwhelming
than that?

Well, he was to know within the week, for though she kept
him a while at bay, left him restless and wretched during a

series of days on each of which he asked about her only again
to have to turn away, she ended his trial by receiving him
where she had always received him. Yet she had been brought
out at some hazard into the presence of so many of the things
that were, consciously, vainly, half their past, and there was
scant service left in the gentleness of her mere desire, all too
visible, to check his obsession and wind up his long trouble.
That was clearly what she wanted; the one thing more, for
her own peace, while she could still put out her hand. He was
so affected by her state that, once seated by her chair, he was
moved to let everything go; it was she herself therefore who
brought him back, took up again, before she dismissed him,
her last word of the other time. She showed how she wished
to leave their affair in order. "I'm not sure you understood.
You've nothing to wait for more. It *has* come."

Oh, how he looked at her! "Really?"

"Really."

"The thing that, as you said, *was* to?"

"The thing that we began in our youth to watch for."

Face to face with her once more he believed her; it was a
claim to which he had so abjectly little to oppose. "You mean
that it has come as a positive, definite occurrence, with a name
and a date?"

"Positive. Definite. I don't know about the 'name,' but,
oh, with a date!"

He found himself again too helplessly at sea. "But come in
the night—come and passed me by?"

May Bartram had her strange, faint smile. "Oh no, it hasn't
passed you by!"

"But if I haven't been aware of it, and it hasn't touched
me——?"

"Ah, your not being aware of it," and she seemed to hesitate an instant to deal with this—"your not being aware of
it is the strangeness *in* the strangeness. It's the wonder *of* the
wonder." She spoke as with the softness almost of a sick child,
yet now at last, at the end of all, with the perfect straightness
of a sibyl. She visibly knew that she knew, and the effect on
him was of something co-ordinate, in its high character, with
the law that had ruled him. It was the true voice of the law;
so on her lips would the law itself have sounded. "It *has*

touched you," she went on. "It has done its office. It has made you all its own."

"So utterly without my knowing it?"

"So utterly without your knowing it." His hand, as he leaned to her, was on the arm of her chair, and, dimly smiling always now, she placed her own on it. "It's enough if *I* know it."

"Oh!" he confusedly sounded, as she herself of late so often had done.

"What I long ago said is true. You'll never know now, and I think you ought to be content. You've *had* it," said May Bartram.

"But had what?"

"Why, what was to have marked you out. The proof of your law. It has acted. I'm too glad," she then bravely added, "to have been able to see what it's *not*."

He continued to attach his eyes to her, and with the sense that it was all beyond him, and that *she* was too, he would still have sharply challenged her, had he not felt it an abuse of her weakness to do more than take devoutly what she gave him, take it as hushed as to a revelation. If he did speak, it was out of the foreknowledge of his loneliness to come. "If you're glad of what it's 'not,' it might then have been worse?"

She turned her eyes away, she looked straight before her with which, after a moment: "Well, you know our fears."

He wondered. "It's something then we never feared?"

On this, slowly, she turned to him. "Did we ever dream, with all our dreams, that we should sit and talk of it thus?"

He tried for a little to make out if they had; but it was as if their dreams, numberless enough, were in solution in some thick, cold mist, in which thought lost itself. "It might have been that we couldn't talk?"

"Well"—she did her best for him—"not from this side. This, you see," she said, "is the *other* side."

"I think," poor Marcher returned, "that all sides are the same to me." Then, however, as she softly shook her head in correction: "We mightn't, as it were, have got across——?"

"To where we are—no. We're *here*"—she made her weak emphasis.

"And much good does it do us!" was her friend's frank comment.

"It does us the good it can. It does us the good that *it* isn't here. It's past. It's behind," said May Bartram. "Before——" but her voice dropped.

He had got up, not to tire her, but it was hard to combat his yearning. She after all told him nothing but that his light had failed—which he knew well enough without her. "Before——?" he blankly echoed.

"Before, you see, it was always to *come*. That kept it present."

"Oh, I don't care what comes now! Besides," Marcher added, "it seems to me I liked it better present, as you say, than I can like it absent with *your* absence."

"Oh, mine!"—and her pale hands made light of it.

"With the absence of everything." He had a dreadful sense of standing there before her for—so far as anything but this proved, this bottomless drop was concerned—the last time of their life. It rested on him with a weight he felt he could scarce bear, and this weight it apparently was that still pressed out what remained in him of speakable protest. "I believe you; but I can't begin to pretend I understand. *Nothing*, for me, is past; nothing *will* pass until I pass myself, which I pray my stars may be as soon as possible. Say, however," he added, "that I've eaten my cake, as you contend, to the last crumb—how can the thing I've never felt at all be the thing I was marked out to feel?"

She met him, perhaps, less directly, but she met him unperturbed. "You take your 'feelings' for granted. You were to suffer your fate. That was not necessarily to know it."

"How in the world—when what is such knowledge but suffering?"

She looked up at him a while, in silence. "No—you don't understand."

"I suffer," said John Marcher.

"Don't, don't!"

"How can I help at least *that*?"

"*Don't!*" May Bartram repeated.

She spoke it in a tone so special, in spite of her weakness, that he stared an instant—stared as if some light, hitherto hidden, had shimmered across his vision. Darkness again closed over it, but the gleam had already become for him an idea. "Because I haven't the right——?"

"Don't *know*—when you needn't," she mercifully urged. "You needn't—for we shouldn't."

"Shouldn't?" If he could but know what she meant!

"No—it's too much."

"Too much?" he still asked—but with a mystification that was the next moment, of a sudden, to give way. Her words, if they meant something, affected him in this light—the light also of her wasted face—as meaning *all*, and the sense of what knowledge had been for herself came over him with a rush which broke through into a question. "Is it of that, then, you're dying?"

She but watched him, gravely at first, as if to see, with this, where he was, and she might have seen something, or feared something, that moved her sympathy. "I would live for you still—if I could." Her eyes closed for a little, as if, withdrawn into herself, she were, for a last time, trying. "But I can't!" she said as she raised them again to take leave of him.

She couldn't indeed, as but too promptly and sharply appeared, and he had no vision of her after this that was anything but darkness and doom. They had parted forever in that strange talk; access to her chamber of pain, rigidly guarded, was almost wholly forbidden him; he was feeling now moreover, in the face of doctors, nurses, the two or three relatives attracted doubtless by the presumption of what she had to "leave," how few were the rights, as they were called in such cases, that he had to put forward, and how odd it might even seem that their intimacy shouldn't have given him more of them. The stupidest fourth cousin had more, even though she had been nothing in such a person's life. She had been a feature of features in *his*, for what else was it to have been so indispensable? Strange beyond saying were the ways of existence, baffling for him the anomaly of his lack, as he felt it to be, of producible claim. A woman might have been, as it were, everything to him, and it might yet present him in no connection that anyone appeared obliged to recognise. If this was the case in these closing weeks it was the case more sharply on the occasion of the last offices rendered, in the great grey

London cemetery, to what had been mortal, to what had been precious, in his friend. The concourse at her grave was not numerous, but he saw himself treated as scarce more nearly concerned with it than if there had been a thousand others. He was in short from this moment face to face with the fact that he was to profit extraordinarily little by the interest May Bartram had taken in him. He couldn't quite have said what he expected, but he had somehow not expected this approach to a double privation. Not only had her interest failed him, but he seemed to feel himself unattended—and for a reason he couldn't sound—by the distinction, the dignity, the propriety, if nothing else, of the man markedly bereaved. It was as if, in the view of society, he had not *been* markedly bereaved, as if there still failed some sign or proof of it, and as if, none the less, his character could never be affirmed, nor the deficiency ever made up. There were moments, as the weeks went by, when he would have liked, by some almost aggressive act, to take his stand on the intimacy of his loss, in order that it *might* be questioned and his retort, to the relief of his spirit, so recorded; but the moments of an irritation more helpless followed fast on these, the moments during which, turning things over with a good conscience but with a bare horizon, he found himself wondering if he oughtn't to have begun, so to speak, further back.

He found himself wondering indeed at many things, and this last speculation had others to keep it company. What could he have done, after all, in her lifetime, without giving them both, as it were, away? He couldn't have made it known she was watching him, for that would have published the superstition of the Beast. This was what closed his mouth now—now that the Jungle had been threshed to vacancy and that the Beast had stolen away. It sounded too foolish and too flat; the difference for him in this particular, the extinction in his life of the element of suspense, was such in fact as to surprise him. He could scarce have said what the effect resembled; the abrupt cessation, the positive prohibition, of music perhaps, more than anything else, in some place all adjusted and all accustomed to sonority and to attention. If he could at any rate have conceived lifting the veil from his image at some moment of the past (what had he done, after all, if not lift it to *her?*), so to do this to-day, to talk to people at large of the jungle cleared and confide to them that he now felt it as safe, would have been not only to see them listen as to a goodwife's tale, but really to hear himself tell one. What it presently came to in truth was that poor Marcher waded through his beaten grass, where no life stirred, where no breath sounded, where no evil eye seemed to gleam from a possible lair, very much as if vaguely looking for the Beast, and still more as if missing it. He walked about in an existence that had grown strangely more spacious, and, stopping fitfully in places where the undergrowth of life struck him as closer, asked himself yearningly, wondered secretly and sorely, if it would have lurked here or there. It would have at all events *sprung*; what was at least complete was his belief in the truth itself of the assurance given him. The change from his old sense to his new was absolute and final: what was to happen *had* so absolutely and finally happened that he was as little able to know a fear for his future as to know a hope; so absent in short was any question of anything still to come. He was to live entirely with the other question, that of his unidentified past, that of his having to see his fortune impenetrably muffled and masked.

The torment of this vision became then his occupation; he couldn't perhaps have consented to live but for the possibility of guessing. She had told him, his friend, not to guess; she had forbidden him, so far as he might, to know, and she had even in a sort denied the power in him to learn: which were so many things, precisely, to deprive him of rest. It wasn't that he wanted, he argued for fairness, that anything that had happened to him should happen over again; it was only that he shouldn't, as an anticlimax, have been taken sleeping so sound as not to be able to win back by an effort of thought the lost stuff of consciousness. He declared to himself at moments that he would either win it back or have done with consciousness for ever; he made this idea his one motive, in fine, made it so much his passion that none other, to compare with it, seemed ever to have touched him. The lost stuff of consciousness became thus for him as a strayed or stolen child to an unappeasable father; he hunted it up and down very much as if he were knocking at doors and inquiring of the police. This was the spirit in which, inevitably, he set himself to travel; he started on a journey that was to be as long as he could make it; it danced before him that, as the other side of the globe couldn't possibly have less to say to him, it might, by a possibility of suggestion, have more. Before he quitted London, however, he made a pilgrimage to May Bartram's grave, took his way to it through the endless avenues of the grim suburban necropolis, sought it out in the wilderness of tombs, and, though he had come but for the renewal of the act of farewell, found himself, when he had at last stood by it, beguiled into long intensities. He stood for an hour, powerless to turn away and yet powerless to penetrate the darkness of death; fixing with his eyes her inscribed name and date, beating his forehead against the fact of the secret they kept, drawing his breath, while he waited as if, in pity of him, some sense would rise from the stones. He kneeled on the stones, however, in vain; they kept what they concealed; and if the face of the tomb did become a face for him it was because her two names were like a pair of eyes that didn't know him. He gave them a last long look, but no palest light broke.

VI

He stayed away, after this, for a year; he visited the depths of Asia, spending himself on scenes of romantic interest, of superlative sanctity; but what was present to him everywhere was that for a man who had known what *he* had known the world was vulgar and vain. The state of mind in which he had lived for so many years shone out to him, in reflection, as a light that coloured and refined, a light beside which the glow of the East was garish, cheap and thin. The terrible truth was that he had lost—with everything else—a distinction as well; the things he saw couldn't help being common when he had become common to look at them. He was simply now one of them himself—he was in the dust, without a peg for the sense of difference; and there were hours when, before the temples of gods and the sepulchres of kings, his spirit turned, for nobleness of association, to the barely discriminated slab in the London suburb. That had become for him, and more intensely with time and distance, his one witness of a past glory. It was all that was left to him for proof or pride, yet the past glories of Pharaohs were nothing to him as he thought of it. Small wonder then that he came back to it on the morrow of his return. He was drawn there this time as irresistibly as the other, yet with a confidence, almost, that was doubtless the effect of the many months that had elapsed. He had lived, in spite of himself, into his change of feeling, and in wandering over the earth had wandered, as might be said, from the circumference to the centre of his desert. He had settled to his safety and accepted perforce his extinction; figuring to himself, with some colour, in the likeness of certain little old men he remembered to have seen, of whom, all meagre and wizened as they might look, it was related that they had in their time fought twenty duels or been loved by ten princesses. They indeed had been wondrous for others, while he was but wondrous for himself; which, however, was exactly the cause of his haste to renew the wonder by getting back, as he might put it, into his own presence. That had quickened his steps and checked his delay. If his visit was prompt it was because he had been separated so long from the part of himself that alone he now valued.

It is accordingly not false to say that he reached his goal with a certain elation and stood there again with a certain assurance. The creature beneath the sod *knew* of his rare experience, so that, strangely now, the place had lost for him its mere blankness of expression. It met him in mildness—not, as before, in mockery; it wore for him the air of conscious greeting that we find, after absence, in things that have closely belonged to us and which seem to confess of themselves to the connection. The plot of ground, the graven tablet, the tended flowers affected him so as belonging to him that he quite felt for the hour like a contented landlord reviewing a piece of property. Whatever had happened—well, had happened. He had not come back this time with the vanity of that question, his former worrying, "What, *what?*" now practically so spent. Yet he would, none the less, never again so cut himself off from the spot; he would come back to it every month, for if he did nothing else by its aid he at least held up his head. It thus grew for him, in the oddest way, a positive resource; he carried out his idea of periodical returns, which took their place at last among the most inveterate of his habits.

What it all amounted to, oddly enough, was that, in his now so simplified world, this garden of death gave him the few square feet of earth on which he could still most live. It was as if, being nothing anywhere else for anyone, nothing even for himself, he were just everything here, and if not for a crowd of witnesses, or indeed for any witness but John Marcher, then by clear right of the register that he could scan like an open page. The open page was the tomb of his friend, and *there* were the facts of the past, there the truth of his life, there the backward reaches in which he could lose himself. He did this, from time to time, with such effect that he seemed to wander through the old years with his hand in the arm of a companion who was, in the most extraordinary manner, his other, his younger self; and to wander, which was more extraordinary yet, round and round a third presence—not wandering she, but stationary, still, whose eyes, turning with his revolution, never ceased to follow him, and whose eyes, turning with his revolution, never ceased to follow him, and whose seat was his point, so to speak, of orientation. Thus in short he settled to live—feeding only on the sense that he once *had* lived, and dependent on it not only for a support but for an identity.

It sufficed him, in its way, for months, and the year elapsed; it would doubtless even have carried him further but for an accident, superficially slight, which moved him, in a quite other direction, with a force beyond any of his impressions of Egypt or of India. It was a thing of the merest chance—the turn, as he afterwards felt, of a hair, though he was indeed to live to believe that if light hadn't come to him in this particular fashion it would still have come in another. He was to live to believe this, I say, though he was not to live, I may not less definitely mention, to do much else. We allow him at any rate the benefit of the conviction, struggling up for him at the end, that, whatever might have happened or not happened, he would have come round of himself to the light. The incident of an autumn day had put the match to the train laid from of old by his misery. With the light before him he knew that even of late his ache had only been smothered. It was strangely drugged, but it throbbed; at the touch it began to bleed. And the touch, in the event, was the face of a fellow-mortal. This face, one grey afternoon when the leaves were thick in the alleys, looked into Marcher's own, at the cemetery, with an expression like the cut of a blade. He felt it, that is, so deep down that he winced at the steady thrust. The person who so mutely assaulted him was a figure he had noticed, on reaching his own goal, absorbed by a grave a short distance away, a grave apparently fresh, so that the emotion of the visitor would probably match it for frankness. This fact alone forbade further attention, though during the time he stayed he remained vaguely conscious of his neighbour, a middle-aged man apparently, in mourning, whose bowed back, among the clustered monuments and mortuary yews, was constantly presented. Marcher's theory that these were elements in contact with which he himself revived, had suffered, on this occasion, it may be granted, a sensible though inscrutable check. The autumn day was dire for him as none had recently been, and he rested with a heaviness he had not yet known on the low stone table that bore May Bartram's name. He rested without power to move, as if some spring in him, some spell vouchsafed, had suddenly been broken forever. If he could have done that moment as he wanted he would simply have stretched himself on the slab that was ready to take him, treating it as a place prepared to receive his last sleep. What in all the wide world had he now to keep awake for? He stared before him with the question, and it was then that, as one of the cemetery walks passed near him, he caught the shock of the face.

His neighbour at the other grave had withdrawn, as he himself, with force in him to move, would have done by now, and was advancing along the path on his way to one of the gates. This brought him near, and his pace was slow, so that—and all the more as there was a kind of hunger in his look—the two men were for a minute directly confronted. Marcher felt him on the spot as one of the deeply stricken—a perception so sharp that nothing else in the picture lived for it, neither his dress, his age, nor his presumable character and class; nothing lived but the deep ravage of the features that he showed. He *showed* them—that was the point; he was moved, as he passed, by some impulse that was either a signal for sympathy or, more possibly, a challenge to another sorrow.

He might already have been aware of our friend, might, at some previous hour, have noticed in him the smooth habit of the scene, with which the state of his own senses so scantly consorted, and might thereby have been stirred as by a kind of overt discord. What Marcher was at all events conscious of was, in the first place, that the imaged of scarred passion presented to him was conscious too—of something that profaned the air; and, in the second, that, roused, startled, shocked, he was yet the next moment looking after it, as it went, with envy. The most extraordinary thing that had happened to him—though he had given that name to other matters as well—took place, after his immediate vague stare, as a consequence of this impression. The stranger passed, but the raw glare of his grief remained, making our friend wonder in pity what wrong, what wound it expressed, what injury not to be healed. What had the man *had* to make him, by the loss of it, so bleed and yet live?

Something—and this reached him with a pang—that *he*, John Marcher, hadn't; the proof of which was precisely John Marcher's arid end. No passion had ever touched him, for this was what passion meant; he had survived and maundered and pined, but where had been *his* deep ravage? The extraordinary thing we speak of was the sudden rush of the result of this question. The sight that had just met his eyes named to him, as in letters of quick flame, something he had utterly, insanely missed, and what he had missed made these things a train of fire, made them mark themselves in an anguish of inward throbs. He had seen *outside* of his life, not learned it within, the way a woman was mourned when she had been loved for herself; such was the force of his conviction of the meaning of the stranger's face, which still flared for him like a smoky torch. It had not come to him, the knowledge, on the wings of experience; it had brushed him, jostled him, upset him, with the disrespect of chance, the insolence of an accident. Now that the illumination had begun, however, it blazed to the zenith, and what he presently stood there gazing at was the sounded void of his life. He gazed, he drew breath, in pain; he turned in his dismay, and, turning, he had before him in sharper incision than ever the open page of his story. The name on the table smote him as the passage of his neighbour

had done, and what it said to him, full in the face, was that
she was what he had missed. This was the awful thought, the
answer to all the past, the vision at the dread clearness of
which he turned as cold as the stone beneath him. Everything
fell together, confessed, explained, overwhelmed; leaving him
most of all stupefied at the blindness he had cherished. The
fate he had been marked for he had met with a vengeance—
he had emptied the cup to the lees; he had been the man of
his time, *the* man, to whom nothing on earth was to have
happened. That was the rare stroke—that was his visitation.
So he saw it, as we say, in pale horror, while the pieces fitted
and fitted. So *she* had seen it, while he didn't, and so she
served at this hour to drive the truth home. It was the truth,
vivid and monstrous, that all the while he had waited the wait
was itself his portion. This the companion of his vigil had at
a given moment perceived, and she had then offered him the
chance to baffle his doom. One's doom, however, was never
baffled, and on the day she had told him that his own had
come down she had seen him but stupidly stare at the escape
she offered him.

The escape would have been to love her; then, *then* he
would have lived. *She* had lived—who could say now with
what passion?—since she had loved him for himself; whereas
he had never thought of her (ah, how it hugely glared at him!)
but in the chill of his egotism and the light of her use. Her
spoken words came back to him, and the chain stretched and
stretched. The beast had lurked indeed, and the beast, at its
hour, had sprung; it had sprung in that twilight of the cold
April when, pale, ill, wasted, but all beautiful, and perhaps
even then recoverable, she had risen from her chair to stand
before him and let him imaginably guess. It had sprung as he
didn't guess; it had sprung as she hopelessly turned from him,
and the mark, by the time he left her, had fallen where it *was*
to fall. He had justified his fear and achieved his fate; he had
failed, with the last exactitude, of all he was to fail of; and a
moan now rose to his lips as he remembered she had prayed
he mightn't know. This horror of waking—*this* was knowledge, knowledge under the breath of which the very tears in
his eyes seemed to freeze. Through them, none the less, he
tried to fix it and hold it; he kept it there before him so that

he might feel the pain. That at least, belated and bitter, had something of the taste of life. But the bitterness suddenly sickened him, and it was as if, horribly, he saw, in the truth, in the cruelty of his image, what had been appointed and done. He saw the Jungle of his life and saw the lurking Beast; then, while he looked, perceived it, as by a stir of the air, rise, huge and hideous, for the leap that was to settle him. His eyes darkened—it was close; and, instinctively turning, in his hallucination, to avoid it, he flung himself, on his face, on the tomb.

The Papers

THERE was a longish period—the dense duration of a London winter, cheered, if cheered it could be called, with lurid electric, with fierce "incandescent" flares and glares—when they repeatedly met, at feeding-time, in a small and not quite savoury pothouse a stone's-throw from the Strand. They talked always of pothouses, of feeding-time—by which they meant any hour between one and four of the afternoon; they talked of most things, even of some of the greatest, in a manner that gave, or that they desired to show as giving, in respect to the conditions of their life, the measure of their detachment, their contempt, their general irony. Their general irony, which they tried at the same time to keep gay and to make amusing at least to each other, was their refuge from the want of savour, the want of napkins, the want, too often, of shillings, and of many things besides that they would have liked to have. Almost all they had with any security was their youth, complete, admirable, very nearly invulnerable, or as yet inattackable; for they didn't count their talent, which they had originally taken for granted and had since then lacked freedom of mind, as well indeed as any offensive reason, to reappraise. They were taken up with other questions and other estimates—the remarkable limits, for instance, of their luck, the remarkable smallness of the talent of their friends. They were above all in that phase of youth and in that state of aspiration in which "luck" is the subject of most frequent reference, as definite as the colour red, and in which it is the elegant name for money when people are as refined as they are poor. She was only a suburban young woman in a sailor hat, and he a young man destitute, in strictness, of occasion for a "topper"; but they felt that they had in a peculiar way the freedom of the town, and the town, if it did nothing else, gave a range to the spirit. They sometimes went, on excursions that they groaned at as professional, far afield from the Strand, but the curiosity with which they came back was mostly greater than any other, the Strand being for them, with its ampler alternative Fleet Street, overwhelmingly the Papers, and the

Papers being, at a rough guess, all the furniture of their consciousness.

The Daily Press played for them the part played by the embowered nest on the swaying bough for the parent birds that scour the air. It was, as they mainly saw it, a receptacle, owing its form to the instinct more remarkable, as they held the journalistic, than that even of the most highly organised animal, into which, regularly, breathlessly, contributions had to be dropped—odds and ends, all grist to the mill, all somehow digestible and convertible, all conveyed with the promptest possible beak and the flutter, often, of dreadfully fatigued little wings. If there had been no Papers there would have been no young friends for us of the figure we hint at, no chance mates, innocent and weary, yet acute even to penetration, who were apt to push off their plates and rest their elbows on the table in the interval between the turn-over of the pint-pot and the call for the awful glibness of their score. Maud Blandy drank beer—and welcome, as one may say; and she smoked cigarettes when privacy permitted, though she drew the line at this in the right place, just as she flattered herself she knew how to draw it, journalistically, where other delicacies were concerned. She was fairly a product of the day—so fairly that she might have been born afresh each morning, to serve, after the fashion of certain agitated ephemeral insects, only till the morrow. It was as if a past had been wasted on her and a future were not to be fitted; she was really herself, so far at least as her great preoccupation went, an edition, an "extra special," coming out at the loud hours and living its life, amid the roar of vehicles, the hustle of pavements, the shriek of newsboys, according to the quantity of shock to be proclaimed and distributed, the quantity to be administered, thanks to the varying temper of Fleet Street, to the nerves of the nation. Maud was a shocker, in short, in petticoats, and alike for the thoroughfare, the club, the suburban train and the humble home; though it must honestly be added that petticoats were not of her essence. This was one of the reasons, in an age of "emancipations," of her intense actuality, as well as, positively, of a good fortune to which, however impersonal she might have appeared, she was not herself in a position to do full justice; the felicity of her having about her naturally so much of the young bachelor that she was saved the disfigurement of any marked straddling or elbowing. It was literally true of her that she would have pleased less, or at least have offended more, had she been obliged, or been prompted, to assert—all too vainly, as it would have been sure to be—her superiority to sex. Nature, constitution, accident, whatever we happen to call it, had relieved her of this care; the struggle for life, the competition with men, the taste of the day, the fashion of the hour had *made* her superior, or had at any rate made her indifferent, and she had no difficulty in remaining so. The thing was therefore, with the aid of an extreme general flatness of person, directness of step and simplicity of motive, quietly enough done, without a grace, a weak inconsequence, a stray reminder to interfere with the success; and it is not too much to say that the success—by which I mean the plainness of the type—would probably never have struck you as so great as at the moments of our young lady's chance comradeship with Howard Bight. For the young man, though his personal signs had not, like his friend's, especially the effect of one of the stages of an evolution, might have been noted as not so fiercely or so freshly a male as to distance Maud in the show.

She presented him in truth, while they sat together, as comparatively girlish. She fell naturally into gestures, tones, expressions, resemblances, that he either suppressed, from sensibility to her personal predominance, or that were merely latent in him through much taking for granted. Mild, sensitive, none too solidly nourished, and condemned, perhaps by a deep delusion as to the final issue of it, to perpetual coming and going, he was so resigned to many things, and so disgusted even with many others, that the least of his cares was the cultivation of a bold front. What mainly concerned him was its being bold enough to get him his dinner, and it was never more void of aggression than when he solicited in person those scraps of information, snatched at those floating particles of news, on which his dinner depended. Had he had time a little more to try his case, he would have made out that if he liked Maud Blandy it was partly by the impression of what she could do for him: what she could do for herself had never entered into his head. The positive quantity, moreover, was vague to his mind; it existed, that is, for the present, but as the proof of how, in spite of the want of encouragement, a fellow could keep going. She struck him in fact as the only encouragement he had, and this altogether by example, since precept, frankly, was deterrent on her lips, as speech was free, judgment prompt, and accent not absolutely pure. The point was that, as the easiest thing to be with her, he was so passive that it almost made him graceful and so attentive that it almost made him distinguished. She was herself neither of these things, and they were not of course what a man had most to be; whereby she contributed to their common view the impatiences required by a proper reaction, forming thus for him a kind of protective hedge behind which he could wait. Much waiting, for either, was, I hasten to add, always in order, inasmuch as their novitiate seemed to them interminable and the steps of their ladder fearfully far apart. It rested—the ladder—against the great stony wall of the public attention—a sustaining mass which apparently wore somewhere, in the upper air, a big, thankless, expressionless face, a countenance equipped with eyes, ears, an uplifted nose and a gaping mouth—all convenient if they could only be reached. The ladder groaned meanwhile, swayed and shook with the weight of the close-pressed climbers, tier upon tier, occupying the upper, the middle, the nethermost rounds and quite preventing, for young persons placed as our young friends were placed, any view of the summit. It was meanwhile moreover only Howard Bight's perverse view—he was confessedly perverse—that Miss Blandy had arrived at a perch superior to his own.

She had hitherto recognised in herself indeed but a tighter clutch and a grimmer purpose; she had recognised, she believed, in keen moments, a vocation; she had recognised that there had been eleven of them at home, with herself as youngest, and distinctions by that time so blurred in her that she might as easily have been christened John. She had recognised truly, most of all, that if they came to talk they both were nowhere; yet this was compatible with her insisting that Howard had as yet comparatively had the luck. When he wrote to people they consented, or at least they answered; almost always, for that matter, they answered with greed, so that he was not without something of some sort to hawk about to buyers. Specimens indeed of human greed—*the* greed, the great one, the eagerness to figure, the snap at the bait of publicity, he had collected in such store as to stock, as to launch, a museum. In this museum the prize object, the high rare specimen, had been for some time established; a celebrity of the day enjoying, uncontested, a glass case all to himself, more conspicuous than any other, before which the arrested visitor might rebound from surprised recognition. Sir A. B. C. Beadel-Muffet K.C.B., M.P., stood forth there as large as life, owing indeed his particular place to the shade of direct acquaintance with him that Howard Bight could boast, yet with his eminent presence in such a collection but too generally and notoriously justified. He was universal and ubiquitous, commemorated, under some rank rubric, on every page of every public print every day in every year, and as inveterate a feature of each issue of any self-respecting sheet as the name, the date, the tariffed advertisements. He had always done something, or was about to do something, round which the honours of announcement clustered, and indeed, as he had inevitably thus become a subject of fallacious report, one half of his chronicle appeared to consist of official contradiction of the other half. His activity—if it had not better been called his passivity—was beyond any other that figured in the public eye, for no other assuredly knew so few or such brief intermittences. Yet, as there was the inside as well as the outside view of his current history, the quantity of it was easy to analyse for the possessor of the proper crucible. Howard Bight, with his arms on the table, took it apart and put it together again most days in the year, so that an amused comparison of notes on the subject often added a mild spice to his colloquies with Maud Blandy. They knew, the young pair, as they considered, many secrets, but they liked to think that they knew none quite so scandalous as the way that, to put it roughly, this distinguished person maintained his distinction.

It was known certainly to all who had to do with the Papers, a brotherhood, a sisterhood of course interested—for what was it, in the last resort, but the interest of their bread and butter?—in shrouding the approaches to the oracle, in not telling tales out of school. They all lived alike on the solemnity, the sanctity of the oracle, and the comings and goings, the doings and undoings, the intentions and retractations of Sir A. B. C. Beadel-Muffet K.C.B., M.P., were in their degree a part of that solemnity. The Papers, taken together the glory of the age, were, though superficially multifold, fundamentally one, so that any revelation of their being procured or procurable to float an object not intrinsically buoyant would very logically convey discredit from the circumference—where the revelation would be likely to be made—to the centre. Of so much as this our grim neophytes, in common with a thousand others, were perfectly aware; but something in the nature of their wit, such as it was, or in the condition of their nerves, such as it easily might become, sharpened almost to acerbity their relish of so artful an imitation of the voice of fame. The fame was *all* voice, as they could guarantee who had an ear always glued to the speaking-tube; the items that made the sum were individually of the last vulgarity, but the accumulation was a triumph—one of the greatest the age could show—of industry and vigilance. It was after all not true that a man had done nothing who for ten years had so fed, so dyked and directed and distributed the fitful sources of publicity. He had laboured, in his way, like a navvy with a spade; he might be said to have earned by each night's work the reward, each morning, of his small spurt of glory. Even for such a matter as its not being true that Sir A. B. C. Beadel-Muffet K.C.B., M.P., was to start on his visit to the Sultan of Samarcand on the 23rd, *but* being true that he was to start on the 29th, the personal attention required was no small affair, taking the legend with the fact, the myth with the meaning, the original artless error with the subsequent earnest truth—allowing in fine for the statement still to come that the visit would have to be relinquished in consequence of the visitor's other pressing engagements, and bearing in mind the countless channels to be successively watered. Our young man, one December afternoon, pushed an evening paper across to his companion, keeping his thumb on a paragraph at which she glanced without eagerness. She might, from her manner, have known by instinct what it would be, and her exclamation had the note of satiety. "Oh, he's working *them* now?"

"If he has begun he'll work them hard. By the time that has gone round the world there'll be something else to say. 'We are authorised to state that the marriage of Miss Miranda Beadel-Muffet to Captain Guy Devereux, of the Fiftieth Rifles, will not take place.' Authorised to state—rather! when every wire in the machine has been pulled over and over. They're authorised to state something every day in the year, and the authorisation is not difficult to get. Only his daughters, now that they're coming on, poor things—and I believe there are many—will have to be chucked into the pot and produced on occasions when other matter fails. How pleasant for them to find themselves hurtling through the air, clubbed by the paternal hand, like golf-balls in a suburb! Not that I suppose they don't like it—why should one suppose anything of the sort?" Howard Bight's impression of the general appetite appeared to-day to be especially vivid, and he and his companion were alike prompted to one of those slightly violent returns on themselves and the work they were doing which none but the vulgar-minded altogether avoid. "People—as I see them—would almost rather be jabbered about unpleasantly than not be jabbered about at all: whenever you try them—whenever, at least, I do—I'm confirmed in that conviction. It isn't only that if one holds out the mere tip of the perch they jump at it like starving fish; it is that they leap straight out of the water themselves, leap in their thousands and come flopping, open-mouthed and goggle-eyed, to one's very door. What is the sense of the French expression about a person's making *des yeux de carpe*? It suggests the eyes that a young newspaper-man seems to see all round him, and I declare I sometimes feel that, if one has the courage not to blink at the show, the gilt is a good deal rubbed off the gingerbread of one's early illusions. They all do it, as the song is at the music-halls, and it's some of one's surprises that tell one most. You've thought there were some high souls that didn't do it—that wouldn't, I mean, to work the oracle, lift a little finger of their own. But, Lord bless you, give them a a chance—you'll find some of the greatest the greediest. I give you my word for it, I haven't a scrap of faith left in a single human creature. Except, of course," the young man added, "the grand creature that *you* are, and the cold, calm, comprehensive one whom you thus admit to your familiarity. *We* face the music. We see, we understand; we know we've got to live, and how we do it. But at least, like this, alone together, we take our intellectual revenge, we escape the indignity of being fools dealing with fools. I don't say we shouldn't enjoy it more if we *were*. But it can't be helped; we haven't the gift— the gift, I mean, of not seeing. We do the worst we can for the money."

"*You* certainly do the worst you can," Maud Blandy soon replied, "when you sit there, with your wanton wiles, and take the spirit out of me. I require a working faith, you know. If one isn't a fool, in our world, where *is* one?"

"Oh, I say!" her companion groaned without alarm. "Don't you fail *me*, mind you."

They looked at each other across their clean platters, and, little as the light of romance seemed superficially to shine in them or about them, the sense was visibly enough in each of being involved in the other. He would have been sharply alone, the softly sardonic young man, if the somewhat dry young woman hadn't affected him, in a way he was even too nervous to put to the test, as saving herself up for him; and the consciousness of absent resources that was on her own side quite compatible with this economy grew a shade or two less dismal with the imagination of his somehow being at costs for her. It wasn't an expense of shillings—there was not much question of that; what it came to was perhaps nothing more than that, being, as he declared himself, "in the know," he kept pulling her in too, as if there had been room for them both. He told her everything, all his secrets. He talked and talked, often making her think of herself as a lean, stiff person, destitute of skill or art, but with ear enough to be performed to, sometimes strangely touched, at moments completely ravished, by a fine violinist. He was her fiddler and genius; she was sure neither of her taste nor of his tunes, but if she could do nothing else for him she could hold the case while he handled the instrument. It had never passed between them that they could draw nearer, for they seemed near, near verily for pleasure, when each, in a decent young life, was so much nearer to the other than to anything else. There was no pleasure known to either that wasn't further off. What held them together was in short that they were in the same boat, a cockle-shell in a great rough sea, and that the movements required for keeping it afloat not only were what the situation safely permitted, but also made for reciprocity and intimacy. These talks over greasy white slabs, repeatedly mopped with moist grey cloths by young women in black uniforms, with inexorable braided "buns" in the nape of weak necks, these sessions, sometimes prolonged, in halls of oilcloth, among penal-looking tariffs and pyramids of scones, enabled them to rest on their oars; the more that they were on terms with the whole families, chartered companies, of food-stations, each a race of innumerable and indistinguishable members, and had mastered those hours of comparative elegance, the earlier and the later, when the little weary ministrants were limply sitting down and the occupants of the red benches bleakly interspaced. So it was, that, at times, they renewed their understanding, and by signs, mannerless and meagre, that would have escaped the notice of witnesses. Maud Blandy had no need to kiss her hand across to him to show she felt what he meant; she had moreover never in her life kissed her hand to anyone, and her companion couldn't have imagined it of her. His romance was so grey that it wasn't romance at all; it was a reality arrived at without stages, shades, forms. If he had been ill or stricken she would have taken him—other resources failing—into her lap; but would that, which would scarce even have been motherly, have been romantic? She nevertheless at this moment put in her plea for the general element. "I can't help it, about Beadel-Muffet; it's too magnificent—it appeals to me. And then I've a particular feeling about him—I'm waiting to see what will happen. It *is* genius, you know, to get yourself so celebrated for nothing—to carry out your idea in the face of everything. I mean your idea of *being* celebrated. It isn't as if he had done even one little thing. What *has* he done when you come to look?"

"Why, my dear chap, he has done everything. He has missed nothing. He has been in everything, *of* everything, *at* everything, *over* everything, *under* everything, that has taken place for the last twenty years. He's *always* present, and, though he never makes a speech, he never fails to get alluded to in the speeches of others. That's doing it cheaper than anyone else does it, but it's thoroughly doing it—which is what we're talking about. And so far," the young man contended, "from its being 'in the face' of anything, it's positively with the help of everything, since the Papers are everything and more. They're made for such people, though no doubt he's the person who has known best how to use them. I've gone through one of the biggest sometimes, from beginning to end—it's quite a thrilling little game—to catch him once out. It has happened to me to think I was near it when, on the last column of the last page—I count 'advertisements,' heaven help us, out!—I've found him as large as life and as true as the needle to the pole. But at last, in a way, it goes, it can't help going, of itself. He comes in, he breaks out, of himself; the letters, under the compositor's hand, form themselves, from the force of habit, into his name—any connection for it, any context, being as good as any other, and the wind, which he has originally 'raised,' but which continues to blow, setting perpetually in his favour. The thing would really be now, don't you see, for him to keep himself out. That would be, on my honour, it strikes me—his *getting* himself out—the biggest fact in his record."

The girl's attention, as her friend developed the picture, had become more present. "He *can't* get himself out. There he is." She had a pause; she had been thinking. "That's just my idea."

"Your idea? Well, an idea's always a blessing. What do you want for it?"

She continued to turn it over as if weighing its value. "Something perhaps *could* be done with it—only it would take imagination."

He wondered, and she seemed to wonder that he didn't see. "Is it a situation for a 'ply'?"

"No, it's too good for a ply—yet it isn't quite good enough for a short story."

"It would do then for a novel?"

"Well, I seem to see it," Maud said—"and with a lot *in* it to be got out. But I seem to see it as a question not of what you or I might be able to do with it, but of what the poor man himself may. That's what I meant just now," she explained, "by my having a creepy sense of what may happen

for him. It has already more than once occurred to me. *Then*,"
she wound up, "we shall have real life, the case itself."

"Do you know *you've* got imagination?" Her friend, rather
interested, appeared by this time to have seized her thought.

"I see him having for some reason, very imperative, to seek
retirement, lie low, to hide, in fact, like a man 'wanted,' but
pursued all the while by the lurid glare that he has himself so
started and kept up, and at last literally devoured ('like Frank-
enstein,' of course!) by the monster he has created."

"I say, you *have* got it!"—and the young man flushed, visibly, artistically, with the recognition of elements which his
eyes had for a minute earnestly fixed. "But it will take a lot
of doing."

"Oh," said Maud, "*we* shan't have to do it. He'll do it
himself."

"I wonder." Howard Bight really wondered. "The fun
would be for him to do it *for* us. I mean for him to want us
to help him somehow to get out."

"Oh, 'us'!" the girl mournfully sighed.

"Why not, when he comes to us to get in?"

Maud Blandy stared. "Do you mean to you personally? You
surely know by this time that no one ever 'comes' to me."

"Why, I went to him in the first instance; I made up to him
straight, I did him 'at home,' somewhere, as I've surely mentioned to you before, three years ago. He liked, I believe—
for he's really a delightful old ass—the way I did it; he knows
my name and has my address, and has written me three or
four times since, with his own hand, a request to be so good
as to make use of my (he hopes) still close connection with
the daily Press to rectify the rumour that he has reconsidered
his opinion on the subject of the blankets supplied to the
Upper Tooting Workhouse Infirmary. He has reconsidered his
opinion on no subject whatever—which he mentions, in the
interest of historic truth, without further intrusion on my
valuable time. And he regards that sort of thing as a commodity that I can dispose of—thanks to my 'close connection'
—for several shillings."

"And can you?"

"Not for several pence. They're all tariffed, but he's tariffed
low—having a value, apparently, that money doesn't repre-

sent. He's always welcome, but he isn't always paid for. The beauty, however, is in his marvellous memory, his keeping us all so apart and not muddling the fellow to whom he has written that he hasn't done this, that or the other with the fellow to whom he has written that he has. He'll write to me again some day about something else—about his alleged position on the date of the next school-treat of the Chelsea Cabmen's Orphanage. I shall seek a market for the precious item, and that will keep us in touch; so that if the complication you have the sense of in your bones does come into play—the thought's too beautiful!—he may once more remember me. Fancy his coming to one with a 'What can you do for me *now*?' " Bight lost himself in the happy vision; it gratified so his cherished consciousness of the "irony of fate"—a consciousness so cherished that he never could write ten lines without use of the words.

Maud showed however at this point a reserve which appeared to have grown as the possibility opened out. "I believe in it—it must come. It can't not. It's the only end. He doesn't know; nobody knows—the simple-minded all: only you and I know. But it won't be nice, remember."

"It won't be funny?"

"It will be pitiful. There'll have to be a reason."

"For his turning round?" the young man nursed the vision. "More or less—I see what you mean. But except for a 'ply' will that so much matter? His reason will concern himself. What will concern us will be his funk and his helplessness, his having to stand there in the blaze, with nothing and nobody to put it out. We shall see him, shrieking for a bucket of water, wither up in the central flame."

Her look had turned sombre. "It makes one cruel. That is it makes *you*. I mean our trade does."

"I dare say—I see too much. But I'm willing to chuck it."

"Well," she presently replied, "I'm not willing to, but it seems pretty well on the cards that I shall have to. *I* don't see too much. I don't see enough. So, for all the good it does me——!"

She had pushed back her chair and was looking round for her umbrella. "Why, what's the matter?" Howard Bight too blankly inquired.

She met his eyes while she pulled on her rusty old gloves. "Well, I'll tell you another time."

He kept his place, still lounging, contented where she had again become restless. "Don't you call it seeing enough to see—to have had so luridly revealed to you—the doom of Beadel-Muffet?"

"Oh, he's not my business, he's yours. You're his man, or one of his men—he'll come back to you. Besides, he's a special case, and, as I say, I'm too sorry for him."

"That's a proof then of what you do see."

Her silence for a moment admitted it, though evidently she was making, for herself, a distinction, which she didn't express. "I don't then see what I want, what I require. And *he*," she added, "if he does have some reason, will have to have an awfully strong one. To be strong enough it will have to be awful."

"You mean he'll have done something?"

"Yes, that may remain undiscovered if he can only drop out of the papers, sit for a while in darkness. You'll know what it is; you'll not be able to help yourself. But I shan't want to, for anything."

She had got up as she said it, and he sat looking at her, thanks to her odd emphasis, with an interest that, as he also rose, passed itself off as a joke. "Ah, then, you sweet sensitive thing, I promise to keep it from you."

II

They met again a few days later, and it seemed the law of their meetings that these should take place mainly within moderate eastward range of Charing Cross. An afternoon performance of a play translated from the Finnish, already several times given, on a series of Saturdays, had held Maud for an hour in a small, hot, dusty theatre where the air hung as heavy about the great "trimmed" and plumed hats of the ladies as over the flora and fauna of a tropical forest; at the end of which she edged out of her stall in the last row, to join a small band of unattached critics and correspondents, spectators with ulterior views and pencilled shirtcuffs, who, coming together in the lobby for an exchange of ideas, were ranging from "Awful rot" to "Rather jolly." Ideas, of this calibre, rumbled and flashed, so that, lost in the discussion, our young woman failed at first to make out that a gentleman on the other side of the group, but standing a little off, had his eyes on her for some extravagant, though apparently quite respectable, purpose. He had been waiting for her to recognise him, and as soon as he had caught her attention he came round to her with an eager bow. She had by this time entirely placed him—placed him as the smoothest and most shining subject with which, in the exercise of her profession, she had yet experimented; but her recognition was accompanied with a pang that his amiable address made but the sharper. She had her reason for awkwardness in the presence of a rosy, glossy, kindly, but discernibly troubled personage whom she had waited on "at home" at her own suggestion—promptly welcomed—and the sympathetic element in whose "personality," the Chippendale, the photographic, the autographic elements in whose flat in the Earl's Court Road, she had commemorated in the liveliest prose of which she was capable. She had described with humour his favourite pug, she had revealed with permission his favourite make of Kodak, she had touched upon his favourite manner of spending his Sundays and had extorted from him the shy confession that he preferred after all the novel of adventure to the novel of subtlety. Her embarrassment was therefore now the greater as, touching to behold, he so clearly had approached her with no intention of asperity, not even at first referring at all to the matter that couldn't have been gracefully explained.

She had seen him originally—had had the instinct of it in making up to him—as one of the happy of the earth, and the impression of him "at home," on his proving so good-natured about the interview, had begotten in her a sharper envy, a hungrier sense of the invidious distinctions of fate, than any her literary conscience, which she deemed rigid, had yet had to reckon with. He must have been rich, rich by such estimates as hers; he at any rate had everything, while she had nothing—nothing but the vulgar need of offering him to brag, on his behalf, for money, if she could get it, about his luck. She hadn't in fact got money, hadn't so much as managed to work in her stuff anywhere; a practical comment sharp

enough on her having represented to him—with wasted pathos, she was indeed soon to perceive—how "important" it
was to her that people should let her get at them. This dim
celebrity had not needed that argument; he had not only, with
his alacrity, allowed her, as she had said, to try her hand, but
had tried *with* her, quite feverishly, and all to the upshot of
showing her that there were even greater outsiders than herself. He could have put down money, could have published,
as the phrase was—a bare two columns—at his own expense;
but it was just a part of his rather irritating luxury that he had
a scruple about that, wanted intensely to taste the sweet, but
didn't want to owe it to any wire-pulling. He wanted the
golden apple straight from the tree, where it yet seemed so
unable to grow for him by any exuberance of its own. He had
breathed to her his real secret—that to be inspired, to work
with effect, he had to feel he was appreciated, to have it all
somehow come back to him. The artist, necessarily sensitive,
lived on encouragement, on knowing and being reminded
that people cared for him a little, cared even just enough to
flatter him a wee bit. They had talked that over, and he had
really, as he called it, quite put himself in her power. He had
whispered in her ear that it might be very weak and silly, but
that positively to be himself, to do anything, certainly to do
his best, he required the breath of sympathy. He did love
notice, let alone praise—there it was. To be systematically
ignored—well, blighted him at the root. He was afraid she
would think he had said too much, but she left him with his
leave, none the less, to repeat a part of it. They had agreed
that she was to bring in prettily, somehow, that he did love
praise; for just the right way he was sure he could trust to her
taste.

She had promised to send him the interview in proof, but
she had been able, after all, to send it but in type-copy. If
she, after all, had had a flat adorned—as to the drawing-
room alone—with eighty-three photographs, and all in plush
frames; if she had lived in the Earl's Court Road, had been
rosy and glossy and well filled out; and if she had looked
withal, as she always made a point of calling it when she
wished to refer without vulgarity to the right place in the

social scale, "unmistakeably gentle"—if she had achieved these things she would have snapped her fingers at all other sweets, have sat as tight as possible and let the world wag, have spent her Sundays in silently thanking her stars, and not have cared to know one Kodak, or even one novelist's "methods," from another. Except for his unholy itch he was in short so just the person she would have liked to be that the last consecration was given for her to his character by his speaking quite as if he had accosted her only to secure her view of the strange Finnish "soul." He had come each time—there had been four Saturdays; whereas Maud herself had had to wait till to-day, though her bread depended on it, for the roundabout charity of her publicly bad seat. It didn't matter *why* he had come—so that he might see it somewhere printed of him that he was "a conspicuously faithful attendant" at the interesting series; it only mattered that he was letting her off so easily, and yet that there was a restless hunger, odd on the part of one of the filled-out, in his appealing eye, which she now saw not to be a bit intelligent, though that didn't matter either. Howard Bight came into view while she dealt with these impressions, whereupon she found herself edging a little away from her patron. Her other friend, who had but just arrived and was apparently waiting to speak to her, would be a pretext for a break before the poor gentleman should begin to accuse her of having failed him. She had failed herself so much more that she would have been ready to reply to him that *he* was scarce the one to complain; fortunately, however, the bell sounded the end of the interval and her tension was relaxed. They all flocked back to their places, and her *camarade*—she knew enough often so to designate him—was enabled, thanks to some shifting of other spectators, to occupy a seat beside her. He had brought with him the breath of business; hurrying from one appointment to another he might have time but for a single act. He had seen each of the others by itself, and the way he now crammed in the third, after having previously snatched the fourth, brought home again to the girl that he was leading the real life. Her own was a dull imitation of it. Yet it happened at the same time that before the curtain rose again he had, with a "Who's your fat friend?" professed to have caught her in the act of making her own brighter.

" 'Mortimer Marshal'?" he echoed after she had, a trifle dryly, satisfied him. "Never heard of him."

"Well, I shan't tell him that. But you *have*," she said; "you've only forgotten. I told you after I had been to him."

Her friend thought—it came back to him. "Oh yes, and showed me what you had made of it. I remember your stuff was charming."

"I see you remember nothing," Maud a little more dryly said. "I didn't show you what I had made of it. I've never made anything. You've not seen my stuff, and nobody has. They won't have it."

She spoke with a smothered vibration, but, as they were still waiting, it had made him look at her; by which she was slightly the more disconcerted. "Who won't?"

"Everyone, everything won't. Nobody, nothing will. He's hopeless, or rather *I* am. I'm no good. And he knows it."

"O—oh!" the young man kindly but vaguely protested. "Has he been making that remark to you?"

"No—that's the worst of it. He's too dreadfully civil. He thinks I can do something."

"Then why do you say he knows you can't?"

She was impatient; she gave it up. "Well, I don't know what he knows—except that he does want to be loved."

"Do you mean he has proposed to you to love him?"

"Loved by the great heart of the public—speaking through its natural organ. He wants to be—well, where Beadel-Muffet is."

"Oh, I hope not!" said Bight with grim amusement.

His friend was struck with his tone. "Do you mean it's coming on for Beadel-Muffet—what we talked about?" And then as he looked at her so queerly that her curiosity took a jump: "It really and truly *is*? Has anything happened?"

"The rummest thing in the world—since I last saw you. We're wonderful, you know, you and I together—we *see*. And what we see always takes place, usually within the week. It wouldn't be believed. But it will do for *us*. At any rate it's high sport."

"Do you mean," she asked, "that his scare has literally begun?"

He meant, clearly, quite as much as he said. "He has written to me again he wants to see me, and we've an appointment for Monday."

"Then why isn't it the old game?"

"Because it isn't. He wants to gather from me, as I *have* served him before, if something can't be done. *On a souvent besoin d'un plus petit que soi.* Keep quiet, and we shall see something."

This was very well; only his manner visibly had for her the effect of a chill in the air. "I hope," she said, "you're going at least to be decent to him."

"Well, you'll judge. Nothing at all can be done—it's too ridiculously late. And it serves him right. I shan't deceive him, certainly, but I might as well enjoy him."

The fiddles were still going, and Maud had a pause. "Well, you know you've more or less lived on him. I mean it's the kind of thing you *are* living on."

"Precisely—that's just why I loathe it."

Again she hesitated. "You mustn't quarrel, you know, with your bread and butter."

He looked straight before him, as if she had been consciously, and the least bit disagreeably, sententious. "What in the world's that but what I shall just be *not* doing? If our bread and butter is the universal push I consult our interest by not letting it trifle with us. They're not to blow hot and cold—it won't do. There he is—let him get out himself. What I call sport is to see if he can."

"And not—poor wretch—to help him?"

But Bight was ominously lucid. "The devil is that he can't *be* helped. His one idea of help, from the day he opened his eyes, has been to be prominently—damn the word!—mentioned: it's the only kind of help that exists in connection with him. What therefore is a fellow to do when he happens to want it to stop—wants a special sort of prominence that will work like a trap in a pantomime and enable him to vanish when the situation requires it? Is one to mention that he wants *not* to be mentioned—never, never, please, any more? Do you see the success of that, all over the place, do you see the headlines in the American papers? No, he must die as he has lived—the Principal Public Person of his time."

"Well," she sighed, "it's all horrible." And then without a transition: "What do you suppose has happened to him?"

"The dreadfulness I wasn't to tell you?"

"I only mean if you suppose him in a really bad hole."

The young man considered. "It can't certainly be that he has had a change of heart—never. It may be nothing worse than that the woman he wants to marry has turned against it."

"But I supposed him—with his children all so boomed—to *be* married."

"Naturally; else he couldn't have got such a boom from the poor lady's illness, death and burial. Don't you remember two years ago?—'We are given to understand that Sir A. B. C. Beadel-Muffet K.C.B., M.P., particularly desires that no flowers be sent for the late Hon. Lady Beadel-Muffet's funeral.' And then, the next day: 'We are authorised to state that the impression, so generally prevailing, that Sir A. B. C. Beadel-Muffet has expressed an objection to flowers in connection with the late Hon. Lady Beadel-Muffet's obsequies, rests on a misapprehension of Sir A. B. C. Beadel-Muffet's markedly individual views. The floral tributes already delivered in Queen's Gate Gardens, and remarkable for number and variety, have been the source of such gratification to the bereaved gentleman as his situation permits.' With a wind-up of course for the following week—the inevitable few heads of remark, on the part of the bereaved gentleman, on the general subject of Flowers at Funerals as a Fashion, vouchsafed, under pressure possibly indiscreet, to a rising young journalist always thirsting for the authentic word."

"I guess now," said Maud, after an instant, "the rising young journalist. You egged him on."

"Dear, no. I panted in his rear."

"It makes you," she added, "more than cynical."

"And what do you call 'more than' cynical?"

"It makes you sardonic. Wicked," she continued; "devilish."

"That's it—that *is* cynical. Enough's as good as a feast." But he came back to the ground they had quitted. "What were you going to say *he's* prominent for, Mortimer Marshal?"

She wouldn't, however, follow him there yet, her curiosity on the other issue not being spent. "Do you know then as a fact, that he's marrying again, the bereaved gentleman?"

Her friend, at this, showed impatience. "My dear fellow, do you *see* nothing? We had it all, didn't we, three months ago, and then we didn't have it, and then we had it again; and goodness knows where we are. But I throw out the possibility. I forget her bloated name, but she may be rich, and she may be decent. She may make it a condition that he keeps out— out, I mean, of the only things he has really ever been 'in.'"

"The Papers?"

"The dreadful, nasty, vulgar Papers. She may put it to him—I see it dimly and queerly, but I see it—that he must get out first, and then they'll talk; then she'll say yes, then he'll have the money. I see it—and much more sharply—that he *wants* the money, needs it, I mean, badly, desperately, so that this necessity may very well make the hole in which he finds himself. Therefore he must do something—what he's trying to do. It supplies the motive that our picture, the other day, rather missed."

Maud Blandy took this in, but it seemed to fail to satisfy her. "It must be something worse. You make it out *that*, so that your practical want of mercy, which you'll not be able to conceal from me, shall affect me as less inhuman."

"I don't make it out anything, and I don't care what it is; the queerness, the grand 'irony' of the case is itself enough for me. You, on your side, however, I think, make it out what you call 'something worse,' because of the romantic bias of your mind. You 'see red.' Yet isn't it, after all, sufficiently lurid that he shall lose his blooming bride?"

"You're sure," Maud appealed, "that he'll lose her?"

"Poetic justice screams for it; and my whole interest in the matter is staked on it."

But the girl continued to brood. "I thought you contend that nobody's half 'decent.' Where do you find a woman to make such a condition?"

"Not easily, I admit." The young man thought. "It will be *his* luck to have found her. That's his tragedy, say, that she can financially save him, but that she happens to be just the one freak, the creature whose stomach has turned. The spark—I mean of decency—has got, after all, somehow to be kept alive; and it may be lodged in this particular female form."

"I see. But why should a female form that's so particular confess to an affinity with a male form that's so fearfully general? As he's *all* self-advertisement, why isn't it much more natural to her simply to loathe him?"

"Well, because, oddly enough, it seems that people don't."

"*You* do," Maud declared. "You'll kill him."

He just turned a flushed cheek to her, and she saw that she had touched something that lived in him. "We *can*," he consciously smiled, "deal death. And the beauty is that it's in a perfectly straight way. We can lead them on. But have you ever seen Beadel-Muffet for yourself?" he continued.

"No. How often, please, need I tell you that I've seen nobody and nothing?"

"Well, if you had you'd understand."

"You mean he's so fetching?"

"Oh, he's great. He's not 'all' self-advertisement—or at least he doesn't seem to be: that's his pull. But I see, you female humbug," Bight pursued, "how much you'd like him yourself."

"I want, while I'm about it, to pity him in sufficient quantity."

"Precisely. Which means, for a woman, with extravagance and to the point of immorality."

"I ain't a woman," Maud Blandy sighed. "I wish I were!"

"Well, about the pity," he went on; "you shall be immoral, I promise you, before you've done. Doesn't Mortimer Marshal," he asked, "take you for a woman?"

"You'll have to ask *him*. How," she demanded, "does one know those things?" And she stuck to her Beadel-Muffet. "If you're to see him on Monday shan't you then get to the bottom of it?"

"Oh, I don't conceal from you that I promise myself larks, but I won't tell you, positively I won't," Bight said, "what I see. You're morbid. If it's only bad enough—I mean his motive—you'll want to save him."

"Well, isn't that what you're to profess to him that *you* want?"

"Ah," the young man returned, "I believe you'd really invent a way."

"I would if I could." And with that she dropped it. "There's my fat friend," she presently added, as the entr'acte still hung heavy and Mortimer Marshal, from a row much in advance of them, screwed himself round in his tight place apparently to keep her in his eye.

"He does then," said her companion, "take you for a woman. I seem to guess he's 'littery.'"

"That's it; so badly that he wrote that 'littery' ply *Corisanda*, you must remember, with Beatrice Beaumont in the principal part, which was given at three matinées in this very place and which hadn't even the luck of being slated. Every creature connected with the production, from the man himself and Beatrice *her*self down to the mothers and grandmothers of the sixpenny young women, the young women of the programmes, was interviewed both before and after, and he promptly published the piece, pleading guilty to the 'littery' charge—which is the great stand he takes and the subject of the discussion."

Bight had wonderingly followed. "Of what discussion?"

"Why, the one he thinks there ought to have been. There hasn't been any, of course, but he wants it, dreadfully misses it. People won't keep it up—whatever they *did* do, though I don't myself make out that they did anything. His state of mind requires something to start with, which has got somehow to be provided. There must have been a noise made, don't you see? to make him prominent; and in order to remain prominent he has got to go for his enemies. The hostility to his ply, and all *because* it's 'littery,' we can do nothing without that; but it's uphill work to come across it. We sit up nights trying, but we seem to get no for'arder. The public attention would seem to abhor the whole matter even as nature abhors a vacuum. We've nothing to go upon, otherwise we might go far. But there we are."

"I see," Bight commented. "You're nowhere at all."

"No; it isn't even that, for we're just where *Corisanda*, on the stage and in the closet, put us at a stroke. Only there we stick fast—nothing seems to happen, nothing seems to come or to be capable of being made to come. We wait."

"Oh, if he waits with *you!*" Bight amicably jibed.

"He may wait for ever?"

"No, but resignedly. You'll make him forget his wrongs."

"Ah, I'm not of that sort, and I could only do it by making him come into his rights. And I recognise now that that's impossible. There are different cases, you see, whole different classes of them, and his is the opposite to Beadel-Muffet's."

Howard Bight gave a grunt. "Why the opposite if you also pity him? I'll be hanged," he added, "if you won't save *him* too."

But she shook her head. She knew. "No; but it's nearly, in its way, as lurid. Do you know," she asked, "what he has done?"

"Why, the difficulty appears to be that he can't have done anything. He should strike once more—hard, and in the same place. He should bring out another ply."

"Why so? You can't be more than prominent, and he *is* prominent. You can't do more than subscribe, in your prominence, to thirty-seven 'press-cutting' agencies in England and America, and, having done so, you can't do more than sit at home with your ear on the postman's knock, looking out for results. *There* comes in the tragedy—there are no results. Mortimer Marshal's postman doesn't knock; the press-cutting agencies can't find anything to cut. With thirty-seven, in the whole English-speaking world, scouring millions of papers for him in vain, and with a big slice of his private income all the while going to it, the 'irony' is too cruel, and the way he looks at one, as in one's degree responsible, does make one wince. He expected, naturally, most from the Americans, but it's they who have failed him worst. Their silence is that of the tomb, and it seems to grow, if the silence of the tomb *can* grow. He won't admit that the thirty-seven look far enough or long enough, and he writes them, I infer, angry letters, wanting to know what the deuce they suppose he has paid them for. But what are they either, poor things, to do?"

"Do? They can print his angry letters. That, at least, will break the silence, and he'll like it better than nothing."

This appeared to strike our young woman. "Upon my word, I really believe he would." Then she thought better of it. "But they'd be afraid, for they do guarantee, you know, that there's something for everyone. They claim it's their strength—that there's enough to go round. They won't want to show that they break down."

"Oh, well," said the young man, "if he can't manage to smash a pane of glass somewhere——!"

"That's what he thought *I* would do. And it's what *I* thought I might," Maud added; "otherwise I wouldn't have approached him. I did it on spec, but I'm no use. I'm a fatal influence. I'm a non-conductor."

She said it with such plain sincerity that it quickly took her companion's attention. "I *say!*" he covertly murmured. "Have you a secret sorrow?"

"Of course I've a secret sorrow." And she stared at it, stiff and a little sombre, not wanting it to be too freely handled, while the curtain at last rose to the lighted stage.

III

She was later on more open about it, sundry other things, not wholly alien, having meanwhile happened. One of these had been that her friend had waited with her to the end of the Finnish performance and that it had then, in the lobby, as they went out, not been possible for her not to make him acquainted with Mr. Mortimer Marshal. This gentleman had clearly waylaid her and had also clearly divined that her companion was of the Papers—papery all through; which doubtless had something to do with his having handsomely proposed to them to accompany him somewhere to tea. They hadn't seen why they shouldn't, it being an adventure, all in their line, like another; and he had carried them, in a four-wheeler, to a small and refined club in a region which was as the fringe of the Piccadilly region, where even their own presence scarce availed to contradict the implication of the exclusive. The whole occasion, they were further to feel, was essentially a tribute to their professional connection, especially that side of it which flushed and quavered, which panted and pined in their host's personal nervousness. Maud Blandy now saw it vain to contend with his delusion that *she*, underfed and unprinted, who had never been so conscious as during these bribed moments of her non-conducting quality, was papery to any purpose—a delusion that exceeded, by her measure, every other form of pathos. The decoration of the tea-room was a pale, æsthetic green, the liquid in the delicate cups a copious potent amber; the bread and butter was thin and golden, the muffins a revelation to her that she was barbarously hungry. There were ladies at other tables with other gentlemen—ladies with long feather boas and hats not of the sailor pattern, and gentlemen whose straight collars were doubled up much higher than Howard Bight's and their hair parted far more at the side. The talk was so low, with pauses somehow so not of embarrassment that it could only have been earnest, and the air, an air of privilege and privacy to our young woman's sense, seemed charged with fine things taken for granted. If it hadn't been for Bight's company she would have grown almost frightened, so much seemed to be offered her for something she couldn't do. That word of Bight's about smashing a window-pane had lingered with her; it had made her afterwards wonder, while they sat in their stalls, if there weren't some brittle surface in range of her own elbow. She had to fall back on the consciousness of how her elbow, in spite of her type, lacked practical point, and that was just why the terms in which she saw her services now, as she believed, bid for, had the effect of scaring her. They came out most, for that matter, in Mr. Mortimer Marshal's dumbly-insistent eyes, which seemed to be perpetually saying: "You know what I mean when I'm too refined—like everything here, don't you see?—to say it out. You know there ought to be something about me somewhere, and that really, with the opportunities, the facilities you enjoy, it wouldn't be so much out of your way just to—well, reward this little attention."

The fact that he was probably every day, in just the same anxious flurry and with just the same superlative delicacy, paying little attentions with an eye to little rewards, this fact by itself but scantily eased her, convinced as she was that no luck but her own was as hopeless as his. He squared the clever young wherever he could get at them, but it was the clever young, taking them generally, who fed from his hand and then forgot him. She didn't forget him; she pitied him too much, pitied herself, and was more and more, as she found, now pitying everyone; only she didn't know how to say to him that she could do, after all, nothing for him. She oughtn't to have come, in the first place, and wouldn't if it hadn't been for her companion. Her companion was increasingly sardonic—which was the way in which, at best, she now increasingly saw him; he was shameless in acceptance, since, as she knew, as she felt at his side, he had come only, at bottom, to mislead and to mystify. *He* was, as she wasn't, on the Papers and of them, and their baffled entertainer knew it without either a hint on the subject from herself or a need, on the young man's own lips, of the least vulgar allusion. Nothing was so much as named, the whole connection was sunk; they talked about clubs, muffins, afternoon performances, the effect of the Finnish soul upon the appetite, quite as if they had met in society. Nothing could have been less like society—she innocently supposed at least—than the real spirit of their meeting; yet Bight did nothing that he might do to keep the affair within bounds. When looked at by their friend so hard and so hintingly, he only looked back, just as dumbly, but just as intensely and, as might be said, portentously; ever so impenetrably, in fine, and ever so wickedly. He didn't smile—as if to cheer—the least little bit; which he might be abstaining from on purpose to make his promises solemn: so, as he tried to smile—she couldn't, it was all too dreadful—she wouldn't meet her friend's eyes, but kept looking, heartlessly, at the "notes" of the place, the hats of the ladies, the tints of the rugs, the intenser Chippendale, here and there, of the chairs and tables, of the very guests, of the very waitresses. It had come to her early: "I've done him, poor man, at home, and the obvious thing now will be to do him at his club." But this inspiration plumped against her fate even as an imprisoned insect against the window-glass. She couldn't do him at his club without decently asking leave; whereby he would know of her feeble feeler, feeble because she was so sure of refusals. She would rather tell him, desperately, what she thought of him than expose him to see again that she was herself nowhere, herself nothing. Her one comfort was that, for the half-hour—it had made the situation quite possible—he seemed fairly hypnotised by her colleague; so that when they took leave he as good as thanked her for what she had this time done for him. It was one of the signs of his infatuated state that he clearly viewed Bight as a mass of helpful cleverness, though the cruel creature, uttering scarce a sound, had only fixed him in a manner that might have been taken for the fascination of deference. He might perfectly have been an idiot for all the poor gentleman knew. But the poor gentleman saw a possible "leg up" in every bush; and nothing but impertinence would have convinced him that she hadn't brought him, compunctiously as to the past, a master of the proper art. Now, more than ever, how he would listen for the postman!

The whole occasion had broken so, for busy Bight, into matters to be attended to before Fleet Street warmed to its work, that the pair were obliged, outside, to part company on the spot, and it was only on the morrow, a Saturday, that they could taste again of that comparison of notes which made for each the main savour, albeit slightly acrid, of their current consciousness. The air was full, as from afar, of the grand indifference of spring, of which the breath could be felt so much before the face could be seen, and they had bicycled side by side out to Richmond Park as with the impulse to meet it on its way. They kept a Saturday, when possible, sacred to the Suburbs as distinguished from the Papers—when possible being largely when Maud could achieve the use of the somewhat fatigued family machine. Many sisters contended for it, under whose flushed pressure it might have been seen spinning in many different directions. Superficially, at Richmond, our young couple rested—found a quiet corner to lounge deep in the Park, with their machines propped by one side of a great tree and their associated backs sustained by another. But agitation, finer than the finest scorching, was in the air for them; it was made sharp, rather abruptly, by a vivid outbreak from Maud. It was very well, she observed, for her friend to be clever at the expense of the general "greed"; he saw it in the light of his own jolly luck, and what she saw, as it happened, was nothing but the general art of letting you starve, yourself, in your hole. At the end of five minutes her companion had turned quite pale with having to face the large extent of her confession. It was a confession for the reason that in the first place it evidently cost her an effort that pride had again and again successfully prevented, and because in the second she had thus the air of having lived overmuch on swagger. She could scarce have said at this moment what, for a good while, she had really lived on, and she didn't let him know now to complain either of her privation or of her disappointments. She did it to show why she couldn't go with him when he was so awfully sweeping. There were at any rate apparently, all over, two wholly different sets of people. If everyone rose to his bait no creature had ever risen to hers; and that was the grim truth of her position, which proved at the least that there were two quite different kinds of luck. They told two different stories of human vanity; they couldn't be reconciled. And the poor girl put it in a nutshell. "There's but one person I've *ever* written to who has so much as noticed my letter."

He wondered, painfully affected—it rather overwhelmed him; he took hold of it at the easiest point. "One person——?"

"The misguided man we had tea with. He alone—*he* rose."

"Well then, you see that when they do rise they *are* misguided. In other words they're donkeys."

"What I see is that I don't strike the right ones and that I haven't therefore your ferocity; that is my ferocity, if I have any, rests on a different ground. You'll say that I go for the wrong people; but I don't, God knows—witness Mortimer Marshal—fly too high. I picked him out, after prayer and fasting, as just the likeliest of the likely—not anybody a bit grand and yet not quite a nobody; and by an extraordinary chance I was justified. Then I pick out others who seem just as good, I pray and fast, and no sound comes back. But I work through my ferocity too," she stiffly continued, "though at first it was great, feeling as I did that when my bread and butter was in it people had no right not to oblige me. It was their duty— what they were prominent *for*—to be interviewed, so as to keep me going; and I did as much for them any day as they would be doing for me."

Bight heard her, but for a moment said nothing. "Did you tell them that? I mean say to them it was your little all?"

"Not vulgarly—I know how. There are ways of saying it's 'important'; and I hint it just enough to see that the importance fetches them no more than anything else. It isn't important to *them*. And I, in their place," Maud went on, "wouldn't answer either; I'll be hanged if ever I would. That's what it comes to, that there *are* two distinct lots, and that my luck, being born so, is always to try the snubbers. You were born to know by instinct the others. But it makes me more tolerant."

"More tolerant of what?" her friend asked.

"Well, of what you described to me. Of what you rail at."

"Thank you for *me*!" Bight laughed.

"Why not? Don't you live on it?"

"Not in such luxury—you surely must see for yourself—as the distinction you make seems to imply. It isn't luxury to be nine-tenths of the time sick of everything. People moreover are worth to me but tuppence apiece; there are too many, confound them—so many that I don't see really how any can be left over for *your* superior lot. It *is* a chance," he pursued—"I've had refusals too—though I confess they've sometimes been of the funniest. Besides, I'm getting out of it," the young man wound up. "God knows I want to. My advice to you," he added in the same breath, "is to sit tight. There are as good fish in the sea——!"

She waited a moment. "You're sick of everything and you're getting out of it; it's not good enough for you, in other words, but it's still good enough for me. Why am I to sit tight when you sit so loose?"

"Because what you want will come—can't help coming. Then, in time, you'll also get out of it. But then you'll have had it, as I have, and the good of it."

"But what, really, if it breeds nothing but disgust," she asked, "do you *call* the good of it?"

"Well, two things. First the bread and butter, and then the fun. I repeat it—sit tight."

"Where's the fun," she asked again, "of learning to despise people?"

"You'll see when it comes. It will all be upon you, it will change for you any day. Sit tight, sit tight."

He expressed such confidence that she might for a minute have been weighing it. "If you get out of it, what will you do?"

"Well, imaginative work. This job has made me at least *see*. It has given me the loveliest tips."

She had still another pause. "It has given me—*my* experience has—a lovely tip too."

"And what's that?"

"I've told you before—the tip of pity. I'm so much sorrier for them all—panting and gasping for it like fish out of water—than I am anything else."

He wondered. "But I thought that was what just isn't your experience."

"Oh, I mean then," she said impatiently, "that my tip is from yours. It's only a different tip. I want to save them."

"Well," the young man replied, and as if the idea had had a meaning for him, "saving them may perhaps work out as a branch. The question is can you be paid for it?"

"Beadel-Muffet would pay me," Maud suddenly suggested.

"Why, that's just what I'm expecting," her companion laughed, "that he will, after to-morrow—directly or indirectly—do *me*."

"Will you take it from him then only to get him in deeper, as that's what you perfectly know you'll do? You won't save him; you'll lose him."

"What then would you, in the case," Bight asked, "do for your money?"

Well, the girl thought. "I'd get him to see me—I should have first, I recognise, to catch my hare—and then I'd work up my stuff. Which would be boldly, quite by a master-stroke, a statement of his fix—of the fix, I mean, of his wanting, his supplicating to be dropped. I'd give out that it would really oblige. Then I'd send my copy about, and the rest of the matter would take care of itself. I don't say *you* could do it that way—you'd have a different effect. But I should be able to trust the thing, being mine, not to be looked at, or, if looked at, chucked straight into the basket. I should so have, to that extent, handled the matter, and I should so, by merely touching it, have broken the spell. That's my one line—I stop things off by touching them. There'd never be a word about him more."

Her friend, with his legs out and his hands locked at the back of his neck, had listened with indulgence. "Then hadn't I better arrange it for you that Beadel-Muffet shall see you?"

"Oh, not after you've damned him!"

"You want to see him first?"

"It will be the only way—to be of any use to him. You ought to wire him in fact not to open his mouth till he has seen me."

"Well, I will," said Bight at last. "But, you know, we shall lose something very handsome—his struggle, all in vain, with his fate. Noble sport, the sight of it all." He turned a little, to rest on his elbow, and, cycling suburban young man as he was, he might have been, outstretched under his tree, melancholy Jacques looking off into a forest glade, even as sailor-hatted Maud, in—for elegance—a new cotton blouse and a long-limbed angular attitude, might have prosefully suggested the mannish Rosalind. He raised his face in appeal to her. "Do you really ask me to sacrifice it?"

"Rather than sacrifice *him*? Of course I do."

He said for a while nothing more; only, propped on his elbow, lost himself again in the Park. After which he turned back to her. "Will you have me?" he suddenly asked.

" 'Have you'——?"

"Be my bonny bride. For better, for worse. I hadn't, upon my honour," he explained with obvious sincerity, "understood you were so down."

"Well, it isn't so bad as that," said Maud Blandy.

"So bad as taking up with *me*?"

"It isn't as bad as having let you know—when I didn't want you to."

He sank back again with his head dropped, putting himself more at his ease. "You're too proud—that's what's the matter with you. And I'm too stupid."

"No, you're not," said Maud grimly. "Not stupid."

"Only cruel, cunning, treacherous, cold-blooded, vile?" He drawled the words out softly, as if they sounded fair.

"And I'm not stupid either," Maud Blandy went on. "We just, poor creatures—well, we just *know*."

"Of course we do. So why do you want us to drug ourselves with rot? to go on as if we didn't know?"

She made no answer for a moment; then she said: "There's good to be known too."

"Of course, again. There are all sorts of things, and some much better than others. That's why," the young man added, "I just put that question to you."

"Oh no, it isn't. You put it to me because you think I feel I'm no good."

"How so, since I keep assuring you that you've only to wait? How so, since I keep assuring you that if you do wait it will all come with a rush? But say I *am* sorry for you," Bight lucidly pursued; "how does that prove either that my motive is base or that I do you a wrong?"

The girl waived this question, but she presently tried another. "Is it your idea that we should live on all the people——?"

"The people we catch? Yes, old man, till we can do better."

"My conviction is," she soon returned, "that if I were to marry you I should dish you. I should spoil the business. It would fall off; and, as I can do nothing myself, then where should we be?"

"Well," said Bight, "we mightn't be quite so high up in the scale of the morbid."

"It's you that are morbid," she answered. "You've, in your way—like everyone else, for that matter, all over the place—'sport' on the brain."

"Well," he demanded, "what is sport but success? What is success but sport?"

"Bring that out somewhere. If it be true," she said, "I'm glad I'm a failure."

After which, for a longish space, they sat together in silence, a silence finally broken by a word from the young man. "But about Mortimer Marshal—how do you propose to save *him?*"

It was a change of subject that might, by its so easy introduction of matter irrelevant, have seemed intended to dissipate whatever was left of his proposal of marriage. That proposal, however, had been somehow both too much in the tone of familiarity to linger and too little in that of vulgarity to drop. It had had no form, but the mild air kept perhaps thereby the better the taste of it. This was sensibly moreover in what the girl found to reply. "I think, you know, that he'd be no such bad friend. I mean that, with his appetite, there would be something to be done. He doesn't half hate me."

"Ah, my dear," her friend ejaculated, "don't, for God's sake, be low."

But she kept it up. "He clings to me. You saw. It's hideous, the way he's able to 'do' himself."

Bight lay quiet, then spoke as with a recall of the Chippendale Club. "Yes, I couldn't 'do' you as he could. But if you don't bring it off——?"

"Why then does he cling? Oh, because, all the same, I'm potentially the Papers still. I'm at any rate the nearest he has got to them. And then I'm other things."

"I see."

"I'm so awfully attractive," said Maud Blandy. She got up with this and, shaking out her frock, looked at her resting bicycle, looked at the distances possibly still to be gained. Her companion paused, but at last also rose, and by that time she was awaiting him, a little gaunt and still not quite cool, as an illustration of her last remark. He stood there watching her, and she followed this remark up. "I do, you know, really pity him."

It had almost a feminine fineness, and their eyes continued to meet. "Oh, you'll work it!" And the young man went to his machine.

IV

It was not till five days later that they again came together, and during these days many things had happened. Maud Blandy had, with high elation, for her own portion, a sharp sense of this; if it had at the time done nothing more intimate for her the Sunday of bitterness just spent with Howard Bight had started, all abruptly, a turn of the tide of her luck. This turn had not in the least been in the young man's having spoken to her of marriage—since she hadn't even, up to the late hour of their parting, so much as answered him straight: she dated the sense of difference much rather from the throb of a happy thought that had come to her while she cycled home to Kilburnia in the darkness. The throb had made her for the few minutes, tired as she was, put on speed, and it had been the cause of still further proceedings for her the first thing the next morning. The active step that was the essence of these proceedings had almost got itself taken before she went to bed; which indeed was what had happened to the extent of her writing, on the spot, a meditated letter. She sat down to it by the light of the guttering candle that awaited her on the dining-room table and in the stale air of family food that only *had* been—a residuum so at the mercy of mere ventilation that she didn't so much as peep into a cupboard; after which she had been on the point of nipping over, as she would have said, to drop it into that opposite pillar-box whose vivid maw, opening out through thick London nights, had received so many of her fruitless little ventures. But she had checked herself and waited, waited to be sure, with the morning, that her fancy wouldn't fade; posting her note in the end, however, with a confident jerk, as soon as she was up. She had, later on, had business, or at least had sought it, among the haunts that she had taught herself to regard as professional; but neither on the Monday nor on either of the days that directly followed had she encountered there the friend whom it would take a difference in more matters than could as yet be dealt with to enable her to regard, with proper assurance or with proper modesty, as a lover. Whatever he was, none the less, it couldn't otherwise have come to her that it was possible to feel lonely in the Strand. That showed, after all, how thick they must constantly have been—which *was* perhaps a thing to begin to think of in a new, in a steadier light. But it showed doubtless still more that her companion was probably up to something rather awful; it made her wonder, holding her breath a little, about Beadel-Muffet, made her certain that he and his affairs would partly account for Bight's whirl of absence.

Ever conscious of empty pockets, she had yet always a penny, or at least a ha'penny, for a paper, and those she now scanned, she quickly assured herself, were edited quite as usual. Sir A. B. C. Beadel-Muffet K.C.B., M.P. had returned on Monday from Undertone, where Lord and Lady Wispers had, from the previous Friday, entertained a very select party; Sir A. B. C. Beadel-Muffet K.C.B., M.P. was to attend on Tuesday the weekly meeting of the society of the Friends of Rest; Sir A. B. C. Beadel-Muffet K.C.B., M.P. had kindly consented to preside on Wednesday, at Samaritan House, at the opening of the Sale of Work of the Middlesex Incurables. These familiar announcements, however, far from appeasing her curiosity, had an effect upon her nerves; she read into them mystic meanings that she had never read before. Her freedom of mind in this direction was indeed at the same time limited, for her own horizon was already, by the Monday night, bristling with new possibilities, and the Tuesday itself—well, what had the Tuesday itself become, with this eruption, from within, of interest amounting really to a revelation, what had the Tuesday itself become but the greatest day yet of her life? Such a description of it would have appeared to apply predominantly to the morning had she not, under the influence, precisely, of the morning's thrill, gone, towards evening, with her design, into the Charing Cross Station. There, at the bookstall, she bought them all, every rag that was hawked; and there, as she unfolded one at a venture, in the crowd and under the lamps, she felt her consciousness further, felt it for the moment quite impressively, enriched. "Personal Peeps—Number Ninety-Three: a Chat with the New Dramatist" needed neither the "H. B." as a terminal signature nor a text spangled, to the exclusion of almost everything else, with Mortimer Marshals that looked as tall as if lettered on posters, to help to account for her young man's use of his time. And yet, as she soon made out, it had been used with an economy that caused her both to wonder and to wince; the "peep" commemorated being none other than their tea with the artless creature the previous Saturday, and the meagre incidents and pale impressions of that occasion furnishing forth the picture.

Bight had solicited no new interview; he hadn't been such a fool—for she saw, soon enough, with all her intelligence, that this was what he would have been, and that a repetition of contact would have dished him. What he *had* done, she found herself perceiving—and perceiving with an emotion that caused her face to glow—was journalism of the intensest essence; a column concocted of nothing, an omelette made, as it were, without even the breakage of the egg or two that might have been expected to be the price. The poor gentleman's whereabouts at five o'clock was the only egg broken, and this light and delicate crash was the sound in the world that would be sweetest to him. What stuff it had to be, since the writer really knew nothing about him, yet how its being just such stuff made it perfectly serve its purpose! She might have marvelled afresh, with more leisure, at such purposes, but she was lost in the wonder of seeing how, without matter, without thought, without an excuse, without a fact and yet at the same time sufficiently without a fiction, he had managed to be as resonant as if he had beaten a drum on the platform of a booth. And he had not been too personal, not made anything awkward for *her*, had given nothing and nobody away, had tossed the Chippendale Club into the air with such a turn that it had fluttered down again, like a blown feather, miles from its site. The thirty-seven agencies would already be posting to their subscriber thirty-seven copies, and their subscriber, on his side, would be posting, to his acquaintance, many times thirty-seven, and thus at least getting something for his money; but this didn't tell her why her friend had taken the trouble—if it had *been* a trouble; why at all events he had taken the time, pressed as he apparently was for that commodity. These things she was indeed presently to learn, but they were meanwhile part of a suspense composed of more elements than any she had yet tasted. And the suspense was prolonged, though other affairs too, that were not part of it, almost equally crowded upon her; the week having almost waned when relief arrived in the form of a cryptic post-card. The post-card bore the H. B., like the precious "Peep," which had already had a wondrous sequel, and it appointed, for the tea-hour, a place of meeting familiar to Maud, with the simple addition of the significant word "Larks!"

When the time he had indicated came she waited for him, at their small table, swabbed like the deck of a steam-packet, nose to nose with a mustard-pot and a price-list, in the consciousness of perhaps after all having as much to tell him as to hear from him. It appeared indeed at first that this might well be the case, for the questions that came up between them when he had taken his place were overwhelmingly those he himself insisted on putting. "What has he done, what *has* he, and what will he?"—that inquiry, not loud but deep, had met him as he sat down; without however producing the least recognition. Then she as soon felt that his silence and his manner were enough for her, or that, if they hadn't been, his wonderful look, the straightest she had ever had from him, would instantly have made them so. He looked at her hard, hard, as if he had meant "I say, mind your eyes!" and it amounted really to a glimpse, rather fearful, of the subject. It was no joke, the subject, clearly, and her friend had fairly gained age, as he had certainly lost weight, in his recent dealings with it. It struck her even, with everything else, that this was positively the way she would have liked him to show if their union had taken the form they hadn't reached the point of discussing; wearily coming back to her from the thick of things, wanting to put on his slippers and have his tea, all prepared by her and in their place, and beautifully to be trusted to regale her in his turn. He was excited, disavowedly, and it took more disavowal still after she had opened her budget—which she did, in truth, by saying to him as her first alternative: "What did you do him *for*, poor Mortimer Marshal? It isn't that he's not in the seventh heaven——!"

"He *is* in the seventh heaven!" Bight quickly broke in. "He doesn't want my blood?"

"Did you do him," she asked, "that he should want it? It's splendid how you could—simply on that show."

"That show? Why," said Howard Bight, "that show was an immensity. That show was volumes, stacks, abysses."

He said it in such a tone that she was a little at a loss. "Oh, you don't want abysses."

"Not much, to knock off such twaddle. There isn't a breath in it of what I saw. What I saw is my own affair. I've got the abysses for myself. They're in my head—it's always something. But the monster," he demanded, "has written you?"

"How couldn't he—that night? I got it the next morning, telling me how much he wanted to thank me and asking me where he might see me. So I went," said Maud, "to see him."

"At his own place again?"

"At his own place again. What do I yearn for but to be received at people's own places?"

"Yes, for the stuff. But when you've had—as you had had from him—the stuff?"

"Well, sometimes, you see, I get more. He gives me all I can take." It was in her head to ask if by chance Bight were jealous, but she gave it another turn. "We had a big palaver, partly about you. He appreciates."

"Me?"

"Me—first of all, I think. All the more that I've had—fancy!—a proof of my stuff, the despised and rejected, as originally concocted, and that he has now seen it. I tried it on again with *Brains*, the night of your thing—sent it off with your thing enclosed as a rouser. They took it, by return, like a shot—you'll see on Wednesday. And if the dear man lives till then, for impatience, I'm to lunch with him that day."

"I see," said Bight. "Well, that was what I did it for. It shows how right I was."

They faced each other, across their thick crockery, with eyes that said more than their words, and that, above all, said, and asked, other things. So she went on in a moment: "I don't know what he doesn't expect. And he thinks I can keep it up."

"Lunch with him *every* Wednesday?"

"Oh, he'd give me my lunch, and more. It was last Sunday that you were right—about my sitting close," she pursued. "I'd have been a pretty fool to jump. Suddenly, I see, the music begins. I'm awfully obliged to you."

"You feel," he presently asked, "quite differently—so differently that I've missed my chance? I don't care for *that* serpent, but there's something else that you don't tell me." The young man, detached and a little spent, with his shoulder against the wall and a hand vaguely playing over the knives, forks and spoons, dropped his succession of sentences without an apparent direction. "Something else has come up, and you're as pleased as Punch. Or, rather, you're not quite entirely so, because you can't goad me to fury. You can't worry me as much as you'd like. Marry me first, old man, and *then* see if I mind. Why shouldn't you keep it up?—I mean lunching with him?" His questions came as in play that was a little pointless, without his waiting more than a moment for answers; though it was not indeed that she might not have answered even in the moment, had not the pointless play been more what she wanted. "Was it at the place," he went on, "that he took us to?"

"Dear no—at his flat, where I've been before. You'll see, in *Brains*, on Wednesday. I don't think I've muffed it—it's really rather there. But he showed me everything this time—

the bathroom, the refrigerator, and the machines for stretching his trousers. He has nine, and in constant use."

"Nine?" said Bight gravely.

"Nine."

"Nine trousers?"

"Nine machines. I don't know how many trousers."

"Ah, my dear," he said, "that's a grave omission; the want
of the information will be felt and resented. But does it all, at
any rate," he asked, "sufficiently fetch you?" After which, as
she didn't speak, he lapsed into helpless sincerity. "Is it really,
you think, his dream to secure you?"

She replied, on this, as if his tone made it too amusing.
"Quite. There's no mistaking it. He sees me as, most days in
the year, pulling the wires and beating the drum somewhere;
that is he sees me of course not exactly as writing about 'our
home'—once I've got one—myself, but as procuring others
to do it through my being (as *you've* made him believe) in
with the Organs of Public Opinion. He doesn't see, if I'm
half decent, why there shouldn't be something about him
every day in the week. He's all right, and he's all ready. And
who, after all, *can* do him so well as the partner of his flat?
It's like making, in one of those big domestic siphons, the
luxury of the poor, your own soda-water. It comes cheaper,
and it's always on the sideboard. '*Vichy chez soi.*' The inter-
viewer at home."

Her companion took it in. "Your place is on *my* sideboard—you're really a first-class fizz! He steps then, at any
rate, into Beadel-Muffet's place."

"That," Maud assented, "is what he would like to do."
And she knew more than ever there was something to
wait for.

"It's a lovely opening," Bight returned. But he still said,
for the moment, nothing else; as if, charged to the brim
though he had originally been, she had rather led his thought
away.

"What have you done with poor Beadel?" she consequently
asked. "What is it, in the name of goodness, you're doing *to*
him? It's worse than ever."

"Of course it's worse than ever."

"He capers," said Maud, "on every housetop—he jumps out of every bush." With which her anxiety really broke out. "*Is* it you that are doing it?"

"If you mean am I seeing him, I certainly am. I'm seeing nobody else. I assure you he's spread thick."

"But you're acting for him?"

Bight waited. "Five hundred people are acting for him; but the difficulty is that what he calls the 'terrific forces of publicity'—by which he means ten thousand *other* persons—are acting against him. We've all in fact been turned on—to turn everything off, and that's exactly the job that makes the biggest noise. It appears everywhere, in every kind of connection and every kind of type, that Sir A. B. C. Beadel-Muffet K.C.B., M.P. desires to cease to appear *anywhere*; and then it appears that his desiring to cease to appear is observed to conduce directly to his more tremendously appearing, or certainly, and in the most striking manner, to his not in the least *dis*appearing. The workshop of silence roars like the Zoo at dinner-time. He *can't* disappear; he hasn't weight enough to sink; the splash the diver makes, you know, tells where he is. If you ask me what I'm doing," Bight wound up, "I'm holding him under water. But we're in the middle of the pond, the banks are thronged with spectators, and I'm expecting from day to day to see stands erected and gate-money taken. There," he wearily smiled, "you have it. Besides," he then added with an odd change of tone, "I rather think you'll see to-morrow."

He had made her at last horribly nervous. "What shall I see?"

"It will all be out."

"Then why shouldn't you tell me?"

"Well," the young man said, "he *has* disappeared. There you are. I mean personally. He's not to be found. But nothing could make more, you see, for ubiquity. The country will ring with it. He vanished on Tuesday night—was then last seen at his club. Since then he has given no sign. How can a man disappear who does *that* sort of thing? It is, as you say, to caper on the housetops. But it will only be known to-night."

"Since when, then," Maud asked, "have you known it?"

"Since three o'clock to-day. But I've kept it. I *am*—a while longer—keeping it."

She wondered; she was full of fears. "What do you expect to get for it?"

"Nothing—if you spoil my market. I seem to make out that you want to."

She gave this no heed; she had her thought. "Why then did you three days ago wire me a mystic word?"

"Mystic——?"

"What do you call 'Larks'?"

"Oh, I remember. Well, it was because I saw larks coming; because I saw, I mean, what has happened. I was sure it would have to happen."

"And what the mischief *is* it?"

Bight smiled. "Why, what I tell you. That he has gone."

"Gone where?"

"Simply bolted to parts unknown. 'Where' is what nobody who belongs to him is able in the least to say, or seems likely to be able."

"Any more than why?"

"Any more than why."

"Only *you* are able to say that?"

"Well," said Bight, "I can say what has so lately stared me in the face, what he has been thrusting at me in all its grotesqueness: his desire for a greater privacy worked through the Papers themselves. He came to me with it," the young man presently added. "I didn't go to *him*."

"And he trusted you," Maud replied.

"Well, you see what I have given him—the very flower of my genius. What more do you want? I'm spent, seedy, sore. I'm sick," Bight declared, "of his beastly funk."

Maud's eyes, in spite of it, were still a little hard. "Is he thoroughly sincere?"

"Good God, no! How *can* he be? Only trying it—as a cat, for a jump, tries too smooth a wall. He drops straight back."

"Then isn't his funk real?"

"As real as he himself is."

Maud wondered. "Isn't his flight——?"

"That's what we shall see!"

"Isn't," she continued, "his reason?"

"Ah," he laughed out, "there you are again!"

But she had another thought and was not discouraged. "Mayn't he be, honestly, mad?"

"Mad—oh yes. But not, I think, honestly. He's not honestly anything in the world but the Beadel-Muffet of our delight."

"Your delight," Maud observed after a moment, "revolts me." And then she said: "When did you last see him?"

"On Tuesday at six, love. I was one of the last."

"Decidedly, too, then, I judge, one of the worst." She gave him her idea. "You hounded him on."

"I reported," said Bight, "success. Told him how it was going."

"Oh, I can see you! So that if he's dead——"

"Well?" asked Bight blandly.

"His blood is on your hands."

He eyed his hands a moment. "They *are* dirty for him! But now, darling," he went on, "be so good as to show me yours."

"Tell me first," she objected, "what you believe. *Is* it suicide?"

"I think that's the thing for us to make it. Till somebody," he smiled, "makes it something else." And he showed how he warmed to the view. "There are weeks of it, dearest, yet."

He leaned more toward her, with his elbows on the table, and in this position, moved by her extreme gravity, he lightly flicked her chin with his finger. She threw herself, still grave, back from his touch, but they remained thus a while closely confronted. "Well," she at last remarked, "I shan't pity you."

"You make it, then, everyone except me?"

"I mean," she continued, "if you do have to loathe yourself."

"Oh, I shan't miss it." And then as if to show how little, "I did mean it, you know, at Richmond," he declared.

"I won't have you if you've killed him," she presently returned.

"You'll decide in that case for the *nine*?" And as the allusion, with its funny emphasis, left her blank: "You want to wear *all* the trousers?"

"You deserve," she said, when light came, "that I should take him." And she kept it up. "It's a lovely flat."

Well, he could do as much. "Nine, I suppose, appeals to you as the number of the muses?"

This short passage, remarkably, for all its irony, brought them together again, to the extent at least of leaving Maud's elbows on the table and of keeping her friend, now a little back in his chair, firm while he listened to her. So the girl came out. "I've seen Mrs. Chorner three times. I wrote that night, after our talk at Richmond, asking her to oblige. And I put on cheek as I had never, never put it. I said the public would be so glad to hear from her 'on the occasion of her engagement.'"

"Do you call that cheek?" Bight looked amused. "She at any rate rose straight."

"No, she rose crooked; but she rose. What you had told me there in the Park—well, immediately happened. She did consent to see me, and so far you had been right in keeping me up to it. But what do you think it was for?"

"To show you *her* flat, *her* tub, *her* petticoats?"

"She doesn't live in a flat; she lives in a house of her own, and a jolly good one, in Green Street, Park Lane; though I did, as happened, see her tub, which is a dream—all marble and silver, like a kind of a swagger sarcophagus, a thing for the Wallace Collection; and though her petticoats, as she first shows, seem all that, if you wear petticoats yourself, you can look at. There's no doubt of her money—given her place and her things, and given her appearance too, poor dear, which would take some doing."

"She squints?" Bight sympathetically asked.

"She's so ugly that she *has* to be rich—she couldn't afford it on less than five thousand a year. As it is, I could well see, she can afford anything—even such a nose. But she's funny and decent; sharp, but a really good sort. And they're *not* engaged."

"She told you so? Then there you are!"

"It all depends," Maud went on; "and you don't know where I am at all. *I* know what it depends on."

"Then there you are again! It's a mine of gold."

"Possibly, but not in your sense. She wouldn't give me the first word of an interview—it wasn't for that she received me. It was for something much better."

Well, Bight easily guessed. "For *my* job?"

"To see what can be done. She loathes his publicity."

The young man's face lighted. "She told you so?"

"She received me on purpose to tell me."

"Then why do you question my 'larks'? What do you want more?"

"I want nothing—with what I have: nothing, I mean, but to help her. We made friends—I like her. And she likes *me*," said Maud Blandy.

"Like Mortimer Marshal, precisely."

"No, precisely not like Mortimer Marshal. I caught, on the spot, her idea—*that* was what took her. Her idea is that I can help her—help her to keep them quiet about Beadel: for which purpose I seem to have struck her as falling from the skies, just at the right moment, into her lap."

Howard Bight followed, yet lingered by the way. "To keep *whom* quiet——?"

"Why, the beastly Papers—what we've been talking about. She wants him straight out of them—*straight*."

"She too?" Bight wondered. "Then *she's* in terror?"

"No, not in terror—or it wasn't that when I last saw her. But in mortal disgust. She feels it has gone too far—which is what she wanted me, as an honest, decent, likely young woman, up to my neck in it, as she supposed, to understand from her. My relation with her is now that I do understand and that if an improvement takes place I shan't have been the worse for it. Therefore you see," Maud went on, "you simply cut my throat when you prevent improvement."

"Well, my dear," her friend returned, "I won't let you bleed to death." And he showed, with this, as confessedly struck. "She doesn't then, you think, *know*——?"

"Know what?"

"Why, what, about him, there may *be* to be known. Doesn't know of his flight."

"She didn't—certainly."

"Nor of anything to make it likely?"

"What you call his queer reason? No—she named it to me no more than you have; though she does mention, distinctly, that he himself hates, or pretends to hate, the exhibition daily made of him."

"She speaks of it," Bight asked, "as pretending——?"

Maud straightened it out. "She feels him—*that* she practically told me—as rather ridiculous. She honestly has her feeling; and, upon my word, it's what I like her for. Her stomach has turned and she has made it her condition. 'Muzzle your Press,' she says; '*then* we'll talk.' She gives him three months—she'll give him even six. And this, meanwhile—when he comes to *you*—is how you forward the muzzling."

"The Press, my child," Bight said, "is the watchdog of civilisation, and the watchdog happens to be—it can't be helped—in a chronic state of *rabies*. Muzzling is easy talk; one can but keep the animal on the run. Mrs. Chorner, however," he added, "seems a figure of fable."

"It's what I told you she would have to be when, some time back, you threw out, as a pure hypothesis, to supply the man with a motive, your exact vision of her. Your motive has come true," Maud went on—"with the difference only, if I understand you, that this doesn't appear the whole of it. That doesn't matter"—she frankly paid him a tribute. "Your forecast was inspiration."

"A stroke of genius"—he had been the first to feel it. But there were matters less clear. "When did you see her last?"

"Four days ago. It was the third time."

"And even then she didn't imagine the truth about him?"

"I don't know, you see," said Maud, "what you *call* the truth."

"Well, that he—quite by that time—didn't know where the deuce to turn. That's truth enough."

Maud made sure. "I don't see how she can have known it and not have been upset. She wasn't," said the girl, "upset. She *isn't* upset. But she's original."

"Well, poor thing," Bight remarked, "she'll have to be."

"Original?"

"Upset. Yes, and original too, if she doesn't give up the job." It had held him an instant—but there were many things. "She sees the wild ass he is, and yet she's willing——?"

" 'Willing' is just what I asked *you* three months ago," Maud returned, "how she *could* be."

He had lost it—he tried to remember. "What then did I say?"

"Well, practically, that women are idiots. Also, I believe, that he's a dazzling beauty."

"Ah yes, he *is*, poor wretch, though beauty to-day in distress."

"Then there you are," said Maud. They had got up, as at the end of their story, but they stood a moment while he waited for change. "If it comes out," the girl dropped, "*that* will save him. If he's dishonoured—as I see her—she'll have him, because then he won't be ridiculous. And I can understand it."

Bight looked at her in such appreciation that he forgot, as he pocketed it, to glance at his change. "Oh, you creatures——!"

"Idiots, aren't we?"

Bight let the question pass, but still with his eyes on her, "You ought to want him to *be* dishonoured."

"I can't want him, then—if he's to get the good of it—to be dead."

Still for a little he looked at her. "And if *you're* to get the good?" But she had turned away, and he went with her to the door, before which, when they had passed out, they had in the side-street, a backwater to the flood of the Strand, a further sharp colloquy. They were alone, the small street for a moment empty, and they felt at first that they had adjourned to a greater privacy, of which, for that matter, he took prompt advantage. "You're to lunch again with the man of the flat?"

"Wednesday, as I say; 1.45."

"Then oblige me by stopping away."

"You don't like it?" Maud asked.

"Oblige me, oblige me," he repeated.

"And disoblige *him*?"

"Chuck him. We've started him. It's enough."

Well, the girl but wanted to be fair. "It's *you* who started him; so I admit you're quits."

"That then started *you*—made *Brains* repent; so you see what you both owe me. I let the creature off, but I hold

you to your debt. There's only one way for you to meet it."
And then as she but looked into the roaring Strand: "With
worship." It made her, after a minute, meet his eyes, but
something just then occurred that stayed any word on the lips
of either. A sound reached their ears, as yet unheeded,
the sound of newsboys in the great thoroughfare shouting
"extra-specials" and mingling with the shout a catch that
startled them. The expression in their eyes quickened as they
heard, borne on the air, "Mysterious Disappearance——!"
and then lost it in the hubbub. It was easy to complete the
cry, and Bight himself gasped. "Beadel-Muffet? Confound
them!"

"Already?" Maud had turned positively pale.

"They've got it first—be hanged to them!"

Bight gave a laugh—a tribute to their push—but her hand
was on his arm for a sign to listen again. It was there, in the
raucous throats; it was there, for a penny, under the lamps and
in the thick of the stream that stared and passed and left it.
They caught the whole thing—"Prominent Public Man!"
And there was something brutal and sinister in the way it was
given to the flaring night, to the other competing sounds, to
the general hardness of hearing and sight which was yet, on
London pavements, compatible with an interest sufficient for
cynicism. He had been, poor Beadel, public and prominent,
but he had never affected Maud Blandy at least as so marked
with this character as while thus loudly committed to extinction. It was horrid—it was tragic; yet her lament for him was
dry. "If he's gone I'm dished."

"Oh, he's gone—now," said Bight.

"I mean if he's dead."

"Well, perhaps he isn't. I see," Bight added, "what you do
mean. If he's dead you can't kill him."

"Oh, she wants him alive," said Maud.

"Otherwise she can't chuck him?"

To which the girl, however, anxious and wondering, made
no direct reply. "Good-bye to Mrs. Chorner. And I owe it
to *you*."

"Ah, my love!" he vaguely appealed.

"Yes, it's you who have destroyed him, and it makes up for
what you've done *for* me."

"I've done it, you mean, against you? I didn't know," he said, "you'd take it so hard."

Again, as he spoke, the cries sounded out: "Mysterious Disappearance of Prominent Public Man!" It seemed to swell as they listened; Maud started with impatience. "I hate it too much," she said, and quitted him to join the crowd.

He was quickly at her side, however, and before she reached the Strand he had brought her again to a pause. "Do you mean you hate it so much you won't have me?"

It had pulled her up short, and her answer was proportionately straight. "I won't have you if he's dead."

"Then will you if he's not?"

At this she looked at him hard. "Do you *know*, first?"

"No—blessed if I do."

"On your honour?"

"On my honour."

"Well," she said after a hesitation, "if *she* doesn't drop me——"

"It's an understood thing?" he pressed.

But again she hung fire. "Well, produce him first."

They stood there striking their bargain, and it was made, by the long look they exchanged, a question of good faith. "I'll produce him," said Howard Bight.

V

If it had not been a disaster, Beadel-Muffet's plunge into the obscure, it would have been a huge success; so large a space did the prominent public man occupy, for the next few days, in the Papers, so near did he come, nearer certainly than ever before, to supplanting other topics. The question of his whereabouts, of his antecedents, of his habits, of his possible motives, of his probable, or improbable, embarrassments, fairly raged, from day to day and from hour to hour, making the Strand, for our two young friends, quite fiercely, quite cruelly vociferous. They met again promptly, in the thick of the uproar, and no other eyes could have scanned the current rumours and remarks so eagerly as Maud's unless it had been those of Maud's companion. The rumours and remarks were mostly very wonderful, and all of a nature to sharpen the excitement produced in the comrades by their being already, as they felt, "in the know." Even for the girl this sense existed, so that she could smile at wild surmises; she struck herself as knowing much more than she did, especially as, with the alarm once given, she abstained, delicately enough, from worrying, from catechising Bight. She only looked at him as to say "See, while the suspense lasts, how generously I spare you," and her attitude was not affected by the interested promise he had made her. She believed he knew more than he said, though he had sworn as to what he didn't; she saw him in short as holding some threads but having lost others, and his state of mind, so far as she could read it, represented in equal measure assurances unsupported and anxieties unconfessed. He would have liked to pass for having, on cynical grounds, and for the mere ironic beauty of it, believed that the hero of the hour was only, as he had always been, "up to" something from which he would emerge more than ever glorious, or at least conspicuous; but, knowing the gentleman was more than anything, more than all else, asinine, he was not deprived of ground in which fear could abundantly grow. If Beadel, in other words, was ass enough, as was conceivable, to be working the occasion, he was by the same token ass enough to have lost control of it, to have committed some folly from which even fools don't rebound. That was the spark of suspicion lurking in the young man's ease, and that, Maud knew, explained something else.

The family and friends had but too promptly been approached, been besieged; yet Bight, in all the promptness, had markedly withdrawn from the game—had had, one could easily judge, already too much to do with it. Who but he, otherwise, would have been so naturally let loose upon the forsaken home, the bewildered circle, the agitated club, the friend who had last conversed with the eminent absentee, the waiter, in exclusive halls, who had served him with five-o'clock tea, the porter, in august Pall Mall, who had called his last cab, the cabman, supremely privileged, who had driven him—where? "The Last Cab" would, as our young woman reflected, have been a heading so after her friend's own heart, and so consonant with his genius, that it took all her discretion not to ask him how he had resisted it. She didn't ask, she but herself noted the title for future use—she would have at least got that, "The Last Cab," out of the business; and, as the days went by and the extra-specials swarmed, the situation between them swelled with all the unspoken. Matters that were grave depended on it for each—and nothing so much, for instance, as her seeing Mrs. Chorner again. To see that lady as things *had* been had meant that the poor woman might have been helped to believe in her. Believing in her she would have paid her, and Maud, disposed as she was, really had felt capable of earning the pay. Whatever, as the case stood, was caused to hang in the air, nothing dangled more free than the profit derivable from muzzling the Press. With the watchdog to whom Bight had compared it barking for dear life, the moment was scarcely adapted for calling afresh upon a person who had offered a reward for silence. The only silence, as we say, was in the girl's not mentioning to her friend how these embarrassments affected her. Mrs. Chorner was a person she liked—a connection more to her taste than any she had professionally made, and the thought of her now on the rack, tormented with suspense, might well have brought to her lips a "See *there* what you've done!"

There was, for that matter, in Bight's face—he couldn't keep it out—precisely the look of seeing it; which was one of her reasons too for not insisting on her wrong. If he couldn't conceal it this was a part of the rest of the unspoken; he didn't allude to the lady lest it might be too sharply said to him that it was on *her* account he should most blush. Last of all he was hushed by the sense of what he had himself said when the news first fell on their ears. His promise to "produce" the fugitive was still in the air, but with every day that passed the prospect turned less to redemption. Therefore if her own promise, on a different head, depended on it, he was naturally not in a hurry to bring the question to a test. So it was accordingly that they but read the Papers and looked at each other. Maud felt in truth that these organs had never been so worth it, nor either she or her friend—whatever the size of old obligations—so much beholden to them. They helped them to wait, and the better, really, the longer the mystery lasted. It grew of course daily richer, adding to its mass as it went and multiplying its features, looming especially larger through the cloud of correspondence, communication, suggestion, supposition, speculation, with which it was presently suffused. Theories and explanations sprouted at night and bloomed in the morning, to be overtopped at noon by a still thicker crop and to achieve by evening the density of a tropical forest. These, again, were the green glades in which our young friends wandered.

Under the impression of the first night's shock Maud had written to Mortimer Marshal to excuse herself from her engagement to luncheon—a step of which she had promptly advised Bight as a sign of her playing fair. He took it, she could see, for what it was worth, but she could see also how little he now cared. He was thinking of the man with whose strange agitation he had so cleverly and recklessly played, and, in the face of the catastrophe of which they were still so likely to have news, the vanities of smaller fools, the conveniences of first-class flats, the memory of Chippendale teas, ceased to be actual or ceased at any rate to be importunate. Her old interview, furbished into freshness, had appeared, on its Wednesday, in *Brains*, but she had not received in person the renewed homage of its author—she had only, once more, had the vision of his inordinate purchase and diffusion of the precious number. It was a vision, however, at which neither Bight nor she smiled; it was funny on so poor a scale compared with their other show. But it befell that when this latter had, for ten days, kept being funny to the tune that so lengthened their faces, the poor gentleman glorified in *Brains* succeeded in making it clear that he was not easily to be dropped. He wanted now, evidently, as the girl said to herself, to live at concert pitch, and she gathered, from three or four notes, to which, at short intervals, he treated her, that he was watching in anxiety for reverberations not as yet perceptible. His expectation of results from what our young couple had done for him would, as always, have been a thing for pity with a young couple less imbued with the comic sense; though indeed it would also have been a comic thing for a young couple less attentive to a different drama. Disappointed of the girl's company at home the author of *Corisanda* had proposed fresh appointments, which she had desired at the moment, and indeed more each time, not to take up; to the extent even that, catching sight of him, unperceived, on one of these occasions, in her inveterate Strand, she checked on the spot a first impulse to make herself apparent. He was before her, in the crowd, and going the same way. He had stopped a little to look at a shop, and it was then that she swerved in time not to pass close to him. She turned and reversed, conscious and convinced that he was, as she mentally put it, on the prowl for her.

She herself, poor creature—as she also mentally put it—she herself was shamelessly on the prowl, but it wasn't, for her self-respect, to get herself puffed, it wasn't to pick up a personal advantage. It was to pick up news of Beadel-Muffet, to be near the extra-specials, and it was, also—as to this she was never blind—to cultivate that nearness by chances of Howard Bight. The blessing of blindness, in truth, at this time, she scantily enjoyed—being perfectly aware of the place occupied, in her present attitude to that young man, by the simple impossibility of not seeing him. She had done with him, certainly, if he *had* killed Beadel, and nothing was now growing so fast as the presumption in favour of some catastrophe, yet shockingly to be revealed, enacted somewhere in desperate darkness—though probably "on lines," as the Papers said, anticipated by none of the theorists in their own columns, any more than by clever people at the clubs, where the betting was so heavy. She had done with him, indubitably, but she had not—it was equally unmistakeable—done with letting him see how thoroughly she *would* have done; or, to feel about it otherwise, she was laying up treasure in time—as against the privations of the future. She was affected moreover—perhaps but half-consciously—by another consideration; her attitude to Mortimer Marshal had turned a little to fright; she wondered, uneasily, at impressions she might have given him; and she had it, finally, on her mind that, whether or no the vain man believed in them, there must be a limit to the belief she had communicated to her friend. He *was* her friend, after all—whatever should happen; and there were things that, even in that hampered character, she couldn't allow him to suppose. It was a queer business now, in fact, for her to ask herself if she, Maud Blandy, had produced on any sane human sense an effect of flirtation.

She saw herself in this possibility as in some grotesque reflector, a full-length looking-glass of the inferior quality that deforms and discolours. It made her, as a flirt, a figure for frank derision, and she entertained, honest girl, none of the self-pity that would have spared her a shade of this sharpened consciousness, have taken an inch from facial proportion where it would have been missed with advantage, or added one in such other quarters as would have welcomed the gift. She might have counted the hairs of her head, for any wish she could have achieved to remain vague about them, just as she might have rehearsed, disheartened, postures of grace, for any dream she could compass of having ever accidentally struck one. Void, in short, of a personal illusion, exempt with an exemption which left her not less helplessly aware of where her hats and skirts and shoes failed, than of where her nose and mouth and complexion, and, above all, where her poor figure, without a scrap of drawing, did, she blushed to bethink herself that she might have affected her young man as really bragging of a conquest. Her *other* young man's pursuit of her, what was it but rank greed—not in the least for her person, but for the connection of which he had formed so preposterous a view? She was ready now to say to herself that she had swaggered to Bight for the joke—odd indeed though the wish to undeceive him at the moment when he would have been more welcome than ever to think what he liked. The only thing she wished him not to think, as she believed, was that she thought Mortimer Marshal thought her—or anyone on earth thought her—intrinsically charming. She didn't want to put to him "Do you suppose I suppose that if it came to the point——?" her reasons for such avoidance being easily conceivable. He was not to suppose that, in any such quarter, she struck herself as either casting a spell or submitting to one; only, while their crisis lasted, rectifications were scarce in order. She couldn't remind him even, without a mistake, that she had but wished to worry him; because in the first place that suggested again a pretension in her (so at variance with the image in the mirror) to put forth arts—suggested possibly even that she used similar ones when she lunched, in bristling flats, with the pushing; and because in the second it would have seemed a sort of challenge to him to renew his appeal.

Then, further and most of all, she had a doubt which by itself would have made her wary, as it distinctly, in her present suspended state, made her uncomfortable; she was haunted by the after-sense of having perhaps been fatuous. A spice of conviction, in respect to what was open to her, an element of elation, in her talk to Bight about Marshal, had there not, after all, been? Hadn't she a little liked to think the wretched man *could* cling to her? and hadn't she also a little, for herself, filled out the future, in fancy, with the picture of the droll relation? She had seen it as droll, evidently; but had she seen it as impossible, unthinkable? It had become unthinkable now, and she was not wholly unconscious of how the change had worked. Such workings were queer—but there they were; the foolish man had become odious to her precisely *because* she was hardening her face for Bight. The latter was no foolish man, but this it was that made it the more a pity he should have placed the impassable between them. That was what, as the days went on, she felt herself take in. It was there, the impassable—she couldn't lucidly have said why, couldn't have explained the thing on the real scale of the wrong her comrade had done. It was a wrong, it was a wrong—she couldn't somehow get out of that; which was a proof, no doubt, that she confusedly tried. The author of *Corisanda* was sacrificed in the effort—for ourselves it may come to that. Great to poor Maud Blandy as well, for that matter, great, yet also attaching, were the obscurity and ambiguity in which some impulses lived and moved—the rich gloom of their combinations, contradictions, inconsistencies, surprises. It rested her verily a little from her straightness—the line of a character, she felt, markedly like the line of the Edgware Road and of Maida Vale—that she *could* be queerly inconsistent, and inconsistent in the hustling Strand, where, if anywhere, you had, under pain of hoofs and wheels, to decide whether or no you would cross. She had moments, before shop-windows, into which she looked without seeing, when all the unuttered came over her. She had once told her friend that she pitied everyone, and at these moments, in sharp unrest, she pitied Bight for their tension, in which nothing was relaxed.

It was all too mixed and too strange—each of them in a different corner with a different impossibility. There was her

own, in far Kilburnia; and there was her friend's, everywhere
—for where didn't he go? and there was Mrs. Chorner's, on
the very edge of Park "Line," in spite of all petticoats and
marble baths; and there was Beadel-Muffet's, the wretched
man, God only knew where—which was what made the whole
show supremely incoherent: he ready to give his head, if, as
seemed so unlikely, he still *had* a head, to steal into cover and
keep under, out of the glare; he having scoured Europe, it
might so well be guessed, for some hole in which the Papers
wouldn't find him out, and then having—what else was there
by this time to presume?—died, in the hole, as the only way
not to see, to hear, to know, let alone *be* known, heard, seen.
Finally, while he lay there relieved by the only relief, here was
poor Mortimer Marshal, undeterred, undismayed, unperceiv-
ing, so hungry to be paragraphed in something like the same
fashion and published on something like the same scale, that,
for the very blindness of it, he couldn't read the lesson that
was in the air, and scrambled, to his utmost, toward the boat
itself that ferried the warning ghost. Just *that*, beyond everything, was the incoherence that made for rather dismal farce,
and on which Bight had put his finger in naming the author
of *Corisanda* as a candidate, in turn, for the comic, the tragic
vacancy. It was a wonderful moment for such an ideal, and
the sight was not really to pass from her till she had seen the
whole of the wonder. A fortnight had elapsed since the night
of Beadel's disappearance, and the conditions attending the
afternoon performances of the Finnish drama had in some
degree reproduced themselves—to the extent, that is, of the
place, the time and several of the actors involved; the audience, for reasons traceable, being differently composed. A lady
of "high social position," desirous still further to elevate that
character by the obvious aid of the theatre, had engaged a
playhouse for a series of occasions on which she was to affront
in person whatever volume of attention she might succeed in
collecting. Her success had not immediately been great, and
by the third or the fourth day the public consciousness was
so markedly astray that the means taken to recover it penetrated, in the shape of a complimentary ticket, even to our
young woman. Maud had communicated with Bight, who
could be sure of a ticket, proposing to him that they should

go together and offering to await him in the porch of the theatre. He joined her there, but with so queer a face—for her subtlety—that she paused before him, previous to their going in, with a straight "You *know* something!"

"About that rank idiot?" He shook his head, looking kind enough; but it didn't make him, she felt, more natural. "My dear, it's all beyond me."

"I mean," she said with a shade of uncertainty, "about poor dear Beadel."

"So do I. So does everyone. No one now, at any moment, means anything about anyone else. But I've lost intellectual control—of the extraordinary case. I flattered myself I still had a certain amount. But the situation at last escapes me. I break down. Non comprenny? I give it up."

She continued to look at him hard. "Then what's the matter with you?"

"Why, just *that*, probably—that I feel like a clever man 'done,' and that your tone with me adds to the feeling. Or, putting it otherwise, it's perhaps only just one of the ways in which I'm so interesting; that, with the life we lead and the age we live in, there's *always* something the matter with me—there can't help being: some rage, some disgust, some fresh amazement against which one hasn't, for all one's experience, been proof. That sense—of having been sold again—produces emotions that may well, on occasion, be reflected in the countenance. There you are."

Well, he might say that, "There you are," as often as he liked without, at the pass they had come to, making her in the least see where she was. She was only just where she stood, a little apart in the lobby, listening to his words, which she found eminently characteristic of him, struck with an odd impression of his talking against time, and, most of all, tormented to recognise that she could fairly do nothing better, at such a moment, than feel he was awfully nice. The moment—that of his most blandly (she would have said in the case of another most impudently) failing, all round, to satisfy her—was appropriate only to some emotion consonant with her dignity. It was all crowded and covered, hustled and interrupted now; but what really happened in this brief passage, and with her finding no words to reply to him, was that dignity quite appeared to collapse and drop from her, to sink to the floor, under the feet of people visibly bristling with "paper," where the young man's extravagant offer of an arm, to put an end and help her in, had the effect of an invitation to leave it lying to be trampled on.

Within, once seated, they kept their places through two intervals, but at the end of the third act—there were to be no less than five—they fell in with a movement that carried half the audience to the outer air. Howard Bight desired to smoke, and Maud offered to accompany him, for the purpose, to the portico, where, somehow, for both of them, the sense was immediately strong that *this*, the squalid Strand, damp yet incandescent, ugly yet eloquent, familiar yet fresh, was life, palpable, ponderable, possible, much more than the stuff, neither scenic nor cosmic, they had quitted. The difference came to them, from the street, in a moist mild blast, which they simply took in, at first, in a long draught, as more amusing than their play, and which, for the moment, kept them conscious of the voices of the air as of something mixed and vague. The next thing, of course, however, was that they heard the hoarse newsmen, though with the special sense of the sound not standing out—which, so far as it did come, made them exchange a look. There was no hawker just then within call.

"What are they crying?"

"Blessed if I care!" Bight said while he got his light—which he had but just done when they saw themselves closely approached. The Papers had come into sight in the form of a small boy bawling the "Winner" of something, and at the same moment they recognised their reprieve they recognised also the presence of Mortimer Marshal.

He had no shame about it. "I fully believed I should find you."

"But you haven't been," Bight asked, "inside?"

"Not at to-day's performance—I only just thought I'd pass. But at each of the others," Mortimer Marshal confessed.

"Oh, you're a devotee," said Bight, whose reception of the poor man contended, for Maud's attention, with this extravagance of the poor man's own importunity. Their friend had sat through the piece three times on the chance of her being there for one or other of the acts, and if he had given that up in discouragement he still hovered and waited. Who now, moreover, was to say he wasn't rewarded? To find her companion as well as at last to find herself gave the reward a character that it took, somehow, for her eye, the whole of this misguided person's curiously large and flat, but distinctly bland, sweet, solicitous countenance to express. It came over the girl with horror that here was a material object—the incandescence, on the edge of the street, didn't spare it—which she had had perverse moments of seeing fixed before her for life. She asked herself, in this agitation, what she would have likened it to; more than anything perhaps to a large clean china plate, with a neat "pattern," suspended, to the exposure of hapless heads, from the centre of the domestic ceiling. Truly she was, as by the education of the strain undergone, learning something every hour—it seemed so to be the case that a strain enlarged the mind, formed the taste, enriched, even, the imagination. Yet in spite of this last fact, it must be added, she continued rather mystified by the actual pitch of her comrade's manner, Bight really behaving as if he enjoyed their visitor's "note." He treated him so decently, as they said, that he might suddenly have taken to liking his company; which was an odd appearance till Maud understood it— whereupon it became for her a slightly sinister one. For the effect of the honest gentleman, she by that time saw, was to make her friend nervous and vicious, and the form taken by his irritation was just this dangerous candour, which encouraged the candour of the victim. She had for the latter a residuum of pity, whereas Bight, she felt, had none, and she didn't want him, the poor man, absolutely to pay with his life.

It was clear, however, within a few minutes, that this was what he was bent on doing, and she found herself helpless before his smug insistence. She had taken his measure; he was *made* incorrigibly to try, irredeemably to fail—to be, in short, eternally defeated and eternally unaware. He wouldn't rage— he *couldn't*, for the citadel might, in that case, have been carried by his assault; he would only spend his life in walking round and round it, asking everyone he met how in the name of goodness one did get in. And everyone would make a fool of him—though no one so much as her companion now— and everything would fall from him but the perfection of his temper, of his tailor, of his manners, of his mediocrity. He evidently rejoiced at the happy chance which had presented him again to Bight, and he lost as little time as possible in proposing, the play ended, an adjournment again to tea. The spirit of malice in her comrade, now inordinately excited, met this suggestion with an amendment that fairly made her anxious; Bight threw out, in a word, the idea that he himself surely, this time, should entertain Mr. Marshal.

"Only I'm afraid I can take you but to a small pothouse that we poor journalists haunt."

"They're just the places I delight in—it would be of an extraordinary interest. I sometimes venture into them—feeling awfully strange and wondering, I do assure you, who people are. But to go there with *you*——!" And he looked from Bight to Maud and from Maud back again with such abysses of appreciation that she knew him as lost indeed.

VI

It was demonic of Bight, who immediately answered that he would tell him with pleasure who everyone was, and she felt this the more when her friend, making light of the rest of the entertainment they had quitted, advised their sacrificing it and proceeding to the other scene. He was really too eager for his victim—she wondered what he wanted to do with him. He could only play him at the most a practical joke—invent appetising identities, once they were at table, for the dull consumers around. No one, at the place they most frequented, had an identity in the least appetising, no one was anyone or anything. It was apparently of the essence of existence on such terms—the terms, at any rate, to which *she* was reduced—that people comprised in it couldn't even minister to each other's curiosity, let alone to envy or awe. She would have wished therefore, for their pursuer, to intervene a little, to warn him against beguilement; but they had moved together along the Strand and then out of it, up a near cross street, without her opening her mouth. Bight, as she felt, was acting to prevent this; his easy talk redoubled, and he led his lamb to the shambles. The talk had jumped to poor Beadel—her friend had startled her by causing it, almost with violence, at a given

moment, to take that direction, and he thus quite sufficiently
stayed her speech. The people she lived with mightn't make
you curious, but there was of course always a sharp exception
for *him*. She kept still, in fine, with the wonder of what he
wanted; though indeed she might, in the presence of their
guest's response, have felt he was already getting it. He was
getting, that is—and *she* was, into the bargain—the fullest illustration of the ravage of a passion; so sublimely Marshal rose
to the proposition, infernally thrown off, that, in whatever
queer box or tight place Beadel might have found himself, it
was something, after all, to have so powerfully interested the
public. The insidious artless way in which Bight made his
point!—"I don't know that I've ever known the public (and
I watch it, as in my trade we have to, day and night) *so* consummately interested." They had that phenomenon—the
present consummate interest—well before them while they sat
at their homely meal, served with accessories so different from
those of the sweet Chippendale (another chord on which the
young man played with just the right effect!), and it would
have been hard to say if the guest were, for the first moments,
more under the spell of the marvellous "hold" on the town
achieved by the great absentee, or of that of the delicious
coarse tablecloth, the extraordinary form of the saltcellars, and
the fact that he had within range of sight, at the other end of
the room, in the person of the little quiet man with blue spectacles and an obvious wig, the greatest authority in London
about the inner life of the criminal classes. Beadel, none the
less, came up again and stayed up—would clearly so have been
kept up, had there been need, by their host, that the girl
couldn't at last fail to see how much it was for herself that his
intention worked. What *was* it, all the same—since it couldn't
be anything so simple as to expose their hapless visitor? What
had she to learn about *him*?—especially at the hour of seeing
what there was still to learn about Bight. She ended by deciding—for his appearance bore her out—that his explosion
was but the form taken by an inward fever. The fever, on this
theory, was the result of the final pang of responsibility. The
mystery of Beadel had grown too dark to be borne—which
they would presently feel; and he was meanwhile in the phase
of bluffing it off, precisely because it was to overwhelm him.

"And do you mean you too would pay with your *life*?" He put the question, agreeably, across the table to his guest; agreeably of course in spite of his eye's dry glitter.

His guest's expression, at this, fairly became beautiful. "Well, it's an awfully nice point. Certainly one would like to *feel* the great murmur surrounding one's name, to *be* there, more or less, so as not to lose the sense of it, and as I really think, you know, the pleasure; the great city, the great empire, the world itself for the moment, hanging literally on one's personality and giving a start, in its suspense, whenever one is mentioned. Big sensation, you know, that," Mr. Marshal pleadingly smiled, "and of course if one were dead one wouldn't enjoy it. One would have to come to life for that."

"Naturally," Bight rejoined—"only that's what the dead don't do. You can't eat your cake and have it. The question is," he good-naturedly explained, "whether you'd be willing, for the certitude of the great murmur you speak of, to part with your life under circumstances of extraordinary mystery."

His guest earnestly fixed it. "Whether *I* would be willing?"

"Mr. Marshal wonders," Maud said to Bight, "if you are, as a person interested in his reputation, definitely proposing to him some such possibility."

He looked at her, on this, with mild, round eyes, and she felt, wonderfully, that he didn't quite see her as joking. He smiled—he always smiled, but his anxiety showed, and he turned it again to their companion. "You mean—a—the knowing how it might be *going* to be felt?"

"Well, yes—call it that. The consciousness of what one's unexplained extinction—given, to start with, one's high position—would mean, wouldn't be able to *help* meaning, for millions and millions of people. The point is—and I admit it's, as you call it, a 'nice' one—if you can think of the impression so made as worth the purchase. *Naturally*, naturally, there's but the impression you make. You don't receive any. You can't. You've only your confidence—so far as that's an impression. Oh, it *is* indeed a nice point; and I only put it to you," Bight wound up, "because, you know, you do like to be recognised."

Mr. Marshal was bewildered, but he was not so bewildered as not to be able, a trifle coyly, but still quite bravely, to confess to that. Maud, with her eyes on her friend, found herself thinking of him as of some plump, innocent animal, more or less of the pink-eyed rabbit or sleek guinea-pig order, involved in the slow spell of a serpent of shining scales. Bight's scales, truly, had never so shone as this evening, and he used to admiration—which was just a part of the lustre—the right shade of gravity. He was neither so light as to fail of the air of an attractive offer, nor yet so earnest as to betray a gibe. He might conceivably have been, as an undertaker of improvements in defective notorieties, placing before his guest a practical scheme. It was really quite as if he were ready to guarantee the "murmur" if Mr. Marshal was ready to pay the price. And the price wouldn't of course be only Mr. Marshal's existence. All this, at least, if Mr. Marshal felt moved to take it so. The prodigious thing, next, was that Mr. Marshal *was* so moved—though, clearly, as was to be expected, with important qualifications. "Do you really mean," he asked, "that one would excite *this* delightful interest?"

"You allude to the charged state of the air on the subject of Beadel?" Bight considered, looking volumes. "It would depend a good deal upon who one *is.*"

He turned, Mr. Marshal, again to Maud Blandy, and his eyes seemed to suggest to her that she should put his question for him. They forgave her, she judged, for having so oddly forsaken him, but they appealed to her now not to leave him to struggle alone. Her own difficulty was, however, meanwhile, that she feared to serve him as he suggested without too much, by way of return, turning his case to the comic; whereby she only looked at him hard and let him revert to their friend. "Oh," he said, with a rich wistfulness from which the comic was not absent, "of course everyone can't pretend to be Beadel."

"Perfectly. But we're speaking, after all, of those who do count."

There was quite a hush, for the minute, while the poor man faltered. "Should you say that *I*—in any appreciable way—count?"

Howard Bight distilled honey. "Isn't it a little a question of how much we should find you *did*, or, for that matter, might, as it were, be made to, in the event of a real catastrophe?"

Mr. Marshal turned pale, yet he met it too with sweetness. "I like the way"—and he had a glance for Maud—"you talk of catastrophes!"

His host did the comment justice. "Oh, it's only because, you see, we're so peculiarly in the presence of one. Beadel shows so tremendously what a catastrophe does for the right person. His absence, you may say, doubles, quintuples, his presence."

"I see, I see!" Mr. Marshal was all there. "It's awfully interesting to be so present. And yet it's rather dreadful to be so absent." It had set him fairly musing; for couldn't the opposites be reconciled? "If he *is*," he threw out, "absent——!"

"Why, he's absent, of course," said Bight, "if he's dead."

"And really dead is what you believe him to be?"

He breathed it with a strange break, as from a mind too full. It was on the one hand a grim vision for his own case, but was on the other a kind of clearance of the field. With Beadel out of the way his own case could live, and he was obviously thinking what it might be to be as dead as that and yet as much alive. What his demand first did, at any rate, was to make Howard Bight look straight at Maud. Her own look met him, but she asked nothing now. She felt him somehow fathomless, and his practice with their infatuated guest created a new suspense. He might indeed have been looking at her to learn how to reply, but even were this the case she had still nothing to answer. So in a moment he had spoken without her. "I've quite given him up."

It sank into Marshal, after which it produced something. "He ought then to come back. I mean," he explained, "to see for himself—to *have* the impression."

"Of the noise he has made? Yes"—Bight weighed it—"that would be the ideal."

"And it would, if one must call it 'noise,'" Marshal limpidly pursued, "make—a—more."

"Oh, but if you *can't*!"

"Can't, you mean, through having already made so much, add to the quantity?"

"Can't"—Bight was a wee bit sharp—"come back, confound it, at all. Can't return from the dead!"

Poor Marshal had to take it. "No—not if you *are* dead."

"Well, that's what we're talking about."

Maud, at this, for pity, held out a perch. "Mr. Marshal, I think, is talking a little on the basis of the possibility of your not being!" He threw her an instant glance of gratitude, and it gave her a push. "So long as you're not quite too utterly, you *can* come back."

"Oh," said Bight, "in time for the fuss?"

"Before"—Marshal met it—"the interest has subsided. It naturally then *wouldn't*—would it?—subside!"

"No," Bight granted; "not if it hadn't, through wearing out—I mean your being lost too long—already died out."

"Oh, of course," his guest agreed, "you mustn't be lost *too* long." A vista had plainly opened to him, and the subject led him on. He had, before its extent, another pause. "About how long, do you think——?"

Well, Bight *had* to think. "I should say Beadel had rather overdone it."

The poor gentleman stared. "But if he can't help him-self——?"

Bight gave a laugh. "Yes; but in case he could."

Maud again intervened, and, as her question was for their host, Marshal was all attention. "Do you consider Beadel has overdone it?"

Well, once more, it took consideration. The issue of Bight's, however, was not of the clearest. "I don't think we can tell unless he *were* to. I don't think that, without seeing it, and judging by the special case, one can quite know how it would be taken. He might, on the one side, have spoiled, so to speak, his market; and he might, on the other, have scored as never before."

"It might be," Maud threw in, "just the making of him."

"Surely"—Marshal glowed—"there's just that chance."

"What a pity then," Bight laughed, "that there isn't some-one to take it! For the light it would throw, I mean, on the laws—so mysterious, so curious, so interesting—that govern the great currents of public attention. They're not wholly whimsical—wayward and wild; they have their strange logic, their obscure reason—if one could only get *at* it! The man who does, you see—and who can keep his discovery to himself!—will make his everlasting fortune, as well, no doubt, as that of a few others. It's *our* branch, *our* preoccupation, in fact, Miss Blandy's and mine—this pursuit of the incalculable, this study, to that end, of the great forces of publicity. Only, of course, it must be remembered," Bight went on, "that in the case we're speaking of—the man disappearing as Beadel has now disappeared, and supplanting for the time every other topic—must have someone on the spot for him, to keep the pot boiling, someone acting, with real intelligence, in his interest. I mean if he's to get the good of it when he does turn up. It would never do, you see, that *that* should be flat!"

"Oh no, not *flat*, never!" Marshal quailed at the thought. Held as in a vise by his host's high lucidity, he exhaled his interest at every pore. "It wouldn't be flat for Beadel, would it?—I mean if he *were* to come."

"Not much! It wouldn't be flat for Beadel—I think I can undertake." And Bight undertook so well that he threw himself back in his chair with his thumbs in the armholes of his waistcoat and his head very much up. "The only thing is that for poor Beadel it's a luxury, so to speak, wasted—and so dreadfully, upon my word, that one quite regrets there's no one to step in."

"To step in?" His visitor hung upon his lips.

"To do the thing better, so to speak—to do it right; to—having raised the whirlwind—really *ride* the storm. To seize the psychological hour."

Marshal met it, yet he wondered. "You speak of the reappearance? I see. But the man of the reappearance would have, wouldn't he?—or perhaps I don't follow?—to be the same as the man of the *dis*appearance. It wouldn't do as well—would it?—for *somebody else* to turn up?"

Bight considered him with attention—as if there were fine possibilities. "No; unless such a person should turn up, say—well, with news of him."

"But what news?"

"With lights—the more lurid the better—*on* the darkness. With the facts, don't you see, *of* the disappearance."

Marshal, on his side, threw himself back. "But he'd have to know them!"

"Oh," said Bight, with prompt portentousness, "that could be managed."

It was too much, by this time, for his victim, who simply turned on Maud a dilated eye and a flushed cheek. "Mr. Marshal," it made her say—"Mr. Marshal would like to turn up."

Her hand was on the table, and the effect of her words, combined with this, was to cause him, before responsive speech could come, to cover it respectfully but expressively with his own. "Do you mean," he panted to Bight, "that you have, amid the general collapse of speculation, facts to give?"

"I've always facts to give."

It begot in the poor man a large hot smile. "But—how shall I say?—authentic, or as I believe you clever people say, 'inspired' ones?"

"If I should undertake such a case as we're supposing, I would of course by that circumstance undertake that my facts should be—well, worthy of it. I would take," Bight on his own part modestly smiled, "pains with them."

It finished the business. "Would you take pains for *me*?"

Bight looked at him now hard. "Would you like to appear?"

"Oh, 'appear'!" Marshal weakly murmured.

"Is it, Mr. Marshal, a real proposal? I mean are you prepared——?"

Wonderment sat in his eyes—an anguish of doubt and desire. "But wouldn't you prepare me——?"

"Would you prepare *me*—that's the point," Bight laughed —"*to* prepare you?"

There was a minute's mutual gaze, but Marshal took it in. "I don't know what you're making me say; I don't know what you're making me *feel*. When one is with people so up in these things——" and he turned to his companions, alternately, a look as of conscious doom lighted with suspicion, a look that was like a cry for mercy—"one feels a little as if one ought to be saved from one's self. For I dare say one's foolish enough with one's poor little wish——"

"The little wish, my dear sir"—Bight took him up—"to stand out in the world! Your wish is the wish of all high spirits."

"It's dear of you to say it." Mr. Marshal was all response. "I shouldn't want, even if it *were* weak or vain, to have lived wholly unknown. And if what you ask is whether I understand you to speak, at it were, professionally——"

"You *do* understand me?" Bight pushed back his chair.

"Oh, but so well!—when I've already seen what you can do. I need scarcely say, that having seen it, I shan't bargain."

"Ah, then, *I* shall," Bight smiled. "I mean with the Papers. It must be half profits."

" 'Profits'?" His guest was vague.

"Our friend," Maud explained to Bight, "simply wants the position."

Bight threw her a look. "Ah, he must take what I give him."

"But what you give me," their friend handsomely contended, "*is* the position."

"Yes; but the terms that I shall get! I don't produce you, of course," Bight went on, "till I've prepared you. But when I do produce you it will be as a value."

"You'll get so much for me?" the poor gentleman quavered.

"I shall be able to get, I think, anything I ask. So we divide." And Bight jumped up.

Marshal did the same, and, while, with his hands on the back of his chair, he steadied himself from the vertiginous view, they faced each other across the table. "Oh, it's too wonderful!"

"You're not afraid?"

He looked at a card on the wall, framed, suspended and marked with the word "Soups." He looked at Maud, who had not moved. "I don't know; I may be; I must feel. What I *should* fear," he added, "would be his coming back."

"Beadel's? Yes, that would dish you. But since he can't——!"

"I place myself," said Mortimer Marshal, "in your hands."

Maud Blandy still hadn't moved; she stared before her at the cloth. A small sharp sound, unheard, she saw, by the others, had reached her from the street, and with her mind instinctively catching at it, she waited, dissimulating a little, for its repetition or its effect. It was the howl of the Strand, it was news of the absent, and it would have a bearing. She had a hesitation, for she winced even now with the sense of Marshal's intensest look at her. He couldn't be saved from himself, but he might be, still, from Bight; though it hung of course, her chance to warn him, on what the news would be. She thought with concentration, while her friends unhooked their overcoats, and by the time these garments were donned she was on her feet. Then she spoke. "I don't want you to be 'dished.'"

He allowed for her alarm. "But how *can* I be?"

"Something has come."

"Something——?" The men had both spoken.

They had stopped where they stood; she again caught the sound. "Listen! They're crying."

They waited then, and it came—came, of a sudden, with a burst and as if passing the place. A hawker, outside, with his "extra," called by someone and hurrying, bawled it as he moved. "Death of Beadel-Muffet—Extraordinary News!"

They all gasped, and Maud, with her eyes on Bight, saw him, to her satisfaction at first, turn pale. But his guest drank it in. "If it's true then"—Marshal triumphed at her—"I'm *not* dished."

But she only looked hard at Bight, who struck her as having, at the sound, fallen to pieces, and as having above all, on the instant, turned cold for his worried game. "Is it true?" she austerely asked.

His white face answered. "It's true."

VII

The first thing, on the part of our friends—after each interlocutor, producing a penny, had plunged into the unfolded "Latest"—was this very evidence of their dispensing with their companion's further attendance on their agitated state, and all the more that Bight was to have still, in spite of agitation, his function with him to accomplish: a result much assisted by the insufflation of wind into Mr. Marshal's sails constituted by the fact before them. With Beadel publicly dead this gentleman's opportunity, on the terms just arranged, opened out; it was quite as if they had seen him, then and there, step, with a kind of spiritual splash, into the empty seat of the boat so launched, scarcely even taking time to master the essentials before he gave himself to the breeze. The essentials indeed he was, by their understanding, to receive in full from Bight at their earliest leisure; but nothing could so vividly have marked his confidence in the young man as the promptness with which he appeared now ready to leave him to his inspiration. The news moreover, as yet, was the rich, grim fact—a sharp flare from an Agency, lighting into blood-colour the locked room, finally, with the police present, forced open, of the first hotel at Frankfort-on-the-Oder; but there was enough of it, clearly, to bear scrutiny, the scrutiny represented in our young couple by the act of perusal prolonged, intensified, repeated, so repeated that it was exactly perhaps with this suggestion of doubt that poor Mr. Marshal had even also a little lost patience. He vanished, at any rate, while his supporters, still planted in the side-street into which they had lately issued, stood extinguished, as to any facial communion, behind the array of printed columns. It was only after he had gone that, whether aware or not, the others lowered, on either side, the absorbing page and knew that their eyes had met. A remarkable thing, for Maud Blandy, then happened, a thing quite as remarkable at least as poor Beadel's suicide, which we recall her having so considerably discounted.

Present as they thus were at the tragedy, present in far Frankfort just where they stood, by the door of their stale pothouse and in the thick of London air, the logic of her situation, she was sharply conscious, would have been an immediate rupture with Bight. He was scared at what he had done—he looked his scare so straight out at her that she might almost have seen in it the dismay of his question of how far his responsibility, given the facts, might, if pried into, be held—and not only at the judgment-seat of mere morals—to reach. The dismay was to that degree illuminating that she had had from him no such avowal of responsibility as this amounted to, and the limit to any laxity on her own side had therefore not been set for her with any such sharpness. It put her at last in the right, his scare—quite richly in the right; and as that was naturally but where she had waited to find herself, everything that now silently passed between them had the

merit, if it had none other, of simplifying. Their hour had
struck, the hour after which she was definitely not to have
forgiven him. Yet what occurred, as I say, was that, if, at the
end of five minutes, she had moved much further, it proved
to be, in spite of logic, not in the sense away from him, but
in the sense nearer. He showed to her, at these strange moments, as blood-stained and literally hunted; the yell of the
hawkers, repeated and echoing round them, was like a cry for
his life; and there was in particular a minute during which,
gazing down into the roused Strand, all equipped both with
mob and with constables, she asked herself whether she had
best get off with him through the crowd, where they would
be least noticed, or get him away through quiet Covent Garden, empty at that hour, but with policemen to watch a furtive
couple, and with the news, more bawled at their heels in the
stillness, acquiring the sound of the very voice of justice. It
was this last sudden terror that presently determined her, and
determined with it an impulse of protection that had somehow to do with pity without having to do with tenderness. It
settled, at all events, the question of leaving him; she couldn't
leave him there and so; she must see at least what would have
come of his own sense of the shock.

The way he took it, the shock, gave her afresh the measure
of how perversely he had played with Marshal—of how he
had tried so, on the very edge of his predicament, to cheat
his fears and beguile his want of ease. He had insisted to his
victim on the truth he had now to reckon with, but had insisted only because he didn't believe it. Beadel, by that attitude, was but lying low; so that he would have no promise
really to redeem. At present he had one, indeed, and Maud
could ask herself if the redemption of it, with the leading of
their wretched friend a further fantastic dance, would be
what he depended on to drug the pain of remorse. By the
time she had covered as much ground as this, however, she
had also, standing before him, taken his special out of his
hand and, folding it up carefully with her own and smoothing it down, packed the two together into such a small tight
ball as she might toss to a distance without the air, which she
dreaded, of having, by any looser proceeding, disowned or
evaded the news. Howard Bight, helpless and passive, putting

on the matter no governed face, let her do with him as she
liked, let her, for the first time in their acquaintance, draw
his hand into her arm as if he were an invalid or as if she
were a snare. She took with him, thus guided and sustained,
their second plunge; led him, with decision, straight to where
their shock was shared and amplified, pushed her way, guarding him, across the dense thoroughfare and through the
great westward current which fairly seemed to meet and challenge them, and then, by reaching Waterloo Bridge with him
and descending the granite steps, set him down at last on the
Embankment. It was a fact, none the less, that she had in
her eyes, all the while, and too strangely for speech, the vision of the scene in the little German city: the smashed door,
the exposed horror, the wondering, insensible group, the
English gentleman, in the disordered room, driven to bay
among the scattered personal objects that only too floridly
announced and emblazoned him, and several of which the
Papers were already naming—the poor English gentleman,
hunted and hiding, done to death by the thing he yet, for so
long, always *would* have, and stretched on the floor with his
beautiful little revolver still in his hand and the effusion of his
blood, from a wound taken, with rare resolution, full in the
face, extraordinary and dreadful.

She went on with her friend, eastward and beside the river,
and it was as if they both, for that matter, had, in their silence,
the dire material vision. Maud Blandy, however, presently
stopped short—one of the connections of the picture so
brought her to a stand. It had come over her, with a force
she couldn't check, that the catastrophe itself would have
been, with all the unfathomed that yet clung to it, just the
thing for her companion's professional hand; so that, queerly
but absolutely, while she looked at him again in reprobation
and pity, it was as much as she could do not to feel it for him
as something missed, not to wish he might have been there
to snatch his chance, and not, above all, to betray to him this
reflection. It had really risen to her lips—"Why aren't *you*, old
man, on the spot?" and indeed the question, had it broken
forth, might well have sounded as a provocation to him to
start without delay. Such was the effect, in poor Maud, for
the moment, of the habit, so confirmed in her, of seeing time

marked only by the dial of the Papers. She had admired in Bight the true journalist that she herself was so clearly not—though it was also not what she had *most* admired in him; and she might have felt, at this instant, the charm of putting true journalism to the proof. She might have been on the point of saying: "Real business, you know, would be for you to start *now*, just as you are, before anyone else, sure as you can so easily be of having the pull"; and she might, after a moment, while they paused, have been looking back, through the river-mist, for a sign of the hour, at the blurred face of Big Ben. That she grazed this danger yet avoided it was partly the result in truth of her seeing for herself quickly enough that the last thing Bight could just then have thought of, even under provocation of the most positive order, was the chance thus failing him, or the train, the boat, the advantage, that the true journalist wouldn't have missed. He quite, under her eyes, while they stood together, ceased to be the true journalist; she saw him, as she felt, put off the character as definitely as she might have seen him remove his coat, his hat, or the contents of his pockets, in order to lay them on the parapet before jumping into the river. Wonderful was the difference that this transformation, marked by no word and supported by no sign, made in the man she had hitherto known. Nothing, again, could have so expressed for her his continued inward dismay. It was as if, for that matter, she couldn't have asked him a question without adding to it; and she didn't wish to add to it, since she was by this time more fully aware that she wished to be generous. When she at last uttered other words it was precisely so that she mightn't press him.

"I think of *her*—poor thing: that's what it makes me do. I think of her there at this moment—just out of the 'Line'—with this stuff shrieked at her windows." With which, having so at once contained and relieved herself, she caused him to walk on.

"Are you talking of Mrs. Chorner?" he after a moment asked. And then, when he had had her quick "Of course—of who else?" he said what she didn't expect. "Naturally one thinks of her. But she has herself to blame. I mean she drove him——" What he meant, however, Bight suddenly dropped, taken as he was with another idea, which had brought them the next minute to a halt. "Mightn't you, by the way, see her?"

"See her *now*——?"

"'Now' or never—for the good of it. Now's just your time."

"But how can it be hers, in the very midst——?"

"*Because* it's in the very midst. She'll tell you things to-night that she'll never tell again. To-night she'll be great."

Maud gaped almost wildly. "You want me, at such an hour, to *call*——?"

"And send up your card with the word—oh, of course the right one!—on it."

"What do you suggest," Maud asked, "as the right one?"

"Well, 'The world *wants* you'—that usually does. I've seldom known it, even in deeper distress than is, after all, here supposable, to fail. Try it, at any rate."

The girl, strangely touched, intensely wondered. "Demand of her, you mean, to let me explain for her?"

"There you are. You catch on. Write *that*—if you like—'Let me explain.' She'll want to explain."

Maud wondered at him more—he had somehow so turned the tables on her. "But she doesn't. It's exactly *what* she doesn't; she never *has*. And that he, poor wretch, was always wanting to——"

"Was precisely what made her hold off? I grant it." He had waked up. "But that was before she had killed him. Trust me, she'll chatter now."

This, for his companion, simply forced it out. "It wasn't *she* who killed him. That, my dear, you know."

"You mean it was I who did? Well then, my child, interview *me*." And, with his hands in his pockets and his idea apparently genuine, he smiled at her, by the grey river and under the high lamps, with an effect strange and suggestive. "*That* would be a go!"

"You mean"—she jumped at it—"you'll tell me what you know?"

"Yes, and even what I've done! But—if you'll take it so—for the Papers. Oh, for the Papers only!"

She stared. "You mean you want me to get it in——?"

"I don't 'want' you to do anything, but I'm ready to help you, ready to get it in for you, like a shot, myself, if it's a thing you yourself want."

"A thing I want—to give you away?"

"Oh," he laughed, "I'm just now worth giving! You'd really do it, you know. And, to help you, here I am. It *would* be for you—only judge!—a leg up."

It would indeed, she really saw; somehow, on the spot, she believed it. But his surrender made her tremble. It wasn't a joke—she *could* give him away; or rather she could sell him for money. Money, thus, was what he offered her, or the value of money, which was the same; it was what he wanted her to have. She was conscious already, however, that she could have it only as he offered it, and she said therefore, but half-heartedly, "I'll keep your secret."

He looked at her more gravely. "Ah, as a secret I can't give it." Then he hesitated. "I'll get you a hundred pounds for it."

"Why don't you," she asked, "get them for yourself?"

"Because I don't care for myself. I care only for you."

She waited again. "You mean for my taking you?" And then as he but looked at her: "How should I take you if I had dealt with you that way?"

"What do I lose by it," he said, "if, by our understanding of the other day, since things have so turned out, you're not to take me at all? So, at least, on my proposal, you get something else."

"And what," Maud returned, "do you get?"

"I *don't* 'get'; I lose. I *have* lost. So I don't matter." The eyes with which she covered him at this might have signified either that he didn't satisfy her or that his last word—*as* his word—rather imposed itself. Whether or no, at all events, she decided that he still did matter. She presently moved again, and they walked some minutes more. He had made her tremble, and she continued to tremble. So unlike anything that had ever come to her was, if seriously viewed, his proposal. The quality of it, while she walked, grew intenser with each step. It struck her as, when one came to look at it, unlike any offer any man could ever have made or any woman ever have received; and it began accordingly, on the instant, to affect her as almost inconceivably romantic, absolutely, in a manner, and quite out of the blue, *dramatic*; immeasurably more so, for example, than the sort of thing she had come out to hear in the afternoon—the sort of thing that was already so far away. If he was joking it was poor, but if he was serious it was, properly, sublime. And he wasn't joking. He was, however, after an interval, talking again, though, trembling still, she had not been attentive; so that she was unconscious of what he had said until she heard him once more sound Mrs. Chorner's name. "If you don't, you know, someone else will, and someone much worse. You told me she likes you." She had at first no answer for him, but it presently made her stop again. It was beautiful, if she would, but it was odd—this pressure for *her* to push at the very hour he himself had renounced pushing. A part of the whole sublimity of his attitude, so far as she was concerned, it clearly was; since, obviously, he was not now to profit by anything she might do. She seemed to see that, as the last service he could render, he wished to launch her and leave her. And that came out the more as he kept it up. "If she likes you, you know, she really wants you. Go to her as a friend."

"And bruit her abroad as one?" Maud Blandy asked.

"Oh, as a friend *from* the Papers—from them and *for* them, and with just your half-hour to give her before you rush back to them. Take it even—oh, you can safely"—the young man developed—"a little high with her. That's the way—the real way." And he spoke the next moment as if almost losing his patience. "You ought by this time, you know, to understand."

There was something in her mind that it still charmed—his mastery of the horrid art. He could see, always, the superior way, and it was as if, in spite of herself, she were getting the truth from him. Only she didn't want the truth—at least not that one. "And if she simply, for my impudence, chucks me out of window? A short way is easy for them, you know, when one doesn't scream or kick, or hang on to the furniture or the banisters. And I usually, you see"—she said it pensively—"don't. I've always, from the first, had my retreat prepared for any occasion, and flattered myself that, whatever hand I might, or mightn't, become at getting in, no one would ever be able so beautifully to get out. Like a flash, simply. And if she does, as I say, chuck me, it's *you* who fall to the ground."

He listened to her without expression, only saying "If you feel for her, as you insist, it's your duty." And then later, as if he had made an impression, "Your duty, I mean, to try. I admit, if you will, that there's a risk, though I don't, with my experience, feel it. Nothing venture, at any rate, nothing have; and it's all, isn't it? at the worst, in the day's work. There's but one thing you can go on, but it's enough. The greatest probability."

She resisted, but she was taking it in. "The probability that she will throw herself on my neck?"

"It will be either one thing or the other," he went on as if he had not heard her. "She'll not receive you, or she will. But if she does your fortune's made, and you'll be able to look higher than the mere *common* form of donkey." She recognised the reference to Marshal, but that was a thing she needn't mind now, and he had already continued. "She'll keep *nothing* back. And you mustn't either."

"Oh, won't I?" Maud murmured.

"Then you'll break faith with her."

And, as if to emphasise it, he went on, though without leaving her an infinite time to decide, for he looked at his watch as they proceeded, and when they came, in their spacious walk, abreast of another issue, where the breadth of the avenue, the expanses of stone, the stretch of the river, the dimness of the distance, seemed to isolate them, he appeared, by renewing their halt and looking up afresh toward the town, to desire to speed her on her way. Many things meanwhile had worked within her, but it was not till she had kept him on past the Temple Station of the Underground that she fairly faced her opportunity. Even then too there were still other things, under the assault of which she dropped, for the moment, Mrs. Chorner. "Did you really," she asked, "believe he'd turn up alive?"

With his hands in his pockets he continued to gloom at her. "Up there, just now, with Marshal—what did you take me as believing?"

"I gave you up. And I do give you. You're beyond me. Only," she added, "I seem to have made you out since then as really staggered. Though I don't say it," she ended, "to bear hard upon you."

"Don't bear hard," said Howard Bight very simply.

It moved her, for all she could have said; so that she had for a moment to wonder if it were bearing hard to mention some features of the rest of her thought. If she was to have him, certainly, it couldn't be without knowing, as she said to herself, something—something she might perhaps mitigate a little the solitude of his penance by possessing. "There were moments when I even imagined that, up to a certain point, you were still in communication with him. Then I seemed to see that you lost touch—though you braved it out for me; that you had begun to be really uneasy and were giving him up. I seemed to see," she pursued after a hesitation, "that it was coming home to you that you had worked him up too high—that you were feeling, if I may say it, that you had better have stopped short. I mean short of *this*."

"You may say it," Bight answered. "I *had* better."

She looked at him a moment. "There was more of him than you believed."

"There was more of him. And now," Bight added, looking across the river, "here's *all* of him."

"Which you feel you have on your heart?"

"I don't know where I have it." He turned his eyes to her. "I must wait."

"For more facts?"

"Well," he returned after a pause, "hardly perhaps for 'more' if—with what we have—this *is* all. But I've things to think out. I must wait to see how I feel. I did nothing but what he wanted. But we were behind a bolting horse—whom neither of us could have stopped."

"And *he*," said Maud, "is the one dashed to pieces."

He had his grave eyes on her. "Would you like it to have been me?"

"Of course not. But you enjoyed it—the bolt; everything up to the smash. Then, with that ahead, you were nervous."

"I'm nervous still," said Howard Bight.

Even in his unexpected softness there was something that escaped her, and it made in her, just a little, for irritation.

"What I mean is that you enjoyed his terror. That was what led you on."

"No doubt—it was so grand a case. But do you call charging me with it," the young man asked, "*not* bearing hard——?"

"No"—she pulled herself up—"it *is*. I don't charge you. Only I feel how little—about what has been, all the while, *behind*—you tell me. Nothing explains."

"Explains what?"

"Why, his act."

He gave a sign of impatience. "Isn't the explanation what I offered a moment ago to give you?"

It came, in effect, back to her. "For use?"

"For use."

"Only?"

"Only." It was sharp.

They stood a little, on this, face to face; at the end of which she turned away. "I'll go to Mrs. Chorner." And she was off while he called after her to take a cab. It was quite as if she were to come upon him, in his strange insistence, for the fare.

VIII

If she kept to herself, from the morrow on, for three days, her adoption of that course was helped, as she thankfully felt, by the great other circumstance and the great public commotion under cover of which it so little mattered what became of private persons. It was not simply that she had her reasons, but she couldn't during this time have descended again to Fleet Street even had she wished, though she said to herself often enough that her behaviour was rank cowardice. She left her friend alone with what he had to face, since, as she found, she could in absence from him a little recover herself. In his presence, the night of the news, she knew she had gone to pieces, had yielded, all too vulgarly, to a weakness proscribed by her original view. Her original view had been that if poor Beadel, worked up, as she inveterately kept seeing him, *should* embrace the tragic remedy, Howard Bight wouldn't be able not to show as practically compromised. He wouldn't be able not to smell of the wretched man's blood, morally speaking,

too strongly for condonations or complacencies. There were
other things, truly, that, during their minutes on the Embankment, he *had* been able to do, but they constituted just
the sinister subtlety to which it was well that she should not
again, yet awhile, be exposed. They were of the order—from
the safe summit of Maida Hill she could make it out—that
had proved corrosive to the muddled mind of the Frankfort
fugitive, deprived, in the midst of them, of any honest issue.
Bight, of course, rare youth, had *meant* no harm; but what
was precisely queerer, what, when you came to judge, less
human, than to be formed for offence, for injury, by the mere
inherent play of the spirit of observation, of criticism, by the
inextinguishable flame, in fine, of the ironic passion? The
ironic passion, in such a world as surrounded one, might assert itself as half the dignity, the decency, of life; yet, none the
less, in cases where one had seen it prove gruesomely fatal
(and not to one's self, which was nothing, but to others, even
the stupid and the vulgar) one was plainly admonished to—
well, stand off a little and think.

This was what Maud Blandy, while the Papers roared and
resounded more than ever with the new meat flung to them,
tried to consider that she was doing; so that the attitude held
her fast during the freshness of the event. The event grew, as
she had felt it would, with every further fact from Frankfort
and with every extra-special, and reached its maximum, inevitably, in the light of comment and correspondence. These
features, before the catastrophe, had indubitably, at the last,
flagged a little, but they revived so prodigiously, under the
well-timed shock, that, for the period we speak of, the poor
gentleman seemed, with a continuance, with indeed an en-
hancement, of his fine old knack, to have the successive editions *all* to himself. They had been always of course, the
Papers, very largely about him, but it was not too much to
say that at this crisis they were about nothing else worth
speaking of; so that our young woman could but groan in
spirit at the direful example set to the emulous. She spared an
occasional moment to the vision of Mortimer Marshal, saw
him drunk, as she might have said, with the mere fragrance
of the wine of glory, and asked herself what art Bight would
now use to furnish him forth as he had promised. The mystery

of Beadel's course loomed, each hour, so much larger and darker that the plan would have to be consummate, or the private knowledge alike beyond cavil and beyond calculation, which should attempt either to sound or to mask the appearances. Strangely enough, none the less, she even now found herself thinking of her rash colleague as attached, for the benefit of his surviving victim, to this idea; she went in fact so far as to imagine him half-upheld, while the public wonder spent itself, by the prospect of the fun he might still have with Marshal. This implied, she was not unconscious, that his notion of fun was infernal, and would of course be especially so were his knowledge as real as she supposed it. He would inflate their foolish friend with knowledge that was false and so start him as a balloon for the further gape of the world. This was the image, in turn, that would yield the last sport—the droll career of the wretched man as wandering forever through space under the apprehension, in time duly gained, that the least touch of earth would involve the smash of his car. Afraid, thus, to drop, but at the same time equally out of conceit of the chill air of the upper and increasing solitudes to which he had soared, he would become such a diminishing speck, though traceably a prey to wild human gyrations, as she might conceive Bight to keep in view for future recreation.

It wasn't however the future that was actually so much in question for them all as the immediately near present, offered to her as the latter was in the haunting light of the inevitably unlimited character of any real inquiry. The inquiry of the Papers, immense and ingenious, had yet for her the saving quality that she didn't take it as real. It abounded, truly, in hypotheses, most of them lurid enough, but a certain ease of mind as to what these might lead to was perhaps one of the advantages she owed to her constant breathing of Fleet Street air. She couldn't quite have said why, but she felt it wouldn't be the Papers that, proceeding from link to link, would arrive vindictively at Bight's connection with his late client. The enjoyment of that consummation would rest in another quarter, and if the young man were as uneasy now as she thought he ought to be even while she hoped he wasn't, it would be from the fear in his eyes of such justice as was shared with the vulgar. The Papers held an inquiry, but the Authorities,

as they vaguely figured to her, would hold an inquest; which
was a matter—even when international, complicated and ar-
rangeable, between Frankfort and London, only on some
system unknown to her—more in tune with possibilities of
exposure. It was not, as need scarce be said, from the exposure of Beadel that she averted herself; it was from the
exposure of the person who had made of Beadel's danger,
Beadel's dread—whatever these really represented—the use
that the occurrence at Frankfort might be shown to certify.
It was well before her, at all events, that if Howard Bight's
reflections, so stimulated, kept pace at all with her own, he
would at the worst, or even at the best, have been glad to
meet her again. It was her knowing that and yet lying low
that she privately qualified as cowardice; it was the instinct of
watching and waiting till she should see how great the danger might become. And she had moreover another reason,
which we shall presently learn. The extra-specials meanwhile
were to be had in Kilburnia almost as soon as in the Strand;
the little ponied and painted carts, tipped at an extraordinary
angle, by which they were disseminated, had for that matter,
she observed, never rattled up the Edgware Road at so fu-
rious a rate. Each evening, it was true, when the flare of Fleet
Street would have begun really to smoke, she had, in resistance to old habit, a little to hold herself; but for three successive days she tided over that crisis. It was not till the
fourth night that her reaction suddenly declared itself, determined as it partly was by the latest poster that dangled free
at the door of a small shop just out of her own street. The
establishment dealt in buttons, pins, tape, and silver bracelets,
but the branch of its industry she patronised was that of
telegrams, stamps, stationery, and the "Edinburgh rock" offered to the appetite of the several small children of her
next-door neighbour but one. "The Beadel-Muffet Mystery,
Startling Disclosures, Action of the Treasury"—at these
words she anxiously gazed; after which she decided. It was
as if from her hilltop, from her very housetop, to which the
window of her little room was contiguous, she had seen the
red light in the east. It *had*, this time, its colour. She went
on, she went far, till she met a cab, which she hailed, "regardless," she felt, as she had hailed one after leaving Bight

by the river. "To Fleet Street" she simply said, and it took her—that she felt too—back into life.

Yes, it was life again, bitter, doubtless, but with a taste, when, having stopped her cab, short of her indication, in Covent Garden, she walked across southward and to the top of the street in which she and her friend had last parted with Mortimer Marshal. She came down to their favoured pothouse, the scene of Bight's high compact with that worthy, and here, hesitating, she paused, uncertain as to where she had best look out. Her conviction, on her way, had but grown; Howard Bight would be looking out—*that* to a certainty; something more, something portentous, had happened (by her evening paper, scanned in the light of her little shop window, she had taken instant possession of it), and this would have made him know that she couldn't keep up what he would naturally call her "game." There were places where they often met, and the diversity of these—not too far apart, however—would be his only difficulty. He was on the prowl, in fine, with his hat over his eyes; and she hadn't known, till this vision of him came, what seeds of romance were in her soul. Romance, the other night, by the river, had brushed them with a wing that was like the blind bump of a bat, but that had been something on *his* part, whereas this thought of bringing him succour as to a Russian anarchist, to some victim of society or subject of extradition, was all her own, and was of this special moment. She *saw* him with his hat over his eyes; she saw him with his overcoat collar turned up; she saw him as a hunted hero cleverly drawn in one of the serialising weeklies or, as they said, in some popular "ply," and the effect of it was to open to her on the spot a sort of happy sense of all her possible immorality. That was the romantic sense, and everything vanished but the richness of her thrill. She knew little enough what she might have to do for him, but her hope, as sharp as a pang, was that, if anything, it would put her in danger too. The hope, as it happened then, was crowned on the very spot; she had never so felt in danger as when, just now, turning to the glazed door of their cookshop, she saw a man, within, close behind the glass, still, stiff and ominous, looking at her hard. The light of the place was behind him, so that his face, in the dusk of the side-street, was dark, but it was visible that she showed for him as an object of interest. The next thing, of course, she had seen more—seen she could be such an object, in such a degree, only to her friend himself, and that Bight had been thus sure of her; and the next thing after that had passed straight in and been met by him, as he stepped aside to admit her, in silence. He *had* his hat pulled down and, quite forgetfully, in spite of the warmth within, the collar of his mackintosh up.

It was his silence that completed the perfection of these things—the perfection that came out most of all, oddly, after he had corrected them by removal and was seated with her, in their common corner, at tea, with the room almost to themselves and no one to consider but Marshal's little man in the obvious wig and the blue spectacles, the great authority on the inner life of the criminal classes. Strangest of all, nearly, was it, that, though now essentially belonging, as Maud felt, to this order, they were not conscious of the danger of his presence. What she had wanted most immediately to learn was how Bight had known; but he made, and scarce to her surprise, short work of that. "I've known every evening—known, that is, that you've wanted to come; and I've been here every evening, waiting just there till I should see you. It was but a question of time. To-night, however, I was sure—for there's, after all, *something* of me left. Besides, besides——!" He had, in short, another certitude. "You've been ashamed—I knew, when I saw nothing come, that you would be. But also that that would pass."

Maud found him, as she would have said, all there. "I've been ashamed, you mean, of being afraid?"

"You've been ashamed about Mrs. Chorner; that is, about *me*. For that you did go to her I know."

"Have you been then yourself?"

"For what do you take me?" He seemed to wonder. "What had I to do with her—except *for* you?" And then before she could say: "Didn't she receive you?"

"Yes, as you said, she 'wanted' me."

"She jumped at you?"

"Jumped at me. She gave me an hour."

He flushed with an interest that, the next moment, had flared in spite of everything into amusement. "So that I was right, in my perfect wisdom, up to the hilt?"

"Up to the hilt. She took it from me."

"That the public wants her?"

"That it won't take a refusal. So she opened up."

"Overflowed?"

"Prattled."

"Gushed?"

"Well, recognised and embraced her opportunity. Kept me there till midnight. Told me, as she called it, everything about everything."

They looked at each other long on it, and it determined in Bight at last a brave clatter of his crockery. "They're stupendous!"

"It's *you* that are," Maud replied, "to have found it out so. You know them down to the ground."

"Oh, what I've found out——!" But it was more than he could talk of then. "If I hadn't really felt sure, I wouldn't so have urged you. Only now, if you please, I don't understand your having apparently but kept her in your pocket."

"Of course you don't," said Maud Blandy. To which she added, "And I don't quite myself. I only know that now that I have her there nothing will induce me to take her out."

"Then you potted her, permit me to say," he answered, "on absolutely false pretences."

"Absolutely; which is precisely why I've been ashamed. I made for home with the whole thing," she explained, "and there, that night, in the hours till morning, when, turning it over, I saw all it really was, I knew that I *couldn't*—that I would rather choose *that* shame, that of not doing for her what I had offered, than the hideous honesty of bringing it out. Because, you see," Maud declared, "it was—well, it was too much."

Bight followed her with a sharpness! "It was so good?"

"Quite beautiful! Awful!"

He wondered. "Really charming?"

"Charming, interesting, horrible. It was *true*—and it was the whole thing. It was herself—and it was *him*, all of him too. Not a bit made up, but just the poor woman melted and overflowing, yet at the same time raging—like the hot-water tap when it boils. I never saw anything like it; everything, as you guaranteed, came out; it has made me know things. So, to have come down here with it, to have begun to hawk it, either through you, as you kindly proposed, or in my own brazen person, to the highest bidder—well, I felt that I didn't *have* to, after all, if I didn't want to, and that if it's the only way I can get money I would much rather starve."

"I see." Howard Bight saw all. "And that's why you're ashamed?"

She hesitated—she was both so remiss and so firm. "I knew that by my not coming back to you, you would have guessed, have found me wanting; just, for that matter, as *she* has found me. And I couldn't explain. I can't—I can't to *her*. So that," the girl went on, "I shall have done, so far as her attitude to me was to be concerned, something more indelicate, something more indecent, than if I had passed her on. I shall have wormed it all out of her, and then, by not having carried it to market, disappointed and cheated her. She was to have heard it cried like fresh herring."

Bight was immensely taken. "Oh, beyond all doubt. You're in a fix. You've played, you see, a most unusual game. The code allows everything *but* that."

"Precisely. So I must take the consequences. I'm dishonoured, but I shall have to bear it. And I shall bear it by getting *out*. Out, I mean, of the whole thing. I shall chuck them."

"Chuck the *Papers*?" he asked in his simplicity.

But his wonder, she saw, was overdone—their eyes too frankly met. "Damn the Papers!" said Maud Blandy.

It produced in his sadness and weariness the sweetest smile that had yet broken through. "We *shall*, between us, if we keep it up, ruin them! And you make nothing," he went on, "of one's having at last so beautifully started you? Your complaint," he developed, "was that you couldn't get in. Then suddenly, with a splendid jump, you *are* in. Only, however, to look round you and say with disgust 'Oh, *here*?' Where the devil do you *want* to be?"

"Ah, that's another question. At least," she said, "I can scrub floors. I can take it out perhaps—my swindle of Mrs. Chorner," she pursued—"in scrubbing *hers*."

He only, after this, looked at her a little. "She has written to you?"

"Oh, in high dudgeon. I was to have attended to the 'press-cutting' people as well, and she was to have seen herself, at the furthest, by the second morning (that was day-before-yesterday) all over the place. She wants to know what I mean."

"And what do you answer?"

"That it's hard, of course, to make her understand, but that I've felt her, since parting with her, simply to be too good."

"Signifying by it, naturally," Bight amended, "that you've felt yourself to be so."

"Well, that too if you like. But she was exquisite."

He considered. "Would she do for a ply?"

"Oh God, no!"

"Then for a tile?"

"Perhaps," said Maud Blandy at last.

He understood, visibly, the shade, as well as the pause; which, together, held him a moment. But it was of something else he spoke. "And you who had found they would never bite!"

"Oh, I was wrong," she simply answered. "Once they've *tasted* blood——!"

"They want to devour," her friend laughed, "not only the bait and the hook, but the line and the rod and the poor fisherman himself? Except," he continued, "that poor Mrs. Chorner hasn't yet even 'tasted.' However," he added, "she obviously will."

Maud's assent was full. "She'll find others. She'll appear."

He waited a moment—his eye had turned to the door of the street. "Then she must be quick. These are things of the hour."

"You hear something?" she asked, his expression having struck her.

He listened again, but it was nothing. "No—but it's some-how in the air."

"What is?"

"Well, that she must hurry. She must get in. She must get out." He had his arms on the table, and, locking his hands and inclining a little, he brought his face nearer to her. "My sense to-night's of an openness——! I don't know what's the matter. Except, that is, that you're great."

She looked at him, not drawing back. "You know everything—so immeasurably more than you admit or than you tell me. You mortally perplex and worry me."

It made him smile. "You're great, you're great," he only repeated. "You know it's quite awfully swagger, what you've done."

"What I haven't, you mean; what I never shall. Yes," she added, but now sinking back—"of course you see that too. What *don't* you see, and what, with such ways, is to be the end of you?"

"You're great, you're great"—he kept it up. "And I like you. That's to be the end of me."

So, for a minute, they left it, while she came to the thing that, for the last half-hour, had most been with her. "What *is* the 'action,' announced to-night, of the Treasury?"

"Oh, they've sent somebody out, partly, it would seem, at the request of the German authorities, to take possession."

"Possession, you mean, of his effects?"

"Yes, and legally, administratively, of the whole matter."

"Seeing, you mean, that there's still more in it——?"

"Than meets the eye," said Bight, "precisely. But it won't be till the case is transferred, as it presently will be, to this country, that they *will* see. Then it will be funny."

"Funny?" Maud Blandy asked.

"Oh, lovely."

"Lovely for *you*?"

"Why not? The bigger the whole thing grows, the lovelier."

"You've odd notions," she said, "of loveliness. Do you expect his situation won't be traced to you? Don't you suppose you'll be forced to speak?"

"To 'speak'——?"

"Why, if it *is* traced. What do you make, otherwise, of the facts to-night?"

"Do you call them facts?" the young man asked.

"I mean the Astounding Disclosures."

"Well, do you only read your headlines? 'The most astounding disclosures are expected'—*that's* the valuable text. Is *it*," he went on, "what fetched you?"

His answer was so little of one that she made her own scant. "What fetched me is that I can't rest."

"No more can I," he returned. "But in what danger do you think me?"

"In any in which you think yourself. Why not, if I don't mean in danger of hanging?"

He looked at her so that she presently took him for serious at last—which was different from his having been either worried or perverse. "Of public discredit, you mean—for having so unmercifully baited him? Yes," he conceded with a straightness that now surprised her, "I've thought of that. But how can the baiting be proved?"

"If they take possession of his effects won't his effects be partly his papers, and won't they, among them, find letters from you, and won't your letters show it?"

"Well, show what?"

"Why, the frenzy to which you worked him—and thereby your connection."

"They won't show it to dunderheads."

"And are they all dunderheads?"

"Every mother's son of them—where anything so beautiful is concerned."

"Beautiful?" Maud murmured.

"Beautiful, my letters are—gems of the purest ray. I'm covered."

She let herself go—she looked at him long. "You're a wonder. But all the same," she added, "you don't like it."

"Well, I'm not sure." Which clearly meant, however, that he almost *was*, from the way in which, the next moment, he had exchanged the question for another. "You haven't anything to tell me of Mrs. Chorner's explanation?"

Oh, as to this, she had already considered and chosen. "What do you want of it when you know so much more? So much more, I mean, than even she has known."

"Then she *hasn't* known——?"

"There you are! What," asked Maud, "are you talking about?"

She had made him smile, even though his smile was perceptibly pale; and he continued. "Of what was behind. Behind any game of mine. Behind everything."

"So am I then talking of that. No," said Maud, "she hasn't known, and she doesn't know I judge, to this hour. Her explanation therefore doesn't bear upon that. It bears upon something else."

"Well, my dear, on what?"

He was not, however, to find out by simply calling her his dear; for she had not sacrificed the reward of her interview in order to present the fine flower of it, unbribed, even to *him*. "You know how little you've ever told me, and you see how, at this instant, even while you press me to gratify you, you give me nothing. I give," she smiled—yet not a little flushed—"nothing *for* nothing."

He showed her he felt baffled, but also that she was perverse. "What you want of me is what, originally, you wouldn't hear of: anything so dreadful, that is, as his predicament must be. You saw that to make him want to keep quiet he must have something to be ashamed of, and that was just what, in pity, you positively objected to learning. You've grown," Bight smiled, "more interested since."

"If I have," said Maud, "it's because *you* have. Now, at any rate, I'm not afraid."

He waited a moment. "Are you very sure?"

"Yes, for my mystification is greater at last than my delicacy. I don't know till I do know"—and she expressed this even with difficulty—"what it has been, all the while, that it was a question of, and what, consequently, all the while, we've been talking about."

"Ah, but why should you know?" the young man inquired. "I can understand your needing to, or somebody's needing to, if we were in a ply, or even, though in a less degree, if we were in a tile. But since, my poor child, we're only in the delicious muddle of life itself——!"

"You may have all the plums of the pudding, and I nothing but a mouthful of cold suet?" Maud pushed back her chair; she had taken up her old gloves; but while she put them on she kept in view both her friend and her grievance. "I don't believe," she at last brought out, "that there *is*, or that there ever was, anything."

"Oh, oh, oh!" Bight laughed.

"There's nothing," she continued, " 'behind.' There's no horror."

"You hold, by that," said Bight, "that the poor man's deed is *all* me? That does make it, you see, bad for me."

She got up and, there before him, finished smoothing her creased gloves. "Then we *are*—if there's such richness—in a ply."

"Well, we are not, at all events—so far as we ourselves are concerned—the spectators." And he also got up. "The spectators must look out for themselves."

"Evidently, poor things!" Maud sighed. And as he still stood as if there might be something for him to come from her, she made her attitude clear—which was quite the attitude now of tormenting him a little. "If you know something about him which she doesn't, and also which *I* don't, she knows something about him—as I do too—which *you* don't."

"Surely: when it's exactly what I'm trying to get out of you. Are you afraid *I'll* sell it?"

But even this taunt, which she took moreover at its worth, didn't move her. "You definitely then won't tell me?"

"You mean that if I will you'll tell *me*?"

She thought again. "Well—yes. But on that condition alone."

"Then you're safe," said Howard Bight. "I *can't*, really, my dear, tell you. Besides, if it's to come out——!"

"I'll wait in that case till it does. But I must warn you," she added, "that *my* facts *won't* come out."

He considered. "Why not, since the rush at her is probably even now being made? Why not, if she receives others?"

Well, Maud could think too. "She'll receive them, but they won't receive *her*. Others are like *your* people—dunderheads. Others won't understand, won't count, won't exist." And she moved to the door. "There *are* no others." Opening the door, she had reached the street with it, even while he replied, overtaking her, that there were certainly none such as herself; but they had scarce passed out before her last remark was, to their somewhat disconcerted sense, sharply enough refuted. There was still the other they had forgotten, and that neglected quantity, plainly in search of them and happy in his instinct of the chase, now stayed their steps in the form of Mortimer Marshal.

IX

He was coming in as they came out; and his "I *hoped* I might find you," an exhalation of cool candour that they took full in the face, had the effect, the next moment, of a great soft carpet, all flowers and figures, suddenly unrolled for them to walk upon and before which they felt a scruple. Their ejaculation, Maud was conscious, couldn't have passed for a welcome, and it wasn't till she saw the poor gentleman checked a little, in turn, by their blankness, that she fully perceived how interesting they had just become to themselves. His face, however, while, in their arrest, they neither proposed to re-enter the shop with him nor invited him to proceed with them anywhere else—his face, gaping there, for Bight's promised instructions, like a fair receptacle, shallow but with all the capacity of its flatness, brought back so to our young woman the fond fancy her companion had last excited in him that he profited just a little—and for sympathy in spite of his folly— by her sense that with her too the latter had somehow amused himself. This placed her, for the brief instant, in a strange fellowship with their visitor's plea, under the impulse of which, without more thought, she had turned to Bight. "Your eager claimant," she, however, simply said, "for the opportunity now so beautifully created."

"I've ventured," Mr. Marshal glowed back, "to come and remind you that the hours are fleeting."

Bight had surveyed him with eyes perhaps equivocal. "You're afraid someone else will step in?"

"Well, with the place so tempting and so empty——!"

Maud made herself again his voice. "Mr. Marshal sees it empty itself perhaps too fast."

He acknowledged, in his large, bright way, the help afforded him by her easy lightness. "I do want to get in, you know, before anything happens."

"And what," Bight inquired, "are you afraid *may* happen?"

"Well, to make sure," he smiled, "I want myself, don't you see, to happen first."

Our young woman, at this, fairly fell, for her friend, into his sweetness. "*Do* let him happen!"

"*Do* let me happen!" Mr. Marshal followed it up.

They stood there together, where they had paused, in their strange council of three, and their extraordinary tone, in connection with their number, might have marked them, for some passer catching it, as persons not only discussing questions supposedly reserved for the Fates, but absolutely enacting some encounter of these portentous forces. "Let you— let you?" Bight gravely echoed, while on the sound, for the moment, immensities might have hung. It was as far, however, as he was to have time to speak, for even while his voice was in the air another, at first remote and vague, joined it there on an ominous note and hushed all else to stillness. It came, through the roar of thoroughfares, from the direction of Fleet Street, and it made our interlocutors exchange an altered look. They recognised it, the next thing, as the howl, again, of the Strand, and then but an instant elapsed before it flared into the night. "Return of Beadel-Muffet! Tremenjous Sensation!"

Tremenjous indeed, so tremenjous that, each really turning as pale with it as they had turned, on the same spot, the other time and with the other news, they stood long enough stricken and still for the cry, multiplied in a flash, again to reach them. They couldn't have said afterwards who first took it up. "Return——?"

"From the *Dead*—I *say*!" poor Marshal piercingly quavered.

"Then he *hasn't* been——?" Maud gasped it with him at Bight.

But that genius, clearly, was not less deeply affected. "He's alive?" he breathed in a long, soft wail in which admiration appeared at first to contend with amazement and then the sense of the comic to triumph over both. Howard Bight uncontrollably—it might have struck them as almost hysterically—laughed.

The others could indeed but stare. "Then who's dead?" piped Mortimer Marshal.

"I'm afraid, Mr. Marshal, that *you* are," the young man returned, more gravely, after a minute. He spoke as if he saw *how* dead.

Poor Marshal was lost. "But someone was killed——!"

"Someone undoubtedly was, but Beadel somehow has survived it."

"Has he, then, been playing the game——?" It baffled comprehension.

Yet it wasn't even that what Maud most wondered. "Have you all the while really known?" she asked of Howard Bight.

He met it with a look that puzzled her for the instant, but that she then saw to mean, half with amusement, half with sadness, that his genius was, after all, simpler. "I wish I had. I really believed."

"All along?"

"No; but after Frankfort."

She remembered things. "You haven't had a notion this evening?"

"Only from the state of my nerves."

"Yes, your nerves must be in a state!" And somehow now she had no pity for him. It was almost as if she were, frankly, disappointed. "*I*," she then boldly said, "didn't believe."

"If you had mentioned that then," Marshal observed to her, "you would have saved me an awkwardness."

But Bight took him up. "She did believe—so that she might punish me."

"Punish you——?"

Maud raised her hand at her friend. "He doesn't understand."

He was indeed, Mr. Marshal, fully pathetic now. "No, I don't understand. Not a wee bit."

"Well," said Bight kindly, "we none of us do. We must give it up."

"You think *I* really must——?"

"You, sir," Bight smiled, "most of all. The places seem so taken."

His client, however, clung. "He won't die again——?"

"If he does he'll again come to life. He'll never die. Only *we* shall die. He's immortal."

He looked up and down, this inquirer; he listened to the

howl of the Strand, not yet, as happened, brought nearer to them by one of the hawkers. And yet it was as if, overwhelmed by his lost chance, he knew himself too weak even for *their* fond aid. He still therefore appealed. "Will *this* be a boom for him?"

"His return? Colossal. For—fancy!—it was exactly what we talked of, you remember, the other day, as the ideal. I mean," Bight smiled, "for a man to be lost, and yet at the same time——"

"To be found?" poor Marshal too hungrily mused.

"To be boomed," Bight continued, "by his smash and yet never to have been too smashed to know how he was booming."

It was wonderful for Maud too. "To have given it all up, and yet to have it all."

"Oh, better than that," said her friend: "to have *more* than all, and more than you gave up. Beadel," he was careful to explain to their companion, "will have more."

Mr. Marshal struggled with it. "More than if he were dead?"

"More," Bight laughed, "than if he weren't! It's what *you* would have liked, as I understand you, isn't it? and what you would have got. It's what *I* would have helped you to."

"But who then," wailed Marshal, "helps *him?*"

"Nobody. His star. His genius."

Mortimer Marshal glared about him as for some sign of such aids in his own sphere. It embraced, his own sphere too, the roaring Strand, yet—mystification and madness!—it was with Beadel the Strand was roaring. A hawker, from afar, at sight of the group, was already scaling the slope. "Ah, but *how* the devil——?"

Bight pointed to this resource. "Go and see."

"But don't *you* want them?" poor Marshal asked as the others retreated.

"The Papers?" They stopped to answer. "No, never again. We've done with them. We give it up."

"I mayn't again see you?"

Dismay and a last clutch were in Marshal's face, but Maud, who had taken her friend's meaning in a flash, found the word to meet them. "We retire from business."

With which they turned again to move in the other sense, presenting their backs to Fleet Street. They moved together up the rest of the hill, going on in silence, not arrested by another little shrieking boy, not diverted by another extra-special, not pausing again till, at the end of a few minutes, they found themselves in the comparative solitude of Covent Garden, encumbered with the traces of its traffic, but now given over to peace. The howl of the Strand had ceased, their client had vanished forever, and from the centre of the empty space they could look up and see stars. One of these was of course Beadel-Muffet's, and the consciousness of that, for the moment, kept down any arrogance of triumph. He still hung above them, he ruled, immortal, the night; they were far beneath, and he now transcended their world; but a sense of relief, of escape, of the light, still unquenched, of their old irony, made them stand there face to face. There was more between them now than there had ever been, but it had ceased to separate them, it sustained them in fact like a deep water on which they floated closer. Still, however, there was something Maud needed. "It had been all the while worked?"

"Ah, not, before God—since I lost sight of him—by *me*."

"Then by himself?"

"I dare say. But there are plenty for him. He's beyond me."

"But you thought," she said, "it *would* be so. You thought," she declared, "something."

Bight hesitated. "I thought it would be great if he *could*. And *as* he could—why, it *is* great. But all the same I too was sold. I *am* sold. That's why I give up."

"Then it's why *I* do. We must do something," she smiled at him, "that requires less cleverness."

"We must love each other," said Howard Bight.

"But can we live by that?"

He thought again; then he decided. "Yes."

"Ah," Maud amended, "we must be 'littery.' We've now got stuff."

"For the dear old ply, for the rattling good tile? Ah, they take better stuff than this—though this too is good."

"Yes," she granted on reflection, "this is good, but it has bad holes. *Who was the dead man in the locked hotel room?*"

"Oh, I don't mean that. *That*," said Bight, "he'll splendidly explain."

"But how?"

"Why, in the Papers. To-morrow."

Maud wondered. "So soon?"

"If he returned to-night, and it's not yet ten o'clock, there's plenty of time. It will be in *all* of them—while the universe waits. He'll hold us in the hollow of his hand. His chance is just there. And there," said the young man, "will be his greatness."

"Greater than ever then?"

"Quadrupled."

She followed; then it made her seize his arm. "*Go* to him!"

Bight frowned. " 'Go'——?"

"This instant. *You* explain!"

He understood, but only to shake his head. "Never again. I bow to him."

Well, she after a little understood; but she thought again. "You mean that the great hole is that he really had no reason, no funk——?"

"I've wondered," said Howard Bight.

"Whether he *had* done anything to make publicity embarrassing?"

"I've wondered," the young man repeated.

"But I thought you knew!"

"So did I. But I thought also I knew he was dead. However," Bight added, "he'll explain that too."

"To-morrow?"

"No—as a different branch. Say day after."

"Ah, then," said Maud, "if he explains——!"

"There's no hole? I don't know!"—and it forced from him at last a sigh. He was impatient of it, for he had done with it; it would soon bore him. So fast they lived. "It will take," he only dropped, "much explaining."

His detachment was logical, but she looked a moment at his sudden weariness. "There's always, remember, Mrs. Chorner."

"Oh yes, Mrs. Chorner; we luckily invented *her*."

"Well, if she drove him to his death——?"

Bight, with a laugh, caught at it. "Is that it? *Did* she drive him?"

It pulled her up, and, though she smiled, they stood again, a little, as on their guard. "Now, at any rate," Maud simply said at last, "she'll marry him. So you see how right I was."

With a preoccupation that had grown in him, however, he had already lost the thread. "How right——?"

"Not to sell my Talk."

"Oh yes,"—he remembered. "Quite right." But it all came to something else. "Whom will *you* marry?"

She only, at first, for answer, kept her eyes on him. Then she turned them about the place and saw no hindrance, and then, further, bending with a tenderness in which she felt so transformed, so won to something she had never been before, that she might even, to other eyes, well have looked so, she gravely kissed him. After which, as he took her arm, they walked on together. "That, at least," she said, "we'll put in the Papers."

Fordham Castle

SHARP LITTLE Madame Massin, who carried on the pleasant
pension and who had her small hard eyes everywhere at
once, came out to him on the terrace and held up a letter
addressed in a manner that he recognised even from afar, held
it with a question in her smile, or a smile, rather a pointed
one, in her question—he could scarce have said which. She
was looking, while so occupied, at the German group engaged
in the garden, near by, with aperitive beer and disputation—
the noonday luncheon being now imminent; and the way in
which she could show prompt lips while her observation
searchingly ranged might have reminded him of the object
placed by a spectator at the theatre in the seat he desires to
keep during the entr'acte. Conscious of the cross-currents of
international passion, she tried, so far as possible, not to mix
her sheep and her goats. The view of the bluest end of the
Lake of Geneva—she insisted in persuasive circulars that it *was*
the bluest—had never, on her high-perched terrace, wanted
for admirers, though thus early in the season, during the first
days of May, they were not so numerous as she was apt to see
them at midsummer. This precisely, Abel Taker could infer,
was the reason of a remark she had made him before the
claims of the letter had been settled. "I shall put you next the
American lady—the one who arrived yesterday. I know you'll
be kind to her; she had to go to bed, as soon as she got here,
with a sick-headache brought on by her journey. But she's
better. Who isn't better as soon as they get here? She's coming
down, and I'm sure she'd like to know you."

Taker had now the letter in his hand—the letter intended
for "Mr. C. P. Addard"; which was not the name inscribed in
the two or three books he had left out in his room, any more
than it matched the initials, "A. F. T." attached to the few
pieces of his modest total of luggage. Moreover, since Madame Massin's establishment counted, to his still somewhat
bewildered mind, so little for an hotel, as hotels were mainly
known to him, he had avoided the act of "registering," and
the missive with which his hostess was practically testing him

639

represented the very first piece of postal matter taken in since his arrival that hadn't been destined to some one else. He had privately blushed for the meagreness of his mail, which made him look unimportant. That however was a detail, an appearance he was used to; indeed the reasons making for such an appearance might never have been so pleasant to him as on this vision of his identity formally and legibly denied. It was denied there in his wife's large straight hand; his eyes, attached to the envelope, took in the failure of any symptom of weakness in her stroke; she at least had the courage of his passing for somebody he wasn't, of his passing rather for nobody at all, and he felt the force of her character more irresistibly than ever as he thus submitted to what she was doing with him. He wasn't used to lying; whatever his faults—and he was used, perfectly, to the idea of his faults—he hadn't made them worse by any perverse theory, any tortuous plea, of innocence; so that probably, with every inch of him giving him away, Madame Massin didn't believe him a bit when he appropriated the letter. He was quite aware he could have made no fight if she had challenged his right to it. That would have come of his making no fight, nowadays, on any ground, with any woman; he had so lost the proper spirit, the necessary confidence. It was true that he had had to do for a long time with no woman in the world but Sue, and of the practice of opposition so far as Sue was concerned the end had been determined early in his career. His hostess fortunately accepted his word, but the way in which her momentary attention bored into his secret like the turn of a gimlet gave him a sense of the quantity of life that passed before her as a dealer with all comers—gave him almost an awe of her power of not wincing. She knew he wasn't, he couldn't be, C. P. Addard, even though she mightn't know, or still less care, who he was; and there was therefore something queer about him if he pretended to be. That was what she didn't mind, there being something queer about him; and what was further present to him was that she would have known when to mind, when really to be on her guard. She attached no importance to his trick; she had doubtless somewhere at the rear, amid the responsive underlings with whom she was sometimes heard volubly, yet so obscurely, to chatter, her clever French amusement about it. He couldn't at all events have said if the whole passage with her most brought home to him the falsity of his position or most glossed it over. On the whole perhaps it rather helped him, since from this moment his masquerade had actively begun.

Taking his place for luncheon, in any case, he found himself next the American lady, as he conceived, spoken of by Madame Massin—in whose appearance he was at first as disappointed as if, a little, though all unconsciously, he had been building on it. Had she loomed into view, on their hostess's hint, as one of the vague alternatives, the possible beguilements, of his leisure—presenting herself solidly where so much else had refused to crystallise? It was certain at least that she presented herself solidly, being a large mild smooth person with a distinct double chin, with grey hair arranged in small flat regular circles, figures of a geometrical perfection; with diamond earrings, with a long-handled eye-glass, with an accumulation of years and of weight and presence, in fine, beyond what his own rather melancholy consciousness acknowledged. He was forty-five, and it took every year of his life, took all he hadn't done with them, to account for his present situation—since you couldn't be, conclusively, of so little use, of so scant an application, to any mortal career, above all to your own, unless you had been given up and cast aside after a long succession of experiments tried with you. But the American lady with the mathematical hair which reminded him in a manner of the old-fashioned "work," the weeping willows and mortuary urns represented by the little glazed-over flaxen or auburn or sable or silvered convolutions and tendrils, the capillary flowers, that he had admired in the days of his innocence—the American lady had probably seen her half-century; all the more that before luncheon was done she had begun to strike him as having, like himself, slipped slowly down over its stretched and shiny surface, an expanse as insecure to fumbling feet as a great cold curved ice-field, into the comparatively warm hollow of resignation and obscurity. She gave him from the first—and he was afterwards to see why—an attaching impression of being, like himself, in exile, and of having like himself learned to butter her bread with a certain acceptance of fate. The only thing that puzzled him on this head was that to parallel his own case she would have had openly to consent to be shelved; which made the difficulty, here, that that was exactly what, as between wife and husband, remained unthinkable on the part of the wife. The necessity for the shelving of one or the other was a case that appeared often to arise, but this wasn't the way he had in general seen it settled. She made him in short, through some influence he couldn't immediately reduce to its elements, vaguely think of her as sacrificed—without blood, as it were; as obligingly and persuadedly passive. Yet this effect, a reflexion of his own state, would doubtless have been better produced for him by a mere melancholy man. She testified unmistakeably to the greater energy of women; for he could think of no manifestation of spirit on his own part that might pass for an equivalent, in the way of resistance, of protest, to the rhythmic though rather wiggy water-waves that broke upon her bald-looking brow as upon a beach bared by a low tide. He had cocked up often enough—and as with the intention of doing it still more under Sue's nose than under his own—the two ends of his half-"sandy" half-grizzled moustache, and he had in fact given these ornaments an extra twist just before coming in to luncheon. That however was but a momentary flourish; the most marked ferocity of which hadn't availed not to land him—well, where he was landed now.

His new friend mentioned that she had come up from Rome and that Madame Massin's establishment had been highly spoken of to her there, and this, slight as it was, straightway contributed in its degree for Abel Taker to the idea that they had something in common. He was in a condition in which he could feel the drift of vague currents, and he knew how highly the place had been spoken of to *him*. There was but a shade of difference in his having had his lesson in Florence. He let his companion know, without reserve, that he too had come up from Italy, after spending three or four months there: though he remembered in time that, being now C. P. Addard, it was only as C. P. Addard he could speak. He tried to think, in order to give himself something to say, what C. P. Addard would have done; but he was doomed to feel always, in the whole connexion, his lack of imagination. He had had many days to come to it and nothing else to do; but he hadn't even yet made up his mind who C. P. Addard was or invested him with any distinguishing marks. He felt like a man who, moving in this, that or the other direction, saw each successively lead him to some danger; so that he began to ask himself why he shouldn't just lie outright, boldly and inventively, and see what that could do for him. There was an excitement, the excitement of personal risk, about it—much the same as would belong for an ordinary man to the first trial of a flying-machine; yet it was exactly such a course as Sue had prescribed on his asking her what he should do. "Anything in the world you like but talk about *me*: think of some other woman, as bad and bold as you please, and say you're married to *her*." Those had been literally her words, together with others, again and again repeated, on the subject of his being free to "kill and bury" her as often as he chose. This was the way she had met his objection to his own death and interment; she had asked him, in her bright hard triumphant way, why he couldn't defend himself by shooting back. The real reason was of course that he was nothing without her, whereas she was everything, could be anything in the wide world she liked, without him. That question precisely had been a part of what was before him while he strolled in the projected green gloom of Madame Massin's plane-trees; he wondered what she *was* choosing to be and how good a time it was helping her to have. He could be sure she was rising to it, on some line or other, and that was what secretly made him say: "Why shouldn't I get something out of it too, just for the harmless fun—?"

It kept coming back to him, naturally, that he hadn't the breadth of fancy, that he knew himself as he knew the taste of ill-made coffee, that he was the same old Abel Taker he had ever been, in whose aggregation of items it was as vain to feel about for latent heroisms as it was useless to rummage one's trunk for presentable clothes that one didn't possess. But did that absolve him (having so definitely Sue's permission) from seeing to what extent he might temporarily make believe? If he were to flap his wings very hard and crow very loud and take as long a jump as possible at the same time— if he were to do all that perhaps he should achieve for half a minute the sensation of soaring. He knew only one thing Sue couldn't do, from the moment she didn't divorce him: she couldn't get rid of his name, unaccountably, after all, as she hated it; she couldn't get rid of it because she would have always sooner or later to come back to it. She might consider that her being a thing so dreadful as Mrs. Abel Taker was a stumbling-block in her social path that nothing but his real, his official, his advertised circulated demise (with "American papers please copy") would avail to dislodge: she would have none the less to reckon with his continued existence as the drop of bitterness in her cup that seasoned undisguiseably each draught. He might make use of his present opportunity to row out into the lake with his pockets full of stones and there quietly slip overboard; but he could think of no shorter cut for her ceasing to be what her marriage and the law of the land had made her. She was not an inch less Mrs. Abel Taker for these days of his sequestration, and the only thing she indeed claimed was that the concealment of the source of her shame, the suppression of the person who had divided with her his inherited absurdity, made the difference of a shade or two for getting honourably, as she called it, "about." How she had originally come to incur this awful inconvenience—*that* part of the matter, left to herself, she would undertake to keep vague; and she wasn't really left to herself so long as he too flaunted the dreadful flag.

This was why she had provided him with another and placed him out at board, to constitute, as it were, a permanent *alibi*; telling him she should quarrel with no colours under which he might elect to sail, and promising to take him back when she had got where she wanted. She wouldn't mind so much then—she only wanted a fair start. It wasn't a fair start—*was* it? she asked him frankly—so long as he was always there, so terribly cruelly there, to speak of what she *had* been. She had been nothing worse, to his sense, than a very pretty girl of eighteen out in Peoria, who had seen at that time no one else she wanted more to marry, nor even any one who had been so supremely struck by her. That, absolutely, was the worst that could be said of her. It was so bad at any rate in her own view—it had grown so bad in the widening light of life—that it had fairly become more than she could bear and that something, as she said, had to be done about it. She hadn't known herself originally any more than she had known him—hadn't foreseen how much better she was going to come out, nor how, for her individually, as distinguished from him, there might be the possibility of a big future. He couldn't be explained away—he cried out with all his dreadful presence that she *had* been pleased to marry him; and what they therefore had to do must transcend explaining. It was perhaps now helping her, off there in London, and especially at Fordham Castle—she was staying last at Fordham Castle, Wilts—it was perhaps inspiring her even more than she had expected, that they were able to try together this particular substitute: news of her progress in fact—her progress on from Fordham Castle, if anything could be higher—would not improbably be contained in the unopened letter he had lately pocketed.

There was a given moment at luncheon meanwhile, in his talk with his countrywoman, when he did try that flap of the wing—did throw off, for a flight into the blue, the first falsehood he could think of. "I stopped in Italy, you see, on my way back from the East, where I had gone—to Constantinople"—he rose actually to Constantinople—"to visit Mrs. Addard's grave." And after they had all come out to coffee in the rustling shade, with the vociferous German tribe at one end of the terrace, the English family keeping silence with an English accent, as it struck him, in the middle, and his direction taken, by his new friend's side, to the other unoccupied corner, he found himself oppressed with what he had on his hands, the burden of keeping up this expensive fiction. He had never been to Constantinople—it could easily be proved against him; he ought to have thought of something better, have got his effect on easier terms. Yet a funnier thing still than this quick repentance was the quite equally fictive ground on which his companion had affected him—when he came to think of it—as meeting him.

"Why you know that's very much the same errand that took me to Rome. I visited the grave of my daughter—whom I lost there some time ago."

She had turned her face to him after making this statement, looked at him with an odd blink of her round kind plain eyes, as if to see how he took it. He had taken it on the spot, for this was the only thing to do; but he had felt how much deeper down he was himself sinking as he replied: "Ah it's a sad pleasure, isn't it? But those are places one doesn't want to neglect."

"Yes—that's what I feel. I go," his neighbour had solemnly pursued, "about every two years."

With which she had looked away again, leaving him really not able to emulate her. "Well, I hadn't been before. You see it's a long way."

"Yes—that's the trying part. It makes you feel you'd have done better—"

"To bring them right home and have it done over there?" he had asked as she let the sad subject go a little. He quite agreed. "Yes—that's what many do."

"But it gives of course a peculiar interest." So they had kept it up. "I mean in places that mightn't have so *very* much."

"Places like Rome and Constantinople?" he had rejoined while he noticed the cautious anxious sound of her "very." The tone was to come back to him, and it had already made him feel sorry for her, with its suggestion of her being at sea like himself. Unmistakeably, poor lady, she too was trying to float—was striking out in timid convulsive movements. Well, he wouldn't make it difficult for her, and immediately, so as not to appear to cast any ridicule, he observed that, wherever great bereavements might have occurred, there was no place so remarkable as not to gain an association. Such memories made at the least another object for coming. It was after this recognition, on either side, that they adjourned to the garden—Taker having in his ears again the good lady's rather troubled or muddled echo: "Oh yes, when you come to all the *objects*—!" The grave of one's wife or one's daughter was an object quite as much as all those that one looked up in Baedeker—those of the family of the Castle of Chillon and the Dent du Midi, features of the view to be enjoyed from different parts of Madame Massin's premises. It was very soon, none the less, rather as if these latter presences, diffusing their reality and majesty, had taken the colour out of all other evoked romance; and to that degree that when Abel's fellow guest happened to lay down on the parapet of the terrace three or four articles she had brought out with her, her fan, a couple of American newspapers and a letter that had obviously come to her by the same post as his own, he availed himself of the accident to jump at a further conclusion. Their coffee, which was "extra," as he knew and as, in the way of benevolence, he boldly warned her, was brought forth to them, and while she was giving her attention to her demitasse he let his eyes rest for three seconds on the superscription of her letter. His mind was by this time made up, and the beauty of it was that he couldn't have said why: the letter was from her daughter, whom she had been burying for him in Rome, and it would be addressed in a name that was really no more hers than the name his wife had thrust upon him was his. Her daughter had put *her* out at cheap board, pending higher issues, just as Sue had put him—so that there was a logic not other than fine in his notifying her of what coffee every day might let her in for. She was addressed on her envelope as "Mrs. Vanderplank," but he had privately arrived, before she so much as put down her cup, at the conviction that this was a borrowed and lawless title, for all the world as if, poor dear innocent woman, she were a bold bad adventuress. He had acquired furthermore the moral certitude that he was on the track, as he would have said, of her true identity, such as it might be. He couldn't think of it as in itself either very mysterious or very impressive; but, whatever it was, her duplicity had as yet mastered no finer art than his own, inasmuch as she had positively not escaped, at table, inadvertently dropping a name which, while it lingered on Abel's ear, gave her quite away. She had spoken, in her solemn sociability and as by the force of old habit, of "Mr. Magaw," and nothing was more to be presumed than that this gentleman was her defunct husband, not so very long defunct, who had permitted her while in life the privilege of association with him, but whose extinction had left her to be worked upon by different ideas.

These ideas would have germed, infallibly, in the brain of the young woman, her only child, under whose rigid rule she now—it was to be detected—drew her breath in pain. Madame Massin would abysmally know, Abel reflected, for he was at the end of a few minutes more intimately satisfied that Mrs. Magaw's American newspapers, coming to her straight from the other side and not yet detached from their wrappers, would not be directed to Mrs. Vanderplank, and that, this being the case, the poor lady would have had to invent some pretext for a claim to goods likely still perhaps to be lawfully called for. And she wasn't formed for duplicity, the large simple scared foolish fond woman, the vague anxiety in whose otherwise so uninhabited and unreclaimed countenance, as void of all history as an expanse of Western prairie seen from a car-window, testified to her scant aptitude for her part. He was far from the desire to question their hostess, however— for the study of his companion's face on its mere inferred merits had begun to dawn upon him as the possible resource of his ridiculous leisure. He might verily have some fun with her—or he would so have conceived it had he not become aware before they separated, half an hour later, of a kind of fellow-feeling for her that seemed to plead for her being spared. She *wasn't* being, in some quarter still indistinct to him—and so no more was he, and these things were precisely a reason. Her sacrifice, he divined, was an act of devotion, a state not yet disciplined to the state of confidence. She had presently, as from a return of vigilance, gathered in her postal property, shuffling it together at her further side and covering it with her pocket-handkerchief—though this very betrayal indeed but quickened his temporary impulse to break out to her, sympathetically, with a "Had you the misfortune to *lose* Magaw?" or with the effective production of his own card and a smiling, an inviting, a consoling "That's who *I* am if you want to know!" He really made out, with the idle human instinct, the crude sense for other people's pains and pleasures that had, on his showing, to his so great humiliation, been found an inadequate outfit for the successful conduct of the coal, the commission, the insurance and, as a last resort, desperate and disgraceful, the book-agency business—he really made out that she didn't want to know, or wouldn't for some little time; that she was decidedly afraid in short, and covertly agitated, and all just because she too, with him, suspected herself dimly in presence of that mysterious "more" than, in the classic phrase, met the eye. They parted accordingly, as if to relieve, till they could recover themselves, the conscious tension of their being able neither to hang back with grace nor to advance with glory; but flagrantly full, at the same time, both of the recognition that they couldn't in such a place avoid each other even if they had desired it, and of the suggestion that they wouldn't desire it, after such subtlety of communion, even were it to be thought of.

Abel Taker, till dinner-time, turned over his little adventure and extracted, while he hovered and smoked and mused, some refreshment from the impression the subtlety of communion had left with him. Mrs. Vanderplank was his senior by several years, and was neither fair nor slim nor "bright" nor truly, nor even falsely, elegant, nor anything that Sue had taught him, in her wonderful way, to associate with the American woman at the American woman's best—that best than which there was nothing better, as he had so often heard her say, on God's great earth. Sue would have banished her to the wildest waste of the unknowable, would have looked over her head in the manner he had often seen her use—as if she were in an exhibition of pictures, were in front of something bad and negligible that had got itself placed on the line, but that had the real thing, the thing of interest for those who *knew* (and when didn't Sue know?) hung above it. In Mrs. Magaw's presence everything would have been of more interest to Sue than Mrs. Magaw; but that consciousness failed to prevent his feeling the appeal of this inmate much rather confirmed than weakened when she reappeared for dinner. It was impressed upon him, after they had again seated themselves side by side, that she was reaching out to him indirectly, guardedly, even as he was to her; so that later on, in the garden, where they once more had their coffee together—it *might* have been so free and easy, so wildly foreign, so almost Bohemian—he lost all doubt of the wisdom of his taking his plunge. This act of resolution was not, like the other he had risked in the morning, an upward flutter into fiction, but a straight and possibly dangerous dive into the very depths of truth. Their instinct was unmistakeably to cling to each other, but it was as if they wouldn't know where to take hold till the air had really been cleared. Actually, in fact, they required a light—the aid prepared by him in the shape of a fresh match for his cigarette after he had extracted, under cover of the scented dusk, one of his cards from his pocket-book.

"There I honestly am, you see—Abel F. Taker; which I think you ought to know." It was relevant to nothing, relevant only to the grope of their talk, broken with sudden silences where they stopped short for fear of mistakes; but as he put the card before her he held out to it the little momentary flame. And this was the way that, after a while and from one thing to another, he himself, in exchange for what he had to give and what he gave freely, heard all about "Mattie"—Mattie Magaw, Mrs. Vanderplank's beautiful and high-spirited daughter, who, as he learned, found her two names, so dreadful even singly, a combination not to be borne, and carried on a quarrel with them no less desperate than Sue's quarrel with—well, with everything. She had, quite as Sue had done, declared her need of a free hand to fight them, and she was, for all the world like Sue again, now fighting them to the death. This similarity of situation was wondrously completed by the fact that the scene of Miss Magaw's struggle was, as her mother explained, none other than that uppermost walk of "high" English life which formed the present field of Mrs. Taker's operations; a circumstance on which Abel presently produced his comment. "Why if they're after the same thing in the same place, I wonder if we shan't hear of their meeting."

Mrs. Magaw appeared for a moment to wonder too. "Well, if they do meet I guess we'll hear. I will say for Mattie that she writes me pretty fully. And I presume," she went on, "Mrs. Taker keeps *you* posted?"

"No," he had to confess—"I don't hear from her in much detail. She knows I back her," Abel smiled, "and that's enough for her. 'You be quiet and I'll let you know when you're wanted'—that's her motto; I'm to wait, wherever I am, till I'm called for. But I guess she won't be in a hurry to call for me"—this reflexion he showed he was familiar with. "I've stood in her light so long—her 'social' light, outside of which everything is for Sue black darkness—that I don't really see the reason she should ever want me back. That at any rate is what I'm doing—I'm just waiting. And I didn't expect the luck of being able to wait in your company. I couldn't suppose—that's the truth," he added—"that there was another, anywhere about, with the same ideas or the same strong character. It had never seemed to be possible," he ruminated, "that there could be any one like Mrs. Taker."

He was to remember afterwards how his companion had appeared to consider this approximation. "Another, you mean, like my Mattie?"

"Yes—like my Sue. Any one that really comes up to her. It will be," he declared, "the first one I've struck."

"Well," said Mrs. Vanderplank, "my Mattie's remarkably handsome."

"I'm sure—! But Mrs. Taker's remarkably handsome too. Oh," he added, both with humour and with earnestness, "if it wasn't for that I wouldn't trust her so! Because, for what she wants," he developed, "it's a great help to be fine-looking."

"Ah it's always a help for a lady!"—and Mrs. Magaw's sigh fluttered vaguely between the expert and the rueful. "But what is it," she asked, "that Mrs. Taker wants?"

"Well, she could tell you herself. I don't think she'd trust me to give an account of it. Still," he went on, "she *has* stated it more than once for my benefit, and perhaps that's what it all finally comes to. She wants to get where she truly belongs."

Mrs. Magaw had listened with interest. "That's just where Mattie wants to get! And she seems to know just where it is."

"Oh Mrs. Taker knows—you can bet your life," he laughed, "on that. It seems to be somewhere in London or in the country round, and I dare say it's the same place as your daughter's. Once she's there, as I understand it, she'll be all right; but she has got to get there—that is to be seen there thoroughly fixed and photographed, and have it in all the papers—first. After she's fixed, she says, we'll talk. We *have* talked a good deal: when Mrs. Taker says 'We'll talk' I know what she means. But this time we'll have it out."

There were communities in their fate that made his friend turn pale. "Do you mean she won't want you to come?"

"Well, for me to 'come,' don't you see? will be for me to come to life. How can I come to life when I've been as dead as I am now?"

Mrs. Vanderplank looked at him with a dim delicacy. "But surely, sir, I'm not conversing with the remains—!"

"You're conversing with C. P. Addard. *He* may be alive—but even this I don't know yet; I'm just trying him," he said: "I'm trying him, Mrs. Magaw, on you. Abel Taker's in his grave, but does it strike you that Mr. Addard is at all above ground?"

He had smiled for the slightly gruesome joke of it, but she looked away as if it made her uneasy. Then, however, as she came back to him, "Are you going to wait here?" she asked.

He held her, with some gallantry, in suspense. "Are you?"

She postponed her answer, visibly not quite comfortable now; but they were inevitably the next day up to their necks again in the question; and then it was that she expressed more of her sense of her situation. "Certainly I feel as if I must wait—as long as I *have* to wait. Mattie likes this place—I mean she likes it for *me*. It seems the right *sort* of place," she opined with her perpetual earnest emphasis.

But it made him sound again the note. "The right sort to pass for dead in?"

"Oh she doesn't want me to pass for *dead*."

"Then what does she want you to pass for?"

The poor lady cast about. "Well, only for Mrs. Vanderplank."

"And who or what is Mrs. Vanderplank?"

Mrs. Magaw considered this personage, but didn't get far. "She isn't any one in particular, I guess."

"That means," Abel returned, "that she isn't alive."

"She isn't more than *half* alive," Mrs. Magaw conceded. "But it isn't what I *am*—it's what I'm passing for. Or rather"—she worked it out—"what I'm just not. I'm not passing—I don't, can't here, where it doesn't matter, you see—for her mother."

Abel quite fell in. "Certainly—she doesn't want to have any mother."

"She doesn't want to have *me*. She wants me to lay low. If I lay low, she says—"

"Oh I know what she says"—Abel took it straight up. "It's the very same as what Mrs. Taker says. If you lie low she can fly high."

It kept disconcerting her in a manner, as well as steadying, his free possession of their case. "I don't feel as if I *was* lying—

I mean as low as she wants—when I talk to you so." She broke it off thus, and again and again, anxiously, responsibly; her sense of responsibility making Taker feel, with his braver projection of humour, quite ironic and sardonic; but as for a week, for a fortnight, for many days more, they kept frequently and intimately meeting, it was natural that the so extraordinary fact of their being, as he put it, in the same sort of box, and of their boxes having so even more remarkably bumped together under Madame Massin's *tilleuls*, shouldn't only make them reach out to each other across their queer coil of communications, cut so sharp off in other quarters, but should prevent their pretending to any real consciousness but that of their ordeal. It was Abel's idea, promptly enough expressed to Mrs. Magaw, that they ought to get something out of it; but when he had said that a few times over (the first time she had met it in silence), she finally replied, and in a manner that he thought quite sublime: "Well, we *shall*—if they do all they want. We shall feel we've helped. And it isn't so *very* much to do."

"You think it isn't so very much to do—to lie down and die for them?"

"Well, if I don't hate it any worse when I'm really dead—!" She took herself up, however, as if she had skirted the profane. "I don't say that if I didn't *believe* in Mat—! But I do believe, you see. That's where she *has* me."

"Oh I see more or less. That's where Sue has *me*."

Mrs. Magaw fixed him with a milder solemnity. "But what has Mrs. Taker against you?"

"It's sweet of you to ask," he smiled; while it really came to him that he was living with her under ever so much less strain than what he had been feeling for ever so long before from Sue. Wouldn't he have liked it to go on and on— wouldn't that have suited C. P. Addard? He seemed to be finding out who C. P. Addard was—so that it came back again to the way Sue fixed things. She had fixed them so that C. P. Addard could become quite interested in Mrs. Vanderplank and quite soothed by her—and so that Mrs. Vanderplank as well, wonderful to say, had lost her impatience for Mattie's summons a good deal more, he was sure, than she confessed. It was from this moment none the less that he began, with a strange but distinct little pang, to see that he couldn't be sure of her. Her question had produced in him a vibration of the sensibility that even the long series of mortifications, of publicly proved inaptitudes, springing originally from his lack of business talent, but owing an aggravation of aspect to an absence of nameable "type" of which he hadn't been left unaware, wasn't to have wholly toughened. Yet it struck him positively as the prettiest word ever spoken to him, so straight a surprise at his wife's dissatisfaction; and he was verily so unused to tributes to his adequacy that this one lingered in the air a moment and seemed almost to create a possibility. He wondered, honestly, what she could see in him, in whom Sue now at last saw really less than nothing; and his fingers instinctively moved to his moustache, a corner of which he twiddled up again, also wondering if it were perhaps only *that*—though Sue had as good as told him that the undue flourish of this feature but brought out to her view the insignificance of all the rest of him. Just to hang in the iridescent ether with Mrs. Vanderplank, to whom he wasn't insignificant, just for them to sit on there together, protected, indeed positively ennobled, by their loss of identity, struck him as the foretaste of a kind of felicity that he hadn't in the past known enough about really to miss it. He appeared to have become aware that he should miss it quite sharply, that he would find how he had already learned to, if she should go; and the very sadness of his apprehension quickened his vision of what would work with her. She would want, with all the roundness of her kind, plain eyes, to see Mattie fixed—whereas he'd be hanged if he wasn't willing, on his side, to take Sue's elevation quite on trust. For the instant, however, he said nothing of that; he only followed up a little his acknowledgment of her having touched him. "What you ask me, you know, is just what I myself was going to ask. What has Miss Magaw got against *you*?"

"Well, if you were to see her I guess you'd know."

"Why I should think she'd like to show you," said Abel Taker.

"She doesn't so much mind their *seeing* me—when once she has had a look at me first. But she doesn't like them to hear me—though I don't talk so very much. Mattie speaks in the real English style," Mrs. Magaw explained.

"But ain't the real English style not to speak at all?"

"Well, she's having the best kind of time, she writes me—so I presume there must be some talk in which she can shine."

"Oh I've no doubt at all Miss Magaw *talks!*"—and Abel, in his contemplative way, seemed to have it before him.

"Well, don't you go and believe she talks too much," his companion rejoined with spirit; and this it was that brought to a head his prevision of his own fate.

"I see what's going to happen. You only want to go to her. You want to get your share, after all. You'll leave me without a pang."

Mrs. Magaw stared. "But won't you be going too? When Mrs. Taker sends for you?"

He shook, as by a rare chance, a competent head. "Mrs. Taker won't send for me. I don't make out the use Mrs. Taker can ever have for me again."

Mrs. Magaw looked grave. "But not to enjoy your seeing—?"

"My seeing where she has come out? Oh that won't be necessary to *her* enjoyment of it. It would be well enough perhaps if I could see without being seen; but the trouble with me—for I'm worse than you," Abel said—"is that it doesn't do for me either to be heard *or* seen. I haven't got *any* side—!" But it dropped; it was too old a story.

"Not any possible side at all?" his friend, in her candour, doubtingly echoed. "Why what do they want over there?"

It made him give a comic pathetic wail. "Ah to know a person who says such things as that to me, and to have to give her up—!"

She appeared to consider with a certain alarm what this might portend, and she really fell back before it. "Would you think I'd be able to give up Mattie?"

"Why not—if she's successful? The thing you wouldn't like—*you* wouldn't, I'm sure—would be to give her up if she should find, or if you should find, she wasn't."

"Well, I guess Mattie will be successful," said Mrs. Magaw.

"Ah you're a worshipper of success!" he groaned. "I'd give Mrs. Taker up, definitely, just to remain C. P. Addard with you."

She allowed it her thought; but, as he felt, superficially. "She's your wife, sir, you know, whatever you do."

" 'Mine'? Ah but whose? She isn't C. P. Addard's."

She rose at this as if they were going too far; yet she showed him, he seemed to see, the first little concession—which was indeed to be the only one—of her inner timidity; something that suggested how she must have preserved as a token, laid away among spotless properties, the visiting-card he had originally handed her. "Well, I guess the one I feel for is Abel F. Taker!"

This, in the end, however, made no difference; since one of the things that inevitably came up between them was that if Mattie had a quarrel with her name her most workable idea would be to get somebody to give her a better. That, he easily made out, was fundamentally what she was after, and, though, delicately and discreetly, as he felt, he didn't reduce Mrs. Vanderplank to so stating the case, he finally found himself believing in Miss Magaw with just as few reserves as those with which he believed in Sue. If it was a question of her "shining" she would indubitably shine; she was evidently, like the wife by whom he had been, in the early time, too provincially, too primitively accepted, of the great radiating substance, and there were times, here at Madame Massin's, while he strolled to and fro and smoked, when Mrs. Taker's distant lustre fairly peeped at him over the opposite mountain-tops, fringing their silhouettes as with the little hard bright rim of a coming day. It was clear that Mattie's mother couldn't be expected not to want to see her married; the shade of doubt bore only on the stage of the business at which Mrs. Magaw might safely be let out of the box. Was she to emerge abruptly *as* Mrs. Magaw?—or was the lid simply to be tipped back so that, for a good look, she might sit up a little straighter? She had got news at any rate, he inferred, which suggested to her that the term of her suppression was in sight; and she even let it out to him that, yes, certainly, for Mattie to be ready for her—and she did look as if she were going to be ready—she must be right down sure. They had had further lights by this time moreover, lights much more vivid always in Mattie's bulletins than in Sue's; which latter, as Abel insistently imaged it, were really each time, on Mrs. Taker's part, as limited as a peep into a death-chamber. The death-chamber was Madame Massin's terrace; and—he completed the image—how could Sue *not* want to know how things were looking for the funeral, which was in any case to be thoroughly "quiet"? *The* vivid thing seemed to pass before Abel's eyes the day he heard of the bright compatriot, just the person to go round with, a charming handsome witty widow, whom Miss Magaw had met at Fordham Castle, whose ideas were, on all important points, just the same as her own, whose means also (so that they could join forces on an equality) matched beautifully, and whose name in fine was Mrs. Sherrington Reeve. "Mattie has felt the want," Mrs. Magaw explained, "of some lady, some real lady like that, to go round with: she says she sometimes doesn't find it very pleasant going round alone."

Abel Taker had listened with interest—this information left him staring. "By Gosh then, she has struck Sue!"

" 'Struck' Mrs. Taker—?"

"She isn't Mrs. Taker now—she's Mrs. Sherrington Reeve." It had come to him with all its force—as if the glare of her genius were, at a bound, high over the summits. "Mrs. Taker's dead: I thought, you know, all the while, she must be, and this makes me sure. She died at Fordham Castle. So we're both dead."

His friend, however, with her large blank face, lagged behind. "At Fordham Castle too—died there?"

"Why she has been as good as *living* there!" Abel Taker emphasised. " 'Address Fordham Castle'—that's about all she has written me. But perhaps she died before she went"—he had it before him, he made it out. "Yes, she must have gone as Mrs. Sherrington Reeve. She had to die to go—as it would be for her like going to heaven. Marriages, sometimes, they say, are made up there; and so, sometimes then, apparently, are friendships—that, you see, for instance, of our two shining ones."

Mrs. Magaw's understanding was still in the shade. "But are you sure—?"

"Why Fordham Castle settles it. If she wanted to get where she truly belongs she has got *there*. She belongs at Fordham Castle."

The noble mass of this structure seemed to rise at his words, and his companion's grave eyes, he could see, to rest on its towers. "But how has she become Mrs. Sherrington Reeve?"

"By my death. And also after that by her own. I had to die first, you see, for *her* to be able to—that is for her to be sure. It's what she has been looking for, as I told you—to *be* sure. But oh—she was sure from the first. She knew I'd die off, when she had made it all right for me—so she felt no risk. She simply became, the day I became C. P. Addard, something as different as possible from the thing she had always so hated to be. She's what she always would have liked to be—so why shouldn't we rejoice for her? Her baser part, her vulgar part, has ceased to be, and she lives only as an angel."

It affected his friend, this elucidation, almost with awe; she took it at least, as she took everything, stolidly. "Do you call Mrs. Taker an angel?"

Abel had turned about, as he rose to the high vision, moving, with his hands in his pockets, to and fro. But at Mrs. Magaw's question he stopped short—he considered with his head in the air. "Yes—now!"

"But do you mean it's her idea to marry?"

He thought again. "Why for all I know she is married."

"With you, Abel Taker, living?"

"But I ain't living. That's just the point."

"Oh you're too dreadful"—and she gathered herself up. "And I won't," she said as she broke off, "help to bury you!"

This office, none the less, as she practically had herself to acknowledge, was in a manner, and before many days, forced upon her by further important information from her daughter, in the light of the true inevitability of which they had, for that matter, been living. She was there before him with her telegram, which she simply held out to him as from a heart too full for words. "Am engaged to Lord Dunderton, and Sue thinks you can come."

Deep emotion sometimes confounds the mind—and Mrs. Magaw quite flamed with excitement. But on the other hand it sometimes illumines, and she could see, it appeared, what Sue meant. "It's because he's so much in love."

"So far gone that she's safe?" Abel frankly asked.

"So far gone that she's safe."

"Well," he said, "if Sue feels it—!" He had so much, he showed, to go by. "Sue *knows*."

Mrs. Magaw visibly yearned, but she could look at all sides. "I'm bound to say, since you speak of it, that I've an idea Sue has helped. She'll like to have her there."

"Mattie will like to have Sue?"

"No, Sue will like to have Mattie." Elation raised to such a point was in fact already so clarifying that Mrs. Magaw could come all the way. "As Lady Dunderton."

"Well," Abel smiled, "one good turn deserves another!" If he meant it, however, in any such sense as that Mattie might be able in due course to render an equivalent of aid, this notion clearly had to reckon with his companion's sense of its strangeness, exhibited in her now at last upheaved countenance. "Yes," he accordingly insisted, "it will work round to that—you see if it doesn't. If that's where they were to come out, and they *have* come—by which I mean if Sue has realised it for Mattie and acted as she acts when she does realise, then she can't neglect it in her own case: she'll just *have* to realise it for herself. And, for that matter, you'll help her too. You'll be able to tell her, you know, that you've seen the last of me." And on the morrow, when, starting for London, she had taken her place in the train, to which he had accompanied her, he stood by the door of her compartment and repeated this idea. "Remember, for Mrs. Taker, that you've seen the last—!"

"Oh but I hope I haven't, sir."

"Then you'll come back to me? If you only will, you know, Sue will be delighted to fix it."

"To fix it—how?"

"Well, she'll tell you how. You've seen how she can fix things, and that will be the way, as I say, you'll help her."

She stared at him from her corner, and he could see she was sorry for him; but it was as if she had taken refuge behind her large high-shouldered reticule, which she held in her lap, presenting it almost as a bulwark. "Mr. Taker," she launched at him over it, "I'm afraid of you."

"Because I'm dead?"

"Oh sir!" she pleaded, hugging her morocco defence. But even through this alarm her finer thought came out. "Do you suppose I shall go to Fordham Castle?"

"Well, I guess that's what they're discussing now. You'll know soon enough."

"If I write you from there," she asked, "won't you come?"

"I'll come as the ghost. Don't old castles always have one?"

She looked at him darkly; the train had begun to move. "I *shall* fear you!" she said.

"Then there you are." And he moved an instant beside the door. "You'll be glad, when you get there, to be able to say—" But she got out of hearing, and, turning away, he felt as abandoned as he had known he should—felt left, in his solitude, to the sense of his extinction. He faced it completely now, and to himself at least could express it without fear of protest. "Why certainly I'm dead."

Julia Bride

S HE HAD WALKED with her friend to the top of the wide
steps of the Museum, those that descend from the galleries of painting, and then, after the young man had left her,
smiling, looking back, waving all gaily and expressively his hat
and stick, had watched him, smiling too, but with a different
intensity—had kept him in sight till he passed out of the great
door. She might have been waiting to see if he would turn
there for a last demonstration; which was exactly what he did,
renewing his cordial gesture and with his look of glad devotion, the radiance of his young face, reaching her across the
great space, as she felt, in undiminished truth. Yes, so she
could feel, and she remained a minute even after he was gone;
she gazed at the empty air as if he had filled it still, asking
herself what more she wanted and what, if it didn't signify
glad devotion, his whole air could have represented.

She was at present so anxious that she could wonder if he
stepped and smiled like that for mere relief at separation; yet
if he wanted in such a degree to break the spell and escape
the danger why did he keep coming back to her, and why, for
that matter, had she felt safe a moment before in letting him
go? She felt safe, felt almost reckless—that was the proof—so
long as he was with her; but the chill came as soon as he had
gone, when she instantly took the measure of all she yet
missed. She might now have been taking it afresh, by the testimony of her charming clouded eyes and of the rigour that
had already replaced her beautiful play of expression. Her radiance, for the minute, had "carried" as far as his, travelling
on the light wings of her brilliant prettiness—he on his side
not being facially handsome, but only sensitive clean and
eager. Then with its extinction the sustaining wings dropped
and hung.

She wheeled about, however, full of a purpose; she passed
back through the pictured rooms, for it pleased her, this idea
of a talk with Mr. Pitman—as much, that is, as anything could
please a young person so troubled. It had happened indeed
that when she saw him rise at sight of her from the settee

where he had told her five minutes before that she would find him, it was just with her nervousness that his presence seemed, as through an odd suggestion of help, to connect itself. Nothing truly would be quite so odd for her case as aid proceeding from Mr. Pitman; unless perhaps the oddity would be even greater for himself—the oddity of her having taken into her head an appeal to him.

She had had to feel alone with a vengeance—inwardly alone and miserably alarmed—to be ready to "meet," that way, at the first sign from him, the successor to her dim father in her dim father's lifetime, the second of her mother's two divorced husbands. It made a queer relation for her; a relation that struck her at this moment as less edifying, less natural and graceful, than it would have been even for her remarkable mother—and still in spite of this parent's third marriage, her union with Mr. Connery, from whom she was informally separated. It was at the back of Julia's head as she approached Mr. Pitman, or it was at least somewhere deep within her soul, that if this last of Mrs. Connery's withdrawals from the matrimonial yoke had received the sanction of the Court (Julia had always heard, from far back, so much about the "Court") she herself, as after a fashion, in that event, a party to it, wouldn't have had the cheek to make up—which was how she inwardly phrased what she was doing—to the long lean loose slightly cadaverous gentleman who was a memory, for her, of the period from her twelfth to her seventeenth year. She had got on with him, perversely, much better than her mother had, and the bulging misfit of his duck waistcoat, with his trick of swinging his eye-glass, at the end of an extraordinarily long string, far over the scene, came back to her as positive features of the image of her remoter youth. Her present age—for her later time had seen so many things happen—gave her a perspective.

Fifty things came up as she stood there before him, some of them floating in from the past, others hovering with freshness: how she used to dodge the rotary movement made by his pince-nez while he always awkwardly, and kindly, and often funnily, talked—it had once hit her rather badly in the eye; how she used to pull down and straighten his waistcoat, making it set a little better, a thing of a sort her mother never did;

how friendly and familiar she must have been with him for that, or else a forward little minx; how she felt almost capable of doing it again now, just to sound the right note, and how sure she was of the way he would take it if she did; how much nicer he had clearly been, all the while, poor dear man, than his wife and the Court had made it possible for him publicly to appear; how much younger too he now looked, in spite of his rather melancholy, his mildly-jaundiced, humorously-determined sallowness and his careless assumption, everywhere, from his forehead to his exposed and relaxed blue socks, almost sky-blue, as in past days, of creases and folds and furrows that would have been perhaps tragic if they hadn't seemed rather to show, like his whimsical black eyebrows, the vague interrogative arch.

Of course he wasn't wretched if he wasn't more sure of his wretchedness than that! Julia Bride would have been sure— had she been through what she supposed *he* had! With his thick loose black hair, in any case, untouched by a thread of grey, and his kept gift of a certain big-boyish awkwardness— that of his taking their encounter, for instance, so amusedly, so crudely, though, as she was not unaware, so eagerly too— he could by no means have been so little his wife's junior as it had been that lady's habit, after the divorce, to represent him. Julia had remembered him as old, since she had so constantly thought of her mother as old; which Mrs. Connery was indeed now, for her daughter, with her dozen years of actual seniority to Mr. Pitman and her exquisite hair, the densest, the finest tangle of arranged silver tendrils that had ever enhanced the effect of a preserved complexion.

Something in the girl's vision of her quondam stepfather as still comparatively young—with the confusion, the immense element of rectification, not to say of rank disproof, that it introduced into Mrs. Connery's favourite picture of her own injured past—all this worked, even at the moment, to quicken once more the clearness and harshness of judgement, the retrospective disgust, as she might have called it, that had of late grown up in her, the sense of all the folly and vanity and vulgarity, the lies, the perversities, the falsification of all life in the interest of who could say what wretched frivolity, what preposterous policy, amid which she had been condemned so ignorantly, so pitifully to sit, to walk, to grope, to flounder, from the very dawn of her consciousness. Didn't poor Mr. Pitman just touch the sensitive nerve of it when, taking her in with his facetious cautious eyes, he spoke to her, right out, of the old, old story, the everlasting little wonder of her beauty?

"Why, you know, you've grown up so lovely—you're the prettiest girl I've ever seen!" Of course she was the prettiest girl he had ever seen; she was the prettiest girl people much more privileged than he had ever seen; since when hadn't she been passing for the prettiest girl any one had ever seen? She had lived in that, from far back, from year to year, from day to day and from hour to hour—she had lived for it and literally *by* it, as who should say; but Mr. Pitman was somehow more illuminating than he knew, with the present lurid light that he cast upon old dates, old pleas, old values and old mysteries, not to call them old abysses: it had rolled over her in a swift wave, with the very sight of him, that her mother couldn't possibly have been right about him—as about what in the world had she ever been right?—so that in fact he was simply offered her there as one more of Mrs. Connery's lies. She might have thought she knew them all by this time; but he represented for her, coming in just as he did, a fresh discovery, and it was this contribution of freshness that made her somehow feel she liked him. It was she herself who, for so long, with her retained impression, had been right about him; and the rectification he represented had *all* shone out of him, ten minutes before, on his catching her eye while she moved through the room with Mr. French. She had never doubted of his probable faults—which her mother had vividly depicted as the basest of vices; since some of them, and the most obvious (not the vices, but the faults) were written on him as he stood there: notably, for instance, the exasperating "business slackness" of which Mrs. Connery had, before the tribunal, made so pathetically much. It might have been, for that matter, the very business slackness that affected Julia as presenting its friendly breast, in the form of a cool loose sociability, to her own actual tension; though it was also true for her, after they had exchanged fifty words, that he had as well his inward fever and that, if he was perhaps wondering what was so particularly the matter with her, she could make out not less that something was the matter with *him*. It had been vague, yet it had been intense, the mute reflexion, "Yes, I'm going to like him, and he's going somehow to help me!" that had directed her steps so straight to him. She was sure even then of this, that he wouldn't put to her a query about his former wife, that he took to-day no grain of interest in Mrs. Connery; that his interest, such as it was—and he couldn't look *quite* like that, to Julia Bride's expert perception, without something in the nature of a new one—would be a thousand times different.

It was as a value of *disproof* that his worth meanwhile so rapidly grew: the good sight of him, the good sound and sense of him, such as they were, demolished at a stroke so blessedly much of the horrid inconvenience of the past that she thought of him, she clutched at him, for a *general* saving use, an application as sanative, as redemptive, as some universal healing wash, precious even to the point of perjury if perjury should be required. That was the terrible thing, that had been the inward pang with which she watched Basil French recede: perjury would have to come in somehow and somewhere—oh so quite certainly!—before the so strange, so rare young man, truly smitten though she believed him, could be made to rise to the occasion, before her measureless prize could be assured. It was present to her, it had been present a hundred times, that if there had only been some one to (as it were) "deny everything" the situation might yet be saved. She so needed some one to lie for her—ah she so needed some one to lie! Her mother's version of everything, her mother's version of anything, had been at the best, as they said, discounted; and she herself could but show of course for an interested party, however much she might claim to be none the less a decent girl—to whatever point, that is, after all that had both remotely and recently happened, presumptions of anything to be called decency could come in.

After what had recently happened—the two or three indirect but so worrying questions Mr. French had put to her—it would only be some thoroughly detached friend or witness who might effectively testify. An odd form of detachment certainly would reside, for Mr. Pitman's evidential character, in her mother's having so publicly and so brilliantly—though, thank the powers, all off in North Dakota!—severed their connexion with him; and yet mightn't it do *her* some good, even if the harm it might do her mother were so little ambiguous? The more her mother had got divorced—with her dreadful cheap-and-easy second performance in that line and her present extremity of alienation from Mr. Connery, which enfolded beyond doubt the germ of a third petition on one side or the other—the more her mother had distinguished herself in the field of folly the worse for her own prospect with the Frenches, whose minds she had guessed to be accessible, and with such an effect of dissimulated suddenness, to some insidious poison.

It was all unmistakeable, in other words, that the more dismissed and detached Mr. Pitman should have come to appear, the more as divorced, or at least as divorcing, his before-time wife would by the same stroke figure—so that it was here poor Julia could but lose herself. The crazy divorces only, or the half-dozen successive and still crazier engagements only—gathered fruit, bitter fruit, of her own incredibly allowed, her own insanely fostered frivolity—either of these two groups of skeletons at the banquet might singly be dealt with; but the combination, the fact of each party's having been so mixed-up with whatever was least presentable for the other, the fact of their having so shockingly amused themselves together, made all present steering resemble the classic middle course between Scylla and Charybdis.

It was not, however, that she felt wholly a fool in having obeyed this impulse to pick up again her kind old friend. *She* at least had never divorced him, and her horrid little filial evidence in Court had been but the chatter of a parrakeet, of precocious plumage and croak, repeating words earnestly taught her and that she could scarce even pronounce. Therefore, as far as steering went, he *must* for the hour take a hand. She might actually have wished in fact that he shouldn't now have seemed so tremendously struck with her; since it was an extraordinary situation for a girl, this crisis of her fortune, this positive wrong that the flagrancy, what she would have been ready to call the very vulgarity, of her good looks might do her at a moment when it was vital she should hang as straight as a picture on the wall. Had it ever yet befallen any young woman in the world to wish with secret intensity that she might have been, for her convenience, a shade less inordinately pretty? She had come to that, to this view of the bane, the primal curse, of their lavishly physical outfit, which had included everything and as to which she lumped herself resentfully with her mother. The only thing was that her mother was, thank goodness, still so much prettier, still so assertively, so publicly, so trashily, so ruinously pretty. Wonderful the small grimness with which Julia Bride put off on this parent the middle-aged maximum of their case and the responsibility of their defect. It cost her so little to recognise in Mrs. Connery at forty-seven, and in spite, or perhaps indeed just by reason, of the arranged silver tendrils which were so like some rare bird's-nest in a morning frost, a facile supremacy for the dazzling effect—it cost her so little that her view even rather exaggerated the lustre of the different maternal items. She would have put it *all* off if possible, all off on other shoulders and on other graces and other morals than her own, the burden of physical charm that had made so easy a ground, such a native favouring air, for the aberrations which, apparently inevitable and without far consequences at the time, had yet at this juncture so much better not have been.

She could have worked it out at her leisure, to the last link of the chain, the way their prettiness had set them trap after trap, all along—had foredoomed them to awful ineptitude. When you were as pretty as that you could, by the whole idiotic consensus, be nothing *but* pretty; and when you were nothing "but" pretty you could get into nothing but tight places, out of which you could then scramble by nothing but masses of fibs. And there was no one, all the while, who wasn't eager to egg you on, eager to make you pay to the last cent the price of your beauty. What creature would ever for a moment help you to behave as if something that dragged in its wake a bit less of a lumbering train would, on the whole, have been better for you? The consequences of being plain were only negative—you failed of this and that; but the consequences of being as *they* were, what were these but endless? though indeed, as far as failing went, your beauty too could let you in for enough of it. Who, at all events, would ever for a moment credit you, in the luxuriance of that beauty, with the study, on your own side, of such truths as these? Julia Bride could, at the point she had reached, positively ask herself this even while lucidly conscious of the inimitable, the triumphant and attested projection, all round her, of her exquisite image. It was only Basil French who had at last, in his doubtless dry but all distinguished way—the way, surely as it was borne in upon her, of all the blood of all the Frenches— stepped out of the vulgar rank. It was only he who, by the trouble she discerned in him, had made her see certain things. It was only for him—and not a bit ridiculously, but just beautifully, almost sublimely—that their being "nice," her mother and she between them, had *not* seemed to profit by their being so furiously handsome.

This had, ever so grossly and ever so tiresomely, satisfied every one else; since every one had thrust upon them, had imposed upon them as by a great cruel conspiracy, their silliest possibilities; fencing them in to these, and so not only shutting them out from others, but mounting guard at the fence, walking round and round outside it to see they didn't escape, and admiring them, talking to them, through the rails, in mere terms of chaff, terms of chucked cakes and apples—as if they had been antelopes or zebras, or even some superior sort of performing, of dancing, bear. It had been reserved for Basil French to strike her as willing to let go, so to speak, a pound or two of this fatal treasure if he might only have got in exchange for it an ounce or so more of their so much less obvious and less published personal history. Yes, it described him to say that, in addition to all the rest of him, and of *his* personal history, and of his family, and of theirs, in addition to their social posture, as that of a serried phalanx, and to their notoriously enormous wealth and crushing respectability, she might have been ever so much less lovely for him if she had been only—well, a little prepared to answer questions. And it wasn't as if, quiet, cultivated, earnest, public-spirited, brought up in Germany, infinitely travelled, awfully like a high-caste Englishman, and all the other pleasant things, it wasn't as if he didn't love to be with her, to look at her, just as she was; for he loved it exactly as much, so far as that footing simply went, as any free and foolish youth who had ever made the last demonstration of it. It was that marriage was for him—and for them all, the serried Frenches—a great matter, a goal to which a man of intelligence, a real shy beautiful man of the world, didn't hop on one foot, didn't skip and jump, as if he were playing an urchins' game, but toward which he proceeded with a deep and anxious, a noble and highly just deliberation.

For it was one thing to stare at a girl till she was bored at it, it was one thing to take her to the Horse Show and the Opera, and to send her flowers by the stack, and chocolates by the ton, and "great" novels, the very latest and greatest, by the dozen; but something quite other to hold open for her, with eyes attached to eyes, the gate, moving on such stiff silver hinges, of the grand square forecourt of the palace of wedlock. The state of being "engaged" represented to him the introduction to this precinct of some young woman with whom his outside parley would have had the duration, distinctly, of his own convenience. That might be cold-blooded if one chose to think so; but nothing of another sort would equal the high ceremony and dignity and decency, above all the grand gallantry and finality, of their then passing in. Poor Julia could have blushed red, before that view, with the memory of the way the forecourt, as she now imagined it, had been dishonoured by her younger romps. She had tumbled over the wall with this, that and the other raw playmate, and had played "tag" and leap-frog, as she might say, from corner to corner. That would be the "history" with which, in case of definite demand, she should be able to supply Mr. French: that she had already, again and again, any occasion offering, chattered and scuffled over ground provided, according to his idea, for walking the gravest of minuets. If that then had been all their *kind* of history, hers and her mother's, at least there was plenty of it: it was the superstructure raised on the other group of facts, those of the order of their having been always so perfectly pink and white, so perfectly possessed of clothes, so perfectly splendid, so perfectly idiotic. These things had been the "points" of antelope and zebra; putting Mrs. Connery for the zebra, as the more remarkably striped or spotted. Such were the data Basil French's enquiry would elicit: her own six engagements and her mother's three nullified marriages—nine nice distinct little horrors in all. What on earth was to be done about them?

II

It was notable, she was afterwards to recognise, that there had been nothing of the famous business slackness in the positive pounce with which Mr. Pitman put it to her that, as soon as he had made her out "for sure," identified her there as old Julia grown-up and gallivanting with a new admirer, a smarter young fellow than ever yet, he had had the inspiration of her being exactly the good girl to help him. She certainly found him strike the hour again with these vulgarities of tone—forms of speech that her mother had anciently described as by themselves, once he had opened the whole battery, sufficient ground for putting him away. Full, however, of the use she should have for him, she wasn't going to mind trifles. What she really gasped at was that, so oddly, he was ahead of her at the start. "Yes, I want something of you, Julia, and I want it right now: you can do me a turn, and I'm blest if my luck—which has once or twice been pretty good, you know—hasn't sent you to me." She knew the luck he meant—that of her mother's having so enabled him to get rid of her; but it was the nearest allusion of the merely invidious kind that he would make. It had thus come to our young woman on the spot and by divination: the service he desired of her matched with remarkable closeness what she had so promptly taken into her head to name to himself—to name in her own interest, though deterred as yet from having brought it right out. She had been prevented by his speaking, the first thing, in that way, as if he had known Mr. French—which surprised her till he explained that every one in New York knew by appearance a young man of his so quoted wealth ("What did she take them all in New York then *for*?") and of whose marked attention to her he had moreover, for himself, round at clubs and places, lately heard. This had accompanied the inevitable free question "Was she engaged to *him* now?"—which she had in fact almost welcomed as holding out to her the perch of opportunity. She was waiting to deal with it properly, but meanwhile he had gone on, and to such effect that it took them but three minutes to turn out, on either side, like a pair of pickpockets comparing, under shelter, their day's booty, the treasures of design concealed about their persons.

"I want you to tell the truth for me—as you only can. I want you to say that I was really all right—as right as you know; and that I simply acted like an angel in a story-book, gave myself away to have it over."

"Why my dear man," Julia cried, "you take the wind straight out of my sails! What I'm here to ask of *you* is that you'll confess to having been even a worse fiend than you were shown up for; to having made it impossible mother should *not* take proceedings." There!—she had brought it out, and with the sense of their situation turning to high excitement for her in the teeth of his droll stare, his strange grin, his characteristic "Lordy, lordy! What good will that do you?" She was prepared with her clear statement of reasons for her appeal, and feared so he might have better ones for his own that all her story came in a flash. "Well, Mr. Pitman, I want to get married this time, by way of a change; but you see we've been such fools that, when something really good at last comes up, it's too dreadfully awkward. The fools we were capable of being—well, you know better than any one; unless perhaps not quite so well as Mr. Connery. It has got to be denied," said Julia ardently—"it has got to be denied flat. But I can't get hold of Mr. Connery—Mr. Connery has gone to China. Besides, if he were here," she had ruefully to confess, "he'd be no good—on the contrary. He wouldn't deny anything—he'd only tell more. So thank heaven he's away—there's *that* amount of good! I'm not engaged yet," she went on—but he had already taken her up.

"You're not engaged to Mr. French?" It was all, clearly, a wondrous show for him, but his immediate surprise, oddly, might have been greatest for that.

"No, not to any one—for the seventh time!" She spoke as with her head held well up both over the shame and the pride. "Yes, the next time I'm engaged I want something to happen. But he's afraid; he's afraid of what may be told him. He's dying to find out, and yet he'd die if he did! He wants to be talked to, but he has got to be talked to right. You could talk to him right, Mr. Pitman—if you only *would*! He can't get over mother—that I feel: he loathes and scorns divorces, and we've had first and last too many. So if he could hear from you that you just made her life a hell—why," Julia concluded, "it would be too lovely. If she *had* to go in for another—after having already, when I was little, divorced father—it would 'sort of' make, don't you see? one less. You'd do the high-toned thing by her: you'd say what a wretch you then were, and that she had had to save her life. In that way he mayn't mind it. Don't you see, you sweet man?" poor Julia pleaded. "Oh," she wound up as if his fancy lagged or his scruple looked out, "of course I want you to *lie* for me!"

It did indeed sufficiently stagger him. "It's a lovely idea for the moment when I was just saying to myself—as soon as I saw you—that you'd speak the truth for *me*!"

"Ah what's the matter with 'you'?" Julia sighed with an impatience not sensibly less sharp for her having so quickly scented some lion in her path.

"Why, do you think there's no one in the world but you who has seen the cup of promised affection, of something really to be depended on, only, at the last moment, by the horrid jostle of your elbow, spilled all over you? I want to provide for my future too as it happens; and my good friend who's to help me to that—the most charming of women this time—disapproves of divorce quite as much as Mr. French. Don't you see," Mr. Pitman candidly asked, "what that by itself must have done toward attaching me to her? *She* has got to be talked to—to be told how little I could help it."

"Oh lordy, lordy!" the girl emulously groaned. It was such a relieving cry. "Well, *I* won't talk to her!" she declared.

"You *won't*, Julia?" he pitifully echoed. "And yet you ask of *me*—!"

His pang, she felt, was sincere, and even more than she had guessed, for the previous quarter of an hour, he had been building up his hope, building it with her aid for a foundation. Yet was he going to see how their testimony, on each side, would, if offered, *have* to conflict? If he was to prove himself for her sake—or, more queerly still, for that of Basil French's high conservatism—a person whom there had been but that one way of handling, how could she prove him, in this other and so different interest, a mere gentle sacrifice to his wife's perversity? She had, before him there, on the instant, all acutely, a sense of rising sickness—a wan glimmer of foresight as to the end of the fond dream. Everything else was against her, everything in her dreadful past—just as if she had been a person represented by some "emotional actress," some desperate erring lady "hunted down" in a play; but was that going to be the case too with her own very decency, the fierce little residuum deep within her, for which she was counting, when she came to think, on so little glory or even credit? Was this also going to turn against her and trip her up—just to show she was really, under the touch and the test, as decent as any one; and with no one but herself the wiser for it meanwhile, and no proof to show but that, as a consequence, she should be unmarried to the end? She put it to Mr. Pitman quite with resentment: "Do you mean to say you're going to be married—?"

"Oh my dear, I too must get engaged first!"—he spoke with his inimitable grin. "But that, you see, is where you come in. I've told her about you. She wants awfully to meet you. The way it happens is too lovely—that I find you just in this place. She's coming," said Mr. Pitman—and as in all the good faith of his eagerness now; "she's coming in about three minutes."

"Coming here?"

"Yes, Julia—right here. It's where we usually meet;" and he was wreathed again, this time as if for life, in his large slow smile. "She loves this place—she's awfully keen on art. Like *you*, Julia, if you haven't changed—I remember how you did love art." He looked at her quite tenderly, as to keep her up to it. "You must still of course—from the way you're here. Just let her *feel* that," the poor man fantastically urged. And then with his kind eyes on her and his good ugly mouth stretched as for delicate emphasis from ear to ear: "Every little helps!"

He made her wonder for him, ask herself, and with a certain intensity, questions she yet hated the trouble of; as whether he were still as moneyless as in the other time—which was certain indeed, for any fortune he ever would have made. His slackness on that ground stuck out of him almost as much as if he had been of rusty or "seedy" aspect—which, luckily for him, he wasn't at all: he looked, in his way, like some pleasant eccentric ridiculous but real gentleman, whose taste might be of the queerest, but his credit with his tailor none the less of the best. She wouldn't have been the least ashamed, had their connexion lasted, of going about with him: so that what a fool, again, her mother had been—since Mr. Connery, sorry as one might be for him, was irrepressibly vulgar. Julia's quickness was, for the minute, charged with all this; but she had none the less her feeling of the right thing to say and the right way to say it. If he was after a future financially assured, even as she herself so frantically was, she wouldn't cast the stone. But if he had talked about her to strange women she couldn't be less than a little majestic. "Who then is the person in question for you—?"

"Why such a dear thing, Julia—Mrs. David E. Drack. Have you heard of her?" he almost fluted.

New York was vast, and she hadn't had that advantage. "She's a widow—?"

"Oh yes: she's not—!" He caught himself up in time. "She's a real one." It was as near as he came. But it was as if he had been looking at her now so pathetically hard. "Julia, she has millions."

Hard, at any rate—whether pathetic or not—was the look she gave him back. "Well, so has—or so *will* have—Basil French. And more of them than Mrs. Drack, I guess," Julia quavered.

"Oh I know what *they've* got!" He took it from her—with the effect of a vague stir, in his long person, of unwelcome embarrassment. But was she going to give up because he was embarrassed? He should know at least what he was costing her. It came home to her own spirit more than ever; but meanwhile he had found his footing. "I don't see how your mother matters. It isn't a question of his marrying *her*."

"No; but, constantly together as we've always been, it's a question of there being so disgustingly much to get over. If we had, for people like them, but the one ugly spot and the one weak side; if we had made, between us, but the one vulgar *kind* of mistake: well, I don't say!" She reflected with a wistfulness of note that was in itself a touching eloquence. "To have our reward in this world we've had too sweet a time.

We've had it all right down here!" said Julia Bride. "I should have taken the precaution to have about a dozen fewer lovers."

"Ah my dear, 'lovers'—!" He ever so comically attenuated.

"Well they *were*!" She quite flared up. "When you've had a ring from each (three diamonds, two pearls and a rather bad sapphire: I've kept them all, and they tell my story!) what are you to call them?"

"Oh rings—!" Mr. Pitman didn't call rings anything. "I've given Mrs. Drack a ring."

Julia stared. "Then aren't you her lover?"

"That, dear child," he humorously wailed, "is what I want you to find out! But I'll handle your rings all right," he more lucidly added.

"You'll 'handle' them?"

"I'll fix your lovers. I'll lie about *them*, if that's all you want."

"Oh about 'them'—!" She turned away with a sombre drop, seeing so little in it. "That wouldn't count—from *you*!" She saw the great shining room, with its mockery of art and "style" and security, all the things she was vainly after, and its few scattered visitors who had left them, Mr. Pitman and herself, in their ample corner, so conveniently at ease. There was only a lady in one of the far doorways, of whom she took vague note and who seemed to be looking at them. "They'd have to lie for themselves!"

"Do you mean he's capable of putting it to them?"

Mr. Pitman's tone threw discredit on that possibility, but she knew perfectly well what she meant. "Not of getting at them directly, not, as mother says, of nosing round himself; but of listening—and small blame to him!—to the horrible things other people say of me."

"But what other people?"

"Why Mrs. George Maule, to begin with—who intensely loathes us, and who talks to his sisters, so that they may talk to *him*: which they do, all the while, I'm morally sure (hating me as they also must). But it's she who's the real reason—I mean of his holding off. She poisons the air he breathes."

"Oh well," said Mr. Pitman with easy optimism, "if Mrs. George Maule's a cat—!"

"If she's a cat she has kittens—four little spotlessly white ones, among whom she'd give her head that Mr. French should make his pick. He could do it with his eyes shut—you can't tell them apart. But she has every name, every date, as you may say, for my dark 'record'—as of course they all call it: she'll be able to give him, if he brings himself to ask her, every fact in its order. And all the while, don't you see? there's no one to speak *for* me."

It would have touched a harder heart than her loose friend's to note the final flush of clairvoyance witnessing this assertion and under which her eyes shone as with the rush of quick tears. He stared at her, and what this did for the deep charm of her prettiness, as in almost witless admiration. "But can't you—lovely as you are, you beautiful thing!—speak for yourself?"

"Do you mean can't I tell the lies? No then, I can't—and I wouldn't if I could. I don't lie myself you know—as it happens; and it could represent to him then about the only thing, the only bad one, I don't do. I *did*—'lovely as I am'!—have my regular time; I wasn't so hideous that I couldn't! Besides, do you imagine he'd come and ask me?"

"Gad, I wish he would, Julia!" said Mr. Pitman with his kind eyes on her.

"Well then I'd tell him!" And she held her head again high. "But he won't."

It fairly distressed her companion. "Doesn't he want then to know—?"

"He wants *not* to know. He wants to be told without asking—told, I mean, that each of the stories, those that have come to him, is a fraud and a libel. *Qui s'excuse s'accuse*, don't they say?—so that do you see me breaking out to him, unprovoked, with four or five what-do-you-call-'ems, the things mother used to have to prove in Court, a set of neat little 'alibis' in a row? How can I get hold of so *many* precious gentlemen, to turn them on? How can *they* want everything fished up?"

She had paused for her climax, in the intensity of these considerations; which gave Mr. Pitman a chance to express his honest faith. "Why, my sweet child, they'd be just glad—!"

It determined in her loveliness almost a sudden glare. "Glad to swear they never had anything to do with such a creature? Then I'd be glad to swear they had lots!"

His persuasive smile, though confessing to bewilderment, insisted. "Why, my love, they've got to swear either one thing or the other."

"They've got to keep out of the way—that's *their* view of it, I guess," said Julia. "Where *are* they, please—now that they *may* be wanted? If you'd like to hunt them up for me you're very welcome." With which, for the moment, over the difficult case, they faced each other helplessly enough. And she added to it now the sharpest ache of her despair. "He knows about Murray Brush. The others"—and her pretty white-gloved hands and charming pink shoulders gave them up— "may go hang!"

"Murray Brush—?" It had opened Mr. Pitman's eyes.

"Yes—yes; I do mind *him*."

"Then what's the matter with his at least rallying—?"

"The matter is that, being ashamed of himself, as he well might, he left the country as soon as he could and has stayed away. The matter is that he's in Paris or somewhere, and that if you expect him to come home for me—!" She had already dropped, however, as at Mr. Pitman's look.

"Why, you foolish thing, Murray Brush is in New York!" It had quite brightened him up.

"He has come back—?"

"Why sure! I saw him—when was it? Tuesday!—on the Jersey boat." Mr. Pitman rejoiced in his news. "*He's* your man!"

Julia too had been affected by it; it had brought in a rich wave her hot colour back. But she gave the strangest dim smile. "He *was*!"

"Then get hold of him, and—if he's a gentleman—he'll prove for you, to the hilt, that he wasn't."

It lighted in her face, the kindled train of this particular sudden suggestion, a glow, a sharpness of interest, that had deepened the next moment, while she gave a slow and sad headshake, to a greater strangeness yet. "He isn't a gentleman."

"Ah lordy, lordy!" Mr. Pitman again sighed. He struggled out of it but only into the vague. "Oh then if he's a pig—!"

"You see there are only a few gentlemen—not enough to go round—and that makes them count so!" It had thrust the girl herself, for that matter, into depths; but whether most of memory or of roused purpose he had no time to judge— aware as he suddenly was of a shadow (since he mightn't perhaps too quickly call it a light) across the heaving surface of their question. It fell upon Julia's face, fell with the sound of the voice he so well knew, but which could only be odd to her for all it immediately assumed.

"There are indeed very few—and one mustn't try *them* too much!" Mrs. Drack, who had supervened while they talked, stood, in monstrous magnitude—at least to Julia's reim- pressed eyes—between them: she was the lady our young woman had descried across the room, and she had drawn near while the interest of their issue so held them. We have seen the act of observation and that of reflexion alike swift in Julia —once her subject was within range—and she had now, with all her perceptions at the acutest, taken in, by a single stare, the strange presence to a happy connexion with which Mr. Pitman aspired and which had thus sailed, with placid majesty, into their troubled waters. She was clearly not shy, Mrs. David E. Drack, yet neither was she ominously bold; she was bland and "good," Julia made sure at a glance, and of a large com- placency, as the good and the bland are apt to be—a large complacency, a large sentimentality, a large innocent ele- phantine archness: she fairly rioted in that dimension of size. Habited in an extraordinary quantity of stiff and lustrous black brocade, with enhancements, of every description, that twin- kled and tinkled, that rustled and rumbled with her least movement, she presented a huge hideous pleasant face, a fea- tureless desert in a remote quarter of which the dispropor- tionately small eyes might have figured a pair of rash adventurers all but buried in the sand. They reduced them- selves when she smiled to barely discernible points—a couple of mere tiny emergent heads—though the foreground of the scene, as if to make up for it, gaped with a vast benevolence. In a word Julia saw—and as if she had needed nothing more; saw Mr. Pitman's opportunity, saw her own, saw the exact nature both of Mrs. Drack's circumspection and of Mrs. Drack's sensibility, saw even, glittering there in letters of gold and as a part of the whole metallic coruscation, the large figure of her income, largest of all her attributes, and (though perhaps a little more as a luminous blur beside all this) the mingled ecstasy and agony of Mr. Pitman's hope and Mr. Pitman's fear.

He was introducing them, with his pathetic belief in the virtue for every occasion, in the solvent for every trouble, of an extravagant genial professional humour; he was naming her to Mrs. Drack as the charming young friend he had told her so much about and who had been as an angel to him in a weary time; he was saying that the loveliest chance in the world, this accident of a meeting in those promiscuous halls, had placed within his reach the pleasure of bringing them together. It didn't indeed matter, Julia felt, what he was saying: he conveyed everything, as far as she was concerned, by a moral pressure as unmistakeable as if, for a symbol of it, he had thrown himself on her neck. Above all, meanwhile, this high consciousness prevailed—that the good lady herself, however huge she loomed, had entered, by the end of a minute, into a condition as of suspended weight and arrested mass, stilled to artless awe by the effect of her vision. Julia had practised almost to lassitude the art of tracing in the people who looked at her the impression promptly sequent; but it was a singular fact that if, in irritation, in depression, she felt that the lighted eyes of men, stupid at their clearest, had given her pretty well all she should ever care for, she could still gather a freshness from the tribute of her own sex, still care to see her reflexion in the faces of women. Never, probably, never would that sweet be tasteless—with such a straight grim spoon was it mostly administered, and so flavoured and strengthened by the competence of their eyes. Women knew so much best *how* a woman surpassed—how and where and why, with no touch or torment of it lost on them; so that as it produced mainly and primarily the instinct of aversion, the sense of extracting the recognition, of gouging out the homage, was on the whole the highest crown one's felicity could wear. Once in a way, however, the grimness beautifully dropped, the jealousy failed: the admiration was all there and the poor plain sister handsomely paid it. It had never been so paid, she was presently certain, as by this great generous object of Mr. Pitman's flame, who without optical aid, it well might have seemed, nevertheless entirely grasped her—might in fact, all benevolently, have been groping her over as by some huge mild proboscis. She gave Mrs. Drack pleasure in short; and who could say of what other pleasures the poor lady hadn't been cheated?

It was somehow a muddled world in which one of her conceivable joys, at this time of day, would be to marry Mr. Pitman—to say nothing of a state of things in which this gentleman's own fancy could invest such a union with rapture. That, however, was their own mystery, and Julia, with each instant, was more and more clear about hers: so remarkably primed in fact, at the end of three minutes, that though her friend, and though *his* friend, were both saying things, many things and perhaps quite wonderful things, she had no free attention for them and was only rising and soaring. She was rising to her value, she was soaring *with* it—the value Mr. Pitman almost convulsively imputed to her, the value that consisted for her of being so unmistakeably the most dazzling image Mrs. Drack had ever beheld. These were the uses, for Julia, in fine, of adversity; the range of Mrs. Drack's experience might have been as small as the measure of her presence was large: Julia was at any rate herself in face of the occasion of her life, and, after all her late repudiations and reactions, had perhaps never yet known the quality of this moment's success. She hadn't an idea of what, on either side, had been uttered—beyond Mr. Pitman's allusion to her having befriended him of old: she simply held his companion with her radiance and knew she might be, for her effect, as irrelevant as she chose. It was relevant to do what he wanted—it was relevant to dish herself. She did it now with a kind of passion, to say nothing of her knowing, with it, that every word of it added to her beauty. She gave him away in short, up to the hilt, for any use of her own, and should have nothing to clutch at now but the possibility of Murray Brush.

"He says I was good to him, Mrs. Drack; and I'm sure I hope I was, since I should be ashamed to be anything else.

If I could be good to him now I should be glad—that's just what, a while ago, I rushed up to him here, after so long, to give myself the pleasure of saying. I saw him years ago very particularly, very miserably tried—and I saw the way he took it. I did see it, you dear man," she sublimely went on—"I saw it for all you may protest, for all you may hate me to talk about you! I saw you behave like a gentleman—since Mrs. Drack agrees with me so charmingly that there are not many to be met. I don't know whether you care, Mrs. Drack"—she abounded, she revelled in the name—"but I've always remembered it of him: that under the most extraordinary provocation he was decent and patient and brave. No appearance of anything different matters, for I speak of what I *know*. Of course I'm nothing and nobody; I'm only a poor frivolous girl, but I was very close to him at the time. That's all my little story—if it *should* interest you at all." She measured every beat of her wing, she knew how high she was going and paused only when it was quite vertiginous. Here she hung a moment as in the glare of the upper blue; which was but the glare—what else could it be?—of the vast and magnificent attention of both her auditors, hushed, on their side, in the splendour she emitted. She had at last to steady herself, and she scarce knew afterwards at what rate or in what way she had still inimitably come down—her own eyes fixed all the while on the very figure of her achievement. She had sacrificed her mother on the altar—proclaimed her false and cruel; and if that didn't "fix" Mr. Pitman, as he would have said—well, it was all she could do. But the cost of her action already somehow came back to her with increase; the dear gaunt man fairly wavered, to her sight, in the glory of it, as if signalling at her, with wild gleeful arms, from some mount of safety, while the massive lady just spread and spread like a rich fluid a bit helplessly spilt. It was really the outflow of the poor woman's honest response, into which she seemed to melt, and Julia scarce distinguished the two apart even for her taking gracious leave of each. "Good-bye, Mrs. Drack; I'm awfully happy to have met you"—like as not it was for this she had grasped Mr. Pitman's hand. And then to him or to her, it didn't matter which, "Good-bye, dear good Mr. Pitman—hasn't it been nice after so long?"

Julia floated even to her own sense swanlike away—she left in her wake their fairly stupefied submission: it was as if she had, by an exquisite authority, now *placed* them, each for each, and they would have nothing to do but be happy together. Never had she so exulted as on this ridiculous occasion in the noted items of her beauty. *Le compte y était*, as they used to say in Paris—every one of them, for her immediate employment, was there; and there was something in it after all. It didn't necessarily, this sum of thumping little figures, imply charm—especially for "refined" people: nobody knew better than Julia that inexpressible charm and quoteable "charms" (quoteable like prices, rates, shares, or whatever, the things they dealt in downtown) are two distinct categories; the safest thing for the latter being, on the whole, that it might include the former, and the great strength of the former being that it might perfectly dispense with the latter. Mrs. Drack wasn't refined, not the least little bit; but what would be the case with Murray Brush now—after his three years of Europe? He had done so what he liked with her—which had seemed so then just the meaning, hadn't it? of their being "engaged"—that he had made her not see, while the absurdity lasted (the absurdity of their pretending to believe they could marry without a cent) how little he was of metal without alloy: this had come up for her, remarkably, but afterwards—come up for her as she looked back. Then she had drawn her conclusion, which was one of the many that Basil French had made her draw. It was a queer service Basil was going to have rendered her, this having made everything she had ever done impossible, if he wasn't going to give her a new chance. If he was it was doubtless right enough. On the other hand Murray might have improved, if such a quantity of alloy, as she called it, *were*, in any man, reducible, and if Paris were the place all happily to reduce it. She had her doubts—anxious and aching on the spot, and had expressed them to Mr. Pitman: certainly, of old, he had been more open to the quoteable than to the inexpressible, to charms than to charm. If she could try the quoteable, however, and with such a grand result, on Mrs. Drack, she couldn't now on Murray—in respect to whom everything had changed. So that if he hadn't a sense for the subtler appeal, the appeal appreciable by people *not* vulgar, on which alone she could depend, what on earth would become of her? She could but yearningly hope, at any rate, as she made up her mind to write to him immediately at his club. It was a question of the right sensibility in him. Perhaps he would have acquired it in Europe.

Two days later indeed—for he had promptly and charmingly replied, keeping with alacrity the appointment she had judged best to propose, a morning hour in a sequestered alley of the Park—two days later she was to be struck well-nigh to alarm by everything he had acquired: so much it seemed to make that it threatened somehow a complication, and her plan, so far as she had arrived at one, dwelt in the desire above all to simplify. She wanted no grain more of extravagance or excess in anything—risking as she had done, none the less, a recall of ancient licence in proposing to Murray such a place of meeting. She had her reasons—she wished intensely to discriminate: Basil French had several times waited on her at her mother's habitation, their horrible flat which was so much too far up and too near the East Side; he had dined there and lunched there and gone with her thence to other places, notably to see pictures, and had in particular adjourned with her twice to the Metropolitan Museum, in which he took a great interest, in which she professed a delight, and their second visit to which had wound up in her encounter with Mr. Pitman, after her companion had yielded, at her urgent instance, to an exceptional need of keeping a business engagement. She mightn't in delicacy, in decency, entertain Murray Brush where she had entertained Mr. French—she was given over now to these exquisite perceptions and proprieties and bent on devoutly observing them; and Mr. French, by good luck, had never been with her in the Park: partly because he had never pressed it, and partly because she would have held off if he had, so haunted were those devious paths and favouring shades by the general echo of her untrammelled past. If he had never suggested their taking a turn there this was because, quite divineably, he held it would commit him further than he had yet gone; and if she on her side had practised a like reserve it was because the place reeked for her, as she inwardly said, with old associations. It reeked with nothing so much perhaps as with the memories evoked by the young man who now awaited her in the nook she had been so competent to indicate; but in what corner of the town, should she look for them, wouldn't those footsteps creak back into muffled life, and to what expedient would she be reduced should she attempt to avoid all such tracks? The Museum was full of tracks, tracks by the hundred—the way really she had knocked about!—but she had to see people somewhere, and she couldn't pretend to dodge every ghost.

All she could do was not to make confusion, make mixtures, of the living; though she asked herself enough what mixture she mightn't find herself to have prepared if Mr. French should, not so very impossibly for a restless roaming man—*her* effect on him!—happen to pass while she sat there with the moustachioed personage round whose name Mrs. Maule would probably have caused detrimental anecdote most thickly to cluster. There existed, she was sure, a mass of luxuriant legend about the "lengths" her engagement with Murray Brush had gone; she could herself fairly feel them in the air, these streamers of evil, black flags flown as in warning, the vast redundancy of so cheap and so dingy social bunting, in fine, that flapped over the stations she had successively moved away from and which were empty now, for such an ado, even to grotesqueness. The vivacity of that conviction was what had at present determined her, while it was the way he listened after she had quickly broken ground, while it was the special character of the interested look in his handsome face, handsomer than ever yet, that represented for her the civilisation he had somehow taken on. Just so it was the quantity of that gain, in its turn, that had at the end of ten minutes begun to affect her as holding up a light to the wide reach of her step. "There was never anything the least serious between us, not a sign or a scrap, do you mind? of anything beyond the merest pleasant friendly acquaintance; and if you're not ready to go to the stake on it for me you may as well know in time what it is you'll probably cost me."

She had immediately plunged, measuring her effect and having thought it well over; and what corresponded to her question of his having become a better person to appeal to was the appearance of interest she had so easily created in him. She felt on the spot the difference that made—it was indeed his form of being more civilised: it was the sense in which Europe in general and Paris in particular had made him develop. By every calculation—and her calculations, based on the intimacy of her knowledge, had been many and deep—he would help her the better the more intelligent he should have become; yet she was to recognise later on that the first chill of foreseen disaster had been caught by her as, at a given moment, this greater refinement of his attention seemed to exhale it. It was just what she had wanted—"if I can only get him interested—!" so that, this proving quite vividly possible, why did the light it lifted strike her as lurid? Was it partly by reason of his inordinate romantic good looks, those of a gallant genial conqueror, but which, involving so glossy a brownness of eye, so manly a crispness of curl, so red-lipped a radiance of smile, so natural a bravery of port, prescribed to any response he might facially, might expressively make a sort of florid disproportionate amplitude? The explanation, in any case, didn't matter; he was going to mean well—that she could feel, and also that he had meant better in the past, presumably, than he had managed to convince her of his doing at the time: the oddity she hadn't now reckoned with was this fact that from the moment he did advertise an interest it should show almost as what she would have called weird. It made a change in him that didn't go with the rest—as if he had broken his nose or put on spectacles, lost his handsome hair or sacrificed his splendid moustache: her conception, her necessity, as she saw, had been that something should be added to him for her use, but nothing for his own alteration.

He had affirmed himself, and his character, and his temper, and his health, and his appetite, and his ignorance, and his obstinacy, and his whole charming coarse heartless personality, during their engagement, by twenty forms of natural emphasis, but never by emphasis of interest. How in fact could you feel interest unless you should know, within you, some dim stir of imagination? There was nothing in the world of which Murray Brush was less capable than of such a dim stir, because you only began to imagine when you felt some approach to a need to understand. *He* had never felt it; for hadn't he been

born, to his personal vision, with that perfect intuition of
everything which reduces all the suggested preliminaries of
judgement to the impertinence—when it's a question of your
entering your house—of a dumpage of bricks at your door?
He had had, in short, neither to imagine nor to perceive,
because he had, from the first pulse of his intelligence, simply
and supremely known: so that, at this hour, face to face with
him, it came over her that she had in their old relation dis-
pensed with any such convenience of comprehension on his
part even to a degree she had not measured at the time. What
therefore must he not have seemed to her as a form of life, a
form of avidity and activity, blatantly successful in its own conceit, that he could have dazzled her so against the interest of
her very faculties and functions? Strangely and richly historic
all that backward mystery, and only leaving for her mind the
wonder of such a mixture of possession and detachment as
they would clearly to-day both know. For each to be so little
at last to the other when, during months together, the idea
of all abundance, all quantity, had been, for each, drawn from
the other and addressed to the other—what was it mon-
strously like but some fantastic act of getting rid of a person
by going to lock yourself up in the *sanctum sanctorum* of that
person's house, amid every evidence of that person's habits
and nature? What was going to happen, at any rate, was that
Murray would show himself as beautifully and consciously understanding—and it would be prodigious that Europe should
have inoculated him with that delicacy. Yes, he wouldn't claim
to know now till she had told him—an aid to performance he
had surely never before waited for or been indebted to from
any one; and then, so knowing, he would charmingly endeavour to "meet," to oblige and to gratify. He would find it, her
case, ever so worthy of his benevolence, and would be literally
inspired to reflect that he must hear about it first.

    She let him hear then everything, in spite of feeling herself
slip, while she did so, to some doom as yet incalculable; she
went on very much as she had done for Mr. Pitman and Mrs.
Drack, with the rage of desperation and, as she was afterwards
to call it to herself, the fascination of the abyss. She didn't
know, couldn't have said at the time, *why* his projected benevolence should have had most so the virtue to scare her: he

would patronise her, as an effect of her vividness, if not of her charm, and would do this with all high intention, finding her case, or rather *their* case, their funny old case, taking on of a sudden such refreshing and edifying life, to the last degree curious and even important; but there were gaps of connexion between this and the intensity of the perception here overtaking her that she shouldn't be able to move in *any* direction without dishing herself. That she couldn't afford it where she had got to—couldn't afford the deplorable vulgarity of having been so many times informally affianced and contracted (putting it only at that, at its being by the new lights and fashions so unpardonably vulgar): he took this from her without turning, as she might have said, a hair; except just to indicate, with his new superiority, that he felt the distinguished appeal and notably the pathos of it. He still took it from her that she hoped nothing, as it were, from any other *alibi*—the people to drag into court being too many and too scattered; but that, as it was with him, Murray Brush, she had been *most* vulgar, most everything she had better not have been, so she depended on him for the innocence it was actually vital she should establish. He blushed or frowned or winced no more at that than he did when she once more fairly emptied her satchel and, quite as if they had been Nancy and the Artful Dodger, or some nefarious pair of that sort, talking things over in the manner of "Oliver Twist," revealed to him the fondness of her view that, could she but have produced a cleaner slate, she might by this time have pulled it off with Mr. French. Yes, he let her in that way sacrifice her honourable connexion with him—all the more honourable for being so completely at an end—to the crudity of her plan for not missing another connexion, so much more brilliant than what he offered, and for bringing another man, with whom she so invidiously and unflatteringly compared him, into her greedy life.

There was only a moment during which, by a particular lustrous look she had never had from him before, he just made her wonder which turn he was going to take; she felt, however, as safe as was consistent with her sense of having probably but added to her danger, when he brought out, the next instant: "Don't you seem to take the ground that we were guilty—that *you* were ever guilty—of something we shouldn't have been? What did we ever do that was secret, or underhand, or any way not to be acknowledged? What did we do but exchange our young vows with the best faith in the world—publicly, rejoicingly, with the full assent of every one connected with us? I mean of course," he said with his grave kind smile, "till we broke off so completely because we found that—practically, financially, on the hard worldly basis—we couldn't work it. What harm, in the sight of God or man, Julia," he asked in his fine rich way, "did we ever do?"

She gave him back his look, turning pale. "Am I talking of *that*? Am I talking of what *we* know? I'm talking of what others feel—of what they *have* to feel; of what it's just enough for them to know not to be able to get over it, once they do really know it. How do they know what *didn't* pass between us, with all the opportunities we had? That's none of their business—if we were idiots enough, on the top of everything! What you may or mayn't have done doesn't count, for *you*; but there are people for whom it's loathsome that a girl should have gone on like that from one person to another and still pretend to be—well, all that a nice girl is supposed to be. It's as if we had but just waked up, mother and I, to such a remarkable prejudice; and now we have it—when we could do so well without it!—staring us in the face. That mother should have insanely *let* me, should so vulgarly have taken it for my natural, my social career—*that's* the disgusting humiliating thing: with the lovely account it gives of both of us! But mother's view of a delicacy in things!" she went on with scathing grimness; "mother's measure of anything, with her grand 'gained cases' (there'll be another yet, she finds them so easy!) of which she's so publicly proud! You see I've no margin," said Julia; letting him take it from her flushed face as much as he would that her mother hadn't left her an inch. It was that he should make use of the spade with her for the restoration of a bit of a margin just wide enough to perch on till the tide of peril should have ebbed a little, it was that he should give her *that* lift—!

Well, it was all there from him after these last words; it was before her that he really took hold. "Oh, my dear child, I can see! Of course there are people—ideas change in our society so fast!—who are not in sympathy with the old American freedom and who read, I dare say, all sorts of uncanny things into it. Naturally you must take them as they are—from the moment," said Murray Brush, who had lighted, by her leave, a cigarette, "your life-path does, for weal or for woe, cross with theirs." He had every now and then such an elegant phrase. "Awfully interesting, certainly, your case. It's enough for me that it *is* yours—I make it my own. I put myself absolutely in your place; you'll understand from me, without professions, won't you? that I do. Command me in every way! What I do like is the sympathy with which you've inspired *him*. I don't, I'm sorry to say, happen to know him personally"—he smoked away, looking off; "but of course one knows all about him generally, and I'm sure he's right for you, I'm sure it would be charming, if you yourself think so. Therefore trust me and even—what shall I say?—leave it to me a little, won't you?" He had been watching, as in his fumes, the fine growth of his possibilities; and with this he turned on her the large warmth of his charity. It was like a subscription of a half a million. "I'll take care of you."

She found herself for a moment looking up at him from as far below as the point from which the school-child, with round eyes raised to the wall, gazes at the particoloured map of the world. Yes, it was a warmth, it was a special benignity, that had never yet dropped on her from any one; and she wouldn't for the first few moments have known how to describe it or even quite what to do with it. Then as it still rested, his fine improved expression aiding, the sense of what had happened came over her with a rush. She was being, yes, patronised; and that was really as new to her—the freeborn American girl who might, if she had wished, have got engaged and disengaged not six times but sixty—as it would have been to be crowned or crucified. The Frenches themselves didn't do it—the Frenches themselves didn't dare it. It was as strange as one would: she recognised it when it came, but anything might have come rather—and it was coming by (of all people in the world) Murray Brush! It overwhelmed her; still she could speak, with however faint a quaver and however sick a smile. "You'll lie for me like a gentleman?"

"As far as that goes till I'm black in the face!" And then while he glowed at her and she wondered if he would pointedly look his lies that way, and if, in fine, his florid gallant knowing, almost winking intelligence, *common* as she had never seen the common vivified, would represent his notion of "blackness": "See here, Julia; I'll do more."

" 'More'—?"

"Everything. I'll take it right in hand. I'll fling over you—"

"Fling over me—?" she continued to echo as he fascinatingly fixed her.

"Well, the biggest *kind* of rose-coloured mantle!" And this time, oh, he did wink: it *would* be the way he was going to wink (and in the grandest good faith in the world) when indignantly denying, under inquisition, that there had been "a sign or a scrap" between them. But there was more to come; he decided she should have it all. "Julia, you've got to know now." He hung fire but an instant more. "Julia, I'm going to be married." His "Julias" were somehow death to her; she could feel that even *through* all the rest. "Julia, I announce my engagement."

"Oh lordy, lordy!" she wailed: it might have been addressed to Mr. Pitman.

The force of it had brought her to her feet, but he sat there smiling up as at the natural tribute of her interest. "I tell you before any one else; it's not to be 'out' for a day or two yet. But we want you to know; *she* said that as soon as I mentioned to her that I had heard from you. I mention to her everything, you see!"—and he almost simpered while, still in his seat, he held the end of his cigarette, all delicately and as for a form of gentle emphasis, with the tips of his fine fingers. "You've not met her, Mary Lindeck, I think: she tells me she hasn't the pleasure of knowing you, but she desires it so much— particularly longs for it. She'll take an interest too," he went on; "you must let me immediately bring her to you. She has heard so much about you and she really wants to see you."

"Oh mercy *me*!" poor Julia gasped again—so strangely did history repeat itself and so did this appear the echo, on Murray Brush's lips, and quite to drollery, of that sympathetic curiosity of Mrs. Drack's which Mr. Pitman, as they said, voiced.

Well, there had played before her the vision of a ledge of safety
in face of a rising tide; but this deepened quickly to a sense
more forlorn, the cold swish of waters already up to her waist
and that would soon be up to her chin. It came really but
from the air of her friend, from the perfect benevolence and
high unconsciousness with which he kept his posture—as if to
show he could patronise her from below upward quite as well
as from above down. And as she took it all in, as it spread to
a flood, with the great lumps and masses of truth it was floating, she knew inevitable submission, not to say submersion,
as she had never known it in her life; going down and down
before it, not even putting out her hands to resist or cling by
the way, only reading into the young man's very face an immense fatality and, for all his bright nobleness, his absence of
rancour or of protesting pride, the great grey blankness of her
doom. It was as if the earnest Miss Lindeck, tall and mild,
high and lean, with eye-glasses and a big nose, but "marked"
in a noticeable way, elegant and distinguished and refined, as
you could see from a mile off, and as graceful, for common
despair of imitation, as the curves of the "copy" set of old by
one's writing-master—it was as if this stately well-wisher,
whom indeed she had never exchanged a word with, but
whom she had recognised and placed and winced at as soon
as he spoke of her, figured there beside him now as also in
portentous charge of her case.

He had ushered her into it in that way, as if his mere right
word sufficed; and Julia could see them throned together,
beautifully at one in all the interests they now shared, and
regard her as an object of almost tender solicitude. It was
positively as if they had become engaged for her good—in
such a happy light as it shed. That was the way people you
had known, known a bit intimately, looked at you as soon as
they took on the high matrimonial propriety that sponged
over the more or less wild past to which you belonged and of
which, all of a sudden, they were aware only through some
suggestion it made them for reminding you definitely that you
still had a place. On her having had a day or two before to
meet Mrs. Drack and to rise to her expectation she had seen
and felt herself act, had above all admired herself, and had at
any rate known what she said, even though losing, at her

altitude, any distinctness in the others. She could have repeated afterwards the detail of her performance—if she hadn't
preferred to keep it with her as a mere locked-up, a mere
unhandled treasure. At present, however, as everything was
for her at first deadened and vague, true to the general effect
of sounds and motions in water, she couldn't have said afterwards what words she spoke, what face she showed, what impression she made—at least till she had pulled herself round
to precautions. She only knew she had turned away, and that
this movement must have sooner or later determined his rising
to join her, his deciding to accept it, gracefully and condoningly—condoningly in respect to her natural emotion, her inevitable little pang—for an intimation that they would be
better on their feet.

They trod then afresh their ancient paths; and though it
pressed upon her hatefully that he must have taken her
abruptness for a smothered shock, the flare-up of her old feeling at the breath of his news, she had still to see herself condemned to allow him this, condemned really to encourage
him in the mistake of believing her suspicious of feminine spite
and doubtful of Miss Lindeck's zeal. She was so far from
doubtful that she was but too appalled at it and at the officious
mass in which it loomed, and this instinct of dread, before
their walk was over, before she had guided him round to one
of the smaller gates, there to slip off again by herself, was
positively to find on the bosom of her flood a plank under aid
of which she kept in a manner and for the time afloat. She
took ten minutes to pant, to blow gently, to paddle dis-
guisedly, to accommodate herself, in a word, to the elements
she had let loose; but as a reward of her effort at least she
then saw how her determined vision accounted for everything.
Beside her friend on the bench she had truly felt all his cables
cut, truly swallowed down the fact that if he still perceived
she was pretty—and *how* pretty!—it had ceased appreciably to
matter to him. It had lighted the folly of her preliminary fear,
the fear of his even yet, to some effect of confusion or other
inconvenience for her, proving more alive to the quoteable in
her, as she had called it, than to the inexpressible. She had
reckoned with the awkwardness of that possible lapse of his
measure of her charm, by which his renewed apprehension of

her grosser ornaments, those with which he had most affinity, might too much profit; but she need have concerned herself as little for his sensibility on one head as on the other. She had ceased personally, ceased materially—in respect, as who should say, to any optical or tactile advantage—to exist for him, and the whole office of his manner had been the more piously and gallantly to dress the dead presence with flowers. This was all to his credit and his honour, but what it clearly certified was that their case was at last not even one of spirit reaching out to spirit. *He* had plenty of spirit—had all the spirit required for his having engaged himself to Miss Lindeck; into which result, once she had got her head well up again, she read, as they proceeded, one sharp meaning after another. It was therefore toward the subtler essence of that mature young woman alone that he was occupied in stretching; what was definite to him about Julia Bride being merely, being entirely—which was indeed thereby quite enough—that she *might* end by scaling her worldly height. They would push, they would shove, they would "boost," they would arch both their straight backs as pedestals for her tiptoe; and at the same time, by some sweet prodigy of mechanics, she would pull them up and up with her.

Wondrous things hovered before her in the course of this walk; her consciousness had become, by an extraordinary turn, a music-box in which, its lid well down, the most remarkable tunes were sounding. It played for her ear alone, and the lid, as she might have figured, was her firm plan of holding out till she got home, of not betraying—to her companion at least—the extent to which she was demoralised. To see him think her demoralised by mistrust of the sincerity of the service to be meddlesomely rendered her by his future wife—she would have hurled herself publicly into the lake there at their side, would have splashed, in her beautiful clothes, among the frightened swans, rather than invite him to that ineptitude. Oh her sincerity, Mary Lindeck's—she would be drenched with her sincerity, and she would be drenched, yes, with *his*; so that, from inward convulsion to convulsion, she had, before they reached their gate, pulled up in the path. There was something her head had been full of these three or four minutes, the intensest little tune of the

music-box, and it had made its way to her lips now; belonging—for all the good it could do her!—to the two or three
sorts of solicitude she might properly express.

"I hope *she* has a fortune, if you don't mind my speaking
of it: I mean some of the money we didn't in *our* time have—
and that we missed, after all, in our poor way and for what
we then wanted of it, so quite dreadfully."

She had been able to wreathe it in a grace quite equal to
any he himself had employed; and it was to be said for him
also that he kept up, on this, the standard. "Oh she's not,
thank goodness, at all badly off, poor dear. We shall do very
well. How sweet of you to have thought of it! May I tell her
that too?" he splendidly glared. Yes, he glared—how couldn't
he, with what his mind was really full of? But, all the same,
he came just here, by her vision, nearer than at any other point
to being a gentleman. He came quite within an ace of it—
with his taking from her thus the prescription of humility of
service, his consenting to act in the interest of her avidity, his
letting her mount that way, on his bowed shoulders, to the
success in which he could suppose she still believed. He
couldn't know, he would never know, that she had then and
there ceased to believe in it—that she saw as clear as the sun
in the sky the exact manner in which, between them, before
they had done, the Murray Brushes, all zeal and sincerity, all
interest in her interesting case, would dish, would ruin, would
utterly destroy her. He wouldn't have needed to go on, for
the force and truth of this; but he did go on—he was as crash-
ingly consistent as a motor-car without a brake. He was visibly
in love with the idea of what they might do for her and of
the rare "social" opportunity that they would, by the same
stroke, embrace. How he had been offhand with it, how he
had made it parenthetic, that he didn't happen "personally"
to know Basil French—as if it would have been at all likely he
should know him, even *im*personally, and as if he could conceal
from her the fact that, since she had made him her overture,
this gentleman's name supremely baited her hook! Oh they
would help Julia Bride if they could—they would do their
remarkable best; but they would at any rate have made his
acquaintance over it, and she might indeed leave the rest to
their thoroughness. He would already have known, he would

already have heard; her appeal, she was more and more sure, wouldn't have come to him as a revelation. He had already talked it over with *her*, with Miss Lindeck, to whom the Frenches, in their fortress, had never been accessible, and his whole attitude bristled, to Julia's eyes, with the betrayal of her hand, her voice, her pressure, her calculation. His tone in fact, as he talked, fairly thrust these things into her face. "But you must see her for yourself. You'll judge her. You'll love her. My dear child"—he brought it all out, and if he spoke of children he might, in his candour, have been himself infantine—"my dear child, she's the person to do it for you. Make it over to her; but," he laughed, "of course see her first! Couldn't you," he wound up—for they were now near their gate, where she was to leave him—"couldn't you just simply make us meet him, at tea, say, informally; just *us* alone, as pleasant old friends of whom you'd have so naturally and frankly spoken to him; and then see what we'd *make* of that?"

It was all in his expression; he couldn't keep it undetected, and his shining good looks couldn't: ah he was so fatally much too handsome for her! So the gap showed just there, in his admirable mask and his admirable eagerness; the yawning little chasm showed where the gentleman fell short. But she took this in, she took everything in, she felt herself do it, she heard herself say, while they paused before separation, that she quite saw the point of the meeting, as he suggested, at her tea. She would propose it to Mr. French and would let them know; and he must assuredly bring Miss Lindeck, bring her "right away," bring her soon, bring *them*, his fiancée and her, together somehow, and as quickly as possible—so that they *should* be old friends before the tea. She would propose it to Mr. French, propose it to Mr. French: that hummed in her ears as she went—after she had really got away; hummed as if she were repeating it over, giving it out to the passers, to the pavement, to the sky, and all as in wild discord with the intense little concert of her music-box. The extraordinary thing too was that she quite believed she should do it, and fully meant to; desperately, fantastically passive—since she almost reeled with it as she proceeded—she was capable of proposing anything to any one: capable too of thinking it likely Mr. French would come, for he had never on her previous proposals declined anything. Yes, she would keep it up to the end, this pretence of owing them salvation, and might even live to take comfort in having done for them what they wanted. What they wanted *couldn't* but be to get at the Frenches, and what Miss Lindeck above all wanted, baffled of it otherwise, with so many others of the baffled, was to get at Mr. French—for all Mr. French would want of either of them!—still more than Murray did. It wasn't till after she had got home, got straight into her own room and flung herself on her face, that she yielded to the full taste of the bitterness of missing a con- nexion, missing the man himself, with power to create such a social appetite, such a grab at what might be gained by them. He could make people, even people like these two and whom there were still other people to envy, he could make them push and snatch and scramble like that—and then remain as incapable of taking her from the hands of such patrons as of receiving her straight, say, from those of Mrs. Drack. It was a high note, too, of Julia's wonderful composition that, even in the long lonely moan of her conviction of her now certain ruin, all this grim lucidity, the perfect clearance of passion, but made her supremely proud of him.

The Jolly Corner

EVERY ONE asks me what I 'think' of everything," said Spencer Brydon; "and I make answer as I can—begging or dodging the question, putting them off with any nonsense. It wouldn't matter to any of them really," he went on, "for, even were it possible to meet in that stand-and-deliver way so silly a demand on so big a subject, my 'thoughts' would still be almost altogether about something that concerns only myself." He was talking to Miss Staverton, with whom for a couple of months now he had availed himself of every possible occasion to talk; this disposition and this resource, this comfort and support, as the situation in fact presented itself, having promptly enough taken the first place in the considerable array of rather unattenuated surprises attending his so strangely belated return to America. Everything was somehow a surprise; and that might be natural when one had so long and so consistently neglected everything, taken pains to give surprises so much margin for play. He had given them more than thirty years—thirty-three, to be exact; and they now seemed to him to have organised their performance quite on the scale of that licence. He had been twenty-three on leaving New York—he was fifty-six to-day: unless indeed he were to reckon as he had sometimes, since his repatriation, found himself feeling; in which case he would have lived longer than is often allotted to man. It would have taken a century, he repeatedly said to himself, and said also to Alice Staverton, it would have taken a longer absence and a more averted mind than those even of which he had been guilty, to pile up the differences, the newnesses, the queernesses, above all the bignesses, for the better or the worse, that at present assaulted his vision wherever he looked.

The great fact all the while however had been the incalculability; since he *had* supposed himself, from decade to decade, to be allowing, and in the most liberal and intelligent manner, for brilliancy of change. He actually saw that he had allowed for nothing; he missed what he would have been sure of finding, he found what he would never have imagined. Proportions and values were upside-down; the ugly things he had expected, the ugly things of his far-away youth, when he had too promptly waked up to a sense of the ugly—these uncanny phenomena placed him rather, as it happened, under the charm; whereas the "swagger" things, the modern, the monstrous, the famous things, those he had more particularly, like thousands of ingenuous enquirers every year, come over to see, were exactly his sources of dismay. They were as so many set traps for displeasure, above all for reaction, of which his restless tread was constantly pressing the spring. It was interesting, doubtless, the whole show, but it would have been too disconcerting hadn't a certain finer truth saved the situation. He had distinctly not, in this steadier light, come over *all* for the monstrosities; he had come, not only in the last analysis but quite on the face of the act, under an impulse with which they had nothing to do. He had come—putting the thing pompously—to look at his "property," which he had thus for a third of a century not been within four thousand miles of; or, expressing it less sordidly, he had yielded to the humour of seeing again his house on the jolly corner, as he usually, and quite fondly, described it—the one in which he had first seen the light, in which various members of his family had lived and had died, in which the holidays of his overschooled boyhood had been passed and the few social flowers of his chilled adolescence gathered, and which, alienated then for so long a period, had, through the successive deaths of his two brothers and the termination of old arrangements, come wholly into his hands. He was the owner of another, not quite so "good"—the jolly corner having been, from far back, superlatively extended and consecrated; and the value of the pair represented his main capital, with an income consisting, in these later years, of their respective rents which (thanks precisely to their original excellent type) had never been depressingly low. He could live in "Europe," as he had been in the habit of living, on the product of these flourishing New York leases, and all the better since, that of the second structure, the mere number in its long row, having within a twelvemonth fallen in, renovation at a high advance had proved beautifully possible.

These were items of property indeed, but he had found himself since his arrival distinguishing more than ever between them. The house within the street, two bristling blocks westward, was already in course of reconstruction as a tall mass of flats; he had acceded, some time before, to overtures for this conversion—in which, now that it was going forward, it had been not the least of his astonishments to find himself able, on the spot, and though without a previous ounce of such experience, to participate with a certain intelligence, almost with a certain authority. He had lived his life with his back so turned to such concerns and his face addressed to those of so different an order that he scarce knew what to make of this lively stir, in a compartment of his mind never yet penetrated, of a capacity for business and a sense for construction. These virtues, so common all round him now, had been dormant in his own organism—where it might be said of them perhaps that they had slept the sleep of the just. At present, in the splendid autumn weather—the autumn at least was a pure boon in the terrible place—he loafed about his "work" undeterred, secretly agitated; not in the least "minding" that the whole proposition, as they said, was vulgar and sordid, and ready to climb ladders, to walk the plank, to handle materials and look wise about them, to ask questions, in fine, and challenge explanations and really "go into" figures.

It amused, it verily quite charmed him; and, by the same stroke, it amused, and even more, Alice Staverton, though perhaps charming her perceptibly less. She wasn't however going to be better-off for it, as *he* was—and so astonishingly much: nothing was now likely, he knew, ever to make her better-off than she found herself, in the afternoon of life, as the delicately frugal possessor and tenant of the small house in Irving Place to which she had subtly managed to cling through her almost unbroken New York career. If he knew the way to it now better than to any other address among the dreadful multiplied numberings which seemed to him to reduce the whole place to some vast ledger-page, overgrown, fantastic, of ruled and criss-crossed lines and figures—if he had formed, for his consolation, that habit, it was really not a little because of the charm of his having encountered and recognised, in the vast wilderness of the wholesale, breaking through the mere gross generalisation of wealth and force and success, a small still scene where items and shades, all delicate things, kept the sharpness of the notes of a high voice perfectly trained, and where economy hung about like the scent of a garden. His old friend lived with one maid and herself dusted her relics and trimmed her lamps and polished her silver; she stood off, in the awful modern crush, when she could, but she sallied forth and did battle when the challenge was really to "spirit," the spirit she after all confessed to, proudly and a little shyly, as to that of the better time, that of *their* common, their quite far-away and antediluvian social period and order. She made use of the street-cars when need be, the terrible things that people scrambled for as the panic-stricken at sea scramble for the boats; she affronted, inscrutably, under stress, all the public concussions and ordeals; and yet, with that slim mystifying grace of her appearance, which defied you to say if she were a fair young woman who looked older through trouble, or a fine smooth older one who looked young through successful indifference; with her precious reference, above all, to memories and histories into which he could enter, she was as exquisite for him as some pale pressed flower (a rarity to begin with), and, failing other sweetnesses, she was a sufficient reward of his effort. They had communities of knowledge, "their" knowledge (this discriminating possessive was always on her lips) of presences of the other age, presences all overlaid, in his case, by the experience of a man and the freedom of a wanderer, overlaid by pleasure, by infidelity, by passages of life that were strange and dim to her, just by "Europe" in short, but still unobscured, still exposed and cherished, under that pious visitation of the spirit from which she had never been diverted.

She had come with him one day to see how his "apartment-house" was rising; he had helped her over gaps and explained to her plans, and while they were there had happened to have, before her, a brief but lively discussion with the man in charge, the representative of the building-firm that had undertaken his work. He had found himself quite "standing-up" to this personage over a failure on the latter's part to observe some detail of one of their noted conditions, and had so lucidly argued his case that, besides ever so prettily flushing, at the time, for sympathy in his triumph, she had afterwards said to him (though to a slightly greater effect of irony) that he had clearly for too many years neglected a real gift. If he had but stayed at home he would have anticipated the inventor of the sky-scraper. If he had but stayed at home he would have discovered his genius in time really to start some new variety of awful architectural hare and run it till it burrowed in a gold-mine. He was to remember these words, while the weeks elapsed, for the small silver ring they had sounded over the queerest and deepest of his own lately most disguised and most muffled vibrations.

It had begun to be present to him after the first fortnight, it had broken out with the oddest abruptness, this particular wanton wonderment: it met him there—and this was the image under which he himself judged the matter, or at least, not a little, thrilled and flushed with it—very much as he might have been met by some strange figure, some unexpected occupant, at a turn of one of the dim passages of an empty house. The quaint analogy quite hauntingly remained with him, when he didn't indeed rather improve it by a still intenser form: that of his opening a door behind which he would have made sure of finding nothing, a door into a room shuttered and void, and yet so coming, with a great suppressed start, on some quite erect confronting presence, something planted in the middle of the place and facing him through the dusk. After that visit to the house in construction he walked with his companion to see the other and always so much the better one, which in the eastward direction formed one of the corners, the "jolly" one precisely, of the street now so generally dishonoured and disfigured in its westward reaches, and of the comparatively conservative Avenue. The Avenue still had pretensions, as Miss Staverton said, to decency; the old people had mostly gone, the old names were unknown, and here and there an old association seemed to stray, all vaguely, like some very aged person, out too late, whom you might meet and feel the impulse to watch or follow, in kindness, for safe restoration to shelter.

They went in together, our friends; he admitted himself with his key, as he kept no one there, he explained, preferring, for his reasons, to leave the place empty, under a simple arrangement with a good woman living in the neighbourhood and who came for a daily hour to open windows and dust and sweep. Spencer Brydon had his reasons and was growingly aware of them; they seemed to him better each time he was there, though he didn't name them all to his companion, any more than he told her as yet how often, how quite absurdly often, he himself came. He only let her see for the present, while they walked through the great blank rooms, that absolute vacancy reigned and that, from top to bottom, there was nothing but Mrs. Muldoon's broomstick, in a corner, to tempt the burglar. Mrs. Muldoon was then on the premises, and she loquaciously attended the visitors, preceding them from room to room and pushing back shutters and throwing up sashes—all to show them, as she remarked, how little there was to see. There was little indeed to see in the great gaunt shell where the main dispositions and the general apportionment of space, the style of an age of ampler allowances, had nevertheless for its master their honest pleading message, affecting him as some good old servant's, some lifelong retainer's appeal for a character, or even for a retiring-pension; yet it was also a remark of Mrs. Muldoon's that, glad as she was to oblige him by her noonday round, there was a request she greatly hoped he would never make of her. If he should wish her for any reason to come in after dark she would just tell him, if he "plased," that he must ask it of somebody else.

The fact that there was nothing to see didn't militate for the worthy woman against what one *might* see, and she put it frankly to Miss Staverton that no lady could be expected to like, could she? "craping up to thim top storeys in the ayvil hours." The gas and the electric light were off the house, and she fairly evoked a gruesome vision of her march through the great grey rooms—so many of them as there were too!—with her glimmering taper. Miss Staverton met her honest glare with a smile and the profession that she herself certainly would recoil from such an adventure. Spencer Brydon meanwhile held his peace—for the moment; the question of the "evil" hours in his old home had already become too grave for him. He had begun some time since to "crape," and he knew just why a packet of candles addressed to that pursuit had been

stowed by his own hand, three weeks before, at the back of a
drawer of the fine old sideboard that occupied, as a "fixture,"
the deep recess in the dining-room. Just now he laughed at
his companions—quickly however changing the subject; for
the reason that, in the first place, his laugh struck him even
at that moment as starting the odd echo, the conscious human
resonance (he scarce knew how to qualify it) that sounds made
while he was there alone sent back to his ear or his fancy; and
that, in the second, he imagined Alice Staverton for the instant on the point of asking him, with a divination, if he ever
so prowled. There were divinations he was unprepared for,
and he had at all events averted enquiry by the time Mrs.
Muldoon had left them, passing on to other parts.

There was happily enough to say, on so consecrated a spot,
that could be said freely and fairly; so that a whole train of
declarations was precipitated by his friend's having herself
broken out, after a yearning look round: "But I hope you
don't mean they want you to pull *this* to pieces!" His answer
came, promptly, with his re-awakened wrath: it was of course
exactly what they wanted, and what they were "at" him for,
daily, with the iteration of people who couldn't for their life
understand a man's liability to decent feelings. He had found
the place, just as it stood and beyond what he could express,
an interest and a joy. There were values other than the beastly
rent-values, and in short, in short—! But it was thus Miss
Staverton took him up. "In short you're to make so good a
thing of your sky-scraper that, living in luxury on *those* ill-
gotten gains, you can afford for a while to be sentimental
here!" Her smile had for him, with the words, the particular
mild irony with which he found half her talk suffused; an irony
without bitterness and that came, exactly, from her having so
much imagination—not, like the cheap sarcasms with which
one heard most people, about the world of "society," bid for
the reputation of cleverness, from nobody's really having any.
It was agreeable to him at this very moment to be sure that
when he had answered, after a brief demur, "Well yes: so,
precisely, you may put it!" her imagination would still do him
justice. He explained that even if never a dollar were to come
to him from the other house he would nevertheless cherish
this one; and he dwelt, further, while they lingered and wan-

dered, on the fact of the stupefaction he was already exciting, the positive mystification he felt himself create.

He spoke of the value of all he read into it, into the mere sight of the walls, mere shapes of the rooms, mere sound of the floors, mere feel, in his hand, of the old silver-plated knobs of the several mahogany doors, which suggested the pressure of the palms of the dead; the seventy years of the past in fine that these things represented, the annals of nearly three generations, counting his grandfather's, the one that had ended there, and the impalpable ashes of his long-extinct youth, afloat in the very air like microscopic motes. She listened to everything; she was a woman who answered intimately but who utterly didn't chatter. She scattered abroad therefore no cloud of words; she could assent, she could agree, above all she could encourage, without doing that. Only at the last she went a little further than he had done himself. "And then how do you know? You may still, after all, want to live here." It rather indeed pulled him up, for it wasn't what he had been thinking, at least in her sense of the words. "You mean I may decide to stay on for the sake of it?"

"Well, *with* such a home—!" But, quite beautifully, she had too much tact to dot so monstrous an *i*, and it was precisely an illustration of the way she didn't rattle. How could any one—of any wit—insist on any one else's "wanting" to live in New York?

"Oh," he said, "I *might* have lived here (since I had my opportunity early in life); I might have put in here all these years. Then everything would have been different enough— and, I dare say, 'funny' enough. But that's another matter. And then the beauty of it—I mean of my perversity, of my refusal to agree to a 'deal'—is just in the total absence of a reason. Don't you see that if I had a reason about the matter at all it would *have* to be the other way, and would then be inevitably a reason of dollars? There are no reasons here *but* of dollars. Let us therefore have none whatever—not the ghost of one."

They were back in the hall then for departure, but from where they stood the vista was large, through an open door, into the great square main saloon, with its almost antique felicity of brave spaces between windows. Her eyes came back from that reach and met his own a moment. "Are you very sure the 'ghost' of one doesn't, much rather, serve—?"

He had a positive sense of turning pale. But it was as near as they were then to come. For he made answer, he believed, between a glare and a grin: "Oh ghosts—of course the place must swarm with them! I should be ashamed of it if it didn't. Poor Mrs. Muldoon's right, and it's why I haven't asked her to do more than look in."

Miss Staverton's gaze again lost itself, and things she didn't utter, it was clear, came and went in her mind. She might even for the minute, off there in the fine room, have imagined some element dimly gathering. Simplified like the death-mask of a handsome face, it perhaps produced for her just then an effect akin to the stir of an expression in the "set" commemorative plaster. Yet whatever her impression may have been she produced instead a vague platitude. "Well, if it were only furnished and lived in—!"

She appeared to imply that in case of its being still furnished he might have been a little less opposed to the idea of a return. But she passed straight into the vestibule, as if to leave her words behind her, and the next moment he had opened the house-door and was standing with her on the steps. He closed the door and, while he re-pocketed his key, looking up and down, they took in the comparatively harsh actuality of the Avenue, which reminded him of the assault of the outer light of the Desert on the traveller emerging from an Egyptian tomb. But he risked before they stepped into the street his gathered answer to her speech. "For me it *is* lived in. For me it *is* furnished." At which it was easy for her to sigh "Ah yes—!" all vaguely and discreetly; since his parents and his favourite sister, to say nothing of other kin, in numbers, had run their course and met their end there. That represented, within the walls, ineffaceable life.

It was a few days after this that, during an hour passed with her again, he had expressed his impatience of the too flattering curiosity—among the people he met—about his appreciation of New York. He had arrived at none at all that was socially producible, and as for that matter of his "thinking" (thinking the better or the worse of anything there) he was wholly taken up with one subject of thought. It was mere vain egoism, and it was moreover, if she liked, a morbid obsession. He found all things come back to the question of what he personally might have been, how he might have led his life and "turned out," if he had not so, at the outset, given it up. And confessing for the first time to the intensity within him of this absurd speculation—which but proved also, no doubt, the habit of too selfishly thinking—he affirmed the impotence there of any other source of interest, any other native appeal. "What would it have made of me, what would it have made of me? I keep for ever wondering, all idiotically; as if I could possibly know! I see what it has made of dozens of others, those I meet, and it positively aches within me, to the point of exasperation, that it would have made something of me as well. Only I can't make out *what*, and the worry of it, the small rage of curiosity never to be satisfied, brings back what I remember to have felt, once or twice, after judging best, for reasons, to burn some important letter unopened. I've been sorry, I've hated it—I've never known what was in the letter. You may of course say it's a trifle—!"

"I don't say it's a trifle," Miss Staverton gravely interrupted.

She was seated by her fire, and before her, on his feet and restless, he turned to and fro between this intensity of his idea and a fitful and unseeing inspection, through his single eyeglass, of the dear little old objects on her chimney-piece. Her interruption made him for an instant look at her harder. "I shouldn't care if you did!" he laughed, however; "and it's only a figure, at any rate, for the way I now feel. *Not* to have followed my perverse young course—and almost in the teeth of my father's curse, as I may say; not to have kept it up, so, 'over there,' from that day to this, without a doubt or a pang; not, above all, to have liked it, to have loved it, so much, loved it, no doubt, with such an abysmal conceit of my own preference: some variation from *that*, I say, must have produced some different effect for my life and for my 'form.' I should have stuck here—if it had been possible; and I was too young, at twenty-three, to judge, *pour deux sous*, whether it *were* possible. If I had waited I might have seen it was, and then I might have been, by staying here, something nearer to one of these types who have been hammered so hard and made so keen by their conditions. It isn't that I admire them so much—the question of any charm in them, or of any charm, beyond that of the rank money-passion, exerted by their conditions *for* them, has nothing to do with the matter: it's only a question of what fantastic, yet perfectly possible, development of my own nature I mayn't have missed. It comes over me that I had then a strange *alter ego* deep down somewhere within me, as the full-blown flower is in the small tight bud, and that I just took the course, I just transferred him to the climate, that blighted him for once and for ever."

"And you wonder about the flower," Miss Staverton said. "So do I, if you want to know; and so I've been wondering these several weeks. I believe in the flower," she continued, "I feel it would have been quite splendid, quite huge and monstrous."

"Monstrous above all!" her visitor echoed; "and I imagine, by the same stroke, quite hideous and offensive."

"You don't believe that," she returned; "if you did you wouldn't wonder. You'd know, and that would be enough for you. What you feel—and what I feel *for* you—is that you'd have had power."

"You'd have liked me that way?" he asked.

She barely hung fire. "How should I not have liked you?"

"I see. You'd have liked me, have preferred me, a billionaire!"

"How should I not have liked you?" she simply again asked.

He stood before her still—her question kept him motionless. He took it in, so much there was of it; and indeed his not otherwise meeting it testified to that. "I know at least what I am," he simply went on; "the other side of the medal's clear enough. I've not been edifying—I believe I'm thought in a hundred quarters to have been barely decent. I've followed strange paths and worshipped strange gods; it must have come to you again and again—in fact you've admitted to me as much—that I was leading, at any time these thirty years, a selfish frivolous scandalous life. And you see what it has made of me."

She just waited, smiling at him. "You see what it has made of *me*."

"Oh you're a person whom nothing can have altered. You were born to be what you are, anywhere, anyway: you've the perfection nothing else could have blighted. And don't you see how, without my exile, I shouldn't have been waiting till now—?" But he pulled up for the strange pang.

"The great thing to see," she presently said, "seems to me to be that it has spoiled nothing. It hasn't spoiled your being here at last. It hasn't spoiled this. It hasn't spoiled your speaking—" She also however faltered.

He wondered at everything her controlled emotion might mean. "Do you believe then—too dreadfully!—that I *am* as good as I might ever have been?"

"Oh no! Far from it!" With which she got up from her chair and was nearer to him. "But I don't care," she smiled.

"You mean I'm good enough?"

She considered a little. "Will you believe it if I say so? I mean will you let that settle your question for you?" And then as if making out in his face that he drew back from this, that he had some idea which, however absurd, he couldn't yet bargain away: "Oh you don't care either—but very differently: you don't care for anything but yourself."

Spencer Brydon recognised it—it was in fact what he had absolutely professed. Yet he importantly qualified. "*He* isn't myself. He's the just so totally other person. But I do want to see him," he added. "And I can. And I shall."

Their eyes met for a minute while he guessed from something in hers that she divined his strange sense. But neither of them otherwise expressed it, and her apparent understanding, with no protesting shock, no easy derision, touched him more deeply than anything yet, constituting for his stifled perversity, on the spot, an element that was like breatheable air. What she said however was unexpected. "Well, *I've* seen him."

"You—?"

"I've seen him in a dream."

"Oh a 'dream'—!" It let him down.

"But twice over," she continued. "I saw him as I see you now."

"You've dreamed the same dream—?"

"Twice over," she repeated. "The very same."

This did somehow a little speak to him, as it also gratified him. "You dream about me at that rate?"

"Ah about *him*!" she smiled.

His eyes again sounded her. "Then you know all about him." And as she said nothing more: "What's the wretch like?"

She hesitated, and it was as if he were pressing her so hard that, resisting for reasons of her own, she had to turn away. "I'll tell you some other time!"

II

It was after this that there was most of a virtue for him, most of a cultivated charm, most of a preposterous secret thrill, in the particular form of surrender to his obsession and of address to what he more and more believed to be his privilege. It was what in these weeks he was living for—since he really felt life to begin but after Mrs. Muldoon had retired from the scene and, visiting the ample house from attic to cellar, making sure he was alone, he knew himself in safe possession and, as he tacitly expressed it, let himself go. He sometimes came twice in the twenty-four hours; the moments he liked best were those of gathering dusk, of the short autumn twilight; this was the time of which, again and again, he found himself hoping most. Then he could, as seemed to him, most intimately wander and wait, linger and listen, feel his fine attention, never in his life before so fine, on the pulse of the great vague place: he preferred the lampless hour and only wished he might have prolonged each day the deep crepuscular spell. Later—rarely much before midnight, but then for a considerable vigil—he watched with his glimmering light; moving slowly, holding it high, playing it far, rejoicing above all, as much as he might, in open vistas, reaches of communication between rooms and by passages; the long straight chance or show, as he would have called it, for the revelation he pretended to invite. It was a practice he found he could perfectly "work" without exciting remark; no one was in the least the wiser for it; even Alice Staverton, who was moreover a well of discretion, didn't quite fully imagine.

He let himself in and let himself out with the assurance of calm proprietorship; and accident so far favoured him that, if a fat Avenue "officer" had happened on occasion to see him entering at eleven-thirty, he had never yet, to the best of his belief, been noticed as emerging at two. He walked there on the crisp November nights, arrived regularly at the evening's end; it was as easy to do this after dining out as to take his way to a club or to his hotel. When he left his club, if he hadn't been dining out, it was ostensibly to go to his hotel; and when he left his hotel, if he had spent a part of the evening there, it was ostensibly to go to his club. Everything was easy in fine; everything conspired and promoted: there was truly even in the strain of his experience something that glossed over, something that salved and simplified, all the rest of consciousness. He circulated, talked, renewed, loosely and pleasantly, old relations—met indeed, so far as he could, new expectations and seemed to make out on the whole that in spite of the career, of such different contacts, which he had spoken of to Miss Staverton as ministering so little, for those who might have watched it, to edification, he was positively rather liked than not. He was a dim secondary social success— and all with people who had truly not an idea of him. It was all mere surface sound, this murmur of their welcome, this popping of their corks—just as his gestures of response were the extravagant shadows, emphatic in proportion as they meant little, of some game of *ombres chinoises*. He projected himself all day, in thought, straight over the bristling line of hard unconscious heads and into the other, the real, the waiting life; the life that, as soon as he had heard behind him the click of his great house-door, began for him, on the jolly corner, as beguilingly as the slow opening bars of some rich music follows the tap of the conductor's wand.

He always caught the first effect of the steel point of his stick on the old marble of the hall pavement, large black-and-white squares that he remembered as the admiration of his childhood and that had then made in him, as he now saw, for the growth of an early conception of style. This effect was the dim reverberating tinkle as of some far-off bell hung who should say where?—in the depths of the house, of the past, of that mystical other world that might have flourished for him had he not, for weal or woe, abandoned it. On this impression he did ever the same thing; he put his stick noiselessly away in a corner—feeling the place once more in the likeness of some great glass bowl, all precious concave crystal, set delicately humming by the play of a moist finger round its edge. The concave crystal held, as it were, this mystical other world, and the indescribably fine murmur of its rim was the sigh there, the scarce audible pathetic wail to his strained ear, of all the old baffled forsworn possibilities. What he did therefore by this appeal of his hushed presence was to wake them into such measure of ghostly life as they might still enjoy. They were shy, all but unappeasably shy, but they weren't really sinister; at least they weren't as he had hitherto felt them—before they had taken the Form he so yearned to make them take, the Form he at moments saw himself in the light of fairly hunting on tiptoe, the points of his evening-shoes, from room to room and from storey to storey.

That was the essence of his vision—which was all rank folly, if one would, while he was out of the house and otherwise occupied, but which took on the last verisimilitude as soon as he was placed and posted. He knew what he meant and what he wanted; it was as clear as the figure on a cheque presented in demand for cash. His *alter ego* "walked"—that was the note of his image of him, while his image of his motive for his own odd pastime was the desire to waylay him and meet him. He roamed, slowly, warily, but all restlessly, he himself did—Mrs. Muldoon had been right, absolutely, with her figure of their "craping"; and the presence he watched for would roam restlessly too. But it would be as cautious and as shifty; the conviction of its probable, in fact its already quite sensible, quite audible evasion of pursuit grew for him from night to night, laying on him finally a rigour to which nothing in his life had been comparable. It had been the theory of many superficially-judging persons, he knew, that he was wasting that life in a surrender to sensations, but he had tasted of no pleasure so fine as his actual tension, had been introduced to no sport that demanded at once the patience and the nerve of this stalking of a creature more subtle, yet at bay perhaps more formidable, than any beast of the forest. The terms, the comparisons, the very practices of the chase positively came again

into play; there were even moments when passages of his occasional experience as a sportsman, stirred memories, from his
younger time, of moor and mountain and desert, revived for
him—and to the increase of his keenness—by the tremendous
force of analogy. He found himself at moments—once he had
placed his single light on some mantel-shelf or in some recess—stepping back into shelter or shade, effacing himself behind a door or in an embrasure, as he had sought of old the
vantage of rock and tree; he found himself holding his breath
and living in the joy of the instant, the supreme suspense created by big game alone.

He wasn't afraid (though putting himself the question as
he believed gentlemen on Bengal tiger-shoots or in close
quarters with the great bear of the Rockies had been known
to confess to having put it); and this indeed—since here at
least he might be frank!—because of the impression, so intimate and so strange, that he himself produced as yet a dread,
produced certainly a strain, beyond the liveliest he was likely
to feel. They fell for him into categories, they fairly became
familiar, the signs, for his own perception, of the alarm his
presence and his vigilance created; though leaving him always
to remark, portentously, on his probably having formed a relation, his probably enjoying a consciousness, unique in the
experience of man. People enough, first and last, had been in
terror of apparitions, but who had ever before so turned the
tables and become himself, in the apparitional world, an incalculable terror? He might have found this sublime had he
quite dared to think of it; but he didn't too much insist, truly,
on that side of his privilege. With habit and repetition he
gained to an extraordinary degree the power to penetrate the
dusk of distances and the darkness of corners, to resolve back
into their innocence the treacheries of uncertain light, the evil-
looking forms taken in the gloom by mere shadows, by accidents of the air, by shifting effects of perspective; putting
down his dim luminary he could still wander on without it,
pass into other rooms and, only knowing it was there behind
him in case of need, see his way about, visually project for his
purpose a comparative clearness. It made him feel, this acquired faculty, like some monstrous stealthy cat; he wondered
if he would have glared at these moments with large shining

yellow eyes, and what it mightn't verily be, for the poor hard-pressed *alter ego*, to be confronted with such a type.

He liked however the open shutters; he opened everywhere those Mrs. Muldoon had closed, closing them as carefully afterwards, so that she shouldn't notice: he liked—oh this he did like, and above all in the upper rooms!—the sense of the hard silver of the autumn stars through the window-panes, and scarcely less the flare of the street-lamps below, the white electric lustre which it would have taken curtains to keep out. This was human actual social; this was of the world he had lived in, and he was more at his ease certainly for the countenance, coldly general and impersonal, that all the while and in spite of his detachment it seemed to give him. He had support of course mostly in the rooms at the wide front and the prolonged side; it failed him considerably in the central shades and the parts at the back. But if he sometimes, on his rounds, was glad of his optical reach, so none the less often the rear of the house affected him as the very jungle of his prey. The place was there more subdivided; a large "extension" in particular, where small rooms for servants had been multiplied, abounded in nooks and corners, in closets and passages, in the ramifications especially of an ample back staircase over which he leaned, many a time, to look far down—not deterred from his gravity even while aware that he might, for a spectator, have figured some solemn simpleton playing at hide-and-seek. Outside in fact he might himself make that ironic *rapprochement*; but within the walls, and in spite of the clear windows, his consistency was proof against the cynical light of New York.

It had belonged to that idea of the exasperated consciousness of his victim to become a real test for him; since he had quite put it to himself from the first that, oh distinctly! he could "cultivate" his whole perception. He had felt it as above all open to cultivation—which indeed was but another name for his manner of spending his time. He was bringing it on, bringing it to perfection, by practice; in consequence of which it had grown so fine that he was now aware of impressions, attestations of his general postulate, that couldn't have broken upon him at once. This was the case more specifically with a phenomenon at last quite frequent for him in the upper rooms, the recognition—absolutely unmistakeable, and by a turn dating from a particular hour, his resumption of his campaign after a diplomatic drop, a calculated absence of three nights—of his being definitely followed, tracked at a distance carefully taken and to the express end that he should the less confidently, less arrogantly, appear to himself merely to pursue. It worried, it finally quite broke him up, for it proved, of all the conceivable impressions, the one least suited to his book. He was kept in sight while remaining himself—as regards the essence of his position—sightless, and his only recourse then was in abrupt turns, rapid recoveries of ground. He wheeled about, retracing his steps, as if he might so catch in his face at least the stirred air of some other quick revolution. It was indeed true that his fully dislocalised thought of these manœuvres recalled to him Pantaloon, at the Christmas farce, buffeted and tricked from behind by ubiquitous Harlequin; but it left intact the influence of the conditions themselves each time he was re-exposed to them, so that in fact this association, had he suffered it to become constant, would on a certain side have but ministered to his intenser gravity. He had made, as I have said, to create on the premises the baseless sense of a reprieve, his three absences; and the result of the third was to confirm the after-effect of the second.

On his return, that night—the night succeeding his last intermission—he stood in the hall and looked up the staircase with a certainty more intimate than any he had yet known. "He's *there*, at the top, and waiting—not, as in general, falling back for disappearance. He's holding his ground, and it's the first time—which is a proof, isn't it? that something has happened for him." So Brydon argued with his hand on the banister and his foot on the lowest stair; in which position he felt as never before the air chilled by his logic. He himself turned cold in it, for he seemed of a sudden to know what now was involved. "Harder pressed?—yes, he takes it in, with its thus making clear to him that I've come, as they say, 'to stay.' He finally doesn't like and can't bear it, in the sense, I mean, that his wrath, his menaced interest, now balances with his dread. I've hunted him till he has 'turned': that, up there, is what has happened—he's the fanged or the antlered animal brought at last to bay." There came to him, as I say—but determined by an influence beyond my notation!—the acuteness of this certainty; under which however the next moment he had broken into a sweat that he would as little have consented to attribute to fear as he would have dared immediately to act upon it for enterprise. It marked none the less a prodigious thrill, a thrill that represented sudden dismay, no doubt, but also represented, and with the selfsame throb, the strangest, the most joyous, possibly the next minute almost the proudest, duplication of consciousness.

"He has been dodging, retreating, hiding, but now, worked up to anger, he'll fight!"—this intense impression made a single mouthful, as it were, of terror and applause. But what was wondrous was that the applause, for the felt fact, was so eager, since, if it was his other self he was running to earth, this ineffable identity was thus in the last resort not unworthy of him. It bristled there—somewhere near at hand, however unseen still—as the hunted thing, even as the trodden worm of the adage *must* at last bristle; and Brydon at this instant tasted probably of a sensation more complex than had ever before found itself consistent with sanity. It was as if it would have shamed him that a character so associated with his own should triumphantly succeed in just skulking, should to the end not risk the open; so that the drop of this danger was, on the spot, a great lift of the whole situation. Yet with another rare shift of the same subtlety he was already trying to measure by how much more he himself might now be in peril of fear; so rejoicing that he could, in another form, actively inspire that fear, and simultaneously quaking for the form in which he might passively know it.

The apprehension of knowing it must after a little have grown in him, and the strangest moment of his adventure perhaps, the most memorable or really most interesting, afterwards, of his crisis, was the lapse of certain instants of concentrated conscious *combat*, the sense of a need to hold on to something, even after the manner of a man slipping and slipping on some awful incline; the vivid impulse, above all, to move, to act, to charge, somehow and upon something—to show himself, in a word, that he wasn't afraid. The state of "holding-on" was thus the state to which he was momentarily reduced; if there had been anything, in the great vacancy, to

seize, he would presently have been aware of having clutched
it as he might under a shock at home have clutched the nearest chair-back. He had been surprised at any rate—of this he
was aware—into something unprecedented since his original
appropriation of the place; he had closed his eyes, held them
tight, for a long minute, as with that instinct of dismay and
that terror of vision. When he opened them the room, the
other contiguous rooms, extraordinarily, seemed lighter—so
light, almost, that at first he took the change for day. He stood
firm, however that might be, just where he had paused; his
resistance had helped him—it was as if there were something
he had tided over. He knew after a little what this was—it had
been in the imminent danger of flight. He had stiffened his
will against going; without this he would have made for the
stairs, and it seemed to him that, still with his eyes closed, he
would have descended them, would have known how, straight
and swiftly, to the bottom.

Well, as he had held out, here he was—still at the top,
among the more intricate upper rooms and with the gauntlet
of the others, of all the rest of the house, still to run when it
should be his time to go. He would go at his time—only at
his time: didn't he go every night very much at the same hour?
He took out his watch—there was light for that: it was scarcely
a quarter past one, and he had never withdrawn so soon. He
reached his lodgings for the most part at two—with his walk
of a quarter of an hour. He would wait for the last quarter—
he wouldn't stir till then; and he kept his watch there with his
eyes on it, reflecting while he held it that this deliberate wait,
a wait with an effort, which he recognised, would serve perfectly for the attestation he desired to make. It would prove
his courage—unless indeed the latter might most be proved
by his budging at last from his place. What he mainly felt now
was that, since he hadn't originally scuttled, he had his dignities—which had never in his life seemed so many—all to
preserve and to carry aloft. This was before him in truth as a
physical image, an image almost worthy of an age of greater
romance. That remark indeed glimmered for him only to glow
the next instant with a finer light; since what age of romance,
after all, could have matched either the state of his mind or,
"objectively," as they said, the wonder of his situation? The

only difference would have been that, brandishing his dignities over his head as in a parchment scroll, he might then—
that is in the heroic time—have proceeded downstairs with a
drawn sword in his other grasp.

At present, really, the light he had set down on the mantel
of the next room would have to figure his sword; which uten-
sil, in the course of a minute, he had taken the requisite number of steps to possess himself of. The door between the
rooms was open, and from the second another door opened
to a third. These rooms, as he remembered, gave all three
upon a common corridor as well, but there was a fourth, beyond them, without issue save through the preceding. To have
moved, to have heard his step again, was appreciably a help;
though even in recognising this he lingered once more a little
by the chimney-piece on which his light had rested. When he
next moved, just hesitating where to turn, he found himself
considering a circumstance that, after his first and comparatively vague apprehension of it, produced in him the start that
often attends some pang of recollection, the violent shock of
having ceased happily to forget. He had come into sight of
the door in which the brief chain of communication ended
and which he now surveyed from the nearer threshold, the
one not directly facing it. Placed at some distance to the left
of this point, it would have admitted him to the last room of
the four, the room without other approach or egress, had it
not, to his intimate conviction, been closed *since* his former
visitation, the matter probably of a quarter of an hour before.
He stared with all his eyes at the wonder of the fact, arrested
again where he stood and again holding his breath while he
sounded its sense. Surely it had been *subsequently* closed—that
is it had been on his previous passage indubitably open!

He took it full in the face that something had happened
between—that he couldn't not have noticed before (by which
he meant on his original tour of all the rooms that evening)
that such a barrier had exceptionally presented itself. He had
indeed since that moment undergone an agitation so extraordinary that it might have muddled for him any earlier view;
and he tried to convince himself that he might perhaps then
have gone into the room and, inadvertently, automatically, on
coming out, have drawn the door after him. The difficulty

was that this exactly was what he never did; it was against his whole policy, as he might have said, the essence of which was to keep vistas clear. He had them from the first, as he was well aware, quite on the brain: the strange apparition, at the far end of one of them, of his baffled "prey" (which had become by so sharp an irony so little the term now to apply!) was the form of success his imagination had most cherished, projecting into it always a refinement of beauty. He had known fifty times the start of perception that had afterwards dropped; had fifty times gasped to himself "There!" under some fond brief hallucination. The house, as the case stood, admirably lent itself; he might wonder at the taste, the native architecture of the particular time, which could rejoice so in the multiplication of doors—the opposite extreme to the modern, the actual almost complete proscription of them; but it had fairly contributed to provoke this obsession of the presence encountered telescopically, as he might say, focussed and studied in diminishing perspective and as by a rest for the elbow.

It was with these considerations that his present attention was charged—they perfectly availed to make what he saw portentous. He *couldn't*, by any lapse, have blocked that aperture; and if he hadn't, if it was unthinkable, why what else was clear but that there had been another agent? Another agent?—he had been catching, as he felt, a moment back, the very breath of him; but when had he been so close as in this simple, this logical, this completely personal act? It was so logical, that is, that one might have *taken* it for personal; yet for what did Brydon take it, he asked himself, while, softly panting, he felt his eyes almost leave their sockets. Ah this time at last they *were*, the two, the opposed projections of him, in presence; and this time, as much as one would, the question of danger loomed. With it rose, as not before, the question of courage—for what he knew the blank face of the door to say to him was "Show us how much you have!" It stared, it glared back at him with that challenge; it put to him the two alternatives: should he just push it open or not? Oh to have this consciousness was to *think*—and to think, Brydon knew, as he stood there, was, with the lapsing moments, not to have acted! Not to have acted—that was the misery and the pang—was even still not to act; was in fact *all* to feel the thing in another, in a new and terrible way. How long did he pause and how long did he debate? There was presently nothing to measure it; for his vibration had already changed—as just by the effect of its intensity. Shut up there, at bay, defiant, and with the prodigy of the thing palpably proveably *done*, thus giving notice like some stark signboard—under that accession of accent the situation itself had turned; and Brydon at last remarkably made up his mind on what it had turned to.

It had turned altogether to a different admonition; to a supreme hint, for him, of the value of Discretion! This slowly dawned, no doubt—for it could take its time; so perfectly, on his threshold, had he been stayed, so little as yet had he either advanced or retreated. It was the strangest of all things that now when, by his taking ten steps and applying his hand to a latch, or even his shoulder and his knee, if necessary, to a panel, all the hunger of his prime need might have been met, his high curiosity crowned, his unrest assuaged—it was amazing, but it was also exquisite and rare, that insistence should have, at a touch, quite dropped from him. Discretion—he jumped at that; and yet not, verily, at such a pitch, because it saved his nerves or his skin, but because, much more valuably, it saved the situation. When I say he "jumped" at it I feel the consonance of this term with the fact that—at the end indeed of I know not how long—he did move again, he crossed straight to the door. He wouldn't touch it—it seemed now that he might *if* he would: he would only just wait there a little, to show, to prove, that he wouldn't. He had thus another station, close to the thin partition by which revelation was denied him; but with his eyes bent and his hands held off in a mere intensity of stillness. He listened as if there had been something to hear, but this attitude, while it lasted, was his own communication. "If you won't then—good: I spare you and I give up. You affect me as by the appeal positively for pity: you convince me that for reasons rigid and sublime—what do I know?—we both of us should have suffered. I respect them then, and, though moved and privileged as, I believe, it has never been given to man, I retire, I renounce—never, on my honour, to try again. So rest for ever—and let *me*!"

That, for Brydon was the deep sense of this last demonstration—solemn, measured, directed, as he felt it to be. He
brought it to a close, he turned away; and now verily he knew
how deeply he had been stirred. He retraced his steps, taking
up his candle, burnt, he observed, well-nigh to the socket,
and marking again, lighten it as he would, the distinctness of
his footfall; after which, in a moment, he knew himself at the
other side of the house. He did here what he had not yet
done at these hours—he opened half a casement, one of those
in the front, and let in the air of the night; a thing he would
have taken at any time previous for a sharp rupture of his spell.
His spell was broken now, and it didn't matter—broken by
his concession and his surrender, which made it idle henceforth that he should ever come back. The empty street—its
other life so marked even by the great lamplit vacancy—was
within call, within touch; he stayed there as to be in it again,
high above it though he was still perched; he watched as for
some comforting common fact, some vulgar human note, the
passage of a scavenger or a thief, some night-bird however
base. He would have blessed that sign of life; he would have
welcomed positively the slow approach of his friend the policeman, whom he had hitherto only sought to avoid, and was
not sure that if the patrol had come into sight he mightn't
have felt the impulse to get into relation with it, to hail it, on
some pretext, from his fourth floor.

The pretext that wouldn't have been too silly or too compromising, the explanation that would have saved his dignity
and kept his name, in such a case, out of the papers, was not
definite to him: he was so occupied with the thought of recording his Discretion—as an effect of the vow he had just
uttered to his intimate adversary—that the importance of this
loomed large and something had overtaken all ironically his
sense of proportion. If there had been a ladder applied to the
front of the house, even one of the vertiginous perpendiculars
employed by painters and roofers and sometimes left standing
overnight, he would have managed somehow, astride of the
window-sill, to compass by outstretched leg and arm that
mode of descent. If there had been some such uncanny thing
as he had found in his room at hotels, a workable fire-escape
in the form of notched cable or a canvas shoot, he would have

availed himself of it as a proof—well, of his present delicacy. He nursed that sentiment, as the question stood, a little in vain, and even—at the end of he scarce knew, once more, how long—found it, as by the action on his mind of the failure of response of the outer world, sinking back to vague anguish. It seemed to him he had waited an age for some stir of the great grim hush; the life of the town was itself under a spell— so unnaturally, up and down the whole prospect of known and rather ugly objects, the blankness and the silence lasted. Had they ever, he asked himself, the hard-faced houses, which had begun to look livid in the dim dawn, had they ever spoken so little to any need of his spirit? Great builded voids, great crowded stillnesses put on, often, in the heart of cities, for the small hours, a sort of sinister mask, and it was of this large collective negation that Brydon presently became conscious— all the more that the break of day was, almost incredibly, now at hand, proving to him what a night he had made of it.

He looked again at his watch, saw what had become of his time-values (he had taken hours for minutes—not, as in other tense situations, minutes for hours) and the strange air of the streets was but the weak, the sullen flush of a dawn in which everything was still locked up. His choked appeal from his own open window had been the sole note of life, and he could but break off at last as for a worse despair. Yet while so deeply demoralised he was capable again of an impulse denoting—at least by his present measure—extraordinary resolution; of re-tracing his steps to the spot where he had turned cold with the extinction of his last pulse of doubt as to there being in the place another presence than his own. This required an effort strong enough to sicken him; but he had his reason, which overmastered for the moment everything else. There was the whole of the rest of the house to traverse, and how should he screw himself to that if the door he had seen closed were at present open? He could hold to the idea that the closing had practically been for him an act of mercy, a chance offered him to descend, depart, get off the ground and never again profane it. This conception held together, it worked; but what it meant for him depended now clearly on the amount of forbearance his recent action, or rather his recent inaction, had engendered. The image of the "presence," whatever it was, waiting there for him to go—this image had not yet been so concrete for his nerves as when he stopped short of the point at which certainty would have come to him. For, with all his resolution, or more exactly with all his dread, he did stop short—he hung back from really seeing. The risk was too great and his fear too definite: it took at this moment an awful specific form.

He knew—yes, as he had never known anything—that, *should* he see the door open, it would all too abjectly be the end of him. It would mean that the agent of his shame—for his shame was the deep abjection—was once more at large and in general possession; and what glared him thus in the face was the act that this would determine for him. It would send him straight about to the window he had left open, and by that window, be long ladder and dangling rope as absent as they would, he saw himself uncontrollably insanely fatally take his way to the street. The hideous chance of this he at least could avert; but he could only avert it by recoiling in time from assurance. He had the whole house to deal with, this fact was still there; only he now knew that uncertainty alone could start him. He stole back from where he had checked himself—merely to do so was suddenly like safety— and, making blindly for the greater staircase, left gaping rooms and sounding passages behind. Here was the top of the stairs, with a fine large dim descent and three spacious landings to mark off. His instinct was all for mildness, but his feet were harsh on the floors, and, strangely, when he had in a couple of minutes become aware of this, it counted somehow for help. He couldn't have spoken, the tone of his voice would have scared him, and the common conceit or resource of "whistling in the dark" (whether literally or figuratively) have appeared basely vulgar; yet he liked none the less to hear him-self go, and when he had reached his first landing—taking it all with no rush, but quite steadily—that stage of success drew from him a gasp of relief.

The house, withal, seemed immense, the scale of space again inordinate; the open rooms, to no one of which his eyes deflected, gloomed in their shuttered state like mouths of cav-erns; only the high skylight that formed the crown of the deep well created for him a medium in which he could advance, but which might have been, for queerness of colour, some watery under-world. He tried to think of something noble, as that his property was really grand, a splendid possession; but this nobleness took the form too of the clear delight with which he was finally to sacrifice it. They might come in now, the builders, the destroyers—they might come as soon as they would. At the end of two flights he had dropped to another zone, and from the middle of the third, with only one more left, he recognised the influence of the lower windows, of half-drawn blinds, of the occasional gleam of streetlamps, of the glazed spaces of the vestibule. This was the bottom of the sea, which showed an illumination of its own and which he even saw paved—when at a given moment he drew up to sink a long look over the banisters—with the marble squares of his childhood. By that time indubitably he felt, as he might have said in a commoner cause, better; it had allowed him to stop and draw breath, and the ease increased with the sight of the old black-and-white slabs. But what he most felt was that now surely, with the element of impunity pulling him as by hard firm hands, the case was settled for what he might have seen above had he dared that last look. The closed door, blessedly remote now, was still closed—and he had only in short to reach that of the house.

He came down further, he crossed the passage forming the access to the last flight; and if here again he stopped an instant it was almost for the sharpness of the thrill of assured escape. It made him shut his eyes—which opened again to the straight slope of the remainder of the stairs. Here was impunity still, but impunity almost excessive; inasmuch as the sidelights and the high fan-tracery of the entrance were glimmering straight into the hall; an appearance produced, he the next instant saw, by the fact that the vestibule gaped wide, that the hinged halves of the inner door had been thrown far back. Out of that again the *question* sprang at him, making his eyes, as he felt, half-start from his head, as they had done, at the top of the house, before the sign of the other door. If he had left that one open, hadn't he left this one closed, and wasn't he now in *most* immediate presence of some inconceivable occult activity? It was as sharp, the question, as a knife in his side, but the answer hung fire still and seemed to lose itself in the vague darkness to which the thin admitted dawn, glimmering archwise over the whole outer door, made a semicircular margin, a cold silvery nimbus that seemed to play a little as he looked—to shift and expand and contract.

It was as if there had been something within it, protected by indistinctness and corresponding in extent with the opaque surface behind, the painted panels of the last barrier to his escape, of which the key was in his pocket. The indistinctness mocked him even while he stared, affected him as somehow shrouding or challenging certitude, so that after faltering an instant on his step he let himself go with the sense that here *was* at last something to meet, to touch, to take, to know— something all unnatural and dreadful, but to advance upon which was the condition for him either of liberation or of supreme defeat. The penumbra, dense and dark, was the virtual screen of a figure which stood in it as still as some image erect in a niche or as some black-vizored sentinel guarding a treasure. Brydon was to know afterwards, was to recall and make out, the particular thing he had believed during the rest of his descent. He saw, in its great grey glimmering margin, the central vagueness diminish, and he felt it to be taking the very form toward which, for so many days, the passion of his curiosity had yearned. It gloomed, it loomed, it was something, it was somebody, the prodigy of a personal presence.

Rigid and conscious, spectral yet human, a man of his own substance and stature waited there to measure himself with his power to dismay. This only could it be—this only till he recognised, with his advance, that what made the face dim was the pair of raised hands that covered it and in which, so far from being offered in defiance, it was buried as for dark deprecation. So Brydon, before him, took him in; with every fact of him now, in the higher light, hard and acute—his planted stillness, his vivid truth, his grizzled bent head and white masking hands, his queer actuality of evening-dress, of dangling double eye-glass, of gleaming silk lappet and white linen, of pearl button and gold watch-guard and polished shoe. No portrait by a great modern master could have presented him with more intensity, thrust him out of his frame with more art, as if there had been "treatment," of the consummate sort, in his every shade and salience. The revulsion, for our friend, had become, before he knew it, immense—this drop, in the act of apprehension, to the sense of his adversary's inscrutable manœuvre. That meaning at least, while he gaped, it offered him; for he could but gape at his other self in this other anguish, gape as a proof that *he*, standing there for the achieved, the enjoyed, the triumphant life, couldn't be faced in his triumph. Wasn't the proof in the splendid covering hands, strong and completely spread?—so spread and so intentional that, in spite of a special verity that surpassed every other, the fact that one of these hands had lost two fingers, which were reduced to stumps, as if accidentally shot away, the face was effectually guarded and saved.

"Saved," though, *would* it be?—Brydon breathed his wonder till the very impunity of his attitude and the very insistence of his eyes produced, as he felt, a sudden stir which showed the next instant as a deeper portent, while the head raised itself, the betrayal of a braver purpose. The hands, as he looked, began to move, to open; then, as if deciding in a flash, dropped from the face and left it uncovered and presented. Horror, with the sight, had leaped into Brydon's throat, gasping there in a sound he couldn't utter; for the bared identity was too hideous as *his*, and his glare was the passion of his protest. The face, *that* face, Spencer Brydon's?—he searched it still, but looking away from it in dismay and denial, falling straight from his height of sublimity. It was unknown, inconceivable, awful, disconnected from any possibility—! He had been "sold," he inwardly moaned, stalking such game as this: the presence before him was a presence, the horror within him a horror, but the waste of his nights had been only grotesque and the success of his adventure an irony. Such an identity fitted his at *no* point, made its alternative monstrous. A thousand times yes, as it came upon him nearer now—the face was the face of a stranger. It came upon him nearer now, quite as one of those expanding fantastic images projected by the magic lantern of childhood; for the stranger, whoever he might be, evil, odious, blatant, vulgar, had advanced as for aggression, and he knew himself give ground. Then harder pressed still, sick with the force of his shock, and falling back as under the hot breath and the roused passion of a life larger than his own, a rage of personality before which his own collapsed, he felt the whole vision turn to darkness and his very feet give way. His head went round; he was going; he had gone.

III

What had next brought him back, clearly—though after how long?—was Mrs. Muldoon's voice, coming to him from quite near, from so near that he seemed presently to see her as kneeling on the ground before him while he lay looking up at her; himself not wholly on the ground, but half-raised and upheld—conscious, yes, of tenderness of support and, more particularly, of a head pillowed in extraordinary softness and fainly refreshing fragrance. He considered, he wondered, his wit but half at his service; then another face intervened, bending more directly over him, and he finally knew that Alice Staverton had made her lap an ample and perfect cushion to him, and that she had to this end seated herself on the lowest degree of the staircase, the rest of his long person remaining stretched on his old black-and-white slabs. They were cold, these marble squares of his youth; but *he* somehow was not, in this rich return of consciousness—the most wonderful hour, little by little, that he had ever known, leaving him, as it did, so gratefully, so abysmally passive, and yet as with a treasure of intelligence waiting all round him for quiet appropriation; dissolved, he might call it, in the air of the place and producing the golden glow of a late autumn afternoon. He had come back, yes—come back from further away than any man but himself had ever travelled; but it was strange how with this sense what he had come back *to* seemed really the great thing, and as if his prodigious journey had been all for the sake of it. Slowly but surely his consciousness grew, his vision of his state thus completing itself: he had been miraculously *carried* back—lifted and carefully borne as from where he had been picked up, the uttermost end of an interminable grey passage. Even with this he was suffered to rest, and what had now brought him to knowledge was the break in the long mild motion.

It had brought him to knowledge, to knowledge—yes, this was the beauty of his state; which came to resemble more and more that of a man who has gone to sleep on some news of a great inheritance, and then, after dreaming it away, after profaning it with matters strange to it, has waked up again to serenity of certitude and has only to lie and watch it grow. This was the drift of his patience—that he had only to let it shine on him. He must moreover, with intermissions, still have been lifted and borne; since why and how else should he have known himself, later on, with the afternoon glow intenser, no longer at the foot of his stairs—situated as these now seemed at that dark other end of his tunnel—but on a deep window-bench of his high saloon, over which had been spread, couch-fashion, a mantle of soft stuff lined with grey fur that was familiar to his eyes and that one of his hands kept fondly feeling as for its pledge of truth. Mrs. Muldoon's face had gone, but the other, the second he had recognised, hung over him in a way that showed how he was still propped and pillowed. He took it all in, and the more he took it the more it seemed to suffice: he was as much at peace as if he had had food and drink. It was the two women who had found him, on Mrs. Muldoon's having plied, at her usual hour, her latch-key—and on her having above all arrived while Miss Staverton still lingered near the house. She had been turning away, all anxiety, from worrying the vain bell-handle—her calculation having been of the hour of the good woman's visit; but the latter, blessedly, had come up while she was still there, and they had entered together. He had then lain, beyond the vestibule, very much as he was lying now—quite, that is, as he appeared to have fallen, but all so wondrously without bruise or gash; only in a depth of stupor. What he most took in, however, at present, with the steadier clearance, was that Alice Staverton had for a long unspeakable moment not doubted he was dead.

"It must have been that I *was*." He made it out as she held him. "Yes—I can only have died. You brought me literally to life. Only," he wondered, his eyes rising to her, "only, in the name of all the benedictions, how?"

It took her but an instant to bend her face and kiss him, and something in the manner of it, and in the way her hands clasped and locked his head while he felt the cool charity and virtue of her lips, something in all this beatitude somehow answered everything. "And now I keep you," she said.

"Oh keep me, keep me!" he pleaded while her face still hung over him: in response to which it dropped again and stayed close, clingingly close. It was the seal of their situation—of which he tasted the impress for a long blissful moment in silence. But he came back. "Yet how did you know—?"

"I was uneasy. You were to have come, you remember—and you had sent no word."

"Yes, I remember—I was to have gone to you at one to-day." It caught on to their "old" life and relation—which were so near and so far. "I was still out there in my strange darkness—where was it, what was it? I must have stayed there so long." He could but wonder at the depth and the duration of his swoon.

"Since last night?" she asked with a shade of fear for her possible indiscretion.

"Since this morning—it must have been: the cold dim dawn of to-day. Where have I been," he vaguely wailed, "where have I been?" He felt her hold him close, and it was as if this helped him now to make in all security his mild moan. "What a long dark day!"

All in her tenderness she had waited a moment. "In the cold dim dawn?" she quavered.

But he had already gone on piecing together the parts of the whole prodigy. "As I didn't turn up you came straight—?"

She barely cast about. "I went first to your hotel—where they told me of your absence. You had dined out last evening and hadn't been back since. But they appeared to know you had been at your club."

"So you had the idea of *this*—?"

"Of what?" she asked in a moment.

"Well—of what has happened."

"I believed at least you'd have been here. I've known, all along," she said, "that you've been coming."

" 'Known' it—?"

"Well, I've believed it. I said nothing to you after that talk we had a month ago—but I felt sure. I knew you *would*," she declared.

"That I'd persist, you mean?"

"That you'd see him."

"Ah but I didn't!" cried Brydon with his long wail. "There's somebody—an awful beast; whom I brought, too horribly, to bay. But it's not me."

At this she bent over him again, and her eyes were in his eyes. "No—it's not you." And it was as if, while her face hovered, he might have made out in it, hadn't it been so near, some particular meaning blurred by a smile. "No, thank heaven," she repeated—"it's not you! Of course it wasn't to have been."

"Ah but it *was*," he gently insisted. And he stared before him now as he had been staring for so many weeks. "I was to have known myself."

"You couldn't!" she returned consolingly. And then reverting, and as if to account further for what she had herself done, "But it wasn't only *that*, that you hadn't been at home," she went on. "I waited till the hour at which we had found Mrs. Muldoon that day of my going with you; and she arrived, as I've told you, while, failing to bring any one to the door, I lingered in my despair on the steps. After a little, if she hadn't come, by such a mercy, I should have found means to hunt her up. But it wasn't," said Alice Staverton, as if once more with her fine intention—"it wasn't only that."

His eyes, as he lay, turned back to her. "What more then?"

She met it, the wonder she had stirred. "In the cold dim dawn, you say? Well, in the cold dim dawn of this morning I too saw you."

"Saw *me*—?"

"Saw *him*," said Alice Staverton. "It must have been at the same moment."

He lay an instant taking it in—as if he wished to be quite reasonable. "At the same moment?"

"Yes—in my dream again, the same one I've named to you. He came back to me. Then I knew it for a sign. He had come to you."

At this Brydon raised himself; he had to see her better. She helped him when she understood his movement, and he sat up, steadying himself beside her there on the window-bench and with his right hand grasping her left. "*He* didn't come to me."

"You came to yourself," she beautifully smiled.

"Ah I've come to myself now—thanks to you, dearest. But this brute, with his awful face—this brute's a black stranger. He's none of *me*, even as I *might* have been," Brydon sturdily declared.

But she kept the clearness that was like the breath of infallibility. "Isn't the whole point that you'd have been different?"

He almost scowled for it. "As different as *that*—?"

Her look again was more beautiful to him than the things of this world. "Haven't you exactly wanted to know *how* different? So this morning," she said, "you appeared to me."

"Like *him*?"

"A black stranger!"

"Then how did you know it was I?"

"Because, as I told you weeks ago, my mind, my imagination, had worked so over what you might, what you mightn't have been—to show you, you see, how I've thought of you. In the midst of that you came to me—that my wonder might be answered. So I knew," she went on; "and believed that, since the question held you too so fast, as you told me that day, you too would see for yourself. And when this morning I again saw I knew it would be because you had—and also then, from the first moment, because you somehow wanted me. *He* seemed to tell me of that. So why," she strangely smiled, "shouldn't I like him?"

It brought Spencer Brydon to his feet. "You 'like' that horror—?"

"I *could* have liked him. And to me," she said, "he was no horror. I had accepted him."

" 'Accepted'—?" Brydon oddly sounded.

"Before, for the interest of his difference—yes. And as *I* didn't disown him, as *I* knew him—which you at last, confronted with him in his difference, so cruelly didn't, my dear— well, he must have been, you see, less dreadful to me. And it may have pleased him that I pitied him."

She was beside him on her feet, but still holding his hand— still with her arm supporting him. But though it all brought for him thus a dim light, "You 'pitied' him?" he grudgingly, resentfully asked.

"He has been unhappy, he has been ravaged," she said.

"And haven't I been unhappy? Am not I—you've only to look at me!—ravaged?"

"Ah I don't say I like him *better*," she granted after a thought. "But he's grim, he's worn—and things have happened to him. He doesn't make shift, for sight, with your charming monocle."

"No"—it struck Brydon: "I couldn't have sported mine 'downtown.' They'd have guyed me there."

"His great convex pince-nez—I saw it, I recognised the kind—is for his poor ruined sight. And his poor right hand—!"

"Ah!" Brydon winced—whether for his proved identity or for his lost fingers. Then, "He has a million a year," he lucidly added. "But he hasn't you."

"And he isn't—no, he isn't—*you*!" she murmured as he drew her to his breast.

"The Velvet Glove"

H E THOUGHT he had already, poor John Berridge, tasted in their fulness the sweets of success; but nothing yet had been more charming to him than when the young Lord, as he irresistibly and, for greater certitude, quite correctly figured him, fairly sought out, in Paris, the new literary star that had begun to hang, with a fresh red light, over the vast, even though rather confused, Anglo-Saxon horizon; positively approaching that celebrity with a shy and artless appeal. The young Lord invoked on this occasion the celebrity's prized judgment of a special literary case; and Berridge could take the whole manner of it for one of the "quaintest" little acts displayed to his amused eyes, up to now, on the stage of European society—albeit these eyes were quite aware, in general, of missing everywhere no more of the human scene than possible, and of having of late been particularly awake to the large extensions of it spread before him (since so he could but fondly read his fate) under the omen of his prodigious "hit." It was because of his hit that he was having rare opportunities—of which he was so honestly and humbly proposing, as he would have said, to make the most: it was because every one in the world (so far had the thing gone) was reading "The Heart of Gold" as just a slightly too fat volume, or sitting out the same as just a fifth-act too long play, that he found himself floated on a tide he would scarce have dared to show his favourite hero sustained by, found a hundred agreeable and interesting things happen to him which were all, one way or another, affluents of the golden stream.

The great renewed resonance—renewed by the incredible luck of the play—was always in his ears without so much as a conscious turn of his head to listen; so that the queer world of his fame was not the mere usual field of the Anglo-Saxon boom, but positively the bottom of the *whole* theatric sea, unplumbed source of the wave that had borne him in the course of a year or two over German, French, Italian, Russian, Scandinavian foot-lights. Paris itself really appeared for the hour the centre of his cyclone, with reports and "returns," to say nothing of agents and emissaries, converging from the minor capitals; though his impatience was scarce the less keen to get back to London, where his work had had no such critical excoriation to survive, no such lesson of anguish to learn, as it had received at the hand of supreme authority, of that French authority which was in such a matter the only one to be artistically reckoned with. If his spirit indeed had had to reckon with it his fourth act practically hadn't: it continued to make him blush every night for the public more even than the inimitable *feuilleton* had made him blush for himself.

This had figured, however, after all, the one bad drop in his cup; so that, for the rest, his high-water mark might well have been, that evening at Gloriani's studio, the approach of his odd and charming applicant, vaguely introduced at the latter's very own request by their hostess, who, with an honest, helpless, genial gesture, washed her fat begemmed hands of the name and identity of either, but left the fresh, fair, ever so habitually assured, yet ever so easily awkward Englishman with his plea to put forth. There was that in this pleasant personage which could still make Berridge wonder what conception of profit from him might have, all incalculably, taken form in such a head—these being truly the last intrenchments of our hero's modesty. He wondered, the splendid young man, he wondered awfully, he wondered (it was unmistakable) quite nervously, he wondered, to John's ardent and acute imagination, quite beautifully, if the author of "The Heart of Gold" would mind just looking at a book by a friend of his, a great friend, which he himself believed rather clever, and had in fact found very charming, but as to which—if it really wouldn't bore Mr. Berridge—he should so like the verdict of some one who knew. His friend was awfully ambitious, and he thought there was something in it—with all of which might he send the book to any address?

Berridge thought of many things while the young Lord thus charged upon him, and it was odd that no one of them was any question of the possible worth of the offered achievement—which, for that matter, was certain to be of the quality of *all* the books, to say nothing of the plays, and the projects for plays, with which, for some time past, he had seen his daily post-bag distended. He had made out, on looking at these things, no difference at all from one to the other. Here, however, was something more—something that made his fellow-guest's overture *independently* interesting and, as he might imagine, important. He smiled, he was friendly and vague; said "A work of fiction, I suppose?" and that he didn't pretend ever to pronounce, that he in fact quite hated, always, to have to, not "knowing," as he felt, any better than any one else; but would gladly look at anything, under that demur, if it would give any pleasure. Perhaps the very brightest and most diamond-like twinkle he had yet seen the star of his renown emit was just the light brought into his young Lord's eyes by this so easy consent to oblige. It was easy because the presence before him was from moment to moment referring itself back to some recent observation or memory; something caught somewhere, within a few weeks or months, as he had moved about, and that seemed to flutter forth at this stir of the folded leaves of his recent experience very much as a gathered, faded flower, placed there for "pressing," might drop from between the pages of a volume opened at hazard.

He had seen him before, this splendid and sympathetic person—whose flattering appeal was by no means *all* that made him sympathetic; he had met him, had noted, had wondered about him, had in fact imaginatively, intellectually, so to speak, quite yearned over him, in some conjunction lately, though ever so fleetingly, apprehended: which circumstance constituted precisely an association as tormenting, for the few minutes, as it was vague, and set him to sounding, intensely and vainly, the face that itself figured everything agreeable except recognition. He couldn't remember, and the young man didn't; distinctly, yes, they had been in presence, during the previous winter, by some chance of travel, through Sicily, through Italy, through the south of France, but his *Seigneurie* —so Berridge liked exotically to phrase it—had then (in ignorance of the present reasons) not noticed *him*. It was positive for the man of established identity, all the while too, and through the perfect lucidity of his sense of achievement in an air "conducting" nothing but the loudest bang, that this was fundamentally much less remarkable than the fact of his being made up to in such a quarter now. That was the disservice, in a manner, of one's having so much imagination: the mysterious values of other types kept looming larger before you than the doubtless often higher but comparatively familiar ones of your own, and if you had anything of the artist's real feeling for life the attraction and amusement of possibilities so projected were worth more to you, in nineteen moods out of twenty, than the sufficiency, the serenity, the felicity, whatever it might be, of your stale personal certitudes. You were intellectually, you were "artistically" rather abject, in fine, if your curiosity (in the grand sense of the term) wasn't worth more to you than your dignity. What *was* your dignity, "anyway," but just the consistency of your curiosity, and what moments were ever so ignoble for you as, under the blighting breath of the false gods, stupid conventions, traditions, examples, your lapses from that consistency? His *Seigneurie*, at all events, delightfully, hadn't the least real idea of what any John Berridge was talking about, and the latter felt that if he had been less beautifully witless, and thereby less true to his right figure, it might scarce have been forgiven him.

His right figure was that of life in irreflective joy and at the highest thinkable level of prepared security and unconscious insolence. What was the pale page of fiction compared with the intimately personal adventure that, in almost any direction, he would have been all so stupidly, all so gallantly, all so instinctively and, by every presumption, so prevailingly ready for? Berridge would have given six months' "royalties" for even an hour of his looser dormant consciousness—since one was oneself, after all, no worm, but an heir of all the ages too—and yet without being able to supply chapter and verse for the felt, the huge difference. His *Seigneurie* was tall and straight, but so, thank goodness, was the author of "The Heart of Gold," who had no such vulgar "mug" either; and there was no intrinsic inferiority in being a bit inordinately, and so it might have seemed a bit strikingly, black-browed instead of being fair as the morning. Again while his new friend delivered himself our own tried in vain to place him; he indulged in plenty of pleasant, if rather restlessly headlong sound, the confessed incoherence of a happy mortal who had always many things "on," and who, while waiting at any moment for connections and consummations, had fallen into the way of talking, as they said, all artlessly, and a trifle more betrayingly, against time. He would always be having appointments, and somehow of a high "romantic" order, to keep, and the imperfect punctualities of others to wait for—though who would be of a quality to make such a pampered personage wait very much our young analyst could only enjoy asking himself. There were women who might be of a quality—half a dozen of those perhaps, of those alone, about the world; our friend was as sure of this, by the end of four minutes, as if he knew all about it.

After saying he would send him the book the young Lord indeed dropped that subject; he had asked where he might send it, and had had an "Oh, I shall remember!" on John's mention of an hotel; but he had made no further dash into literature, and it was ten to one that this would be the last the distinguished author might hear of the volume. Such again was a note of these high existences—that made one content to ask of them no whit of other consistency than that of carrying off the particular occasion, whatever it might be, in a dazzle of amiability and felicity and leaving *that* as a sufficient trace of their passage. Sought and achieved consistency was but an angular, a secondary motion; compared with the air of complete freedom it might have an effect of deformity. There was no placing this figure of radiant ease, for Berridge, in any relation that didn't appear not good enough—that is among the relations that hadn't been too good for Berridge himself. He was all right where he was; the great Gloriani somehow made that law; his house, with his supreme artistic position, was good enough for any one, and to-night in especial there were charming people, more charming than our friend could recall from any other scene, as the natural train or circle, as he might say, of such a presence. For an instant he thought he had got the face as a specimen of imperturbability watched, with wonder, across the hushed rattle of roulette at Monte-Carlo; but this quickly became as improbable as any question of a vulgar *table d'hôte*, or a steam-boat deck, or a herd of fellow-pilgrims cicerone-led, or even an opera-box serving, during a performance, for frame of a type observed from the stalls. One placed young gods and goddesses only when one placed them on Olympus, and it met the case, always, that they were of Olympian race, and that they glimmered for one,

at the best, through their silver cloud, like the visiting apparitions in an epic.

This was brief and beautiful indeed till something happened
that gave it, for Berridge, on the spot, a prodigious extension—an extension really as prodigious, after a little, as if he
had suddenly seen the silver clouds multiply and then the
whole of Olympus presently open. Music, breaking upon the
large air, enjoined immediate attention, and in a moment he
was listening, with the rest of the company, to an eminent
tenor, who stood by the piano; and was aware, with it, that
his Englishman had turned away and that in the vast, rich,
tapestried room where, in spite of figures and objects so numerous, clear spaces, wide vistas, and, as they might be called,
becoming situations abounded, there had been from elsewhere, at the signal of unmistakable song, a rapid accession
of guests. At first he but took this in, and the way that several
young women, for whom seats had been found, looked
charming in the rapt attitude; while even the men, mostly
standing and grouped, "composed," in their stillness, scarce
less impressively, under the sway of the divine voice. It ruled
the scene, to the last intensity, and yet our young man's fine
sense found still a resource in the range of the eyes, without
sound or motion, while all the rest of consciousness was held
down as by a hand mailed in silver. It was better, in this way,
than the opera—John alertly thought of that: the composition
sung might be Wagnerian, but no Tristram, no Iseult, no Parsifal and, no Kundry of them all could ever show, could ever
"act" to the music, as our friend had thus the power of seeing
his dear contemporaries of either sex (armoured *they* so otherwise than in cheap Teutonic tinsel!) just continuously and
inscrutably sit to it.

It made, the whole thing together, an enchantment amid
which he had in truth, at a given moment, ceased to distinguish parts—so that he was himself certainly at last soaring as
high as the singer's voice and forgetting, in a lost gaze at the
splendid ceiling, everything of the occasion but what his intelligence poured into it. This, as happened, was a flight so
sublime that by the time he had dropped his eyes again a
cluster of persons near the main door had just parted to give
way to a belated lady who slipped in, through the gap made

for her, and stood for some minutes full in his view. It was a proof of the perfect hush that no one stirred to offer her a seat, and her entrance, in her high grace, had yet been so noiseless that she could remain at once immensely exposed and completely unabashed. For Berridge, once more, if the scenic show before him so melted into the music, here precisely might have been the heroine herself advancing to the foot-lights at her cue. The interest deepened to a thrill, and everything, at the touch of his recognition of this personage, absolutely the most beautiful woman now present, fell exquisitely together and gave him what he had been wanting from the moment of his taking in his young Englishman.

It was there, the missing connection: her arrival had on the instant lighted it by a flash. Olympian herself, supremely, divinely Olympian, she had arrived, could *only* have arrived, for the one person present of really equal race, our young man's late converser, whose flattering demonstration might now stand for one of the odd extravagant forms taken by nervous impatience. This charming, this dazzling woman had been one member of the couple disturbed, to his intimate conviction, the autumn previous, on his being pushed by the officials, at the last moment, into a compartment of the train that was to take him from Cremona to Mantua—where, failing a stop, he had had to keep his place. The other member, by whose felt but unseized identity he had been haunted, was the unconsciously insolent form of guaranteed happiness he had just been engaged with. The sense of the admirable intimacy that, having taken its precautions, had not reckoned with his irruption—this image had remained with him; to say nothing of the interest of aspect of the associated figures, so stamped somehow with rarity, so beautifully distinct from the common occupants of padded corners, and yet on the subject of whom, for the romantic structure he was immediately to raise, he had not had a scrap of evidence.

If he had imputed to them conditions it was all his own doing: it came from his inveterate habit of abysmal imputation, the snatching of the ell wherever the inch peeped out, without which where would have been the tolerability of life? It didn't matter now what he had imputed—and he always held that his expenses of imputation were, at the worst, a compliment to those inspiring them. It only mattered that each of the pair had been then what he really saw each now—full, that is, of the pride of their youth and beauty and fortune and freedom, though at the same time particularly preoccupied: preoccupied, that is, with the affairs, and above all with the passions, of Olympus. Who had they been, and what? Whence had they come, whither were they bound, what tie united them, what adventure engaged, what felicity, tempered by what peril, magnificently, dramatically attended? These had been his questions, all so inevitable and so impertinent, at the time, and to the exclusion of any scruples over his not postulating an inane honeymoon, his not taking the "tie," as he should doubtless properly have done, for the mere blest matrimonial; and he now retracted not one of them, flushing as they did before him again with their old momentary life. To feel his two friends renewedly in presence—friends of the fleeting hour though they had but been, and with whom he had exchanged no sign save the vaguest of salutes on finally relieving them of his company—was only to be conscious that he hadn't, on the spot, done them, so to speak, half justice, and that, for his superior entertainment, there would be ever so much more of them to come.

II

It might already have been coming indeed, with an immense stride, when, scarce more than ten minutes later, he was aware that the distinguished stranger had brought the Princess straight across the room to speak to him. He had failed in the interval of any glimpse of their closer meeting; for the great tenor had sung another song and then stopped, immediately on which Madame Gloriani had made his pulse quicken to a different, if not to a finer, throb by hovering before him once more with the man in the world he most admired, as it were, looking at him over her shoulder. The man in the world he most admired, the greatest then of contemporary Dramatists—and bearing, independently, the name inscribed if not in deepest incision at least in thickest gilding on the rich re-creative roll—this prodigious personage was actually to suffer "presentation" to him at the good lady's generous but inef-

fectual hands, and had in fact the next instant, left alone with
him, bowed, in formal salutation, the massive, curly, witty
head, so "romantic" yet so modern, so "artistic" and ironic
yet somehow so civic, so Gallic yet somehow so cosmic, his
personal vision of which had not hitherto transcended that of
the possessor of a signed and framed photograph in a consecrated quarter of a writing-table.

It was positive, however, that poor John was afterward to
remember of this conjunction nothing whatever but the fact
of the great man's looking at him very hard, straight in the
eyes, and of his not having himself scrupled to do as much,
and with a confessed intensity of appetite. It was improbable,
he was to recognise, that they had, for the few minutes, only
stared and grimaced, like pitted boxers or wrestlers; but what
had abode with him later on, none the less, was just the cherished memory of his not having so lost presence of mind as
to fail of feeding on his impression. It was precious and precarious, that was perhaps all there would be of it; and his
subsequent consciousness was quite to cherish this queer view
of the silence, neither awkward nor empty nor harsh, but on
the contrary quite charged and brimming, that represented
for him his use, his unforgettable enjoyment in fact, of his
opportunity. Had nothing passed in words? Well, no misery
of murmured "homage," thank goodness; though something
must have been said, certainly, to lead up, as they put it at the
theatre, to John's having asked the head of the profession,
before they separated, if he by chance knew who the so radiantly handsome young woman might be, the one who had
so lately come in and who wore the pale yellow dress, of the
strange tone, and the magnificent pearls. They must have separated soon, it was further to have been noted; since it was
before the advance of the pair, their wonderful dazzling
charge upon him, that he had distinctly seen the great man,
at a distance again, block out from his sight the harmony of
the faded gold and the pearls—to speak only of that—and
plant himself there (the mere high Atlas-back of renown to
Berridge now) as for communion with them. He had blocked
everything out, to this tune, effectually; with nothing of the
matter left for our friend meanwhile but that, as he had said,
the beautiful lady was the Princess. What Princess, or the Prin-

cess of what?—our young man had afterward wondered; his companion's reply having lost itself in the prelude of an outburst by another vocalist who had approached the piano.

It was after these things that she so incredibly came to him, attended by her adorer—since he took it for absolute that the young Lord was her adorer, as who indeed mightn't be?—and scarce waiting, in her bright simplicity, for any form of introduction. It may thus be said in a word that this was the manner in which she made our hero's acquaintance, a satisfaction that she on the spot described to him as really wanting of late to her felicity. "I've read everything, you know, and 'The Heart of Gold' three times": she put it all immediately on that ground, while the young Lord now smiled, beside her, as if it were quite the sort of thing he had done too; and while, further, the author of the work yielded to the consciousness that whereas in general he had come at last scarce to be able to bear the iteration of those words, which affected him as a mere vain vocal convulsion, so not a breath of this association now attended them, so such a person as the Princess could make of them what she would. Unless it was to be really what *he* would!—this occurred to him in the very thick of the prodigy, no single shade of possibility of which was less prodigious than any other. It was a declaration, simply, the admirable young woman was treating him to, a profession of "artistic sympathy"—for she was in a moment to use this very term that made for them a large, clear, common ether, an element all uplifted and rare, of which they could equally partake.

If she was Olympian—as in her rich and regular young beauty, that of some divine Greek mask over-painted say by Titian, she more and more appeared to him—this offered air was that of the gods themselves: she might have been, with her long rustle across the room, Artemis decorated, hung with pearls, for her worshippers, yet disconcerting them by having, under an impulse just faintly fierce, snatched the cup of gold from Hebe. It was to him, John Berridge, she thus publicly offered it; and it was his over-topping *confrère* of shortly before who was the worshipper most disconcerted. John had happened to catch, even at its distance, after these friends had joined him, the momentary deep, grave estimate, in the great

Dramatist's salient watching eyes, of the Princess's so singular performance: the touch perhaps this, in the whole business, that made Berridge's sense of it most sharp. The sense of it as *prodigy* didn't in the least entail his feeling abject—any more, that is, than in the due dazzled degree; for surely there would have been supreme wonder in the eagerness of her exchange of mature glory for thin notoriety, hadn't it still exceeded everything that an Olympian of such race should have found herself bothered, as they said, to "read" at all—and most of all to read three times!

With the turn the matter took as an effect of this meeting, Berridge was more than once to find himself almost ashamed for her—since it seemed never to occur to her to be so for herself: he was jealous of the type where she might have been taken as insolently careless of it; his advantage (unless indeed it had been his ruin) being that he could inordinately reflect upon it, could wander off thereby into kinds of licence of which she was incapable. He hadn't, for himself, waited till now to be sure of what he would do were *he* an Olympian: he would leave his own stuff snugly unread, to begin with; that would be a beautiful start for an Olympian career. He should have been as unable to write those works in short as to make anything else of them; and he should have had no more arithmetic for computing fingers than any perfect-headed marble Apollo mutilated at the wrists. He should have consented to know but the grand personal adventure on the grand personal basis: nothing short of this, no poor cognisance of confusable, pettifogging things, the sphere of earth-grubbing questions and two-penny issues, would begin to be, on any side, Olympian enough.

Even the great Dramatist, with his tempered and tested steel and his immense "assured" position, even he was not Olympian: the look, full of the torment of earth, with which he had seen the Princess turn her back, and for such a purpose, on the prized privilege of his notice, testified sufficiently to that. Still, comparatively, it was to be said, the question of a personal relation with an authority so eminent on the subject of the passions—to say nothing of the rest of his charm—might have had for an ardent young woman (and the Princess was unmistakably ardent) the absolute attraction of romance:

unless, again, prodigy of prodigies, she were looking for her romance very particularly elsewhere. Yet where could she have been looking for it, Berridge was to ask himself with private intensity, in a manner to leave her so at her ease for appearing to offer *him* everything?—so free to be quite divinely gentle with him, to hover there before him in all her mild, bright, smooth sublimity and to say: "I should be so very grateful if you'd come to see me."

There succeeded this a space of time of which he was afterward to lose all account, was never to recover the history; his only coherent view of it being that an interruption, some incident that kept them a while separate, had then taken place, yet that during their separation, of half an hour or whatever, they had still somehow not lost sight of each other, but had found their eyes meeting, in deep communion, all across the great peopled room; meeting and wanting to meet, wanting— it was the most extraordinary thing in the world for the suppression of stages, for confessed precipitate intensity—to use together every instant of the hour that might be left them. Yet to use it for what?—unless, like beautiful fabulous figures in some old-world legend, for the frankest and almost the crudest avowal of the impression they had made on each other. He couldn't have named, later on, any other person she had during this space been engaged with, any more than he was to remember in the least what he had himself ostensibly done, who had spoken to him, whom he had spoken to, or whether he hadn't just stood and publicly gaped or languished.

Ah, Olympians were unconventional indeed—that was a part of their high bravery and privilege; but what it also appeared to attest in this wondrous manner was that they could communicate to their chosen in three minutes, by the mere light of their eyes, the same shining cynicism. He was to wonder of course, tinglingly enough, whether he had really made an ass of himself, and there was this amount of evidence for it that there certainly *had* been a series of moments each one of which glowed with the lucid sense that, as she couldn't like him as much as *that* either for his acted clap-trap or for his printed verbiage, what it must come to was that she liked him, and to such a tune, just for himself and quite after no other fashion than that in which every goddess in the calendar had, when you came to look, sooner or later liked some prepossessing young shepherd. The question would thus have been, for him, with a still sharper eventual ache, of whether he positively *had*, as an effect of the miracle, been petrified, before fifty pair of eyes, to the posture of a prepossessing shepherd— and would perhaps have left him under the shadow of some such imputable fatuity if his consciousness hadn't, at a given moment, cleared up to still stranger things.

The agent of the change was, as quite congruously happened, none other than the shining youth whom he now seemed to himself to have been thinking of for ever so long, for a much longer time than he had ever in his life spent at an evening party, as the young Lord: which personage suddenly stood before him again, holding him up an odd object and smiling, as if in reference to it, with a gladness that at once struck our friend as almost too absurd for belief. The object was incongruous by reason of its being, to a second and less preoccupied glance, a book; and what had befallen Berridge within twenty minutes was that they—the Princess and he, that is—had got such millions of miles, or at least such thousands of years, away from *those* platitudes. The book, he found himself assuming, could only be *his* book (it seemed also to have a tawdry red cover); and there came to him memories, dreadfully false notes sounded so straight again by his new acquaintance, of certain altogether different persons who at certain altogether different parties had flourished volumes before him very much with that insinuating gesture, that arch expression, and that fell intention. The meaning of these things—of all possible breaks of the charm at such an hour!— was that he should "signature" the ugly thing, and with a characteristic quotation or sentiment: that was the way people simpered and squirmed, the way they mouthed and beckoned, when animated by such purposes; and it already, on the spot, almost broke his heart to see such a type as that of the young Lord brought, by the vulgarest of fashions, so low. This state of quick displeasure in Berridge, however, was founded on a deeper question—the question of how in the world he was to remain for himself a prepossessing shepherd if he should consent to come back to these base actualities. It was true that

even while this wonderment held him, his aggressor's perfect
good conscience had placed the matter in a slightly different
light.

"By an extraordinary chance I've found a copy of my
friend's novel on one of the tables here—I see by the inscription that she has presented it to Gloriani. So if you'd like to
glance at it—!" And the young Lord, in the pride of his association with the eminent thing, held it out to Berridge as
artlessly as if it had been a striking natural specimen of some
sort, a rosy round apple grown in his own orchard, or an
exceptional precious stone, to be admired for its weight and
lustre. Berridge accepted the offer mechanically—relieved at
the prompt fading of his worst fear, yet feeling in himself a
tell-tale facial blankness for the still absolutely anomalous
character of his friend's appeal. He was even tempted for a
moment to lay the volume down without looking at it—only
with some extemporised promise to borrow it of their host
and take it home, to give himself to it at an easier moment.
Then the very expression of his fellow-guest's own countenance determined in him a different and a still more dreadful
view; in fact an immediate collapse of the dream in which he
had for the splendid previous space of time been living. The
young Lord himself, in his radiant costly barbarism, figured
far better than John Berridge could do the prepossessing
shepherd, the beautiful mythological mortal "distinguished"
by a goddess; for our hero now saw that his whole manner of
dealing with his ridiculous tribute was marked exactly by the
grand simplicity, the prehistoric good faith, as one might call
it, of far-off romantic and "plastic" creatures, figures of exquisite Arcadian stamp, glorified rustics like those of the train
of peasants in "A Winter's Tale," who thought nothing of
such treasure-trove, on a Claude Lorrain sea-strand, as a royal
infant wrapped in purple: something in that fabulous style of
exhibition appearing exactly what his present demonstration
might have been prompted by.

"The Top of the Tree, by Amy Evans"—scarce credible
words floating before Berridge after he had with an anguish
of effort dropped his eyes on the importunate title-page—
represented an object as alien to the careless grace of goddess-
haunted Arcady as a washed-up "kodak" from a wrecked ship

might have been to the appreciation of some islander of wholly unvisited seas. Nothing could have been more in the tone of an islander deplorably diverted from his native interests and dignities than the glibness with which John's own child of nature went on. "It's her pen-name, Amy Evans"— he couldn't have said it otherwise had he been a blue-chinned penny-a-liner; yet marking it with a disconnectedness of intelligence that kept up all the poetry of his own situation and only crashed into that of other persons. The reference put the author of "The Heart of Gold" quite into *his* place, but left the speaker absolutely free of Arcady. "Thanks awfully"—Berridge somehow clutched at that, to keep everything from swimming. "Yes, I should like to look at it," he managed, horribly grimacing now, he believed, to say; and there was in fact a strange short interlude after this in which he scarce knew what had become of any one or of anything; in which he only seemed to himself to stand alone in a desolate place where even its desolation didn't save him from having to stare at the greyest of printed pages. Nothing here helped anything else, since the stamped greyness didn't even in itself make it impossible his eyes should follow such sentences as: "The loveliness of the face, which was that of the glorious period in which Pheidias reigned supreme, and which owed its most exquisite note to that shell-like curl of the upper lip which always somehow recalls for us the smile with which wind-blown Astarte must have risen from the salt sea to which she owed her birth and her terrible moods"; or "It was too much for all the passionate woman in her, and she let herself go, over the flowering land that had been, but was no longer their love, with an effect of blighting desolation that might have proceeded from one of the more physical, though not more awful, convulsions of nature."

He seemed to know later on that other and much more natural things had occurred; as that, for instance, with now at last a definite intermission of the rare music that for a long time past, save at the briefest intervals, had kept all participants ostensibly attentive and motionless, and that in spite of its high quality and the supposed privilege of listening to it he had allowed himself not to catch a note of, there was a great rustling and shifting and vociferous drop to a lower

plane, more marked still with the quick clearance of a way to
supper and a lively dispersal of most of the guests. Hadn't he
made out, through the queer glare of appearances, though
they yet somehow all came to him as confused and unreal,
that the Princess was no longer there, wasn't even only
crowded out of his range by the immediate multiplication of
her court, the obsequious court that the change of pitch had
at once permitted to close round her; that Gloriani had offered her his arm, in a gallant official way, as to the greatest
lady present, and that he was left with half a dozen persons
more knowing than the others, who had promptly taken,
singly or in couples, to a closer inspection of the fine small
scattered treasures of the studio?

He himself stood there, rueful and stricken, nursing a silly
red-bound book under his arm very much as if he might have
been holding on tight to an upright stake, or to the nearest
piece of furniture, during some impression of a sharp earth-
quake-shock or of an attack of dyspeptic dizziness; albeit indeed that he wasn't conscious of this absurd, this instinctive
nervous clutch till the thing that was to be more wonderful
than any yet suddenly flared up for him—the sight of the Princess again on the threshold of the room, poised there an instant, in her exquisite grace, for recovery of some one or of
something, and then, at recognition of him, coming straight
to him across the empty place as if he alone, and nobody and
nothing else, were what she incredibly wanted. She was there,
she was radiantly *at* him, as if she had known and loved him
for ten years—ten years during which, however, she had never
quite been able, in spite of undiscouraged attempts, to cure
him, as goddesses *had* to cure shepherds, of his mere mortal
shyness.

"Ah no, not *that* one!" she said at once, with her divine
familiarity; for she had in the flash of an eye "spotted" the
particular literary production he seemed so very fondly to
have possessed himself of and against which all the Amy Evans
in her, as she would doubtless have put it, clearly wished on
the spot to discriminate. She pulled it away from him; he let
it go; he scarce knew what was happening—only made out
that she distinguished the right one, the one that should have
been shown him, as blue or green or purple, and intimated

that her other friend, her fellow-Olympian, as Berridge had thought of him from the first, really did too clumsily bungle matters, poor dear, with his officiousness over the red one! She went on really as if she had come for that, some such rectification, some such eagerness of reunion with dear Mr. Berridge, some talk, after all the tiresome music, of questions really urgent; while, thanks to the supreme strangeness of it, the high tide of golden fable floated him afresh, and her pretext and her plea, the queerness of her offered motive, melted away after the fashion of the enveloping clouds that do their office in epics and idylls.

"You didn't perhaps know I'm Amy Evans," she smiled, "or even perhaps that I write in English—which I love, I assure you, as much as you can yourself do, and which gives one (doesn't it? for who should know if not you?) the biggest of publics. I 'just love'—don't they say?—your American millions; and all the more that they really *take* me for Amy Evans, as I've just wanted to be taken, to be loved too for myself, don't you know?—that they haven't seemed to try at all to 'go behind' (don't you say?) my poor dear little *nom de guerre*. But it's the new one, my last, 'The Velvet Glove,' that I should like you to judge me by—if such a *corvée* isn't too horrible for you to think of; though I admit it's a move straight in the romantic direction—since after all (for I might as well make a clean breast of it) it's dear old discredited romance that I'm most in sympathy with. I'll send you 'The Velvet Glove' to-morrow, if you *can* find half an hour for it; and then—and *then*—!" She paused as for the positive bright glory of her meaning.

It could only be so extraordinary, her meaning, whatever it was, that the need in him that would—whatever it was again!—meet it most absolutely formed the syllables on his lips as: "Will you be very, *very* kind to me?"

"Ah 'kind,' dear Mr. Berridge? 'Kind,'" she splendidly laughed, "is nothing to what—!" But she pulled herself up again an instant. "Well, to what I want to be! Just *see*," she said, "how I want to be!" It was exactly, he felt, what he couldn't *but* see—in spite of books and publics and pen-names, in spite of the really "decadent" perversity, recalling that of the most irresponsibly insolent of the old Romans and

Byzantines, that could lead a creature so formed for living and breathing her Romance, and so committed, up to the eyes, to the constant fact of her personal immersion in it and genius for it, the dreadful amateurish dance of ungrammatically scribbling it, with editions and advertisements and reviews and royalties and every other futile item: since what was more of the deep essence of throbbing intercourse itself than this very act of her having broken away from people, in the other room, to whom he was as nought, of her having, with her *crânerie* of audacity and indifference, just turned her back on them all as soon as she had begun to miss him? What was more of it than her having forbidden them, by a sufficient curt ring of her own supremely silver tone, to attempt to check or criticise her freedom, than her having looked him up, at his distance, under all the noses he had put out of joint, so as to let them think whatever they might—not of herself (much she troubled to care!) but of the new champion to be reckoned with, the invincible young lion of the day? What was more of it in short than her having perhaps even positively snubbed for him the great mystified Sculptor and the great bewildered Dramatist, treated to this queer experience for the first time of their lives?

It all came back again to the really great ease of really great ladies, and to the perfect facility of everything when once they were great enough. *That* might become the delicious thing to him, he more and more felt, as soon as it should be supremely attested; it was ground he had ventured on, scenically, representationally, in the artistic sphere, but without ever dreaming he should "realise" it thus in the social. Handsomely, gallantly just now, moreover, he didn't so much as let it occur to him that the social experience would perhaps on some future occasion richly profit further scenic efforts; he only lost himself in the consciousness of all she invited him to believe. It took licence, this consciousness, the next moment, for a tremendous further throb, from what she had gone on to say to him in so many words—though indeed the words were nothing and it was all a matter but of the implication that glimmered through them: "Do you *want* very much your supper here?" And then while he felt himself glare, for charmed response, almost to the point of his tears rising with it: "Because if you don't——!"

"Because if I don't—?" She had paused, not from the faintest shade of timidity, but clearly for the pleasure of making him press.

"Why shouldn't we go together, letting me drive you home?"

"You'll come home with me?" gasped John Berridge while the perspiration on his brow might have been the morning dew on a high lawn of Mount Ida.

"No—you had better come with *me*. That's what I mean; but I certainly will come to you with pleasure some time if you'll let me."

She made no more than that of the most fatuous of freedoms, as he felt directly he had spoken that it might have seemed to her; and before he had even time to welcome the relief of not having then himself, for beastly contrition, to make more of it, she had simply mentioned, with her affectionate ease, that she wanted to get away, that of the bores there she might easily, after a little, have too much, and that if he'd but say the word they'd nip straight out together by an independent door and be sure to find her motor in the court. What word he had found to say, he was afterward to reflect, must have little enough mattered; for he was to have kept, of what then occurred, but a single other impression, that of her great fragrant rustle beside him over the rest of the ample room and toward their nearest and friendliest resource, the door by which he had come in and which gave directly upon a staircase. This independent image was just that of the only other of his fellow-guests with whom he had been closely concerned; he had thought of him rather indeed, up to that moment, as the Princess's fellow-Olympian—but a new momentary vision of him seemed now to qualify it.

The young Lord had reappeared within a minute on the threshold, that of the passage from the supper-room, lately crossed by the Princess herself, and Berridge felt him there, saw him there, wondered about him there, all, for the first minute, without so much as a straight look at him. He would have come to learn the reason of his friend's extraordinary public demonstration—having more right to his curiosity, or his anxiety or whatever, than any one else; he would be taking in the remarkable appearances that thus completed it, and would perhaps be showing quite a different face for them, at the point they had reached, than any that would have hitherto consorted with the beautiful security of his own position. So much, on our own young man's part, for this first flush of a presumption that he might have stirred the germs of ire in a celestial breast; so much for the moment during which nothing would have induced him to betray, to a possibly rueful member of an old aristocracy, a vulgar elation or a tickled, unaccustomed glee. His inevitable second thought was, however, it has to be confessed, another matter, which took a different turn—for, frankly, all the conscious conqueror in him, as Amy Evans would again have said, couldn't forego a probably supreme consecration. He treated himself to no prolonged reach of vision, but there was something he nevertheless fully measured for five seconds—the sharp truth of the fact, namely, of how the interested observer in the doorway must really have felt about him. Rather disconcertingly, hereupon, the sharp truth proved to be that the most amused, quite the most encouraging and the least invidious of smiles graced the young Lord's handsome countenance—forming, in short, his final contribution to a display of high social candour unprecedented in our hero's experience. No, he wasn't jealous, didn't do John Berridge the honour to be, to the extent of the least glimmer of a spark of it, but was so happy to see his immortal mistress do what she liked that he could positively beam at the odd circumstance of her almost lavishing public caresses on a gentleman not, after all, of negligible importance.

III

Well, it was all confounding enough, but this indication in particular would have jostled our friend's grasp of the presented cup had he had, during the next ten minutes, more independence of thought. That, however, was out of the question when one positively felt, as with a pang somewhere deep within, or even with a smothered cry for alarm, one's whole sense of proportion shattered at a blow and ceasing to serve. "Not *straight*, and not too fast, shall we?" was the ineffable young woman's appeal to him, a few minutes later, beneath the wide glass porch-cover that sheltered their brief wait for their chariot of fire. It was there even as she spoke; the capped charioteer, with a great clean curve, drew up at the steps of the porch, and the Princess's footman, before rejoining him in front, held open the door of the car. She got in, and Berridge was the next instant beside her; he could only say: "As you like, Princess—where you will; certainly let us prolong it; let us prolong everything; don't let us have it over—strange and beautiful as it can only be!—a moment sooner than we must." So he spoke, in the security of their intimate English, while the perpendicular imperturbable *valet-de-pied*, white-faced in the electric light, closed them in and then took his place on the box where the rigid liveried backs of the two men, presented through the glass, were like a protecting wall; such a guarantee of privacy as might come—it occurred to Berridge's inexpugnable fancy—from a vision of tall guards erect round Eastern seraglios.

His companion had said something, by the time they started, about their taking a turn, their looking out for a few of the night-views of Paris that were so wonderful; and after that, in spite of his constantly prized sense of knowing his enchanted city and his way about, he ceased to follow or measure their course, content as he was with the particular exquisite assurance it gave him. *That* was knowing Paris, of a wondrous bland April night; that was hanging over it from vague consecrated lamp-studded heights and taking in, spread below and afar, the great scroll of all its irresistible story, pricked out, across river and bridge and radiant *place*, and along quays and boulevards and avenues, and around monumental circles and squares, in syllables of fire, and sketched and summarised, further and further, in the dim fire-dust of endless avenues; that was all of the essence of fond and thrilled and throbbing recognition, with a thousand things understood and a flood of response conveyed, a whole familiar possessive feeling appealed to and attested.

"From you, you know, it *would* be such a pleasure, and I think—in fact I'm sure—it would do so much for the thing in America." Had she gone on as they went, or had there been pauses of easy and of charmed and of natural silence, breaks and drops from talk, but only into greater confidence and sweetness?—such as her very gesture now seemed a part of; her laying her gloved hand, for emphasis, on the back of his own, which rested on his knee and which took in from the act he scarce knew what melting assurance. The emphasis, it was true—this came to him even while for a minute he held his breath—seemed rather that of Amy Evans; and if her talk, while they rolled, had been in the sense of these words (he had really but felt that they were shut intimately in together, all his consciousness, all his discrimination of meanings and indications being so deeply and so exquisitely merged in that) the case wasn't as surely and sublimely, as extravagantly, as fabulously romantic for him as his excited pulses had been seeming to certify. Her hand was there on his own, in precious living proof, and splendid Paris hung over them, as a conse- crating canopy, her purple night embroidered with gold; yet he waited, something stranger still having glimmered for him, waited though she left her hand, which expressed emphasis and homage and tenderness, and anything else she liked in- deed—since it was all then a matter of what he next heard and what he slowly grew cold as he took from her.

"You know they do it here so charmingly—it's a compli- ment a clever man is always so glad to pay a literary friend, and sometimes, in the case of a great name like yours, it renders such a service to a poor little book like mine!" She spoke ever so humbly and yet ever so gaily—and still more than before with this confidence of the sincere admirer and the comrade. That, yes, through his sudden sharpening chill, was what first became distinct for him; she was mentioning somehow her explanation and her conditions—her motive, in fine, disconcerting, deplorable, dreadful, in respect to the experience, otherwise so boundless, that he had taken her as having opened to him; and she was doing it, above all, with the clearest coolness of her general privilege. What in particular she was talking about he as yet, still holding his breath, wondered; it was something she wanted him to do for her—which was exactly what he had hoped, but some- thing of what trivial and, heaven forgive them both, of what dismal order? Most of all, meanwhile, he felt the dire pen- etration of two or three of the words she had used; so that after a painful minute the quaver with which he repeated them resembled his drawing, slowly, carefully, timidly, some barbed dart out of his flesh.

"A 'literary friend'?" he echoed as he turned his face more to her; so that, as they sat, the whites of her eyes, near to his own, gleamed in the dusk like some silver setting of deep sapphires.

It made her smile—which in their relation now was like the breaking of a cool air-wave over the conscious sore flush that maintained itself through his general chill. "Ah, of course you don't allow that I *am* literary—and of course if you're awfully cruel and critical and incorruptible you won't let it say for me what I so want it should!"

"Where are we, where, in the name of all that's damnably, of all that's grotesquely delusive, are we?" he said, without a sign, to himself; which was the form of his really being quite at sea as to what she was talking about. That uncertainty indeed he could but frankly betray by taking her up, as he cast about him, on the particular ambiguity that his voice perhaps already showed him to find most irritating. "Let *it* show? 'It,' dear Princess——?"

"Why, my dear man, let your Preface show, the lovely, friendly, irresistible log-rolling Preface that I've been asking you if you wouldn't be an angel and write for me."

He took it in with a deep long gulp—he had never, it seemed to him, had to swallow anything so bitter. "You've been asking me if I wouldn't write you a Preface?"

"To 'The Velvet Glove'—after I've sent it to you and you've judged if you really can. Of course I don't want you to perjure yourself; but"—and she fairly brushed him again, at their close quarters, with her fresh fragrant smile—"I do want you so to like me, and to say it all out beautifully and publicly."

"You want me to like you, Princess?"

"But, heaven help us, haven't you understood?"

Nothing stranger could conceivably have been, it struck him—if he was right now—than this exquisite intimacy of her manner of setting him down on the other side of an abyss. It was as if she had lifted him first in her beautiful arms, had raised him up high, high, high, to do it, pressing him to her immortal young breast while he let himself go, and then, by some extraordinary effect of her native force and her alien quality, setting him down exactly where she wanted him to be—which was a thousand miles away from her. Once more, so preposterously face to face with her for these base issues, he took it all in; after which he felt his eyes close, for amazement, despair and shame, and his head, which he had some time before, baring his brow to the mild night, eased of its crush-hat, sink to confounded rest on the upholstered back of the seat. The act, the ceasing to see, and if possible to hear, was for the moment a retreat, an escape from a state that he felt himself fairly flatter by thinking of it as "awkward"; the state of really wishing that his humiliation might end, and of wondering in fact if the most decent course open to him mightn't be to ask her to stop the motor and let him down.

He spoke no word for a long minute, or for considerably more than that; during which time the motor went and went, now even somewhat faster, and he knew, through his closed eyes, that the outer lights had begun to multiply and that they were getting back somewhere into the spacious and decorative quarters. He knew this, and also that his retreat, for all his attitude as of accommodating thought, his air—*that* presently and quickly came to him—of having perhaps gathered himself in, for an instant, at her behest, to turn over, in his high ingenuity, some humbugging "rotten" phrase or formula that he might place at her service and make the note of such an effort; he became aware, I say, that his lapse was but a half-retreat, with her strenuous presence and her earnest pressure and the close cool respiration of her good faith absolutely timing the moments of his stillness and the progress of the car. Yes, it was wondrous well, he had all but made the biggest of all fools of himself, almost as big a one as *she* was still, to every appearance, in her perfect serenity, trying to make of him; and the one straight answer to it *would* be that he should reach forward and touch the footman's shoulder and demand that the vehicle itself should make an end.

That would be an answer, however, he continued intensely to see, only to inanely importunate, to utterly superfluous Amy Evans—not a bit to his at last exquisitely patient companion, who was clearly now quite taking it from him that what kept him in his attitude was the spring of the quick desire to oblige her, the charming loyal impulse to consider a little what he could do for her, say "handsomely yet conscientiously" (oh the loveliness!) before he should commit himself. She was enchanted—*that* seemed to breathe upon him; she waited, she hung there, she quite bent over him, as Diana over the sleeping Endymion, while all the conscientious man of letters in him, as she might so supremely have phrased it, struggled with the more peccable, the more muddled and "squared," though, for her own ideal, the so much more *banal* comrade. Yes, he could keep it up now—that is he could hold out for his real reply, could meet the rather marked tension of the rest of their passage as well as she; he should be able somehow or other to make his wordless detachment, the tribute of his ostensibly deep consideration of her request, a retreat in good order. She *was*, for herself, to the last point of her guileless fatuity, Amy Evans and an asker for "lifts," a conceiver of twaddle both in herself and in him; or at least, so far as she fell short of all this platitude, it was no fault of the really affecting folly of her attempt to become a mere magazine mortal after the only fashion she had made out, to the intensification of her self-complacency, that she might.

Nothing might thus have touched him more—if to be touched, beyond a certain point, hadn't been to be squared— than the way she failed to divine the bearing of his thoughts; so that she had probably at no one small crisis of her life felt so much a promise in the flutter of her own as on the occasion of the beautiful act she indulged in at the very moment, he was afterward to recognise, of their sweeping into her great smooth, empty, costly street—a desert, at that hour, of lavish lamplight and sculptured stone. She raised to her lips the hand she had never yet released and kept it there a moment pressed close against them; he himself closing his eyes to the deepest detachment he was capable of while he took in with a smothered sound of pain that this was the conferred bounty by which Amy Evans sought most expressively to encourage, to sustain and to reward. The motor had slackened and in a moment would stop; and meanwhile even after lowering his hand again she hadn't let it go. This enabled it, while he after a further moment roused himself to a more confessed consciousness, to form with his friend's a more active relation, to possess him of hers, in turn, and with an intention the straighter that her glove had by this time somehow come off. Bending over it without hindrance, he returned as firmly and fully as the application of all his recovered wholeness of feeling, under his moustache, might express, the consecration the bareness of his own knuckles had received; only after which it was that, still thus drawing out his grasp of her, and having let down their front glass by his free hand, he signified to the footman his view of their stopping short.

They had arrived; the high, closed *porte-cochère*, in its crested stretch of wall, awaited their approach; but his gesture took effect, the car pulled up at the edge of the pavement, the man, in an instant, was at the door and had opened it; quickly moving across the walk, the next moment, to press the bell at the gate. Berridge, as his hand now broke away, felt he had cut his cable; with which, after he had stepped out, he raised again the glass he had lowered and closed, its own being already down, the door that had released him. During these motions he had the sense of his companion, still radiant and splendid, but somehow momentarily suppressed, suspended, silvered over and celestially blurred, even as a summer moon by the loose veil of a cloud. So it was he saw her while he leaned for farewell on the open window-ledge; he took her in as her visible intensity of bright vagueness filled the circle that the interior of the car made for her. It was such a state as she would have been reduced to—he felt this, was certain of it—for the first time in her life; and it was he, poor John Berridge, after all, who would have created the condition.

"Good-night, Princess. I sha'n't see you again."

Vague was indeed no word for it—shine though she might, in her screened narrow niche, as with the liquefaction of her pearls, the glimmer of her tears, the freshness of her surprise. "You won't come in—when you've had no supper?"

He smiled at her with a purpose of kindness that could never in his life have been greater; and at first but smiled without a word. He presently shook his head, however—doubtless also with as great a sadness. "I seem to have supped to my fill, Princess. Thank you, I won't come in."

It drew from her, while she looked at him, a long low anxious wail. "And you won't do my Preface?"

"No, Princess, I won't do your Preface. Nothing would induce me to say a word in print about you. I'm in fact not sure I shall ever mention you in any manner at all as long as ever I live."

He had felt for an instant as if he were speaking to some miraculously humanised idol, all sacred, all jewelled, all votively hung about, but made mysterious, in the recess of its shrine, by the very thickness of the accumulated lustre. And "Then you don't like me—?" was the marvellous sound from the image.

"Princess," was in response the sound of the worshipper, "Princess, I adore you. But I'm ashamed for you."

"Ashamed——?"

"You *are* Romance—as everything, and by what I make out every one, about you is; so what more do you want? Your Preface—the only one worth speaking of—was written long ages ago by the most beautiful imagination of man."

Humanised at least for these moments, she could understand enough to declare that she didn't. "I don't, I don't!"

"You don't need to understand. Don't attempt such base things. Leave those to us. Only live. Only be. *We'll* do the rest."

She moved over—she had come close to the window. "Ah, but Mr. Berridge——!"

He raised both hands; he shook them at her gently, in deep and soft deprecation. "Don't sound my dreadful name. Fortunately, however, you can't help yourself."

"Ah, *voyons*! I so want——!"

He repeated his gesture, and when he brought down his hands they closed together on both of hers, which now quite convulsively grasped the window-ledge. "Don't speak, because when you speak you really say things—!" You *are* Romance," he pronounced afresh and with the last intensity of conviction and persuasion. "That's all you have to do with it," he continued while his hands, for emphasis, pressed hard on her own.

Their faces, in this way, were nearer together than ever, but with the effect of only adding to the vividness of that dire non-intelligence from which, all perversely and incalculably, her very beauty now appeared to gain relief. This made for

him a pang and almost an anguish; the fear of her saying
something yet again that would wretchedly prove how little
he moved her perception. So his eyes, of remonstrant, of sup-
pliant intention, met hers close, at the same time that these,
so far from shrinking, but with their quite other swimming
plea all bedimmed now, seemed almost to wash him with the
tears of her failure. He soothed, he stroked, he reassured her
hands, for tender conveyance of his meaning, quite as she had
just before dealt with his own for brave demonstration of hers.
It was during these instants as if the question had been which
of them *could* most candidly and fraternally plead. Full but
of that she kept it up. "Ah, if you'd only think, if you'd
only try——!"

He couldn't stand it—she was capable of believing he had
edged away, excusing himself and trumping up a factitious
theory, because he hadn't the wit, hadn't the hand, to knock
off the few pleasant pages she asked him for and that any
proper Frenchman, master of the *métier*, would so easily and
gallantly have promised. Should she so begin to commit herself he'd, by the immortal gods, anticipate it in the manner
most admirably effective—in fact he'd even thus make her further derogation impossible. Their faces were so close that he
could practise any rich freedom—even though for an instant,
while the back of the chauffeur guarded them on that side
and his own presented breadth, amplified by his loose mantle,
filled the whole window-space, leaving him no observation
from any quarter to heed, he uttered, in a deep-drawn final
groan, an irrepressible echo of his pang for what might have
been, the muffled cry of his insistence. "You *are* Romance!"—he drove it intimately, inordinately home, his lips,
for a long moment, sealing it, with the fullest force of authority, on her own; after which, as he broke away and the
car, starting again, turned powerfully across the pavement, he
had no further sound from her than if, all divinely indulgent
but all humanly defeated, she had given the question up, falling back to infinite wonder. He too fell back, but could still
wave his hat for her as she passed to disappearance in the great
floridly framed aperture whose wings at once came together
behind her.

Mora Montravers

THEY were such extraordinary people to have been so odiously stricken that poor Traffle himself, always, at the best—though it was indeed just now at the worst—what his wife called horribly philosophic, fairly grimaced back, in private, at so flagrant a show of the famous, the provokedly vicious, "irony," the thing he had so often read about in clever stories, with which the usually candid countenance of their fate seemed to have begun of a sudden to bristle. Ah, that irony of fate often admired by him as a phrase and recognised as a truth—so that if he himself ever wrote a story it should certainly and most strikingly *be* about that—he fairly saw it leer at them now, could quite positively fancy it guilty of a low wink at them, in their trouble, out of that vast visage of the world that was made up for them of the separate stony stares or sympathising smirks presented by the circle of their friends. When he could get away from Jane he would pause in his worried walk—about the house or the garden, always, since he could now seldom leave her to brood alone for longer than that—and, while he shook his keys or his loose coin restlessly and helplessly in the pockets into which his hands had come to be inveterately and foolishly thrust, suffer his own familiar face, or the chance reflection of it in some gloomy glass, to respond distortedly to the grim and monstrous joke. He moved from room to room—as he easily could, at present, since their catastrophe; for when he thus sounded the depths of slumbering mirrors it was more than ever as if they were all "spare" rooms, dreary and unapplied, and as if Jane and he were quartered in them, even year after year, quite as on some dull interminable visit.

The joke was at all events in its having befallen *them*, him and his admirable, anxious, conscientious wife, who, living on their sufficient means in their discreet way, liked, respected, and even perhaps a bit envied, in the Wimbledon world (with so much good old mahogany and so many Bartolozzis, to say nothing of their collection of a dozen family miniatures) to have to pick up again as best they could—which was the way

Jane put it—the life that Miss Montravers, their unspeakable niece, though not, absolutely not and never, as every one would have it, their adopted daughter, had smashed into smithereens by leaving their roof, from one day to the other, to place herself immediately under the protection, or at least under the inspiration, of a little painter-man commonly called Puddick, who had no pretensions to being a gentleman and had given her lessons. If she had acted, unquestionably, according to her remarkable nature, this added no grace to the turn of the wheel of their fortune—which was, so deplorably, that any fledgling of their general nest (and Mora was but gone twenty-one and really clever with her brush) should *have* such a nature. It wasn't that, since her coming to them at fifteen, they had been ever, between themselves, at their ease about her—glossed over as everything had somehow come to be by the treacherous fact of her beauty. She had been such a credit to them that way that if it hadn't put them, as earnest observers, quite off their guard, the dazzle and charm of it appeared mostly to have misled their acquaintance. That was the worst cruelty for them, that with such a personal power to please she shouldn't, even on some light irregular line, have flown, as might have been conceived, higher. These things were dreadful, were even grotesque, to say; but what wasn't so now—after his difficult, his critical, his distinctly conclusive and, above all, as he secretly appraised it, his unexpectedly and absurdly interesting interview with Mr. Puddick? This passage, deplorably belated by Mora's own extraordinarily artful action, had but just taken place, and it had sent him back to Jane saddled with the queerest and most difficult errand of his life.

He hadn't, however, on his return, at once sought her in the drawing-room—though her plan of campaign had been that they should fly their flag as high as ever, and, changing none of their refined habits, sit in that bow-windowed place of propriety, even as in a great glazed public cage, as much as ever—he had sneaked away again to tip-toe, with his pensive private humour, over the whole field; observing in her society, for the most part, the forms of black despair and grim participation, if even at the same time avoiding inconsiderate grossness; but at bottom, since his moments with Puddick, almost

ready to take, as a man of the world, the impartial, the detached, in fact—hang it!—even the amused view. It hadn't as
yet made a shade of difference in his tone that Mora was
Jane's niece, and not even her very own, but only the child
of her half-sister, whose original union with Malcolm Montravers had moreover made a break between them that had
waited for healing till after the ill-starred husband's death and
the eve of that of the perfectly disillusioned wife; but in these
slightly rueful, though singularly remedial, dips into thoughtful solitude he had begun at last to treat himself to luxuries
that he could feel he was paying for. Mora was, accurately
speaking, no sharer of his blood, and he absolutely denied her
the right not alone socially to dishonour, but, beyond a mere
ruffle of the surface, morally to discompose him; mixed with
which rather awkwardly, not to say perhaps a bit perversely,
was the sense that as the girl was showing up, unmistakably,
for one of the most curious of "cases"—the term Puddick
himself had used about her—she wouldn't be unlikely to reward some independent, some intelligent notice.

He had never from the first, to do himself—or to do *her*—
justice, felt he had really known her, small, cool, supposedly
childish, yet not a bit confiding, verily not a bit appealing,
presence as she was; but clearly he should know her now, and
to do so might prove indeed a job. Not that he wanted to be
too cold-blooded about her—that is in the way of enlightened
appreciation, the detachment of the simply scandalised state
being another matter; for this was somehow to leave poor
Jane, and poor Jane's gloom of misery, in the lurch. But once
safely back from the studio, Puddick's own—where he hadn't
been sure, upon his honour, that some coarse danger mightn't
crop up—he indulged in a surreptitious vow that if any "fun,"
whether just freely or else more or less acutely speaking, was
to come of the matter, he'd be blamed if he'd be wholly deprived of it. The possibility of an incalculable sort of interest—
in fact, quite a refined sort, could there be refinement in such
doings—had somehow come out with Puddick's at once saying: "Certainly sir, I'll marry her if you and Mrs. Traffle absolutely insist—and if Mora herself (the great point!) can be
brought round to look at it in that way. But I warn you that
if I do, and that if she makes that concession, I shall probably

lose my hold of her—which won't be best, you know, for any one concerned. You don't suppose I don't *want* to make it all right, do you?" the surprising young man had gone on. "The question's only of what *is* right—or what will be if we keep our heads and take time—with such an extraordinary person as Mora, don't you see? to deal with. You must grant me," Mr. Puddick had wound up, "that she's a rum case."

II

What he had first felt, of course, was the rare coolness of it, the almost impudent absence of any tone of responsibility; which had begun by seeming to make the little painter-man's own case as "rum," surely, as one could imagine it. He had gone, poor troubled Traffle, after the talk, straight to his own studio, or to the rather chill and vague, if scrupulously neat, pavilion at the garden-end, which he had put up eight years ago in the modest hope that it would increasingly inspire him; since it wasn't making preparations and invoking facilities that constituted swagger, but, much rather, behaving as if one's powers could boldly dispense with them. He was certain Jane would come to him there on hearing of him from the parlour-maid, to whom he had said a word in the hall. He wasn't afraid—no—of having to speak a little as he felt; but, though well aware of his wife's impatience, he wasn't keen, either, for any added intensity of effort to abound only in Mrs. Traffle's sense. He required space and margin, he required a few minutes' time, to say to himself frankly that this dear dismal lady *had* no sense—none at least of their present wretched question—that was at all worth developing: since he of course couldn't possibly remark it to poor Jane. He had perhaps never remarked for his own private benefit so many strange things as between the moment of his letting himself again into the perpetually swept and garnished temple of his own per-functory æsthetic rites, where everything was ready to his hand and only that weak tool hung up, and his glimpse of Jane, from the smaller window, as she came down the garden walk. Puddick's studio had been distinctly dirty, and Puddick himself, from head to foot, despite his fine pale little face and bright, direct, much more searching than shifting eyes, almost

as spotty as the large morsel of rag with which he had so oddly
begun to rub his fingers while standing there to receive
Mora's nearest male relative; but the canvas on his easel, the
thing that even in the thick of his other adventure was making
so straight a push for the Academy, almost embarrassed that
relative's eyes, not to say that relative's conscience, by the
cleanness of its appeal. Traffle hadn't come to admire his picture or to mark how he didn't muddle where not muddling
was vital; he had come to denounce his conduct, and yet now,
perhaps most of all, felt the strain of having pretended so to
ignore what would intensely have interested him. Thanks to
this barren artifice, to the after-effect of it on his nerves, his
own preposterous place, all polish and poverty, pointed such
a moral as he had never before dreamed of. Spotless it might
be, unlike any surface or aspect presented under the high hard
Puddick north-light, since it showed no recording trace, no
homely smear—since it had had no hour of history. That was
the way truth showed and history came out—in spots: by
them, and by nothing else, you knew the real, as you knew
the leopard, so that the living creature and the living life
equally had to have them. Stuffed animals and weeping
women were—well, another question. He had gathered, on
the scene of his late effort, that Mora didn't weep, that she
was still perfectly pleased with her shocking course; her complacency indeed remained at such a pitch as to make any question of her actual approach, on whatever basis, or any rash
direct challenge of her, as yet unadvisable. He was at all
events, after another moment, in presence of Jane's damp severity; *she* never ceased crying, but her tears froze as they fell—
though not, unfortunately, to firm ice, any surface that would
bear the weight of large argument. The only thing for him,
none the less, was to carry the position with a rush, and he
came at once to the worst.

"He'll do it—he's willing; but he makes a most striking
point—I mean given the girl as we know her and as he of
course by this time must. He keeps his advantage, he thinks,
by not forcing the note—don't you see?" Traffle himself—
under the quick glow of his rush—actually saw more and
more. "He's feeling his way—he used that expression to me;

and again I haven't to tell you, any more than he really had to tell me, that with Mora one has to sit tight. He puts on us, in short, the responsibility.''

He had felt how more than ever her "done" yellow hair—done only in the sense of an elaborately unbecoming conformity to the spasmodic prescriptions, undulations and inflations of the day, not in that of any departure from its pale straw-coloured truth—was helped by her white invalidical shawl to intensify those reminders of their thin ideals, their bloodless immunity, their generally compromised and missed and forfeited frankness, that every other feature of their domestic scene had just been projecting for him. "Responsibility—we responsible?" She gaped with the wonder of it.

"I mean that we should be if anything were to happen by our trying to impose on her *our* view of her one redemption. I give it you for his own suggestion—and thereby worth thinking of.''

But Jane could take nothing in. "He suggests that he needn't marry her, and you agree with him? Pray what is there left to 'happen,' '' she went on before he could answer, "after her having happened so completely to disgrace herself?''

He turned his back a moment—he had shortly before noticed a framed decoration, a "refined" Japanese thing that gave accent, as he would have said, to the neatness of his mouse-grey wall, and that needed straightening. Those spare apprehensions had somehow, it was true, suddenly been elbowed out of his path by richer ones; but he obeyed his old habit. "She can leave him, my dear; that's what she can do—and not, you may well believe, to come back to us.''

"If she *will* come I'll take her—even now," said Jane Traffle; "and who can ask of me more than that?''

He slid about a little, sportively, on his polished floor, as if he would have liked to skate, while he vaguely, inaudibly hummed. "Our difficulty is that she doesn't ask the first blessed thing of us. We've been, you see, too stupid about her. Puddick doesn't say it, but he knows it—that I felt. She feels what she is—and so does he.''

"What she is? She's an awful little person"—and Mrs. Traffle stated it with a cold finality she had never yet used.

"Well then, that's what she feels!—even though it's probably not the name she employs in connection with it. She has tremendously the sense of life."

"That's bad," cried Jane, "when you haven't—not even feebly!—the sense of decency."

"How do you know, my dear," he returned, "when you've never had it?" And then as she but stared, since he couldn't mean she hadn't the sense of decency, he went on, really quite amazed at himself: "People must have both if possible, but if they can only have one I'm not sure that that one, as we've had it—not at all 'feebly,' as you say!— is the better of the two. What do we know about the sense of life—when it breaks out with real freedom? It has never broken out here, my dear, for long enough to leave its breath on the window-pane. But they've got it strong down there in Puddick's studio."

She looked at him as if she didn't even understand his language, and she flopped thereby into the trap set for her by a single word. "Is she living *in* the studio?"

He didn't avoid her eyes. "I don't know where she's living."

"And do I understand that you didn't ask him?"

"It was none of my business—I felt that there in an unexpected way; I couldn't somehow *not* feel it—and I suggest, my dear, accordingly, that it's also none of yours. I wouldn't answer, if you really want to know," he wound up, hanging fire an instant, but candidly bringing it out—"I wouldn't answer, if you really want to know, for their relations."

Jane's eyebrows mounted and mounted. "Whoever in the world would?"

He waited a minute, looking off at his balanced picture— though not as if now really seeing it. "I'm not talking of what the vulgar would say—or *are* saying, of course, to their fill. I'm not talking of what those relations may be. I'm talking— well," he said, "of what they mayn't."

"You mean they may be innocent?"

"I think it possible. They're, as he calls it, a 'rum' pair. They're not like us."

"If we're not like them," she broke in, "I grant you I hope not."

"We've no imagination, you see," he quietly explained— "whereas they have it on tap, for the sort of life they lead down there, all the while." He seemed wistfully to figure it out. "For us only one kind of irregularity is possible—for them, no doubt, twenty kinds."

Poor Jane listened this time—and so intently that after he had spoken she still rendered his obscure sense the tribute of a wait. "You think it's possible she's not living with him?"

"I think anything possible."

"Then what in the world did she want?"

"She wanted in the first place to get away from *us*. We didn't like her——"

"Ah, we never let her see it!"—Jane could triumphantly make *that* point.

It but had for him, however, an effect of unconscious comedy. "No, that was it—and she wanted to get away from everything we did to prevent her; from our solemn precautions *against* her seeing it. We didn't understand her, or we should have understood how much she must have wanted to. We were afraid of her in short, and she wanted not to see our contortions over it. Puddick isn't beautiful—though he has a fine little head and a face with some awfully good marks; but he's a Greek god, for statuesque calm, compared with us. He isn't afraid of her."

Jane drew herself elegantly up. "I understood you just now that it's exactly what he *is*!"

Traffle reflected. "That's only for his having to deal with her in our way. Not if he handles her in his own."

"And what, pray, is his own?"

Traffle, his hands in his pockets, resumed his walk, touching with the points of his shoes certain separations between the highly-polished planks of his floor. "Well, why should we have to know?"

"Do you mean we're to wash our hands of her?"

He only circulated at first—but quite sounding a low whistle of exhilaration. He felt happier than for a long time; broken as at a blow was the formation of ice that had somehow covered, all his days, the whole ground of life, what he would have called the things under. There they were, the things under. He could see them now; which was practically what he after a little replied. "It will be so interesting." He pulled up, none the less, as he turned, before her poor scared and mottled face, her still suffused eyes, her "dressed" head parading above these miseries.

She vaguely panted, as from a dance through bush and briar. "But *what*, Sidney, will be?"

"To see what becomes of her. Without our muddling." Which was a term, however, that she so protested against his use of that he had on the spot, with more kindness than logic, to attenuate, admitting her right to ask him who could do less—less than take the stand she proposed; though indeed coming back to the matter that evening after dinner (they never really got away from it; but they had the consciousness now of false starts in other directions, followed by the captive returns that were almost as ominous of what might still be before them as the famous tragic *rentrée* of Louis XVI and Marie Antoinette from Varennes); when he brought up, for their common relief, the essential fact of the young woman's history as they had suffered it to shape itself: her coming to them bereft and homeless, addressed, packed and registered after the fashion of a postal packet; their natural flutter of dismay and apprehension, but their patient acceptance of the charge; the five flurried governesses she had had in three years, who had so bored her and whom she had so deeply disconcerted; the remarkable disposition for drawing and daubing that she had shown from the first and that had led them to consent to her haunting of a class in town, that had made her acquainted with the as yet wholly undistinguished young artist, Walter Puddick, who, with a couple of other keen and juvenile adventurers of the brush, "criticised," all at their ease, according to the queer new licence of the day, and with nobody to criticise *them*, eighty supposed daughters of gentlemen; the uncontrolled spread of her social connection in London, on the oddest lines, as a proof of this prosecution of her studies; her consequent prolonged absences, her strange explanations and deeper duplicities, and presently her bolder defiances; with her staying altogether, at last, one fine day, under pretext of a visit at Highgate, and writing them at the end of a week, during which they had been without news of her, that her visit was to Mr. Puddick and his "set," and was likely to be of long duration, as he was "looking after her," and there were plenty of people in the set to help, and as she, above all, wanted nothing more: nothing more, of course, than her two hundred and seventy a year, the scant remainder of her mother's fortune that she had come into the use of, under that battered lady's will, on her eighteenth birthday, and through which her admirers, every member of the set, no doubt, wouldn't have found her least admirable. Puddick wouldn't be paying for her, by the blessing of heaven—*that*, Traffle recognised, would have been ground for anything; the case rather must be the other way round. She was "treating" the set, probably, root and branch—magnificently; so no wonder she was having success and liking it. Didn't Jane recognise, therefore, how in the light of this fact almost any droll *different* situation—different from the common and less edifying turn of such affairs—might here prevail? He could imagine even a fantastic delicacy; not on the part of the set at large perhaps, but on that of a member or two.

What Jane most promptly recognised, she showed him in answer to this, was that, with the tone he had so extraordinarily begun to take on the subject, his choice of terms left her staring. Their ordeal would have to be different indeed from anything she had yet felt it for it to affect her as droll, and Mora's behaviour to repudiate at every point and in some scarce conceivable way its present appearance for it to strike her either as delicate or as a possible cause of delicacy. In fact she could have but her own way—Mora was a monster.

"Well," he laughed—quite brazen about it now—"if she is it's because she has paid for it! Why the deuce did her stars, unless to make her worship gods entirely other than Jane Traffle's, rig her out with a name that puts such a premium on adventures? 'Mora Montravers'—it paints the whole career for you. She *is*, one does feel, her name; but how couldn't she be? She'd dishonour it and its grand air if she weren't."

"Then by that reasoning you admit," Mrs. Traffle returned with more of an argumentative pounce than she had perhaps ever achieved in her life, "that she *is* misconducting herself."

It pulled him up but ten seconds. "It isn't, love, that she's misconducting herself—it's that she's conducting, positively, and by her own lights doubtless quite responsibly, Miss Montravers through the preappointed circle of that young lady's experience." Jane turned on this a desolate back; but he only went on. "It would have been better for us perhaps if she could have been a Traffle—but, failing that, I think I should, on the ground that sinning at all one should sin boldly, have elected for Montravers outright. That *does* the thing—it gives the unmistakable note. And if 'Montravers' made it probable 'Mora'—don't you see, dearest?—made it sure. Would you *wish* her to change to Puddick?" This brought her round again, but as the affirmative hadn't quite leaped to her lips he found time to continue. "Unless indeed they can make some arrangement by which he takes *her* name. Perhaps we can work it that way!"

His suggestion was thrown out as for its positive charm; but Jane stood now, to do her justice, as a rock. "She's doing something that, surely, no girl in the world ever did before— in preferring, as I so strangely understand you, that her lover *shouldn't* make her the obvious reparation. But is her reason her dislike of his vulgar name?"

"That has no weight for *you*, Jane?" Traffle asked in reply.

Jane dismally shook her head. "Who, indeed, as you say, are *we*? Her reason—if it is her reason—is vulgarer still."

He didn't believe it could be Mora's reason, and though he had made, under the impression of the morning, a brave fight, he had after reflection to allow still for much obscurity in their question. But he had none the less retained his belief in the visibly uncommon young man, and took occasion to make of his wife an inquiry that hadn't hitherto come up in so straight a form and that sounded of a sudden rather odd. "Are you at all *attached* to her? Can you give me your word for *that*?"

She faced him again like a waning wintry moon. "Attached to Mora? Why she's my sister's child."

"Ah that, my dear, is no answer! Can you assure me on your honour that you're conscious of anything you can call real affection for her?"

Jane blankly brooded. "What has that to do with it?"

"I think it has everything. If we don't feel a tenderness."

"*You* certainly strike me as feeling one!" Mrs. Traffle sarcastically cried.

He weighed it, but to the effect of his protesting. "No, not enough for me to demand of her to marry to spare my sensibility."

His wife continued to gloom. "What is there in what she has done to *make* us tender?"

"Let us admit then, if there's nothing, that it has made us tough! Only then we must *be* tough. If we're having the strain and the pain of it let us also have the relief and the fun."

"Oh the 'fun'!" Jane wailed; but adding soon after: "If she'll marry him I'll forgive her."

"Ah, that's not enough!" he pronounced as they went to bed.

III

Yet he was to feel too the length that even forgiving her would have to go—for Jane at least—when, a couple of days later, they both, from the drawing-room window, saw, to their liveliest astonishment, the girl alight at the gate. She had taken a fly from the station, and their attention caught her as she paused apparently to treat with the cabman of the question of his waiting for her or coming back. It seemed settled in a moment that he should wait; he didn't remount his box, and she came in and up the garden-path. Jane had already flushed, and with violence, at the apparition, and in reply to her companion's instant question had said: "Yes, I'll see her if she has come back."

"Well, she *has* come back."

"She's keeping her cab—she hasn't come to stay." Mrs. Traffle had gained a far door of retreat.

"You won't speak to her?"

"Only if she has come to stay. *Then*—volumes!"

He had remained near the window, held fast there by the weight of indefinite obligation that his wife's flight from the field shifted to his shoulders. "But if she comes back to stay what can Puddick do?"

This kept her an instant. "To stay till he marries her is what I mean."

"Then if she asks for you—as she only must—am I to tell her that?"

Flushed and exalted, her hand on the door, Jane had for this question a really grand moment. "Tell her that if he will she shall come in—with your assent—for my four hundred."

"Oh, oh!" he ambiguously sounded while she whisked away and the door from the hall was at the same time thrown open by the parlour-maid. "Miss Montravers!" announced, with a shake of anguish, that domestic, whose heightened colour and scared eyes conformed to her mistress's example. Traffle felt his own cheek, for that matter, unnaturally glow, and the very first of his observations as Mora was restored to his sight might have been that she alone of them all wore her complexion with no difference. There was little doubt moreover that this charming balance of white and pink couldn't have altered but to its loss; and indeed when they were left alone the whole immediate effect for him of the girl's standing there in immediate bright silence was that of her having come simply to reaffirm her extraordinary prettiness. It might have been just to say: "You've thought, and you think, all sorts of horrible things about me, but observe how little my appearance matches them, and in fact keep up coarse views if you can in the light of my loveliness." Yet it wasn't as if she had changed, either, even to the extent of that sharper emphasis: he afterward reflected, as he lived over this passage, that he must have taken for granted in her, with the life she was leading, so to call it, some visibility of boldness, some significant surface—of which absurd supposition her presence, at the end of three minutes, had disabused him to the point of making all the awkwardness his and leaving none at all for her. That was a side of things, the awkward, that she clearly meant never again to recognise in conversation—though certainly from the first, ever, she had brushed it by lightly enough. She was in truth exactly the same—except for her hint that they might have forgotten how pretty she *could* be; and he further made sure she would incur neither pains nor costs for any new attempt on them. The Mora they had always taken her for would serve her perfectly still; that young woman was bad enough, in all conscience, to hang together through anything that might yet happen.

So much he was to feel she had conveyed, and that it was the little person presenting herself, at her convenience, on

these terms who had been all the while, in their past, their
portentous inmate—since what had the portent been, by the
same token, but exactly of this? By the end of three minutes
more our friend's sole thought was to conceal from her that
he had looked for some vulgar sign—such as, reported to
Wimbledon tea-tables, could be confidentially mumbled
about: he was almost as ashamed of that elderly innocence as
if she had caught him in the fact of disappointment at it.
Meanwhile she had expressed her errand very simply and serenely. "I've come to see you because I don't want to lose
sight of you—my being no longer with you is no reason for
that." She was going to ignore, he saw—and she would put
it through: she was going to ignore everything that suited her,
and the quantity might become prodigious. Thus it would rest
upon *them*, poor things, to disallow, if they must, the grace
of these negatives—in which process she would watch them
flounder without help. It opened out before him—a vertiginous view of a gulf; the abyss of what the ignoring would
include for the convenient general commerce; of what might
lie behind, in fine, should the policy foreshadow the lurking
quantity. He knew the vague void for one he should never
bridge, and that to put on emphasis where Mora chose to
neglect it would be work only for those who "gathered samphire" like the unfortunates in "King Lear," or those who,
by profession, planted lightning-rods at the tips of tremendous towers. He was committed to pusillanimity, which would
yet have to figure for him, before he had done with it, he
knew, as a gallant independence, by letting ten minutes go
without mention of Jane. Mora had put him somehow into
the position of having to explain that her aunt wouldn't see
her—precisely that was the mark of the girl's attitude. But
he'd be hanged if he'd do anything of the sort.

It was therefore like giving poor Jane basely away, his not,
to any tune, speaking for her—and all the more that their
visitor sat just long enough to let his helplessness grow and
reach perfection. By this facility it was he who showed—and
for her amusement and profit—all the change she kept him
from imputing to herself. He presented her—she held him up
to himself as presenting her—with a new uncle, made over,
to some loss of dignity, on purpose for her; and nothing could

less have suited their theory of his right relation than to have
a private understanding with her at his wife's expense. However, gracefully grave and imperturbable, inimitably armed by
her charming correctness, as she sat there, it would be her line
in life, he was certain, to reduce many theories, solemn Wimbledon theories about the scandalous person, to the futility of
so much broken looking-glass. Not naming her aunt—since
he didn't—she had of course to start, for the air of a morning
call, some other hare or two; she asked for news of their few
local friends quite as if these good people mightn't ruefully
have "cut" her, by what they had heard, should they have
met her out on the road. She spoke of Mr. Puddick with perfect complacency, and in particular held poor Traffle very
much as some master's fiddle-bow might have made him hang
on the semi-tone of a silver string when she referred to the
visit he had paid the artist and to the latter's having wondered
whether he liked what he saw. *She* liked, more and more, Mora
intimated, what was offered to her own view; Puddick was
going to do, she was sure, such brilliant work—so that she
hoped immensely he would come again. Traffle found himself,
yes—it was positive—staying his breath for this; there was in
fact a moment, that of her first throwing off her free "Puddick," when it wouldn't have taken much more to make him
almost wish that, for rounded perfection, she'd say "Walter"
at once. He would scarce have guaranteed even that there
hadn't been just then some seconds of his betraying that
imagination in the demoralised eyes that her straight, clear,
quiet beams sounded and sounded, against every presumption
of what might have been. What essentially happened, at any
rate, was that by the time she went she had not only settled
him in the sinister attitude of having lost all interest in her
aunt, but had made him give her for the profane reason of it
that he was gaining so much in herself.

He rushed in again, for that matter, to a frank clearance the
moment he had seen the girl off the premises, attended her,
that is, back to her fly. He hadn't at this climax remarked to
her that she must come again—which might have meant either of two or three incoherencies and have signified thereby
comparatively little; he had only fixed on her a rolling eye—
for it rolled, he strangely felt, without leaving her; which had

the air of signifying heaven knew what. She took it, clearly, during the moment she sat there before her start, for the most rather than for the least it might mean; which again made him gape with the certitude that ever thereafter she would make him seem to have meant what she liked. She had arrived in a few minutes at as wondrous a recipe or as quick an inspiration for this as if she had been a confectioner using some unprecedented turn of the ladle for some supersubtle cream. He was a proved conspirator from that instant on, which was practically what he had qualified Jane, within ten minutes—if Jane had only been refreshingly sharper—to pronounce him. For what else in the world did it come to, his failure of ability to attribute any other fine sense to Mora's odd "step" than the weird design of just giving them a lead? They were to leave her alone, by her sharp prescription, and she would show them once for all how to do it. Cutting her dead wasn't leaving her alone, any idiot could do that; conversing with her affably was the privilege she offered, and the one he had so effectually embraced—he made a clean breast of this—that he had breathed to her no syllable of the message left with him by her aunt.

"Then you mean," this lady now inquired, "that I'm to go and call upon her, at that impossible place, just as if she were the pink of propriety and we had no exception whatever to take to her conduct? Then you mean," Mrs. Traffle had pursued with a gleam in her eye of more dangerous portent than any he had ever known himself to kindle there—"then you mean that I'm to grovel before a chit of a creature on whom I've lavished every benefit, and to whom I've actually offered every indulgence, and who shows herself, in return for it all, by what I make out from your rigmarole, a fiend of insolence as well as of vice?"

The danger descried by Sidney Traffle was not that of any further act of violence from Jane than this freedom of address to him, unprecedented in their long intercourse—this sustained and, as he had in a degree to allow, not unfounded note of sarcasm; such a resort to which, on his wife's part, would, at the best, mark the prospect for him, in a form flushed with novelty, of much conscious self-discipline. What looked out of her dear foolish face, very much with the effect of a new and strange head boldly shown at an old and familiar pacific window, was just the assurance that he might hope for no abashed sense in her of differing from him on all this ground as she had never differed on any. It was as if now, unmistakably, she *liked* to differ, the ground being her own and he scarce more than an unwarranted poacher there. Of course it *was* her own, by the fact, first, of Mora's being her, not his, sister's child; and, second, by all the force with which her announced munificence made it so. He took a moment to think how he could best meet her challenge, and then reflected that there was, happily, nothing like the truth—*his* truth, of which it was the insidious nature to prevail. "What she wanted, I make out, was but to give us the best pleasure she could think of. The pleasure, I mean, of our not only recognising how little we need worry about her, but of our seeing as well how pleasant it may become for us to keep in touch with her."

These words, he was well aware, left his wife—given her painful narrowness—a bristling quiver of retorts to draw from; yet it was not without a silent surprise that he saw her, with her irritated eyes on him, extract the bolt of finest point. He had rarely known her to achieve that discrimination before. "The pleasure then, in her view, you 'make out'—since you make out such wonders!—is to be all for us only?"

He found it fortunately given him still to smile. "That will depend, dear, on our appreciating it enough to make things agreeable to *her* in order to get it. But as she didn't inquire for you," he hastened to add, "I don't—no I don't—advise your going to see her *even* for the interest I speak of!" He bethought himself. "We must wait a while."

"Wait till she gets worse?"

He felt after a little that he should be able now always to command a kindly indulgent tone. "I'll go and see her if you like."

"Why in the world should I like it? Is it your idea—for the pleasure you so highly appreciate, and heaven knows what you mean by it!—to cultivate with her a free relation of your own?"

"No"—he promptly returned—"I suggest it only as acting *for* you. Unless," he went on, "you decidedly wish to act altogether for yourself."

For some moments she made no answer; though when she at last spoke it was as if it *were* an answer. "I shall send for Mr. Puddick."

"And whom will you send?"

"I suppose I'm capable of a note," Jane replied.

"Yes, or you might even telegraph. But are you sure he'll come?"

"Am I sure, you mean," she asked, "that his companion will let him? I can but try, at all events, and shall at any rate have done what I can."

"I think he's afraid of her——"

Traffle had so begun, but she had already taken him up. "And you're not, you mean—and that's why you're so eager?"

"Ah, my dear, my dear?" He met it with his strained grimace. "Let us by all means," he also, however, said, "have him if we can."

On which it was, for a little, that they strangely faced each other. She let his accommodation lie while she kept her eyes on him, and in a moment she had come up, as it were, elsewhere. "If I thought you'd see her——!"

"That I'd see her?"—for she had paused again.

"See her and go on with her—well, without my knowledge," quavered poor Jane, "I assure you you'd seem to me even worse than her. So will you promise me?" she ardently added.

"Promise you what, dear?" He spoke quite mildly.

"Not to see her in secret—which I believe would kill me."

"Oh, oh, oh, love!" Traffle smiled while she positively glared.

IV

Three days having elapsed, however, he had to feel that things had considerably moved on his being privileged to hear his wife, in the drawing-room, where they entertained Mr. Puddick at tea, put the great question straighter to that visitor than he himself, Sidney Traffle, could either have planned or presumed to do. Flushed to a fever after they had beat about the bush a little, Jane didn't flinch from her duty. "What I want to know in plain terms, if you please, is whether or no you're Mora's lover?" "Plain terms"—she did have inspirations! so that under the shock he turned away, humming, as ever, in his impatience, and, the others being seated over the vain pretence of the afternoon repast, left the young man to say what he might. It was a fool's question, and there was always a gape for the wisest (the greater the wisdom and the greater the folly) in any apprehension of such. As if he were going to say, remarkable Puddick, not less remarkable in his way than Mora—to say, that is, anything that would suit Jane; and as if it didn't give her away for a goose that she should assume he was! Traffle had never more tiptoed off to the far end of the room, whether for pretence of a sudden interest in his precious little old Copley Fielding or on any other extemporised ground, than while their guest momentarily hung fire; but though he winced it was as if he now liked to wince—the occasions she gave him for doing so were such a sign of his abdication. He had wholly stepped aside, and she could flounder as she would: he had found exactly the formula that saved his dignity, that expressed his sincerity, and that yet didn't touch his curiosity. "I see it would be indelicate for me to go further—yes, love, I do see *that*:" such was the concession he had resorted to for a snap of the particular tension of which we a moment ago took the measure. This had entailed Jane's gravely pronouncing him, for the first time in her life, ridiculous; as if, in common sense—! She used that term also with much freedom now; at the same time that it hadn't prevented her almost immediately asking him if *he* would mind writing her letter. Nothing could suit him more, from the moment she was ostensibly to run the show—as for her benefit he promptly phrased the matter—than that she should involve herself in as many inconsistencies as possible; since if he did such things in spite of his scruple this was as nothing to her needing him at every step in spite of her predominance.

His delicacy was absurd for her because Mora's indecency had made this, by her logic, the only air they could now breathe; yet he knew how it nevertheless took his presence to wind her up to her actual challenge of their guest. Face to face with that personage alone she would have failed of the assurance required for such crudity; deeply unprepared as she really was, poor dear, for the crudity to which she might, as a consequence, have opened the gates. She lived altogether thus—and nothing, to her husband's ironic view, he flattered himself, could be droller—in perpetual yearning, deprecating, in bewildered and muddled communion with the dreadful law of crudity; as if in very truth, to *his* amused sense, the situation hadn't of necessity to be dressed up to the eyes for them in every sort of precaution and paraphrase. Traffle had privately reached the point of seeing it, at its high pitch of mystery and bravery, absolutely defy any common catchword. The one his wife had just employed struck him, while he hunched his shoulders at the ominous pause she had made inevitable for sturdy Puddick, as the vulgarest, and he had time largely to blush before an answer came. He had written, explicitly on Jane's behalf, to request the favour of an interview, but had been careful not to intimate that it was to put that artless question. To have dragged a busy person, a serious person, out from town on the implication of his being treated for reward to so *bête* an appeal—no, one surely couldn't appear to have been concerned in that. Puddick had been under no obligation to come—one might honestly have doubted whether he would even reply. However, his power of reply proved not inconsiderable, as consorted with his having presented himself not a bit ruefully or sulkily, but all easily and coolly, and even to a visible degree in a spirit of unprejudiced curiosity. It was as if he had practically forgotten Traffle's own invasion of him at his studio—in addition to which who indeed knew what mightn't have happened between the Chelsea pair in a distracting or freshly epoch-making way since then?— and was ready to show himself for perfectly good-natured, but for also naturally vague about what they could want of him again. "It depends, ma'am, on the sense I understand you to attach to that word," was in any case the answer to which he at his convenience treated Jane.

"I attach to it the only sense," she returned, "that could force me—by *my* understanding of it—to anything so painful as this inquiry. I mean are you so much lovers as to make it indispensable you should immediately marry?"

"Indispensable to who, ma'am?" was what Traffle heard their companion now promptly enough produce. To which, as it appeared to take her a little aback, he added: "Indispensable to *you*, do you mean, Mrs. Traffle? Of course, you see, I haven't any measure of *that*."

"Should you have any such measure"—and with it she had for her husband the effect now of quite "speaking up"—"if I were to give you my assurance that my niece will come into money when the proper means are taken of making her connection with you a little less—or perhaps I should say altogether less—distressing and irregular?"

The auditor of this exchange rocked noiselessly away from his particular point of dissociation, throwing himself at random upon another, before Mr. Puddick appeared again to have made up his mind, or at least to have adjusted his intelligence; but the movement had been on Traffle's part but the instinct to stand off more and more—a vague effort of retreat that didn't prevent the young man's next response to pressure from ringing out in time to overtake him. "Is what you want me to understand then that you'll handsomely pay her if she marries me? Is it to tell me that that you asked me to come?" It was queer, Sidney felt as he held his breath, how he kept liking this inferior person the better—the better for his carrying himself so little like any sort of sneak—on every minute spent in his company. They had brought him there at the very best to patronise him, and now would simply have to reckon with his showing clearly for so much more a person "of the world" than they. Traffle, it was true, was becoming, under the precious initiation opened to him by Mora, whether directly or indirectly, much more a man of the world than ever yet: as much as that at least he could turn over in his secret soul while their visitor pursued. "Perhaps you also mean, ma'am, that you suppose me to require that knowledge to determine my own behaviour—in the sense that if she comes in for money I may clutch at the way to come into it too?" He put this as the straightest of questions; yet he also, it was marked, followed up that side-issue further, as if to fight shy of what Jane wanted most to know. "Is it your idea of me that I haven't married her because she isn't rich enough, and that on what you now tell me I may think better of it? Is that how you see me, Mrs. Traffle?" he asked, at his quiet pitch, without heat.

It might have floored his hostess a little, to her husband's vision, but she seemed at once to sit up, on the contrary, so much straighter, that he, after hearing her, immediately turned round. "Don't you *want*, Mr. Puddick, to be able to marry a creature so beautiful and so clever?"

This was somehow, suddenly, on Jane's part, so prodigious, for art and subtlety, Traffle recognised, that he had come forward again and a remarkable thing had followed. Their guest had noticed his return and now looked up at him from over the tea-table, looked in a manner so direct, so intelligent, so quite amusedly critical, that, afresh, before he knew it, he had treated the little fact as the flicker of a private understanding between them, and had just cynically—for it was scarce covertly—smiled back at him in the independence of it. So there he was again, Sidney Traffle; after having tacitly admitted to Mora that her aunt was a goose of geese—compared to himself and *her*—he was at present putting that young woman's accomplice up to the same view of his conjugal loyalty, which might be straightway reported to the girl. Well, what was he, all the same, to do? Jane *was*, on all the ground that now spread immeasurably about them, a goose of geese: all that had occurred was that she more showily displayed it; and that she might indeed have had a momentary sense of triumph when the best that their friend first found to meet her withal proved still another evasion of the real point. "I don't think, if you'll allow me to say so, Mrs. Traffle, that you've any right to ask me, in respect to Miss Montravers, what I 'want'—or that I'm under any obligation to tell you. I've come to you, quite in the dark, because of Mr. Traffle's letter, and so that you shouldn't have the shadow of anything to complain of. But please remember that I've neither appealed to you in any way nor put myself in a position of responsibility toward you."

So far, but only so far, however, had he successfully proceeded before Jane was down upon him in her new trenchant form. "It's not of your responsibility to us I'm talking, but all of your responsibility to *her*. We efface ourselves," she all effectively bridled, "and we're prepared for every reasonable sacrifice. But we do still a little care what becomes of the child to whom we gave up years of our life. If you care enough for her to live with her, don't you care enough to work out some way of making her your very own by the aid of such help as we're eager to render? Or are we to take from you, as against that, that, even thus with the way made easy, she's so amazingly constituted as to prefer, in the face of the world, your actual terms of intercourse?"

The young man had kept his eyes on her without flinching, and so he continued after she had spoken. He then drank down what remained of his tea and, pushing back his chair, got up. He hadn't the least arrogance, not the least fatuity of type—save so far as it might be offensive in such a place to show a young head modelled as with such an intention of some one of the finer economic uses, and a young face already a little worn as under stress of that economy—but he couldn't help his looking, while he pulled down his not very fresh waistcoat, just a trifle like a person who had expected to be rather better regaled. This came indeed, for his host, to seeing that he looked bored; which was again, for that gentleman, a source of humiliation. What style of conversation, comparatively, on the showing of it, wouldn't he and Mora meanwhile be having together? If they would only invite *him*, their uncle—or rather no, when it came to that, not a bit, worse luck, their uncle—if they would only invite him, their humble admirer, to tea! During which play of reflection and envy, at any rate, Mr. Puddick had prepared to take his leave. "I don't think I can talk to you, really, about my 'terms of intercourse' with any lady." He wasn't superior, exactly—wasn't so in fact at all, but was nevertheless crushing, and all the more that his next word seemed spoken, in its persistent charity, for their help. "If it's important you should get at that sort of thing it strikes me you should do so by the lady herself."

Our friend, at this, no longer stayed his hand. "Mrs. Traffle doesn't see her," he explained to their companion—"as the situation seems to present itself."

"You mean Mora doesn't see me, my dear!" Mrs. Traffle replied with spirit.

He met it, however, with a smile and a gallant inclination. "Perhaps I mean that she only unsuccessfully tries to."

"She doesn't then take the right way!" Mora's aunt tossed off.

Mr. Puddick looked at her blandly. "Then you lose a good deal, ma'am. For if you wish to learn from me how much I admire your niece," he continued straight, "I don't in the least mind answering to that that you may put my sentiments at the highest. I *adore* Miss Montravers," he brought out, after a slight catch of his breath, roundly and impatiently. "I'd do anything in the world for her."

"Then do you pretend," said Jane with a rush, as if to break through this opening before she was checked, "then do you pretend that you're living with her in innocence?"

Sidney Traffle had a groan for it—a hunched groan in which he exhaled the anguish, as he would have called it, of his false position; but Walter Puddick only continued, in his fine un-blinking way, to meet Jane's eyes. "I repudiate absolutely your charge of my 'living' with her or of her living with me. Miss Montravers is irreproachable and immaculate."

"All appearances to the contrary notwithstanding?" Mrs. Traffle cried. "You'd do anything in the world for her, and she'd by the same token, I suppose, do anything in the world for you, and yet you ask me to believe that, all the while, you are, together, in this extraordinary way, doing nothing in the world—?" With which, to his further excruciation, her husband, with eyes averted from her, felt her face turn, as for a strained and unnatural intensity of meaning, upon himself. "He attempts, dear, to prove too much! But I only desire," she continued to their guest, "that you should definitely understand how far I'm willing to go."

"It *is* rather far you know," Sidney, at this, in spite of everything, found himself persuasively remarking to Puddick.

It threw his wife straight upon him, and he felt her there, more massively weighted than he had ever known her, while she said: "I'll make it four hundred and fifty. Yes, a year," she then exaltedly pursued to their visitor. "I pass you my word of honour for it. That's what I'll allow Mora as your wife."

Traffle watched him, under this—and the more that an odd spasm or shade had come into his face; which in turn made

our friend wish the more to bridge somehow the dark oddity
of their difference. What was all the while at bottom sharpest
for him was that they might somehow pull more together.
"That, you see," he fluted for conciliation, "is her aunt's really,
you know, I think, rather magnificent message for her."

The young man took in clearly, during a short silence, the
material magnificence—while Traffle again noted how almost
any sort of fineness of appreciation could show in his face.
"I'm sure I'm much obliged to you," he presently said.

"You don't refuse to let her have it, I suppose?" Mrs. Traffle further proceeded.

Walter Puddick's clear eyes—clear at least as his host had
hitherto judged them—seemed for the minute attached to the
square, spacious sum. "I don't refuse anything. I'll give her
your message."

"Well," said Jane, "that's the assurance we've wanted."
And she gathered herself as for relief, on her own side, at his
departure.

He lingered but a moment—which was long enough, however, for her husband to see him, as with an intenser twinge
of the special impatience just noted in him, look, all unhappily,
from Mora's aunt to Mora's uncle. "Of course I can't mention to her such a fact. But I wish, all the same," he said with
a queer sick smile, "that you'd just simply let us alone."

He turned away with it, but Jane had already gone on.
"Well, you certainly seem in sufficient possession of the right
way to make us!"

Walter Puddick, picking up his hat and with his distinctly
artistic and animated young back presented—though how it
came to show so strikingly for such Sidney Traffle couldn't
have said—reached one of the doors of the room which was
not right for his egress; while Sidney stood divided between
the motion of correcting and guiding him and the irresistible
need of covering Jane with a last woeful reproach. For he had
seen something, had caught it from the sharp flicker of trouble
finally breaking through Puddick's face, caught it from the
fact that—yes, positively—the upshot of their attack on him
was a pair of hot tears in his eyes. They stood for queer, deep
things, assuredly, these tears; they spoke portentously, since
that was her note, of wonderful Mora; but there was an in-

delicacy in the pressure that had thus made the source of them public. "You *have* dished us now!" was what, for a Parthian shot, Jane's husband would have liked to leave with her, and what in fact he would have articulately phrased if he hadn't rather given himself to getting their guest with the least discomfort possible out of the room. Into the hall he ushered him, and there—absurd, incoherent person as he had again to know himself for—vaguely yet reassuringly, with an arm about him, patted him on the back. The full force of this victim's original uttered warning came back to him; the probable perfect wisdom of his plea that, since he had infinitely to manage, *their* line, the aunt's and the uncle's, was just to let him feel his way; the gage of his sincerity as to this being the fact of his attachment. Sidney Traffle seemed somehow to feel the fullest force of both these truths during the moment his young friend recognised the intention of his gesture; and thus for a little, at any rate, while the closed door of the drawing-room and the shelter of the porch kept them unseen and unheard from within, they faced each other for the embarrassment that, as Traffle would have been quite ready to put it, they had in common. Their eyes met their eyes, their conscious grin their grin; hang it, yes, the screw *was* on Mora's lover. Puddick's recognition of his sympathy—well, proved that he needed something, though he didn't need interference from the outside; which couldn't, any way they might arrange it, seem delicate enough. Jane's obtrusion of her four hundred and fifty affected Traffle thus as singularly gross; though part of that association might proceed for him, doubtless, from the remark in which his exasperated sensibility was, the next thing, to culminate.

"I'm afraid I can't explain to you," he first said, however, "why it is that in spite of my indoctrination, my wife fails to see that there's only one answer a gentleman may make to the so intimate question she put to you."

"I don't know anything about that; I wasn't at all making her a conventional reply. But I don't mind assuring you, on my sacred honour——"

So Walter Puddick was going on, but his host, with a firm touch of his arm, and very handsomely, as that host felt, or at least desired to feel, wouldn't have it. "Ah, it's none of my business; I accept what you've said, and it wouldn't matter to you if I didn't. Your situation's evidently remarkable," Traffle all sociably added, "and I don't mind telling you that I, for one, have confidence in your tact. I recognised, that day I went to see you, that this was the only thing to do, and have done my best, ever since, to impress it on Mrs. Traffle. She replies to me that I talk at my ease, and the appearances *are* such, I recognise, that it would be odd she shouldn't mind them. In short she has shown you how much she does mind them. I tell her," our friend pursued, "that we mustn't weigh appearances too much against realities—and that *of* those realities," he added, balancing again a little on his toes and clasping his waist with his hands, which at the same time just worked down the back of his waistcoat, "you must be having your full share." Traffle liked, as the effect of this, to see his visitor look at him harder; he felt how the ideal turn of their relation would be that he should show all the tact he *was* so incontestably showing, and yet at the same time not miss anything that would be interesting. "You see of course for yourself how little, after all, she knows Mora. She doesn't appreciate the light hand that you must have to have with her—and that, I take it," Sidney Traffle smiled, "is what you contend for with us."

"I don't contend for anything with you, sir," said Walter Puddick.

"Ah, but you do want to be let alone," his friend insisted.

The young man turned graver in proportion to this urbanity. "Mrs. Traffle has closed my mouth."

"By laying on you, you mean, the absolute obligation to report her offer—?" That lady's representative continued to smile, but then it was that he yet began to see where fine freedom of thought—translated into act at least—would rather grotesquely lodge him. He hung fire, none the less, but for an instant; even though not quite saying what he had been on the point of. "I should like to feel at liberty to put it to you that if, in your place, I felt that a statement of Mrs. Traffle's overture would probably, or even possibly, dish me, I'm not sure I should make a scruple of holding my tongue about it. But of course I see that I can't very well go so far without looking to you as if my motive might be mixed. You might naturally say that I can't *want* my wife's money to go out of the house."

Puddick had an undissimulated pause for the renewed effort to do justice to so much elegant arrangement of the stiff truth of his case; but his intelligence apparently operated, and even to the extent of showing him that his companion really meant, more and more, as well—as well, that is, to *him*—as it was humanly conceivable that Mrs. Traffle's husband *could* mean. "Your difficulty's different from mine, and from the appearance I incur in carrying Miss Montravers her aunt's message as a clear necessity and at any risk."

"You mean that your being conscientious about it may look as if the risk you care least to face is that of not with a little patience coming in yourself for the money?" After which, with a glitter fairly sublime in its profession of his detachment from any stupid course: "You can be sure, you know, that *I'd* be sure——!"

"Sure I'm not a pig?" the young man asked in a manner that made Traffle feel quite possessed at last of his confidence.

"Even if you keep quiet I shall know you're not, and shall believe also you won't have thought me one." To which, in the exaltation produced by this, he next added: "Isn't she, with it all—with all she has done for you I mean—splendidly fond of you?"

The question proved, however, but one of those that seemed condemned to cast, by their action, a chill; which was expressed, on the young man's part, with a certain respectful dryness. "How do you know, sir, what Miss Montravers has done for me?"

Sidney Traffle felt himself enjoy, on this, a choice of replies—one of which indeed would have sprung easiest from his lips. "Oh now, come!" seemed for the instant what he would have liked most to hear himself say; but he renounced the pleasure—even though making up for it a little by his actual first choice. "Don't I know at least that she left the honourable shelter of this house for you?"

Walter Puddick had a wait. "I never asked it of her."

"You didn't seduce her, no—and even her aunt doesn't accuse you of it. But that she should have given up—well, what she *has* given up, moderately as you may estimate it,"

Traffle again smiled—"surely has *something* to say about her case?"

"What has more to say than anything else," Puddick promptly returned to this, "is that she's the very cleverest and most original and most endowed, and in every way most wonderful, person I've known in all my life."

His entertainer fairly glowed, for response, with the light of it. "Thank you then!" Traffle thus radiated.

" 'Thank you for nothing!' " cried the other with a short laugh and set into motion down the steps and the garden walk by this final attestation of the essential impenetrability even of an acutest young artist's *vie intime* with a character sketchable in such terms.

Traffle accompanied him to the gate, but wondering, as they went, if it was quite inevitable one should come back to feeling, as the result of every sort of brush with people who were really living, like so very small a boy. No, no, one must stretch to one's tallest again. It restored one's stature a little then that one didn't now mind that this demonstration would prove to Jane, should she be waiting in the drawing-room and watching for one's return, that one had detained their guest for so much privacy in the porch. "Well, take care what you do!" Traffle bravely brought out for good-bye.

"Oh, I shall tell her," Puddick replied under the effect of his renewed pat of the back; and even, standing there an instant, had a further indulgence. "She loathes my unfortunate name of course; but she's such an incalculable creature that my information possibly may fetch her."

There was a final suddenness of candour in it that made Traffle gape. "Oh, our names, and hers—! But is her loathing of yours then all that's the matter?"

Walter Puddick stood some seconds; he might, in pursuance of what had just passed, have been going to say things. But he had decided again the next moment for the fewest possible. "No!" he tossed back as he walked off.

V

"We seem to have got so beautifully used to it," Traffle remarked more than a month later to Jane—"we seem to have lived into it and through it so, and to have suffered and surmounted the worst, that, upon my word, I scarce see what's the matter now, or what, that's so very dreadful, it's doing or has done for us. We haven't the interest of her, no," he had gone on, slowly pacing and revolving things according to his wont, while the sharer of his life, tea being over and the service removed, reclined on a sofa, perfectly still and with her eyes rigidly closed; "we've lost that, and I agree that it was great—I mean the interest of the number of ideas the situation presented us with. That has dropped—by our own act, evidently; we must have simply settled the case, a month ago, in such a way as that we shall have no more acquaintance with it; by which I mean no more of the fun of it. I, for one, confess I miss the fun—put it only at the fun of our having had to wriggle so with shame, or, call it if you like, to live so under arms, against prying questions and the too easy exposure of our false explanations; which only proves, however, that, as I say, the worst that has happened to us appears to be that we're going to find life tame again—as tame as it was before ever Mora came into it so immensely to enrich and agitate it. She has gone out of it, obviously, to leave it flat and forlorn—tasteless after having had for so many months the highest flavour. If, by her not thanking you even though she declines, by her not acknowledging in any way your—as I admit—altogether munificent offer, it seems indicated that we shall hold her to have definitely enrolled herself in the deplorable 'flaunting' class, we must at least recognise that she doesn't flaunt at *us*, at whomever else she may; and that she has in short cut us as neatly and effectively as, in the event of her conclusive, her supreme contumacy, we could have aspired to cut *her*. Never was a scandal, therefore, less scandalous—more naturally a disappointment, that is, to our good friends, whose resentment of this holy calm, this absence of any echo of any convulsion, of any sensation of any kind to be picked up, strikes me as ushering in the only form of ostracism our dissimulated taint, our connection with lurid facts that *might* have gone on making us rather eminently worth while, will have earned for us. But aren't custom and use breaking us in to the sense even of *that* anticlimax, and preparing for us future years of wistful, rueful, regretful thought of the time when everything was nice and dreadful?"

Mrs. Traffle's posture was now, more and more, certainly, this recumbent sightless stillness; which she appeared to have resorted to at first—after the launching, that is, of her ultimatum to Mr. Puddick—as a sign of the intensity with which she awaited results. There had been no results, alas, there were none from week to week; never was the strain of suspense less gratefully crowned; with the drawback, moreover, that they could settle to nothing—not even to the alternative, that of the cold consciousness of slighted magnanimity, in which Jane had assumed beforehand that she should find her last support. Her husband circled about her couch, with his eternal dim whistle, at a discreet distance—as certain as if he turned to catch her in the act that when his back was presented in thoughtful retreat her tightened eyes opened to rest on it with peculiar sharpness. She waited for the proof that she had intervened to advantage—the advantage of Mora's social future—and she had to put up with Sidney's watching her wait. So he, on his side, lived under her tacit criticism of that attention; and had they asked themselves, the comfortless pair— as it's in fact scarce conceivable that they didn't—what it would practically have cost them to receive their niece without questions, they might well have judged their present ordeal much the dearer. When Sidney had felt his wife glare at him undetectedly for a fortnight he knew at least what it meant, and if she had signified how much he might have to pay for it should he presume again to see Mora alone, she was now, in their community of a quietude that had fairly soured on their hands, getting ready to quarrel with him for his poverty of imagination about that menace. Absolutely, the conviction grew for him, she would have liked him better to do something, even something inconsiderate of her to the point of rudeness, than simply parade there in the deference that left her to languish. The fault of this conspicuous propriety, which gave on her nerves, was that it did nothing to refresh their decidedly rather starved sense of their case; so that Traffle was frankly merciless—frankly, that is, for himself—in his application of her warning. There was nothing he would indeed have liked better than to call on Mora—quite, as who should say, in the friendly way to which her own last visit at Wimbledon had set so bright an example. At the same time, though he revelled in his acute reflection as to the partner of his home— "I've only to go, and then come back with some 'new fact,' *à la Dreyfus*, in order to make her sit up in a false flare that will break our insufferable spell"—he was yet determined that the flare, certain to take place sooner or later, should precede his act; so large a licence might he then obviously build upon it. His excursions to town were on occasion, even, in truth, not other than perverse—determined, that is, he was well aware, by their calculated effect on Jane, who could imagine in his absence, each time, that he might be "following some-thing up" (an expression that had in fact once slipped from her), might be having the gumption, in other words, to glean a few straws for their nakeder nest; imagine it, yes, only to feel herself fall back again on the mere thorns of consistency.

It wasn't, nevertheless, that he took all his exercise to this supersubtle tune; the state of his own nerves treated him at moments to larger and looser exactions; which is why, though poor Jane's sofa still remained his centre of radiation, the span of his unrest sometimes embraced half London. He had never been on such fidgety terms with his club, which he could neither not resort to, from his suburb, with an unnatural fre-quency, nor make, in the event, any coherent use of; so that his suspicion of his not remarkably carrying it off there was confirmed to him, disconcertingly, one morning when his dash townward had been particularly wild, by the free address of a fellow-member prone always to overdoing fellowship and who had doubtless for some time amusedly watched his vague gyrations—"I say, Traff, old man, what in the world, this time, have you got 'on'?" It had never been anything but easy to answer the ass, and was easier than ever now—" 'On'? You don't suppose I dress, do you, to come to meet *you*?"—yet the effect of the nasty little mirror of his unsatisfied state so flashed before him was to make him afresh wander wide, if wide half the stretch of Trafalgar Square could be called. He turned into the National Gallery, where the great masters were tantalising more by their indifference than by any offer of company, and where he could take up again his personal tra-dition of a lawless range. One couldn't be a *raffiné* at Wimbledon—no, not with any comfort; but he quite liked to think how he had never been anything less in the great museum, distinguished as he thus was from those who gaped impartially and did the place by schools. *His* sympathies were special and far-scattered, just as the places of pilgrimage he most fondly reverted to were corners unnoted and cold, where the idol in the numbered shrine sat apart to await him.

So he found himself at the end of five minutes in one of the smaller, one of the Dutch rooms—in a temple bare in very fact at that moment save for just one other of the faithful. This was a young person—visibly young, from the threshold of the place, in spite of the back presented for an instant while a small picture before which she had stopped continued to hold her; but who turned at sound of his entering footfall, and who then again, as by an alertness in this movement, engaged his eyes. With which it was remarkably given to Traffle to feel himself recognise even almost to immediate, to artless extravagance of display, two things; the first that his fellow-votary in the unprofaned place and at the odd morning hour was none other than their invincible Mora, surprised, by this extraordinary fluke, in her invincibility, and the second (oh his certainty of *that*!) that she was expecting to be joined there by no such pale fellow-adventurer as her whilom uncle. It amazed him, as it also annoyed him, on the spot, that his heart, for thirty seconds, should be standing almost still; but he wasn't to be able afterward to blink it that he had at once quite gone to pieces, any slight subsequent success in recovering himself to the contrary notwithstanding. Their happening thus to meet was obviously a wonder—it made him feel unprepared; but what especially did the business for him, he subsequently reflected, was again the renewed degree, and for that matter the developed kind, of importance that the girl's beauty gave her. Dear Jane, at home, as he knew—and as Mora herself probably, for that matter, did—was sunk in the conviction that she was leading a life; but whatever she was doing it was clearly the particular thing she might best be occupied with. How could anything be better for a lovely creature than thus to grow from month to month in loveliness?—so that she was able to stand there before him with no more felt inconvenience than the sense of the mere tribute of his eyes could promptly rectify.

That ministered positively to his weakness—the justice he did on the spot to the rare shade of human felicity, human impunity, human sublimity, call it what one would, surely dwelling in such a consciousness. How could a girl have to think long, have to think more than three-quarters of a second, under any stress whatever, of anything in the world but that her presence was an absolute incomparable value? The prodigious thing, too, was that it had had in the past, and the comparatively recent past that one easily recalled, to content itself with counting twenty times less: a proof precisely that any conditions so determined could only as a matter of course have been odious and, at the last, outrageous to her. Goodness knew with what glare of graceless inaction this rush of recognitions was accompanied in poor Traffle; who was later on to ask himself whether he had showed to less advantage in the freshness of his commotion or in the promptly enough subsequent rage of his coolness. The commotion, in any case, had doubtless appeared more to paralyse than to agitate him, since Mora had had time to come nearer while he showed for helplessly planted. He hadn't even at the moment been proud of his presence of mind, but it was as they afterward haunted his ear that the echoes of what he at first found to say were most odious to him.

"I'm glad to take your being here for a sign you've not lost your interest in Art"—that might have passed if he hadn't so almost feverishly floundered on. "I hope you keep up your painting—with such a position as you must be in for serious work; I always thought, you know, that you'd do something if you'd stick to it. In fact we quite miss your not bringing us something to admire as you sometimes did; we haven't, you see, much of an art-atmosphere now. I'm glad you're fond of the Dutch—that little Metsu over there that I think you were looking at is a pet thing of my own; and, if my living to do something myself hadn't been the most idiotic of dreams, something in *his* line—though of course a thousand miles behind him—was what I should have tried to go in for. You see at any rate where—missing as I say our art-atmosphere—I have to come to find one. Not such a bad place certainly"— so he had hysterically gabbled; "especially at this quiet hour—

as I see you yourself quite feel. I just turned in—though it does discourage! I hope, however, it hasn't that effect on *you*," he knew himself to grin with the last awkwardness; making it worse the next instant by the gay insinuation: "I'm bound to say it isn't how you look—discouraged!"

It reeked for him with reference even while he said it—for the truth was but too intensely, too insidiously, somehow, that her confidence implied, that it in fact bravely betrayed, grounds. He was to appreciate this wild waver, in retrospect, as positive dizziness in a narrow pass—the abyss being naturally on either side; that abyss of the facts of the girl's existence which he must thus have seemed to rush into, a smirking, a disgusting tribute to them through his excessive wish to show how clear he kept of them. The terrible, the fatal truth was that she made everything too difficult—or that this, at any rate, was how she enjoyed the exquisite privilege of affecting him. She watched him, she saw him splash to keep from sinking, with a pitiless cold sweet irony; she gave him rope as a syren on a headland might have been amused at some bather beyond his depth and unable to swim. It was all the fault—his want of ease was—of the real extravagance of his idea of not letting her spy even the tip of the tail of any "freedom" with her; thanks to which fatality she had indeed the game in her own hands. She exhaled a distinction—it glanced out of every shade of selection, every turn of expression, in her dress, though she had always, for that matter, had the genius of felicity there—which was practically the "new fact" all Wimbledon had been awaiting; and yet so perverse was their relation that to mark at all any special consideration for it was to appear just to make the allusion he was most forbidding himself. It was hard, his troubled consciousness told him, to be able neither to overlook her new facts without brutality nor to recognise them without impertinence; and he was frankly at the end of his resources by the time he ceased beating the air. Then it was, yes, then it was perfectly, as if she had patiently let him show her each of his ways of making a fool of himself; when she still said nothing a moment—and yet still managed to keep him ridiculous—as if for certainty on that head. It was true that when she at last spoke she swept everything away.

"It's a great chance my meeting you—for what you so kindly think of me."

She brought that out as if he had been uttering mere vain sounds—to which she preferred the comparative seriousness of the human, or at least of the mature, state, and her unexpectedness it was that thus a little stiffened him up. "What I think of you? How do you know what I think?"

She dimly and charmingly smiled at him, for it wasn't really that she was harsh. She was but infinitely remote—the syren on her headland dazzlingly in view, yet communicating, precisely, over such an abyss. "Because it's so much more, you mean, than you know yourself? If you don't know yourself, if you know as little as, I confess, you strike me as doing," she, however, at once went on, "I'm more sorry for you than anything else; even though at the best, I dare say, it must seem odd to you to hear me so patronising." It was borne in upon him thus that she would now make no difference, to his honour—to that of his so much more emancipated spirit at least—between her aunt and her uncle; so much should the poor uncle enjoy for his pains. He should stand or fall with fatal Jane—for at this point he was already sure Jane had been fatal; it was in fact with fatal Jane tied as a millstone round his neck that he at present knew himself sinking. "You try to make grabs at some idea, but the simplest never occurs to you."

"What do you call the simplest, Mora?" he at this heard himself whine.

"Why, my being simply a good girl. You gape at it"—he was trying exactly not to—"as if it passed your belief; but it's really all the while, to my own sense, what has been the matter with me. I mean, you see, a good creature—wanting to live at peace. Everything, however, occurs to you but that—and in spite of my trying to show you. You never understood," she said with her sad, quiet lucidity, "what I came to see you for two months ago." He was on the point of breaking in to declare that the reach of his intelligence at the juncture of which she spoke had been quite beyond expression; but he checked himself in time, as it would strike her but as a vague weak effort to make exactly the distinction that she held cheap. No, he wouldn't give Jane away now—he'd suffer anything instead; the taste of what he should have to suffer was already there on his lips: it came over him, to the strangest effect of desolation, of desolation made certain, that they should have lost Mora for ever, and that this present scant passage must count for them as her form of rupture. Jane had treated her the other day—treated her, that is, through Walter Puddick, who would have been, when all was said, a faithful agent—to *their* form, their form save on the condition attached, much too stiff a one, no doubt; so that he was actually having the extraordinary girl's answer. What they thought of her was that she was Walter Puddick's mistress—the only difference between them being that whereas her aunt fixed the character upon her as by the act of tying a neatly inscribed luggage-tag to a bandbox, he himself flourished about with *his* tag in his hand and a portentous grin for what he could do with it if he would. She brushed aside alike, however, vulgar label and bewildered formula; she but took Jane's message as involving an insult, and if she treated him, as a participant, with any shade of humanity, it was indeed that she was the good creature for whom she had a moment ago claimed credit. Even under the sense of so supreme a pang poor Traffle could value his actual, his living, his wonderful impression, rarest treasure of sense, as what the whole history would most have left with him. It was all he should have of her in the future—the mere memory of these dreadful minutes in so noble a place, minutes that were shining easy grace on her part and helpless humiliation on his; wherefore, tragically but instinctively, he gathered in, as for preservation, every grain of the experience. That was it; they had given her, without intending it, still wider wings of freedom; the clue, the excuse, the pretext, whatever she might call it, for shaking off any bond that had still incommoded her. She was spreading her wings—that was what he saw—as if she hovered, rising and rising, like an angel in a vision; it was the picture that he might, if he chose, or mightn't, make Jane, on his return, sit up to. Truths, these, that for our interest in him, or for our grasp of them, press on us in succession, but that within his breast were quick and simultaneous; so that it was virtually without a wait he heard her go on. "Do try—that's really all I want to say—to keep hold of my husband."

"Your husband—?" He *did* gape.

She had the oddest charming surprise—her nearest approach to familiarity. "Walter Puddick. Don't you know I'm married?" And then as for the life of him he still couldn't but stare: "Hasn't he told you?"

"Told us? Why, we haven't seen him——"

"Since the day you so put the case to him? Oh, I should have supposed—!" She would have supposed, obviously, that he might in some way have communicated the fact; but she clearly hadn't so much as assured herself of it. "Then there exactly he is—he doesn't seem, poor dear, to know what to do." And she had on his behalf, apparently, a moment of beautiful anxious, yet at the same time detached and all momentary thought. "That's just then what I mean."

"My dear child," Traffle gasped, "what on earth *do* you mean?"

"Well"—and she dropped for an instant comparatively to within his reach—"that it's where you *can* come in. Where in fact, as I say, I quite wish you would!"

All his wondering attention for a moment hung upon her. "Do you ask me, Mora, to *do* something for you?"

"Yes"—and it was as if no "good creature" had ever been so beautiful, nor any beautiful creature ever so good—"to make him your care. To see that he does get it."

"Get it?" Traffle blankly echoed.

"Why, what you promised him. My aunt's money."

He felt his countenance an exhibition. "She promised it, Mora, to *you*."

"If I married him, yes—because I wasn't fit for her to speak to till I should. But if I'm now proudly Mrs. Puddick——!"

He had already, however, as with an immense revulsion, a long jump, taken her up: "You are, you *are*—?" He gaped at the difference it made and in which then, immensely, they seemed to recover her.

"Before all men—and the Registrar."

"The Registrar?" he again echoed; so that, with another turn of her humour, it made her lift her eyebrows at him.

"You mean it doesn't hold if *that's* the way——?"

"It holds, Mora, I suppose, any way—that makes a real marriage. It is," he hopefully smiled, "real?"

"Could anything be more real," she asked, "than to have become such a thing?"

"Walter Puddick's wife?" He kept his eyes on her pleadingly. "Surely, Mora, it's a *good* thing—clever and charming as he is." Now that Jane had succeeded his instinct, of a sudden, was to back her up.

Mrs. Puddick's face—and the fact was it was strange, in the light of her actual aspect, to think of her and name her so—showed, however, as ready a disposition. "If he's as much as that then why were you so shocked by my relations with him?"

He panted—he cast about. 'Why, we didn't doubt of his distinction—of what it was at any rate likely to become."

"You only doubted of mine?" she asked with her harder look.

He threw up helpless arms, he dropped them while he gazed at her. "It doesn't seem to me possible any one can ever have questioned your gift for doing things in your own way. And if you're now married," he added with his return of tentative presumption and his strained smile, "your own way opens out for you, doesn't it? as never yet."

Her eyes, on this, held him a moment, and he couldn't have said now what was in them. "I think it does. I'm seeing," she said—"I shall see. Only"—she hesitated but for an instant—"for that it's necessary you shall look after him."

They stood there face to face on it—during a pause that, lighted by her radiance, gave him time to take from her, somehow, larger and stranger things than either might at all intelligibly or happily have named. "Do you ask it of me?"

"I ask it of you," said Mrs. Puddick after a wait that affected him as giving his contribution to her enjoyment of that title as part of her reason.

He held out, however—contribution or no contribution—another moment. "Do you beg me very hard?"

Once more she hung fire—but she let him have it. "I beg you very hard."

It made him turn pale. "Thank you," he said; and it was as if now he didn't care what monstrous bargain he passed with her—which was fortunate, for that matter, since, when she next spoke, the quantity struck him as looming large.

"I want to be free."

"How can you not?" said Sidney Traffle, feeling, to the most extraordinary tune, at one and the same time both sublime and base; and quite vague, as well as indifferent, as to which character prevailed.

"But I don't want him, you see, to suffer."

Besides the opportunity that this spread before him, he could have blessed her, could have embraced her, for "you see." "Well, I promise you he sha'n't suffer if I can help it."

"Thank you," she said in a manner that gave him, if possible, even greater pleasure yet, showing him as it did, after all, what an honest man she thought him. He even at that point had his apprehension of the queerness of the engagement that, as an honest man, he was taking—the engagement, since she so "wanted to be free," to relieve her, so far as he devotedly might, of any care hampering this ideal; but his perception took a tremendous bound as he noticed that their interview had within a moment become exposed to observation. A reflected light in Mora's face, caught from the quarter behind him, suddenly so advised him and caused him to turn, with the consequence of his seeing a gentleman in the doorway by which he had entered—a gentleman in the act of replacing the hat raised to salute Mrs. Puddick and with an accompanying smile still vivid in a clear, fresh, well-featured face. Everything took for Sidney Traffle a sharper sense from this apparition, and he had, even while the fact of the nature of his young friend's business there, the keeping of an agreeable appointment in discreet conditions, stood out for him again as in its odd insolence of serenity and success, the consciousness that whatever his young friend was doing, whatever she was "up to," he was now quite as much in the act of backing her as the gentleman in the doorway, a slightly mature, but strikingly well-dressed, a pleasantly masterful-looking gentleman, a haunter of the best society, one could be sure, was waiting for him to go. Mora herself, promptly, had that apprehension, and conveyed it to him, the next thing, in words that amounted, with their sweet conclusive look, to a decent dismissal. "Here's what's of *real* importance to me,"

she seemed to say; "so, though I count on you, I needn't
keep you longer." But she took time in fact just to revert.
"I've asked him to go to you; and he will, I'm sure, he *will*:
by which you'll have your chance, don't fear! Good-bye." She
spoke as if this "chance" were what he would now at once be
most yearning for; and thus it was that, while he stayed but
long enough to let his eyes move again to the new, the impatient and distinctly "smart," yes, unmistakably, this time,
not a bit Bohemian candidate for her attention, and then let
them come back to herself as for some grasp of the question
of a relation already so developed, there might have hung
itself up there the prospect of an infinite future of responsibility about Walter Puddick—if only as a make-weight perhaps
to the extinction of everything else. When he had turned his
back and begun humbly to shuffle, as it seemed to him,
through a succession of shining rooms where the walls bristled
with eyes that watched him for mockery, his sense was of
having seen the last of Mora as completely as if she had just
seated herself in the car of a rising balloon that would never
descend again to earth.

VI

It was before that aspect of the matter, at any rate, that Sidney
Traffle made a retreat which he would have had to regard as
the most abject act of his life hadn't he just savingly been able
to regard it as the most lucid. The aftertaste of that quality of
an intelligence in it sharp even to soreness was to remain with
him, intensely, for hours—to the point in fact (which says all)
of rendering necessary a thoughtful return to his club rather
than a direct invocation of the society of his wife. He ceased,
for the rest of the day there, to thresh about; that phase, sensibly, was over for him; he dropped into a deep chair, really
exhausted, quite spent, and in this posture yielded to reflections too grave for accessory fidgets. They were so grave, or
were at least so interesting, that it was long since he had been
for so many hours without thinking of Jane—of whom he
didn't even dream after he had at last inevitably, reacting from
weeks of tension that were somehow ended for ever, welcomed a deep foodless doze which held him till it was time

to order tea. He woke to partake, still meditatively, of that repast—yet, though late the hour and quite exceptional the length of his absence, with his domestic wantonness now all gone and no charm in the thought of how Jane would be worried. He probably shouldn't be wanton, it struck him, ever again in his life; that tap had run dry—had suffered an immense, a conclusive diversion from the particular application of its flow to Jane.

This truth indeed, I must add, proved of minor relevance on his standing before that lady, in the Wimbledon drawing-room, considerably after six o'clock had struck, and feeling himself in presence of revelations prepared not only to match, but absolutely to ignore and override, his own. He hadn't put it to himself that if the pleasure of stretching her on the rack appeared suddenly to have dropped for him this was because "it"—by which he would have meant everything else—was too serious; but *had* he done so he would at once have indulged in the amendment that he himself certainly was. His wife had in any case risen from the rack, the "bed of steel" that, in the form of her habitual, her eternal, her plaintive, aggressive sofa, had positively a pushed-back and relegated air—an air to the meaning of which a tea-service that fairly seemed to sprawl and that even at such an hour still almost unprecedentedly lingered, added the very accent of recent agitations. He hadn't been able not to consult himself a little as to the strength of the dose, or as to the protraction of the series of doses, in which he should administer the squeezed fruit, the expressed and tonic liquor, of his own adventure; but the atmosphere surrounding Jane herself was one in which he felt questions of that order immediately drop. The atmosphere surrounding Jane had been, in fine, on no occasion that he could recall, so perceptibly thick, so abruptly rich, so charged with strange aromas; he could really almost have fancied himself snuff up from it a certain strength of transient tobacco, the trace of a lately permitted cigarette or two at the best—rarest of accidents and strangest of discords in that harmonious whole. Had she, gracious goodness, been smoking with somebody?—a possibility not much less lurid than this conceived extravagance of the tolerated, the independent pipe.

Yes, absolutely, she eyed him through a ranker medium than had ever prevailed between them by any perversity of his; eyed him quite as if prepared, in regular tit-for-tat fashion, to stretch *him*, for a change, on his back, to let him cool his heels in that posture while she sauntered in view pointedly enough for him to tell her how he liked it. Something had happened to her in his absence that made her quite indifferent, in other words, to what might have happened to any one else at all; and so little had he to fear asperity on the score of his selfish day off that she didn't even see the advantage to her, for exasperation of his curiosity, of holding him at such preliminary arm's-length as would be represented by a specious "scene." She would have liked him, he easily recognized, to burst with curiosity, or, better still, to grovel with it, before she should so much as throw him a sop; but just this artless pride in her it was that, by the very candour of its extravagance, presently helped him to a keen induction. He had only to ask himself what could have occurred that would most of all things conduce to puffing her up with triumph, and then to reflect that, thoroughly to fill that bill, as who should say, she must have had a contrite call from Mora. He knew indeed, consummately, how superior a resource to morbid contrition that young woman was actually cultivating; in accordance with which the next broadest base for her exclusive command of the situation—and she clearly claimed nothing less—would be the fact that Walter Puddick had been with her and that she had had him (and to the tune of odd revelry withal to which their disordered and unremoved cups glaringly testified) all to herself. Such an interview with him as had so uplifted her that she distractedly had failed to ring for the parlour-maid, with six o'clock ebbing in strides—this did tell a story, Traffle ruefully recognised, with which it might well verily yet be given her to work on him. He was promptly to feel, none the less, how he carried the war across her border, poor superficial thing, when he decided on the direct dash that showed her she had still to count with him.

He didn't offer her, as he looked about, the mere obvious "I see you've had visitors, or a visitor, and have smoked a pipe with them and haven't bored yourself the least mite"—he broke straight into: "He has come out here again then, the

wretch, and you've done him more justice? You've done him
a good deal, my dear," he laughed in the grace of his advantage, "if you've done him even half as much as he appears to
have done your tea-table!" For this the quick flash-light of his
imagination—that's what it *was* for her to have married an
imaginative man—was just the drop of a flying-machine into
her castle court while she stood on guard at the gate. She
gave him a harder look, and he feared he might kindle by too
great an ease—as he was far from prematurely wishing to do—
her challenge of his own experience. Her flush of presumption
turned in fact, for the instant, to such a pathetically pale glare
that, before he knew it, conscious of his resources and always
coming characteristically round to indulgence as soon as she
at all gave way, he again magnanimously abdicated. "He came
to say it's no use?" he went on, and from that moment knew
himself committed to secrecy. It had tided him over the few
seconds of his danger—that of Jane's demanding of him what
he had been up to. He didn't want to be asked, no; and his
not being asked guarded his not—yes—positively lying; since
what most of all now filled his spirit was that he shouldn't
himself positively *have* to speak. His not doing so would be
his keeping something all to himself—as Jane would have
liked, for the six-and-a-half minutes of her strained, her poor
fatuous chance, to keep her passage with Puddick; or to do
this, in any case, till he could feel her resist what would certainly soon preponderantly make for her wish to see him stare
at her producible plum. It wasn't, moreover, that he could on
his own side so fully withstand wonder; the wonder of this
new singular ground of sociability between persons hitherto
seeing so little with the same eyes. There were things that
fitted—fitted somehow the fact of the young man's return,
and he could feel in his breast-pocket, when it came to that,
the presence of the very key to almost any blind or even wild
motion, as a sign of trouble, on poor Puddick's part; but what
and where was the key to the mystery of Jane's sudden pride
in his surely at the best very queer communication? The eagerness of this pride it was, at all events, that after a little so
worked as to enable him to breathe again for his own momentarily menaced treasure. "They're married—they've been
married a month; not a bit as one would have wished, or by

any form decent people recognise, but with the effect, at least, he tells me, that she's now legally his wife and he legally her husband, so that neither can marry any one else, and that— and that——"

"And that she has taken his horrid name, under our pressure, in exchange for her beautiful one—the one that so fitted her and that we ourselves, when all was said, did like so to keep repeating, in spite of everything, you won't deny, for the pleasant showy thing, compared with our own and most of our friends', it was to have familiarly about?" He took her up with this, as she had faltered a little over the other sources of comfort provided for them by the union so celebrated; in addition to which his ironic speech gained him time for the less candid, and thereby more cynically indulgent, profession of entire surprise. And he immediately added: "They've gone in for the mere civil marriage?"

"She appears to have consented to the very least of one that would do: they looked in somewhere, at some dingy office, jabbered a word or two to a man without h's and with a pen behind his ear, signed their names, and then came out as good as you and me; very much as you and I the other day sent off that little postal-packet to Paris from our grocer's back-shop."

Traffle showed his interest—he took in the news. "Well, you know, you didn't make Church a condition."

"No—fortunately not. I was clever enough," Jane bridled, "for that."

She had more for him, her manner showed—she had that to which the bare fact announced was as nothing; but he saw he must somehow, yes, pay by knowing nothing more than he could catch at by brilliant guesses. That had after an instant become a comfort to him: it would legitimate dissimulation, just as this recognised necessity would make itself quickly felt as the mere unregarded underside of a luxury. "And they're at all events, I take it," he went on, "sufficiently tied to be divorced."

She kept him—but only for a moment. "Quite sufficiently, I gather; and that," she said, "may come."

She made him, with it, quite naturally start. "Are they thinking of it already?"

She looked at him another instant hard, as with the rich expression of greater stores of private knowledge than she could adapt all at once to his intelligence. "You've no conception—not the least!—of how he feels."

Her husband hadn't hereupon, he admitted to himself, all artificially to gape. "Of course I haven't, love." Now that he had decided not to give his own observation away—and this however Puddick might "feel"—he should find it doubtless easy to be affectionate. "But he has been telling *you* all about it?"

"He has been here nearly two hours—as you of course, so far as that went, easily guessed. Nominally—at first—he had come out to see you; but he asked for me on finding you absent, and when I had come in to him seemed to want nothing better——"

"Nothing better than to stay and stay, Jane?" he smiled as he took her up. "Why in the world should he? What I ask myself," Traffle went on, "is simply how in the world you yourself could bear it." She turned away from him, holding him now, she judged, in a state of dependence; she reminded him even of himself, at similar moments of her own *asservissement*, when he turned his back upon her to walk about and keep her unsatisfied; an analogy markedly perceptible on her pausing a moment as under her first impression of the scattered tea-things and then ringing to have them attended to. Their domestic, retarded Rebecca, almost fiercely appeared, and her consequent cold presence in the room and inevitably renewed return to it, by the open door, for several minutes, drew out an interval during which he felt nervous again lest it should occur to his wife to wheel round on him with a question. She did nothing of the sort, fortunately; she was as stuffed with supersessive answers as if she were the latest number of a penny periodical: it was only a matter still of his continuing to pay his penny. She wasn't, moreover, his attention noted, trying to be portentous; she was much rather secretly and perversely serene—the basis of which condition did a little tax his fancy. What on earth had Puddick done to her—since he hadn't been able to bring her out Mora—that had made her distinguishably happier, beneath the mere grimness of her finally scoring at home, than she

had been for so many months? The best she could have
learned from him—Sidney might even at this point have
staked his life upon it—wouldn't have been that she could
hope to make Mrs. Puddick the centre of a grand rehabili-
tative tea-party. "Why then," he went on again, "if they were
married a month ago and he was so ready to stay with you
two hours, hadn't he come sooner?"

"He didn't come to tell me they were married—not on
purpose for that," Jane said after a little and as if the fact itself
were scarce more than a trifle—compared at least with others
she was possessed of, but that she didn't yet mention.

"Well"—Traffle frankly waited now—"what in the world
did he come to tell you?"

She made no great haste with it. "His fears."

"What fears—at present?" he disingenuously asked.

" 'At present?' Why, it's just 'at present' that he feels he has
got to look out." Yes, she was distinctly, she was strangely
placid about it. "It's worse to have to have them now that
she's his wife, don't you understand?" she pursued as if he
were really almost beginning to try her patience. "His difficulties aren't over," she nevertheless condescended further to
mention.

She was irritating, decidedly; but he could always make the
reflection that if she had been truly appointed to wear him
out she would long since have done so. "What difficulties,"
he accordingly continued, "are you talking about?"

"Those my splendid action—for he grants perfectly that it
is and will remain splendid—have caused for him." But her
calmness, her positive swagger of complacency over it, *was*
indeed amazing.

"Do you mean by your having so forced his hand?" Traffle
had now no hesitation in risking.

"By my having forced *hers*," his wife presently returned.
"By my glittering bribe, as he calls it."

He saw in a moment how she liked what her visitor had
called things; yet it made him, himself, but want more. "She
found your bribe so glittering that she couldn't resist it?"

"She couldn't resist it." And Jane sublimely stalked. "She
consented to perform the condition attached—as I've mentioned to you—for enjoying it."

Traffle artfully considered. "If she has met you on that arrangement where do the difficulties come in?"

Jane looked at him a moment with wonderful eyes. "For me? They don't come in!" And she again turned her back on him.

It really tempted him to permit himself a certain impatience—which in fact he might have shown hadn't he by this time felt himself more intimately interested in Jane's own evolution than in Mr. Puddick's, or even, for the moment, in Mora's. That interest ministered to his art. "You must tell me at your convenience about yours, that is about your apparently feeling yourself now so beautifully able to sink yours. What I'm asking you about is his—if you've put them so at your ease."

"I haven't put them a bit at their ease!"—and she was at him with it again almost as in a glow of triumph.

He aimed at all possible blankness. "But surely four hundred and fifty more a year——!"

"Four hundred and fifty more is nothing to her."

"Then why the deuce did she marry him for it?—since she apparently couldn't bring herself to without it."

"She didn't marry him that she herself should get my allowance—she married him that *he* should."

At which Traffle had a bit genuinely to wonder. "It comes at any rate to the same if you pay it to her."

Nothing, it would seem, could possibly have had on Jane's state of mind a happier effect. "I sha'n't pay it to her."

Her husband could again but stare. "You *won't*, dear?" he deprecated.

"I don't," she nobly replied. And then as at last for one of her greater cards: "I pay it to *him*."

"But if he pays it to *her*——?"

"He doesn't. He explains."

Traffle cast about. "Explains—a—to Mora?"

"Explains to me. He *has*," she almost defiantly bridled, "perfectly explained."

Her companion smiled at her. "Ah, *that* then is what took him two hours!" He went on, however, before she could either attenuate or amplify: "It must have taken him that of course to arrange with you—as I understand?—for his monopolising the money?"

She seemed to notify him now that from her high command of the situation she could quite look down on the spiteful sarcastic touch. "We have plenty to arrange. We have plenty to discuss. We shall often—if you want to know—have occasion to meet." After which, "Mora," she quite gloriously brought forth, "hates me worse than ever."

He opened his eyes to their widest. "For settling on her a substantial fortune?"

"For having"—and Jane had positively a cold smile for it—"believed her not respectable."

"Then *was* she?" Traffle gaped.

It did turn on him the tables! "Mr. Puddick continues to swear it." But even though so gracefully patient of him she remained cold.

"You yourself, however, haven't faith?"

"No," said Mrs. Traffle.

"In his word, you mean?"

She had a fine little wait. "In her conduct. In his knowledge of it."

Again he had to rise to it. "With other persons?"

"With other persons. Even then."

Traffle thought. "But even when?"

"Even from the first," Jane grandly produced.

"Oh, oh, oh!" he found himself crying with a flush. He had had occasion to colour in the past for her flatness, but never for such an audacity of point. Wonderful, all round, in the light of reflection, seemed what Mora was doing for them. "It won't be her husband, at all events, who has put you up to *that*!"

She took this in as if it might have been roguishly insinuating in respect to her own wit—though not, as who should say, to make any great use of it. "It's what I read——"

"What you 'read'—?" he asked as she a little hung fire.

"Well, into the past that from far back so troubled me. I had plenty to tell *him*!" she surprisingly went on.

"Ah, my dear, to the detriment of his own wife?" our friend broke out.

It earned him, however, but her at once harder and richer look. Clearly she was at a height of satisfaction about something—it spread and spread more before him. "For all that really, you know, she *is* now his wife!"

He threw himself amazedly back. "You mean she practically isn't?" And then as her eyes but appeared to fill it out: "Is that what you've been having from him?—and is that what we've done?"

She looked away a little—she turned off again. "Of course I've wanted the full truth—as to what I've done."

Our friend could imagine that, at strict need; but wondrous to him with it was this air in her as of the birth of a new detachment. "What you've 'done,' it strikes me, might be a little embarrassing for us; but you speak as if you really quite enjoyed it!"

This was a remark, he had to note, by which she wasn't in the least confounded; so that if he had his impression of that odd novelty in her to which allusion has just been made, it might indeed have been quite a new Jane who now looked at him out of her conscious eyes. "He likes to talk to me, poor dear."

She treated his observation as if that quite met it—which couldn't but slightly irritate him; but he hadn't in the least abjured self-control, he was happy to feel, on his returning at once: "And you like to talk with *him*, obviously—since he appears so beautifully and quickly to have brought you round from your view of him as merely low."

She flushed a little at this reminder, but it scarcely pulled her up. "I never thought him low"—she made no more of it than that; "but I admit," she quite boldly smiled, "that I did think him wicked."

"And it's now your opinion that people can be wicked without being low?"

Prodigious really, he found himself make out while she just hesitated, the opinions over the responsibility of which he should yet see her—and all as a consequence of this one afternoon of his ill-inspired absence—ready thus unnaturally to smirk at him. "It depends," she complacently brought out, "on the kind."

"On the kind of wickedness?"

"Yes, perhaps. And"—it didn't at all baffle her—"on the kind of people."

"I see. It's all, my dear, I want to get at—for a proper understanding of the extraordinary somersault you appear to have turned. Puddick has just convinced you that *his* immoralities are the right ones?"

"No, love—nothing will ever convince me that any immoralities deserve that name. But some," she went on, "only seem wrong till they're explained."

"And those are the ones that, as you say, he has been explaining?" Traffle asked with a glittering cheerful patience.

"He has explained a great deal, yes"—Jane bore up under it; "but I think that, by the opportunity for a good talk with him, I've at last understood even more. We weren't, you see, before," she obligingly added, "in his confidence."

"No, indeed," her husband opined, "we could scarcely be said to be. But now we are, and it makes the difference?"

"It makes the difference to *me*," Jane nobly contented herself with claiming. "If I've been remiss, however," she showed herself prepared to pursue, "I must make it up. And doubtless I *have* been."

" 'Remiss,' " he stared, "when you're in full enjoyment of my assent to our making such sacrifices for her?"

She gave it, in her superior way, a moment's thought. "I don't mean remiss in act; no, that, thank goodness, we haven't been. But remiss in feeling," she quite unbearably discriminated.

"Ah, that, *par exemple*," he protested, "I deny that I've been for a moment!"

"No"—and she fairly mused at him; "you seemed to have all sorts of ideas; while I," she conceded, "had only one, which, so far as it went, was good. But it didn't go far enough."

He watched her a moment. "I doubtless don't know what idea you mean," he smiled, "but how far does it go now?"

She hadn't, with her preoccupied eyes on him, so much as noticed the ironic ring of it. "Well, you'll see for yourself. I mustn't abandon him."

"Abandon Puddick? Who the deuce then ever said you must?"

"Didn't *you* a little," she blandly inquired, "all the while you were so great on our not 'interfering'?"

"I was great—if great you call it—only," he returned, "so far as I was great for our just a little understanding."

"Well, what I'm telling you is that I think I do at present just a little understand."

"And doesn't it make you feel just a little badly?"

"No"—she serenely shook her head; "for my intention was so good. He does justice now," she explained, "to my intention; or he will very soon—he quite let me *see* that, and it's why I'm what you call 'happy.' With which," she wound up, "there's so much more I can still do. There are bad days, you see, before him—and then he'll have only me. For if she *was* respectable," Jane proceeded, reverting as imperturbably to their question of a while back, "she's certainly not nice now."

He'd be hanged, Traffle said to himself, if he wouldn't look at her hard. "Do you mean by not coming to thank you?" And then as she but signified by a motion that this she had now made her terms with: "What else then is the matter with her?"

"The matter with her," said Jane on the note of high deliberation and competence, and not without a certain pity for his own want of light, "the matter with her is that she's quite making her preparations, by what he's convinced, for leaving him."

"Leaving him?"—he met it with treasures of surprise.

These were nothing, however, he could feel, to the wealth of authority with which she again gave it out. "Leaving him."

"A month after marriage?"

"A month after—their form; and she seems to think it handsome, he says, that she waited the month. *That*," she added, "is what he came above all that we should know."

He took in, our friend, many things in silence; but he presently had his comment. "We've done our job then to an even livelier tune than we could have hoped!"

Again this moral of it all didn't appear to shock her. "He doesn't reproach me," she wonderfully said.

"I'm sure it's very good of him then!" Traffle cried.

But her blandness, her mildness, was proof. "My dear Sidney, Walter *is* very good."

She brought it out as if she had made, quite unaided, the discovery; though even this perhaps was not what he most stared at. "Do you call him Walter?"

"Surely"—and she returned surprise for surprise—"isn't he my nephew?"

Traffle bethought himself. "You recognise the Registrar then for *that*."

She could perfectly smile back. "I don't know that I would if our friend weren't so interesting."

It was quite for Sidney Traffle, at this, as if he hadn't known up to that moment, filled for him with her manner of intimating her reason, what sort of a wife—for coolness and other things—he rejoiced in. Really he had to take time—and to throw himself, while he did so, into pretences. "The Registrar?"

"Don't be a goose, dear!"—she showed she could humour him at last; and it was perhaps the most extraordinary impression he had ever in his life received. "But you'll see," she continued in this spirit. "I mean how I shall interest you." And then as he but seemed to brood at her: "Interest you, I mean, in my interest—for I sha'n't content myself," she beautifully professed, "with your simply not minding it."

"Minding your interest?" he frowned.

"In my poor ravaged, lacerated, pathetic nephew. I shall expect you in some degree to share it."

"Oh, I'll share it if you like, but you must remember how little I'm responsible."

She looked at him abysmally. "No—it *was* mainly me. He brings that home to me, poor dear. Oh, he doesn't scare me!"—she kept it up; "and I don't know that I want him to, for it seems to clear the whole question, and really to ease me a little, that he should put everything before me, his grievance with us, I mean, and that I should know just how he has seen our attitude, or at any rate mine. I was stupid the other day when he came—he saw but a part of it then. It's settled," she further mentioned, "that I shall go to him."

"Go to him—?" Traffle blankly echoed.

"At his studio, dear, you know," Jane promptly supplied. "I want to see his work—for we had some talk about that too. He has made me care for it."

Her companion took these things in—even so many of them as there now seemed to be: they somehow left him, in point of fact, so stranded. "Why not call on *her* at once?"

"That will be useless when she won't receive me. Never, never!" said Jane with a sigh so confessedly superficial that her husband found it peculiarly irritating.

"He has brought *that* 'home' to you?" he consequently almost jibed.

She winced no more, however, than if he had tossed her a flower. "Ah, what he has made me realise is that if he has definitely lost her, as he feels, so we ourselves assuredly have, for ever and a day. But he doesn't mean to lose sight of her, and in that way——"

"In that way?"—Traffle waited.

"Well, I shall always hear whatever there may be. And there's no knowing," she developed as with an open and impartial appetite, "what that mayn't come to."

He turned away—with his own conception of this possible expansive quantity and a sore sense of how the combinations of things were appointed to take place without his aid or presence, how they kept failing to provide for him at all. It was his old irony of fate, which seemed to insist on meeting him at every turn. Mora had testified in the morning to no further use for him than might reside in his making her shuffled-off lover the benevolent business of his life; but even in this cold care, clearly, he was forestalled by a person to whom it would come more naturally. It was by his original and independent measure that the whole case had become interesting and been raised above the level of a mere vulgar scandal; in spite of which he could now stare but at the prospect of exclusion, and of his walking round it, through the coming years—to walk vaguely round and round announcing itself thus at the best as the occupation of his future—in wider and remoter circles. As against this, for warmth, there would nestle in his breast but a prize of memory, the poor little secret of the passage at the Gallery that the day had bequeathed him. He might propose to hug this treasure of consciousness, to make it, by some ingenuity he couldn't yet forecast, his very own; only it was a poor thing in view of their positive privation, and what Jane was getting out of the whole business—*her* ingenuity it struck him he could quite forecast—would certainly be a comparative riot of sympathy. He stood with his hands in his pockets and gazed a little, very sightlessly—that is with an other than ranging vision, even though not other than baffled one too—out of the glimmering square of the window. Then, however, he recalled himself, slightly shook himself, and the next moment had faced about with a fresh dissimulation. "If you talk of her leaving him, and he himself comes in for all your bounty, what then is she going to live upon?"

"On her wits, he thinks and fears; on her beauty, on her audacity. Oh, it's a picture—!" Jane was now quite unshrinkingly able to report from her visitor. Traffle, morally fingering, as it were, the mystic medal under his shirt, was at least equally qualified, on his side, to gloom all yearningly at her; but she had meanwhile testified further to her consistent command of their position. "He believes her to be more than ever—*not* 'respectable.'"

"How, 'more than ever,' if respectable was what she *was*?"

"It was what she wasn't!" Jane returned.

He had a prodigious shrug—it almost eased him for the moment of half his impatience. "I understood that you told me a moment ago the contrary."

"Then you understood wrong. All I said was that he says she was—but that I don't believe him."

He wondered, following. "Then how does he come to describe her as less so?"

Jane straightened it out—Jane surpassed herself. "He doesn't describe her as less so than she 'was'—I only put her at that. *He*"—oh, she was candid and clear about it!—"simply puts her at less so than she might be. In order, don't you see," she luminously reasoned, "that we shall have it on our conscience that we took the case out of his hands."

"And you allowed to him then that that's how we do have it?"

To this her face lighted as never yet. "Why, it's just the point of what I tell you—that I feel I *must*."

He turned it over. "But why so if you're right?"

She brought up her own shoulders for his density. "I haven't been right. I've been wrong."

He could only glare about. "In holding her then already to have fallen——?"

"Oh dear no, not that! In having let it work me up. Of course I can but take from him now," she elucidated, "what he insists on."

Her husband measured it. "Of course, in other words, you can but believe she was as bad as possible, and yet pretend to him he has persuaded you of the contrary?"

"Exactly, love—so that it shall make us worse. As bad as he wants us," she smiled.

"In order," Traffle said after a moment, "that he may comfortably take the money?"

She welcomed this gleam. "In order that he may comfortably take it."

He could but gaze at her again. "You *have* arranged it!"

"Certainly I have—and that's why I'm calm. He considers, at any rate," she continued, "that it will probably be Sir Bruce. I mean that she'll leave him for."

"And who in the world is Sir Bruce?"

She consulted her store of impressions. "Sir Bruce Bagley, Bart., I think he said."

Traffle fitted it in silence. "A soldier?" he then asked.

"I'm uncertain—but, as I seem to remember, a patron. He buys pictures."

Traffle could privately imagine it. "And that's how she knows him?"

Jane allowed for his simplicity. "Oh, how she 'knows' people——!"

It still held him, however, an instant. "What sort of a type?"

She seemed to wonder a little at his press of questions, but after just facing it didn't pretend to more than she knew. She was, on this basis of proper relations that she had settled, more and more willing, besides, to oblige. "I'll find out for you."

It came in a tone that made him turn off. "Oh, I don't mind." With which he was back at the window.

She hovered—she didn't leave him; he felt her there behind
him as if she had noted a break in his voice or a moisture in
his eyes—a tribute to a natural pang even for a not real niece.
He wouldn't renew with her again, and would have been glad
now had she quitted him; but there grew for him during the
next moments the strange sense that, with what had so bravely
happened for her—to the point of the triumph of displaying
it to him inclusive—the instinct of compassion worked in her;
though whether in respect of the comparative solitude to
which her duties to "Walter" would perhaps more or less rel-
egate him, or on the score of his having brought home to
him, as she said, so much that was painful, she hadn't yet
made up her mind. This, after a little, however, she discreetly
did; she decided in the sense of consideration for his nerves.
She lingered—he felt her more vaguely about; and in the silence that thus lasted between them he felt also, with its importance, the determination of their life for perhaps a long
time to come. He was wishing she'd go—he was wanting not
then again to meet her eyes; but still more than either of these
things he was asking himself, as from time to time during the
previous months he had all subtly and idly asked, what would
have been the use, after all, of so much imagination as constantly worked in him. Didn't it let him into more deep holes
than it pulled him out of? Didn't it make for him more tight
places than it saw him through? Or didn't it at the same time,
not less, give him all to himself a life, exquisite, occult, dangerous and sacred, to which everything ministered and which
nothing could take away?

He fairly lost himself in that aspect—which it was clear only
the vision and the faculty themselves could have hung there,
of a sudden, so wantonly, before him; and by the moment
attention for nearer things had re-emerged he seemed to
know how his wife had interpreted his air of musing melancholy absence. She had dealt with it after her own fashion;
had given him a moment longer the benefit of a chance to
inquire or appeal afresh; and then, after brushing him good-
humouredly, in point of fact quite gaily, with her skirts, after
patting and patronising him gently with her finger-tips, very
much as he had patted and patronised Walter Puddick that
day in the porch, had put him in his place, on the whole

matter of the issue of their trouble, or at least had left him in it, by a happy last word. She had judged him more upset, more unable to conclude or articulate, about Mora and Sir Bruce, than she, with her easier power of rebound, had been; and her final wisdom, indeed her final tenderness, would be to show him cheerful and helpful mercy. "No then, I see I mustn't rub it in. You sha'n't be worried. I'll keep it all to myself, dear." With which she would have floated away—with which and some other things he was sensibly, relievingly alone. But he remained staring out at the approach of evening—and it was of the other things he was more and more conscious while the vague grey prospect held him. Even while he had looked askance in the greyness at the importunate fiend of fancy it was riding him again as the very genius of twilight; it played the long reach of its prompt lantern over Sir Bruce Bagley, the patron of promising young lives. He wondered about Sir Bruce, recalling his face and his type and his effect— his effect, so immediate, on Mora; wondered how he had proceeded, how he would still proceed, how far perhaps even they had got by that time. Lord, the fun some people did have! Even Jane, with her conscientious new care—even Jane, unmistakably, was in for such a lot.

Crapy Cornelia

THREE TIMES within a quarter of an hour—shifting the while his posture on his chair of contemplation—had he looked at his watch as for its final sharp hint that he should decide, that he should get up. His seat was one of a group fairly sequestered, unoccupied save for his own presence, and from where he lingered he looked off at a stretch of lawn freshened by recent April showers and on which sundry small children were at play. The trees, the shrubs, the plants, every stem and twig just ruffled as by the first touch of the light finger of the relenting year, struck him as standing still in the blest hope of more of the same caress; the quarter about him held its breath after the fashion of the child who waits with the rigour of an open mouth and shut eyes for the promised sensible effect of his having been good. So, in the windless, sun-warmed air of the beautiful afternoon, the Park of the winter's end had struck White-Mason as waiting; even New York, under such an impression, was "good," good enough— for *him*; its very sounds were faint, were almost sweet, as they reached him from so seemingly far beyond the wooded horizon that formed the remoter limit of his large shallow glade. The tones of the frolic infants ceased to be nondescript and harsh—were in fact almost as fresh and decent as the frilled and puckered and ribboned garb of the little girls, which had always a way, in those parts, of so portentously flaunting the daughters of the strange native—that is of the overwhelmingly alien—populace at him.

Not that these things in particular were his matter of meditation now; he had wanted, at the end of his walk, to sit apart a little and think—and had been doing that for twenty minutes, even though as yet to no break in the charm of procrastination. But he had looked without seeing and listened without hearing: all that had been positive for him was that he hadn't failed vaguely to feel. He had felt in the first place, and he continued to feel—yes, at forty-eight quite as much as at any point of the supposed reign of younger intensities—the great spirit of the air, the fine sense of the season, the supreme appeal of Nature, he might have said, to his time of life; quite as if she, easy, indulgent, indifferent, cynical Power, were offering him the last chance it would rest with his wit or his blood to embrace. Then with that he had been entertaining, to the point and with the prolonged consequence of accepted immobilization, the certitude that if he did call on Mrs. Worthingham and find her at home he couldn't in justice to himself not put to her the question that had lapsed the other time, the last time, through the irritating and persistent, even if accidental, presence of others. What friends she had—the people who so stupidly, so wantonly stuck! If they *should*, he and she, come to an understanding, that would presumably have to include certain members of her singularly ill-composed circle, in whom it was incredible to him that he should ever take an interest. This defeat, to do himself justice—he had bent rather predominantly on *that*, you see; ideal justice to *her*, with her possible conception of what it should consist of, being another and quite a different matter—he had had the fact of the Sunday afternoon to thank for; she didn't "keep" that day for him, since they hadn't, up to now, quite begun to cultivate the appointment or assignation founded on explicit sacrifices. He might at any rate look to find this pleasant practical Wednesday—should he indeed, at his actual rate, stay it before it ebbed—more liberally and intendingly given him.

The sound he at last most wittingly distinguished in his nook was the single deep note of half-past five borne to him from some high-perched public clock. He finally got up with the sense that the time from then on *ought* at least to be felt as sacred to him. At this juncture it was—while he stood there shaking his garments, settling his hat, his necktie, his shirt-cuffs, fixing the high polish of his fine shoes as if for some reflection in it of his straight and spare and grizzled, his refined and trimmed and dressed, his altogether distinguished person, that of a gentleman abundantly settled, but of a bachelor markedly nervous—at this crisis it was, doubtless, that he at once most measured and least resented his predicament. If he should go he would almost to a certainty find her, and if he should find her he would almost to a certainty come to the point. He wouldn't put it off again—there was that high consideration for him of justice at least to himself. He had never yet denied himself anything so apparently fraught with possibilities as the idea of proposing to Mrs. Worthingham— never yet, in other words, denied himself anything he had so distinctly wanted to do; and the results of that wisdom had remained for him precisely the precious parts of experience. Counting only the offers of his honourable hand, these had been on three remembered occasions at least the consequence of an impulse as sharp and a self-respect as reasoned; a self-respect that hadn't in the least suffered, moreover, from the failure of each appeal. He had been met in the three cases— the only ones he at all compared with his present case—by the frank confession that he didn't somehow, charming as he was, cause himself to be superstitiously believed in; and the lapse of life, afterward, had cleared up many doubts.

It *wouldn't* have done, he eventually, he lucidly saw, each time he had been refused; and the candour of his nature was such that he could live to think of these very passages as a proof of how right he had been—right, that is, to have put himself forward always, by the happiest instinct, only in im- possible conditions. He had the happy consciousness of hav- ing exposed the important question to the crucial test, and of having escaped, by that persistent logic, a grave mistake. What better proof of his escape than the fact that he was now free to renew the all-interesting inquiry, and should be exactly, about to do so in different and better conditions? The con- ditions were better by as much more—as much more of his career and character, of his situation, his reputation he could even have called it, of his knowledge of life, of his somewhat extended means, of his possibly augmented charm, of his cer- tainly improved mind and temper—as was involved in the actual impending settlement. Once he had got into motion, once he had crossed the Park and passed out of it, entering, with very little space to traverse, one of the short new streets that abutted on its east side, his step became that of a man young enough to find confidence, quite to find felicity, in the sense, in almost any sense, of action. He could still enjoy almost anything, absolutely an unpleasant thing, in default of a better, that might still remind him he wasn't so old. The standing newness of everything about him would, it was true, have weakened this cheer by too much presuming on it; Mrs.

Worthingham's house, before which he stopped, had that gloss of new money, that glare of a piece fresh from the mint and ringing for the first time on any counter, which seems to claim for it, in any transaction, something more than the "face" value.

This could but be yet more the case for the impression of the observer introduced and committed. On our friend's part I mean, after his admission and while still in the hall, the sense of the general shining immediacy, of the still unhushed clamour of the shock, was perhaps stronger than he had ever known it. That broke out from every corner as the high pitch of interest, and with a candour that—no, certainly—he had never seen equalled; every particular expensive object shrieking at him in its artless pride that it had just "come home." He met the whole vision with something of the grimace produced on persons without goggles by the passage from a shelter to a blinding light; and if he had—by a perfectly possible chance—been "snap-shotted" on the spot, would have struck you as showing for his first tribute to the temple of Mrs. Worthingham's charming presence a scowl almost of anguish. He wasn't constitutionally, it may at once be explained for him, a goggled person; and he was condemned, in New York, to this frequent violence of transition—having to reckon with it whenever he went out, as who should say, from himself. The high pitch of interest, to his taste, was the pitch of history, the pitch of acquired and earned suggestion, the pitch of association, in a word; so that he lived by preference, incontestably, if not in a rich gloom, which would have been beyond his means and spirits, at least amid objects and images that confessed to the tone of time.

He had ever felt that an indispensable presence—with a need of it moreover that interfered at no point with his gentle habit, not to say his subtle art, of drawing out what was left him of his youth, of thinly and thriftily spreading the rest of that choicest jam-pot of the cupboard of consciousness over the remainder of a slice of life still possibly thick enough to bear it; or in other words of moving the melancholy limits, the significant signs, constantly a little further on, very much as property-marks or staked boundaries are sometimes stealthily shifted at night. He positively cherished in fact, as against the too inveterate gesture of distressfully guarding his eye-balls—so many New York aspects seemed to keep him at it—an ideal of adjusted appreciation, of courageous curiosity, of fairly letting the world about him, a world of constant breath-less renewals and merciless substitutions, make its flaring as-sault on its own inordinate terms. Newness *was* value in the piece—for the acquisitor, or at least sometimes might be, even though the act of "blowing" hard, the act marking a heated freshness of arrival, or other form of irruption, could never minister to the peace of those already and long on the field; and this if only because maturer tone was after all most ap-preciable and most consoling when one staggered back to it, wounded, bleeding, blinded, from the riot of the raw—or, to put the whole experience more prettily, no doubt, from ex-cesses of light.

II

If he went in, however, with something of his more or less inevitable scowl, there were really, at the moment, two rather valid reasons for screened observation; the first of these being that the whole place seemed to reflect as never before the lustre of Mrs. Worthingham's own polished and prosperous little person—to smile, it struck him, with her smile, to twin-kle not only with the gleam of her lovely teeth, but with that of all her rings and brooches and bangles and other gewgaws, to curl and spasmodically cluster as in emulation of her charm-ing complicated yellow tresses, to surround the most animated of pink-and-white, of ruffled and ribboned, of frilled and fes-tooned Dresden china shepherdesses with exactly the right system of rococo curves and convolutions and other flour-ishes, a perfect bower of painted and gilded and moulded con-ceits. The second ground of this immediate impression of scenic extravagance, almost as if the curtain rose for him to the first act of some small and expensively mounted comic opera, was that she hadn't, after all, awaited him in fond sin-gleness, but had again just a trifle inconsiderately exposed him to the drawback of having to reckon, for whatever design he might amiably entertain, with the presence of a third and quite superfluous person, a small black insignificant but none the less oppressive stranger. It was odd how, on the instant, the little lady engaged with her did affect him as comparatively black—very much as if that had absolutely, in such a medium, to be the graceless appearance of any item not positively of some fresh shade of a light colour or of some pretty pretension to a charming twist. Any witness of their meeting, his hostess should surely have felt, would have been a false note in the whole rosy glow; but what note so false as that of the dingy little presence that she might actually, by a refinement of her perhaps always too visible study of effect, have provided as a positive contrast or foil? whose name and intervention, more-over, she appeared to be no more moved to mention and account for than she might have been to "present"—whether as stretched at her feet or erect upon disciplined haunches—some shaggy old domesticated terrier or poodle.

Extraordinarily, after he had been in the room five minutes—a space of time during which his fellow-visitor had neither budged nor uttered a sound—he had made Mrs. Worthingham out as all at once perfectly pleased to see him, completely aware of what he had most in mind, and sin-gularly serene in face of his sense of their impediment. It was as if for all the world she didn't take it for one, the immobility, to say nothing of the seeming equanimity, of their tactless companion; at whom meanwhile indeed our friend himself, after his first ruffled perception, no more ad-ventured a look than if advised by his constitutional kind-ness that to notice her in any degree would perforce be ungraciously to glower. He talked after a fashion with the woman as to whose power to please and amuse and serve him, as to whose really quite organised and indicated fitness for lighting up his autumn afternoon of life his conviction had lately strained itself so clear; but he was all the while carrying on an intenser exchange with his own spirit and trying to read into the charming creature's behaviour, as he could only call it, some confirmation of his theory that she also had her inward flutter and anxiously counted on him. He found support, happily for the conviction just named, in the idea, at no moment as yet really repugnant to him, the idea bound up in fact with the finer essence of her appeal, that she had her own vision too of her quality and her price,

and that the last appearance she would have liked to bristle
with was that of being forewarned and eager.

He had, if he came to think of it, scarce definitely warned
her, and he probably wouldn't have taken to her so consciously in the first instance without an appreciative sense that,
as she was a little person of twenty superficial graces, so she
was also a little person with her secret pride. She might just
have planted her mangy lion—not to say her muzzled house-
dog—there in his path as a symbol that she wasn't cheap and
easy; which would be a thing he couldn't possibly wish his
future wife to have shown herself in advance, even if to him
alone. That she could make him put himself such questions
was precisely part of the attaching play of her iridescent surface, the shimmering interfusion of her various aspects; that
of her youth with her independence—her pecuniary perhaps
in particular, that of her vivacity with her beauty, that of her
facility above all with her odd novelty; the high modernity, as
people appeared to have come to call it, that made her so
much more "knowing" in some directions than even he, man
of the world as he certainly was, could pretend to be, though
all on a basis of the most unconscious and instinctive and
luxurious assumption. She was "up" to everything, aware of
everything—if one counted from a short enough time back
(from week before last, say, and as if quantities of history had
burst upon the world within the fortnight); she was likewise
surprised at nothing, and in that direction one might reckon
as far ahead as the rest of her lifetime, or at any rate as the
rest of his, which was all that would concern him: it was as if
the suitability of the future to her personal and rather pampered tastes was what she most took for granted, so that he
could see her, for all her Dresden-china shoes and her flutter
of wondrous befrilled contemporary skirts, skip by the side of
the coming age as over the floor of a ball-room, keeping step
with its monstrous stride and prepared for every figure of the
dance.

Her outlook took form to him suddenly as a great square
sunny window that hung in assured fashion over the immensity of life. There rose toward it as from a vast swarming *plaza*
a high tide of motion and sound; yet it was at the same time
as if even while he looked her light gemmed hand, flashing

on him in addition to those other things the perfect polish of the prettiest pink finger-nails in the world, had touched a spring, the most ingenious of recent devices for instant ease, which dropped half across the scene a soft-coloured mechanical blind, a fluttered, fringed awning of charmingly toned silk, such as would make a bath of cool shade for the favoured friend leaning with her there—that is for the happy couple itself—on the balcony. The great view would be the prospect and privilege of the very state he coveted—since didn't he covet it?—the state of being so securely at her side; while the wash of privacy, as one might count it, the broad fine brush dipped into clear umber and passed, full and wet, straight across the strong scheme of colour, would represent the security itself, all the uplifted inner elegance, the condition, so ideal, of being shut out from nothing and yet of having, so gaily and breezily aloft, none of the burden or worry of anything. Thus, as I say, for our friend, the place itself, while his vivid impression lasted, portentously opened and spread, and what was before him took, to his vision, though indeed at so other a crisis, the form of the "glimmering square" of the poet; yet, for a still more remarkable fact, with an incongruous object usurping at a given instant the privilege of the frame and seeming, even as he looked, to block the view.

The incongruous object was a woman's head, crowned with a little sparsely feathered black hat, an ornament quite unlike those the women mostly noticed by White-Mason were now "wearing," and that grew and grew, that came nearer and nearer, while it met his eyes, after the manner of images in the kinematograph. It had presently loomed so large that he saw nothing else—not only among the things at a considerable distance, the things Mrs. Worthingham would eventually, yet unmistakably, introduce him to, but among those of this lady's various attributes and appurtenances as to which he had been in the very act of cultivating his consciousness. It was in the course of another minute the most extraordinary thing in the world: everything had altered, dropped, darkened, disappeared; his imagination had spread its wings only to feel them flop all grotesquely at its sides as he recognised in his hostess's quiet companion, the oppressive alien who hadn't indeed interfered with his fanciful flight, though she had prevented his immediate declaration and brought about the thud, not to say the felt violent shock, of his fall to earth, the perfectly plain identity of Cornelia Rasch. It was she who had remained there at attention; it was she their companion hadn't introduced; it was she he had forborne to face with his fear of incivility. He stared at her—everything else went.

"Why it has been *you* all this time?"

Miss Rasch fairly turned pale. "I was waiting to see if you'd know me."

"Ah, my dear Cornelia"—he came straight out with it—"rather!"

"Well, it isn't," she returned with a quick change to red now, "from having taken much time to look at me!"

She smiled, she even laughed, but he could see how she had felt his unconsciousness, poor thing; the acquaintance, quite the friend of his youth, as she had been, the associate of his childhood, of his early manhood, of his middle age in fact, up to a few years back, not more than ten at the most; the associate too of so many of his associates and of almost all of his relations, those of the other time, those who had mainly gone for ever; the person in short whose noted disappearance, though it might have seemed final, had been only of recent seasons. She was present again now, all unexpectedly—he had heard of her having at last, left alone after successive deaths and with scant resources, sought economic salvation in Europe, the promised land of American thrift—she was present as this almost ancient and this oddly unassertive little rotund figure whom one seemed no more obliged to address than if she had been a black satin ottoman "treated" with buttons and gimp; a class of object as to which the policy of blindness was imperative. He felt the need of some explanatory plea, and before he could think had uttered one at Mrs. Worthingham's expense. "Why, you see we weren't introduced——!"

"No—but I didn't suppose I should have to be named to you."

"Well, my dear woman, you haven't—do me that justice!" He could at least make this point. "I felt all the while—!" However, it would have taken him long to say what he had been feeling; and he was aware now of the pretty projected light of Mrs. Worthingham's wonder. She looked as if, out for a walk with her, he had put her to the inconvenience of his stopping to speak to a strange woman in the street.

"I never supposed you knew her!"—it was to him his hostess excused herself.

This made Miss Rasch spring up, distinctly flushed, distinctly strange to behold, but not vulgarly nettled—Cornelia was incapable of that; only rather funnily bridling and laughing, only showing that this was all she had waited for, only saying just the right thing, the thing she could make so clearly a jest. "Of course if you *had* you'd have presented him."

Mrs. Worthingham looked while answering at White-Mason. "I didn't want you to go—which you see you do as soon as he speaks to you. But I never dreamed——!"

"That there was anything between us? Ah, there are no end of things!" He, on his side, though addressing the younger and prettier woman, looked at his fellow-guest; to whom he even continued: "When did you get back? May I come and see you the very first thing?"

Cornelia gasped and wriggled—she practically giggled; she had lost every atom of her little old, her little young, though always unaccountable prettiness, which used to peep so, on the bare chance of a shot, from behind indefensible features, that it almost made watching her a form of sport. He had heard vaguely of her, it came back to him (for there had been no letters; their later acquaintance, thank goodness, hadn't involved that) as experimenting, for economy, and then as settling, to the same rather dismal end, somewhere in England, at one of those intensely English places, St. Leonards, Cheltenham, Bognor, Dawlish—which, awfully, *was* it?—and she now affected him for all the world as some small squirming, exclaiming, genteelly conversing old maid of a type vaguely associated with the three-volume novels he used to feed on (besides his so often encountering it in "real life") during a far-away stay of his own at Brighton. Odder than any element of his ex-gossip's identity itself, however, was the fact that she somehow, with it all, rejoiced his sight. Indeed the supreme oddity was that the manner of her reply to his request for leave to call should have absolutely charmed his attention. She didn't look at him; she only, from under her frumpy,

crapy, curiously exotic hat, and with her good little near-
sighted insinuating glare, expressed to Mrs. Worthingham,
while she answered him, wonderful arch things, the overdone
things of a shy woman. "Yes, you may call—but only when
this dear lovely lady has done with you!" The moment after
which she had gone.

III

Forty minutes later he was taking his way back from the queer
miscarriage of his adventure; taking it, with no conscious positive felicity, through the very spaces that had witnessed
shortly before the considerable serenity of his assurance. He
had said to himself then, or had as good as said it, that, since
he might do perfectly as he liked, it couldn't fail for him that
he must soon retrace those steps, humming, to all intents, the
first bars of a wedding-march; so beautifully had it cleared up
that he was "going to like" letting Mrs. Worthingham accept
him. He was to have hummed no wedding-march, as it
seemed to be turning out—he had none, up to now, to hum;
and yet, extraordinarily, it wasn't in the least because she had
refused him. Why then hadn't he liked as much as he had
intended to like it putting the pleasant act, the act of not
refusing him, in her power? Could it all have come from the
awkward minute of his failure to decide sharply, on Cornelia's
departure, whether or no he would attend her to the door?
He hadn't decided at all—what the deuce had been in him?—
but had danced to and fro in the room, thinking better of
each impulse and then thinking worse. He had hesitated like
an ass erect on absurd hind legs between two bundles of hay;
the upshot of which must have been his giving the falsest
impression. In what way that was to be for an instant considered had their common past committed him to crapy Cornelia? He repudiated with a whack on the gravel any ghost of
an obligation.

What he could get rid of with scanter success, unfortunately,
was the peculiar sharpness of his sense that, though mystified
by his visible flurry—and yet not mystified enough for a sympathetic question either—his hostess had been, on the whole,
even more frankly diverted: which was precisely an example

of that newest, freshest, finest freedom in her, the air and the candour of assuming, not "heartlessly," not viciously, not even very consciously, but with a bright pampered confidence which would probably end by affecting one's nerves as the most impertinent stroke in the world, that every blest thing coming up for her in any connection was somehow matter for her general recreation. There she was again with the innocent egotism, the gilded and overflowing anarchism, really, of her doubtless quite unwitting but none the less rabid modern note. Her grace of ease was perfect, but it was all grace of ease, not a single shred of it grace of uncertainty or of difficulty—which meant, when you came to see, that, for its happy working, not a grain of provision was left by it to mere manners. This was clearly going to be the music of the future—that if people were but rich enough and furnished enough and fed enough, exercised and sanitated and manicured and generally advised and advertised and made "knowing" enough, *avertis* enough, as the term appeared to be nowadays in Paris, all they had to do for civility was to take the amused ironic view of those who might be less initiated. In *his* time, when he was young or even when he was only but a little less middle-aged, the best manners had been the best kindness, and the best kindness had mostly been some art of not insisting on one's luxurious differences, of concealing rather, for common humanity, if not for common decency, a part at least of the intensity or the ferocity with which one might be "in the know."

Oh, the "know"—Mrs. Worthingham was in it, all instinctively, inevitably, and as a matter of course, up to her eyes; which didn't, however, the least little bit prevent her being as ignorant as a fish of everything that really and intimately and fundamentally concerned *him*, poor dear old White-Mason. She didn't, in the first place, so much as know who he was—by which he meant know who and what it was to *be* a White-Mason, even a poor and a dear and old one, "anyway." That indeed—he did her perfect justice—was of the very essence of the newness and freshness and beautiful, brave, social irresponsibility by which she had originally dazzled him: just exactly that circumstance of her having no instinct for any old quality or quantity or identity, a single historic or social value,

as he might say, of the New York of his already almost legendary past; and that additional one of his, on his side, having,
so far as this went, cultivated blankness, cultivated positive
prudence, as to her own personal background—the vagueness, at the best, with which all honest gentlefolk, the New
Yorkers of his approved stock and conservative generation,
were content, as for the most part they were indubitably wise,
to surround the origins and antecedents and queer unimaginable early influences of persons swimming into their ken from
those parts of the country that quite necessarily and naturally
figured to their view as "God-forsaken" and generally impossible.

The few scattered surviving representatives of a society once
"good"—*rari nantes in gurgite vasto*—were liable, at the pass
things had come to, to meet, and even amid old shades once
sacred, or what was left of such, every form of social impossibility, and, more irresistibly still, to find these apparitions
often carry themselves (often at least in the case of the
women) with a wondrous wild gallantry, equally imperturbable and inimitable, the sort of thing that reached its maximum in Mrs. Worthingham. Beyond that who ever wanted to
look up their annals, to reconstruct their steps and stages, to
dot their i's in fine, or to "go behind" anything that was
theirs? One wouldn't do that for the world—a rudimentary
discretion forbade it; and yet this check from elementary un-
discussable taste quite consorted with a due respect for them,
or at any rate with a due respect for oneself in connection
with them; as was just exemplified in what would be his own,
what would be poor dear old White-Mason's, insurmountable
aversion to having, on any pretext, the doubtless very queer
spectre of the late Mr. Worthingham presented to him. No
question had he asked, or would he ever ask, should his life—
that is should the success of his courtship—even intimately
depend on it, either about that obscure agent of his mistress's
actual affluence or about the happy head-spring itself, and the
apparently copious tributaries, of the golden stream.

From all which marked anomalies, at any rate, what was the
moral to draw? He dropped into a Park chair again with that
question, he lost himself in the wonder of why he had come
away with his homage so very much unpaid. Yet it didn't seem

at all, actually, as if he could say or conclude, as if he could do anything but keep on worrying—just in conformity with his being a person who, whether or no familiar with the need to make his conduct square with his conscience and his taste, was never wholly exempt from that of making his taste and his conscience square with his conduct. To this latter occupation he further abandoned himself, and it didn't release him from his second brooding session till the sweet spring sunset had begun to gather and he had more or less cleared up, in the deepening dusk, the effective relation between the various parts of his ridiculously agitating experience. There were vital facts he seemed thus to catch, to seize, with a nervous hand, and the twilight helping, by their vaguely whisked tails; unquiet truths that swarmed out after the fashion of creatures bold only at eventide, creatures that hovered and circled, that verily brushed his nose, in spite of their shyness. Yes, he had practically just sat on with his "mistress"—heaven save the mark!—as if *not* to come to the point; as if it had absolutely come up that there would be something rather vulgar and awful in doing so. The whole stretch of his stay after Cornelia's withdrawal had been consumed by his almost ostentatiously treating himself to the opportunity of which he was to make nothing. It was as if he had sat and watched himself—that came back to him: Shall I now or sha'n't I? Will I now or won't I? "Say within the next three minutes, say by a quarter past six, or by twenty minutes past, at the furthest—always if nothing more comes up to prevent."

What had already come up to prevent was, in the strangest and drollest, or at least in the most preposterous, way in the world, that not Cornelia's presence, but her very absence, with its distraction of his thoughts, the thoughts that lumbered after her, had made the difference; and without his being the least able to tell why and how. He put it to himself after a fashion by the image that, this distraction once created, his working round to his hostess again, his reverting to the matter of his errand, began suddenly to represent a return from so far. That was simply all—or rather a little less than all; for something else had contributed. "I never dreamed you knew her," and "I never dreamed *you* did," were inevitably what had been exchanged between them—supplemented by

Mrs. Worthingham's mere scrap of an explanation: "Oh yes—
to the small extent you see. Two years ago in Switzerland
when I was at a high place for an 'aftercure,' during twenty
days of incessant rain, she was the only person in an hotel full
of roaring, gorging, smoking Germans with whom I could
have a word of talk. She and I were the only speakers of English, and were thrown together like castaways on a desert
island and in a raging storm. She was ill besides, and she had
no maid, and mine looked after her, and she was very grateful—writing to me later on and saying she should certainly
come to see me if she ever returned to New York. She *has*
returned, you see—and there she was, poor little creature!"
Such was Mrs. Worthingham's tribute—to which even his asking her if Miss Rasch had ever happened to speak of him
caused her practically to add nothing. Visibly she had never
thought again of any one Miss Rasch had spoken of or anything Miss Rasch had said; right as she was, naturally, about
her being a little clever queer creature. This was perfectly true,
and yet it was probably—by being *all* she could dream of
about her—what had paralysed his proper gallantry. Its effect
had been not in what it simply stated, but in what, under his
secretly disintegrating criticism, it almost luridly symbolised.

He had quitted his seat in the Louis Quinze drawing-room
without having, as he would have described it, done anything
but give the lady of the scene a superior chance not to betray
a defeated hope—not, that is, to fail of the famous "pride"
mostly supposed to prop even the most infatuated women at
such junctures; by which chance, to do her justice, she had
thoroughly seemed to profit. But he finally rose from his later
station with a feeling of better success. He had by a happy
turn of his hand got hold of the most precious, the least obscure of the flitting, circling things that brushed his ears. What
he wanted—as justifying for him a little further consideration—was there before him from the moment he could put it
that Mrs. Worthingham had no data. He almost hugged that
word—it suddenly came to mean so much to him. No data,
he felt, for a conception of the sort of thing the New York of
"his time" had been in his personal life—the New York so
unexpectedly, so vividly and, as he might say, so perversely
called back to all his senses by its identity with that of poor

Cornelia's time: since even she had had a time, small show as it was likely to make now, and his time and hers had been the same. Cornelia figured to him while he walked away as, by contrast and opposition, a massive little bundle of data; his impatience to go to see her sharpened as he thought of this: so certainly should he find out that wherever he might touch her, with a gentle though firm pressure, he would, as the fond visitor of old houses taps and fingers a disfeatured, over-papered wall with the conviction of a wainscot-edge beneath, recognise some small extrusion of history.

IV

There would have been a wonder for us meanwhile in his continued use, as it were, of his happy formula—brought out to Cornelia Rasch within ten minutes, or perhaps only within twenty, of his having settled into the quite comfortable chair that, two days later, she indicated to him by her fireside. He had arrived at her address through the fortunate chance of his having noticed her card, as he went out, deposited, in the good old New York fashion, on one of the rococo tables of Mrs. Worthingham's hall. His eye had been caught by the pencilled indication that was to affect him, the next instant, as fairly placed there for his sake. This had really been his luck, for he shouldn't have liked to write to Mrs. Worthingham for guidance—*that* he felt, though too impatient just now to an-alyze the reluctance. There was nobody else he could have approached for a clue, and with this reflection he was already aware of how it testified to their rare little position, his and Cornelia's—position as conscious, ironic, pathetic survivors together of a dead and buried society—that there would have been, in all the town, under such stress, not a member of their old circle left to turn to. Mrs. Worthingham had practically, even if accidentally, helped him to knowledge; the last nail in the coffin of the poor dear extinct past had been planted for him by his having thus to reach his antique contemporary through perforation of the newest newness. The note of this particular recognition was in fact the more prescribed to him that the ground of Cornelia's return to a scene swept so bare of the associational charm was certainly inconspicuous. What had she then come back for?—he had asked himself that; with the effect of deciding that it probably would have been, a little, to "look after" her remnant of property. Perhaps she had come to save what little might still remain of that shrivelled interest; perhaps she had been, by those who took care of it for her, further swindled and despoiled, so that she wished to get at the facts. Perhaps on the other hand—it was a more cheerful chance—her investments, decently administered, were making larger returns, so that the rigorous thrift of Bognor could be finally relaxed.

He had little to learn about the attraction of Europe, and rather expected that in the event of his union with Mrs. Worthingham he should find himself pleading for it with the competence of one more in the "know" about Paris and Rome, about Venice and Florence, than even she could be. He could have lived on in *his* New York, that is in the sentimental, the spiritual, the more or less romantic visitation of it; but had it been positive for him that he could live on in hers?—unless indeed the possibility of this had been just (like the famous *vertige de l'abîme*, like the solicitation of danger, or otherwise of the dreadful) the very hinge of his whole dream. However that might be, his curiosity was occupied rather with the conceivable hinge of poor Cornelia's: it was perhaps thinkable that even Mrs. Worthingham's New York, once it should have become possible again at all, might have put forth to this lone exile a plea that wouldn't be in the chords of Bognor. For himself, after all, too, the attraction had been much more of the Europe over which one might move at one's ease, and which therefore could but cost, and cost much, right and left, than of the Europe adapted to scrimping. He saw himself on the whole scrimping with more zest even in Mrs. Worthingham's New York than under the inspiration of Bognor. Apart from which it was yet again odd, not to say perceptibly pleasing to him, to note where the emphasis of his interest fell in this fumble of fancy over such felt oppositions as the new, the latest, the luridest power of money and the ancient reserves and moderations and mediocrities. These last struck him as showing by contrast the old brown surface and tone as of velvet rubbed and worn, shabby, and even a bit dingy, but all soft and subtle and still velvety—which meant still dignified;

whereas the angular facts of current finance were as harsh and
metallic and bewildering as some stacked "exhibit" of ugly
patented inventions, things his mediæval mind forbade his taking in. He had for instance the sense of knowing the pleasant
little old Rasch fortune—pleasant as far as it went; blurred
memories and impressions of what it had been and what it
hadn't, of how it had grown and how languished and how
melted; they came back to him and put on such vividness that
he could almost have figured himself testify for them before
a bland and encouraging Board. The idea of taking the field
in any manner on the subject of Mrs. Worthingham's resources would have affected him on the other hand as an odious ordeal, some glare of embarrassment and exposure in a
circle of hard unhelpful attention, of converging, derisive, un-
suggestive eyes.

In Cornelia's small and quite cynically modern flat—the
house had a grotesque name, "The Gainsborough," but at
least wasn't an awful boarding-house, as he had feared, and
she could receive him quite honourably, which was so much
to the good—he would have been ready to use at once to her
the greatest freedom of friendly allusion: "Have you still your
old 'family interest' in those two houses in Seventh Avenue?—
one of which was next to a corner grocery, don't you know?
and was occupied as to its lower part by a candy-shop where
the proportion of the stock of suspectedly stale popcorn to
that of rarer and stickier joys betrayed perhaps a modest capital
on the part of your father's, your grandfather's, or whoever's
tenant, but out of which I nevertheless remember once to
have come as out of a bath of sweets, with my very garments,
and even the separate hairs of my head, glued together. The
other of the pair, a tobacconist's, further down, had before it
a wonderful huge Indian who thrust out wooden cigars at an
indifferent world—you could buy candy cigars too, at the
pop-corn shop, and I greatly preferred them to the wooden;
I remember well how I used to gape in fascination at the
Indian and wonder if the last of the Mohicans was like him;
besides admiring so the resources of a family whose 'property'
was in such forms. I haven't been round there lately—we must
go round together; but don't tell me the forms have utterly
perished!" It was after *that* fashion he might easily have been

moved, and with almost no transition, to break out to Cornelia—quite as if taking up some old talk, some old community of gossip, just where they had left it; even with the consciousness perhaps of overdoing a little, of putting at its maximum, for the present harmony, recovery, recapture (what should he call it?) the pitch and quantity of what the past had held for them.

He didn't in fact, no doubt, dart straight off to Seventh Avenue, there being too many other old things and much nearer and long subsequent; the point was only that for everything they spoke of after he had fairly begun to lean back and stretch his legs, and after she had let him, above all, light the first of a succession of cigarettes—for everything they spoke of he positively cultivated extravagance and excess, piling up the crackling twigs as on the very altar of memory; and that by the end of half an hour she had lent herself, all gallantly, to their game. It was the game of feeding the beautiful iridescent flame, ruddy and green and gold, blue and pink and amber and silver, with anything they could pick up, anything that would burn and flicker. Thick-strown with such gleanings the occasion seemed indeed, in spite of the truth that they perhaps wouldn't have proved, under cross-examination, to have rubbed shoulders in the other life so very hard. Casual contacts, qualified communities enough, there had doubtless been, but not particular "passages," nothing that counted, as he might think of it, for their "very own" together, for nobody's else at all. These shades of historic exactitude didn't signify; the more and the less that there had been made perfect terms—and just by his being there and by her rejoicing in it—with their present need to have *had* all their past could be made to appear to have given them. It was to this tune they proceeded, the least little bit as if they knowingly pretended—he giving her the example and setting her the pace of it, and she, poor dear, after a first inevitable shyness, an uncertainty of wonder, a breathlessness of courage, falling into step and going whatever length he would.

She showed herself ready for it, grasping gladly at the perception of what he must mean; and if she didn't immediately and completely fall in—not in the first half-hour, not even in the three or four others that his visit, even whenever he consulted his watch, still made nothing of—she yet understood enough as soon as she understood that, if their finer economy hadn't so beautifully served, he might have been conveying this, that, and the other incoherent and easy thing by the comparatively clumsy method of sound and statement. "No, I never made love to you; it would in fact have been absurd, and I don't care—though I almost know, in the sense of almost remembering!—who did and who didn't; but you were always about, and so was I, and, little as you may yourself care who *I* did it to, I dare say you remember (in the sense of having known of it!) any old appearances that told. But we can't afford at this time of day not to help each other to have had—well, everything there was, since there's no more of it now, nor any way of coming by it *except so*; and therefore let us make together, let us make over and recreate, our lost world; for which we have after all and at the worst such a lot of material. You were in particular my poor dear sisters' friend—they thought you the funniest little brown thing possible; so isn't that again to the good? You were mine only to the extent that you were so much in and out of the house— as how much, if we come to that, wasn't one in and out, south of Thirtieth Street and north of Washington Square, in those days, those spacious, sociable, Arcadian days, that we flattered ourselves we filled with the modern fever, but that were so different from any of these arrangements of pretended hourly Time that dash themselves forever to pieces as from the fiftieth floors of sky-scrapers."

This was the kind of thing that was in the air, whether he said it or not, and that could hang there even with such quite other things as more crudely came out; came in spite of its being perhaps calculated to strike us that these last would have been rather and most the unspoken and the indirect. They were Cornelia's contribution, and as soon as she had begun to talk of Mrs. Worthingham—*he* didn't begin it!—they had taken their place bravely in the centre of the circle. There they made, the while, their considerable little figure, but all within the ring formed by fifty other allusions, fitful but really intenser irruptions that hovered and wavered and came and went, joining hands at moments and whirling round as in chorus, only then again to dash at the slightly huddled centre

with a free twitch or peck or push or other taken liberty, after
the fashion of irregular frolic motions in a country dance or
a Christmas game.

"You're so in love with her and want to marry her!"—
she said it all sympathetically and yearningly, poor crapy
Cornelia; as if it were to be quite taken for granted that she
knew all about it. And then when he had asked how she
knew—why she took so informed a tone about it; all on the
wonder of her seeming so much more "in" it just at that
hour than he himself quite felt he could figure for: "Ah,
how but from the dear lovely thing herself? Don't you suppose *she* knows it?"

"Oh, she absolutely 'knows' it, does she?"—he fairly heard
himself ask that; and with the oddest sense at once of sharply
wanting the certitude and yet of seeing the question, of hearing himself say the words, through several thicknesses of
some wrong medium. He came back to it from a distance;
as he would have had to come back (this was again vivid to
him) should he have got round again to his ripe intention
three days before—after his now present but then absent
friend, that is, had left him planted before his now absent but
then present one for the purpose. "Do you mean she—at all
confidently!—expects?" he went on, not much minding if it
couldn't but sound foolish; the time being given it for him
meanwhile by the sigh, the wondering gasp, all charged with
the unutterable, that the tone of his appeal set in motion.
He saw his companion look at him, but it might have been
with the eyes of thirty years ago; when—very likely!—he had
put her some such question about some girl long since dead.
Dimly at first, then more distinctly, didn't it surge back on
him for the very strangeness that there had been some such
passage as this between them—yes, about Mary Cardew!—in
the autumn of '68?

"Why, don't you realise your situation?" Miss Rasch struck
him as quite beautifully wailing—above all to such an effect
of deep interest, that is, on her own part and in him.

"My situation?"—he echoed, he considered; but reminded
afresh, by the note of the detached, the far-projected in it, of
what he had last remembered of his sentient state on his once
taking either at the dentist's.

"Yours and hers—the situation of her adoring you. I suppose you at least know it," Cornelia smiled.

Yes, it was like the other time and yet it wasn't. *She* was like—poor Cornelia was—everything that used to be; that somehow was most definite to him. Still he could quite reply "Do you call it—her adoring me—*my* situation?"

"Well, it's a part of yours, surely—if you're in love with her."

"Am I, ridiculous old person! in love with her?" White-Mason asked.

"I may be a ridiculous old person," Cornelia returned—"and, for that matter, of course I am! But she's young and lovely and rich and clever: so what could be more natural?"

"Oh, I was applying that opprobrious epithet—!" He didn't finish, though he meant he had applied it to himself. He had got up from his seat; he turned about and, taking in, as his eyes also roamed, several objects in the room, serene and sturdy, not a bit cheap-looking, little old New York objects of '68, he made, with an inner art, as if to recognise them—made so, that is, for himself; had quite the sense for the moment of asking them, of imploring them, to recognise *him*, to be for him things of his own past. Which they truly were, he could have the next instant cried out; for it meant that if three or four of them, small sallow carte-de-visite photographs, faithfully framed but spectrally faded, hadn't in every particular, frames and balloon skirts and false "property" balustrades of unimaginable terraces and all, the tone of time, the secret for warding and easing off the perpetual imminent ache of one's protective scowl, one would verily but have to let the scowl stiffen, or to take up seriously the question of blue goggles, during what might remain of life.

V

What he actually took up from a little old Twelfth-Street table that piously preserved the plain mahogany circle, with never a curl nor a crook nor a hint of a brazen flourish, what he paused there a moment for commerce with, his back presented to crapy Cornelia, who sat taking that view of him, during this opportunity, very protrusively and frankly and fondly, was one of the wasted mementos just mentioned, over which he both uttered and suppressed a small comprehensive cry. He stood there another minute to look at it, and when he turned about still kept it in his hand, only holding it now a little behind him. "You *must* have come back to stay—with all your beautiful things. What else does it mean?"

" 'Beautiful'?" his old friend commented with her brow all wrinkled and her lips thrust out in expressive dispraise. They might at that rate have been scarce more beautiful than she herself. "Oh, don't talk so—after Mrs. Worthingham's! *They're* wonderful, if you will: such things, such things! But one's own poor relics and odds and ends are one's own at least; and one *has*—yes—come back to them. They're all I have in the world to come back to. They were stored, and what I was paying—!" Miss Rasch wofully added.

He had possession of the small old picture; he hovered there; he put his eyes again to it intently; then again held it a little behind him as if it might have been snatched away or the very feel of it, pressed against him, was good to his palm. "Mrs. Worthingham's things? You think them beautiful?"

Cornelia did now, if ever, show an odd face. "Why certainly prodigious, or whatever. Isn't that conceded?"

"No doubt every horror, at the pass we've come to, is conceded. That's just what I complain of."

"Do you *complain*?"—she drew it out as for surprise: she couldn't have imagined such a thing.

"To me her things are awful. They're the newest of the new."

"Ah, but the old forms!"

"Those are the most blatant. I mean the swaggering reproductions."

"Oh but," she pleaded, "we can't all be *really* old."

"No, we can't, Cornelia. But *you* can—!" said White-Mason with the frankest appreciation.

She looked up at him from where she sat as he could imagine her looking up at the curate at Bognor.

"Thank you, sir! If that's all you want——!"

"It *is*," he said, "all I want—or almost."

"Then no wonder such a creature as that," she lightly moralised, "won't suit you!"

He bent upon her, for all the weight of his question, his smoothest stare. "You hold she certainly won't suit me?"

"Why, what can I tell about it? Haven't you by this time found out?"

"No, but I think I'm finding." With which he began again to explore.

Miss Rasch immensely wondered. "You mean you don't expect to come to an understanding with her?" And then as even to this straight challenge he made at first no answer: "Do you mean you give it up?"

He waited some instants more, but not meeting her eyes—only looking again about the room. "What do you think of my chance?"

"Oh," his companion cried, "what has what I think to do with it? How can I think anything but that she must like you?"

"Yes—of course. But how much?"

"Then don't you really know?" Cornelia asked.

He kept up his walk, oddly preoccupied and still not looking at her. "Do you, my dear?"

She waited a little. "If you haven't really put it to her I don't suppose she knows."

This at last arrested him again. "My dear Cornelia, she doesn't know——!"

He had paused as for the desperate tone, or at least the large emphasis of it, so that she took him up. "The more reason then to help her to find it out."

"I mean," he explained, "that she doesn't know anything."

"Anything?"

"Anything else, I mean—even if she does know *that*."

Cornelia considered of it. "But what else need she—in particular—know? Isn't that the principal thing?"

"Well"—and he resumed his circuit—"she doesn't know anything that *we* know. But nothing," he re-emphasised—"nothing whatever!"

"Well, can't she do without that?"

"Evidently she can—and evidently she does, beautifully. But the question is whether *I* can!"

He had paused once more with his point—but she glared, poor Cornelia, with her wonder. "Surely if you know for yourself——!"

"Ah, it doesn't seem enough for me to know for myself! One wants a woman," he argued—but still, in his prolonged tour, quite without his scowl—"to know *for* one, to know *with* one. That's what you do now," he candidly put to her.

It made her again gape. "Do you mean you want to marry *me*?"

He was so full of what he did mean, however, that he failed even to notice it. "She doesn't in the least know, for instance, how old I am."

"That's because you're so young!"

"Ah, there you are!"—and he turned off afresh and as if almost in disgust. It left her visibly perplexed—though even the perplexed Cornelia was still the exceedingly pointed; but he had come to her aid after another turn. "Remember, please, that I'm pretty well as old as you."

She had all her point at least, while she bridled and blinked, for this. "You're exactly a year and ten months older."

It checked him there for delight. "You remember my birthday?"

She twinkled indeed like some far-off light of home. "I remember every one's. It's a little way I've always had—and that I've never lost."

He looked at her accomplishment, across the room, as at some striking, some charming phenomenon. "Well, *that's* the sort of thing I want!" All the ripe candour of his eyes confirmed it.

What could she do therefore, she seemed to ask him, but repeat her question of a moment before?—which indeed presently she made up her mind to. "Do you want to marry *me*?"

It had this time better success—if the term may be felt in any degree to apply. All his candour, or more of it at least, was in his slow, mild, kind, considering head-shake. "No, Cornelia—not to *marry* you."

His discrimination was a wonder; but since she was clearly treating him now as if everything about him was, so she could as exquisitely meet it. "Not at least," she convulsively smiled, "until you've honourably tried Mrs. Worthingham. Don't you really *mean* to?" she gallantly insisted.

He waited again a little; then he brought out: "I'll tell you presently." He came back, and as by still another mere glance over the room, to what seemed to him so much nearer. "That table *was* old Twelfth-Street?"

"Everything here was."

"Oh, the pure blessings! With you, ah, with you, I haven't to wear a green shade." And he had retained meanwhile his small photograph, which he again showed himself. "Didn't we talk of Mary Cardew?"

"Why, do you remember it?" She marvelled to extravagance.

"You make me. You connect me with it. You connect it with *me*." He liked to display to her this excellent use she thus had, the service she rendered. "There are so many connections—there will *be* so many. I feel how, with you, they must all come up again for me: in fact you're bringing them out already, just while I look at you, as fast as ever you can. The fact that you knew every one—!" he went on; yet as if there were more in that too than he could quite trust himself about.

"Yes, I knew every one," said Cornelia Rasch; but this time with perfect simplicity. "I knew, I imagine, more than you do—or more than you did."

It kept him there, it made him wonder with his eyes on her. "Things about *them*—our people?"

"Our people. Ours only now."

Ah, such an interest as he felt in this—taking from her while, so far from scowling, he almost gaped, all it might mean! "Ours indeed—and it's awfully good they are; or that we're still here for them! Nobody else is—nobody but you: not a cat!"

"Well, I *am* a cat!" Cornelia grinned.

"Do you mean you can tell me things—?" It was too beautiful to believe.

"About what really *was*?" she artfully considered, holding him immensely now. "Well, unless they've come to you with time; unless you've learned—or found out."

"Oh," he reassuringly cried—reassuringly, it most seemed, for himself—"nothing has come to me with time, everything has gone from me. How can I find out now! What creature has an idea——?"

She threw up her hands with the shrug of old days—the sharp little shrug his sisters used to imitate and that she hadn't had to go to Europe for. The only thing was that he blessed her for bringing it back. "Ah, the ideas of people now——!"

"Yes, their ideas are certainly not about *us.*" But he ruefully faced it. "We've none the less, however, to live with them."

"With their ideas—?" Cornelia questioned.

"With *them*—these modern wonders; such as they are!" Then he went on: "It must have been to help me you've come back."

She said nothing for an instant about that, only nodding instead at his photograph. "What has become of yours? I mean of *her.*"

This time it made him turn pale. "You remember I *have* one?"

She kept her eyes on him. "In a 'pork-pie' hat, with her hair in a long net. That was so 'smart' then; especially with one's skirt looped up, over one's hooped magenta petticoat, in little festoons, and a row of very big onyx beads over one's braided velveteen sack—braided quite plain and very broad, don't you know?"

He smiled for her extraordinary possession of these things—she was as prompt as if she had had them before her. "Oh, rather—'don't I know?' You wore brown velveteen, and, on those remarkably small hands, funny gauntlets—like mine."

"Oh, do *you* remember? But like yours?" she wondered.

"I mean like hers in my photograph." But he came back to the present picture. "This is better, however, for really showing her lovely head."

"Mary's head was a perfection!" Cornelia testified.

"Yes—it was better than her heart."

"Ah, don't say that!" she pleaded. "You weren't fair."

"Don't you think I was fair?" It interested him immensely—and the more that he indeed mightn't have been; which he seemed somehow almost to hope.

"She didn't think so—to the very end."

"She didn't?"—ah the right things Cornelia said to him! But before she could answer he was studying again closely the small faded face. "No, she doesn't, she doesn't. Oh, her charming sad eyes and the way they *say* that, across the years, straight into mine! But I don't know, I don't know!" White-Mason quite comfortably sighed.

His companion appeared to appreciate this effect. "That's just the way you used to flirt with her, poor thing. Wouldn't you like to have it?" she asked.

"This—for my very own?" He looked up delighted. "I really may?"

"Well, if you'll give me yours. We'll exchange."

"That's a charming idea. We'll exchange. But you must come and get it at my rooms—where you'll see my things."

For a little she made no answer—as if for some feeling. Then she said: "You asked me just now why I've come back."

He stared as for the connection; after which with a smile: "Not to do *that*——?"

She waited briefly again, but with a queer little look. "I can do those things now; and—yes!—that's in a manner why. I came," she then said, "because I knew of a sudden one day—knew as never before—that I was old."

"I see. I see." He quite understood—she had notes that so struck him. "And how did you like it?"

She hesitated—she decided. "Well, if I liked it, it was on the principle perhaps on which some people like high game!"

"High game—that's good!" he laughed. "Ah, my dear, we're 'high'!"

She shook her head. "No, not you—yet. I at any rate didn't want any more adventures," Cornelia said.

He showed their small relic again with assurance. "You wanted *us*. Then here we are. Oh how we can talk!—with all those things you know! You *are* an invention. And you'll see there are things *I* know. I shall turn up here—well, daily."

She took it in, but only after a moment answered. "There was something you said just now you'd tell me. Don't you mean to try——?"

"Mrs. Worthingham?" He drew from within his coat his pocket-book and carefully found a place in it for Mary Cardew's carte-de-visite, folding it together with deliberation over which he put it back. Finally he spoke. "No—I've decided. I can't—I don't want to."

Cornelia marvelled—or looked as if she did. "Not for all she has?"

"Yes—I know all she has. But I also know all she hasn't. And, as I told you, she herself doesn't—hasn't a glimmer of a suspicion of it; and never will have."

Cornelia magnanimously thought. "No—but she knows other things."

He shook his head as at the portentous heap of them. "Too many—too many. And other indeed—*so* other! Do you know," he went on, "that it's as if *you*—by turning up for me—had brought that home to me?"

" 'For you,' " she candidly considered. "But what—since you can't marry me!—can you do with me?"

Well, he seemed to have it all. "Everything. I can live with you—just this way." To illustrate which he dropped into the other chair by her fire; where, leaning back, he gazed at the flame. "I can't give you up. It's very curious. It has come over me as it did over you when you renounced Bognor. That's it—I know it at last, and I see one can like it. I'm 'high.' You needn't deny it. That's my taste. I'm old." And in spite of the considerable glow there of her little household altar he said it without the scowl.

The Bench of Desolation

S HE HAD practically, he believed, conveyed the intimation, the horrid, brutal, vulgar menace, in the course of their last dreadful conversation, when, for whatever was left him of pluck or confidence—confidence in what he would fain have called a little more aggressively the strength of his position— he had judged best not to take it up. But this time there was no question of not understanding, or of pretending he didn't; the ugly, the awful words, ruthlessly formed by her lips, were like the fingers of a hand that she might have thrust into her pocket for extraction of the monstrous object that would serve best for—what should he call it?—a gage of battle.

"If I haven't a very different answer from you within the next three days I shall put the matter into the hands of my solicitor, whom it may interest you to know I've already seen. I shall bring an action for 'breach' against you, Herbert Dodd, as sure as my name's Kate Cookham."

There it was, straight and strong—yet he felt he could say for himself, when once it had come, or even, already, just as it was coming, that it turned on, as if she had moved an electric switch, the very brightest light of his own very reasons. There *she* was, in all the grossness of her native indelicacy, in all her essential excess of will and destitution of scruple; and it was the woman capable of that ignoble threat who, his sharper sense of her quality having become so quite deterrent, was now making for him a crime of it that he shouldn't wish to tie himself to her for life. The vivid, lurid thing was the reality, all unmistakable, of her purpose; she had thought her case well out; had measured its odious, specious presentability; had taken, he might be sure, the very best advice obtainable at Properley, where there was always a first-rate promptitude of everything fourth-rate; it was disgustingly certain, in short, that she'd proceed. She was sharp and adroit, moreover—distinctly in certain ways a masterhand; how otherwise, with her so limited mere attractiveness, should she have entangled him? He couldn't shut his eyes to the very probable truth that if she should try it she'd pull it off. She *knew* she would—precisely; and her assurance was thus the very proof of her cruelty. That she had pretended she loved him was comparatively nothing; other women had pretended it, and other women too had really done it; but that she had pretended he could possibly have been right and safe and blest in loving *her*, a creature of the kind who could sniff that squalor of the law-court, of claimed damages and brazen lies and published kisses, of love-letters read amid obscene guffaws, as a positive tonic to resentment, as a high incentive to her course—this was what put him so beautifully in the right. It was what might signify in a woman all through, he said to himself, the mere imagination of such machinery. Truly what a devilish conception and what an appalling nature!

But there was no doubt, luckily, either, that he *could* plant his feet the firmer for his now intensified sense of these things. He was to live, it appeared, abominably worried, he was to live consciously rueful, he was to live perhaps even what a scoffing world would call abjectly exposed; but at least he was to live saved. In spite of his clutch of which steadying truth, however, and in spite of his declaring to her, with many other angry protests and pleas, that the line of conduct she announced was worthy of a vindictive barmaid, a lurking fear in him, too deep to counsel mere defiance, made him appear to keep open a little, till he could somehow turn round again, the door of possible composition. He had scoffed at her claim, at her threat, at her thinking she could hustle and bully him— "Such a way, my eye, to call back to life a dead love!"—yet his instinct was ever, prudentially but helplessly, for gaining time, even if time only more wofully to quake, and he gained it now by not absolutely giving for his ultimatum that he wouldn't think of coming round. He didn't in the smallest degree mean to come round, but it was characteristic of him that he could for three or four days breathe a little easier by having left her under the impression that he perhaps might. At the same time he couldn't not have said—what had con-duced to bring out, in retort, her own last word, the word on which they had parted—"Do you mean to say you yourself would now be *willing* to marry and live with a man of whom you could feel, the thing done, that he'd be all the while thinking of you in the light of a hideous coercion?" "Never you mind about *my* willingness," Kate had answered; "you've known what that has been for the last six months. Leave that to me, my willingness—I'll take care of it all right; and just see what conclusion you can come to about your own."

He was to remember afterward how he had wondered whether, turned upon her in silence while her odious lucidity reigned unchecked, his face had shown her anything like the quantity of hate he felt. Probably not at all; no man's face *could* express that immense amount; especially the fair, re-fined, intellectual, gentlemanlike face which had had—and by her own more than once repeated avowal—so much to do with the enormous fancy she had originally taken to him. "Which—frankly now—would you personally *rather* I should do," he had at any rate asked her with an intention of supreme irony: "just sordidly marry you on top of this, or leave you the pleasure of your lovely appearance in court and of your so assured (since that's how you feel it) big haul of damages? Sha'n't you be awfully disappointed, in fact, if I don't let you get something better out of me than a poor plain ten-shilling gold ring and the rest of the blasphemous rubbish, as we should make it between us, pronounced at the altar? I take it of course," he had swaggered on, "that your pretension wouldn't be for a moment that I should—after the act of profanity—take up my life with you."

"It's just as much my dream as it ever was, Herbert Dodd, to take up mine with *you*! Remember for me that I can do with it, my dear, that my idea is for even as much as that of you!" she had cried; "remember that for me, Herbert Dodd; remember, remember!"

It was on this she had left him—left him frankly under a mortal chill. There might have been the last ring of an appeal or a show of persistent and perverse tenderness in it, however preposterous any such matter; but in point of fact her large, clean, plain, brown face—so much too big for her head, he now more than ever felt it to be, just as her head was so much too big for her body, and just as her hats had an irritating way of appearing to decline choice and conformity in respect to *any* of her dimensions—presented itself with about as much expression as his own shop-window when the broad, blank, sallow blind was down. He was fond of his shop-window with some good show on; he had a fancy for a good show and was master of twenty different schemes of taking arrangement for the old books and prints, "high-class rarities" his modest catalogue called them, in which he dealt and which his maternal uncle, David Geddes, had, as he liked to say, "handed down" to him. His widowed mother had screwed the whole thing, the stock and the connection and the rather bad little house in the rather bad little street, out of the ancient worthy, shortly before his death, in the name of the youngest and most interesting, the "delicate" one and the literary, of her five scattered and struggling children. He could enjoy his happiest collocations and contrasts and effects, his harmonies and varieties of toned and faded leather and cloth, his sought color-notes and the high clearnesses, here and there, of his white and beautifully figured price-labels, which pleased him enough in themselves almost to console him for not oftener having to break, on a customer's insistence, into the balanced composition. But the dropped expanse of time-soiled canvas, the thing of Sundays and holidays, with just his name, "Herbert Dodd, Successor," painted on below his uncle's antique style, the feeble penlike flourishes already quite archaic—this ugly vacant mask, which might so easily be taken for the mask of failure, somehow always gave him a chill.

That had been just the sort of chill—the analogy was complete—of Kate Cookham's last look. He supposed people doing an awfully good and sure and steady business, in whatever line, could see a whole front turned to vacancy that way and merely think of the hours off represented by it. Only for this— nervously to bear it, in other words, and Herbert Dodd, quite with the literary temperament himself, was capable of that amount of play of fancy, or even of morbid analysis—you had to be on some footing, you had to feel some confidence, pretty different from his own up to now. He had never *not* enjoyed passing his show on the other side of the street and taking it in thence with a casual obliquity; but he had never held optical commerce with the drawn blind for a moment longer than he could help. It *always* looked horribly final and as if it never would come up again. Big and bare, with his name staring at him from the middle, it thus offered in its grimness a turn of comparison for Miss Cookham's ominous visage. She never wore pretty, dotty, transparent veils, as Nan Drury did, and the words "Herbert Dodd"—save that she had sounded them at him there two or three times more like a Meg Merrilies or the bold bad woman in one of the melodramas of high life given during the fine season in the pavilion at the end of Properley Pier—were dreadfully, were permanently, seated on her lips. *She* was grim, no mistake.

That evening, alone in the back room above the shop, he saw so little what he could do that, consciously demoralised for the hour, he gave way to tears about it. Her taking a stand so incredibly "low," that was what he couldn't get over. The particular bitterness of his cup was his having let himself in for a struggle on such terms—the use, on her side, of the vulgarest process known to the law: the vulgarest, the vulgarest, he kept repeating that, clinging to the help rendered him by this imputation to his terrorist of the vice he sincerely believed he had ever, among difficulties (for oh he recognised the difficulties!) sought to keep most alien to him. He knew what he was, in a dismal, down-trodden sphere enough—the lean young proprietor of an old business that had itself rather shrivelled with age than ever grown fat, the purchase and sale of second-hand books and prints, with the back street of a long-fronted south-coast watering-place (Old Town by good luck) for the dusky field of his life. But he had gone in for all the education he could get—his educated customers would often hang about for more talk by the half-hour at a time, he actually feeling himself, and almost with a scruple, hold them there; which meant that he had had (he couldn't be blind to that) natural taste and had lovingly cultivated and formed it. Thus, from as far back as he could remember, there had been things all round him that he suffered from when other people didn't; and he had kept most of his suffering to himself— which had taught him, in a manner, *how* to suffer, and how almost to like to.

So, at any rate, he had never let go his sense of certain differences, he had done everything he could to keep it up— whereby everything that was vulgar was on the wrong side of his line. He had believed, for a series of strange, oppressed months, that Kate Cookham's manners and tone were on the right side; she had been governess—for young children—in

two very good private families, and now had classes in literature and history for bigger girls who were sometimes brought
by their mammas; in fact, coming in one day to look over his
collection of students' manuals, and drawing it out, as so
many did, for the evident sake of his conversation, she had
appealed to him that very first time by her apparently pronounced intellectual side—goodness knew she didn't even
then by the physical!—which she had artfully kept in view till
she had entangled him past undoing. And it had all been but
the cheapest of traps—when he came to take the pieces apart
a bit—laid over a brazen avidity. What he now collapsed for,
none the less—what he sank down on a chair at a table and
nursed his weak, scared sobs in his resting arms for—was the
fact that, whatever the trap, it held him as with the grip of
sharp murderous steel. There he was, there he was; alone in
the brown summer dusk—brown through *his* windows—he
cried and he cried. He shouldn't get out without losing a
limb. The only question was which of his limbs it should be.

Before he went out, later on—for he at last felt the need
to—he could, however, but seek to remove from his face and
his betraying eyes, over his washing-stand, the traces of his
want of fortitude. He brushed himself up; with which, catching his stricken image a bit spectrally in an old dim toilet-
glass, he knew again, in a flash, the glow of righteous
resentment. Who should be assured against coarse usage if a
man of his really elegant, perhaps in fact a trifle over-refined
or "effete" appearance, his absolutely gentlemanlike type,
couldn't be? He never went so far as to rate himself, with
exaggeration, a gentleman; but he would have maintained
against all comers, with perfect candour and as claiming a high
advantage, that he was, in spite of that liability to blubber,
"like" one; which he *was* no doubt, for that matter, at several
points. Like what lady then, who could ever possibly have
been taken for one, was Kate Cookham, and therefore how
could one have anything—anything of the intimate and private order—out with her fairly and on the plane, the only
possible one, of common equality? He might find himself crippled for life; he believed verily, the more he thought, that that
was what was before him. But he ended by seeing this doom
in the almost redeeming light of the fact that it would all have

been because he was, comparatively, too aristocratic. Yes, a man in his station couldn't afford to carry that so far—it must sooner or later, in one way or another, spell ruin. Never mind—it was the only thing he could be. Of course he should exquisitely suffer—but when hadn't he exquisitely suffered? How was he going to get through life by *any* arrangement without that? No wonder such a woman as Kate Cookham had been keen to annex so rare a value. The right thing would have been that the highest price should be paid for it—by such a different sort of logic from this nightmare of *his* having to pay.

II

Which was the way, of course, he talked to Nan Drury—as he had felt the immediate wild need to do; for he should perhaps be able to bear it all somehow or other with *her*—while they sat together, when time and freedom served, on one of the very last, the far westward, benches of the interminable sea-front. It wasn't every one who walked so far, especially at that flat season—the only ghost of a bustle now, save for the gregarious, the obstreperous haunters of the fluttering, far-shining Pier, being reserved for the sunny Parade of midwinter. It wasn't every one who cared for the sunsets (which you got awfully well from there and which were a particular strong point of the lower, the more "sympathetic," as Herbert Dodd liked to call it, Properley horizon) as he had always intensely cared, and as he had found Nan Drury care; to say nothing of his having also observed how little they directly spoke to Miss Cookham. He had taught this oppressive companion to notice them a bit, as he had taught her plenty of other things, but that was a different matter; for the reason that the "land's end" (stretching a point it carried off that name) had been, and had had to be, by their lack of more sequestered resorts and conveniences, the scene of so much of what she styled their wooing-time—or, to put it more properly, of the time during which she had made the straightest and most un-abashed love to *him*: just as it could henceforth but render possible, under an equal rigour, that he should enjoy there periods of consolation from beautiful, gentle, tender-souled

Nan, to whom he was now at last, after the wonderful way they had helped each other to behave, going to make love, absolutely unreserved and abandoned, absolutely reckless and romantic love, a refuge from poisonous reality, as hard as ever he might.

The league-long, paved, lighted, garden-plotted, seated and refuged Marina renounced its more or less celebrated attractions to break off short here; and an inward curve of the kindly westward shore almost made a wide-armed bay, with all the ugliness between town and country, and the further casual fringe of the coast, turning, as the day waned, to rich afternoon blooms of grey and brown and distant—it might fairly have been beautiful Hampshire—blue. Here it was that, all that blighted summer, with Nan—from the dreadful May-day on—he gave himself up to the reaction of intimacy with the *kind* of woman, at least, that he liked; even if of everything else that might make life possible he was to be, by what he could make out, forever starved. Here it was that—as well as on whatever other scraps of occasions they could manage— Nan began to take off and fold up and put away in her pocket her pretty, dotty, becoming veil; as under the logic of his having so tremendously ceased, in the shake of his dark storm-gust, to be engaged to another woman. Her removal of that obstacle to a trusted friend's assuring himself whether the peachlike bloom of her finer facial curves bore the test of such further inquiry into their cool sweetness as might reinforce a mere baffled gaze—her momentous, complete surrender of so much of her charm, let us say, both marked the change in the situation of the pair and established the record of their perfect observance of every propriety for so long before. They afterward in fact could have dated it, their full clutch of their freedom and the bliss of their having so little henceforth to consider save their impotence, their poverty, their ruin; dated it from the hour of his recital to her of the—at the first blush—quite appalling upshot of his second and conclusive "scene of violence" with the mistress of his fortune, when the dire terms of his release had had to be formally, and oh! so abjectly, acceded to. She "compromised," the cruel brute, for Four Hundred Pounds down—for not a farthing less would she stay her strength from "proceedings." No jury in the land but would give her six, on the nail ("Oh she knew quite where she was, thank you!") and he might feel lucky to get off with so whole a skin. This was the sum, then, for which he had grovellingly compounded—under an agreement sealed by a supreme exchange of remarks.

" 'Where in the name of lifelong ruin are you to *find* Four Hundred?' " Miss Cookham had mockingly repeated after him while he gasped as from the twist of her grip on his collar. "That's *your* look-out, and I should have thought you'd have made sure you knew before you decided on your base perfidy." And then she had mouthed and minced, with ever so false a gentility, her consistent, her sickening conclusion. "Of course—I may mention again—if you too distinctly object to the trouble of looking, you know where to find *me*."

"I had rather starve to death than ever go within a mile of you!" Herbert described himself as having sweetly answered; and that was accordingly where *they* devotedly but desperately were—he and she, penniless Nan Drury. Her father, of Drury & Dean, was, like so far too many other of the anxious characters who peered through the dull window-glass of dusty offices at Properley, an Estate and House Agent, Surveyor, Valuer and Auctioneer; she was the prettiest of six, with two brothers, neither of the least use, but, thanks to the manner in which their main natural protector appeared to languish under the accumulation of his attributes, they couldn't be said very particularly or positively to live. Their continued collective existence was a good deal of a miracle even to themselves, though they had fallen into the way of not unnecessarily, or too nervously, exchanging remarks upon it, and had even in a sort, from year to year, got used to it. Nan's brooding pinkness when he talked to her, her so very parted lips, considering her pretty teeth, her so very parted eyelids, considering her pretty eyes, all of which might have been those of some waxen image of uncritical faith, cooled the heat of his helplessness very much as if he were laying his head on a tense silk pillow. She had, it was true, forms of speech, familiar watchwords, that affected him as small scratchy perforations of the smooth surface from within; but his pleasure in her and need of her were independent of such things and really almost altogether determined by the fact of the happy, even if all so lonely, forms and instincts in her which claimed kinship with his own. With her natural elegance stamped on her as by a die, with her dim and disinherited individual refinement of grace, which would have made any one wonder who she was anywhere—hat and veil and feather-boa and smart umbrella-knob and all—with her regular God-given distinction of type, in fine, she couldn't abide vulgarity much more than he could.

Therefore it didn't seem to him, under his stress, to matter particularly, for instance, if she *would* keep on referring so many things to the time, as she called it, when she came into his life—his own great insistence and contention being that she hadn't in the least entered there till his mind was wholly made up to eliminate his other friend. What that methodical fury was so fierce to bring home to him was the falsity to herself involved in the later acquaintance; whereas just his precious right to hold up his head to everything—before himself at least—sprang from the fact that she couldn't make dates fit anyhow. He hadn't so much as heard of his true beauty's existence (she had come back but a few weeks before from her two years with her terribly trying deceased aunt at Swindon, previous to which absence she had been an unnoticeable chit) till days and days, ever so many, upon his honour, after he had struck for freedom by his great first backing-out letter—the precious document, the treat for a British jury, in which, by itself, Miss Cookham's firm instructed her to recognise the prospect of a fortune. The way the ruffians had been "her" ruffians—it appeared as if she had posted them behind her from the first of her beginning her game!—and the way "instructions" bounced out, with it, at a touch, larger than life, as if she had arrived with her pocket full of them! The date of the letter, taken with its other connections, and the date of *her* first give-away for himself, his seeing her get out of the Brighton train with Bill Frankle that day he had gone to make the row at the Station parcels' office about the miscarriage of the box from Wales—those were the facts it sufficed him to point to, as he had pointed to them for Nan Drury's benefit, goodness knew, often and often enough. If he didn't seek occasion to do so for any one else's—in open court as they said—that was his own affair, or at least his and Nan's.

It little mattered, meanwhile, if on their bench of desolation, all that summer—and it may be added for summers and summers, to say nothing of winters, there and elsewhere, to come—she did give way to her artless habit of not contradicting him enough, which led to her often trailing up and down before him, too complacently, the untimely shreds and patches of his own glooms and desperations. "Well, I'm glad I *am* in your life, terrible as it is, however or whenever I did come in!" and "*Of course* you'd rather have starved—and it seems pretty well as if we shall, doesn't it?—than have bought her off by a false, abhorrent love, wouldn't you?" and "It isn't as if she hadn't made up to you the way she did before you had so much as looked at her, is it? or as if you hadn't shown her what you felt her really to be before you had so much as looked at *me*, is it either?" and "Yes, how on earth, pawning the shoes on your feet, you're going to raise another shilling—*that's* what you want to know, poor darling, don't you?"

III

His creditor, at the hour it suited her, transferred her base of operations to town, to which impenetrable scene she had also herself retired; and his raising of the first Two Hundred, during five exasperated and miserable months, and then of another Seventy piece-meal, bleedingly, after long delays and under the epistolary whiplash cracked by the London solicitor in his wretched ear even to an effect of the very report of Miss Cookham's tongue—these melancholy efforts formed a scramble up an arduous steep where steps were planted and missed, and bared knees were excoriated, and clutches at wayside tufts succeeded and failed, on a system to which poor Nan could have intelligently entered only if she had been somehow less ladylike. She kept putting into his mouth the sick quaver of where he should find the rest, the always inextinguishable rest, long after he had in silent rage fallen away from any further payment at all—at first, he had but too blackly felt, for himself, to the still quite possible non-exclusion of some penetrating ray of "exposure." He didn't care a tuppenny damn now, and in point of fact, after he had by hook and by crook succeeded in being able to unload to the tune of Two-Hundred-and-Seventy, and then simply returned the newest reminder of his outstanding obligation unopened, this latter belated but real sign of fight, the first he had risked, remarkably caused nothing at all to happen; nothing at least but his being moved to quite tragically rueful wonder as to whether exactly some such demonstration mightn't have served his turn at an earlier stage.

He could by this time at any rate measure his ruin—with three fantastic mortgages on his house, his shop, his stock, and a burden of interest to carry under which his business simply stretched itself inanimate, without strength for a protesting kick, without breath for an appealing groan. Customers lingering for further enjoyment of the tasteful remarks he had cultivated the unobstrusive art of throwing in, would at this crisis have found plenty to repay them, might his wit have strayed a little more widely still, toward a circuitous egotistical outbreak, from the immediate question of the merits of this and that author or of the condition of this and that volume. He had come to be conscious through it all of strangely glaring at people when they tried to haggle—and not, as formerly, with the glare of derisive comment on their overdone humour, but with that of fairly idiotised surrender—as if they were much mistaken in supposing, for the sake of conversation, that he might take himself for saveable by the difference between sevenpence and ninepence. He watched everything impossible and deplorable happen as in an endless prolongation of his nightmare; watched himself proceed, that is, with the finest, richest incoherence, to the due preparation of his catastrophe. Everything came to seem *equally* part of this—in complete defiance of proportion; even his final command of detachment, on the bench of desolation (where each successive fact of his dire case regularly cut itself out black, yet of senseless silhouette, against the red west) in respect to poor Nan's flat infelicities, which for the most part kept no pace with the years or with change, but only shook like hard peas in a child's rattle, the same peas always, of course, so long as the rattle didn't split open with usage or from somebody's act of irritation. They represented, or they had long done so, her contribution to the more superficial of the two branches of intimacy—the intellectual alternative, the one that didn't merely consist of her preparing herself for his putting his arm round her waist.

There were to have been moments, nevertheless, all the first couple of years, when she did touch in him, though to his actively dissimulating it, a more or less sensitive nerve—moments as they were too, to do her justice, when she treated him not to his own wisdom, or even folly, served up cold, but to a certain small bitter fruit of her personal, her unnatural, plucking. "I wonder that since *she* took legal advice so freely, to come down on you, you didn't take it yourself, a little, before being so sure you stood no chance. Perhaps *your* people would have been sure of something quite different— *perhaps*, I only say, you know." She "only" said it, but she said it, none the less, in the early time, about once a fortnight. In the later, and especially after their marriage, it had a way of coming up again to the exclusion, as it seemed to him, of almost everything else; in fact during the most dismal years, the three of the loss of their two children, the long stretch of sordid embarrassment ending in her death, he was afterward to think of her as having generally said it several times a day. He was then also to remember that his answer, before she had learnt to discount it, had been inveterately at hand: "What would any solicitor have done or wanted to do but drag me just into the hideous public arena"—he had always so put it— "that it has been at any rate my pride and my honour, the one rag of self-respect covering my nakedness, to have loathed and avoided from every point of view?"

That had disposed of it so long as he cared, and by the time he had ceased to care for anything it had also lost itself in the rest of the vain babble of home. After his wife's death, during his year of mortal solitude, it awoke again as an echo of far-off things—far-off, very far-off, because he felt then not ten but twenty years older. That was by reason simply of the dead weight with which his load of debt had settled—the persistence of his misery dragging itself out. With all that had come and gone the bench of desolation was still there, just as the immortal flush of the westward sky kept hanging its indestructible curtain. He had never got away—everything had left him, but he himself had been able to turn his back on nothing—and now, his day's labour before a dirty desk at the Gas

Works ended, he more often than not, almost any season at temperate Properley serving his turn, took his slow straight way to the Land's End and, collapsing there to rest, sat often for an hour at a time staring before him. He might in these sessions, with his eyes on the grey-green sea, have been counting again and still recounting the beads, almost all worn smooth, of his rosary of pain—which had for the fingers of memory and the recurrences of wonder the same felt break of the smaller ones by the larger that would have aided a pious mumble in some dusky altar-chapel.

If it has been said of him that when once full submersion, as from far back, had visibly begun to await him, he watched himself, in a cold lucidity, *do* punctually and necessarily each of the deplorable things that were inconsistent with his keeping afloat, so at present again he might have been held agaze just by the presented grotesqueness of that vigil. Such ghosts of dead seasons were all he *had* now to watch—such a recaptured sense for instance as that of the dismal unavailing awareness that had attended his act of marriage. He had let submersion final and absolute become the signal for it—a mere minor determinant having been the more or less contemporaneously unfavourable effect on the business of Drury & Dean of the sudden disappearance of Mr. Dean with the single small tin box into which the certificates of the firm's credit had been found to be compressible. That had been his only form—or had at any rate seemed his only one. He couldn't not have married, no doubt, just as he couldn't not have suffered the last degree of humiliation and almost of want, or just as his wife and children couldn't not have died of the little he was able, under dire reiterated pinches, to do for them; but it *was* "rum," for final solitary brooding, that he hadn't appeared to see his way definitely to undertake the support of a family till the last scrap of his little low-browed, high-toned business, and the last figment of "property" in the old tiled and timbered shell that housed it, had been sacrificed to creditors mustering six rows deep.

Of course what had counted too in the odd order was that even at the end of the two or three years he had "allowed" her, Kate Cookham, gorged with his unholy tribute, had become the subject of no successful siege on the part either of

Bill Frankle or, by what he could make out, of any one else. She had judged decent—he could do her that justice—to take herself personally out of his world, as he called it, for good and all, as soon as he had begun regularly to bleed; and, to whatever lucrative practice she might be devoting her great talents in London or elsewhere, he felt his conscious curiosity about her as cold, with time, as the passion of vain protest that she had originally left him to. He could recall but two direct echoes of her in all the bitter years—both communicated by Bill Frankle, disappointed and exposed and at last quite remarkably ingenuous sneak, who had also, from far back, taken to roaming the world, but who, during a period, used fitfully and ruefully to reappear. Herbert Dodd had quickly seen, at their first meeting—every one met every one sooner or later at Properley, if meeting it could always be called, either in the glare or the gloom of the explodedly attractive Embankment—that no silver stream of which he himself had been the remoter source could have played over the career of this all but repudiated acquaintance. That hadn't fitted with his first, his quite primitive raw vision of the probabilities, and he had further been puzzled when, much later on, it had come to him in a round-about way that Miss Cookham was supposed to be, or to have been, among them for a few days "on the quiet," and that Frankle, who had seen her and who claimed to know more about it than he said, was cited as authority for the fact. But he hadn't himself at this juncture seen Frankle; he had only wondered, and a degree of mystification had even remained.

That memory referred itself to the dark days of old Drury's smash, the few weeks between his partner's dastardly flight and Herbert's own comment on it in the form of his standing up with Nan for the nuptial benediction of the Vicar of St. Bernard's on a very cold, bleak December morning and amid a circle of seven or eight long-faced, red-nosed and altogether dowdy persons. Poor Nan herself had come to affect him as scarce other than red-nosed and dowdy by that time, but this only added, in his then, and indeed in his lasting view, to his general and his particular morbid bravery. He had cultivated ignorance, there were small inward immaterial luxuries he could scrappily cherish even among other, and the harshest, destitutions; and one of them was represented by this easy refusal of his mind to render to certain passages of his experience, to various ugly images, names, associations, the homage of continued attention. That served him, that helped him; but what happened when, a dozen dismal years having worn themselves away, he sat single and scraped bare again, as if his long wave of misfortune had washed him far beyond everything and then conspicuously retreated, was that, thus stranded by tidal action, deposited in the lonely hollow of his fate, he felt even sustaining pride turn to nought and heard no challenge from it when old mystifications, stealing forth in the dusk of the day's work done, scratched at the door of speculation and hung about, through the idle hours, for irritated notice.

The evenings of his squalid clerkship were all leisure now, but there was nothing at all near home on the other hand, for his imagination, numb and stiff from its long chill, to begin to play with. Voices from far off would quaver to him therefore in the stillness; where he knew for the most recurrent, little by little, the faint wail of his wife. He had become deaf to it in life, but at present, after so great an interval, he listened again, listened and listened, and seemed to hear it sound as by the pressure of some weak broken spring. It phrased for his ear her perpetual question, the one she had come to at the last as under the obsession of a discovered and resented wrong, a wrong withal that had its source much more in his own action than anywhere else. "That you didn't make *sure* she could have done anything, that you didn't make sure and that you were too afraid!"—this commemoration had ended by playing such a part of Nan's finally quite contracted consciousness as to exclude everything else.

At the time, somehow, he had made his terms with it; he had then more urgent questions to meet than that of the poor creature's taste in worrying pain; but actually it struck him—not the question, but the fact itself of the taste—as the one thing left over from all that had come and gone. So it was; nothing remained to him in the world, on the bench of desolation, but the option of taking up that echo—together with an abundance of free time for doing so. That he hadn't made sure of what might and what mightn't have been done to him, that he had been too afraid—had the proposition a possible bearing on his present apprehension of things? To reply indeed he would have had to be able to say what his present apprehension of things, left to itself, amounted to; an uninspiring effort indeed he judged it, sunk to so poor a pitch was his material of thought—though it might at last have been the feat he sought to perform as he stared at the grey-green sea.

IV

It was seldom he was disturbed in any form of sequestered speculation, or that at his times of predilection, especially that of the long autumn blankness between the season of trippers and the season of Bath-chairs, there were westward stragglers enough to jar upon his settled sense of priority. For himself his seat, the term of his walk, was consecrated; it had figured to him for years as the last (though there were others, not immediately near it, and differently disposed, that might have aspired to the title); so that he could invidiously distinguish as he approached, make out from a distance any accident of occupation, and never draw nearer while that unpleasantness lasted. What he disliked was to compromise on his tradition, whether for a man, a woman or a connoodling couple; it was to idiots of this last composition he most objected, he having sat there, in the past, alone, having sat there interminably with Nan, having sat there with—well, with other women when women, at hours of ease, could still care or count for him, but having never shared the place with any shuffling or snuffling stranger.

It was a world of fidgets and starts, however, the world of his present dreariness—he alone possessed in it, he seemed to make out, of the secret, of the dignity of sitting still with one's fate; so that if he took a turn about or rested briefly elsewhere even foolish philanderers—though this would never have been his and Nan's way—ended soon by some adjournment as visibly pointless as their sprawl. Then, their backs turned, he would drop down on it, the bench of desolation—which was what he, and he only, made it by sad adoption; where, for that matter, moreover, once he had settled at his end, it was marked that nobody else ever came to sit. He saw people, along the Marina, take this liberty with other resting presences; but his own struck them perhaps in general as either of too grim or just of too dingy a vicinage. He might have affected the fellow-lounger as a man evil, unsociable, possibly engaged in working out the idea of a crime; or otherwise, more probably—for on the whole he surely looked harmless—devoted to the worship of some absolutely unpractical remorse.

On a certain October Saturday he had got off, as usual, early; but the afternoon light, his pilgrimage drawing to its aim, could still show him, at long range, the rare case of an established usurper. His impulse was then, as by custom, to deviate a little and wait, all the more that the occupant of the bench was a lady, and that ladies, when alone, were—at that austere end of the varied frontal stretch—markedly discontinuous; but he kept on at sight of this person's rising, while he was still fifty yards off, and proceeding, her back turned, to the edge of the broad terrace, the outer line of which followed the interspaced succession of seats and was guarded by an iron rail from the abruptly lower level of the beach. Here she stood before the sea, while our friend on his side, recognising no reason to the contrary, sank into the place she had quitted. There were other benches, eastward and off by the course of the drive, for vague ladies. The lady indeed thus thrust upon Herbert's vision might have struck an observer either as not quite vague or as vague with a perverse intensity suggesting design.

Not that our own observer at once thought of these things; he only took in, and with no great interest, that the obtruded presence was a "real" lady; that she was dressed—he noticed such matters—with a certain elegance of propriety or intention of harmony; and that she remained perfectly still for a good many minutes; so many in fact that he presently ceased to heed her, and that as she wasn't straight before him, but as far to the left as was consistent with his missing her profile, he had turned himself to one of his sunsets again (though it wasn't quite one of his best) and let it hold him for a time that enabled her to alter her attitude and present a fuller view. Without other movement, but her back now to the sea and her face to the odd person who had appropriated her corner, she had taken a sustained look at him before he was aware she had stirred. On that apprehension, however, he became also promptly aware of her direct, her applied observation. As his sense of this quickly increased he wondered who she was and what she wanted—what, as it were, was the matter with her; it suggested to him, the next thing, that she had, under some strange idea, actually been waiting for him. Any idea about him to-day on the part of any one could only be strange.

Yes, she stood there with the ample width of the Marina between them, but turned to him, for all the world, as to show frankly that she was concerned with him. And she *was*—oh yes—a real lady: a middle-aged person, of good appearance and of the best condition, in quiet but "handsome" black, save for very fresh white kid gloves, and with a pretty, dotty, becoming veil, predominantly white, adjusted to her countenance; which through it somehow, even to his imperfect sight, showed strong fine black brows and what he would have called on the spot character. But she was pale; her black brows were the blacker behind the flattering tissue; she still kept a hand, for support, on the terrace-rail, while the other, at the end of an extended arm that had an effect of rigidity, clearly pressed hard on the knob of a small and shining umbrella, the lower extremity of whose stick was equally, was sustainingly, firm on the walk. So this mature, qualified, important person stood and looked at the limp, undistinguished—oh his values of aspect now!—shabby man on the bench.

It was extraordinary, but the fact of her interest, by immensely surprising, by immediately agitating him, blinded him at first to her identity and, for the space of his long stare, diverted him from it; with which even then, when recognition did break, the sense of the shock, striking inward, simply consumed itself in gaping stillness. He sat there motionless and weak, fairly faint with surprise, and there was no instant, in all the succession of so many, at which Kate Cookham could have caught the special sign of his intelligence. Yet that she did catch something he saw—for he saw her steady herself, by her two supported hands, to meet it; while, after she had done so, a very wonderful thing happened, of which he could scarce, later on, have made a clear statement, though he was to think it over again and again. She moved toward him, she reached him, she stood there, she sat down near him, he merely passive and wonderstruck, unresentfully "impressed," gaping and taking it in—and all as with an open allowance on the part of each, so that they positively and quite intimately met in it, of the impertinence for their case, this case that brought them again, after horrible years, face to face, of the vanity, the profanity, the impossibility, of anything between them but silence.

Nearer to him, beside him at a considerable interval (oh she was immensely considerate!) she presented him, in the sharp terms of her transformed state—but thus the more amply, formally, ceremoniously—with the reasons that would serve him best for not having precipitately known her. She was simply another and a totally different person, and the exhibition of it to which she had proceeded with this solemn anxiety was all, obviously, for his benefit—once he had, as he appeared to be doing, provisionally accepted her approach. He had remembered her as inclined to the massive and disowned by the graceful; but this was a spare, fine, worn, almost wasted lady—who had repaired waste, it was true, however, with something he could only appreciate as a rich accumulation of manner. She was strangely older, so far as that went—marked by experience and as if many things had happened to her; her face had suffered, to its improvement, contraction and concentration; and if he had granted, of old and from the first, that her eyes were remarkable, had they yet ever had for him this sombre glow? Withal, something said, she had flourished—he felt it, wincing at it, as that; she had had a life, a career, a history—something that her present waiting air and nervous consciousness couldn't prevent his noting there as a deeply latent assurance. She had flourished, she had flourished—though to learn it after this fashion was somehow at the same time not to feel she flaunted it. It wasn't thus execration that she revived in him; she made in fact, exhibitively, as he could only have put it, the matter of long ago irrelevant, and these extraordinary minutes of their reconstituted relation—how many? how few?—addressed themselves altogether to new possibilities.

Still it after a little awoke in him as with the throb of a touched nerve that his own very attitude was supplying a connection; he knew presently that he wouldn't have had her go, *couldn't* have made a sign to her for it—which was what she had been uncertain of—without speaking to him; and that therefore he was, as at the other, the hideous time, passive to whatever she might do. She was even yet, she was always, in possession of him; she had known how and where to find him and had appointed that he should see her, and, though he had never dreamed it was again to happen to him, he was meeting it already as if it might have been the only thing that the least humanly *could*. Yes, he had come back there to flop, by long custom, upon the bench of desolation *as* the man in the whole place, precisely, to whom nothing worth more than tuppence could happen; whereupon, in the grey desert of his consciousness, the very earth had suddenly opened and flamed. With this, further, it came over him that he hadn't been prepared and that his wretched appearance must show it. He wasn't fit to receive a visit—any visit; a flush for his felt misery, in the light of her opulence, broke out in his lean cheeks. But if he coloured he sat as he was—she should at least, as a visitor, be satisfied. His eyes only, at last, turned from her and resumed a little their gaze at the sea. That, however, didn't relieve him, and he perpetrated in the course of another moment the odd desperate gesture of raising both his hands to his face and letting them, while he pressed it to them, cover and guard it. It was as he held them there that she at last spoke.

"I'll go away if you wish me to." And then she waited a moment. "I mean now—now that you've seen I'm here. I wanted you to know it, and I thought of writing—I was afraid of our meeting accidentally. Then I was afraid that if I wrote you might refuse. So I thought of this way—as I knew you must come out here." She went on with pauses, giving him a chance to make a sign. "I've waited several days. But I'll do what you wish. Only I should like in that case to come back." Again she stopped; but strange was it to him that he wouldn't have made her break off. She held him in boundless wonder. "I came down—I mean I came from town—on purpose. I'm staying on still, and I've a great patience and will give you time. Only may I say it's important? Now that I do see you," she brought out in the same way, "I see how inevitable it was—I mean that I should have wanted to come. But you must feel about it as you can," she wound up—"till you get used to the idea."

She spoke so for accommodation, for discretion, for some ulterior view already expressed in her manner, that, after taking well in, from behind his hands, that this was her very voice—oh ladylike!—heard, and heard in deprecation of displeasure, after long years again, he uncovered his face and freshly met her eyes. More than ever he couldn't have known her. Less and less remained of the figure all the facts of which had long ago so hardened for him. She was a handsome, grave, authoritative, but refined and, as it were, physically rearranged person—she, the outrageous vulgarity of whose prime assault had kept him shuddering so long as a shudder was in him. That atrocity in her was what everything had been built on, but somehow, all strangely, it was slipping from him; so that, after the oddest fashion conceivable, when he felt he mustn't let her go, it was as if he were putting out his hand to *save* the past, the hideous real unalterable past, exactly as she had been the cause of its being and the cause of his undergoing it. He should have been too awfully "sold" if he wasn't going to have been right about her.

"I don't mind," he heard himself at last say. Not to mind had seemed for the instant the length he was prepared to go; but he was afterward aware of how soon he must have added: "You've come on purpose to see me?" He was on the point of putting to her further: "What then do you want of me?" But he would keep—yes, in time—from appearing to show he cared. If he showed he cared, where then would be his revenge? So he was already, within five minutes, thinking his revenge uncomfortably over instead of just comfortably knowing it. What came to him, at any rate, as they actually fell to talk, was that, with such precautions, considerations, reduplications of consciousness, almost avowed feelings of her way on her own part, and light fingerings of his chords of sensibility, she was understanding, she *had* understood, more things than all the years, up to this strange eventide, had given him an inkling of. They talked, they went on—he hadn't let her retreat, to whatever it committed him and however abjectly it did so; yet keeping off and off, dealing with such surface facts as involved ancient acquaintance but held abominations at bay. The recognition, the attestation that she *had* come down for him, that there would be reasons, that she had even hovered and watched, assured herself a little of his habits (which she managed to speak of as if, on their present ampler development, they were much to be deferred to), detained them enough to make vivid how, listen as stiffly or as serenely as he might, she sat there in fear, just as she had so stood there at first, and that her fear had really to do with her calculation of some sort of chance with him. What chance could it possibly be? Whatever it might have done, on this prodigious showing, with Kate Cookham, it made the present witness to the state of his fortunes simply exquisite: he ground his teeth secretly together as he saw he should have to take *that*. For what did it mean but that she would have liked to pity him if she could have done it with safety? Ah, however, he must give her no measure of safety!

By the time he had remarked, with that idea, that she probably saw few changes about them there that weren't for the worse—the place was going down, down and down, so fast that goodness knew where it would stop—and had also mentioned that in spite of this he himself remained faithful, with all its faults loving it still; by the time he had, after that fashion, superficially indulged her, adding a few further light and just sufficiently dry reflections on local matters, the disappearance of landmarks and important persons, the frequency of gales, the low policy of the town-council in playing down to cheap excursionists: by the time he had so acquitted himself, and she had observed, of her own motion, that she was staying at the Royal, which he knew for the time-honoured, the conservative and exclusive hotel, he had made out for himself one thing at least, the amazing fact that he had been landed by his troubles, at the end of time, in a "social relation," of all things in the world, and how of that luxury he was now having unprecedented experience. He had but once in his life had his nose in the Royal, on the occasion of his himself delivering a parcel during some hiatus in his succession of impossible small boys and meeting in the hall the lady who had bought of him, in the morning, a set of Crabbe, largely, he flattered himself, under the artful persuasion of his acute remarks on that author, gracefully associated by him, in this colloquy, he remembered, with a glance at Charles Lamb as well, and who went off in a day or two without settling, though he received her cheque from London three or four months later.

That hadn't been a social relation; and truly, deep within his appeal to himself to be remarkable, to be imperturbable and impenetrable, to be in fact quite incomparable now, throbbed the intense vision of his drawing out and draining dry the sensation he had begun to taste. He would do it, moreover—that would be the refinement of his art—not only without the betraying anxiety of a single question, but just even by seeing her flounder (since she must, in a vagueness deeply disconcerting to her) as to her real effect on him. She was distinctly floundering by the time he had brought her— it had taken ten minutes—down to a consciousness of absurd and twaddling topics, to the reported precarious state, for instance, of the syndicate running the Bijou Theatre at the Pierhead—all as an admonition that she might want him to want to know why she was thus waiting on him, might want it for all she was worth, before he had ceased to be so remarkable as not to ask her. He didn't—and this assuredly was wondrous enough—want to do anything worse to her than let her flounder; but he was willing to do that so long as it mightn't prevent his seeing at least where *he* was. He seemed still to see where he was even at the minute that followed her final break- off, clearly intended to be resolute, from make-believe talk.

"I wonder if I might prevail on you to come to tea with me to-morrow at five."

He didn't so much as answer it—though he could scarcely believe his ears. To-morrow was Sunday, and the proposal referred, clearly, to the custom of "five-o'clock" tea, known to him only by the contemporary novel of manners and the catchy advertisement of table-linen. He had never in his life been present at any such luxurious rite, but he was offering practical indifference to it as a false mark of his sense that his social relation had already risen to his chin. "I gave up my very modest, but rather interesting little old book business, perhaps you know, ever so long ago."

She floundered so that she could say nothing—meet *that* with no possible word; all the less too that his tone, casual

and colourless, wholly defied any apprehension of it as a reverse. Silence only came; but after a moment she returned to
her effort. "If you *can* come I shall be at home. To see you
otherwise than thus was in fact what, as I tell you, I came
down for. But I leave it," she returned, "to your feeling."

He had at this, it struck him, an inspiration; which he required however a minute or two to decide to carry out; a
minute or two during which the shake of his foot over his
knee became an intensity of fidget. "Of course I know I still
owe you a large sum of money. If it's about *that* you wish to
see me," he went on, "I may as well tell you just here that I
shall be able to meet my full obligation in the future as little
as I've met it in the past. I can never," said Herbert Dodd,
"pay up that balance."

He had looked at her while he spoke, but on finishing
looked off at the sea again and continued to agitate his foot.
He knew now what he had done and why; and the sense of
her fixed dark eyes on him during his speech and after didn't
alter his small contentment. Yet even when she still said nothing he didn't turn round; he simply kept his corner as if *that*
were his point made, should it even be the last word between
them. It might have been, for that matter, from the way in
which she presently rose, gathering herself, her fine umbrella
and her very small smart reticule, in the construction of which
shining gilt much figured, well together, and, after standing
another instant, moved across to the rail of the terrace as she
had done before and remained, as before, with her back to
him, though this time, it well might be, under a different fear.
A quarter of an hour ago she hadn't tried him, and had had
that anxiety; now that she had tried him it wasn't easier—but
she was thinking what she still could do. He left her to think—
nothing in fact more interesting than the way she might decide had ever happened to him; but it was a part of this also
that as she turned round and came nearer again he didn't rise,
he gave her no help. If she got any, at least, from his looking
up at her only, meeting her fixed eyes once more in silence,
that was her own affair. "You must think," she said—"you
must take all your time, but I shall be at home." She left it
to him thus—she insisted, with her idea, on leaving him something too. And on her side as well she showed an art—which

resulted, after another instant, in his having to rise to his feet. He flushed afresh as he did it—it exposed him so shabbily the more; and now if she took him in, with each of his seedy items, from head to foot, he didn't and couldn't and wouldn't know it, attaching his eyes hard and straight to something quite away from them.

It stuck in his throat to say he'd come, but she had so curious a way with her that he still less could say he wouldn't, and in a moment had taken refuge in something that was neither. "Are you married?"—he put it to her with that plainness, though it had seemed before he said it to do more for him than while she waited before replying.

"No, I'm not married," she said; and then had another wait that might have amounted to a question of what this had to do with it.

He surely couldn't have told her; so that he had recourse, a little poorly as he felt, but to an "Oh!" that still left them opposed. He turned away for it—that is for the poorness, which, lingering in the air, had almost a vulgar platitude; and when he presently again wheeled about she had fallen off as for quitting him, only with a pause, once more, for a last look. It was all a bit awkward, but he had another happy thought, which consisted in his silently raising his hat as for a sign of dignified dismissal. He had cultivated of old, for the occasions of life, the right, the discriminated bow, and now, out of the grey limbo of the time when he could care for such things, this flicker of propriety leaped and worked. She might, for that matter, herself have liked it; since, receding further, only with her white face toward him, she paid it the homage of sub-mission. He remained dignified, and she almost humbly went.

V

Nothing in the world, on the Sunday afternoon, could have prevented him from going; he was not after all destitute of three or four such articles of clothing as, if they wouldn't particularly grace the occasion, wouldn't positively dishonour it. That deficiency might have kept him away, but no voice of the spirit, no consideration of pride. It sweetened his impa-tience in fact—for he fairly felt it a long time to wait—that his pride would really most find its account in his acceptance of these conciliatory steps. From the moment he could put it in that way—that he couldn't refuse to hear what she might have, so very elaborately, to say for herself—he ought certainly to be at his ease; in illustration of which he whistled odd snatches to himself as he hung about on that cloud-dappled autumn Sunday, a mild private minstrelsy that his lips hadn't known since when? The interval of the twenty-four hours, made longer by a night of many more revivals than oblivions, had in fact dragged not a little; in spite of which, however, our extremely brushed-up and trimmed and polished friend knew an unprecedented flutter as he was ushered, at the Royal Hotel, into Miss Cookham's sitting-room. Yes, it was an adventure, and he had never had an adventure in his life; the term, for him, was essentially a term of high appreciation—such as disqualified for that figure, under due criticism, every single passage of his past career.

What struck him at the moment as qualifying in the highest degree this actual passage was the fact that at no great distance from his hostess in the luxurious room, as he apprehended it, in which the close of day had begun to hang a few shadows, sat a gentleman who rose as she rose, and whose name she at once mentioned to him. He had for Herbert Dodd all the air of a swell, the gentleman—rather red-faced and bald-headed, but moustachioed, waistcoated, necktied to the highest pitch, with an effect of chains and rings, of shining teeth in a glassily monocular smile; a wondrous apparition to have been asked to "meet" him, as in contemporary fiction, or for him to have been asked to meet. "Captain Roper, Mr. Herbert Dodd"— their entertainer introduced them, yes; but with a sequel immediately afterward more disconcerting apparently to Captain Roper himself even than to her second and more breathless visitor; a "Well then, good-bye till the next time," with a hand thrust straight out, which allowed the personage so addressed no alternative but to lay aside his teacup, even though Herbert saw there was a good deal left in it, and glare about him for his hat. Miss Cookham had had her tea-tray on a small table before her, she had served Captain Roper while waiting for Mr. Dodd; but she simply dismissed him now, with a high sweet unmistakable decision, a knowledge of what she was about, as our hero would have called it, which enlarged at a stroke the latter's view of the number of different things and sorts of things, in the sphere of the manners and ways of those living at their ease, that a social relation would put before one. Captain Roper would have liked to remain, would have liked more tea, but Kate signified in this direct fashion that she had had enough of him. Herbert had seen things, in his walk of life—rough things, plenty; but never things smoothed with that especial smoothness, carried out as it were by the fine form of Captain Roper's own retreat, which included even a bright convulsed leave-taking cognisance of the plain, vague individual, of no lustre at all and with the very low-class guard of an old silver watch buttoned away under an ill-made coat, to whom he was sacrificed.

It came to Herbert as he left the place a shade less remarkable—though there was still wonder enough and to spare—that he had been even publicly and designedly sacrificed; exactly so that, as the door closed behind him, Kate Cookham, standing there to wait for it, could seem to say, across the room, to the friend of her youth, only by the expression of her fine eyes: "There—see what I do for you!" "For" him—that was the extraordinary thing, and not less so that he was already, within three minutes, after this fashion, taking it in as by the intensity of a new light; a light that was one somehow with this rich inner air of the plush-draped and much-mirrored hotel, where the fire-glow and the approach of evening confirmed together the privacy, and the loose curtains at the wide window were parted for a command of his old lifelong Parade—the field of life so familiar to him from below and in the wind and the wet, but which he had never in all the long years hung over at this vantage.

"He's an acquaintance, but a bore," his hostess explained in respect to Captain Roper. "He turned up yesterday, but I didn't invite him, and I had said to him before you came in that I was expecting a gentleman with whom I should wish to be alone. I go quite straight at my idea that way, as a rule; but you know," she now strikingly went on, "how straight I go. And he had had," she added, "his tea."

Dodd had been looking all round—had taken in, with the rest, the brightness, the distinguished elegance, as he supposed it, of the tea-service with which she was dealing and the variously tinted appeal of certain savoury edibles on plates. "Oh but he *hadn't* had his tea!" he heard himself the next moment earnestly reply; which speech had at once betrayed, he was then quickly aware, the candour of his interest, the unsophisticated state that had survived so many troubles. If he was so interested how could he be proud, and if he was proud how could he be so interested?

He had made her at any rate laugh outright, and was further conscious, for this, both that it was the first time of that since their new meeting, and that it didn't affect him as harsh. It affected him, however, as free, for she replied at once, still smiling and as a part of it: "Oh, I think we shall get on!"

This told him he had made some difference for her, shown her the way, or something like it, that she hadn't been sure of yesterday; which moreover wasn't what he had intended—he had come armed for showing her nothing; so that after she had gone on with the same gain of gaiety, "You must at any rate comfortably have yours," there was but one answer for him to make.

His eyes played again over the tea-things—they seemed strangely to help him; but he didn't sit down. "I've come, as you see—but I've come, please, to understand; and if you require to be alone with me, and if I break bread with you, it seems to me I should first know exactly where I am and to what you suppose I so commit myself." He had thought it out and over and over, particularly the turn about breaking bread; though perhaps he didn't give it, in her presence—this was impossible, her presence altered so many things—quite the full sound or the weight he had planned.

But it had none the less come to his aid—it had made her perfectly grave. "You commit yourself to nothing. You're perfectly free. It's only I who commit myself."

On which, while she stood there as if all handsomely and deferentially waiting for him to consider and decide, he would have been naturally moved to ask her what she committed herself then *to*—so moved, that is, if he hadn't, before saying it, thought more sharply still of something better. "Oh, that's another thing."

"Yes, that's another thing," Kate Cookham returned. To which she added, "So *now* won't you sit down?" He sank with deliberation into the seat from which Captain Roper had risen; she went back to her own and while she did so spoke again. "I'm *not* free. At least," she said over her tea-tray, "I'm free only for this."

Everything was there before them and around them, everything massive and shining, so that he had instinctively fallen back in his chair as for the wondering, the resigned acceptance of it; where her last words stirred in him a sense of odd deprecation. Only for "that"? "That" was everything, at this moment, to his long inanition, and the effect, as if she had suddenly and perversely mocked him, was to press the spring of a protest. "Isn't 'this' then riches?"

"Riches?" she smiled over, handing him his cup—for she had triumphed in having struck from him a question.

"I mean haven't you a lot of money?" He didn't care now that it was out; his cup was in his hand, and what was that but proved interest? He had succumbed to the social relation.

"Yes, I've money. Of course you wonder—but I've wanted you to wonder. It was to make you take that in that I came. So now you know," she said, leaning back where she faced him, but in a straighter chair and with her arms closely folded, after a fashion characteristic of her, as for some control of her nerves.

"You came to show you've money?"

"That's one of the things. Not a lot—not even very much. But enough," said Kate Cookham.

"Enough? I should think so!" he again couldn't help a bit crudely exhaling.

"Enough for what I wanted. I don't always live like this— not at all. But I came to the best hotel on purpose. I wanted to show you I could. Now," she asked, "do you understand?"

"Understand?" He only gaped.

She threw up her loosed arms, which dropped again beside her. "I did it *for* you—I did it *for* you!"

" 'For' me——?"

"What I did—what I did here of old."

He stared, trying to see it. "When you made me pay you?"

"The Two Hundred and Seventy—all I could get from you, as you reminded me yesterday, so that I had to give up the rest. It was my idea," she went on—"it was my idea."

"To bleed me quite to death?" Oh, his ice was broken now!

"To make you raise money—since you could, you *could*. You did, you did—so what better proof?"

His hands fell from what he had touched; he could only stare—her own manner for it was different now too. "I did. I did indeed—!" And the woful weak simplicity of it, which seemed somehow all that was left him, fell even on his own ear.

"Well then, here it is—it isn't lost!" she returned with a graver face.

" 'Here' it is," he gasped, "my poor agonised old money—my blood?"

"Oh, it's *my* blood too, you must know now!" She held up her head as not before—as for her right to speak of the thing to-day most precious to her. "I took it, but this—my being here this way—is what I've made of it! That was the idea I had!"

Her "ideas," as things to boast of, staggered him. "To have everything in the world, like this, at my wretched expense?"

She had folded her arms back again—grasping each elbow she sat firm; she knew he could see, and had known well from the first, what she had wanted to say, difficult, monstrous though it might be. "No more than at my own—but to do something with your money that you'd never do yourself."

"Myself, myself?" he wonderingly wailed. "Do you know—or don't you?—what my life has been?"

She waited, and for an instant, though the light in the room had failed a little more and would soon be mainly that of the flaring lamps on the windy Parade, he caught from her dark eye a silver gleam of impatience. "You've suffered and you've worked—which, God knows, is what I've done! *Of course* you've suffered," she said—"you inevitably had to! We have to," she went on, "to do or to be or to get anything."

"And pray what have I done or been or got?" Herbert Dodd found it almost desolately natural to demand.

It made her cover him again as with all she was thinking of. "Can you imagine nothing, or can't you conceive—?" And then as her challenge struck deeper in, deeper down than it had yet reached, and with the effect of a rush of the blood to his face, "It was *for* you, it was *for* you!" she again broke out—"and for what or whom else could it have been?"

He saw things to a tune now that made him answer straight: "I thought at one time it might be for Bill Frankle."

"Yes—that was the way you treated me," Miss Cookham as plainly replied.

But he let this pass; his thought had already got away from it. "What good then—its having been for me—has that ever done me?"

"Doesn't it do you any good *now*?" his friend returned. To which she added, with another dim play of her tormented brightness, before he could speak: "But if you won't even have your tea——!"

He had in fact touched nothing and, if he could have explained, would have pleaded very veraciously that his appetite, keen when he came in, had somehow suddenly failed. It was beyond eating or drinking, what she seemed to want him to take from her. So if he looked, before him, over the array, it was to say, very grave and graceless: "Am I to understand that you offer to repay me?"

"I offer to repay you with interest, Herbert Dodd"—and her emphasis of the great word was wonderful.

It held him in his place a minute, and held his eyes upon her; after which, agitated too sharply to sit still, he pushed back his chair and stood up. It was as if mere distress or dismay at first worked in him, and was in fact a wave of deep and irresistible emotion which made him, on his feet, sway as in a great trouble and then, to correct it, throw himself stiffly toward the window, where he stood and looked out unseeing. The road, the wide terrace beyond, the seats, the eternal sea beyond that, the lighted lamps now flaring in the October night-wind, with the few dispersed people abroad at the tea-hour; these things, meeting and melting into the firelit hospitality at his elbow—or was it that portentous amenity that melted into *them*?—seemed to form round him and to put before him, all together, the strangest of circles and the

newest of experiences, in which the unforgettable and the unimaginable were confoundingly mixed. "Oh, oh, oh!"—he
could only almost howl for it.

And then, while a thick blur for some moments mantled
everything, he knew she had got up, that she stood watching
him, allowing for everything, again all "cleverly" patient with
him, and he heard her speak again as with studied quietness
and clearness. "I wanted to take care of you—it was what I
first wanted—and what you first consented to. I'd have done
it, oh I'd have done it, I'd have loved you and helped you
and guarded you, and you'd have had no trouble, no bad
blighting ruin, in all your easy, yes, just your quite jolly and
comfortable life. I showed you and proved to you this—I
brought it home to you, as I fondly fancied, and it made me
briefly happy. You swore you cared for me, you wrote it and
made me believe it—you pledged me your honour and your
faith. Then you turned and changed suddenly from one day
to another; everything altered, you broke your vows, you as
good as told me you only wanted it off. You faced me with
dislike, and in fact tried not to face me at all; you behaved as
if you hated me—you had seen a girl, of great beauty, I admit,
who made me a fright and a bore."

This brought him straight round. "No, Kate Cookham."

"Yes, Herbert Dodd." She but shook her head, calmly and
nobly, in the now gathered dusk, and her memories and
her cause and her character—or was it only her arch-subtlety,
her line and her "idea"?—gave her an extraordinary large
assurance.

She had touched, however, the treasure of his own case—
his terrible own case that began to live again at once by the
force of her talking of hers, and which could always all cluster
about his great asseveration. "No, no, never, never; I had
never seen her then and didn't dream of her; so that when
you yourself began to be harsh and sharp with me, and to
seem to want to quarrel, I could have but one idea—which
was an appearance you didn't in the least, as I saw it then,
account for or disprove."

"An appearance—?" Kate desired, as with high astonishment, to know which one.

"How *shouldn't* I have supposed you really to care for Bill

Frankle?—as thoroughly believing the motive of your claim for my money to be its help to your marrying him, since you couldn't marry me. I was only surprised when, time passing, I made out that that hadn't happened; and perhaps," he added the next instant with something of a conscious lapse from the finer style, "hadn't been in question."

She had listened to this only staring, and she was silent after he had said it, so silent for some instants that while he considered her something seemed to fail him, much as if he had thrown out his foot for a step and not found the place to rest it. He jerked round to the window again, and then she answered, but without passion unless it was that of her weariness for something stupid and forgiven in him, "Oh, the blind, the pitiful folly!"—to which, as it might perfectly have applied to her own behaviour, he returned nothing. She had moreover at once gone on. "Have it then that there wasn't much to do—between your finding that you loathed me for another woman or discovering only, when it came to the point, that you loathed me quite enough for myself."

Which, as she put it in that immensely effective fashion, he recognised that he must just unprotestingly and not so very awkwardly—not so *very*!—take from her; since, whatever he had thus come to her for, it wasn't to perjure himself with any pretence that, "another woman" or no other woman, he hadn't, for years and years, abhorred her. Now he was taking tea with her—or rather, literally, seemed not to be; but this made no difference, and he let her express it as she would while he distinguished a man he knew, Charley Coote, outside on the Parade, under favour of the empty hour and one of the flaring lamps, making up to a young woman with whom (it stuck out grotesquely in his manner) he had never before conversed. Dodd's own position was that of acquiescing in this recall of what had so bitterly been—but he hadn't come back to her, of himself, to stir up, to recall or to recriminate, and for *her* it could but be the very lesson of her whole present act that if she touched anything she touched everything. Soon enough she *was* indeed, and all overwhelmingly, touching everything—with a hand of which the boldness grew.

"But I didn't let *that*, even, make a difference in what I wanted—which was all," she said, "and had only and passionately been, to take care of you. I had *no* money whatever —nothing then of my own, not a penny to come by anyhow; so it wasn't with mine I could do it. But I could do it with yours," she amazingly wound up—"if I could once get yours out of you."

He faced straight about again—his eyebrows higher than they had ever been in his life. "Mine? What penny of it was mine? What scrap beyond a bare, mean little living had I ever pretended to have?"

She held herself still a minute, visibly with force; only her eyes consciously attached to the seat of a chair the back of which her hands, making it tilt toward her a little, grasped as for support. "You pretended to have enough to marry me— and that was all I afterward claimed of you when you wouldn't." He was on the point of retorting that he had absolutely pretended to nothing—least of all to the primary desire that such a way of stating it fastened on him; he was on the point for ten seconds of giving her full in the face: "I never *had* any such dream till you yourself—infatuated with me as, frankly, you on the whole appeared to be—got round me and muddled me up and made me behave as if in a way that went against the evidence of my senses." But he was to feel as quickly that, whatever the ugly, the spent, the irrecoverable truth, he might better have bitten his tongue off: there beat on him there this strange and other, this so prodigiously different beautiful and dreadful truth that no far remembrance and no abiding ache of his own could wholly falsify, and that was indeed all out with her next words. "That—*using* it for you and using you yourself for your own future—was my motive. I've led my life, which has been an affair, I assure you; and, as I've told you without your quite seeming to understand, I've brought everything fivefold back to you."

The perspiration broke out on his forehead. "Everything's mine?" he quavered as for the deep piercing pain of it.

"Everything!" said Kate Cookham.

So it told him how she had loved him—but with the tremendous effect at once of its only glaring out at him from the whole thing that it was verily she, a thousand times over, who, in the exposure of his youth and his vanity, had, on the bench of desolation, the scene of yesterday's own renewal, left for him no forward steps to take. It hung there for him tragically vivid again, the hour she had first found him sequestered and accessible after making his acquaintance at his shop. And from this, by a succession of links that fairly clicked to his ear as with their perfect fitting, the fate and the pain and the payment of others stood together in a great grim order. Everything there then was *his*—to make him ask what had been Nan's, poor Nan's of the constant question of whether he need have collapsed. She was before him, she was between them, his little dead dissatisfied wife; across all whose final woe and whose lowly grave he was to reach out, it appeared, to take gifts. He saw them too, the gifts; saw them—she bristled with them—in his actual companion's brave and sincere and authoritative figure, her strangest of demonstrations. But the other appearance was intenser, as if their ghost had waved wild arms; so that half a minute hadn't passed before the one poor thing that remained of Nan, and that yet thus became a quite mighty and momentous poor thing, was sitting on his lips as for its sole opportunity.

"Can you give me your word of honour that I mightn't, under decent advice, have defied you?"

It made her turn very white; but now that she had said what she *had* said she could still hold up her head. "Certainly you might have defied me, Herbert Dodd."

"They would have told me you had no legal case?"

Well, if she was pale she was bold. "You talk of decent advice—!" She broke off, there was too much to say, and all needless. What she said instead was: "They would have told you I had nothing."

"I didn't so much as ask," her sad visitor remarked.

"Of course you didn't so much as ask."

"I couldn't be so outrageously vulgar," he went on.

"*I* could, by God's help!" said Kate Cookham.

"Thank you." He had found at his command a tone that made him feel more gentlemanlike than he had ever felt in his life or should doubtless ever feel again. It might have been enough—but somehow as they stood there with this immense clearance between them it wasn't. The clearance was like a sudden gap or great bleak opening through which there blew upon them a deadly chill. Too many things had fallen away, too many new rolled up and over him, and they made something within shake him to his base. It upset the full vessel, and though she kept her eyes on him he let that consequence come, bursting into tears, weakly crying there before her even as he had cried to himself in the hour of his youth when she had made him groundlessly fear. She turned away then—*that* she couldn't watch, and had presently flung herself on the sofa and, all responsively wailing, buried her own face on the cushioned arm. So for a minute their smothered sobs only filled the room. But he made out, through this disorder, where he had put down his hat; his stick and his new tan-coloured gloves—they had cost two-and-thruppence and would have represented sacrifices—were on the chair beside it. He picked these articles up and all silently and softly—gasping, that is, but quite on tiptoe—reached the door and let himself out.

VI

Off there on the bench of desolation a week later she made him a more particular statement, which it had taken the remarkably tense interval to render possible. After leaving her at the hotel that last Sunday he had gone forth in his reaggravated trouble and walked straight before him, in the teeth of the west wind, close to the iron rails of the stretched Marina and with his telltale face turned from persons occasionally met, and toward the surging sea. At the Land's End, even in the confirmed darkness and the perhaps imminent big blow, his immemorial nook, small shelter as it yielded, had again received him; and it was in the course of this heedless session, no doubt, where the agitated air had nothing to add to the commotion within him, that he began to look his extraordinary fortune a bit straighter in the face and see it confess itself at once a fairy-tale and a nightmare. That, visibly, confoundingly, she was still attached to him (attached in fact was a mild word!) and that the unquestionable proof of it was in this offered pecuniary salve, of the thickest composition, for his wounds and sores and shames—these things were the fantastic fable, the tale of money in handfuls, that he seemed to have only to stand there and swallow and digest and feel himself full-fed by; but the whole of the rest was nightmare, and most of all nightmare his having thus to thank one through whom Nan and his little girls had known torture.

He didn't care for himself now, and this unextinguished and apparently inextinguishable charm by which he had held her was a fact incredibly romantic; but he gazed with a longer face than he had ever had for anything in the world at his potential acceptance of a great bouncing benefit from the person he intimately, if even in a manner indirectly, associated with the conditions to which his lovely wife and his children (who would have been so lovely too) had pitifully succumbed. He had accepted the social relation—which meant he had taken even that on trial—without knowing what it so dazzlingly masked; for a social relation it had become with a vengeance when it drove him about the place as now at his hours of freedom (and he actually and recklessly took, all demoralised and unstrung and unfit either for work or for anything else, other liberties that would get him into trouble) under this queer torment of irreconcilable things, a bewildered consciousness of tenderness and patience and cruelty, of great evident mystifying facts that were as little to be questioned as to be conceived or explained, and that were yet least, withal, to be lost sight of.

On that Sunday night he had wandered wild, incoherently ranging and throbbing, but this became the law of his next days as well, since he lacked more than ever all other resort or refuge and had nowhere to carry, to deposit, or contractedly let loose and lock up, as it were, his swollen consciousness, which fairly split in twain the raw shell of his sordid little boarding-place. The arch of the sky and the spread of sea and shore alone gave him space; he could roam with himself anywhere, in short, far or near—he could only never take himself back. That certitude—that this was impossible to him even should she wait there among her plushes and bronzes ten years—was the thing he kept closest clutch of; it did wonders for what he would have called his self-respect. Exactly as he had left her so he would stand off—even though at moments when he pulled up sharp somewhere to put himself an intensest question his heart almost stood still. The days of the week went by, and as he had left her she stayed; to the extent, that is, of his having neither sight nor sound of her, and of the failure of every sign. It took nerve, he said, not to return to her, even for curiosity—since how, after all, in the name of wonder, had she invested the fruits of her extortion to such advantage, there being no chapter of all the obscurity of the years to beat that for queerness? But he dropped, tired to death, on benches, half a dozen times an evening—exactly on purpose to recognise that the nerve required was just the nerve he had.

As the days without a token from her multiplied he came in as well for hours—and these indeed mainly on the bench of desolation—of sitting stiff and stark in presence of the probability that he had lost everything for ever. When he passed the Royal he never turned an eyelash, and when he met Captain Roper on the Front, three days after having been introduced to him, he "cut him dead"—another privileged consequence of a social relation—rather than seem to himself to make the remotest approach to the question of whether Miss Cookham had left Properley. He had cut people in the days of his life before, just as he had come to being himself cut—since there had been no time for him wholly without one or other face of that necessity—but had never effected such a severance as of this rare connection, which helped to give him thus the measure of his really precious sincerity. If he had lost what had hovered before him he had lost it, his only tribute to which proposition was to grind his teeth with one of those "scrunches," as he would have said, of which the violence fairly reached his ear. It wouldn't make him lift a finger, and in fact if Kate had simply taken herself off on the Tuesday or the Wednesday she would have been reabsorbed again into the darkness from which she had emerged—and no lifting of fingers, the unspeakable chapter closed, would evermore avail. That at any rate was the kind of man he still was—even after all that had come and gone, and even if for a few dazed hours certain things had seemed pleasant. The dazed hours had passed, the surge of the old bitterness had dished him (shouldn't he have been shamed if it hadn't?), and he might sit there as before, as always, with nothing at all on earth to look to. He had therefore wrongfully believed himself to be degraded; and the last word about him would be that he *couldn't* then, it appeared, sink to vulgarity as he had tried to let his miseries make him.

And yet on the next Sunday morning, face to face with him again at the Land's End, what she very soon came to was: "As if I believed you didn't *know* by what cord you hold me!" Absolutely too, and just that morning in fact, above all, he wouldn't, he quite couldn't have taken his solemn oath that he hadn't a sneaking remnant, as he might have put it to himself—a remnant of faith in tremendous things still to come of their interview. The day was sunny and breezy, the sea of a cold purple; he wouldn't go to church as he mostly went of Sunday mornings, that being in its way too a social relation—and not least when two-and-thruppenny tan-coloured gloves were new; which indeed he had the art of keeping them for ages. Yet he would dress himself as he scarce mustered resources for even to figure on the fringe of Society, local and transient, at St. Bernard's, and in this trim he took his way westward; occupied largely, as he went, it might have seemed to any person pursuing the same course and happening to observe him, in a fascinated study of the motions of his shadow, the more or less grotesque shape projected, in front of him and mostly a bit to the right, over the blanched asphalt of the Parade and dandling and dancing at such a rate, shooting out and then contracting, that, viewed in themselves, its eccentricities might have formed the basis of an interesting challenge: "Find the state of mind, guess the nature of the agitation, possessing the person so remarkably represented!" Herbert Dodd, for that matter, might have been himself attempting to make by the sun's sharp aid some approach to his immediate horoscope.

It had at any rate been thus put before him that the dandling and dancing of his image occasionally gave way to perfect immobility, when he stopped and kept his eyes on it. "Suppose she should come, suppose she *should*!" it is revealed at least to ourselves that he had at these moments audibly breathed—breathed with the intensity of an arrest between hope and fear. It had glimmered upon him from early, with the look of the day, that, given all else that could happen, this would be rather, as he put it, in her line; and the possibility lived for him, as he proceeded, to the tune of a suspense almost sickening. It was, from one small stage of his pilgrimage to another, the "For ever, never!" of the sentimental case the playmates of his youth used to pretend to settle by plucking the petals of a daisy. But it came to his truly turning faint— so "queer" he felt—when, at the gained point of the long stretch from which he could always tell, he arrived within positive sight of his immemorial goal. His seat was taken and she was keeping it for him—it could only be *she* there in possession; whereby it shone out for Herbert Dodd that if he hadn't been quite sure of her recurrence she had at least been quite sure of his. *That* pulled him up to some purpose, where recognition began for them—or to the effect, in other words, of his pausing to judge if he could bear, for the sharpest note of their intercourse, this inveterate demonstration of her making him do what she liked. What settled the question for him then—and just while they avowedly watched each other, over the long interval, before closing, as if, on either side, for the major advantage—what settled it was this very fact that what she liked she liked so terribly. If it were simply to "use" him, as she had said the last time, and no matter to the profit of which of them she called it, one might let it go for that; since it could make her wait over, day after day, in that fashion, and with such a spending of money, on the hazard of their meeting again. How could she be the least sure he would ever again consent to it after the proved action on him, a week ago, of her last monstrous honesty? It was indeed positively as if he were now himself putting this influence—and for their common edification—to the supreme, to the finest test. He had a sublime, an ideal flight, which lasted about a minute. "Suppose, now that I see her there and what she has taken so characteristically for granted, suppose I just show her that she *hasn't* only confidently to wait or whistle for me, and that the length of my leash is greater than she measures, and that everything's impossible always?—show it by turning my back on her now and walking straight away. She won't be able not to understand *that*!"

Nothing had passed, across their distance, but the mute apprehension of each on the part of each; the whole expanse, at the church hour, was void of other life (he had scarce met a creature on his way from end to end), and the sun-seasoned gusts kept brushing the air and all the larger prospect clean. It was through this beautiful lucidity that he watched her watch him, as it were—watch him for what he would do. Neither moved at this high tension; Kate Cookham, her face fixed on him, only waited with a stiff appearance of leaving him, not for dignity but—to an effect of even deeper perversity— for kindness, free to choose. It yet somehow affected him at present, this attitude, as a gage of her *knowing too*—knowing, that is, that he wasn't really free, that this was the thinnest of vain parades, the poorest of hollow heroics, that his need, his solitude, his suffered wrong, his exhausted rancour, his foredoomed submission to any shown interest, all hung together too heavy on him to let the weak wings of his pride do more than vaguely tremble. They couldn't, they didn't carry him a single beat further away; according to which he stood rooted, neither retreating nor advancing, but presently correcting his own share of the bleak exchange by looking off at the sea. Deeply conscious of the awkwardness this posture gave him, he yet clung to it as the last shred of his honour, to the clear argument that it was one thing for him to have felt beneath all others, the previous days, that she was to be counted on, but quite a different for her to have felt that *he* was. His checked approach, arriving thus at no term, could in these odd conditions have established that he wasn't only if Kate Cookham had, as either of them might have said, taken it so— if she had given up the game at last by rising, by walking away and adding to the distance between them, and he had then definitely let her vanish into space. It became a fact that when she did finally rise—though after how long our record scarce takes on itself to say—it was not to confirm their separation but to put an end to it; and this by slowly approaching him till she had come within earshot. He had wondered, once aware of it in spite of his averted face, what she would say and on what note, as it were, she would break their week's silence; so that he had to recognise anew, her voice reaching him, that remarkable quality in her which again and again came up for him as her art.

"There are twelve hundred and sixty pounds, to be definite, but I have it all down for you—and you've only to draw."

They lost themselves, these words, rare and exquisite, in the wide bright genial medium and the Sunday stillness, but even while that occurred and he was gaping for it she was herself there, in her battered ladylike truth, to answer for them, to represent them, and, if a further grace than their simple syllabled beauty were conceivable, almost embarrassingly to cause them to materialise. Yes, she let her smart and tight little reticule hang as if it bulged, beneath its clasp, with the whole portentous sum, and he felt himself glare again at this vividest of her attested claims. She might have been ready, on the spot, to open the store to the plunge of his hand, or, with the situation otherwise conceived, to impose on his pauperised state an acceptance of alms on a scale unprecedented in the annals of street charity. Nothing so much counted for him, however, neither grave numeral nor elegant fraction, as the short, rich, rounded word that the breeze had picked up as it dropped and seemed now to blow about between them. "To draw—to draw?" Yes, he gaped it as if it had no sense; the fact being that even while he did so he was reading into her use of the term more romance than any word in the language had ever had for him. He, Herbert Dodd, was to live to "draw," like people, scarce hampered by the conditions of earth, whom he had remotely and circuitously heard about, and in fact when he walked back with her to where she had been sitting it was very much, for his strained nerves, as if the very bench of desolation itself were to be the scene of that exploit and he mightn't really live till he reached it.

When they had sat down together she did press the spring of her reticule, from which she took, not a handful of gold nor a packet of crisp notes, but an oblong sealed letter, which she had thus waited on him, she remarked, on purpose to deliver, and which would certify, with sundry particulars, to the credit she had opened for him at a London bank. He received it without looking at it—he held it, in the same manner, conspicuous and unassimilated, for most of the rest of the immediate time, appearing embarrassed with it, nervously twisting and flapping it, yet thus publicly retaining it even while aware, beneath everything, of the strange, the quite dreadful, wouldn't it be? engagement that such inaction practically stood for. He could accept money to that amount, yes—but not for nothing in return. For what then in return? He kept asking himself for what, while she said other things and made above all, in her high, shrewd, successful way the point that, no, he needn't pretend that his conviction of her continued personal interest in him wouldn't have tided him over any question besetting him since their separation. She put it to him that the deep instinct of where he should at last find her must confidently have worked for him, since she confessed to her instinct of where she should find *him*; which meant—oh it came home to him as he fingered his sealed treasure!—neither more nor less than that she had now created between them an equality of experience. He wasn't to have done all the suffering, *she* was to have "been through" things he couldn't even guess at; and, since he was bargaining away his right ever again to allude to the unforgettable, so much there was of it, what her tacit proposition came to was that they were "square" and might start afresh.

He didn't take up her charge, as his so compromised "pride" yet in a manner prompted him, that he had enjoyed all the week all those elements of ease about her; the most he achieved for that was to declare, with an ingenuity contributing to float him no small distance further, that of course he had turned up at their old place of tryst, which had been, through the years, the haunt of his solitude and the goal of his walk any Sunday morning that seemed too beautiful for church; but that he hadn't in the least built on her presence there—since that supposition gave him, she would understand, wouldn't she? the air, disagreeable to him, of having come in search of her. Her quest of himself, once he had been seated there, would have been another matter—but in short "Of course after all you did come to me, just now, didn't you?" He felt himself, too, lamely and gracelessly grin, as for the final kick of his honour, in confirmation of the record that he had then yielded but to her humility. Her humility became for him at this hour and to this tune, on the bench of desolation, a quantity more prodigious and even more mysterious than that other guaranteed quantity the finger-tips of his left hand could feel the tap of by the action of his right; though what was in especial extraordinary was the manner in which she could keep making him such allowances and yet meet him again, at some turn, as with her residuum for her clever self so great.

"Come to you, Herbert Dodd?" she imperturbably echoed. "I've been coming to you for the last ten years!"

There had been for him just before this sixty supreme seconds of intensest aspiration—a minute of his keeping his certificate poised for a sharp thrust back at her, the thrust of the wild freedom of his saying: "No, no, I *can't* give them up; I can't simply sink them deep down in my soul forever, with no cross in all my future to mark *that* burial; so that if this is what our arrangement means I must decline to have anything to do with it." The words none the less hadn't come, and when she had herself, a couple of minutes later, spoken those others, the blood rose to his face as if, given his stiffness and her extravagance, he had just indeed saved himself.

Everything in fact stopped, even his fidget with his paper; she imposed a hush, she imposed at any rate the conscious decent form of one, and he couldn't afterward have told how long, at this juncture, he must have sat simply gazing before him. It was so long, at any rate, that Kate herself got up— and quite indeed, presently, as if her own forms were now at an end. He had returned her nothing—so what was she waiting for? She had been on the two other occasions momentarily at a loss, but never so much so, no doubt, as was thus testified to by her leaving the bench and moving over once more to the rail of the terrace. She could carry it off, in a manner, with her resources, that she was waiting with so little to wait for; she could face him again, after looking off at the sea, as if this slightly stiff delay, not wholly exempt from awkwardness, had been but a fine scruple of her courtesy. She had gathered herself in; after giving him time to appeal she could take it that he had decided and that nothing was left for her to do. "Well then," she clearly launched at him across the broad walk— "well then, good-bye."

She had come nearer with it, as if he might rise for some show of express separation; but he only leaned back motionless, his eyes on her now—he kept her a moment before him.

"Do you mean that we don't—that we don't—?" But he broke down.

"Do I 'mean'—?" She remained as for questions he might ask, but it was wellnigh as if there played through her dotty veil an irrepressible irony for that particular one. "I've meant, for long years, I think, all I'm capable of meaning. I've meant so much that I can't mean more. So there it is."

"But if you go," he appealed—and with a sense as of final flatness, however he arranged it, for his own attitude—"but if you go sha'n't I see you again?"

She waited a little, and it was strangely for him now as if—though at last so much more gorged with her tribute than she had ever been with his—something still depended on her. "Do you *like* to see me?" she very simply asked.

At this he did get up; that was easier than to say—at least with responsive simplicity; and again for a little he looked hard and in silence at his letter; which at last, however, raising his eyes to her own for the act, while he masked their conscious ruefulness, to his utmost, in some air of assurance, he slipped into the inner pocket of his coat, letting it settle there securely. "You're too wonderful." But he frowned at her with it as never in his life. "Where does it all come from?"

"The wonder of poor me?" Kate Cookham said. "It comes from *you*."

He shook his head slowly—feeling, with his letter there against his heart, such a new agility, almost such a new range of interest. "I mean so *much* money—so extraordinarily much."

Well, she held him a while blank. "Does it seem to you extraordinarily much—twelve-hundred-and-sixty? Because, you know," she added, "it's all."

"It's enough!" he returned with a slight thoughtful droop of his head to the right and his eyes attached to the far horizon as through a shade of shyness for what he was saying. He felt all her own lingering nearness somehow on his cheek.

"It's enough? Thank you then!" she rather oddly went on.

He shifted a little his posture. "It was more than a hundred a year—for you to get together."

"Yes," she assented, "that was what year by year I tried for."

"But that you could live all the while and save that—!" Yes, he was at liberty, as he hadn't been, quite pleasantly to marvel. All his wonderments in life had been hitherto unanswered— and didn't the change mean that here again was the social relation?

"Ah, I didn't live as you saw me the other day."

"Yes," he answered—and didn't he the next instant feel he must fairly have smiled with it?—"the other day you *were* going it!"

"For once in my life," said Kate Cookham. "I've left the hotel," she after a moment added.

"Ah, you're in—a—lodgings?" he found himself inquiring as for positive sociability.

She had apparently a slight shade of hesitation, but in an instant it was all right; as what he showed he wanted to know she seemed mostly to give him. "Yes—but far of course from here. Up on the hill." To which, after another instant, "At The Mount, Castle Terrace," she subjoined.

"Oh, I *know* The Mount. And Castle Terrace is awfully sunny and nice."

"Awfully sunny and nice," Kate Cookham took from him.

"So that if it isn't," he pursued, "like the Royal, why you're at least comfortable."

"I shall be comfortable anywhere now," she replied with a certain dryness.

It was astonishing, however, what had become of his own. "Because I've accepted——?"

"Call it that!" she dimly smiled.

"I hope then at any rate," he returned, "you can now thoroughly rest." He spoke as for a cheerful conclusion and moved again also to smile, though as with a poor grimace, no doubt; since what he seemed most clearly to feel was that since he "accepted" he mustn't, for his last note, have accepted in sulkiness or gloom. With that, at the same time, he couldn't but know, in all his fibres, that with such a still-watching face as the dotty veil didn't disguise for him there was no possible concluding, at least on his part. On hers, on hers it was—as he had so often for a week had reflectively to pronounce things—another affair. Ah, somehow, both formidably and helpfully, her face concluded—yet in a sense so strangely enshrouded in things she didn't tell him. What *must* she, what mustn't she, have done? What she had said—and she had really told him nothing—was no account of her life; in the midst of which conflict of opposed recognitions, at any rate, it was as if, for all he could do, he himself now considerably floundered. "But I can't think—I can't think——!"

"You can't think I can have made so much money in the time and been honest?"

"Oh, you've been *honest*!" Herbert Dodd distinctly allowed.

It moved her stillness to a gesture—which, however, she had as promptly checked; and she went on the next instant as for further generosity to his failure of thought. "Everything was possible, under my stress, with my hatred."

"Your hatred—?" For she had paused as if it were after all too difficult.

"Of what I should for so long have been doing to you."

With this, for all his failures, a greater light than any yet shone upon him. "It made you think of ways——?"

"It made me think of everything. It made me work," said Kate Cookham. She added, however, the next moment: "But that's my story."

"And I mayn't hear it?"

"No—because I mayn't hear yours."

"Oh, mine—!" he said with the strangest, saddest, yet after all most resigned sense of surrender of it; which he tried to make sound as if he couldn't have told it, for its splendor of sacrifice and of misery, even if he would.

It seemed to move in her a little, exactly, that sense of the invidious. "Ah, mine too, I assure you——!"

He rallied at once to the interest. "Oh, we *can* talk then?"

"Never," she all oddly replied. "Never," said Kate Cookham.

They remained so, face to face; the effect of which for him was that he had after a little understood why. That was fundamental. "Well, I see."

Thus confronted they stayed; and then, as he saw with a contentment that came up from deeper still, it was indeed she who, with her worn fine face, would conclude. "But I can take care of you."

"You *have*!" he said as with nothing left of him but a beautiful appreciative candour.

"Oh, but you'll want it now in a way—!" she responsibly answered.

He waited a moment, dropping again on the seat. So, while she still stood, he looked up at her; with the sense somehow that there were too many things and that they were all together, terribly, irresistibly, doubtless blessedly, in her eyes and her whole person; which thus affected him for the moment as more than he could bear. He leaned forward, dropping his elbows to his knees and pressing his head on his hands. So he stayed, saying nothing; only, with the sense of her own sustained, renewed and wonderful action, knowing that an arm had passed round him and that he was held. She was beside him on the bench of desolation.

A Round of Visits

H E HAD been out but once since his arrival, Mark Monteith; that was the next day after—he had disembarked
by night on the previous; then everything had come at once,
as he would have said, everything had changed. He had got
in on Tuesday; he had spent Wednesday for the most part
down town, looking into the dismal subject of his anxiety—
the anxiety that, under a sudden decision, had brought him
across the unfriendly sea at mid-winter, and it was through
information reaching him on Wednesday evening that he had
measured his loss, measured above all his pain. These were
two distinct things, he felt, and, though both bad, one much
worse than the other. It wasn't till the next three days had
pretty well ebbed, in fact, that he knew himself for so badly
wounded. He had waked up on Thursday morning, so far as
he had slept at all, with the sense, together, of a blinding New
York blizzard and of a deep sore inward ache. The great white
savage storm would have kept him at the best within doors,
but his stricken state was by itself quite reason enough.

He so felt the blow indeed, so gasped, before what had
happened to him, at the ugliness, the bitterness, and, beyond
these things, the sinister strangeness, that, the matter of his
dismay little by little detaching and projecting itself, settling
there face to face with him as something he must now live
with always, he might have been in charge of some horrid
alien thing, some violent, scared, unhappy creature whom
there was small joy, of a truth, in remaining with, but whose
behaviour wouldn't perhaps bring him under notice, nor otherwise compromise him, so long as he should stay to watch
it. A young jibbering ape of one of the more formidable sorts,
or an ominous infant panther, smuggled into the great gaudy
hotel and whom it might yet be important he shouldn't advertise, couldn't have affected him as needing more domestic
attention. The great gaudy hotel—The Pocahontas, but carried out largely on "Du Barry" lines—made all about him,
beside, behind, below, above, in blocks and tiers and super-
positions, a sufficient defensive hugeness; so that, between the

massive labyrinth and the New York weather, life in a light-
house during a gale would scarce have kept him more apart.
Even when in the course of that worse Thursday it had occurred to him for vague relief that the odious certified facts
couldn't be all his misery, and that, with his throat and a
probable temperature, a brush of the epidemic, which was
for ever brushing him, accounted for something, even then
he couldn't resign himself to bed and broth and dimness,
but only circled and prowled the more within his high cage,
only watched the more from his tenth story the rage of the
elements.

In the afternoon he had a doctor—the caravanserai, which
supplied everything in quantities, had one for each group of
so many rooms—just in order to be assured that he was *grippé*
enough for anything. What his visitor, making light of his
attack, perversely told him was that he was, much rather,
"blue" enough, and from causes doubtless known to himself—which didn't come to the same thing; but he "gave him
something," prescribed him warmth and quiet and broth and
courage, and came back the next day as to readminister this
last dose. He then pronounced him better, and on Saturday
pronounced him well—all the more that the storm had abated
and the snow had been dealt with as New York, at a push,
knew how to deal with things. Oh, how New York knew how
to deal—to deal, that is, with other accumulations lying passive to its hand—was exactly what Mark now ached with his
impression of; so that, still threshing about in this consciousness, he had on the Saturday come near to breaking out as to
what was the matter with him. The Doctor brought in somehow the air of the hotel—which, cheerfully and conscientiously, by his simple philosophy, the good man wished to
diffuse; breathing forth all the echoes of other woes and
worries and pointing the honest moral that, especially with
such a thermometer, there were enough of these to go round.
Our sufferer, by that time, would have liked to tell some one;
extracting, to the last acid strain of it, the full strength of his
sorrow, taking it all in as he could only do by himself and with
the conditions favourable at least to this, had been his natural
first need. But now, he supposed, he *must* be better; there was
something of his heart's heaviness he wanted so to give out.

He had rummaged forth on the Thursday night half a dozen old photographs stuck into a leather frame, a small show-case that formed part of his usual equipage of travel—he mostly set it up on a table when he stayed anywhere long enough; and in one of the neat gilt-edged squares of this convenient portable array, as familiar as his shaving-glass or the hair-brushes, of backs and monograms now so beautifully toned and wasted, long ago given him by his mother, Phil Bloodgood handsomely faced him. Not contemporaneous, and a little faded, but so saying what it said only the more dreadfully, the image seemed to sit there, at an immemorial window, like some long effective and only at last exposed "decoy" of fate. It was *because* he was so beautifully good-looking, because he was so charming and clever and frank—besides being one's third cousin, or whatever it was, one's early school-fellow and one's later college classmate—that one had abjectly trusted him. To live thus with his unremoved, undestroyed, engaging, treacherous face, had been, as our traveller desired, to live with all of the felt pang; had been to consume it in such a single hot, sore mouthful as would so far as possible dispose of it and leave but cold dregs. Thus, if the Doctor, casting about for pleasantness, had happened to notice him there, salient since he was, and possibly by the same stroke even to know him, as New York—and more or less to its cost now, mightn't one say?—so abundantly and agreeably had, the cup would have overflowed and Monteith, for all he could be sure of the contrary, would have relieved himself positively in tears.

"Oh *he's* what's the matter with me—that, looking after some of my poor dividends, as he for the ten years of my absence had served me by doing, he has simply jockeyed me out of the whole little collection, such as it was, and taken the opportunity of my return, inevitably at last bewildered and uneasy, to 'sail,' ten days ago, for parts unknown and as yet unguessable. It isn't the beastly values themselves, however; that's only awkward and I can still live, though I don't quite know how I shall turn round; it's the horror of *his* having done it, and done it to *me*—without a mitigation or, so to speak, a warning or an excuse." That, at a hint or a jog, is what he would have brought out—only to feel afterward, no doubt, that he had wasted his impulse and profaned even a little his sincerity. The Doctor didn't in the event so much as glance at his cluster of portraits—which fact quite put before our friend the essentially more vivid range of imagery that a pair of eyes transferred from room to room and from one queer case to another, in such a place as that, would mainly be adjusted to. It wasn't for *him* to relieve himself touchingly, strikingly or whatever, to such a man: such a man might much more pertinently—save for professional discretion—have emptied out there his own bag of wonders; prodigies of observation, flowers of oddity, flowers of misery, flowers of the monstrous, gathered in current hotel practice. Countless possibilities, making doctors perfunctory, Mark felt, swarmed and seethed at their doors; it showed for an incalculable world, and at last, on Sunday, he decided to leave his room.

II

Everything, as he passed through the place, went on—all the offices of life, the whole bustle of the market, and withal, surprisingly, scarce less that of the nursery and the playground; the whole sprawl in especial of the great gregarious fireside: it was a complete social scene in itself, on which types might figure and passions rage and plots thicken and dramas develop, without reference to any other sphere, or perhaps even to anything at all outside. The signs of this met him at every turn as he threaded the labyrinth, passing from one extraordinary masquerade of expensive objects, one portentous "period" of decoration, one violent phase of publicity, to another: the heavy heat, the luxuriance, the extravagance, the quantity, the colour, gave the impression of some wondrous tropical forest, where vociferous, bright-eyed, and feathered creatures, of every variety of size and hue, were half smothered between undergrowths of velvet and tapestry and ramifications of marble and bronze. The fauna and the flora startled him alike, and among them his bruised spirit drew in and folded its wings. But he roamed and rested, exploring and in a manner enjoying the vast rankness—in the depth of which he suddenly encountered Mrs. Folliott, whom he had last seen, six months before, in London, and who had spoken to him then, pre-

cisely, of Phil Bloodgood, for several years previous her con-
fidential American agent and factotum too, as she might say,
but at that time so little in her good books, for the extraordinary things he seemed to be doing, that she was just hurrying home, she had made no scruple of mentioning, to take
everything out of his hands.

Mark remembered how uneasy she had made him—how
that very talk with her had wound him up to fear, as so acute
and intent a little person she affected him; though he had
affirmed with all emphasis and flourish his own confidence and
defended, to iteration, his old friend. This passage had remained with him for a certain pleasant heat of intimacy, his
partner, of the charming appearance, being what she was; he
liked to think how they had fraternised over their difference
and called each other idiots, or almost, without offence. It
was always a link to have scuffled, failing a real scratch, with
such a character; and he had at present the flutter of feeling
that something of this would abide. *He* hadn't been hurrying
home, at the London time, in any case; he was doing nothing
then, and had continued to do it; he would want, before
showing suspicion—that had been his attitude—to have more,
after all, to go upon. Mrs. Folliott also, and with a great actual
profession of it, remembered and rejoiced; and, also staying
in the house as she was, sat with him, under a spreading palm,
in a wondrous rococo salon, surrounded by the pinkest, that
is the fleshiest, imitation Boucher panels, and wanted to know
if he *now* stood up for his swindler. She would herself have
tumbled on a cloud, very passably, in a fleshy Boucher manner, hadn't she been over-dressed for such an exercise; but she
was quite realistically aware of what had so naturally happened—she was prompt about Bloodgood's "flight."

She had acted with energy, on getting back—she had saved
what she could; which hadn't, however, prevented her losing
all disgustedly some ten thousand dollars. She was lovely,
lively, friendly, interested, she connected Monteith perfectly
with their discussion that day during the water-party on the
Thames; but, sitting here with him half an hour, she talked
only of her peculiar, her cruel sacrifice—since she should never
get a penny back. He had felt himself, on their meeting, quite
yearningly reach out to her—so decidedly, by the morning's

end, and that of his scattered sombre stations, had he been sated with meaningless contacts, with the sense of people all about him intensely, though harmlessly, animated, yet at the same time raspingly indifferent. *They* would have, he and she at least, their common pang—through which fact, somehow, he should feel less stranded. It wasn't that he wanted to be pitied—he fairly didn't pity himself; he winced, rather, and even to vicarious anguish, as it rose again, for poor shamed Bloodgood's doom-ridden figure. But he wanted, as with a desperate charity, to give some easier turn to the mere ugliness of the main facts; to work off his obsession from them by mixing with it some other blame, some other pity, it scarce mattered what—if it might be some other experience; as an effect of which larger ventilation it would have, after a fashion and for a man of free sensibility, a diluted and less poisonous taste.

By the end of five minutes of Mrs. Folliott, however, he felt his dry lips seal themselves to a makeshift simper. She could *take* nothing—no better, no broader perception of anything than fitted her own small faculty; so that though she must have recalled or imagined that he had still, up to lately, had interests at stake, the rapid result of her egotistical little chatter was to make him wish he might rather have conversed with the French waiter dangling in the long vista that showed the oriental café as a climax, or with the policeman, outside, the top of whose helmet peeped above the ledge of a window. She bewailed her wretched money to excess—she who, he was sure, had quantities more; she pawed and tossed her bare bone, with her little extraordinarily gemmed and manicured hands, till it acted on his nerves; she rang all the changes on the story, the dire fatality, of her having wavered and mud-dled, thought of this and but done that, of her stupid failure to have pounced, when she had first meant to, in season. She abused the author of their wrongs—recognising thus too Monteith's right to loathe him—for the desperado he assur-edly had proved, but with a vulgarity of analysis and an in-capacity for the higher criticism, as her listener felt it to be, which made him determine resentfully, almost grimly, that she shouldn't have the benefit of a grain of *his* vision or *his* version of what had befallen them, and of how, in particular, it had come; and should never dream thereby (though much would she suffer from that!) of how interesting he might have been. She had, in a finer sense, no manners, and to be concerned with her in any retrospect was—since their discourse was of losses—to feel the dignity of history incur the very gravest. It was true that such fantasies, or that any shade of inward irony, would be Greek to Mrs. Folliott.

It was also true, however, and not much more strange, when she had presently the comparatively happy thought of "Lunch with *us*, you poor dear!" and mentioned three or four of her "crowd"—a new crowd, rather, for her, all great Sunday lunchers there and immense fun, who would in a moment be turning up—that this seemed to him as easy as anything else; so that after a little, deeper in the jungle and while, under the temperature as of high noon, with the crowd complete and "ordering," he wiped the perspiration from his brow, he felt he was letting himself go. He did that certainly to the extent of leaving far behind any question of Mrs. Folliott's manners. They didn't matter there—nobody's did; and if she ceased to lament her ten thousand it was only because, among higher voices, she couldn't make herself heard. Poor Bloodgood didn't have a show, as they might have said, didn't get through at any point; the crowd was so new that—there either having been no hue and cry for him, or having been too many others, for other absconders, in the intervals—they had never so much as heard of him and would have no more of Mrs. Folliott's true inwardness, on that subject at least, than she had lately cared to have of Monteith's.

There was nothing like a crowd, this unfortunate knew, for making one feel lonely, and he felt so increasingly during the meal; but he got thus at least in a measure away from the terrible little lady; after which, and before the end of the hour, he wanted still more to get away from every one else. He was in fact about to perform this manœuvre when he was checked by the jolly young woman he had been having on his left and who had more to say about the Hotels, up and down the town, than he had ever known a young woman to have to say on any subject at all; she expressed herself in hotel terms exclusively, the names of those establishments playing through her speech as the *leit-motif* might have recurrently flashed and romped through a piece of profane modern music. She wanted to present him to the pretty girl she had brought with her, and who had apparently signified to her that she must do so.

"I think you know my brother-in-law, Mr. Newton Winch," the pretty girl had immediately said; she moved her head and shoulders together, as by a common spring, the effect of a stiff neck or of something loosened in her back hair; but becoming, queerly enough, all the prettier for doing so. He had seen in the papers, her brother-in-law, Mr. Monteith's arrival—Mr. Mark P. Monteith, wasn't it?—and where he was, and she had been with him, three days before, at the time; whereupon he had said "Hullo, what can have brought old Mark back?" He seemed to have believed—Newton had seemed—that that shirker, as he called him, never *would* come; and she guessed that if she had known she was going to meet such a former friend ("Which he claims you are, sir," said the pretty girl) he would have asked her to find out what the trouble could be. But the real satisfaction would just be, she went on, if his former friend would himself go and see him and tell him; he had appeared of late so down.

"Oh, I remember him"—Mark didn't repudiate the friendship, placing him easily; only then he wasn't married and the pretty girl's sister must have come in later: which showed, his not knowing such things, how they had lost touch. The pretty girl was sorry to have to say in return to this that her sister wasn't living—had died two years after marrying; so that Newton was up there in Fiftieth Street alone; where (in explanation of his being "down") he had been shut up for days with bad *grippe*; though now on the mend, or she wouldn't have gone to him, not she, who had had it nineteen times and didn't want to have it again. But the horrid poison just seemed to have entered into poor Newton's soul.

"That's the way it *can* take you, don't you know?" And then as, with her single twist, she just charmingly hunched her eyes at our friend, "Don't you want to go to see him?"

Mark bethought himself: "Well, I'm going to see a lady——"

She took the words from his mouth. "Of course you're going to see a lady—every man in New York is. But Newton isn't a lady, unfortunately for him, to-day; and Sunday after-noon in this place, in this weather, alone——!"

"Yes, isn't it awful?"—he was quite drawn to her.

"Oh, *you've* got your lady!"

"Yes, I've got my lady, thank goodness!" The fervour of which was his sincere tribute to the note he had had on Friday morning from Mrs. Ash, the only thing that had a little tem-pered his gloom.

"Well then, feel for others. Fit him in. Tell him why!"

"Why I've come back? I'm glad I *have*—since it was to see *you*!" Monteith made brave enough answer, promising to do what he could. He liked the pretty girl, with her straight attack and her free awkwardness—also with her difference from the others through something of a sense and a distinction given her by so clearly having Newton on her mind. Yet it was odd to him, and it showed the lapse of the years, that Winch—as he had known him of old—could *be* to that degree on any one's mind.

III

Outside in the intensity of the cold—it was a jump from the Tropics to the Pole—he felt afresh the force of what he had just been saying; that if it weren't for the fact of Mrs. Ash's good letter of welcome, despatched, characteristically, as soon as she had, like the faithful sufferer in Fiftieth Street, observed his name, in a newspaper, on one of the hotel-lists, he should verily, for want of a connection and an abutment, have scarce dared to face the void and the chill together, but have sneaked back into the jungle and there tried to lose himself. He made, as it was, the opposite effort, resolute to walk, though hov-ering now and then at vague crossways, radiations of roads to nothing, or taking cold counsel of the long but still sketchy vista, as it struck him, of the northward Avenue, bright and bleak, fresh and harsh, rich and evident somehow, a perspec-tive like a page of florid modern platitudes. He didn't quite know what he had expected for his return—not certainly ser-enades and deputations; but without Mrs. Ash his mail would have quite lacked geniality, and it was as if Phil Bloodgood had gone off not only with so large a slice of his small *pecu-*

lium, but with all the broken bits of the past, the loose ends of old relationships, that he had supposed he might pick up again. Well, perhaps he should still pick up a few—by the sweat of his brow; no motion of their own at least, he by this time judged, would send them fluttering into his hand.

Which reflections but quickened his forecast of this charm of the old Paris inveteracy renewed—the so-prized custom of nine years before, when he still believed in results from his fond frequentation of the Beaux Arts; that of walking over the river to the Rue de Marignan, precisely, every Sunday without exception, and sitting at her fireside, and often all offensively, no doubt, outstaying every one. How he had used to want those hours then, and how again, after a little, at present, the Rue de Marignan might have been before him! He had gone to her there at that time with his troubles, such as they were, and they had always worked for her amusement—which had been her happy, her clever way of taking them: she couldn't have done anything better for them in that phase, poor innocent things compared with what they might have been, than be amused by them. Perhaps that was what she would still be—with those of his present hour; now too they might inspire her with the touch she best applied and was most instinctive mistress of: this didn't at all events strike him as what he should most resent. It wasn't as if Mrs. Folliott, to make up for boring him with her own plaint, for example, had had so much as a gleam of conscious diversion over his.

"I'm *so* delighted to see you, I've such immensities to tell you!"—it began with the highest animation twenty minutes later, the very moment he stood there, the sense of the Rue de Marignan in the charming room and in the things about all reconstituted, regrouped, wonderfully preserved, down to the very sitting-places in the same relations, and down to the faint sweet mustiness of generations of cigarettes; but everything else different, and even vaguely alien, and by a measure still other than that of their own stretched interval and of the dear delightful woman's just a little pathetic alteration of face. He had allowed for the nine years, and so, it was to be hoped, had she; but the last thing, otherwise, that would have been touched, he immediately felt, was the quality, the intensity, of her care to see him. She cared, oh so visibly and touchingly and almost radiantly—save for her being, yes, distinctly, a little *more* battered than from even a good nine years' worth; nothing could in fact have perched with so crowning an impatience on the heap of what she had to "tell" as that special shade of revived consciousness of having him in particular to tell it to. It wasn't perhaps much to matter how soon she brought out and caused to ring, as it were, on the little recognised marqueterie table between them (such an anciently envied treasure), the heaviest gold-piece of current history she was to pay him with for having just so felicitously come back: he knew already, without the telling, that intimate domestic tension must lately, within those walls, have reached a climax and that he could serve supremely—oh how he was going to serve!— as the most sympathetic of all pairs of ears.

The whole thing was upon him, in any case, with the minimum of delay: Bob had had it from her, definitely, the first of the week, and it was absolutely final now, that they must set up avowedly separate lives—without horrible "proceedings" of any sort, but with her own situation, her independence, secured to her once for all. She had been coming to it, taking her time, and she had gone through—well, so old a friend would guess enough what; but she was at the point, oh blessedly now, where she meant to stay, he'd see if she didn't; with which, in this wonderful way, he himself had arrived for the cream of it and she was just selfishly glad. Bob had gone to Washington—ostensibly on business, but really to recover breath; she had, speaking vulgarly, knocked the wind out of him and was allowing him time to turn round. Mrs. Folliott moreover, she was sure, would have gone—was certainly believed to have been seen there five days ago; and of course his first necessity, for public use, would be to patch up something with Mrs. Folliott. Mark knew about Mrs. Folliott?—who was only, for that matter, one of a regular "bevy." Not that it signified, however, if he didn't: she would tell him about *her* later.

He took occasion from the first fraction of a break not quite to know what he knew about Mrs. Folliott—though perhaps he could imagine a little; and it was probably at this minute that, having definitely settled to a position, and precisely in his very own tapestry *bergère*, the one with the delicious little spectral "subjects" on the back and seat, he partly exhaled, and yet managed partly to keep to himself, the deep resigned sigh of a general comprehension. He knew what he was "in" for, he heard her go on—she said it again and again, seemed constantly to be saying it while she smiled at him with her peculiar fine charm, her positive gaiety of sensibility, scarce dimmed: "I'm just selfishly glad, just selfishly glad!" Well, she was going to have reason to be; she was going to put the whole case to him, all her troubles and plans, and each act of the tragi-comedy of her recent existence, as to the dearest and safest sympathiser in all the world. There would be no chance for *his* case, though it was so much for his case he had come; yet there took place within him but a mild, dumb convulsion, the momentary strain of his substituting, by the turn of a hand, one prospect of interest for another.

Squaring himself in his old *bergère*, and with his lips, during the effort, compressed to the same passive grimace that had an hour or two before operated for the encouragement of Mrs. Folliott—just as it was to clear the stage completely for the present more prolonged performance—he shut straight down, as he even in the act called it to himself, on any personal claim for social consideration and rendered a perfect little agony of justice to the grounds of his friend's vividness. For it was all the justice that could be expected of him that, though, secretly, he wasn't going to be interested in her being interesting, she was yet going to be so, all the same, by the very force of her lovely material (Bob Ash *was* such a pure pearl of a donkey!) and he was going to keep on knowing she was—yes, to the very end. When after the lapse of an hour he rose to go, the rich fact that she *had* been was there between them, and with an effect of the frankly, fearlessly, harmlessly intimate fireside passage for it that went beyond even the best memories of the pleasant past. He hadn't "amused" her, no, in quite the same way as in the Rue de Marignan time—it had then been he who for the most part took frequent turns, emphatic, explosive, elocutionary, over that wonderful waxed parquet while she laughed as for the young perversity of him from the depths of the second, the matching *bergère*. To-day she herself held and swept the floor, putting him merely to the trouble of his perpetual "Brava!" But that was all through the change of basis—the amusement, another name only for the thrilled absorption, having been inevitably for *him*; as how could it have failed to be with such a regular "treat" to his curiosity? With the tea-hour now other callers were turning up, and he got away on the plea of his wanting so to think it all over. He hoped again he hadn't too queer a grin with his assurance to her, as if she would quite know what he meant, that he had been thrilled to the core. But she returned, quite radiantly, that he had carried *her* completely away; and her sincerity was proved by the final frankness of their temporary parting. "My pleasure of you is selfish, horribly, I admit; so that if *that* doesn't suit you—!" Her faded beauty flushed again as she said it.

IV

In the street again, as he resumed his walk, he saw how perfectly it would *have* to suit him and how he probably for a long time wouldn't be suited otherwise. Between them and that time, however, what mightn't, for him, poor devil, on his new basis, have happened? She wasn't at any rate within any calculable period going to care so much for anything as for the so quaintly droll terms in which her rearrangement with her husband—thanks to that gentleman's inimitable fatuity—would have to be made. This was what it was to own, exactly, her special grace—the brightest gaiety in the finest sensibility; *such* a display of which combination, Mark felt as he went (if he could but have done it still more justice) she must have regaled him with! That exquisite last flush of her fadedness could only remain with him; yet while he presently stopped at a street-corner in a district redeemed from desolation but by the passage just then of a choked trolley-car that howled, as he paused for it, beneath the weight of its human accretions, he seemed to know the inward "sinking" that had been determined in a hungry man by some extravagant sight of the preparation of somebody else's dinner. Florence Ash was dining, so to speak, off the feast of appreciation, appreciation of what she had to "tell" him, that he had left her seated at; and she was welcome, assuredly—welcome, welcome, welcome, he musingly, he wistfully, and yet at the same time a trifle mechanically, repeated, stayed as he was a moment longer by the suffering shriek of another public vehicle and a sudden odd automatic return of his mind to the pretty girl, the flower of Mrs. Folliott's crowd, who had spoken to him of Newton Winch. It was extraordinarily as if, on the instant, she reminded him, from across the town, that *she* had offered him dinner: it was really quite strangely, while he stood there, as if she had told him where he could go and get it. With which, none the less, it was apparently where he wouldn't find her—and what was there, after all, of nutritive in the image of Newton Winch? He made up his mind in a moment that it owed that property, which the pretty girl had somehow made imputable, to the fact of its simply being just then the one image of anything known to him that the terrible place had to offer. Nothing, he a minute later reflected, could have been so "rum" as that, sick and sore, of a bleak New York eventide, he should have had nowhere to turn if not to the said Fiftieth Street.

That was the direction he accordingly took, for when he found the number given him by the same remarkable agent of fate also present to his memory he recognised the direct intervention of Providence and how it absolutely required a miracle to explain his so precipitately embracing this loosest of connections. The miracle indeed soon grew clearer: Providence had, on some obscure system, chosen this very ridiculous hour to save him from cultivation of the sin of selfishness, the obsession of egotism, and was breaking him to its will by constantly directing his attention to the claims of others. Who could say what at that critical moment mightn't have become of Mrs. Folliott (otherwise too then so sadly embroiled!) if she hadn't been enabled to air to him her grievance and her rage?—just as who could deny that it must have done Florence Ash a world of good to have put her thoughts about Bob in order by the aid of a person to whom the vision of Bob in the light of those thoughts (or in other words to whom *her* vision of Bob and nothing else) would mean so delightfully much? It was on the same general lines that poor Newton Winch, bereft, alone, ill, perhaps dying, and with the drawback of a not very sympathetic personality—as Mark remembered it at least—to contend against in almost any con-

ceivable appeal to human furtherance, it was on these lines,
very much, that the luckless case in Fiftieth Street was offered
him as a source of salutary discipline. The moment for such
a lesson might strike him as strange, in view of the quite special and independent opportunity for exercise that his spirit
had during the last three days enjoyed there in his hotel bed-
room; but evidently his languor of charity needed some admonition finer than any it might trust to chance for, and by
the time he at last, Winch's residence recognised, was duly
elevated to his level and had pressed the electric button at his
door, he felt himself acting indeed as under stimulus of a sharp
poke in the side.

V

Within the apartment to which he had been admitted, moreover, the fine intelligence we have imputed to him was in the
course of three minutes confirmed; since it took him no
longer than that to say to himself, facing his old acquaintance,
that he had never seen any one so improved. The place, which
had the semblance of a high studio light as well as a general
air of other profusions and amplitudes, might have put him
off a little by its several rather glaringly false accents, those of
contemporary domestic "art" striking a little wild. The scene
was smaller, but the rich confused complexion of the Pocahontas, showing through Du Barry paint and patches, might
have set the example—which had been followed with the cost-
liest candour—so that, clearly, Winch was in these days rich,
as most people in New York seemed rich; as, in spite of Bob's
depredations, Florence Ash was, as even Mrs. Folliott was in
spite of Phil Bloodgood's, as even Phil Bloodgood himself
must have been for reasons too obvious; as in fine every one
had a secret for being, or for feeling, or for looking, every
one at least but Mark Monteith.

These facts were as nothing, however, in presence of his
quick and strong impression that his pale, nervous, smiling,
clean-shaven host had undergone since their last meeting
some extraordinary process of refinement. He had been ill,
unmistakably, and the effects of a plunge into plain clean living, where any fineness had remained, were often startling,

sometimes almost charming. But independently of this, and for a much longer time, some principle of intelligence, some art of life, would discernibly have worked in him. Remembered from college years and from those two or three luckless and faithless ones of the Law School as constitutionally common, as consistently and thereby doubtless even rather powerfully coarse, clever only for uncouth and questionable things, he yet presented himself now as if he had suddenly and mysteriously been educated. There was a charm in his wide, "drawn," convalescent smile, in the way his fine fingers—had he anything like fine fingers of old?—played, and just fidgeted, over the prompt and perhaps a trifle incoherent offer of cigars, cordials, ashtrays, over the question of his visitor's hat, stick, fur coat, general best accommodation and ease; and how the deuce, accordingly, had charm, for coming out so on top, Mark wondered, "squared" the other old elements? For the short interval so to have dealt with him what force had it turned on, what patented process, of the portentous New York order in which there were so many, had it skilfully applied? Were these the things New York did when you just gave her *all* her head, and that he himself then had perhaps too complacently missed? Strange almost to the point of putting him positively off at first—quite as an exhibition of the uncanny—this sense of Newton's having all the while neither missed nor muffed anything, and having, as with an eye to the *coup de théâtre* to come, lowered one's expectations, at the start, to that abject pitch. It might have been taken verily for an act of bad faith—really for such a rare stroke of subtlety as could scarce have been achieved by a straight or natural aim.

So much as this at least came and went in Monteith's agitated mind; the oddest intensity of apprehension, admiration, mystification, which the high north-light of the March afternoon and the quite splendidly vulgar appeal of fifty overdone decorative effects somehow fostered and sharpened. Everything had already gone, however, the next moment, for wasn't the man he had come so much too intelligently himself to patronise absolutely bowling him over with the extraordinary speech: "See here, you know—you must be ill, or have had a bad shock, or some beastly upset: are you very sure you ought to have come out?" Yes, he after an instant believed his ears; coarse common Newton Winch, whom he had called on because he could, as a gentleman, after all afford to, coarse common Newton Winch, who had had troubles and been epidemically poisoned, lamentably sick, who bore in his face and in the very tension, quite exactly the "charm," of his manner, the traces of his late ordeal, and, for that matter, of scarce completed gallant emergence—this astonishing ex-comrade was simply writing himself at a stroke (into our friend's excited imagination at all events) the most distinguished of men. Oh, *he* was going to be interesting, if Florence Ash had been going to be; but Mark felt how, under the law of a lively present difference, that would be as an effect of one's having one's self thoroughly rallied. He knew within the minute that the tears stood in his eyes; he stared through them at his friend with a sharp "Why, how do you know? How *can* you?" To which he added before Winch could speak: "I met your charming sister-in-law a couple of hours since—at luncheon, at the Pocahontas; and heard from her that you were badly laid up and had spoken of me. So I came to minister to you."

The object of this design hovered there again, considerably restless, shifting from foot to foot, changing his place, beginning and giving up motions, striking matches for a fresh cigarette, offering them again, redundantly, to his guest and then not lighting himself—but all the while with the smile of another creature than the creature known to Mark; all the while with the history of something that had happened to him ever so handsomely shining out. Mark was conscious within himself from this time on of two quite distinct processes of notation—that of his practically instant surrender to the consequences of the act of perception in his host of which the two women trained supposably in the art of pleasing had been altogether incapable; and that of some other condition on Newton's part that left his own poor power of divination nothing less than shamed. This last was signally the case on the former's saying, ever so responsively, almost radiantly, in answer to his account of how he happened to come: "Oh then it's very interesting!" *That* was the astonishing note, after what he had been through: neither Mrs. Folliott nor Florence

Ash had so much as hinted or breathed to him that *he* might have incurred that praise. No wonder therefore he was now taken—with this fresh party's instant suspicion and imputation of it; though it was indeed for some minutes next as if each tried to see which could accuse the other of the greater miracle of penetration. Mark was so struck, in a word, with the extraordinarily straight guess Winch had had there in reserve for him that, other quick impressions helping, there was nothing for him but to bring out, himself: "There must be, my dear man, something rather wonderful the matter with you!" The quite more intensely and more irresistibly drawn grin, the quite unmistakably deeper consciousness in the dark, wide eye, that accompanied the not quite immediate answer to which remark he was afterward to remember.

"How do you know that—or why do you think it?"

"Because there *must* be—for you to see! I shouldn't have expected it."

"Then you take me for a damned fool?" laughed wonderful Newton Winch.

VI

He could say nothing that, whether as to the sense of it or as to the way of it, didn't so enrich Mark's vision of him that our friend, after a little, as this effect proceeded, caught himself in the act of almost too curiously gaping. Everything, from moment to moment, fed his curiosity; such a question, for instance, as whether the quite ordinary peepers of the Newton Winch of their earlier youth could have looked, under any provocation, either dark or wide; such a question, above all, as how *this* incalculable apparition came by the whole startling power of play of its extravagantly sensitive labial connections—exposed, so to its advantage (he now jumped at one explanation) by the removal of what had probably been one of the vulgarest of moustaches. With this, at the same time, the oddity of that particular consequence was vivid to him; the glare of his curiosity fairly lasting while he remembered how he had once noted the very opposite turn of the experiment for Phil Bloodgood. He would have said in advance that poor Winch couldn't have afforded to risk showing his "real" mouth; just as he would have said that in spite of the fine ornament that so considerably muffled it Phil could only have gained by showing his. But to have seen Phil shorn—as he once had done—was earnestly to pray that he might promptly again bristle; beneath Phil's moustache lurked nothing to "make up" for it in case of removal. While he thought of which things the line of grimace, as he could only have called it, the mobile, interesting, ironic line the great double curve of which connected, in the face before him, the strong nostril with the lower cheek, became the very key to his first idea of Newton's capture of refinement. He had shaved and was happily transfigured. Phil Bloodgood had shaved and been wellnigh lost; though why should he just now too precipitately drag the reminiscence in?

That question too, at the queer touch of association, played up for Mark even under so much proof that the state of his own soul was being with the lapse of every instant registered. Phil Bloodgood had brought about the state of his soul—there was accordingly that amount of connection; only it became further remarkable that from the moment his companion had sounded him, and sounded him, he knew, down to the last truth of things, his disposition, his necessity to talk, the desire that had in the morning broken the spell of his confinement, the impulse that had thrown him so defeatedly into Mrs. Folliott's arms and into Florence Ash's, these forces seemed to feel their impatience ebb and their discretion suddenly grow. His companion was talking again, but just then, incongruously, made his need to communicate lose itself. It was as if his personal case had already been touched by some tender hand—and that, after all, was the modest limit of its greed. "I know now why you came back—did Lottie mention how I had wondered? But sit down, sit down—only let me, nervous beast as I am, take it standing!—and believe me when I tell you that I've now ceased to wonder. My dear chap, I *have* it! It can't but have been for poor Phil Bloodgood. He sticks out of you, the brute—as how, with what he has done to you, shouldn't he? There was a man to see me yesterday—Tim Slater, whom I don't think you know, but who's 'on' everything within about two minutes of its happening (I never saw such a fellow!) and who confirmed my supposition, all my

own, however, mind you, at first, that you're one of the suf-
ferers. So how the devil can you *not* feel knocked? Why *should*
you look as if you were having the time of your life? What a
hog to have played it on *you*, on *you*, of all his friends!" So
Newton Winch continued, and so the air between the two
men might have been, for a momentary watcher—which is
indeed what I can but invite the reader to become—that of a
nervously displayed, but all considerate, as well as most acute,
curiosity on the one side, and that on the other, after a little,
of an eventually fascinated acceptance of so much free and in
especial of so much right attention. "Do you *mind* my asking
you? Because if you do I won't press; but as a man whose
own responsibilities, some of 'em at least, don't differ much,
I gather, from some of his, one would like to know how
he was ever allowed to get to the point—! But I *do* plough
you up?"

Mark sat back in his chair, moved but holding himself, his
elbows squared on each arm, his hands a bit convulsively in-
terlocked across him—very much in fact as he had appeared
an hour ago in the old tapestry *bergère*; but as his rigour was
all then that of the grinding effort to profess and to give, so
it was considerably now for the fear of too hysterically gush-
ing. Somehow too—since his wound was to that extent
open—he winced at hearing the author of it branded. He
hadn't so much minded the epithets Mrs. Folliott had applied,
for they were to the appropriator of *her* securities. As the appropriator of his own he didn't so much want to brand him
as—just more "amusingly" even, if one would!—to make out,
perhaps, with intelligent help, how such a man, in such a relation, *could* come to tread such a path: which was exactly the
interesting light that Winch's curiosity and sympathy were
there to assist him to. He pleaded at any rate immediately his
advertising no grievance. "I feel sore, I admit, and it's a horrid
sort of thing to have had happen; but when you call him a
brute and a hog I rather squirm, for brutes and hogs never
live, I guess, in the sort of hell in which he now must be."

Newton Winch, before the fireplace, his hands deep in his
pockets, where his guest could see his long fingers beat a tat-
too on his thighs, Newton Winch dangled and swung himself,
and threw back his head and laughed. "Well, I must say you

take it amazingly!—all the more that to see you again this way is to feel that if, all along, there was a man whose delicacy and confidence and general attitude might have marked him for a particular consideration, you'd have been the man." And they were more directly face to face again; with Newton smiling and smiling *so* appreciatively; making our friend in fact almost ask himself when before a man had ever grinned from ear to ear to the effect of its so becoming him. What he replied, however, was that Newton described in those flattering terms a client temptingly fatuous; after which, and the exchange of another protest or two in the interest of justice and decency, and another plea or two in that of the still finer contention that even the basest misdeeds had always somewhere or other, could one get at it, their propitiatory side, our hero found himself on his feet again, under the influence of a sudden failure of everything but horror—a horror determined by some turn of their talk and indeed by the very fact of the freedom of it. It was as if a far-borne sound of the hue and cry, a vision of his old friend hunted and at bay, had suddenly broken in—this other friend's, this irresistibly intelligent other companion's, practically vivid projection of that making the worst ugliness real. "Oh, it's just making my wry face to somebody, and your letting me and caring and wanting to know: that," Mark said, "is what does me good; not any other hideous question. I mean I don't take any interest in *my* case—what one wonders about, you see, is what can be done for him. I mean, that is"—for he floundered a little, not knowing at last quite what he did mean, a great rush of mere memories, a great humming sound as of thick, thick echoes, rising now to an assault that he met with his face indeed contorted. If he didn't take care he should howl; so he more or less successfully took care—yet with his host vividly watching him while he shook the danger temporarily off. "I don't mind—though it's rather *that*; my having felt this morning, after three dismal dumb bad days, that one's friends perhaps would be thinking of one. All I'm conscious of now—I give you my word—is that I'd like to see him."

"You'd like to see him?"

"Oh, I don't say," Mark ruefully smiled, "that I should like him to see *me*——!"

Newton Winch, from where he stood—and they were to-gether now, on the great hearth-rug that was a triumph of modern orientalism—put out one of the noted fine hands and, with an expressive headshake, laid it on his shoulder. "Don't wish him that, Monteith—don't wish him that!"

"Well, but,"—and Mark raised his eyebrows still higher—"he'd see I bear up; pretty well!"

"God forbid he should see, my dear fellow!" Newton cried as for the pang of it.

Mark had for his idea, at any rate, the oddest sense of an exaltation that grew by this use of frankness. "I'd go to him. Hanged if I wouldn't—anywhere!"

His companion's hand still rested on him. "You'd go to him?"

Mark stood up to it—though trying to sink solemnity as pretentious. "I'd go like a shot." And then he added: "And it's probably what—when we've turned round—I *shall* do."

"When 'we' have turned round?"

"Well"—he was a trifle disconcerted at the tone—"I say that because you'll have helped me."

"Oh, I do nothing but want to help you!" Winch replied—which made it right again; especially as our friend still felt himself reassuringly and sustainingly grasped. But Winch went on: "You *would* go to him—in kindness?"

"Well—to understand."

"To understand how he could swindle you?"

"Well," Mark kept on, "to try and make out with him how, after such things—!" But he stopped; he couldn't name them.

It was as if his companion knew. "Such things as you've done for him of course—such services as you've rendered him."

"Ah, from far back. If I could tell you," our friend vainly wailed—"if I could tell you!"

Newton Winch patted his shoulder. "Tell me—tell me!"

"The sort of relation, I mean; ever so many things of a kind—!" Again, however, he pulled up; he felt the tremor of his voice.

"Tell me, tell me," Winch repeated with the same move-ment.

The tone in it now made their eyes meet again, and with this presentation of the altered face Mark measured as not before, for some reason, the extent of the recent ravage. "You must have been ill indeed."

"Pretty bad. But I'm better. And you do me good"—with which the light of convalescence came back.

"I don't awfully bore you?"

Winch shook his head. "You keep me up—and you see how no one else comes near me."

Mark's eyes made out that he *was* better—though it wasn't yet that nothing was the matter with him. If there was ever a man with whom there was still something the matter—! Yet one couldn't insist on that, and meanwhile he clearly did want company. "Then there we are. I myself had no one to go to."

"You save my life," Newton renewedly grinned.

VII

"Well, it's your own fault," Mark replied to that, "if you make me take advantage of you." Winch had withdrawn his hand, which was back, violently shaking keys or money, in his trousers pocket; and in this position he had abruptly a pause, a sensible, absence, that might have represented either some odd drop of attention, some turn-off to another thought, or just simply the sudden act of listening. His guest had indeed himself—under suggestion—the impression of a sound. "Mayn't you perhaps—if you hear something—have a call?"

Mark had said it so lightly, however, that he was the more struck with his host's appearing to turn just paler; and, with it, the latter now *was* listening. "You hear something?"

"I thought *you* did." Winch himself, on Mark's own pressure of the outside bell, had opened the door of the apartment—an indication then, it sufficiently appeared, that Sunday afternoons were servants', or attendants', or even trained nurses' holidays. It had also marked the stage of his convalescence, and to that extent—after his first flush of surprise—had but smoothed Monteith's way. At present he barely gave further attention; detaching himself as under some odd cross-impulse, he had quitted the spot and then taken, in the wide room, a restless turn—only, however, to revert in a moment to his friend's just-uttered deprecation of the danger of boring him. "If I make you take advantage of me—that is blessedly talk to me—it's exactly what I want to do. Talk to me—talk to me!" He positively waved it on; pulling up again, however, in his own talk, to say with a certain urgency: "Hadn't you better sit down?"

Mark, who stayed before the fire, couldn't but excuse himself. "Thanks—I'm very well so. I think of things and I fidget."

Winch stood a moment with his eyes on the ground. "Are you very sure?"

"Quite—I'm all right if you don't mind."

"Then as you like!" With which, shaking to extravagance again his long legs, Newton had swung off—only with a movement that, now his back was turned, affected his visitor as the most whimsical of all the forms of his rather unnatural manner. He was curiously different with his back turned, as Mark now for the first time saw it—dangling and somewhat wavering, as from an excess of uncertainty of gait; and this impression was so strange, it created in our friend, uneasily and on the spot, such a need of explanation, that his speech was stayed long enough to give Winch time to turn round again. The latter had indeed by this moment reached one of the limits of the place, the wide studio bay, where he paused, his back to the light and his face afresh presented, to let his just passingly depressed and quickened eyes take in as much as possible of the large floor, range over it with such brief freedom of search as the disposition of the furniture permitted. He was looking for something, though the betrayed reach of vision was but of an instant. Mark caught it, however, and with his own sensibility all in vibration, found himself feeling at once that it meant something and that what it meant was connected with his entertainer's slightly marked appeal to him, the appeal of a moment before, not to remain standing. Winch knew by this time quite easily enough that he was hanging fire; which meant that they were suddenly facing each other across the wide space with a new consciousness.

Everything had changed—changed extraordinarily with the mere turning of that gentleman's back, the treacherous aspect of which its owner couldn't surely have suspected. If the question was of the pitch of their sensibility, at all events, it wouldn't be Mark's that should vibrate to least purpose. Visibly it had come to his host that something had within the few instants remarkably happened, but there glimmered on him an induction that still made him keep his own manner. Newton himself might now resort to any manner he liked. His eyes had raked the floor to recover the position of something dropped or misplaced, and something, above all, awkward or compromising; and he had wanted his companion not to command this scene from the hearth-rug, the hearth-rug where he had been just before holding him, hypnotising him to blindness, *because* the object in question would there be most exposed to sight. Mark embraced this with a further drop—while the apprehension penetrated—of his power to go on, and with an immense desire at the same time that his eyes should seem only to look at his friend; who broke out now, for that matter, with a fresh appeal. "Aren't you going to take advantage of me, man—aren't you going to *take* it?"

Everything had changed, we have noted, and nothing could more have proved it than the fact that, by the same turn, sincerity of desire had dropped out of Winch's chords, while irritation, sharp and almost imperious, had come in. "That's because he sees I see something!" Mark said to himself; but he had no need to add that it shouldn't prevent his seeing more—for the simple reason that, in a miraculous fashion, this was exactly what he did do in glaring out the harder. It was beyond explanation, but the very act of blinking thus in an attempt at showy steadiness became one and the same thing with an optical excursion lasting the millionth of a minute and making him aware that the edge of a rug, at the point where an arm-chair, pushed a little out of position, overstraddled it, happened just not wholly to have covered in something small and queer, neat and bright, crooked and compact, in spite of the strong toe-tip surreptitiously applied to giving it the right lift. Our gentleman, from where he hovered, and while looking straight at the master of the scene, yet saw, as by the tiny flash of a reflection from fine metal, *under* the chair. What he recognised, or at least guessed at, as sinister, made him for a moment turn cold, and that chill was on him while Winch again addressed him—as differently as possible from any manner yet used. "I beg of you in God's name to talk to me—to *talk* to me!"

It had the ring of pure alarm and anguish, but was by this turn at least more human than the dazzling glitter of intelligence to which the poor man had up to now been treating him. "It's you, my good friend, who are in deep trouble," Mark was accordingly quick to reply, "and I ask your pardon for being so taken up with my own sorry business."

"Of course I'm in deep trouble"—with which Winch came nearer again; "but turning you on was exactly what I wanted."

Mark Monteith, at this, couldn't, for all his rising dismay, but laugh out; his sense of the ridiculous so swallowed up, for that brief convulsion, his sense of the sinister. Of such convenience in pain, it seemed, was the fact of another's pain, and of so much worth again disinterested sympathy! "Your interest was then——?"

"My interest was in your being interesting. For you *are*! And my nerves—!" said Newton Winch with a face from which the mystifying smile had vanished, yet in which distinction, as Mark so persistently appreciated it, still sat in the midst of ravage.

Mark wondered and wondered—he made strange things out. "Your nerves have needed company." He could lay his hand on him now, even as shortly before he had felt Winch's own pressure of possession and detention. "As good for you yourself, that—or still better," he went on—"than I and my grievance were to have found you. Talk to *me*, talk to *me*, Newton Winch!" he added with an immense inspiration of charity.

"That's a different matter—that others but too much can do! But I'll say this. If you want to go to Phil Bloodgood——!"

"Well?" said Mark as he stopped. He stopped, and Mark had now a hand on each of his shoulders and held him at arm's-length, held him with a fine idea that was not disconnected from the sight of the small neat weapon he had been fingering in the low luxurious morocco chair—it was of the finest orange colour—and then had laid beside him on the carpet; where, after he had admitted his visitor, his presence of mind coming back to it and suggesting that he couldn't pick it up without making it more conspicuous, he had thought, by some swing of the foot or other casual manœuvre, to dissimulate its visibility.

They were at close quarters now as not before and Winch perfectly passive, with eyes that somehow had no shadow of a secret left and with the betrayal to the sentient hands that grasped him of an intense, an extraordinary general tremor. To Mark's challenge he opposed afresh a brief silence, but the very quality of it, with his face speaking, was that of a gaping wound. "Well, you needn't take *that* trouble. You see I'm such another."

"Such another as Phil——?"

He didn't blink. "I don't know for sure, but I guess I'm worse."

"Do you mean you're guilty——?"

"I mean I shall be wanted. Only I've stayed to take it."

Mark threw back his head, but only tightened his hands. He inexpressibly understood, and nothing in life had ever been so strange and dreadful to him as his thus helping himself by a longer and straighter stretch, as it were, to the monstrous sense of his friend's "education." It had been, in its immeasurable action, the education of business, of which the fruits were all around them. Yet prodigious was the interest, for prodigious truly—it seemed to loom before Mark—must have been the system. "To 'take' it?" he echoed; and then, though faltering a little, "To take what?"

He had scarce spoken when a long sharp sound shrilled in from the outer door, seeming of so high and peremptory a pitch that with the start it gave him his grasp of his host's shoulders relaxed an instant, though to the effect of no movement in *them* but what came from just a sensibly intenser vibration of the whole man. "For *that*!" said Newton Winch.

"Then you've known——?"

"I've expected. You've helped me to wait." And then as Mark gave an ironic wail: "You've tided me over. My condition has *wanted* somebody or something. Therefore, to complete this service, will you be so good as to open the door?"

Deep in the eyes Mark looked him, and still to the detection of no glimmer of the earlier man in the depths. The earlier man had been what he invidiously remembered—yet would *he* had been the whole simpler story! Then he moved his own eyes straight to the chair under which the revolver lay and which was but a couple of yards away. He felt his companion take this consciousness in, and it determined in them another long, mute exchange. "What do you mean to do?"

"Nothing."

"On your honour?"

"*My* 'honour'?" his host returned with an accent that he felt even as it sounded he should never forget.

It brought to his own face a crimson flush—he dropped his guarding hands. Then as for a last look at him: "You're wonderful!"

"We *are* wonderful," said Newton Winch, while, simultaneously with the words, the pressed electric bell again and for a longer time pierced the warm cigaretted air.

Mark turned, threw up his arms, and it was only when he had passed through the vestibule and laid his hand on the door-knob that the horrible noise dropped. The next moment he was face to face with two visitors, a nondescript personage in a high hat and an astrakhan collar and cuffs, and a great belted constable, a splendid massive New York "officer" of the type he had had occasion to wonder at much again in the course of his walk, the type so by itself—his wide observation quite suggested—among those of the peacemakers of the earth. The pair stepped straight in—no word was said; but as he closed the door behind them Mark heard the infallible crack of a discharged pistol and, so nearly with it as to make all one violence, the sound of a great fall; things the effect of which was to lift him, as it were, with his company, across the threshold of the room in a shorter time than that taken by this record of the fact. But their rush availed little; Newton was stretched on his back before the fire; he had held the weapon horribly to his temple, and his upturned face was disfigured. The emissaries of the law, looking down at him, exhaled simultaneously a gruff imprecation, and then while the worthy in the high hat bent over the subject of their visit the one in the helmet raised a severe pair of eyes to Mark. "Don't you think, sir, you might have prevented it?"

Mark took a hundred things in, it seemed to him—things of the scene, of the moment, and of all the strange moments before; but one appearance more vividly even than the others stared out at him. "I really think I must practically have caused it."

Chronology

1843 Born April 15 at 21 Washington Place, New York City, the second child (after William, born January 11, 1842, N.Y.C.) of Henry James of Albany and Mary Robertson Walsh of New York. Father lives on inheritance of $10,000 a year, his share of litigated $3,000,000 fortune of his Albany father, William James, an Irish immigrant who came to the U.S. immediately after the Revolution.

1843–45 Accompanied by mother's sister, Catharine Walsh, and servants, the James parents take infant children to England and later to France. Reside at Windsor, where father has nervous collapse ("vastation") and experiences spiritual illumination. He becomes a Swedenborgian (May 1844), devoting his time to lecturing and religious-philosophical writings. James later claimed his earliest memory was a glimpse, during his second year, of the Place Vendôme in Paris with its Napoleonic column.

1845–47 Family returns to New York. Garth Wilkinson James (Wilky) born July 21, 1845. Family moves to Albany at 50 N. Pearl St., a few doors from grandmother Catharine Barber James. Robertson James (Bob or Rob) born August 29, 1846.

1847–55 Family moves to a large house at 58 W. 14th St., New York. Alice James born August 7, 1848. Relatives and father's friends and acquaintances—Horace Greeley, George Ripley, Charles Anderson Dana, William Cullen Bryant, Bronson Alcott, and Ralph Waldo Emerson ("I knew he was great, greater than any of our friends")—are frequent visitors. Thackeray calls during his lecture tour on the English humorists. Summers at New Brighton on Staten Island and Fort Hamilton on Long Island's south shore. On steamboat to Fort Hamilton August 1850, hears Washington Irving tell his father of Margaret Fuller's drowning in shipwreck off Fire Island. Frequently visits Barnum's American Museum on free days. Taken to art shows and theaters; writes and draws stage scenes. Described by father as "a devourer of libraries." Taught in assorted private

925

schools and by tutors in lower Broadway and Greenwich Village. But father claims in 1848 that American schooling fails to provide "sensuous education" for his children and plans to take them to Europe.

1855–58 Family (with Aunt Kate) sails for Liverpool, June 27. James is intermittently sick with malarial fever as they travel to Paris, Lyon, and Geneva. After Swiss summer, leaves for London where Robert Thomson (later Robert Louis Stevenson's tutor) is engaged. Early summer 1856, family moves to Paris. Another tutor engaged and children attend experimental Fourierist school. Acquires fluency in French. Family goes to Boulogne-sur-mer in summer, where James contracts typhoid. Spends late October in Paris, but American crash of 1857 returns family to Boulogne where they can live more cheaply. Attends public school (fellow classmate is Coquelin, the future French actor).

1858–59 Family returns to America and settles in Newport, Rhode Island. Goes boating, fishing, and riding. Attends the Reverend W. C. Leverett's Berkeley Institute, and forms friendship with classmate Thomas Sergeant Perry. Takes long walks and sketches with the painter John La Farge.

1859–60 Father, still dissatisfied with American education, returns family to Geneva in October. James attends a pre-engineering school, Institution Rochette, because parents, with "a flattering misconception of my aptitudes," feel he might benefit from less reading and more mathematics. After a few months withdraws from all classes except French, German, and Latin, and joins William as a special student at the Academy (later the University of Geneva) where he attends lectures on literary subjects. Studies German in Bonn during summer 1860.

1860–62 Family returns to Newport in September where William studies with William Morris Hunt, and James sits in on his classes. La Farge introduces him to works of Balzac, Mérimée, Musset, and Browning. Wilky and Bob attend Frank Sanborn's experimental school in Concord with children of Hawthorne and Emerson and John Brown's daughter. Early in 1861, orphaned Temple cousins come to live in Newport. Develops close friendship with cousin

Mary (Minnie) Temple. Goes on a week's walking tour in July in New Hampshire with Perry. William abandons art in autumn 1861 and enters Lawrence Scientific School at Harvard. James suffers back injury in a stable fire while serving as a volunteer fireman. Reads Hawthorne ("an American could be an artist, one of the finest").

1862–63   Enters Harvard Law School (Dane Hall). Wilky enlists in the Massachusetts 44th Regiment, and later in Colonel Robert Gould Shaw's 54th, one of the first black regiments. Summer 1863, Bob joins the Massachusetts 55th, another black regiment, under Colonel Hollowell. James withdraws from law studies to try writing. Sends unsigned stories to magazines. Wilky is badly wounded and brought home to Newport in August.

1864   Family moves from Newport to 13 Ashburton Place, Boston. First tale, "A Tragedy of Error" (unsigned), published in *Continental Monthly* (Feb. 1864). Stays in Northampton, Massachusetts, early August–November. Begins writing book reviews for *North American Review* and forms friendship with its editor, Charles Eliot Norton, and his family, including his sister Grace (with whom he maintains a long-lasting correspondence). Wilky returns to his regiment.

1865   First signed tale, "The Story of a Year," published in *Atlantic Monthly* (March 1865). Begins to write reviews for the newly founded *Nation* and publishes anonymously in it during next fifteen years. William sails on a scientific expedition with Louis Agassiz to the Amazon. During summer James vacations in the White Mountains with Minnie Temple and her family; joined by Oliver Wendell Holmes Jr. and John Chipman Gray, both recently demobilized. Father subsidizes plantation for Wilky and Bob in Florida with black hired workers. (The idealistic but impractical venture fails in 1870.)

1866–68   Continues to publish reviews and tales in Boston and New York journals. William returns from Brazil and resumes medical education. James has recurrence of back ailment and spends summer in Swampscott, Massachusetts. Begins friendship with William Dean Howells. Family moves to 20 Quincy St., Cambridge. William, suffering from nervous ailments, goes to Germany in spring 1867. "Poor Richard," James's longest story to date, published in *Atlantic Monthly* (June–Aug. 1867). William begins intermittent criticism of Henry's story-telling and style (which will continue throughout their careers). Momentary meeting with Charles Dickens at Norton's house. Vacations in Jefferson, New Hampshire, summer 1868. William returns from Europe.

1869–70   Sails in February for European tour. Visits English towns and cathedrals. Through Nortons meets Leslie Stephen, William Morris, Dante Gabriel Rossetti, Edward Burne-Jones, John Ruskin, Charles Darwin, and George Eliot (the "one marvel" of his stay in London). Goes to Paris in May, then travels in Switzerland in summer and hikes into Italy in autumn, where he stays in Milan, Venice (Sept.), Florence, and Rome (Oct. 30–Dec. 28). Returns to England to drink the waters at Malvern health spa in Worcestershire because of digestive troubles. Stays in Paris en route and has first experience of Comédie Française. Learns that his beloved cousin, Minnie Temple, has died of tuberculosis.

1870–72   Returns to Cambridge in May. Travels to Rhode Island, Vermont, and New York to write travel sketches for *The Nation*. Spends a few days with Emerson in Concord. Meets Bret Harte at Howells' home April 1871. *Watch and Ward*, his first novel, published in *Atlantic Monthly* (Aug.–Dec. 1871). Serves as occasional art reviewer for the *Atlantic* January–March 1872.

1872–74   Accompanies Aunt Kate and sister Alice on tour of England, France, Switzerland, Italy, Austria, and Germany from May through October. Writes travel sketches for *The Nation*. Spends autumn in Paris, becoming friends with James Russell Lowell. Escorts Emerson through the Louvre. (Later, on Emerson's return from Egypt, will show him the Vatican.) Goes to Florence in December and from there to Rome, where he becomes friends with actress Fanny Kemble, her daughter Sarah Butler Wister, and William Wetmore Story and his family. In Italy sees old family friend Francis Boott and his daughter Elizabeth (Lizzie), expatriates who have lived for many years in Florentine villa on Bellosguardo. Takes up horseback riding on the Campagna. Encounters Matthew Arnold in April 1873 at Story's. Moves from Rome hotel to rooms of his own. Continues writing and now earns enough to support himself. Leaves Rome in June, spends summer in Bad Homburg. In October goes to Florence, where William joins him. They also visit Rome, William returning to America in March. In Baden-Baden June–August and returns to America September 4, with *Roderick Hudson* all but finished.

1875   *Roderick Hudson* serialized in *Atlantic Monthly* from January (published by Osgood at the end of the year). First book, *A Passionate Pilgrim and Other Tales*, published January 31. Tries living and writing in New York, in rooms at 111 E. 25th Street. Earns $200 a month from novel installments and continued reviewing, but finds New York too expensive. *Transatlantic Sketches*, published in April, sells almost 1,000 copies in three months. In Cambridge in July decides to return to Europe; arranges with John Hay, assistant to the publisher, to write Paris letters for the *New York Tribune*.

1875–76   Arriving in Paris in November, he takes rooms at 29 Rue de Luxembourg (since renamed Cambon). Becomes friend of Ivan Turgenev and is introduced by him to Gustave Flaubert's Sunday parties. Meets Edmond de Goncourt, Émile Zola, G. Charpentier (the publisher), Catulle Mendès, Alphonse Daudet, Guy de Maupassant, Ernest Renan, Gustave Doré. Makes friends with Charles Sanders Peirce, who is in Paris. Reviews (unfavorably) the early Impressionists at the Durand-Ruel gallery. By midsummer has received $400 for *Tribune* pieces, but editor asks for more Parisian gossip and James resigns. Travels in France during July, visiting Normandy and the Midi, and in September crosses to San Sebastian, Spain, to see a bullfight ("I thought the bull, in any case, a finer fellow than any of his tormentors"). Moves to London in December, taking rooms at 3 Bolton Street, Piccadilly, where he will live for the next decade.

1877   *The American* published. Meets Robert Browning and George du Maurier. Leaves London in midsummer for visit to Paris and then goes to Italy. In Rome rides again in Campagna and hears of an episode that inspires "Daisy

Miller." Back in England, spends Christmas at Stratford with Fanny Kemble.

1878   Publishes first book in England, *French Poets and Novelists* (Macmillan). Appearance of "Daisy Miller" in *Cornhill Magazine*, edited by Leslie Stephen, is international success, but by publishing it abroad loses American copyright and story is pirated in U.S. *Cornhill* also prints "An International Episode." *The Europeans* is serialized in *Atlantic*. Now a celebrity, he dines out often, visits country houses, gains weight, takes long walks, fences, and does weightlifting to reduce. Elected to Reform Club. Meets Tennyson, George Meredith, and James McNeill Whistler. William marries Alice Howe Gibbens.

1879   Immersed in London society (". . . dined out during the past winter 107 times!"). Meets Edmund Gosse and Robert Louis Stevenson, who will later become his close friends. Sees much of Henry Adams and his wife, Marian (Clover), in London and later in Paris. Takes rooms in Paris, September–December. *Confidence* is serialized in *Scribner's* and published by Chatto & Windus. *Hawthorne* appears in Macmillan's "English Men of Letters" series.

1880–81   Stays in Florence March–May to work on *The Portrait of a Lady*. Meets Constance Fenimore Woolson, American novelist and grandniece of James Fenimore Cooper. Returns to Bolton Street in June, where William visits him. *Washington Square* serialized in *Cornhill Magazine* and published in U.S. by Harper & Brothers (Dec. 1880). *The Portrait of a Lady* serialized in *Macmillan's Magazine* (Oct. 1880–Nov. 1881) and *Atlantic Monthly*, published by Macmillan and Houghton, Mifflin (Nov. 1881). Publication both in United States and in England yields him the then-large income of $500 a month, though book sales are disappointing. Leaves London in February for Paris, the south of France, the Italian Riviera, and Venice, and returns home in July. Sister Alice comes to London with her friend Katharine Loring. James goes to Scotland in September.

1881–83   In November revisits America after absence of six years. Lionized in New York. Returns to Quincy Street for Christmas and sees ailing brother Wilky for the first time in ten years. In January visits Washington and the Henry Adamses and meets President Chester A. Arthur. Summoned to Cambridge by mother's death January 29 ("the sweetest, gentlest, most beneficent human being I have ever known"). All four brothers are together for the first time in fifteen years at her funeral. Alice and father move from Cambridge to Boston. Prepares a stage version of "Daisy Miller" and returns to England in May. William, now a Harvard professor, comes to Europe in September. Proposed by Leslie Stephen, James becomes member, without the usual red tape, of the Atheneum Club. Travels in France in October to write *A Little Tour in France* (published 1884) and has last visit with Turgenev, who is dying. Returns to England in December and learns of father's illness. Sails for America but Henry James Sr. dies December 18, 1882, before his arrival. Made executor of father's will. Visits brothers Wilky and Bob in Milwaukee in January. Quarrels with William over division of property—James wants to restore Wilky's share. Macmillan publishes a collected pocket edition of James's novels and tales in fourteen volumes. *Siege of London* and *Portraits of Places* published. Returns to Bolton Street in September. Wilky dies in November. Constance Fenimore Woolson comes to London for the winter.

1884–86   Goes to Paris in February and visits Daudet, Zola, and Goncourt. Again impressed with their intense concern with "art, form, manner" but calls them "mandarins." Misses Turgenev, who had died a few months before. Meets John Singer Sargent and persuades him to settle in London. Returns to Bolton Street. Sargent introduces him to young Paul Bourget. During country visits encounters many British political and social figures, including W. E. Gladstone, John Bright, and Charles Dilke. Alice, suffering from nervous ailment, arrives in England for visit in November but is too ill to travel and settles near her brother. *Tales of Three Cities* ("The Impressions of a Cousin," "Lady Barbarina," "A New England Winter") and "The Art of Fiction" published 1884. Alice goes to Bournemouth in late January. James joins her in May and becomes an intimate of Robert Louis Stevenson, who resides nearby. Spends August at Dover and is visited by Paul Bourget. Stays in Paris for the next two months. Moves into a flat at 34 De Vere Gardens in Kensington early in March 1886. Alice takes rooms in London. *The Bostonians* serialized in *Century* (Feb. 1885–Feb. 1886; published 1886), *The Princess Casamassima* serialized in *Atlantic Monthly* (Sept. 1885–Oct. 1886; published 1886).

1886–87   Leaves for Italy in December for extended stay, mainly in Florence and Venice. Sees much of Constance Fenimore Woolson and stays in her villa. Writes "The Aspern Papers" and other tales. Returns to De Vere Gardens in July and begins work on *The Tragic Muse*. Pays several country visits. Dines out less often ("I know it all—all that one sees by 'going out'—today, as if I had made it. But if I had, I would have made it better!").

1888   *The Reverberator*, *The Aspern Papers*, *Louisa Pallant*, *The Modern Warning*, and *Partial Portraits* published. Elizabeth Boott Duveneck dies. Robert Louis Stevenson leaves for the South Seas. Engages fencing teacher to combat "symptoms of a portentous corpulence." Goes abroad in October to Geneva (where he visits Woolson), Genoa, Monte Carlo, and Paris.

1889–90   Catharine Walsh (Aunt Kate) dies March 1889. William comes to England to visit Alice in August. James goes to Dover in September and then to Paris for five weeks. Writes account of Robert Browning's funeral in Westminster Abbey. Dramatizes *The American* for the Compton Comedy Company. Meets and becomes close friends with American journalist William Morton Fullerton and young American publisher Wolcott Balestier. Goes to Italy for the summer, staying in Venice and Florence, and takes a brief walking tour in Tuscany with W. W. Baldwin, an American physician practicing in Florence. Miss Woolson moves to Cheltenham, England, to be near James. *Atlantic Monthly* rejects his story "The Pupil," but it appears in England. Writes series of drawing-room comedies for theater. Meets Rudyard Kipling. *The Tragic Muse* serialized in *Atlantic Monthly* (Jan. 1889–May 1890; published 1890). *A London Life* (including "The Patagonia," "The Liar," "Mrs. Temperly") published 1889.

1891   *The American* produced at Southport is a success during road tour. After residence in Leamington, Alice returns to London, cared for by Katharine Loring. Doctors discover she has breast cancer. James circulates comedies (*Mrs. Vibert*, later called *Tenants*, and *Mrs. Jasper*, later named *Disengaged*) among theater managers who are cool to his work. Unimpressed at first by Ibsen, writes an appreciative review after seeing a performance of *Hedda Gabler* with Elizabeth Robins, a young Kentucky actress; persuades her to take the part of Mme. de Cintré in the London production of *The American*. Recuperates from flu in Ireland. James Russell Lowell dies. *The American* opens in London, September 26, and runs for seventy nights. Wolcott Balestier dies, and James attends his funeral in Dresden in December.

1892   Alice James dies March 6. James travels to Siena to be near the Paul Bourgets, and Venice, June–July, to visit the Daniel Curtises, then to Lausanne to meet William and his family, who have come abroad for sabbatical. Attends funeral of Tennyson at Westminster Abbey. Augustin Daly agrees to produce *Mrs. Jasper*. *The American* continues to be performed on the road by the Compton Company. *The Lesson of the Master* (with a collection of stories including "The Marriages," "The Pupil," "Brooksmith," "The Solution," and "Sir Edmund Orme") published.

1893   Fanny Kemble dies in January. Continues to write unproduced plays. In March goes to Paris for two months. Sends Edward Compton first act and scenario for *Guy Domville*. Meets William and family in Lucerne and stays a month, returning to London in June. Spends July completing *Guy Domville* in Ramsgate. George Alexander, actor-manager, agrees to produce the play. Daly stages first reading of *Mrs. Jasper*, and James withdraws it, calling the rehearsal a mockery. *The Real Thing and Other Tales* (including "The Wheel of Time," "Lord Beaupré," "The Visit") published.

1894   Constance Fenimore Woolson dies in Venice, January. Shocked and upset, James prepares to attend funeral in Rome but changes his mind on learning she is a suicide. Goes to Venice in April to help her family settle her affairs. Receives one of four copies, privately printed by Miss Loring, of Alice's diary. Finds it impressive but is concerned that so much gossip he told Alice in private has been included (later burns his copy). Robert Louis Stevenson dies in the South Pacific. *Guy Domville* goes into rehearsal. *Theatricals: Two Comedies* and *Theatricals: Second Series* published.

1895   *Guy Domville* opens January 5 at St. James's Theatre. At play's end James is greeted by a fifteen-minute roar of boos, catcalls, and applause. Horrified and depressed, abandons the theater. Play earns him $1,300 after five-week run. Feels he can salvage something useful from playwriting for his fiction ("a key that, working in the same *general* way fits the complicated chambers of *both* the dramatic and the narrative lock"). Writes scenario for *The Spoils of Poynton*. Visits Lord Wolseley and Lord Houghton in Ireland. In the summer goes to Torquay in Devonshire and stays until November while electricity is being installed in De Vere Gardens flat. Friendship with W. E. Norris, who resides at Torquay. Writes a one-act play ("Mrs. Gracedew") at request of Ellen Terry. *Terminations* (containing "The Death of the Lion," "The Coxon Fund," "The Middle Years," "The Altar of the Dead") published.

1896–97 Finishes *The Spoils of Poynton* (serialized in *Atlantic Monthly* April–Oct. 1896 as *The Old Things*; published 1897). *Embarrassments* ("The Figure in the Carpet," "Glasses," "The Next Time," "The Way It Came") published. Takes a house on Point Hill, Playden, opposite the old town of Rye, Sussex, August–September. Ford Madox Hueffer (later Ford Madox Ford) visits him. Converts play *The Other House* into novel and works on *What Maisie Knew* (published Sept. 1897). George du Maurier dies early in October. Because of increasing pain in wrist, hires stenographer William MacAlpine in February and then purchases a typewriter; soon begins direct dictation to MacAlpine at the machine. Invites Joseph Conrad to lunch at De Vere Gardens and begins their friendship. Goes to Bournemouth in July. Serves on jury in London before going to Dunwich, Suffolk, to spend time with Temple-Emmet cousins. In late September 1897 signs a twenty-one-year lease for Lamb House in Rye for £70 a year ($350). Takes on extra work to pay for setting up his house—the life of William Wetmore Story ($1,250 advance) and will furnish an "American Letter" for new magazine *Literature* (precursor of *Times Literary Supplement*) for $200 a month. Howells visits.

1898   "The Turn of the Screw" (serialized in *Collier's* Jan.–April; published with "Covering End" under the title *The Two Magics*) proves his most popular work since "Daisy Miller." Sleeps in Lamb House for first time June 28. Soon after is visited by William's son, Henry James Jr. (Harry), followed by a stream of visitors: future Justice Oliver Wendell Holmes, Mrs. J. T. Fields, Sarah Orne Jewett, the Paul Bourgets, the Edward Warrens, the Daniel Curtises, the Edmund Gosses, and Howard Sturgis. His witty friend Jonathan Sturges, a young, crippled New Yorker, stays for two months during autumn. *In the Cage* published. Meets neighbors Stephen Crane and H. G. Wells.

1899   Finishes *The Awkward Age* and plans trip to the Continent. Fire in Lamb House delays departure. To Paris in March and then visits the Paul Bourgets at Hyères. Stays with the Curtises in their Venice palazzo, where he meets and becomes friends with Jessie Allen. In Rome meets young American-Norwegian sculptor Hendrik C. Andersen; buys one of his busts. Returns to England in July and Andersen comes for three days in August. William, his wife, Alice, and daughter, Peggy, arrive at Lamb House in October. First meeting of brothers in six years. William now has confirmed heart condition. James B. Pinker becomes literary agent and for first time James's professional relations are systematically organized; he reviews copyrights, finds new publishers, and obtains better prices for work ("the germ of a new career"). Purchases Lamb House for $10,000 with an easy mortgage.

1900   Unhappy at whiteness of beard which he has worn since the Civil War, he shaves it off. Alternates between Rye and London. Works on *The Sacred Fount*. Works on and then sets aside *The Sense of the Past* (never finished). Begins *The Ambassadors*. *The Soft Side*, a collection of twelve tales, published. Niece Peggy comes to Lamb House for Christmas.

1901   Obtains permanent room at the Reform Club for London visits and spends eight weeks in town. Sees funeral of Queen Victoria. Decides to employ a typist, Mary Weld, to replace the more expensive overqualified shorthand stenographer, MacAlpine. Completes *The Ambassadors* and begins *The Wings of the Dove*. *The Sacred Fount* published.

Has meeting with George Gissing. William James, much improved, returns home after two years in Europe. Young Cambridge admirer Percy Lubbock visits. Discharges his alcoholic servants of sixteen years (the Smiths). Mrs. Paddington is new housekeeper.

1902   In London for the winter but gout and stomach disorder force him home earlier. Finishes *The Wings of the Dove* (published in August). William James Jr. (Billy) visits in October and becomes a favorite nephew. Writes "The Beast in the Jungle" and "The Birthplace."

1903   *The Ambassadors, The Better Sort* (a collection of eleven tales), and *William Wetmore Story and His Friends* published. After another spell in town, returns to Lamb House in May and begins work on *The Golden Bowl*. Meets and establishes close friendship with Dudley Jocelyn Persse, a nephew of Lady Gregory. First meeting with Edith Wharton in December.

1904–05   Completes *The Golden Bowl* (published Nov. 1904). Rents Lamb House for six months, and sails in August for America after twenty-year absence. Sees new Manhattan skyline from New Jersey on arrival and stays with Colonel George Harvey, president of Harper's, in Jersey shore house with Mark Twain as fellow guest. Goes to William's country house at Chocorua in the White Mountains, New Hampshire. Re-explores Cambridge, Boston, Salem, Newport, and Concord, where he visits brother Bob. In October stays with Edith Wharton in the Berkshires and motors with her through Massachusetts and New York. Later visits New York, Philadelphia (where he delivers lecture "The Lesson of Balzac"), and then Washington, D.C., as a guest in Henry Adams' house. Meets (and is critical of) President Theodore Roosevelt. Returns to Philadelphia to lecture at Bryn Mawr. Travels to Richmond, Charleston, Jacksonville, Palm Beach, and St. Augustine. Then lectures in St. Louis, Chicago, South Bend, Indianapolis, Los Angeles (with a short vacation at Coronado Beach near San Diego), San Francisco, Portland, and Seattle. Returns to explore New York City ("the terrible town"), May–June. Lectures on "The Question of Our Speech" at Bryn Mawr commencement. Elected to newly founded American Academy of Arts and Letters

(William declines). Returns to England in July; lectures had more than covered expenses of his trip. Begins revision of novels for the New York Edition.

1906–08   Writes "The Jolly Corner" and *The American Scene* (published 1907). Writes eighteen prefaces for the New York Edition (twenty-four volumes published 1907–09). Visits Paris and Edith Wharton in spring 1907 and motors with her in Midi. Travels to Italy for the last time, visiting Hendrik Andersen in Rome, and goes on to Florence and Venice. Engages Theodora Bosanquet as his typist in autumn. Again visits Edith Wharton in Paris, spring 1908. William comes to England to give a series of lectures at Oxford and receives an honorary Doctor of Science degree. James goes to Edinburgh in March to see a tryout by the Forbes-Robertsons of his play *The High Bid*, a rewrite in three acts of the one-act play originally written for Ellen Terry (revised earlier as the story "Covering End"). Play gets only five special matinees in London. Shocked by slim royalties from sales of the New York Edition.

1909   Growing acquaintance with young writers and artists of Bloomsbury, including Virginia and Vanessa Stephen and others. Meets and befriends young Hugh Walpole in February. Goes to Cambridge in June as guest of admiring dons and undergraduates and meets John Maynard Keynes. Feels unwell and sees doctors about what he believes may be heart trouble. They reassure him. Late in year burns forty years of his letters and papers at Rye. Suffers severe attacks of gout. *Italian Hours* published.

1910   Very ill in January ("food-loathing") and spends much time in bed. Nephew Harry comes to be with him in February. In March is examined by Sir William Osler, who finds nothing physically wrong. James begins to realize that he has had "a sort of nervous breakdown." William, in spite of now severe heart trouble, and his wife, Alice, come to England to give him support. Brothers and Alice go to Bad Nauheim for cure, then travel to Zurich, Lucerne, and Geneva, where they learn Robertson (Bob) James has died in America of heart attack. James's health begins to improve but William is failing. Sails with William and Alice for America in August. William dies at Chocorua soon after arrival, and James remains with the family for the winter. *The Finer Grain* and *The Outcry* published.

1911   Honorary degree from Harvard in spring. Visits with Howells and Grace Norton. Sails for England July 30. On return to Lamb House, decides he will be too lonely there and starts search for a London flat. Theodora Bosanquet obtains two work rooms adjoining her flat in Chelsea and he begins autobiography, *A Small Boy and Others*. Continues to reside at the Reform Club.

1912   Delivers "The Novel in *The Ring and the Book*," on the 100th anniversary of Browning's birth, to the Royal Society of Literature. Honorary Doctor of Letters from Oxford University June 26. Spends summer at Lamb House. Sees much of Edith Wharton ("the Firebird"), who spends summer in England. (She secretly arranges to have Scribner's put $8,000 into James's account.) Takes 21 Carlyle Mansions, in Cheyne Walk, Chelsea, as London quarters. Writes a long admiring letter for William Dean Howells' seventy-fifth birthday. Meets André Gide. Contracts bad case of shingles and is ill four months, much of the time not able to leave bed.

1913   Moves into Cheyne Walk flat. Two hundred and seventy friends and admirers subscribe for seventieth birthday portrait by Sargent and present also a silver-gilt Charles II porringer and dish ("golden bowl"). Sargent turns over his payment to young sculptor Derwent Wood, who does a bust of James. Autobiography *A Small Boy and Others* published. Goes with niece Peggy to Lamb House for the summer.

1914   *Notes of a Son and Brother* published. Works on "The Ivory Tower." Returns to Lamb House in July. Niece Peggy joins him. Horrified by the war ("this crash of our civilisation," "a nightmare from which there is no waking"). In London in September participates in Belgian Relief, visits wounded in St. Bartholomew's and other hospitals; feels less "finished and useless and doddering" and recalls Walt Whitman and his Civil War hospital visits. Accepts chairmanship of American Volunteer Motor Ambulance Corps in France. *Notes on Novelists* (essays on Balzac, Flaubert, Zola) published.

1915–16   Continues work with the wounded and war relief. Has occasional lunches with Prime Minister Asquith and family, and meets Winston Churchill and other war leaders. Discovers that he is considered an alien and has to report to police before going to coastal Rye. Decides to become a British national and asks Asquith to be one of his sponsors. Receives Certificate of Naturalization on July 26. H. G. Wells satirizes him in *Boon* ("leviathan retrieving pebbles") and James, in the correspondence that follows, writes: "Art *makes* life, makes interest, makes importance." Burns more papers and photographs at Lamb House in autumn. Has a stroke December 2 in his flat, followed by another two days later. Develops pneumonia and during delirium gives his last confused dictation (dealing with the Napoleonic legend) to Theodora Bosanquet, who types it on the familiar typewriter. Mrs. William James arrives December 13 to care for him. On New Year's Day, George V confers the Order of Merit. Dies February 28. Funeral services held at the Chelsea Old Church. The body is cremated and the ashes are buried in Cambridge Cemetery family plot.

Note on the Texts

This volume, one of five collecting the complete stories of Henry James, presents in the approximate chronological order of their completion 31 stories that were first published between 1898 and 1910. James considered periodical publication as an intermediate step in the composition of his stories and always revised them for book publication, making changes in wording as well as eliminating commas introduced by periodical editors; he consistently requested that publishers follow his lighter use of commas and that American publishers retain his British spellings. During this period James was living in England, and when his stories were to be published in both American and English book editions, his practice was to correct and revise the proofs of only one publisher and to have corrected proofs sent to the other publisher. He did not read the subsequent proofs for the other edition.

Collations show that the editions for which James corrected and revised proofs follow his wishes, both in punctuation and in wording, more closely than the other editions. James read proofs of the English typesettings for *The Soft Side* (1900) and *The Better Sort* (1903). Three of the stories from this period were first collected in *The Novels and Tales of Henry James*, the 1907-9 New York Edition of his works published by Scribner, which was proofread carefully by James. (One of these stories, "Julia Bride," was published separately by Harper and Brothers later in 1909, but collation shows that James' proofreading of this separate edition was less careful than that of the New York Edition.) He read proofs of the American setting for *The Finer Grain* (1910).

The following list gives the sources of the stories included in this volume and the dates of their first periodical and first American and English book publications. (James later included 15 stories from *The Soft Side* and *The Better Sort* in the 1907-9 New York Edition of his collected works.)

"John Delavoy" (*Cosmopolis*, January–February 1898), "The Given Case" (*Collier's Weekly*, December 31, 1898–January 7, 1899, and *Black & White*, March 11–18, 1899), " 'Europe' " (*Scribner's Magazine*, June 1899), "The Great Condition" (*The Anglo-Saxon Review*, June 1899), "The Real Right Thing" (*Collier's Weekly*, December 16, 1899), "Paste" (*Frank Leslie's Popular Monthly*, December 1899), "The Great Good Place" (*Scribner's Magazine*, January 1900), "Maud-Evelyn" (*Atlantic Monthly*, April 1900), and "Miss Gunton of Poughkeepsie" (*Cornhill Magazine*, May 1900, and *Truth*, May–June 1900) appeared in *The Soft Side*, published in London by Methuen

& Co. on August 30, 1900, and in New York by Macmillan Co. in September 1900. "The Tree of Knowledge," "The Abasement of the Northmores," and "The Third Person" were published for the first time in *The Soft Side*. The texts printed in this volume are from the Methuen edition.

"The Special Type" (*Collier's Weekly*, June 16, 1900), "The Tone of Time" (*Scribner's Magazine*, November 1900), "Broken Wings" (*Century Magazine*, December 1900), "The Two Faces" (published as "The Faces" in *Harper's Bazaar*, December 15, 1900, and as "The Two Faces" in *Cornhill Magazine*, June 1901), "Mrs. Medwin" (*Punch*, August 28–September 18, 1901), "The Beldonald Holbein" (*Harper's New Monthly Magazine*, October 1901), "The Story in It" (*The Anglo-American Magazine*, January 1902), and "Flickerbridge" (*Scribner's Magazine*, February 1902) appeared in *The Better Sort*, published in London by Methuen & Co. and in New York by Charles Scribner's Sons on February 26, 1903. "The Birthplace," "The Beast in the Jungle," and "The Papers" were published for the first time in *The Better Sort*. The texts printed in this volume are from the Methuen edition.

"Fordham Castle" (*Harper's Monthly Magazine*, December 1904) appeared in volume 16 (*The Author of "Beltraffio"* . . . , 1909) of *The Novels and Tales of Henry James*, the New York Edition, published in 24 volumes in New York by Charles Scribner's Sons from 1907 to 1909. "Julia Bride" (*Harper's Monthly Magazine*, March–April 1908) appeared in volume 17 (*The Altar of the Dead* . . . , published before July 1909) of the New York Edition and in *Julia Bride*, published in New York by Harper and Brothers in September 1909; "The Jolly Corner" (*The English Review*, December 1908) appeared in volume 17 of the New York Edition. The texts printed in this volume are from the New York Edition.

" 'The Velvet Glove' " (*The English Review*, March 1909), "Mora Montravers" (*The English Review*, August–September 1909), "Crapy Cornelia" (*Harper's Monthly Magazine*, October 1909), "The Bench of Desolation" (*Putnam's Magazine*, October 1909–January 1910), and "A Round of Visits" (*The English Review*, April–May 1910) appeared in *The Finer Grain*, published in New York by Charles Scribner's Sons on October 6, 1910, and in London by Methuen & Co., Ltd., on October 13, 1910. The texts printed in this volume are from the Scribner edition.

This volume presents the texts of the printings chosen for inclusion here but does not attempt to reproduce features of their typographic design. Spelling, punctuation, and capitalization often are expressive features and they are not altered, even when inconsistent or irregular. The following is a list of typographical errors corrected, cited by page and line number: 16.23, made wait for; 19.10, Do; 100.39, back.; 101.3, her"; 140.7, Therefore; 145.20, then if; 209.37, that; 231.21, himself; 244.34, anything,; 312.27, it,"; 326.7, and thirty; 332.34, greatnesss,; 432.30, Wenhan; 460.38, There are; 490.24, away."; 634.16, Frankfort,"; 669.19, choose; 709.22, be found; 754.1, his-drawing; 757.2, hinderance; 757.9, *porte-cochère*; 775.33, described; 799.34, gentlemen; 824.39, emotion; 825.3, ecent; 827.30, it?"; 827.34, life,"; 852.39, But be; 866.5, o the; 872.27, worked; 883.34, nightmare; 898.26, agreeable; 921.14–15, covenience.

Notes

In the notes below, the reference numbers denote page and line of this volume (the line count includes titles and headings). No note is made for material included in standard desk-reference books such as Webster's *Collegiate*, *Biographical*, and *Geographical* dictionaries. Quotations from Shakespeare are keyed to *The Riverside Shakespeare*, ed. G. Blakemore Evans (Boston: Houghton Mifflin, 1974). For further background than is provided in the notes, see *Henry James Letters*, ed. Leon Edel (Cambridge: The Belknap Press of Harvard University Press, Vol. I—1843–1875 [1974]; Vol. II—1875–1883 [1975]; Vol. III—1883–1895 [1980]; Vol. IV—1895–1916 [1984]) and *The Complete Notebooks of Henry James*, ed. Leon Edel and Lyall H. Powers (New York and Oxford: Oxford University Press, 1987).

23.20   *par exemple*]   Upon my word.

26.22   *demi-jour*]   Twilight.

41.30   *"Comme . . . trouve!"*]   "Precisely!"

63.9–10   date . . . Waterloo.]   The last battle of the Napoleonic Wars, fought on June 18, 1815.

68.13   "dark backward."]   Shakespeare, *The Tempest*, I.ii.49–50: "What seest thou else / In the dark backward and abysm of time?"

69.26   Falstaff . . . fields.]   Cf. Shakespeare, *Henry V*, II.iii.16–17, where Hostess describes Falstaff's dying: " . . . for his nose was as sharp as a pen, and 'a / babbl'd of green fields."

80.16   *seconde jeunesse*]   Second youth.

87.35   Temple]   Area of London, site of the Inner and Middle Temple Inns of Court, societies for students and practitioners of law.

144.36–37   *Speriamo*]   Let's hope.

155.25   'There is a happy . . . away!']   Hymn (1838) by Scottish poet Andrew Young (1807–89).

158.40–159.1   Monte Cassino . . . Grande Chartreuse]   Respectively, the Benedictine monastery on Monte Cassino, Italy (destroyed by Allied bombing in 1944), and the motherhouse of the Carthusian monks, in a valley of the French Alps about 15 miles from Grenoble.

163.4   *où donner de la tête*]   What to do next.

166.33   "the vision . . . divine."]   William Wordsworth (1770–1850), "The Excursion," I.79: "Oh! many are the Poets that are sown / By Nature; men endowed with highest gifts, / The vision and the faculty divine . . . "

202.27–30   'John . . . foot?]   Cf. the last lines of "John Anderson my jo, John," untitled poem about two aging lovers that Robert Burns (1759–96) adapted from an old song (jo means "sweetheart").

212.12   *caro*]   Darling.

217.6   *Tirez-vous de là.*]   Explain that.

224.16–17   ignorance . . . bliss.]   Thomas Gray, "On a Distant Prospect of Eton College" (1742), stanza 10: "Yet, ah! why should they know their fate, / Since sorrow never comes too late, / And happiness too swiftly flies? / Thought would destroy their paradise. / No more; where ignorance is bliss, / 'Tis folly to be wise."

230.26   *là-bas.*]   Over there.

251.33   *inédit*]   Unpublished.

255.14   Tauchnitz novel]   One of a series of cheap reprints published by Tauchnitz (Leipzig, Germany) beginning in 1841. For copyright reasons, the series, eventually called "Collection of British and American Authors," was specified for sale only on the Continent.

294.17–18   'Thou . . . did it!']   Macbeth to the ghost of Banquo, whom his assassins had murdered, in Shakespeare, *Macbeth*, III.iv.49.

300.10   *affichage*]   Display (literally, placarding).

307.31   *très-bel homme*]   Very handsome man.

307.36   *Connais pas!*]   Don't know her!

343.27–28   "Nous . . . coupés,"]   "We'll go no more to the woods; / The laurels are cut down," opening of an untitled poem by Théodore de Banville (1823–91); the lines are from an old children's rhyme.

354.5   *procédé*]   Behavior, conduct.

367.2   "collar-work."]   Uphill work (from the drag of a heavy load on the collar of a horse).

387.32   "*Bonté . . . belle!*"]   "Good gracious, my dear—what a beautiful old woman she turns out to be!"

388.12   *Où . . . donc?*]   So where is she?

388.39–40   *c'est . . . faire.*]   That's a head to be painted.

422.9   Carolus]   Painter and portraitist Carolus Duran (1837–1917; born Charles Durand) was a leader of the new French school and head of one of the principal ateliers in Paris.

427.30   *impayable*]   Priceless, inimitable.

434.28–29 "Miss Harriet"] Story (1884) about an elderly English spinster who mistakes a young artist's attentions as amorous and commits suicide when she finds him kissing another woman.

446.27 Bradshaw] *Bradshaw's Monthly Railway Guide*, a series begun in 1839 by English engraver and printer George Bradshaw (1801–53).

464.25 Casa Santa] Name of the legendary home of the Virgin Mary in Loreto, Italy; it was supposedly transported by angels from Nazareth in 1291.

472.32 'The play's the thing.'] Shakespeare, *Hamlet*, II.ii.604.

475.23–24 *compris*] Included in the price.

499.39 lazzarone] Neapolitan usage for a vagabond, beggar.

548.28 making . . . *carpe*] Making carp's eyes; ogling.

559.8–9 *On . . . soi.*] One often needs someone lesser than oneself.

597.14 Non comprenny?] Anglicized French: "Don't you understand?"

608.33 dish] Defeat, utterly ruin, cheat, circumvent.

653.9 *tilleuls*] Linden trees.

682.7 *Le compte y était*] Everything added up.

706.37 *pour deux sous*] Two cents worth.

710.26 *ombres chinoises.*] Shadow play.

713.27 *rapprochement*] Comparison.

734.32 *Seigneurie*] Lordship.

737.26–27 Tristram . . . Kundry] The lovers in Richard Wagner's *Tristan und Isolde* (1865; Tristam and Iseult are versions of the names in English legends) and the youth and the temptress Kundry in his *Parsifal* (1882).

748.22 *corvée*] Chore; unpleasant job.

749.9 *crânerie*] Showing off.

756.5 Endymion] A mythological shepherd, the most beautiful of men, who falls into a perpetual sleep and is visited nightly by Diana.

758.28 *voyons!*] Come, come! Surely! Now then!

773.23–24 gathered samphire] Shakespeare, *King Lear*, IV.vi.15: "Half way down / Hangs one that gathers sampire, dreadful trade!" Samphire (or sea-fennel), a plant used for pickling, grows on sea cliffs.

779.23 *bête*] Stupid, silly, nonsensical.

785.2 dished] See note 608.33.

788.12 *vie intime*] Private life.

791.40   *raffiné*]   Refined, cultivated person; swell, dandy.

805.21–22   *asservissement*]   Subservience.

825.20   "glimmering square"]   Alfred Tennyson, *The Princess, A Medley* (in the lyric "Tears, idle tears"), IV.34: "Ah, sad and strange, as in dark summer dawns / The earliest pipe of half awaken'd birds / To dying ears, when unto dying eyes / The casement slowly grows a glimmering square; / So sad, so strange, the days that are no more."

829.18   *avertis*]   Informed.

830.14   *rari . . . vasto*]   Virgil, *Aeneid*, I.118: " . . . only a few scattered swimmers in the vast whirlpool."

834.20   *vertige de l'abîme*]   Vertigo at the edge of the abyss.

851.4   Meg Merrilies]   An old "gypsy" involved in the kidnapping, and later the restoration, of Bertram in Walter Scott's *Guy Mannering* (1815).

896.35   "Du Barry"]   A reference to the lavish style of Jeanne Bécu, Countess du Barry (1743–93), last mistress of Louis XV.

904.38–905.1   *peculium*]   Small savings.

906.40   *bergère*]   Wing-back chair.

CATALOGING INFORMATION

James, Henry, 1843–1916.
    Complete stories 1898–1910/Henry James.
        p.   cm. — (The Library of America ; 83)
1. Manners and customs—Fiction.   I. Title.   II. Series.
PS 2110   1996   95–23462
813′.4—dc20
ISBN 1–883011–10–8

THE LIBRARY OF AMERICA SERIES

1. Herman Melville, *Typee, Omoo, Mardi* (1982)
2. Nathaniel Hawthorne, *Tales and Sketches* (1982)
3. Walt Whitman, *Poetry and Prose* (1982)
4. Harriet Beecher Stowe, *Three Novels* (1982)
5. Mark Twain, *Mississippi Writings* (1982)
6. Jack London, *Novels and Stories* (1982)
7. Jack London, *Novels and Social Writings* (1982)
8. William Dean Howells, *Novels 1875–1886* (1982)
9. Herman Melville, *Redburn, White-Jacket, Moby-Dick* (1983)
10. Nathaniel Hawthorne, *Collected Novels* (1983)
11. Francis Parkman, *France and England in North America* vol. I, (1983)
12. Francis Parkman, *France and England in North America* vol. II, (1983)
13. Henry James, *Novels 1871–1880* (1983)
14. Henry Adams, *Novels, Mont Saint Michel, The Education* (1983)
15. Ralph Waldo Emerson, *Essays and Lectures* (1983)
16. Washington Irving, *History, Tales and Sketches* (1983)
17. Thomas Jefferson, *Writings* (1984)
18. Stephen Crane, *Prose and Poetry* (1984)
19. Edgar Allan Poe, *Poetry and Tales* (1984)
20. Edgar Allan Poe, *Essays and Reviews* (1984)
21. Mark Twain, *The Innocents Abroad, Roughing It* (1984)
22. Henry James, *Essays, American & English Writers* (1984)
23. Henry James, *European Writers & The Prefaces* (1984)
24. Herman Melville, *Pierre, Israel Potter, The Confidence-Man, Tales & Billy Budd* (1985)
25. William Faulkner, *Novels 1930–1935* (1985)
26. James Fenimore Cooper, *The Leatherstocking Tales* vol. I, (1985)
27. James Fenimore Cooper, *The Leatherstocking Tales* vol. II, (1985)
28. Henry David Thoreau, *A Week, Walden, The Maine Woods, Cape Cod* (1985)
29. Henry James, *Novels 1881–1886* (1985)
30. Edith Wharton, *Novels* (1986)
31. Henry Adams, *History of the United States during the Administrations of Jefferson* (1986)
32. Henry Adams, *History of the United States during the Administrations of Madison* (1986)
33. Frank Norris, *Novels and Essays* (1986)
34. W. E. B. Du Bois, *Writings* (1986)
35. Willa Cather, *Early Novels and Stories* (1987)
36. Theodore Dreiser, *Sister Carrie, Jennie Gerhardt, Twelve Men* (1987)
37. Benjamin Franklin, *Writings* (1987)
38. William James, *Writings 1902–1910* (1987)
39. Flannery O'Connor, *Collected Works* (1988)
40. Eugene O'Neill, *Complete Plays 1913–1920* (1988)
41. Eugene O'Neill, *Complete Plays 1920–1931* (1988)
42. Eugene O'Neill, *Complete Plays 1932–1943* (1988)
43. Henry James, *Novels 1886–1890* (1989)
44. William Dean Howells, *Novels 1886–1888* (1989)
45. Abraham Lincoln, *Speeches and Writings 1832–1858* (1989)
46. Abraham Lincoln, *Speeches and Writings 1859–1865* (1989)
47. Edith Wharton, *Novellas and Other Writings* (1990)
48. William Faulkner, *Novels 1936–1940* (1990)
49. Willa Cather, *Later Novels* (1990)
50. Ulysses S. Grant, *Personal Memoirs and Selected Letters* (1990)
51. William Tecumseh Sherman, *Memoirs* (1990)
52. Washington Irving, *Bracebridge Hall, Tales of a Traveller, The Alhambra* (1991)
53. Francis Parkman, *The Oregon Trail, The Conspiracy of Pontiac* (1991)
54. James Fenimore Cooper, *Sea Tales: The Pilot, The Red Rover* (1991)

55. Richard Wright, *Early Works* (1991)
56. Richard Wright, *Later Works* (1991)
57. Willa Cather, *Stories, Poems, and Other Writings* (1992)
58. William James, *Writings 1878–1899* (1992)
59. Sinclair Lewis, *Main Street & Babbitt* (1992)
60. Mark Twain, *Collected Tales, Sketches, Speeches, & Essays 1852–1890* (1992)
61. Mark Twain, *Collected Tales, Sketches, Speeches, & Essays 1891–1910* (1992)
62. *The Debate on the Constitution: Part One* (1993)
63. *The Debate on the Constitution: Part Two* (1993)
64. Henry James, *Collected Travel Writings: Great Britain & America* (1993)
65. Henry James, *Collected Travel Writings: The Continent* (1993)
66. *American Poetry: The Nineteenth Century,* Vol. 1 (1993)
67. *American Poetry: The Nineteenth Century,* Vol. 2 (1993)
68. Frederick Douglass, *Autobiographies,* (1994)
69. Sarah Orne Jewett, *Novels and Stories* (1994)
70. Ralph Waldo Emerson, *Collected Poems and Translations* (1994)
71. Mark Twain, *Historical Romances* (1994)
72. John Steinbeck, *Novels and Stories 1932–1937* (1994)
73. William Faulkner, *Novels 1942–1954* (1994)
74. Zora Neale Hurston, *Novels and Stories* (1995)
75. Zora Neale Hurston, *Folklore, Memoirs, and Other Writings* (1995)
76. Thomas Paine, *Collected Writings* (1995)
77. *Reporting World War II: American Journalism 1938–1944* (1995)
78. *Reporting World War II: American Journalism 1944–1946* (1995)
79. Raymond Chandler, *Stories and Early Novels* (1995)
80. Raymond Chandler, *Later Novels and Other Writings* (1995)
81. Robert Frost, *Collected Poems, Prose, & Plays* (1995)
82. Henry James, *Complete Stories 1892–1898* (1996)
83. Henry James, *Complete Stories 1898–1910* (1996)
84. William Bartram, *Travels and Other Writings* (1996)

This book is set in 10 point Linotron Galliard,
a face designed for photocomposition by Matthew Carter
and based on the sixteenth-century face Granjon. The paper is
acid-free Ecusta Nyalite and meets the requirements for permanence
of the American National Standards Institute. The binding
material is Brillianta, a woven rayon cloth made by
Van Heek-Scholco Textielfabrieken, Holland.
The composition is by The Clarinda
Company. Printing and binding by
R.R.Donnelley & Sons Company.
Designed by Bruce Campbell.

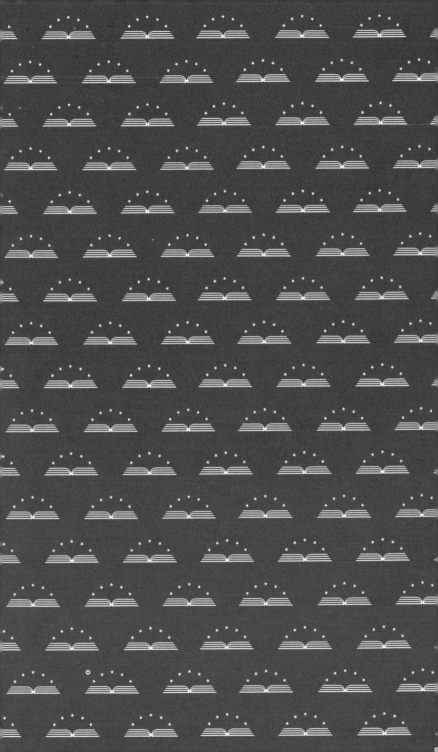